The CAUL

Published and Distributed throughout the World by
J. A. M. Publications in cooperation with
BookSurge, LLC
An Amazon.com Company

J. A. M. PUBLICATIONS
43 Brookside Drive
Williamsville, New York 14221-6915
Tel: (716) 634-6645—Fax: (716) 634-7204
E-Mail: editor@jampublications.com
Website URL: http://www.jampublications.com

BOOKSURGE PUBLISHING
5341 Dorchester Road, Suite 16
North Charleston, SC 29418
Tel: (866) 308-6235, Ext 120—Fax: (843) 577-7506
E-Mail: order@booksurge.com
Website URL: http://www.booksurge.com

Real events and the author's experiences have inspired the
creation of the characters in this fictitious epic story. Except
for historical and public figures, the characters and events in
this trilogy are fictional and any resemblance to real persons is
purely coincidental.

Photo of G-41 Gozzard yacht on front cover, courtesy of
North Castle Marine, Ltd., Goderich, Ontario, Canada.
http://www.gozzard.com

Cover art by Parrinello Printing, Inc., Cheektowaga, NY.
http://www.parrinelloprinting.com

Library of Congress Control Number: 2006901524

JAMES
ALLAN MATTE

The CAUL
A Trilogy
Part I
Born With A Mission

J. A. M. Publications in cooperation with
BookSurge, LLC
An Amazon.com Company
2006

CONTENTS

PART 1

BORN WITH A MISSION

PART II

TRUTH and DECEPTION

PART III

GOOD vs. EVIL

GOODNESS and KINDNESS
You Shall Reap What You Sow.

PROLOGUE

This is the story of a man burdened with the Caul of Destiny who suffers the tribulations of a predestined life filled with unending challenges that benefit a world that forsakes him. This epic novel, based on the life experiences of the author who was born with the CAUL: a protective membrane that shields the infant from all kinds of diseases and endows him with a certain clairvoyance and safety from nature's perils, will take you, the reader, on an incredible journey through the last seven decades of the twentieth century. From the United States to Canada, England, Scotland, France, Germany, Luxembourg, Holland, Spain, Malta, Italy, Croatia, Korea, Libya, Israel, and Saudi Arabia. You will learn what it was like to be a member of the Armed Forces of the United States shortly after the Second World War in Europe and the Far East at a time when American Servicemen were the envy of foreign nationals, many of whom resented their extended presence. You will witness the raw combativeness of airmen and soldiers amongst themselves and their courage when confronted with the enemy. The protagonist must suffer through all of these challenges in order to grow into a man whose strength and convictions are strong enough to permit his right of passage into the world of intrigue and danger that will test his morality as a Special Agent of the Office of Special Investigations (OSI), United States Air Force, and the United States Army Criminal Investigations Division (CID). However, these were just the stepping stones to a greater challenge that required all of his training and experience to fulfill the role of the ultimate interrogator as a polygraphist, and the beginning of a new career as a scientist in the field of forensic psychophysiology that eventually brought him prominence as the world's leading authority on scientific truth verification and lie detection.

This incredible, true-to-life story will appeal to and inspire people of all ages and levels of maturity with its central theme of goodness over evil that takes the protagonist to the far corners of the earth as a Federal Agent. You will see this man of destiny grow from the poverty of the Great Depression to become the world's leading authority on forensic psychophysiology using the polygraph, leaving the world with the greatest written works on the topic of scientific truth verification and lie detection, that paves the way for the courts of the world to be free from mendacity and injustice. This novel portrays the best and exposes the worst in people at all levels of society, and its ending clearly invokes the beginning to bring this epic story to an extraordinary conclusion when the protagonist, unaware of his true destiny, fulfills his final role as the Biblical Truth-Seeker who must confront the Anti-Christ.

Throughout history, there have been men and women who appeared destined to change the course of humanity, some for the better and others for the worse. A few of the former entered this world with a protective shield against all kinds of disease and the endowment of a certain clairvoyance and safety from nature's perils. Those seemingly fortunate few, saddled with the burden of their destiny, were born with the *Caul*.

CHAPTER I

The Arrival

It was a cloudy evening and the temperature was just above freezing. The cold wintry wind carried its last snow of the season across the Greater South Bay entrance to the Hudson River onto the Brooklyn shores at Fort Hamilton, New York. Suddenly the bright side of the moon appeared through an opening in the clouds, illuminating the Small Harbour Hospital in witness to a most extraordinary event about to take place.

Inside the hospital's second story labor room where the moon's glow had entered through the north window, lay a twenty-four year-old, auburn-haired woman dressed only in a white gown pulled up to her waist as she rested her feet in stirrups. She had been in labor for thirteen hours and the attending nurse who had been comforting her took her hand in hers, and with an empathic smile said "You're doing fine Mrs. Markham."

Doctor Ronald Goldstein, a friend of Mrs. Markham's husband, suddenly exclaimed "Push Nora, push, the baby is almost here, oh my God, I don't believe it." But Nora Markham couldn't see what was happening because her head was lying back and her view was blocked by the gown across her thighs.

The baby emerged from the womb completely covered by a clear, thin veil of skin. It was 9:30 PM, the 10th of March 1931, during Prohibition and the Great Depression. As Doctor Goldstein slit the veil open to extract the baby from its protective sack, he told the nurse "This baby doesn't need a bath; this baby is protected by the *caul* from the most contagious disease." Then looking at Mrs. Markham he said, "It's a beautiful, healthy boy Nora."

"I've been a nurse for nineteen years and I've never assisted a birth like this, and I never heard of anything like a *caul*."

Doctor Goldstein explained. "That thin membrane which covered and protected this baby is known as a *caul*. Some believe it's a sign of clairvoyance. Others believe that such a child has a special destiny and is protected until his destiny is fulfilled."

Doctor Goldstein mused about the path this child would take and the contributions he would make to this world, then he placed the caul into a container and told the nurse to label it and place it aside for him. "What name will you give your baby?" he asked Nora.

"James...he's so beautiful," as she held him beside her for a moment, then he was taken away by the nurse.

That evening Nora telephoned her mother in Montreal, Canada and told her the circumstances surrounding the birth of her son. "You should have asked for the caul, Nora...it brings good luck to whomever possesses it. A ship's Captain would pay a lot of money for that caul because it brings luck to his vessel."

"It's too late for me to ask for it now, Maman," said Nora, sounding a bit annoyed but also disappointed.

"Has your husband Herc seen the baby yet?" asked her mother, Nancy Boivin.

"No Mom, he hasn't been at the hospital yet today. He told me he had to attend an important meeting with someone at the publishing house...but his mother Eloisa sent me flowers...they're gorgeous."

Nora, a petite woman with hazel eyes and dark red curly hair, was a Capricorn woman who lived up to her astrological sign of being wise beyond her years and practical without sacrificing her romantic dreams, but her fiery temper and stubbornness would often be her undoing.

Her mother Nancy, born in New Hampshire to French-Canadian parents domiciled in Montreal, felt that Hercules couldn't be trusted. Musicians, especially Italians, have such big egos she thought, and with him being center stage as a concert pianist and talented music arranger for the top bands, women flocked at his side, waiting to be picked. No wonder he changed his name from Hercules Giammatteo to Anthony Markham. Too many Italians in the music business he had said. But she couldn't share her suspicions with her daughter Nora. She hoped that with the birth of James, his first born, he would perhaps settle down and make Nora happy.

But that wasn't to be. Three years later, while cleaning the apartment, Nora found two letters tucked inside a compartment of the phonograph cabinet. They were addressed to Nora's husband from a woman named Joyce Bellamy. As she read them her stomach started to ache and tears welled in her eyes, but then she read that Joyce Bellamy was pregnant with his child and at that point Nora broke down and cried for the longest time. Her attractive face betrayed a sadness at life's persistent unfairness.

Nora had not heard from her husband for three days and had no money to buy food for her or her son James, who was now forty months old. She depended upon the generosity of her mother-in-law Eloisa for the necessities of life. Eloisa was the daughter of an Italian Baroness who had eloped with the lead cellist from the Rome Philharmonic Orchestra to New York City. Eloisa's parents had disapproved of their daughter's choice, Antonio, and had threatened to disown her if she married him. Antonio and Eloisa decided to make a new start in the United States and settled in Brooklyn, New York. Eloisa felt great empathy for Nora whose isolation from her parents in Montreal, Canada reminded Eloisa of her own isolation from her parents in Rome, Italy. The humble, submissive position of Italian wives, especially from the old country, prohibited her from asserting herself with her son Hercules who had obviously embraced New York City's night life at the expense of his wife and son.

Eventually her husband Hercules made an appearance and Nora confronted him with Joyce Bellamy's love letters. He grabbed the letters from her and stormed out of the apartment. "May the best woman win" said Joyce Bellamy in one of her letters. Nora knew that she had lost when shortly thereafter, Eloisa, her only supportive ally in the Giammatteo family, took ill and died.

Shortly thereafter, Herc moved his Nora and their son James into another apartment in Sunnyside, Long Island because he had not been paying the rent at the previous one. Herc moved them in and left, apparently to live with the other woman Joyce Bellamy. Two days passed without a word from Herc. Nora had no money nor any food for herself or her son and was becoming desperate. She had nowhere to turn. Overwhelmed with fear and despair she dropped to her knees and with her elbows on the bed where little Jimmy lay, she held her hands together against her forehead in prayer. "Please dear God, please help us, I have no food to feed my child. I know these are hard times; I'm not asking anything for myself, but my child is starving and I know you love children, please, please help us…" Then Nora started reciting "Our Father who art in heaven, hallowed be thy name, thy kingdom come, thy will be done, on earth as it is in heaven, give us this day our daily bread and forgive us our trespasses…" Suddenly she heard what sounded like a knock on the door to the apartment. She couldn't believe it. She waited…then another knock on the door. Could it be her husband she thought…that would surely be a miracle. She wiped the tears from her eyes with her hands then answered the door. To her surprise there stood Herc, a heavyset man at two hundred and ten pounds on a five feet and ten inch frame, dressed in his usual gray pinstriped suit, white shirt and tie. "I don't know what came over me," he said. "I had this strange urge to come and see you. Is Jimmy alright?"

"We don't have any food, Herc. We haven't had anything to eat in two days. Can you give us any money at all, anything?"

Herc thought for a moment. "All I can spare is fifty cents, Nora."

Nora thankfully took the fifty cents and asked Herc to watch Jimmy while she ran down to the store to buy milk and bread. When she returned to the apartment, Herc was gone. At least she and Jimmy would have something to eat for another day, she thought.

That evening, Nora received another visitor. This time it was from a middle aged woman who lived with her husband in the upstairs apartment. As Nora opened the door, the woman introduced herself. "I'm Susan…I'm your neighbor upstairs." She hesitated, feeling a bit uneasy. "I know what's been going on, and I've brought you and your son some food."

"Oh! thank you, you're so kind. But my husband was just here this afternoon and I was able to buy a loaf of bread and milk."

Susan looked at Nora sorrowfully. "Please take this. It's homemade meatloaf. Your son needs nourishment and so do you."

Susan then looked pensively at Nora. "You know, it's none of my business Nora, but you know, my husband is a musician and he knows your husband." Susan then added, "My husband told me that your husband Herc plays around, and I don't mean with his music."

Nora just stared at Susan in disbelief, but deep down inside, she knew Susan was right. She said nothing. The tears in her eyes said it all.

Susan added, "Look Nora, you and your son are starving. You've got to do something, take him to court or contact your parents."

"Yes, I know you're right. I must do something soon," said Nora. "Thank you so much for all of your help. I will never forget your kindness. God bless you."

As Nora closed the door to her apartment while carrying the meat loaf, she thought how miraculously her prayers had been answered, and she had come to a decision.

It was late evening when Nora boarded the sleeper train with her curly blond-haired son Jimmy at New York's Grand Central Station. For the first time since the birth of her son, she felt a sense of security and peace. She was going home to her parents and sisters in Montreal. With her son fast asleep, Nora lay in her bunk in the small sleeping compartment, reliving the highlights and the trauma of her failed marriage, wondering if there was anything she could have done to save it. She had gone to New York City to take voice lessons as an aspiring radio singer when she was spotted by Hercules who owned and operated a music publishing house next door to the studio. He had asked to be introduced to her, but she felt that he was too sophisticated for her and refused to accept his lavish offers of entertainment. But his persistence finally paid off and to her chagrin she fell in love and married him. After James was born, she occasionally heard from people associated with musicians that Hercules was consorting with other women, but the thought of his infidelity was too painful. It was better not to worry about things that had not been proven. Here was a man who was given everything. He came from an affluent family of professionals and he himself was the youngest graduate of the New York Conservatory of Music, a talented concert pianist and a published composer and music arranger. But he lacked the capacity to love and care for his wife and child. If only she had listened to her initial instinct. But out of all this misery and suffering, she was a wiser woman with a gift from God, her son James. Then Nora remembered her father's words on the telephone when she had called her parents for help. "We'll be more than happy to have you and your son live with us, but you must raise your son as a French-Canadian," she was told by her father. "And to avoid prejudice you'll have to change his first name to Jacques, which is simply the French translation for James," he had added.

Nora knew her father Joseph Boivin was right. He was a college-educated French—Canadian businessman who had married Nancy Labelle, an American born French woman from Nashua, New Hampshire. Nancy gave birth to a son Ernest and two daughters, Genevieve and Nora, while residing at Nashua, then catastrophe struck the Boivin family when Joe Boivin's American business partner cheated Joe and caused their Import-Export business to fail. After Joe and Nancy moved to Montreal, Canada, Joe's birthplace, Nancy gave birth to two more daughters, Louella and Pauline. Ernest had joined the United States Marine Corps and Genevieve had moved to Pennsylvania. Therefore Nora expected to see only her sisters Louella and Pauline with her parents when she arrived in Montreal.

A taxi pulled up to the front entrance of La Gare Windsor, Montreal's largest train station. The driver stepped out of the taxi and opened the rear passenger door allowing a tall, lean and distinguished looking gentleman dressed in a dark three-piece suit, top coat and brim hat to descend, followed by two chique young ladies wearing fur lined boots, fur collared coats and fur hats that caught some of the light snow still falling after the night's flurries. The man paid the taxi driver then the two young ladies each grabbed one of their father's arms and entered the train station.

"Papa, what time is Nora's train due to arrive?" asked Louella, who seemed to have this perpetual smile with her round cheeks and bright eyes.

"Huit heures," replied Joseph Boivin, insisting on speaking in French, although bilingual.

"I'm going to check with the train master to see if the train is arriving on time," said Pauline, who left in quick step. Of his three daughters, Genevieve was living in New York City; Pauline was the feistiest and there didn't seem to be any similarity between them. Yet they all got along marvelously; they shared close family ties.

"This is a big train station, ha! Papa," Louella exclaimed to her father in French.

"The biggest in Montreal…the largest in Canada," replied her father. "But this is nothing compared to Grand Central Station in New York."

Pauline returned exuberant. "The train is arriving on time at eight o'clock." Then she put her arm inside her father's arm and the three of them walked very slowly along the platform looking at the people milling around in their various attires.

Joe was so proud escorting his two grownup daughters. But he was also worried about their future. He had given his children the best upbringing a man could provide. He had even acquiesced to his wife's demand that his daughters attend Saint Ambrose Primary English School so that they could be completely bilingual, inasmuch as the French-Canadian schools taught little or no English. He had encouraged them to be independent and self-sufficient. He did not interfere when his daughter Nora decided to study music in New York City. He felt that the moral values and cautionary teachings instilled in them at home and by the nuns would protect them against undesirable people. But that was with Canadians. Americans are different.

Look what happened to me, he thought. *I was cheated out of my business by my partner, an American. Now my daughter Nora has been cheated by a New Yorker, the fastest of Americans. I certainly can't blame her*, he told himself. *It's good that she's coming home to Canada. Here she can meet a decent French-Canadian who has been taught the same values.* He felt satisfied and pleased that Nora had agreed to have her son Jacques attend French—Canadian schools. *Hopefully that will compensate for his Italian-American genes, and his Boivin blood will dominate. For sure I'm not going to let Pauline and Louella leave Montreal*, he promised himself, *and Nancy will agree I'm sure.*

"I think the train is arriving," said Louella, straining her neck to see through the crowd of people.

"Well, I see a train too, but is it the right one?" exclaimed Pauline.

Joseph Boivin, who stood a foot taller than his daughters, looked attentively at the train as it approached then said in French "Yes, that's Nora's train alright, but let's stay together so no one gets lost in the crowd. We'll walk towards the center train and watch for her." Then in a serious voice he said, "You must remember never to mention Jacques' father to him or in his presence."

As the train came to a stop, people started crowding along the platform near the train exits searching for debarking relatives or friends, impeding porters' access to those passengers with heavy luggage. But Joseph didn't move from his position and flanked by his two daughters he kept his gaze on the primary train exits, then suddenly exclaimed, "There she is, there's Nora and Jacques." He raised his hand in the air and waved to her until she saw him.

Nora was standing on the top exit step with Jacques in her arms. Although he could walk, she was afraid he might get trampled in the crowd. She had two large suitcases which she could not manage, but she saw that her father had hired a porter who came to her aid. She was rushed by her two sisters who hugged her and took little Jacques from her arms. Nora stepped up to her father and threw her arms around him with tears of happiness and thankfulness. At that moment, Joseph experienced such deep emotion that he had to fight back his own tears, which if seen, he felt would diminish his image as the family's pillar of strength. He now realized that the return of his daughter and her child to his care and protection was not only his moral obligation, but a blessing to his family.

They all started walking along the platform with little Jacques himself walking between his two aunts while Nora walked arm in arm with her father with the porter following them with the luggage outside to the taxi stand where they embarked for the short trip from lower Montreal to the Boivin home in mid-city Montreal.

The taxi finally stopped on Rue St. Hubert next to a three-story brick building with wooden stairs and porches at each level. As the passengers descended the taxi, a smiling, rosy cheeked woman no more than four feet eleven inches tall, wearing her wavy gray hair in a pompadour to make herself look taller, stood in the open doorway to the downstairs apartment. The harsh Quebec weather aged women much quicker than their southern sisters. Nancy Labelle Boivin had been Nashua's queen, weighing only one hundred and five pounds at age seventeen. Bearing five children took its toll, but there still remained signs of youth in her beautiful complexion, large blue eyes and positive, exuberant personality. With Joe trailing behind with Nora's suitcases, the three daughters led by Nora with her son in hand mounted the porch steps and Nora embraced her mother who then turned her attention to Jacques while they all looked on.

Nancy held Jacques' hands in hers and leaning towards him with a big smile she said, "So finally I get to meet my Grandson. He's got such beautiful curly hair…I'm your Grandma Nancy…" Jacques just stood staring at his Grandma, taking her all in, then he smiled back at her. Nancy hugged Jacques and kissed him on the cheek. "I cooked a nice dinner and some delicious apple pie just for you Jacques," she said as they walked into the house. The inside of the apartment house was deceptively large with four bedrooms. Jacques was shown his room which was small but comfortable and warm. Jacques knew he would like it here. He was finally home with his family.

Dinner was served in the dining room with Grandpa Joe seated at the head of the table flanked by his three daughters and his Grandson Jacques. Grandma was busy serving the food with occasional help from Louella or Pauline. The talk, mostly in French, centered around Nora, her trip, and her plans for the future. All being bilingual, their conversation would unconsciously move from French to English to French, easily confusing Jacques with his adolescent English so he remained very quiet, but watched them all in wonderment, smiling occasionally when one of his aunts or Grandma would run their hand through his blond hair or compliment him.

"You know Christmas is only two weeks away Jacques," said Aunt Pauline.

"Yeah, and we told Santa Claus that you were here, that this is your home now and to leave you lots of presents," Aunt Louella said laughingly watching Jacques' face light up. "And tomorrow Grandpa is going to get a Christmas three…would you like to come with us?"

Jacques nodded, and said, "Oh! Yes." Then he turned toward Grandpa and asked, "May I be excused, I have to go to the bathroom?"

Smiling at Jacques' politeness, Grandpa replied, "Certainly young man." Then turning to Nora as Jacques left the table Grandpa said, "I'm astonished at such good manners from such a young boy; you did a splendid job with him Nora."

"Well, I lost my husband, not my culture," replied Nora. "You had always told us Papa that the first years are the formative ones, and if you want them to learn good habits, start them young."

"And on that note we ought to make plans to enter Jacques into a French school as soon as they will accept him," replied Grandpa.

"I think Jacques should attend l'Ecole St. Sacrament," said Grandma Nancy. "The Soeur Sainte Croix are exceptional teachers."

"Jacques doesn't know any French whatsoever, so he has a lot of catching up to do. It'll take the nuns at least a year for them to get Jimmy to catch up to the other kids, don't you think so Papa?" said Nora.

"That depends on Jacques to a great extent. If the child has a musical ear, he will learn another language quickly," said Joseph.

Louella thought of saying that with Jacques' parents both being musicians, it would be expected that Jacques would also have a musical ear, but then she remembered Papa's admonition not to bring up the topic of Jacques' father. "I think Jacques will do just fine," she said. "Where is Jacques? Is he still in the bathroom?"

"I'll go check on him," said Grandmaman, getting up from the table.

"I'll go visit the Soeur Sainte Croix tomorrow and find out more about their school," said Nora.

Grandma Nancy appeared in the dining room smiling. "Jacques must be exhausted from his train ride because he's fast asleep on his bed."

"I'll go in his bedroom and undress him into his pajamas and tuck him in," said Nora.

"You don't have to Nora," said Grandma Nancy. "I took care of it. He's alright."

"Does Jacques ask about his father?" asked Louella to Nora.

"I told him that his father died of double pneumonia," answered Nora, turning her head towards her father and mother to see their reaction.

Joseph remained silent, but Grandmaman replied, "It will probably help him put the past behind and concentrate on the present and the future. But eventually when he gets older, he'll have to be told the truth."

"Are you going to read to us Papa, the next chapter of the Comte de Monte Christo?" asked Louella, changing the subject.

Papa hesitated, then looked at Nancy for direction.

"Oh please Papa, it's getting so interesting," pleaded Pauline.

"OK, but let's clear the table first," said Nancy.

Grandpa Joseph loved to read the French classics to his wife and children. They would all settle in the living room on sofas and couches around Grandpa who would read in his melodious, baritone voice the classics from Victor Hugo, Jules Verne, Honore de Balzac, Alexander Dumas and other French authors who captured their imagination and sense of adventure. The intimacy of those shared adventures was to be cherished long after the contents of the stories were to be remembered.

That summer Nora took Jacques to Mount Royal, at the foot of the city of Montreal where during the winter she had taken Jacques tobogganing. A trolley took them all the way to the top of the mountain where a huge cross cast its religious spell over the entire city. From there they walked to a small lake called Lac du Castor. There was a stone and cement walkway around the lake perimeter for visitors to enjoy the wildlife of the lake and some could be seen feeding the ducks. Jacques had brought his birthday gift with him and was anxious to use it. He went to the edge of the water and placed his sixteen inch sailboat in the water, then he picked up the reel of string attached to the boat tiller and gave his sailboat a nudge towards open water, controlling its direction by moving the tiller with the string which he had borrowed from his kite. He watched his white hulled sailboat heel to leeward and Jacques imagined himself aboard sailing into the unknown world of adventure. He sailed for a couple of hours totally lost in reverie, until Nora gently reminded him that they had to return home. That sailing experience was never to be forgotten.

The summer was over and the children of Montreal were getting ready for their first day of school. That September morning, Nora appeared with her son Jacques at l'Ecole St. Sacrament where they were greeted by Sister Marie, who asked them to be seated in the foyer while she fetched Sister Blanche. After a few minutes, the inner foyer door opened and Sister Blanche appeared so silently, dressed in a full black habit completely covering her hair and ears, exposing only her broad pale face which was surrounded by a wimple consisting of a large starched white pleated fan, which accented her naturally beautiful skin and large blue eyes.

"I'm Sister Blanche," she said in a calm, soft voice. "Your son Jacques is going to be in my class and I've also been assigned tutorial duties to bring Jacques up to the rest of the class." Then Sister Blanche turned to Jacques, and bent over, her face ever so near to Jacques' and with a warm smile she said, "I'm Sister Blanche...I guess I must be your very first teacher...but I'm going to be your dearest friend too," while still smiling at Jacques who was completely mesmerized by her haloed face. Sister Blanche took an instant liking to this curly blond-haired five-year-old boy whose handsomeness reminded her of a son she was ordained not to bear. Yes, she thought, I'm going to care for this boy as if he were my own. Sister Blanche said her farewells to Nora then turned towards Jacques who shyly took her outstretched hand in his and accompanied her down the hall to his first classroom.

It was spring and some neighborhood children were using axes to chop the thick winter ice that had formed over the sidewalks on Rue St. Hubert, also known by anglophones as St. Hubert Street. Nora was late for her meeting with Sister Blanche at l'Ecole St. Sacrament. Jacques had been her pupil for eight months and she was anxious to learn of his progress. Sister Blanche invited Nora into a room adjoining the principal's office. Although there was a small desk with a chair, Sister Blanche showed Nora to one of the three chairs near the wall where she joined her.

"I've been out of town visiting my sister Genevieve," said Nora in French. "But I am concerned about my son's progress in school. His Grandmother tells me that he has been very quiet at home, probably because she will only speak to him in French, and so do my sisters. We figured that he'd learn the language faster that way."

"Jacques has also been very quiet in class," said Sister Blanche, also in French. "He sat in front of the class like 'le petit bonhome dans la lune', the little boy on the moon. For the first six months he never said a word. Then one day, I asked him to read a passage from his textbook and he amazed everyone with the speed of his fluency. He's now the fastest and best reader in the class. I predict he will be first in his class this year."

"Oh! I'm so happy to hear that, I was getting worried," said Nora with a sigh of relief. "You've been very kind to Jacques and I would like to give you something as an expression of my gratitude." Nora then pulled out a gift-wrapped package from her bag.

Sister Blanche quietly protested. "It's very gracious of you Mrs. Markham, but I cannot accept any gifts."

"Oh! It's only a box of chocolates…you can share them with the other sisters…please." Then Nora got up and placed the box of chocolates on the corner of the desk.

Sister Blanche smiled at Nora's determination. Jacques has that silent determination too, she thought.

Jacques finished first in his class at l'Ecole St. Sacrament. He then transferred to l'ecole St. Hubert, another Catholic school run by Marist Brothers. For the next three years Jacques finished first in his class, skipping the second grade. His ability at writing in French earned him the nickname of *Poet* by his language teacher. But then his grades started to diminish and Jacques couldn't understand why he was ranking only second or third in his class. When he received his grades he just sat there, staring at the teacher with bewilderment in his eyes, which did not go unnoticed by the teacher who made no attempt to give any explanation. That was Jacques' first dose of humility. Then he moved residence.

The Boivin family and the Markhams moved from St. Hubert Street to St. Denis Street which provided transportation from downtown Montréal to upper Montreal by electric trolleys. That same year, Pauline started dating Roland, a dashingly handsome French-Canadian whose pride and joy was his 1936 Royal Chrysler. Jacques liked Roland for his kindness and obvious love for Pauline, and his sincere interest in Jacques' activities. Jacques was especially fond of Pauline's nickname "Pony," which the Boivin family had given her because whenever she got mad, she would stomp her heel into the ground repeatedly.

But Louella was not to be outdone. She met and started dating Martin, a quiet man, Irish-Canadian, and before Pauline could recover from the shock, Louella married Martin and moved out of the Boivin house into an apartment on Bloomfield Street Park Extension about five miles away. Louella was not like her sister Pauline, the high spirited wild pony. She loved a good laugh, but her sweet and gentle personality gave comfort to all those who came in contact with her. She was so scared on the day of her marriage when she and Martin drove away from the church as newlyweds on their honeymoon, that she started crying and asking for her mother Nancy, to the consternation of Martin who was looking forward to this long awaited honeymoon. But Martin was equally as sensitive as Louella and would prove to be the perfect husband and father to their children.

The impact of the religious teachings by the nuns and the Marist brothers on Jacques was so profound that one day when Nora came home unexpectedly, she found Jacques standing in the corner of the dining room facing the wall.

"What are you doing standing in the corner, Jacques?" asked Nora.

"I've been a bad boy," replied Jacques remorsefully.

"Well, what have you done to merit that?" asked Nora in astonishment.

"I found a nickel on the floor in the kitchen and I used it to buy myself an ice-cream cone," replied Jacques with tears in his eyes.

"Oh! Jacques, come here my dear boy," she said, hugging him for his honesty, and most of all for his repentance and self-discipline.

"You're an honest boy Jacques…I'm proud of you," said Nora with admiration.

Nora privately told Grandmaman of the incident and Grandmaman didn't seem surprised considering the number of religious retreats sponsored by the Catholic Church that Jacques and other students had attended which preached fire and brimstone to the point that students were afraid to spit on the sidewalk for fear that lightning might strike them.

As the seasons passed, Jacques' transition from an American child to a young French-Canadian boy manifested itself quite fluently in his command of the French language, which now far surpassed what limited English he possessed upon arrival in Montreal.

Jacques was now eleven years old and quickly made friends with the neighborhood hockey players.

One day, Jacques came home holding a handkerchief to his nose, which was still bleeding.

"What happened?" asked Grandmaman.

"I took a short-cut through the English neighborhood to get to school and two big boys came up to me and one of them punched me on the nose," said Jacques.

"I told you to stay away from those English bums," said Nancy with anger not directed at Jacques. "Here Jacot, let me take care of this." She washed the blood from his face. "Well, nothing is broken; you'll live," she laughed. She often called him 'Jacot,' which is the equivalent of 'Jim' instead of Jacques. "Did you hit him back?" Nancy asked.

"No, he was much bigger and older than me and there were two of them."

"Listen Jacot, if somebody hits you, you hit him back, no matter how big he is. I don't want you to come crying to me because someone hit you. You understand?" But Nancy didn't mean it. She had a soft spot for her Jacot, but she didn't want him to grow up a softy. Her son Ernest was a United States Marine rough rider whom she often talked about to Jacques and had showed him a picture of Ernest on horseback. She knew Jacques was a good-natured boy who wouldn't dream of hurting anyone. But she knew that he would be easy prey for the bullies of the world, and needed to be tough to protect himself.

"Yes, Grandmaman, don't worry, I'll take care of myself. You won't ever see me crying," said Jacques, who knew that his Grandmaman loved him and had only his best interests at heart. But he didn't want to disappoint her. He couldn't understand why anyone would want to punch a complete stranger who had done him no harm. Then the thought struck him. Those English bullies thought I was a French-Canadian and they must harbor the same hatred for the French as the French-Canadians do for the English, whom they feel stole their country in a major battle at the Plains of Abraham in Quebec.

Jacques' thoughts drifted to what he had learned in French-Canadian History about the English and French conflict between British Major General James Wolfe and French Lieutenant General the Marquis de Montcalm, which ended with the English conquest of Quebec City and the rest of Canada, and the apparent bitterness that still remained with the French-Canadians over the loss of their country, but their language and culture were yet unconquered. Jacques remembered what one of his Marist Brother teachers had recently told the class. "The Canadian government has just minted a new octagonal nickel which doesn't have a word of French on it. If a store keeper gives you one of those nickels for change, give it back to him and tell him that you won't accept Canadian money that doesn't have French on it."

The next afternoon, Jacques met his friends Jean-Guy and Pierrot. "Hey! what happened to your nose?" asked Jean-Guy, staring at Jacques' still swollen nose.

"Yeah! Looks like you forgot to duck, hey!" said Pierrot, laughing.

Jacques remained silent.

"Well, tell us what happened," said Pierrot anxiously.

Jacques related how he had taken a shortcut through the English neighborhood and was accosted by two teenagers and the one with red hair punched him on the nose without provocation.

"That's probably the same guy that beat me up last year on that same street; he had red hair too, sort of burly. I heard some of the other guys refer to him as the 'lapin' because his nose and ears reminded them of a rabbit," said Jean-Guy with a touch of angry sarcasm. "I'd like to meet him again when I get to be his age," he added. Jean-Guy had grown a few inches since then and promised to be a big, tall adult.

"Yeah! I've been taking wrestling lessons at the school gymnasium…I'd like to see him try something with me," said Pierrot who was shorter than Jean-Guy and Jacques, but stockier.

"My Grandmother told me that everything comes to he who waits," said Jacques passively.

"Your Grandmother has more quotations than the Bible has prayers, I swear," said Pierrot, laughing. "Hey! I hear they're building an outdoor ice skating rink a couple of blocks from the English High School, right across from the empty field at the flour mill. Let's go take a look."

"But there'll be a lot of English guys in the school yard…if they see us they'll kill us…there're too many; we won't stand a chance," said Jean-Guy, a bit worried.

"Naw! We can bypass the school yard by cutting across the empty field. It's got high weeds and nobody can see us crossing it," said Pierrot bravely. "What do you think Jacques?"

"Yeah! Sure, let's go see how they're putting up the hockey rink," said Jacques matter-of-factly.

The three boys walked through the high weeds in the field adjacent to the flour mill with Pierrot leading the way followed by Jacques and Jean-Guy. As they approached the end of the field still shielded from view by the high weeds, Jacques could see the English school yard to his front left. The gate was wide open and at the center of the yard Jacques spotted Lapin with his unmistakable red hair talking to a dozen classmates around him. Jacques quickly surveyed the yard and noticed that there were about fifty other students mostly at the far end of the yard.

Jacques had stopped walking and was staring at the people in the school yard while Pierrot and Jean-Guy had continued walking towards the empty, almost completed ice rink.

"Hey! Jacques, c'mon, let's go," said Jean-Guy anxiously.

Noticing Jacques' unresponsiveness to Jean-Guy, Pierrot doubled back towards Jacques and in an understanding tone said, "Forget it Jacques; don't even think about it; remember what your Grandmother told you; you'll get your chance."

"I can't wait that long," replied Jacques sternly, and he walked out of the cover of the tall weeds towards the school yard in plain sight. Pierrot and Jean-Guy hid in the weeds in total disbelief watching Jacques as he continued his agile walk directly towards the entrance to the school yard. Jacques realized that he wasn't old or big enough to beat Lapin, but he was the fastest runner in his age group, and he had to prove to himself that he could overcome his fear.

Lapin and his friends were now aware of Jacques' approach as he entered the school yard. They all separated to either side of Lapin who stood at the middle of the student horseshoe. Lapin suddenly recognized Jacques from his earlier encounter and couldn't understand the nerve of this kid walking right into the enemy camp. Lapin grinned with anticipation at beating up a French-Canadian in front of his English classmates.

Jacques was about thirty feet from Lapin and never slowed his pace. His anger had overcome his fear at the sight of Lapin and he was trying to decide where to punch Lapin: in the stomach or in the face or the tip of his jaw. He knew he would only get one punch in and he wanted to make it count, but he had no experience at this.

With unanticipated speed, Jacques lunged and struck Lapin with a right punch on the chin knocking him back and just as quickly Jacques had turned about and was running like a deer out of the school yard with a trail of about fifteen students running behind him trying to catch him, while Pierrot and Jean-Guy, crouched in the weeds, watched in terror, praying that Jacques would not be caught.

Jacques was running with amazing speed towards St. Denis Street and would have to cover about a mile before reaching his house. Jacques never looked back, but kept on running at top speed with the soles of his feet rising high behind him parallel to the ground until he reached St. Denis Street, then he looked back quickly and saw that he had outdistanced his nearest opponent, and resumed a more reasonable pace until he reached Jean-Guy's house where he rested on the wooden steps to wait for their eventual arrival. He felt redeemed and the risk had been well worth it. But he decided not to tell his Grandmother about it. This was a personal challenge.

The following day, the three boys took a walk to the Mount Royal Mountain where Jacques found a long tree branch that he thought would make an excellent bow. Pierrot and Jean-Guy found smaller branches to make arrows and upon their return to Jacques' backyard, they all went to work sanding down the small branches into arrows while Jacques shaped the bow.

"That waxed string is not strong enough to take the pressure of this bow which is as tall as I am," said Jacques to Pierrot and Jean-Guy. "But I've got an idea that might work," added Jacques who then went into the house, returning with a tennis racket.

"Whose racket is that?" asked Jean-Guy.

"My mother's," replied Jacques. "But she never uses it, so she won't miss it…I hope."

Jacques started to unravel the network of the tennis racket.

"You know," said Jacques. "That stuff is catgut. It's very tough and flexible. It ought to drive those arrows a hundred yards, maybe farther. But we're going to have to weigh down the tip by wrapping it with wire."

"Why don't we cut off the head of a nail, then drive that end of the nail into the tip of the arrow, then we can go hunting," suggested Pierrot.

"OK, but we'll have to balance the arrow with a feather or two at the other end. I know, I'll pull some of the small feathers from my mother's old hats." With that, Jacques disappeared once more inside the house and a short time later reappeared with several small colorful feathers which he gave to Jean-Guy to fasten to the three arrows they were working on.

Jacques completed the bow and was trying it out by pulling on the catgut at its center while holding the big bow with his left hand and arm extended.

"Boy! That takes a lot of pulling, but the catgut is holding strong," said Jacques. "You got one arrow finished yet Pierrot?"

"Yeah as a matter of fact, Jean-Guy is finishing the last one."

"Let's go to the fields, we can try it out there, plenty of open space and there's woods with some wildlife," said Perrot.

"You done Jean-Guy?" asked Jacques with anticipation.

"Yeah! All done. Let's go."

Each boy carried an arrow, but Jacques carried the bow. When they arrived at the field, they observed an old dilapidated wooden shed and Pierrot asked Jacques if he could use the bow to shoot his arrow at the shed.

"Sure, but that's quite a distance. Are you sure you don't want to get closer before you shoot?" asked Jacques, handing Pierrot the bow.

"There's only one way to find out," said Pierrot, then pulled hard and steady on the catgut holding the arrow in its groove. The arrow's red feather was almost touching his cheek, then Pierrot let the arrow fly with the three boys watching it travel more than seventy yards penetrating through the glassless window of the old shed. There was a big smile of satisfaction across Pierrot's face as the other two boys looked on in awe.

"Wow! Did you see that arrow go!" exclaimed Jean-Guy.

"Yeah!" answered Jacques. "I hope there's nobody inside that shed. Let's go find that arrow."

They all ran to the shed. Jacques opened the battered door and they walked in, one after the other. There on the opposite wall of the window the boys stared at the arrow imbedded into the very center of a newspaper picture of Hitler pasted on the wall.

"Look at that. You think we uncovered the hideout of Nazi spies?" asked Pierrot.

"No," answered Jacques. "Kids like us used this shed as their club house. That's just a newspaper clipping of Hitler."

"Look at that, the arrow went right into Hitler's mouth," said Jean-Guy. "Poetic justice, hey!"

"Boy, this place is a mess; let's get out of here," said Pierrot.

"Let's leave the arrow where it is as a symbol of our having been here," said Jacques, taking the bow back from Pierrot.

"What, and waste a good arrow?" asked Pierrot.

"The tip is damaged and if you pull it out of the wall, it will split…leave it," said Jacques impatiently.

They all left the shed with two arrows remaining. As they walked towards the wooded area, Jean-Guy spotted a bird's nest in the fork of a nearby tree.

"Pass me the bow Jacques. I'm going to see if I can hit that bird's nest over there," said Jean-Guy.

"I don't think that's right. Those birds are helpless in that nest. C'mon, pick another target Jean-Guy," said Jacques, refusing to give him the bow.

"We said we were going to hunt, didn't we? That's the reason we made the bow and arrows," said Jean-Guy with Pierrot agreeing.

"Yeah! Something that has a chance to fight back or escape," said Jacques, annoyed.

"OK! Pass me the bow. I'll only shoot at a rabbit or a squirrel or something that can run fast, alright," said Jean-Guy.

Jacques handed Jean-Guy the bow and Jean-Guy placed his arrow at the ready. As they neared the woods, Jean-Guy spotted a squirrel running up a tree just ahead of him. He took quick aim and fired his arrow, missing the squirrel by inches, sinking the arrow into the tree.

They all walked to the tree to retrieve the arrow and Jean-Guy pulled on the arrow, which broke. "Well, I can save the feathers for another arrow," said Jean-Guy, disappointed.

"Don't feel bad Jean-Guy, those squirrels are fast," said Pierrot.

Jacques took back the bow and placed his arrow on the bow at the ready as they walked into the woods. Suddenly they all heard a loud grunt.

"Sounds like a bull," said Pierrot.

"Well if it is, I don't think a bow and arrow is going to be enough to bring it down," said Jean-Guy.

"Quiet you guys, I'm trying to figure out where that sound is coming from," said Jacques with his bow and arrow at the ready, walking forward with his two companions on either side of him.

Suddenly a big beast appeared through the brush. Jacques had his arrow pointed and aimed at the beast.

"Go on shoot Jacques, shoot," shouted Pierrot.

"C'mon Jacques, don't miss," said Jean-Guy.

"It's a harmless cow," said Jacques lowering and relaxing his bow. "I can't shoot a helpless animal."

"What's a cow doing here in the woods?" asked Jean-Guy.

"Who knows, let's get out of here," said Jacques.

"Aren't you going to use your arrow?" asked Pierrot.

"Yeah! Some other time," answered Jacques, but he never did.

That winter, Grandpapa Joseph became very ill and it was determined that his recovery would be very slow. This was especially difficult for Grandmaman Nancy who was suffering from varicose veins that had her legs swollen twice their normal size. Canadian winters were long and hard on people's health and longevity, but they provided the whitest and most picturesque Christmases nature could present. That biggest and most blessed event of the year was quickly approaching with only two weeks left before Midnight Mass and the celebrated reveillon where the entire family clan and all of their children taste the assorted dishes of French-Canadian cuisine prepared by all of the women in the family. Gathered in the dining room after a delicious meal of Grandmaman's ragout, (including the mixture of lamb, pork and beef meatballs,) Grandmaman, Pauline, Nora and Jacques sat around the table, some drinking tea, while discussing preparations for Christmas Eve. The only family member missing at the table was Grandpapa Joseph who was still in the hospital recovering from his illness.

"Jacques, this is your third helping of the ragout…you're a real gourmand," said Nora annoyed.

Jacques smiled without looking up and kept eating one of his favorite meals. Not only did he like the flavor of those three meats, lamb, beef and pork, rolled into meatballs with the accompanying potatoes in heavy brown gravy, but it stuck to his ribs for a long period which helped to sustain him when playing hockey in the ice cold weather of the north.

"Jacques is a gourmet, not a gourmand…he appreciates his Grandmother's cooking," said Grandmaman, smiling at Jacques.

"Yeah, you think he knows the difference," said Nora cajolingly.

"I hope you mind your manners, Jacques, when we go to the Reveillon. There'll be a lot of people there," said Nora.

"Of course he will. Stop picking on him Nora," said Grandmaman.

"King Dodo. He can do no wrong according to Grandmaman," said Nora, annoyed that Grandmaman was taking Jacques' side.

"Roland is driving us down to Longueuil for the Reveillon," said Pauline. "But we must plan on a snowy Christmas which might take us an hour to get there, hey!"

"We don't want to arrive at the Reveillon any later than one thirty, hey, because we have a lot of food to bring and set up," said Nora, a bit concerned.

"Well, that means we would have to leave here no later than twelve-thirty," said Grandmaman. "Midnight Mass at L'Eglise St. Denis doesn't end until about one fifteen. Besides, Jacques is the soloist this year for the Christmas Choir."

"We don't have to stay the whole Mass. We can leave around twelve-thirty or twelve-forty and I can go upstairs where the choir is and explain to Father Tournois that Jacques has to leave early to join the family Reveillon at Longueuil," said Nora, who didn't seem to fear the wrath of Father Tournois.

Jacques couldn't believe his ears. How could his mother have such little regard for the amount of practice, time and effort on his part and the part of Father Tournois and the church choir for such an important event involving the whole parish. In spite of his good manners and what he had been taught about not interrupting adults in conversation, Jacques felt compelled to argue his case.

"Maman, if you pull me out of the choir before the end of the Mass, I'll never be able to sing in the choir again. Father Tournois has devoted a lot of time training me for this event."

"Look, Jacques, it's either that or I'll visit Father Tournois tomorrow and tell him he has two weeks to find someone else to take your place. What will it be?"

"I don't think it's fair, Nora, to pull him out of the choir like that. Martin and Louella are driving to Longueuil in their own car and they could leave a little later and pick up Jacques right after Mass," said Pauline.

"I can't ask Lou to do that. Besides, why should they be inconvenienced because of Jacques' singing in the choir?" said Nora.

"I'd rather not go to the Reveillon than leave the choir, Maman," said Jacques.

"You'll go with us when we decide to go, Jacques, and that's that," said Nora.

"But I can sing with the Choir and then I can come back to the house and go to bed. Why can't I do that, Maman?"

"Listen Jacques. I'm your mother and while you're living in this house you will do as you're told, understand?"

"No, I don't understand how you can do this, and I'm not going to stay in this house if I can't stay in the choir," said Jacques angrily.

"What are you going to do, leave? Go ahead leave," said Nora defiantly, knowing that she had the upper hand.

"Fine," said Jacques, standing up. "And I'm not coming back."

Jacques stormed out the back door wearing only a sweater into subzero snowy weather. He was angry at his mother's disregard for his wants and even more so at her assuredness that he would not leave. He knew where he had to go, and that was to his aunt Louella who lived about five miles away. He was driven there only once, but he knew he could find her place, and he knew she would welcome him with open arms as she was his favorite aunt.

Jacques pulled up the collar of his shirt and pulled down the sleeves over his closed fists to keep his hands warm as he braved the cold wind and blinding snow. He knew he could make it or he would die trying, but there was no turning back, ever.

"It's been a half hour and Jacques' not back. Pauline, why don't you go out back and see if he's there and tell him to come back in," said Grandmaman.

"Alright Maman," said Pauline, putting on her boots, fur jacket and hat.

As Pauline left the house, Nora told her mother, "You know Maman, you spoil him too much. Now if he doesn't get his own way he goes into a tantrum, and I'm just not going to let him get away with it, and I wish you would not interfere, Maman. When he gets back in, I'm going to ground him for a week, no hockey, no playing outside."

"He's just a boy, Nora. Singing in that choir, especially as the soloist is an honor that he worked very hard to attain, and you capriciously swept aside his first major accomplishment. You have a lot yet to learn, Nora."

"He's my son, Maman."

"And may I remind you that this is my house, Nora, and Jacques is my grandson, and I'm not going to watch you make another serious mistake, not when it comes to my grandson."

The back door opened and Pauline entered, her hat and shoulders covered with snow. "I can't find him anywhere. I checked with Jean-Guy at his house and our new neighbors next door, the Carons, with whose son Marcel I saw Jacques playing a few days ago. But he just vanished."

"What about Pierrot; what's his family name?" said Nora.

"I think it's Bertrand. Yes, I believe it's Bertrand," said Grandmaman. "Look it up in the phone book, Nora, and let's call them because it's too far to walk over there in this weather."

While Nora was telephoning the Bertrands, Pauline discussed the various possibilities of Jacques' whereabouts with Grandmaman.

"I think I'll call Roland in case he went there. It's about a mile from here and Jacques knows where he lives," said Pauline.

"But Roland would have called us if Jacques had gone there," said Grandmaman.

"Where else could he have gone to? Louella lives about five or six miles from here and in this cold there's no way he would ever attempt to go there, and I'm not sure he even knows how to get there," said Pauline.

"Well, he's not at the Bertrand's," said Nora. "But Pierrot's mother said she would call us if he shows up there."

"It's nearly an hour since Jacques' been gone. I think I'm going to ask Roland to come over in his car, and Roland and I will ride around looking for him."

"He must be freezing, the poor kid," said Grandmaman, obviously worried.

"He didn't have to go out there; that was stupid. Why does he have to worry me so?" said Nora.

"He's never challenged your authority before Nora, and I don't think he ever wanted to, but you attempted to take away his self-esteem. I think Jacques is showing the early signs of manhood, independence. If I were you, I wouldn't push this issue any further when he returns," said Grandmaman.

"I deliberately kept Jacques from learning to play the piano or any other musical instrument because I don't want him to become a musician like his father. I want him to be a civil engineer or have some other respectable profession, not a womanizing musician. But in spite of all my efforts, his musical genes still found a way to manifest themselves in that choir. I'm afraid of where that might lead to, don't you understand Maman? I'm doing this for his own good."

"Quest sera, sera! He's at the age where you must cut the apron strings. Let him be who he is meant to be, Nora. We both love him, and we both want what's best for him."

The telephone rang and Nora answered it. "It's Lou," she said to Grandmaman. "Oh! He's there, thank God. Is he alright? Good. A good night's sleep will take care of him. So Martin will drive him back here tomorrow morning. Alright Lou, thanks for calling us right away. I'll talk to you tomorrow, goodnight."

"He was a very lucky boy; he could have frozen to death," said Grandmaman. "When he comes back here tomorrow, I don't want you to bring the matter up again. It's Christmas and in that spirit I will myself tell him that he's to give the performance of his life at Midnight Mass. Martin and Lou will pick him up afterwards for the Reveillon," said Grandmaman in a voice that Nora knew too well to challenge.

That Christmas eve, Jacques' voice was as clear as a bell and his high notes were effortless. His main concern was remembering the lyrics, especially those hymns in Latin which he was required to memorize. The choir master wanted him to sing without the aid of a music sheet, an arduous task for Jacques who couldn't understand Latin. To avoid embarrassment for both the choir and himself, Jacques had written each Latin hymn on narrow strips of paper which he had slipped inside his sleeve for instant retrieval into his palm when needed.

Downstairs in the main body of the church, packed to the limit with parishioners, sat Grandmaman, her three daughters, Martin and Roland. Grandpapa was still in the hospital and his condition was not improving.

"Listen to that beautiful voice Nora, he got it from you no doubt," whispered Grandmaman who was sitting next to her. "You should be proud of him."

"Yes, but his voice is due to change soon." Nora then thought about the singing career she had aspired to in New York City. *I could have been a singing star on the radio if I hadn't listened to Hercules.* "One musician in the family is enough," he had said to her. *Oh well, no sense harboring bitterness, life goes on.*

Jacques played ice hockey at the school's outdoor ice skating rink, even when temperatures were below zero. On his birthday in March, as usual, he had been playing hockey when he entered the Boivin residence in full hockey gear and skates, careful to stand on the indoor mat over the linoleum floor when he was greeted by his cousin Elaine who was accompanied by her fiancé Gus Davis.

"Jacques, this is your cousin Elaine; she's my sister Genevieve's daughter, and this is Gus, her fiancé. Gus is a Second Lieutenant in the U. S. Army stationed at the Quartermaster Corps in New York City and Elaine works for the War Department there," said Nora excitedly.

Jacques took off his big hockey gloves and his woolen beanie, then kissed Elaine on both cheeks and shook Gus' hand. "I'm very pleased to meet you," Jacques said in French, not knowing that Gus only spoke English.

"My God, your hockey gloves are so big; they look like boxing gloves. You know Jacques, Gus was the unofficial boxing champ at the University of California," said Elaine. "Maybe he can give you some tips, hey!"

Jacques was impressed by the clean-cut, all-American athletic appearance that Gus portrayed as a middleweight boxer and Jacques was anxious to learn all he could about boxing during Gus' short stay there. He soon learned that Gus could only speak and understand English, but Jacques had not completely forgotten the limited amount of English he had when he arrived in Montreal, and soon engaged Gus in a fragmented conversation about boxing, although Gus did most of the talking.

"It's very important to know how to close and hold your fist," said Gus to Jacques after some prodding by Jacques to give him some pointers.

"Close your right fist. Now bend your thumb over your index finger and your middle finger and make sure your thumb is tucked over them so you don't break it, that's it," said Gus, showing Jacques his closed fist in case Jacques didn't understand his English explanation.

"Now straighten out your wrist. The back of your fist should be straight in line with your forearm," said Gus, showing his own fist and forearm. "Good," said Gus.

"Now when you stand to face your opponent, keep both your fists up, clenched like I showed you. That's it. Now tuck your elbows in to protect your ribs. That's right. Good," said Gus, looking pleased.

"You're a quick study," commented Gus to Jacques.

"Now, never lead with your right. Use your left fist and jab your opponent wherever there's an opening. In the solar plexus," pointing to his stomach. "Or in the face," pointing to his nose.

"Now let me show you a combination," said Gus. Then Gus slowly moved his left fist resting it on Jacques' right kidney area. Then Gus withdrew his left fist and slowly moved it out again and placed it on Jacques' right cheek then withdrew it, then slowly threw his right fist directly to Jacques' chin. "That's the combination you should learn," said Gus.

"When you throw your left to his kidney, your opponent will drop his right arm lowering his right fist which will leave his head unprotected on that side. So you quickly throw our left again, this time to the right side of his face which should stun him long enough for you to then hit him with a straight right punch to the jaw or the nose. You can practice that combination on a punching bag. Hitting him on the nose will usually draw a lot of blood and that will have a devastating psychological effect on your opponent. Take it from me, I know," said Gus confidently.

"You know Jacques, you can give a boxer all the training in the world, but you can't improve his speed. That's something you're born with, and that's what distinguishes the winners from the losers."

Jacques was ever so grateful to Gus for that boxing lesson, as he knew that some day he would surely need it to defend himself against the bullies that are present in every school.

Gus stayed in the spare bedroom and Elaine stayed in Louella's former bedroom. This was not for mere appearances as Elaine was a devout Catholic with strong moral values and still a virgin. But three days later they were gone, back to New York, and Jacques would never see Gus again.

Soon spring followed winter and Jacques and his friends were busy chopping the ice from the sidewalks with axes to expose the cement for their wooden tops to spin against each other. Then that glorious but short summer arrived and Jacques decided to build a full size airplane. He had no plans, no tools and no materials, just a memory of one he had seen in a book at the school library and the rare occasion when one flew high over Montreal. Grandmaman would not allow him the use of Grandpapa's hammer because Jacques had previously used it to practice tomahawk throwing against a drawn bulls eye on the backyard fence nearly destroying it.

"Hey! Jacques, where're you going?" shouted Jean-Guy while descending the stairs to his upper apartment house.

"To the field next to the Ogilvy flour mill to see if I can pick up some scrap wood."

"Wait, I'll go with you," he said, catching up to Jacques.

"What are you going to do with it?" asked Jean-Guy.

"I'm going to build an airplane," Jacques replied in a serious tone.

"Really! That's a great idea, but what'll we use for tools?"

"We'll find a rock that has a flat edge to it and use that for a hammer. Then there are plenty of rusty nails lying on the ground and the last time I was there, I saw several orange crates where the workers at Ogilvy dump their trash. Don't worry, we'll find what we need."

Jacques and Jean-Guy worked that whole morning carrying two large planks from the field down to the lane that separated Jacques' back yard fence and the Carmelite Convent wall which stood three stories high and ran the length of a whole city block. Jacques often wondered what was hidden behind that immense wall that denied public access to the cloistered Carmelite nuns. The boys filled their pockets with rusty nails and brought one large wooden crate and a small one from discarded boxes left by Ogilvy employees. They also brought several pieces of wood of various sizes, one of which contained a knot in it near the center.

Jacques pounded at the knot with the sharp edge of his stone and knocked it out leaving a half-inch hole in the board. "That's where we'll put that short pipe through for the propeller shaft," said Jacques, and he proceeded to nail the board against the front of the larger orange crate. He then nailed the crate to the front of the long wooden, weathered plank.

"Jean-Guy, why don't you nail down the small crate right here," he said, pointing to the board about a foot back from the front crate. "That'll be the pilot seat, while I carve out the propeller," he said, pulling out his boy scout knife.

It wasn't long before they had a rough propeller installed against the pipe sticking out of the front crate with an inside handle adapted from a scrap metal rod which they had bent by inserting it into a crevice in the Carmelite wall. The tail had been nailed on, but had to be strengthened with the aid of metal coat hangers.

"It looks good," said Jean-Guy. "But what do we use for wheels?"

"That's easy," said Jacques. "We'll cut one of my roller skates in half and nail both halves underneath the front of the board as far apart as we can, and then we'll nail the other skate at the back of the board underneath the tail, et voila!"

"You sure have some imagination," said Jean-Guy admiringly. "But how are we going to cut your skate?"

"What we need is an ax," said Jacques, thinking and looking around for an alternative. "We could stick the skate upside down on the trolley tracks but I think the wheels are too wide…they would probably destroy the skate." Then Jacques and Jean-Guy noticed a blond straight-haired bespectacled boy about their age emerging from the neighbor's back yard.

"Bonjour, I'm Marcel Caron. We just moved in last week. Is that plane really going to fly?"

"We'll find out as soon as we get some wheels on it. You wouldn't happen to have an ax handy, by any chance?" asked Jacques. "Our parents have locked theirs up until next winter. By the way, I'm Jacques and this is Jean-Guy." They shook hands with each other.

"Let me see if there is one in our shed; I'll be right back," said Marcel.

A couple of minutes later, Marcel appeared with his father's ax, which he carefully handed to Jacques.

Jacques placed his skate upside down on a piece of scrap wood and with a measured swing of the ax, split the skate into two halves. He then thankfully returned the ax to Marcel and proceeded to hammer the two halves to the front, underneath the board which ran the length of the fuselage. The front wings had not yet been installed. Jean-Guy and Jacques then picked up the largest and widest weathered plank they had found and nailed its center to the top of the orange crate, giving it a fourteen feet wing span. In addition, they ran two pieces of old rusty wire from the tip of the wings to the bottom of the crate at the center cockpit.

The two boys then pushed the airplane to the center of the cement paved lane which was to serve as the runway, with Marcel looking on. They stood there for a moment admiring their creation. Suddenly their reverie was broken by the sudden appearance of Grandmaman who had opened the door to the backyard's wooden fence to see what all the commotion was about.

"Did you build this yourself, Jacques?" asked Grandmaman.

"No, Jean-Guy helped me."

Grandmaman stared at the airplane for a moment then asked, "What did you use to build it with?"

"Well, we used this rock for a hammer, and we straightened out a bunch of rusty nails that we found in the field, and nailed together scrap wood and boxes, and now we're ready for takeoff." said Jacques, hoping that she would not notice the roller skates underneath the fuselage.

"Hey! Bien! Jean-Guy, you be the pilot and I'll push the plane," said Jacques with exuberance.

Jean-Guy sat on the small box seat, and turned the handle from inside the front crate causing the propeller to rotate. "OK, ready for takeoff," yelled Jean-Guy.

"Can I help push the plane?" asked Marcel pleadingly.

"Sure, you grab the left side of the plane and I'll grab the right."

Grandmaman looked incredulously at these boys as if they were the Wright Brothers, and so confident was Jacques' demeanor that she half expected the plane might just take off.

"Alright," yelled Jacques. "Let's start pushing." The plane started moving forward slowly at first, then it began to pick up speed as Marcel and Jacques were running, pushing the plane ever faster while Jean-Guy was frantically hand turning the propeller.

Had their hopes had any lifting power, the airplane would have soared, but alas, the airplane never left the ground, although it traveled the entire length of the lane. The boys pushed the plane back to its departure point with Grandmaman looking on. Jacques then walked towards her, still breathing hard from the effort.

"I guess it needs a motor, hey!" Jacques said, laughing.

"Never mind, Jacques, that was quite an accomplishment. Someday you will do something really great; I just know it." She smiled at him and returned to the house.

"Well, the plane won't fly," said Jean-Guy. "But it rides nice. What do we do with it now?"

"We can't get it into my yard because of its wings. So let's remove the wings and we'll use the fuselage as a scooter," said Jacques.

"That's a great idea," said Jean-Guy with Marcel agreeing, and they all got busy transforming the airplane into a scooter.

Suddenly, Jacques heard the doorbell to his Grandmother's house ring and then heard talking from within. Curious as to who would be visiting them at this hour, Jacques walked to the back door of the house and heard Grandmaman telling the iceman to bring in one block of ice for the icebox. Jacques quickly ran back to the back yard and summoned his two friends.

"Hey guys, the iceman is here. Let's go to the street out front where the ice carriage is and pick up some pieces of ice to chew on." The three of them excused themselves as they entered the house past Grandmaman and out into the street in front of the house. Sure enough, there was a large four-wheel cart pulled by a horse, standing at the curb with the back panel of the cart open. The iceman wore a rubber apron and with a large metal pincer, grabbed a block of ice about one square foot in size which he pulled from the carriage and carried into Grandmaman's house for deposit into her icebox. While the iceman was inside the house, Jacques and his two friends grabbed several small pieces of ice that had broken off the ice blocks and went over to Jean-Guy's stoop where they sat and chewed on their frozen booty. As they sat there, a boy of about 12 years of age climbed out of the cab of the carriage to meet with the iceman, who now had exited Grandmaman's residence with his empty pincer, and pointed to Jacques and his friends with his deformed, miniaturized hand that had only three small fingers.

"I think the kid is turning us in for stealing some ice chips," exclaimed Jean-Guy.

"Yeah! Did you see his hand?" said Marcel .

"Both of his hands are deformed," said Jacques. "I've never seen anything like it."

"Boy! I wonder how he got that way?" said Marcel .

"I guess he was born that way. A freak of nature I guess," said Jean-Guy.

Yes, they all thought. *We are sure glad it didn't happen to any of us. Nature can be cruel.*

The iceman ignored the kids and both he and his son got back into the carriage and ordered the horse to move on.

Jacques left his friends and entered the house and told Grandmaman about the boy with the deformed hands.

"You should have seen his hands, Grandmaman. Both of his hands were really small and he had only three small fingers on each hand. How can that be Grandmaman?"

asked Jacques with incredulity.

"Apparently this is the first time you have seen anyone with a handicap, Jacques. Well, let me tell you that life can be very unjust to some people and children especially. And it is usually children that are the most cruel to them because they do not understand God's plan that tests those who are exposed to the handicap as well as the handicapped children of this world. You must never make fun of someone like that Jacques, or else God will punish you and make you the same way. Instead, you should be kind to them and help them through their ordeal. I want you to always remember that Jacques." Indeed, Jacques remembered those words for the rest of his life.

That summer was filled with activities that boys thrive on, such as Jacques' trip with Roland to the family cottage at St. Emile, sixty miles north of Montreal to help Roland build a short road from the cottage to the main country road. After three days of fighting the huge Canadian mosquitoes, Jacques had to be driven back to Montreal because the mosquitoes had bitten his eyelids so bad, they swelled shut after assaulting the rest of his uncovered body.

Upon his recovery from the mosquito assault, Jacques then returned to the family cottage at St. Emile near the Lake of Fourteen Islands where a Boy Scout camp was located. When Jacques returned home to the city, he discovered that all of his friends but Marcel were vacationing with their family. Bored, Jacques went to call upon Marcel who lived next door at the upper apartment. He rang the doorbell, hoping Marcel would be at home, but a blue eyed, blonde-haired girl of Jacques' age answered the door.

"Are you looking for Marcel?" she asked quizzingly.

"Yes, is he here?" asked Jacques, admiring her beautiful features without appearing to do so.

"Yes, please come in," she said, opening the door wider, allowing Jacques to enter into the vestibule. "I'm his sister Juliette," she added. "I'll get my brother for you."

Jacques watched Juliette's long blonde hair flowing over her shoulders as she pranced away and realized how pleasurable she was and how isolated he had been all of his young life from girls his age, attending all boys' schools. He wanted to see more of her, but Marcel showed up, alone.

"Hiya Jacques, I see you're back from the country. I'm glad you came over because my sister is driving me crazy. Let's get out of here."

As they walked out of Marcel's house and down the wooden stairs to the street below, Jacques suggested that they go to the Convent of the Carmelites which was protected by the gigantic, large wall running the entire length of the lane in back of their houses.

"Let's go to the Carmelites' convent and buy a bag of host cuttings, it's only a nickel," said Jacques.

"You mean the bread of the Eucharist?" replied Marcel.

"Yeah! It comes in white sheets from which they punch out the circular hosts, and that's what you get at communion. What's left from those sheets they put into paper bags and sell for a nickel."

"Are those leftovers blessed too?" asked Marcel.

"I don't think so, but they taste just the same. I love it."

"But I didn't bring any money with me," complained Marcel.

"That's OK, I've got a dime, enough for two bags," replied Jacques.

Upon arrival at the Convent of the Carmelites, Jacques opened the unlocked door and entered the small vestibule followed by Marcel. To the left of a small corridor was a window with a basket weave sliding door through which you could barely see shadows. There was a hand bell sitting on its ledge. Jacques rang the bell and in an instant the window door slid open, revealing one of the novice Carmelites who had not yet taken her vows and was therefore permitted to be seen and act as liaison between the Carmelites and the public.

"What can I do for you boys?" she asked.

"We'd like to buy two bags of host cuttings, please," answered Jacques.

The sister looked at Jacques curiously. "You've been here before to purchase host cuttings, haven't you?" she said smilingly.

"Yes," nodding his head.

"Perhaps you'd like to become a priest someday," she said quizzingly. "You'd then get more than just cuttings; you'd receive the blessed host each and every morning, wouldn't you like that?" she asked.

Jacques knew that he had a lot more of life to explore, especially after meeting Juliette, before he could settle for the reclusiveness of the priesthood. "Thank you sister, but I think I'll stick to the cuttings for now."

The Sister smiled at the two boys and left for a moment then returned with two brown paper bags full of host cuttings. Jacques gave her a dime, thanked the sister and the boys left. As they were walking down the street eating the host cuttings, Marcel asked Jacques, "Did you ever think of becoming a priest?"

"No, not me. I think it takes a special person. You have to receive the call from God," answered Jacques.

"You really believe that?" replied Marcel. "My father told me that influential families hide their handicapped relatives from the public by encouraging them and even forcing them to enter convents or monasteries."

"Maybe that's true in some cases, but the majority of people in the clergy are there to serve God," answered Jacques.

"Oh! Yeah. Just look at Sister Agnes. Who'd want to marry that old witch? And Brother Etienne at Ecole St. Denis, he has six toes and three fingers and walks like the hunchback of Notre Dame; how would you like to have him for a father?" said Marcel sarcastically.

"You should never make fun of people's handicaps, less you end up just like them," Jacques replied, remembering his Grandmother's warning.

"I've never seen Brother Etienne use the strap or the blackboard pointer on any of his students like some of the others," added Jacques.

"Yeah! That's because they're all scared to death of him," retorted Marcel.

"If you'd only get over your fear of him and talked to him just once after class, you'd find him to be the kindest and most helpful teacher in school."

"Hey! Maybe you can put in a good word for me then, 'cause I don't do so well in his class," replied Marcel.

"I won't be there this fall," said Jacques.

"What do you mean you won't be there this fall? Where're you going?"

"I just found out yesterday. My mother is sending me to boarding school."

"You're kidding, really. Where?"

"At the College Saint-Paul in Varennes. It's on the other side of the St. Lawrence river about fifty miles north of Montreal, maybe further."

"You don't look too happy about it; do you have to go Jacques?"

"I've got no choice. My Grandfather is terminally ill and my Grandmother's health is not great either, and my mother is joining her sister Genevieve in the United States to see what job opportunities are out there. But I hear that it's a great high school with a terrific hockey team; besides, Patrick O'Reilly is going too, so at least I'll know someone there."

"Who's Patrick O'Reilly?"

"Oh! He and his widowed father live next door to ma Tante Lu-Lu. That's my aunt Louella," said Jacques laughingly.

"So Jean-Guy and Pierrot don't know you're leaving in the fall, then."

"No, they don't."

"Boy, we're all going to miss you Jacques."

"Not half as much as I'm going to miss you guys," replied Jacques, arriving at the bottom of the wooden stairway leading up to Marcel's residence. The door opened and Juliette hesitantly walked down the stairs towards them.

"What are you guys eating?" she said with a mischievous smile.

"Host cuttings," replied Marcel nonchalantly.

"Can I taste it?" she asked her brother.

"I hardly have any left," he replied, a bit annoyed.

"You can have some of mine," said Jacques, extending his opened bag to her admiringly.

"Thanks," she said and reached into the bag and pulled out a long cutting which she broke off with a laugh.

Jacques admired her perfect, unblemished skin and rosy cheeks. He felt he could look into her big blue eyes forever. He knew she was the love of his young life, and in barely four weeks summer would be over and he would be leaving for boarding school. Jacques suddenly felt very sad and became silent, just watching her placing pieces of host cuttings on her tongue as if repeatedly receiving communion. She looked so beautifully pure and angelic.

Suddenly, a black 1936 Royal Chrysler convertible pulled up to the curb and stopped. It was Aunt Pauline with her fiancé Roland.

As they walked towards the Boivin residence, they greeted Jacques and his friends, and Pauline called out to Jacques.

"Dinner will be ready soon Jacques, so why don't you come on in and clean up before dinner, oui?"

"OK! Pat, I'll be right over," said Jacques, reluctant to leave his newfound love.

"Here," said Jacques giving his bag of host cuttings to Juliette. "I've got to go in. I'll see you Marcel." And he left without looking back.

Juliette's angelic face kept Jacques company through the first hours of the night, followed by an erotic dream which seemed so real when he awoke that morning with the scent of his spent passion.

After breakfast that day, Jacques went out to find his friends and noticed that Jean-Guy, Pierrot and Marcel were sitting on Jean-Guy's outside stairway, talking to two teenagers that Jacques had never seen before. One of them was tall and burly; the other was short and stocky. Jacques approached them and Jean-Guy introduced him to the two newcomers.

"Meet Robert and Maurice," Jean-Guy said to Jacques, motioning to the tall black haired teenager and the short light haired one respectively. They didn't hold out their hand in customary friendship and Jacques felt that they were sizing him up, especially the tall one, which made Jacques feel uncomfortable. Jacques sat next to Marcel on one of the steps and listened to the continued conversation between the boys.

"Robert and Maurice were visiting Robert's father who works at the flour mill across the street where my father works, ain't that a coincidence?" said Jean-Guy to Jacques.

Jacques nodded his head affirmatively, but didn't say anything. He sensed that Robert was a trouble maker, a bully. He didn't like his demeanor and wished that he and his friend would just go away.

At that moment Robert, who was standing facing the stairs, turned his gaze to his right and a grin came over his face as he stared at Juliette descending the stairs to her house. Juliette paid no attention to the boys as she turned and walked in the opposite direction.

"Hey! She's not bad, that petite peteuse ('little farter' referring to her derriere). Has she got a name?"

"That's Marcel's sister Juliette," said Jean-Guy to Robert.

"Oh! Yeah!...Hey! How about introducing her to me?" said Robert to Marcel with a devilish grin.

Marcel remained silent, afraid to say anything that might provoke Robert into a fight which Marcel felt sure Robert would enjoy abusing him with his greater weight and height. Marcel never had a fight in his young life. His father was a professional pianist and organist and his mother was a kind, soft-spoken homemaker who created an atmosphere of love throughout the household. There simply was no room in their lives for altercations. Marcel was an intelligent, talented and sensitive young man whose temperament would never entertain his involvement in a fist fight.

Marcel's silence irritated Robert who stepped closer to the stairs where Marcel was seated in between Pierrot and Jacques.

"Whatsa matter, ain't I good enough for her?"

Jacques sensed Marcel's fear of Robert and his reluctance to answer him confirmed it. Jacques' feelings for Juliette and her brother Marcel compelled him to react to Robert's threat in spite of Jacques' fear of him.

"Why don't you leave him alone," said Jacques to Robert in a firm but non-threatening voice.

"You going to make me, curly?" asked Robert, looking directly at Jacques.

Jacques understood the implication that his curly hair was a sign of femininity, weakness.

"Look, we're not looking for a fight, so why don't you just go back to your own neighborhood," said Jacques.

"Whatsa matter, you're too yellow to fight me?"

Jacques' fear turned to anger. He sprung from where he was sitting to the pavement clearing three steps, then facing Robert, he remembered the punch combination he had learned from Gus, but he realized this guy might be too big to test such a close range, untested tactic. He thought it might be more effective, if not safer, to test the French Savate used by one his adventure heroes, which required agility but was devastatingly effective, in the stories at least. He thought it was worth a try.

Marcel was relieved that Robert's attention was now on Jacques and although he detested fighting, he admired Jacques for his courage and survival instincts, and dearly wanted to see Robert pulverized.

Jean-Guy and Pierrot stood next to Robert's friend Maurice to keep him from interfering with the bout. As Jacques' friends they knew of Jacques' dislike for conflict, but relished the opportunity to observe his swiftness in action.

Robert threw a round house with his right fist missing Jacques who had ducked under it throwing a left jab to Robert's stomach, then he withdrew quickly to avoid a left punch from Robert who seemed unaffected by the stomach blow. Jacques stepped quickly aside to avoid a rushing left punch, then followed up with a right punch to Robert's kidney, then stepped back to evaluate his opponent. Robert was grinning, moving his fists in circles, when Jacques took three quick steps towards Robert then leaped high into the air with both feet tucked in which he suddenly straightened out, hitting Robert squarely on the chest. The impact drove Robert back off his feet, hitting the sidewalk flat on his back with his head hitting the pavement. Following the impact, Jacques' feet landed him firmly upright like a cat, ready for further battle. But Robert wasn't getting up. Instead he was moaning and his friend Maurice went to attend to him.

Jacques stood there hoping he hadn't caused Robert any serious injury. Marcel came to his side and reassured Jacques that Robert deserved it, when Robert finally got off the ground with the help of Maurice. Robert looked in Jacques' direction in quiet disbelief of what had happened, then turned around and started to walk away in the company of Maurice.

"Wow! Where did you learn that move?" asked Pierrot with Jean-Guy and Marcel looking on in admiration.

"I read about it; it's called a 'savate'," answered Jacques, a bit embarrassed at all the attention.

"Hey! You got to teach me how to do it," said Pierrot as they all started to walk away towards Jacques' house. But Jacques had no intention of teaching him since he himself would be reluctant to use it again; he might have killed Robert and for a moment he thought he had. He remembered reading in the newspapers about the kid who punched another kid causing him to hit his head on the doorknob of his front door resulting in his death. *No*, he thought, *I've got to stay out of fights.*

The next day Jacques came in for lunch and Grandmaman was especially buoyant as she served Jacques his soup and sandwich.

"Mrs. Caron next door told me this morning all about your fight with that big bully, to save Juliette's honor. I want you to know that I'm really proud of you Jacques," said Grandmaman, looking at him with a warm smile.

"It was nothing Grandmaman, and it was not to save Juliette's honor," said Jacques, embarrassed by the implication.

"Don't be modest, Jacot. You were called upon to exercise your talents to fight evil, and you responded to that call admirably. You know Jacques, we all have a duty in life. Those who are endowed with strength are duty bound to protect the weak, the healthy to help the sick, the rich to help the poor, the smart to help those who are handicapped. That is your solemn duty Jacques, never forget it." Then she walked over to Jacques and gave him a big hug because she loved her 'petit friser'.

A week later, Juliette left Montreal to enter her first year at an all girls' school in Sherbrook, to the dismay of Jacques who had not had a chance to get acquainted with the first love of his life. She departed quietly one morning by car with her parents without saying 'au revoir' to Jacques, apparently unaware of Jacques' feelings for her.

That afternoon, Nora returned from shopping. No one was inside the house except Grandmaman who was baking a chocolate cake.

"Where is Jacques, Maman?" asked Nora.

"He's sitting on the back porch. I've been watching him from the kitchen window. The poor kid's heart is broken over Juliette's departure. So I decided I'd bake him a chocolate cake to cheer him up."

"You know Maman, he'll be leaving also for St. Paul College in two weeks. I feel that now is the time to tell him the truth about his father."

"He just lost his first girlfriend, maybe this is not the right time, Nora."

"I'll be leaving for New York City shortly after he enters boarding school; I'll be gone for about nine months and won't have a chance to explain things and he'll be that much older without knowing the truth. I just can't wait any longer, Maman."

"Well I suppose some things can't wait for ideal conditions. But be gentle with him; he's a lot more sensitive than he lets on."

Nora opened the kitchen door and stepped onto the back porch overlooking the back yard. Jacques was sitting on the porch steps with his chin resting on his right fist.

"You look like Rodin's statue of the 'thinker'—a penny for your thoughts, Jacques."

"Hello Maman," said Jacques, not looking up.

"I know how you feel Jacot; it's your first love. We all feel that way the first time, but it's just an adolescent infatuation. A week after you have entered St. Paul College, you'll forget all about her, and there will be plenty of other girls in your life, you'll see 'mon cher'."

"Maman, I really don't want to talk about her, alright?"

"Alright Jacques, but there is something important that I do want to talk to you about. While you're attending boarding school at Varennes, I'll be working in New York City, but I'll be back for the summer to be with you. In the meantime, I'll write to you every week and I'll send you an allowance, OK?"

"You're going away to New York?"

"Oui, mon cher. There are more job opportunities and the pay is better in New York. You'll be busy studying and playing hockey and by the end of the school term we'll be together again."

Jacques said nothing. He knew that his mother loved him and was doing what was best for the both of them.

"Jacques, you remember a long time ago I told you that your father had died of double pneumonia?"

"Yes," said Jacques, looking up at his mother.

"Well, I think that now you're old enough to understand the truth. Your father is not dead, Jacques. He left us when you were very young."

Jacques took the news with unusual calm. "Where is he living now?"

"Somewhere in New York City. I don't know exactly. I have had no contact with him or his family since your father's mother died. She was my only friend in that family."

"Why did he leave us, Maman?"

Nora thought for a moment, wondering if Jacques was old enough to handle that much truth. His outward calmness gratified her. *Yes*, she thought, *he has the inner strength of the Boivin blood line, even at such a tender age.*

"Your father left us for another woman, Jacques. He was a man of great musical talent, but with a destructive weakness for women. The music profession reeks with lustful temptations. Your father ruined his musical career over women. It's a real shame. We moved to Montreal because Grandpapa and Grandmaman were the only people who would help me raise you. But now Grandpapa is terminally ill and Grandmaman's health is also failing. That's why I entered you into boarding school while I look for a good job in New York City to support us, Jacques."

"Do you have a picture of my father, Maman?"

"I have just one, Jacques. I destroyed all the others. I was very upset you know."

Nora had anticipated Jacques' request and retrieved from her purse a small 3x5 photograph depicting a stocky Italian-American man of about thirty dressed in a light colored suit holding a small curly blond-haired boy in his arms.

"That was taken in the backyard of our apartment in Brooklyn, Jacques," said Nora.

Jacques studied the picture very carefully. He couldn't remember his father. He wondered what sort of a man he was. *It doesn't matter now*, he thought. He handed the photograph back to Nora without saying a word. Two weeks later, Jacques, accompanied by his mother and his aunt Pauline, was driven by Roland in his 1936 black Royal Chrysler to St. Paul College situated along the eastern shore of the St. Lawrence river about 60 miles north of Montreal.

College was the term used to describe a secondary school in the Quebec province. Jacques was now thirteen and the year was 1944. He was aware of the World War with Germany and Japan from newspaper and radio reports on the allies' progress, but he had attended only one public movie in his entire young life. That was because Snow White and the Seven Dwarfs was excluded from the prohibition enacted by the Canadian government against all children under the age of sixteen from attending public theatres. This was the result of a terrible theatre fire at Halifax which claimed the lives of more than five hundred children. But schools occasionally showed classic French movies to its students but nothing about the war.

As they drove north along the shore of the St. Lawrence River, Jacques observed the flat land to his right and the smell of horse manure commonly used as soil fertilizer. It was all farmland, toiled by unmechanized labor. As they approached a small village, Roland announced their arrival at Varennes. St. Paul College was the only large building in the small village, and appeared almost immediately. Its façade overlooked the St. Lawrence River with the main road separating its deep front yard from the shoreline. The building was four stories high and very wide. Two circled cement stairways met at the large front entrance. Classes were not in session yet, and the bulk of the student body had not yet arrived.

"You're going to love it here Jacques, it's a wonderful school, and what a location, hey!" said Nora.

"Yeah! Jacques, the Christian Brothers are excellent teachers, hey!" said Pauline.

Jacques remained silent, observing his surroundings while Roland luckily found a parking space near the front of the college. They all exited the car and Roland handed Jacques one of his two suitcases from the trunk.

"Well Jacques, this should be an interesting experience for you. Make the most of it because before you know it, you'll be graduating and then have to work like the rest of us," said Roland half jokingly.

Nora entered the front lobby of the college followed by her sister Pauline, then Jacques and Roland, each carrying a suitcase.

They were immediately met by a soft spoken Christian Brother of medium height and build, wearing the habitual black robe with the split tab on white collar.

"I'm Brother Michel," he announced with a slight bow and a handshake to Nora.

"I'm Mrs. Markham and this is my son Jacques whom I'm placing under your good care," said Nora with a smile. She then added, "And this is my sister Pauline and her fiancé Roland."

Brother Michel gave a slight bow again as he shook their hands.

"You may leave Jacques' suitcases here," Brother Michel said, pointing to a corner of the room. "As soon as you have said your goodbyes to your family Jacques, I will show you to your quarters."

Jacques placed his suitcase down in the corner and Roland placed the other one next to it, then stood facing Jacques and shook his hand vigorously in genuine friendship.

Pauline then came over and kissed Jacques on the cheeks and hugged him. "You be good and study hard, uui!" she said with a smile.

Jacques looked at Nora with a longing for the only home he had known, in Montreal with Grandmaman. He felt sad, almost abandoned, but he knew that there were no choices, and he would have to make the best of it.

Nora looked up at Jacques who was now taller than her, and said, "I love you Jacques, Bien Gros." She kissed him on the lips and hugged him. Nora then looked up at Jacques again, this time with tears in her eyes and said, "It'll only be for nine months, then you'll be back in Montreal with us. Time will go quickly, you'll see, Jacot. I'll write to you often, oui mon cher." Nora kissed him again, then turned with her head down and walked out of the lobby followed by Aunt Pauline and Roland who waved goodbye.

Jacques walked to the window and watched as they boarded Roland's car and drove away. He felt emptiness. *Will I ever see them again?* he asked himself. *Of course,* he thought. *In any event, I'd better get used to the idea of being on my own, at least for the next nine months anyway.* Jacques took a deep breath as he turned around, and to his surprise noticed Brother Michel quietly standing there near Jacques' suitcases, patiently waiting for him.

"Well, young man, are you ready to see your new home?" said Brother Michel.

"Indeed I am Sir," replied Jacques as he grabbed both his suitcases and followed Brother Michel down a long corridor towards the staircase that led to the dormitory on the fourth floor.

Brother Michel started up the stairs without offering Jacques any assistance with his two suitcases. "The dormitory is on the top floor which houses about one hundred and fifty students," said Brother Michel matter-of-factly.

Jacques did not want to show Brother Michel the enormous effort he had to make to carry the two large suitcases which were pulling at every muscle in his young, immature body, for fear that he would not meet Brother Michel's apparent expectations. Thus he did not reply.

When they reached the top floor, Jacques observed that the dormitory was well-lit by the sunlight which entered through the many large windows facing the St. Lawrence River, and the opposing wall overlooking the school playground. The floors were made of hardwood and the metal spring beds were lined up in rows, military style. In front of each bed was a wooden foot locker painted dark green. There was a square open space at the center of the dormitory which contained a foot high dais upon which sat a large rocking chair. On the dais floor next to it sat a large brass hand bell.

As Brother Michel led the way down the middle aisle past the dais he pointed his left hand towards the rocking chair.

"That's where the Brother in charge of the dormitory sits at bedtime to insure that silence is maintained. The bell is used to wake you up each morning, and you have twenty minutes to wash up, get dressed and be ready to go to the dining hall which is located on the basement floor adjacent to the indoor recreation room."

Brother Michel stopped for a couple of seconds, then turned to his right, walked up to the third aisle and turned around facing Jacques.

"This is your bed for the remainder of your stay here. Note the number on the footlocker, number 35. There are no locks on any of the lockers; there's no need of them here. Larceny is extremely rare and is severely punished when found. I hope that you will learn a great deal during your stay here. It's all up to you. You can unpack your things and put your suitcases under your bed for the time being. There's a wall locker with the same number on it over there." He pointed to the south wall "For those clothes you want to hang. When you're through settling in, come downstairs to the recreation room until supper time." Having said that, Brother Michel turned around and exited the dormitory.

Jacques opened the footlocker and found that it contained an upper insert to put things such as his toilet articles and other non-clothing items. His only valuable was a spring loaded watch given to him by his mother on his last birthday. The insert could be removed simply by lifting it out of the foot locker, revealing a rather large area for folded or rolled underclothing.

Jacques thought, *this is only Friday and school doesn't start until Monday, no wonder there's no one here, at least not in the dormitory. Maybe those who are already here are in the recreation area.*

Jacques hurriedly opened his suitcases and unpacked them in a neat, organized manner as was his customary habit of doing things. He was curious as to whether the students occupying the bunks on either side of him had already arrived, and was tempted to find out by opening their footlockers to see if they had been filled, but thought better of it, less someone think that he may be committing a theft or invading their privacy. *No*, he thought, *I'll simply have to wait and see who is in the recreation room and who will be joining him for supper. Maybe Patrick O'Reilly has arrived.* But Jacques thought it more likely that his father would bring him to the school on Sunday afternoon.

As Jacques entered the recreation room, he was surprised to find several boys playing games he had never seen before. There must have been at least thirty newly arrived students occupied with games and another two dozen engaged in conversation and reading activities. Before descending to the bottom step, Jacques surveyed the entire recreation room and as expected, he did not see Patrick O'Reilly. Jacques decided to observe at close range the games being played and then get involved in the action as a way of meeting his newly found classmates. There were three pool tables, a couple of ping pong tables, at least four shuffle board tables and a punching bag in one of the corners of the recreation room. Jacques walked over to one of the occupied shuffle boards to see how the game was played.

As Jacques was standing by the shuffle board watching two boys sliding their wooden disks towards each other's goal, one of the boys also watching from the other side of the shuffle board appeared more interested in Jacques' presence.

"'Hi! I'm Claude. Just arrived have you?"

"Yes," answered Jacques, looking at Claude quickly then returning his gaze at the shuffle board action. Claude was a couple of inches shorter than Jacques, but had a stocky, muscular build that one usually attains from lifting weights. His unruly, thick black hair resembled a mop that simply could not be combed.

"I'm new too. I got here two days ago, and Brother Antoine gave me a tour of the school. My father knows Brother Antoine's father from their school days."

"Nothing like having political connections," cried one of the shuffle board players, overhearing the conversation.

"Do you know what the school schedule is like?" asked Jacques of Claude.

"As a matter of fact, I do," said Claude with self-importance, hoping that others would also lend an ear to his privileged knowledge, not realizing the presence of senior classmates in the recreation room.

"First we suffer the shock of being awakened by the loud bell of the dormitory Brother-on-Duty who takes copious notes of any stragglers who don't get themselves ready with their bed made up to standards within a total, and I mean a total of twenty minutes," said Claude with emphasis, expecting some kind of a reaction from Jacques who remained non-expressive.

"Then we all assemble into the dining room for the usual breakfast of rolled oats, milk, toast and Chinese tea," said Claude.

"Chinese tea," exclaimed one of the shuffle board players. "How do you know it's Chinese?"

"Because it tastes the same as the tea that is always served in a Chinese restaurant where my parents have sometimes taken me. It's served from a metal kettle into a little cup, plain, no milk or sugar added, just like the Chinese do," said Claude, who had already eaten in the school dining room for the past two days.

"So what happens after that?" said Jacques.

"Well, you can't leave the dining room until the Brothers dismiss us. Then we have half an hour to spend in the recreation room," said Claude.

"Or in the shit house," added the shuffle board player. "Yeah! And you'd better do it then, because the brothers don't like you to do it during the study period or when in class."

"How do you know so much?" inquired Claude of the shuffle board player.

"Because I was here last year junior," replied the shuffle board player.

"Well, what happens if you have to go?" asked Claude.

"You do it once and the Brother might let you go. But if you make a habit of it then he might just let you piss in your pants." said the shuffle board player. "It also depends on which Brother is on *guard* duty," he added.

"You make it sound like we're in a prison," protested Claude.

"The discipline and the penalties for disobedience are just as harsh. You'll find out soon enough," announced the shuffle board player, who then turned his attention to Jacques who had been quietly but attentively listening to the conversation. "My name is Hubert," he said, extending his right hand to Jacques in a friendly gesture.

Hubert was one year older than Jacques and Claude and of course one year ahead of them academically. Hubert had a large, well-padded frame, but was built like a pear; not athletically inclined, but compelled to participate in sports by the enforced school sports schedule and rules.

"I'm Jacques. Do they play a lot of hockey here?"

"From December through May you'll be playing hockey every waking moment that you're not in class or the study hall. Hell, we the students build the three hockey rinks right out there on the school playground. We play after class, and in the evenings as well," said Hubert.

"At night!" exclaimed Claude. "Don't tell me that we have to install flood lights too."

"No, you idiot. They're permanently mounted on telephone poles. But we have to erect the wooden sides to all three rinks, and then when the first full snow falls, the entire school marches over the snow in all three rinks to mat it down. Then the brothers volunteer several of us to take turns watering the snow at nighttime when it's real cold, with fire hoses."

"Sacre Bleu! It must get to twenty below zero at night here," said Claude.

"More like thirty and forty below zero with the wind off the St. Lawrence River," added Hubert. "It's alright when you're moving playing hockey, but when you're stationary, pouring ice-cold water on the packed snow for a couple of hours, the tip of your feet and fingers start to hurt."

"But you must get relief, right," said Claude.

"Oh! Yeah!" replied Hubert. "The next shift of boys comes on to relieve you, and so do the Brothers who are always there to supervise and make sure that it's done right. But it takes two or three nights of hosing to get all the bumps off and get a nice even rink."

"What about the blue and red lines? Do they get those game lines under the ice?" asked Jacques.

"Sure we do. The rinks are the same as the one in the Forum in Montreal," grinned Hubert. "Well, almost. Hey! They're regulation size rinks, and we do play other schools you know."

"You play hockey, Jacques?" asked Hubert.

"Yeah! I've played some," replied Jacques modestly.

"How about you, Claude?" asked Hubert.

"Oh! Yeah! I've been playing hockey since I was five," replied Claude.

"Well, you must be pretty good, hey!" said Hubert. "What position you play?"

"Center or left wing, whichever is needed," replied Claude.

"Well, we'll see when you cut the ice in December," said Hubert.

"Yeah! I can't wait," said Claude eagerly.

Just then, a loud bell went off and a Christian Brother motioned to all the students that it was time to go to the library for an hour before retiring to the dormitory.

"Normally if this was a school day, we would now be going to the study hall to do our homework and study our assigned lessons. But since school hasn't officially started yet, they're sending us to the library to get acquainted with it," said Hubert.

"Not a bad idea," said Jacques who loved to read books of all sorts.

The school library located on the second floor next to the Chapel was of modest size, but every shelf was filled to capacity with hardcover books, all in the French language. Upon entering the library, Jacques became thrilled at the prospect of having access to such a literary treasure. He spent that hour perusing through the library looking for books of interest which he would later enjoy reading. He was especially interested in adventure stories, preferably of epic proportions. Jacques was an especially fast reader for his age, having consistently placed first in reading and writing at previous schools.

Jacques entered the dormitory on the fourth floor with the other students and went to his assigned bed consisting of a metal frame with stretched metal springs upon which lay a four-inch mattress. Clean sheets covered by a dark green colored blanket completed the bed with a pillow at its head. Jacques, as did the other students, went to his wall locker and hung up his clothes and dressed only in his underwear shorts and shirt, took out his soap dish from his footlocker and the towel hung at the foot of the bed and went to the community wash basin at the north end of the dormitory.

Jacques made his way to one of the faucets extending from a long water pipe stretching a good fifty feet over a narrow metal basin of equal length with faucets extending out on both sides of the water pipe to accommodate students on both sides of the basin. With soap in hand, Jacques washed his face and brushed his teeth alongside the other students, when an apparently older student of large build shoved the student across the basin from Jacques out of the way and took his place at the basin. Jacques felt the fear expressed on the face of the victimized student who would not dare challenge this obviously bigger and mean adversary. The poor kid simply moved over behind another student who appeared nearly finished at the basin. Jacques made a mental note of avoiding this bully, but suspected that sooner or later he would have the unpleasant task of facing him as he knew that his conscience would not allow him to stand idly by in the presence of abuse of power. As Jacques was leaving the wash basin, the student who had been washing himself next to him accosted Jacques and in a whispering voice said, "That was Yves the *bear*. He likes to push freshman around. I noticed you gave him a serious look, but stay clear of him, he's trouble."

"Thanks for the warning. My name is Jacques. What's yours?"

"Alain," replied the tall, skinny, bespectacled freshman.

"See you around Alain," said Jacques, carrying his bag of toilet articles and towel.

Jacques got back to his bunk and exchanged greetings with Claude whose bunk was to his right ,and Maurice on the second bunk to his left, when suddenly they heard the sound of the hand bell being waved by Brother Etienne who was standing on the dais at the center of the dormitory near the head of the stairway leading to the lower floors.

"Silence," yelled Brother Etienne. "When I turn off the lights, there will be complete silence. Anyone caught talking after lights out will be made to stand at attention before me for as long as I see fit. Now lights out." However, before Brother Etienne reached the light switch, Brother Julien appeared with Patrick O'Reilly, who was carrying his suitcase and a handbag.

Brother Julien had been raised on a farm not far from Quebec City and must have been kicked by a horse, because he sported a long red scar across the right side of his forehead which descended from the center of his hairline to the end of his right brow. It gave him a mean and threatening look. Brother Julien's coarse black hair parted on the right side, but unevenly cut, failed to soften his appearance as a stern disciplinarian. Brother Julien whispered something to Brother Etienne then asked Patrick to follow him. To Jacques' surprise, Brother Julien walked down the middle aisle towards Jacques' bed and pointing to the unoccupied bunk next to Jacques, told Patrick, "This is your bunk and footlocker. There's a wall locker against the wall with the same number for your use also. Hurry up and get into bed. You can unpack in the morning." With those final words, Brother Julien left the dormitory and Patrick greeted Jacques with subdued joy at seeing a familiar face and quickly undressed and got into bed.

Suddenly, the dormitory was in near total darkness except for the faint light at the north end where the latrine was located and the moonlight penetrated through the several dormitory windows.

Jacques thought that after such a stern warning, no one would dare violate Brother Etienne's instructions, but sure enough, after only thirty minutes of lights out, Brother Etienne had one student standing at attention before him in front of the dais. Brother Etienne moved very slowly in his slightly creaky rocking chair which was the only thing that broke the dormitory silence. Jacques wondered how long this young student would have to stand at attention in front of Brother Etienne, and Jacques could not fall asleep, partially in empathy, but also curiosity. After one hour, Brother Etienne released the student who returned to his bunk. Jacques felt relief and fell asleep.

The next morning, all of the students were marched into the dining room adjoining the recreation room. As the students entered the dining room, they were directed to the various elongated tables by some of the Christian Brothers. Each table accommodated twelve students who sat on a wooden bench attached to the table, six on each side. The food was brought to each table by the kitchen employees. That morning, a bowl of hot rolled oats was brought to each table, along with a pitcher of milk, a loaf of bread and a small butter dish. The bowl of rolled oats was passed around and Jacques took his share and passed it to Patrick, who turned up his long thin nose at it in disdain and passed it to the student to his right. Patrick's high forehead and pronounced chin gave his slightly freckled face with sensitive looking eyes an air of studiousness and intelligence that betrayed his athletic ability.

"What's the matter Pat? You don't like rolled oats?" said Jacques.

"Not particularly, this batch looked lumpy," replied Patrick.

"You might as well get used to it Patrick, because you get rolled oats almost every morning," said Claude sarcastically.

Patrick said nothing, but thought to himself that this was going to be a hell of an experience. He missed home already, but he really didn't have a home because his mother had died and his father's work required a lot of traveling, hence his placement at St. Paul College. Patrick was somewhat encouraged by Jacques' apparent unworried and unaffected behavior as if he knew that better times were ahead. He was glad that Jacques was his friend. Patrick observed that Jacques was not gregarious, but nevertheless attracted the friendship of other students who formed a camaraderie that made life at the college fun and interesting for the group. Patrick thought, *what the hell, so breakfast was not so good, I'll make up for it at lunch time.* When lunch time came around, Jacques noticed that Patrick was not eating his meatloaf.

"Put some of that gravy on it and it will camouflage the taste of the meatloaf. Actually it's not bad tasting at all," said Jacques to Patrick.

Patrick followed Jacques' advice and poured gravy from a large spoon that came with the bowl of gravy onto his meatloaf and grudgingly started eating small pieces of it.

"You're just going to have to adjust to this bland food or you're going to starve," said Jacques.

"Yeah, think of something pleasant while you eat it," said Claude with a sarcastic smile.

Jacques then thought of Grandmaman's ragout, so delicious and filling. How he missed that home cooking. Then his thoughts came back to the reality of his situation. When the food is good, he'll just eat more of it to make up for the poor meals. That's all there is to it. The problem was that there were no snack bars or other sources of food at the college which was isolated on the banks of the St. Lawrence River. That evening the students were served beans, all you could eat. That was a veritable feast for Jacques, who loved beans. He ate three large servings and his companions were astonished at the amount of beans he could eat at one sitting.

"Boy! There is going to be music tonight," exclaimed Claude with a sardonic smile.

"Yeah! Music to be heard, but not smelled," replied Hubert.

"Hey! Jacques, they're going to nickname you 'Le Grand Peteur' (The Great Farter) after tonight," remarked Patrick humourously.

Jacques took the ribbing in stride as he knew they really were his friends who meant no harm. Fortunately for Jacques, beans were served quite often at dinner time along with frankfurters which Jacques found very tasty and nourishing—it stuck to his ribs as the saying went. However, Jacques' elation over the college's 'French cuisine' was short-lived when one morning at breakfast the students were served their usual rolled oats.

As the large bowl of hot rolled oats was placed on the dining table in front of Jacques and his table companions, they just sat there in total silence and shock at what they saw. Large worms formed ridges on the surface of the rolled oats. They all stared at the bowl in disgust. No one would even touch the serving spoon. Jacques got the attention of one of the dining room servers and pointed out the worms in the bowl.

The server matter-of-factly picked up the bowl and brought it back to the kitchen, subsequently returning with another bowl of cooked rolled oats without apology or comment. However, no one at the table dared to even stir the new bowl of oats to see if there were any worms in it. They were all afraid to complain to the Brothers for fear of some type of reprisal. Corporal punishment was alive and well at College St. Paul.

Jacques and Patrick satisfied their appetite with a large glass of milk and bread. It took a long time for Jacques and the other students at that table to ever eat rolled oats again. Jacques thought it best never to mention it to his mother in his letters to her. There was nothing she could really do about it; she couldn't afford to move him to another boarding school, hence the less she knew, the better it would be for all.

As time went by, Jacques received occasional letters from his mother Nora who would always enclose a few dollars for incidentals.

One Sunday afternoon, Patrick's father came to visit him from Montreal and amongst other things, gave him a couple of comic books. Later that evening, Patrick showed the comic books to Jacques and lent him one to read. Jacques noticed on the back cover an advertisement for a crystal radio which sold for $5.00 in United States funds. Jacques was intrigued and mailed the $5.00 he had saved from the dollars he had received from his mother, to the company in Chicago, Illinois.

About ten days later, Jacques received a package in the mail from Chicago. Jacques took the package into the recreation hall where he opened it in the presence of Patrick and Claude. The small crystal radio consisted of a small stone-like rectangular shaped crystal with a wire connected to a needle which was to be used to pick at various locations on the crystal until the signal of a radio station could be heard through the set of headphones. Batteries were not needed. To Jacques' and his friends' disappointment, the short wire antenna severely limited the reception.

"It would be great if we could hear the hockey games played at the Forum in Montreal," exclaimed Claude.

"Yeah, but we need a stronger antenna," replied Patrick.

"I've got an idea," said Jacques. "We could use the bed springs in the dormitory as a huge antenna. We could connect several of the metal beds with wire coat hangers, and attach the crystal radio's antenna to my own bed springs, which connected to three or four other beds would give us one humongous antenna."

"Sacre Bleu! We could probably pick up California stations with that kind of antenna. Let's do it," said Claude enthusiastically.

That night, just before lights went out, Jacques and his two friends connected their three beds with metal coat hangers, and Jacques connected his crystal radio to his own bed springs. He hid the radio from view with his blanket and started picking at the crystal with the antenna's needle. Suddenly he heard the announcer's voice on a Montreal radio station giving a rapid account of the hockey players' actions at the Forum.

"I got the Forum…The Montreal Canadians are playing the Toronto Maple Leafs," whispered Jacques to Patrick lying in the next bed. Patrick whispered the same to Claude who whispered it to the next student to his right.

"What's the score, Jacques?" whispered Patrick anxiously.

"I don't know yet," replied Jacques. "Wait a minute…here it comes."

"It's Montreal two, Toronto nothing," whispered Jacques to Patrick, who repeated the score to his neighbor.

"Shhhhhhhh," whispered Claude. "Brother Julien is coming our way."

Everyone lay silently in their beds, feigning sleep while Brother Julien walked slowly past the foot of their beds. Brother Julien was sure he had heard voices from their location, but seemed satisfied that all was now quiet in the dormitory and returned to his rocking chair.

Jacques listened to the rest of the game, only occasionally passing on the score as the game developed to its end with Montreal winning with a final score of four to one.

That morning, the three boys made sure that the coat hangers were removed from their beds and hidden in their respective foot lockers. Jacques wrapped his small, crystal radio inside a thick woolen sock which he hid in his footlocker. That day, several students gathered around Jacques to learn the details of the previous night's hockey game at the Forum, careful not to be within earshot of any of the Brothers during their conversation about the game. They knew that the discovery of the crystal radio, especially in the dormitory after lights out, would result in forfeiture of the radio and punishment for those involved.

Claude approached Jacques. "Hey! Did you know that the Canucks are playing the New York Rangers Friday night at Madison Square Garden in New York City?"

"No I didn't," replied Jacques.

"You think that you can get that game on your crystal radio?" asked Claude, who now was joined by several other students.

Jacques was worried that with so many students aware of his possession and use of a crystal radio in the dormitory, his secret would leak to the Brothers. Jacques cautiously replied that he really didn't know, and excused himself, saying he had to go to the bathroom.

Later he confided with Patrick and Claude that he would certainly try and there was a good chance that if he picked the crystal long enough, he would probably get that particular station and Friday was definitely on for Madison Square Garden.

Just before dinner, Claude decided to venture those three steps from the Recreation Room into the Dining Room to see what they would be serving that evening, and surprised Brother Julien shaking his fist at a younger student whom he knew as Marcel. Claude felt certain that had he not dropped in on them, Brother Julien would have punched Marcel. Julien dropped his closed fist in embarrassment and Claude quickly exited the dining room and reported what he had seen to Jacques and Patrick.

"I wonder what Marcel did to get Brother Julien so mad at him?" asked Claude rhetorically.

"Marcel is not the kind of kid that usually gets into trouble," replied Patrick.

"You know that his bed is only one bed up from me in the next row," Jacques mused openly.

"He probably knows about the radio," replied Claude.

"Yeah! But he's not the type to snitch on us," said Patrick.

"He's small and timid. It wouldn't take much for Brother Julien to intimidate him into telling him whatever he knows," replied Claude.

"Mon Dieu," exclaimed Jacques. "Let's not worry about it. If Brother Julien knew something, he would already have had us on the carpet with strap in hand. Let's go punch the bag outside." Jacques and his two friends exited the recreation room by climbing four steps to the door leading to the large outside patio which ran nearly the entire length of the school building. The patio was fifteen feet wide and covered by a corrugated metal roof attached to the school building at an angle that allowed the winter snow and rain to drain off of it into the large school playground. As the three boys stepped onto the patio, they immediately turned left in the direction of a punching bag hanging by a short chain fastened to a metal swivel attached to a long horizontal metal bar about seven feet from the cement floor that extended from the wall of the school building to a vertical pillar which supported the patio roof. There were several of those pillars, but only two of them supported a punching bag apparatus.

Jacques stepped to the left side of the hanging bag while Patrick stood to the right side of the bag facing Jacques.

"Double or single rotation?" asked Jacques.

"The usual double rotation," replied Patrick.

Jacques punched the bag with the flat side of his closed fist and wrist driving the bag up and around the horizontal bar and back down for Patrick to strike, but Patrick allowed the bag to go around another turn before hitting the bag with the flat side of his closed fist driving the punching bag in the opposite direction, going around the metal bar twice before Jacques hit the bag again. As each boy struck the bag harder and harder, causing the bag to travel faster and faster, one of them would eventually miss the bag thus compelling him to relinquish his position to the next student in line. These young boys did not dare hit the bag with the knuckle side of the fist as it would most certainly place too much strain on their yet under-developed wrists. Jacques would hit the bag with his flat right fist and on the next rotation of the bag, he used the side of his left fist and wrist, and so conserved energy. Jacques then delivered one tremendous wallop to the punching bag that sped up the rhythm that each player depended on in his timing to strike the bag, inasmuch as the bag traveled too fast for the eye to judge, but the chain and swivel made a particular noise announcing the end of each revolution that a blind man could time perfectly. Patrick did not expect this sudden surge in the bag's rotation and missed the bag at its second rotation. Disappointed, Patrick stepped aside for Claude to take his place against Jacques the victor.

Claude stepped up to the bag facing Jacques and requested they play the less popular single rotation which required more speed and alertness. With the single rotation, the bag did not have time to accelerate to the great speed of double rotation, but the players had less time to deliver their punches which in that instance was more effective if the player could strike the bag with his closed knuckled fist rather than his flat fist and wrist.

These boys had already developed calluses on the knuckles of their fists and especially at the joints of the first phalanges which took the brunt of the punching bag's skin wearing force when it was hit with the flat part of the closed fist. Jacques' hands were unusually thick and well padded; ideal for a bare-knuckle fighter in that the hand bones were well protected. Jacques decided to test the strength of his right wrist by hitting the bag with his closed knuckled fist.

Both Jacques and Claude were hitting the bag in a steady rhythm when suddenly Jacques slapped the bag instead of hitting it with his fist which caused the bag to barely make it over the horizontal bar. Claude threw his fist into thin air, completely missing the bag which was still descending. Claude uttered, "Merde."

"Hey, guys," exclaimed Patrick, "Brother Samuel is starting a game of 'drapeau'. Let's go join them."

"OK, let's do it," replied Jacques enthusiastically, and the three boys walked over to the right field where the main hockey rink was erected each year. The wooden sideboards that circumferenced the ice rink in winter had left their imprint into the ground upon removal in the spring. A whitewash solution had been poured into the two imprinted lines about 85 feet long at each end of the rink. About 25 students comprising Team A were lined up behind the white line where the flag pole known in French as the "drapeau" was located about three feet in front of the line at its middle section. The flag pole (drapeau) was held at a forty-five degree angle inside a hole in a flat wooden board towards the forward line two hundred feet away where Team B was strategizing on a method of stealing the flag pole from Team A without being tagged by one of its members. The rules of the game allowed Team B to assign one of its members to act as a guard who could not be tagged, but also could not steal the drapeau. His role was to prevent any member of Team A from leaving the line and running forward towards any member of Team B that was attempting to steal the drapeau or sliding into the line of Team A without being tagged by a member of Team A. The guard would run in front of the line from one end to the other in an attempt to tag a member of Team A that left the line towards any member of Team B who was getting too close to the drapeau or Team A's line. Once a member of Team B succeeded in invading Team A's line of defense, usually by sliding into the line under the protection of the guard, that member was permitted to situate himself at the line directly behind the drapeau where he had to wait for an opportunity to leap at the drapeau and run with it towards the line of Team B, 200 feet away, without being tagged by a pursuing Team A member who himself had to avoid being tagged by the Guard.

Jacques was assigned to Team A with Claude, but Patrick ended up in Team B. Jacques took a position at the end of the line about forty feet to the right of the drapeau. Jacques reasoned that the guard would be busy keeping Team A members nearest the drapeau at bay, and would have to travel too far in order to tag Jacques who would position himself about 15 to 20 feet away from the line. Each time the guard would advance towards Jacques, he would run back to the line in sufficient time to avoid being tagged by the guard. Jacques kept doing that, exhausting the guard who started to pay less attention to Jacques' transgression into Team B territory. Patrick, one of Team B's members had managed to successfully slip into Team A's defensive line under the protection of the Guard without being tagged, and now was in a position to steal the drapeau. Everyone on both sides knew that Patrick was a fast runner and once afoot with the drapeau, he would be hard to catch. But Jacques had at times as much as a 25 foot lead from the line and was in a position to intercept Patrick should he steal the drapeau, and so Patrick did in a burst of speed that surprised surrounding Team A members.

The moment that Patrick leaped off the line with the drapeau, Jacques took off with such speed that he ended up near the line of Team B waiting for Patrick who was running towards him. Even Jacques was stunned at how fast he got into that position of being in between Patrick and Team B's line which Patrick had to cross with the drapeau. Jacques was standing still, waiting for Patrick who slowed down as he approached him, then like a hockey player on ice, Patrick faked a move to the right then unexpectedly moved left catching Jacques off balance and unable to recover in time to tag Patrick before he crossed the line with the drapeau. Nobody could believe it, most of all Jacques who was embarrassed at being outmaneuvered.

"What happened? You were way ahead of him…you had him cold," exclaimed Claude who had run up to Jacques.

"I don't know. I wasn't expecting that sudden move in the other direction and I lost my balance. By the time I recovered my balance, he was over the line," replied Jacques in disgust. As Jacques glanced in the direction of Team B's line, he could see Patrick laughing with some of his teammates. In a sincere gesture of camaraderie, Jacques walked over to his friend Patrick and congratulated him on his swift move, but reassured him that next time he would be ready for him. Then Jacques walked over to the side of the play field and stood there pensively. Brother Samuel, a tall, slim, dark haired man with thick metal rimmed glasses observed Jacques' demeanor and walked over to him.

"You know that you are the fastest runner in the school. But you just learned a lesson, that speed is not everything and that other factors can decide the winner. You got overconfident and got caught flat footed, that's all. You must not let something like this bother you. So let's get back into the game, Jacques." That was indeed a lesson Jacques would not soon forget. But Brother Samuel also knew that young Jacques was not nearly fully developed, hence still at the awkward stage. The game of drapeau was soon forgotten when the three hockey rinks were erected by the students and faculty in anticipation of the first snow.

No sooner had the three rinks been erected, that a few days later the big white flakes from the north blanketed the school grounds with several inches of snow. That evening, several of the Christian brothers with student volunteers, marched in military fashion up and down the length of each rink, stomping on the snow to create a hard snow surface which would later be hosed with water that would form the ice inside the rink. It would take several evenings of water hosing to obtain an even ice surface upon which to play hockey. The required blue and red lines would be inserted just before the last water hosing so that they would be apparent to the players. Powerful overhead spotlights attached to wooden poles on each side of the rinks permitted night games and general ice skating for the students. The long, cold Quebec winters justified the major effort required in the erection of those three ice rinks which brought great pleasure to both students and faculty.

Each time it snowed, the students would remove the snow from the ice rinks by skating with a four-foot wide hand plow thus driving the snow into piles that were then shoveled over the wooden sides of the rink which were about four feet high. It didn't take too long before the snow over the side of the rinks piled up several feet above the wooden side boards. Each evening, when there was not a scheduled hockey game, the students had a choice of playing in the game room or free skating on the primary ice rink lit up by the flood lights. Some of the students played tag and whoever was tagged would chase after any of the other students in the game until he tagged one of them by touching any part of their body. Some daring students would escape by diving over the side of the rink into the piled up snow, which required a significant leap not without risks.

One wintry evening, Jacques, Patrick, Claude and Alain were joined by several other students in a game of tag. They all wore hockey sweaters bearing the name and symbol of various Canadian major league teams and their hockey skates had metal toe plates which no doubt often contributed to near frozen toes. Most wore two pairs of thick woolen socks. Many students were using skates that were at least one size too big because their parents wanted the skates to last more than one season which required some of them to wear two and even three pairs of socks. Some of the students also wore leather ankle supports that laced very tightly over their socks. As they grew into their skates, the need for extra socks and ankle supports vanished. The blades on the skates required renewed sharpening at least once per week and this was done in the tool room at the college. It was important for the blade to have sharp edges so that the skater could lean sharply on turns and stop on a dime if needed. Jacques loved the game of tag because it tested his speed and agility against the other students.

Several students were already skating counterclockwise around the rink while others were attempting fancy footwork at the center of the rink or else engaged in short-term conversations.

"O.K....who wants to take the tag?" asked Jacques.

"I'll take it," replied Claude. "I'm coming after you after the count of five."

They took off skating in different directions across the ice rink. Alain attempted to hide by mingling with the skaters promenading around the rink. Patrick and Jacques hung out together at the other end of the rink waiting for Claude to make his move, figuring that if Claude came after them, they would wait until he came within a few feet of them and then they would split in opposite directions leaving Claude in the middle to make a decision as to which one of them he would pursue, knowing full well that they were both super fast skaters. Claude decided to go after slower prey and spotted Emile in the middle of the rink talking to Alain. Claude put on a burst of speed towards them and Alain alerted Emile who immediately took off and joined the growing number of students skating counterclockwise around the rink which left Alain as the target.

Alain was back skating all the while watching Claude stalking him when Alain bumped into Yves the Bear who saw Alain backing up, but made no attempt to get out of his way. Yves shoved Alain who fell down on his rear end onto the ice. Yves then stood over Alain with his gloved fists clenched, obviously waiting for Alain to get up so that he could punch him.

"Yves is just looking for a fight, isn't he?" said Jacques to Patrick.

"Yeah! And it's always someone smaller than him so he can be sure he'll win," replied Patrick with disdain.

Without saying another word, Jacques took off skating towards Alain and Yves, with Patrick following him. Alain was still lying on the ice but propped up on his right elbow with his left hand and arm raised to protect himself against Yves who was attempting to punch him by leaning over him. Alain's face displayed fear and a plea for help.

Jacques skated up to Yves' right side knowing he was left handed and blocked him from hitting Alain.

"Why are you picking on him? He barely bumped into you and it was an accident," said Jacques in a stern voice.

Seeing Jacques come to his defense, Alain attempted to stand up at which time Yves threw a left punch at Alain which missed the mark when Jacques shoved Yves back.

Now Yves' full attention was on Jacques and several students were now gathered around the pair giving them a wide berth in which to fight. Yves cautiously advanced towards Jacques who was slowly skating backwards leading Yves into the wooden sides of the rink. With Jacques' back only about four to five feet from the rink side, Jacques threw a left jab with his leather gloved hand at Yves' nose, drawing blood. In a rage, Yves lunged forward at Jacques who side-stepped him and as Yves passed by him, Jacques stuck his left foot out and tripped Yves, who went plunging head first into the wooden rink side, nearly knocking him out. As Yves lay on his back holding his head and moaning from the pain, Brother Julien came running in his black low quarter boots onto the ice rink, occasionally steadying himself by holding onto the wooden side of the rink. As he arrived at the scene, everyone was distancing themselves from Yves and thus stood Jacques a few feet from Yves.

"Did you do this, Jacques?" asked Brother Julien in a loud voice.

"He came after me Sir, and I defended myself," replied Jacques.

"I want you to report to me in the Study Hall," said Brother Julien sternly.

By this time, Yves had managed to stand up, still holding his head. His nose was still bloody.

"All right Yves. Report to the infirmary immediately," ordered Brother Julien.

Patrick and Claude started skating towards Jacques who was slowly skating towards the entrance/exit to the ice rink.

"Hey! Wait for us, Jacques," yelled Patrick.

"That was a nice move on your part Jacques, but Yves won't forget this and you can be sure he will seek revenge when he's not wearing ice skates," warned Patrick.

"Qu'est sera, sera," replied Jacques nonchalantly.

"Yeah! We can handle that bully. We're the three musketeers. One for all and all for one," said Claude jokingly.

The eight o'clock bell rang and all of the students reported to the Study Hall for their one-hour study period before retiring to the dormitory.

"Jacques Markham. Front and center," said Brother Julien in a loud voice.

"Hang tough," whispered Claude, who was sitting next to Jacques.

Patrick watched Jacques walk slowly to the front of the class and felt a nausea of empathy.

"Hold out your right hand," ordered Brother Julien.

Jacques stuck out his right hand and Brother Julien grabbed his wrist with his left hand and with his right hand pulled out a long thick leather strap from a pocket inside his black robe. Brother Julien raised the strap real high and came down hard striking the palm of Jacques' right hand which made a loud noise that made several of the students in the front row wince in horrified terror. But Jacques bit his teeth real tight and the only emotion he showed was the tightening of his jaw muscles. Brother Julien struck Jacques' hand again real hard and evinced no visible emotion from Jacques. Frustrated at not 'breaking' Jacques, he struck his open hand a third time and observed that Jacques' hand was beginning to swell. Brother Julien knew that if he continued to strike his right hand, it could split open; hence he instructed Jacques to now extend his left hand and repeated the process, striking him with all of his might. Jacques was fighting back involuntary tears and hoped that he could remain tearless for the next two strikes. Surprisingly, he was starting to become numb to the pain and endured the remaining strikes without shedding a single tear to the disappointment of Brother Julien who dismissed him back to his seat.

As he sat down at his student desk, Jacques placed both of his abnormally thick hands on his desk to examine them.

"Boy! You had better go to the bathroom and run some cold water over those swollen hands," whispered Claude.

"Next time you'd better wax your hands, Jacques," whispered Patrick.

Jacques chalked it up to experience and licked his wounds silently and privately.

Jacques was to experience at least two other forms of corporal punishment while at the College, and neither of them would be any easier than the first.

While at the school library, Jacques got absorbed into a long novel filled with adventure and a red-headed protagonist whose athletic exploits had seized Jacques' imagination to such an extent that he couldn't part with it until he had finished reading it. He took it out of the library and brought it with him to the Study Hall where he continued reading the book instead of completing his distasteful math homework.

The next morning, Jacques sat in Brother Antoine's math class, hoping that through some miracle, Brother Antoine would not ask for the students' homework. However, to Jacques' chagrin, all students were asked to pass along their completed homework. Brother Antoine checked the students' papers and then asked, "Jacques Markham, I don't see your homework. Did you complete your assignment?"

"I'm sorry sir, but I got engrossed into reading a book and forgot about it," replied Jacques remorsefully.

"Come on up here," ordered Brother Antoine. Brother Antoine had heard from Brother Julien's experience that this boy was tougher than he looked with his refined features, perfect skin and curly hair, and he doubted that corporal punishment would ever be a deterrent for him. Brother Antoine decided to use his "clicker," a six inch long wooden cylinder bulging at the center with a groove at the top which accommodated a rounded stick extending the length of the *clicker* that swiveled up and down. The stick was held inside its groove by a rubber band that circumferenced the bulb slightly forward of its center. Brother Antoine would pull down on the end of the rounded stick of his *clicker* nearest his thumb and then released it causing the other end to hit the base of the *clicker,* thereby producing a distinctive noise. The *clicker* was used to get a student's attention, one way or the other. Brother Antoine often kept his *clicker* inside the wide sleeve of his black robe known as a *habit.*

Jacques walked up to Brother Antoine, who grabbed his left arm, held it under his armpit and placed his shoulder against the podium preventing Jacques from having access to his left hand which by now Brother Antoine was holding by the wrist with palm side down. With his right hand, Brother Antoine raised his *clicker* and brought it down hard against the top of Jacques' left hand where there was little padding. Jacques gritted his teeth, but wanted to yell from the excruciating pain. The second blow to his hand caused it to swell. The third blow produced a significant welt that even Brother Antoine could not disregard. Jacques was ready to attempt to withdraw his hand by whatever means was necessary if Brother Antoine struck him again, but to his relief, Brother Antoine released his hand and Jacques returned to his seat. The top of his left hand had a welt the size of a large grape that still pained him for several hours afterwards. *One thing is for sure,* Jacques thought, *I'm never going to miss homework again.*

The hockey game between the upper classmen and the lower classmen was on for Saturday afternoon. The first line for the lower classmen included Jacques as forward Center, Patrick as his left wingman, and Claude as his right wingman, familiarly known amongst the lower classmen as the three musketeers. The upper classmen included Yves the bear, who always played as a defenseman due to his large size and lack of speed necessary as a forward player.

As the hockey game progressed into the second period, neither team had scored a goal. The play was now in the lower classmen's zone when Patrick managed to get the puck away from one of the upper classmen's control and he shot it to Jacques, who was positioned just below the blue line near mid-center of the rink. Moving the puck forward and from side to side with his hockey stick, Jacques traveled with such speed that no one behind him could hope to catch him. It was up to the two defensemen that stood between Jacques and the goalie to stop him. The two defensemen, Yves and Francois, stood side by side with only a few feet between them. Yves being left handed and Francois right handed caused them to have their hockey sticks nearly crossing each other as they waited, expecting Jacques to attempt to move around them either to their right or left. Jacques was coming at them with tremendous speed and instead of going around them, he leaped in between them over their hockey sticks with the puck having slipped through them. As Jacques landed, he instantly seized the loose puck and now facing only the goalie, faked a move to the right but moved left shooting the puck into the net scoring the only goal so far in the game. Jacques skated around the back of the goalie's net without fanfare and towards his teammates who stood in awe at what they had just seen.

"That boy is a natural," said Brother Samuel to Brother Michel.

"Yeah! And he's not quite yet 15 years old. We could be looking at a future professional hockey player," replied Brother Michel.

"I don't know about that. Have you heard him sing in the choir at Sunday Mass? He's got a great voice that should be developed. I'm considering having him sing as the soloist at the forthcoming graduating class," said Brother Samuel. "Apparently he sang in the choir for the St. Denis Church in Montreal before coming here," added Brother Samuel.

"You'd better hurry up because boys of that age go through a voice change where they can't sing a note for a couple of years," replied Brother Michel.

The game ended with a win for the lower classmen when Patrick scored the other goal assisted by Jacques.

A week later, Jacques experienced the third variety of corporal punishment at the college, but thankfully, it was also to be his last. As Jacques entered the latrine prior to going to Brother Etienne's class, he was surprised to see Claude consoling Emile who appeared frantic and nearly in tears.

"What's the matter?" inquired Jacques, addressing both of them, but primarily directing his question at Claude.

"Emile lost his homework. But I think someone probably stole it from his school bag when he laid it down in the recreation room to play shuffle board. All anyone has to do is either copy the answers and throw the original away or else erase the name or put his own on it since the answers are only in numbers," said Claude.

"Who would do such a thing?" asked Jacques rhetorically.

"You'd be surprised," replied Claude.

"Do you think that Brother Etienne will believe me when I tell him that I did my homework, but somehow it got lost or stolen?" asked Emile in a shaky voice.

"I don't think so," replied Claude in a low voice.

"I've seen him use that blackboard pointer to hit a student in back of the legs till the boy crouched to the floor in agony," said Emile, fearful of the same fate.

"Yeah! That's his favorite method of punishment," replied Claude.

"Never mind that Emile," said Jacques reaching into his school bag. "Here, you take my homework which is in pencil and just erase my name and put yours on it. I'll take care of the rest," said Jacques with a definite and amusing plan in mind.

Claude looked in astonishment at Jacques while Jacques handed his homework to a very receptive and thankful Emile. Claude stepped aside and whispered into Jacques' ear, "We've got an important hockey game in two days. You'll barely be able to walk for a week after Brother Etienne gets through with you."

"Don't worry Claude. I won't let you guys down," replied Jacques confidently.

"Let me borrow your twelve inch ruler, Claude," asked Jacques, thanking him upon receipt of his wooden ruler. Jacques excused himself and entered one of the latrine stalls and closed the door, while Claude and Emile exited the latrine.

Jacques lowered the heavy woolen socks that covered his woolen pants up to his knees. He then pulled up each of his trouser legs and inserted the borrowed twelve inch wooden ruler inside his inner sock which he then covered by pulling down his pants leg. He then pulled up his woolen socks over the pants right up to his knee, then folded it over his calf to add bulk and to give his calf the expected contour. Jacques did the same to his other leg using his own ruler. Now he was ready to take his punishment. The way he reasoned it, he was preventing an injustice from being perpetrated on Emile and he was avoiding the administration of undue punishment.

After the students were all seated in Brother Etienne's classroom, they were instructed to pass forward their completed homework. By this time, Claude had made Patrick aware of Jacques' act of salvation and possible folly. Jacques had not made his friends aware of the ruse because their behavior during and after the punishment phase might betray his act.

"Mr. Markham, I see that you did not hand in your homework. Do you have a plausible explanation?" asked Brother Etienne.

"Not one that you would find plausible, Sir," replied Jacques.

"Alright young man, front and center and be quick about it," said Brother Etienne with impatience at what he considered a sarcastic reply.

"Step up onto the platform," ordered Brother Etienne. The platform was one step up from the classroom floor to give the instructor and the students a certain amount of elevation that permitted the entire class to see what was written on the blackboard. Jacques stood on the edge of the platform facing the blackboard when Brother Etienne grabbed his blackboard pointer, a four foot long cylindrical stick which he swung in a large arc striking the back of Jacques' legs dead center on his calves. Jacques feigned restrained pain by grimacing with the tightening of his lips. Brother Etienne struck the back of Jacques' legs again, causing Jacques to again grimace. Brother Etienne, apparently frustrated by Jacques' resistance to pain, swung the pointer with all of his might at Jacques' calves, breaking the pointer in half which flew across the floor. Jacques faked a wince, pursed his lips and gave a furtive look at Brother Etienne who was staring at the back of Jacques' legs in astonishment at what had happened. For a moment, Jacques feared that Brother Etienne would discover the ruse, but was quickly relieved when Brother Etienne ordered him to return to his seat.

Jacques never told his friends about his insertion of the rulers because he feared that at some point in time, it would get back to the Brothers, who would then revisit the issue.

However, fate has a way of uncovering the truth, and this was to be no exception. Emile, fraught with guilt over the corporal punishment received by Jacques on his behalf, wrote a letter to his father telling him about the entire incident. A few days later, a big strapping man wearing farmer's coveralls appeared at the college in an old pick-up truck.

He demanded to see the Principal, identifying himself as Jean Tremblay, Emile's father.

Mr. Tremblay was invited into the Principal's office where he was greeted by a diminutive man wearing round wire spectacles. After they shook hands, Brother Denis returned to his seat behind a large desk. Although there was a wooden chair facing Brother Denis' desk, Mr. Tremblay remained standing and pulling out his son's letter, handed it to Brother Denis.

"I received this letter from my son Emile yesterday, and frankly I'm very upset about the way it was handled. I can't believe that you are still using such medieval methods of punishment. I know from Emile that his friend Jacques has no father to protect him, but I'll tell you this…if that Brother…Etienne is it…ever uses that stick on my son…I'll break his neck with my bare hands, I tell you."

Brother Denis observed that Mr. Tremblay's blood pressure was rising as he spoke from the increasing redness appearing in his face. His huge stature intimidated Brother Denis, whose mind was racing in an attempt to think of a plausible excuse for Brother Etienne's behavior as related in Emile's letter.

"I can assure you, Mr. Tremblay, that neither I nor this College condones such a method of punishment, and if true, I sincerely apologize and you can be sure that it will be rectified. I will summon Brother Etienne and also Jacques Markham to appear at this office immediately to resolve this matter. Won't you please have a seat? Can I offer you a cup of coffee?"

"No thank you. Maybe later," replied Mr. Tremblay, still visibly upset.

Brother Denis left his office to talk to another Brother, then returned to keep Mr. Tremblay company while they waited for Brother Etienne and Jacques Markham.

Soon there was a knock at the door to the Principal's office.

"Come in," said Brother Denis in a normal tone of voice.

The door opened and Brother Etienne entered, followed by Jacques. Brother Etienne sensed that he was in trouble by the severe look he was given by Mr. Tremblay who was taller and at least fifty pounds heavier than him . *If looks could kill,* Brother Etienne thought, *I'd be a dead duck.*

"This is Brother Etienne and that is Jacques Markham," said Brother Denis, observing that Mr. Tremblay did not make any attempt to shake his hand. However he did acknowledge Jacques presence by extending his hand to him, stating "My son Emile has told me a lot about you, Jacques. I'm glad he has you as a friend."

Jacques nodded in agreement and said, "Thank you Mr. Tremblay."

"Brother Etienne, I will get right to the point of this meeting. Mr. Tremblay has brought to my attention a matter which is spelled out in this letter written by Mr. Tremblay's son Emile. I would like you to read this letter and explain to me and Mr. Tremblay the reason you took such drastic action against Jacques."

Brother Etienne accepted the letter from Brother Denis and as he read it, his face became flushed with anger and embarrassment.

"No one told me that Emile's homework had been stolen or lost," said Brother Etienne in a low voice directed principally at Brother Denis. "We need to maintain discipline in our classrooms and some students seem immune to the strap, therefore stronger measures are required," added Brother Etienne, looking in Jacques' direction.

"How can you justify breaking a stick on that boy's legs?" said Mr. Tremblay to Brother Etienne in a menacing manner, and before Brother Etienne could reply, Mr. Tremblay continued, "You should be ashamed of yourself, a grown man and a member of the clergy, beating up on a youngster like that. Be thankful that it wasn't my son you did that to, or else you'd be lying in a hospital right now."

Brother Etienne did not dare utter a word, for fear that anything he might say might provoke Mr. Tremblay to violence. However, in an attempt to prevent such eminent violence to occur, Jacques seized that short moment of silence to reveal that Brother Etienne did not hurt him after all.

"I have something to confess, Brother Denis," uttered Jacques, avoiding Brother Etienne's eyes.

"Well, what is it Jacques?" replied Brother Denis, with Mr. Tremblay and Brother Etienne staring at him anxiously.

"I knew when I did not turn in my homework that Brother Etienne would hit me in back of the legs with his wooden pointer, because he's used it several times before on other students in his classroom. So I covered the calves of my legs with two wooden rulers which I hid inside my pants and socks. That's probably why his pointer broke into pieces when he hit me," explained Jacques, who now felt relieved.

Brother Etienne started to say something to Jacques when Brother Denis raised his small hand at him indicating for him to remain silent. Mr. Tremblay was smiling from ear to ear at Jacques, whom he was ready to adopt at his own.

"Tell me Jacques," asked Brother Denis. "Do you feel that it was right for you to avoid punishment, even though it was severe?"

"Well, sir. The way I see it, I was merely trying to prevent an injustice from being perpetrated on Emile who was frightened to death at the prospect of being beaten by Brother Etienne, who he was sure wouldn't believe his homework had been stolen."

"If Emile had informed me that his homework had been stolen, I would have asked him to redo the math problems in class to prove that he knew the subject matter. He would then have avoided punishment," replied Brother Etienne with smugness.

"Two weeks ago, you applied the stick to Henri Bouchard, even though he told you that his homework was missing from his bag. That's why Emile didn't think you would believe him," replied Jacques, turning his head towards Brother Denis for a sign of agreement and understanding.

"I am glad that we have cleared up this misunderstanding and that no one was hurt. However, I am directing you Brother Etienne to never again use a blackboard pointer or any other type of stick to hit students. Do I make myself clear on this?" stated Brother Denis, staring directly at Brother Etienne.

"Yes sir. I understand and I will follow your directions Brother Denis."

"I know that you have a class in progress, so you can leave now Brother Etienne. I will talk to you further about this matter at dinner time," said Brother Denis.

After Brother Etienne left the Principal's office, Brother Denis told Jacques to return to his class, thanking him for his candidness.

Alone in the Principal's office, Brother Denis confided with Mr. Tremblay. "Sometimes, my Brothers can get overzealous in the disciplining of students. But those are rare exceptions. Nevertheless, you can now be assured that this will never happen again. You have my promise," said Brother Denis.

"I believe you and I'm quite satisfied at the way you handled this. I must tell you, Brother Denis, that it took a lot of courage for that boy Jacques to do what he did for my son."

"Let's not forget that his courage was aided by his creativity," replied Brother Denis with a smile.

For a moment Mr. Tremblay looked puzzled at Brother Denis' remark.

"Putting those two rulers inside his trousers to absorb the shock was creative to say the least," explained Brother Denis, raising his right eyebrow.

"Very creative indeed," replied Mr. Tremblay with laughter. "I was wondering if I could see my son for a few minutes before I leave. It's a two and a half hour drive to Quebec City."

"Of course. I'll get Brother Michel to get him for you and your son can walk you to your vehicle," replied Brother Denis amicably.

And so ended the use of the wooden pointer as a method of corporal punishment at St. Paul College, although the strap and clicker remained in use throughout Jacques attendance at the college.

On the 9th of May 1945, the faculty of St. Paul College gathered with all of the students at the playground where it was announced that Germany had surrendered to the allies in Rheims, France, and as such, the war in Europe was over. In celebration, the students were made to form a V for victory, and at its point stood a senior student holding a flagpole flying the Canadian flag while the entire student body and faculty sang the Canadian national anthem.

In preparation for the graduation ceremony for the senior classmen, Brother Samuel, who played the piano, spent several sessions training Jacques to sing a song titled 'L'enfant de la montagne' (The mountain boy) for the graduating class, even though Jacques himself was only a junior not yet ready for graduation.

The graduation ceremony was being held in the study hall which was also used to show occasional French movies. Brother Samuel sat at a piano on the stage with sheets of music propped up on the piano in front of him. Jacques stood front and center on the stage waiting for his cue from Brother Samuel to start singing. Facing the large audience of the entire student body, faculty and many parents in attendance at their sons' graduation, Jacques felt intimidated and nervous at the prospect of giving a poor performance. This was different than singing in a church choir where you are usually located in the balcony at the rear of the church, out of sight of the parishioners. Here he was, all alone, facing his peers and instructors, to perform a duty he had never sought nor desired.

Half-way through the song, Jacques' voice faltered at a high note, but he quickly recovered. He had been told that his voice would soon change and he would not be able to sing again for a few years until it matured. Now conscious of his voice change, he became nervous and at one point forgot the lyrics and promptly improvised with his own words that only Brother Samuel detected until he was able to recover the remaining lyrics and finish the song as if no errors had been made. The audience applauded and Jacques left the stage to take his seat in the audience next to Patrick and Claude.

"Hey! That was pretty good," said Patrick to Jacques.

"I didn't think so. I missed a high note and forgot some of the lyrics," replied Jacques.

"Well, I didn't notice it," replied Patrick surprised at Jacques' critical comment.

"I guess my voice is changing," said Jacques.

"Change is inevitable," commented Patrick with finality.

No one at the school celebrated the end of the war in the Pacific with Japan on 14 August 1945, immediately after two atomic bombs were dropped by a lone American bomber on Hiroshima and Nagasaki, inasmuch as the school was closed for the summer and all of the students had left for home, or as in the case of Jacques Markham, to work on a farm.

It was a bright, sunny day in June 1945 when Roland and Aunt Pauline drove up and parked their 1936 Royal Chrysler in front of the circular staircase at the front entrance to the College Saint Paul in Varennes. As they entered the College, they were greeted by Brother Michel who invited them to be seated in the foyer while he fetched their nephew Jacques Markham. A few minutes later, Jacques appeared with his suitcase and a handbag. Jacques dropped his luggage and shook hands with Roland, who was always happy to see him, and then Pauline hugged Jacques and kissed him on both cheeks as is the French custom. Jacques had been informed by letter from his mother that he would be spending the summer with distant cousins of the family who owned a farm near Saint-Jean-Sur-Richelieu located about fifty miles southeast of Montreal. Roland and Pauline were there to drive him to the farm.

Jacques didn't know what to expect as he had never worked on a farm. He felt mixed emotions in that it was an adventure that excited him, but he was being shuttled and displaced again to spend his summer with strangers. He longed to be back in Montreal with his Grandmother, his relatives, and his neighborhood friends. Jacques realized that those same reasons that brought him to Saint

Paul College, also brought him to the farm, because there was no place for him in Montreal. However, Jacques' youthful attitude of eternal hope in the future made life's challenges child's play as he knew deep in his heart that his destiny would eventually take him far away from all of this.

Roland drove off the main road that ran parallel to the Richelieu River, and pulled into the driveway fronting a large two-story wooden house painted white with red shutters. It was a typical large farm house, except that its back yard overlooked the Richelieu River with a wooden planked dock and attached row boat. On the other side of the main road, Jacques observed row after row of potato plants as far as the eye could see, and about one hundred yards from the road stood a large unpainted and weathered barn with a long wooden ramp leading up to two large barn doors. Attached to the right side of the barn was a wooden unpainted shed with large screen windows and a door.

As Roland, Pauline and Jacques descended the vehicle, they were greeted by a large, middle aged woman, accompanied by her 14 year old Grandson Edouard, who was staying at the farm for the summer.

"You must be Roland and Pauline. I'm Antoinette and this is my grandson Edouard," said the dark, gray-haired woman, greeting the two adults. Then turning her attention to Jacques, she said, "I see you're a strapping young man. Just what we need because there's plenty of work this time of year. Edouard, why don't you take Jacques inside the house and get him settled in the upstairs bedroom."

"Bien sur Grandmere," replied Edouard, who took hold of Jacques' lighter bag and proceeded towards the house.

Jacques did not want to follow Edouard until he had a chance to say goodbye to his Aunt and Roland . Jacques stepped forward towards Roland, who shook his hand with both of his hands. "Jacques…you'll like it here. It's a healthy lifestyle and an opportunity to be out in the country. Do write to us if you need anything." Jacques nodded in agreement but remained silent.

Aunt Pauline then embraced Jacques. "Hey Bien Cherie, you'll have a boy your own age to play with. It'll be a lot of fun, you'll see."

"Oui ma tante. I'll be alright," replied Jacques, who then turned, picked up his suitcase and followed Edouard inside the house where he was invited by him to come upstairs into his bedroom.

"We are to share this bedroom. Your bed is next to the window. Mine is nearest the door. You can hang your clothes in that closet over there. The only bathroom in the house is downstairs next to Grandma and Grandpa's bedroom. The half bath downstairs is out of order. My Uncle is supposed to come over and fix it, but he hasn't had time."

Jacques observed that it was a very old house with a radiator heating in the winter plus the fireplace he had noticed upon entering the house. The only means of cooling the room was with an electric fan, but Jacques did not notice any in the room, not that he felt any immediate need for one.

"Today is Sunday, the only day off from work. Tomorrow we have to get up at 5:30 AM, eat breakfast and then Grandpa will take us out to the barn. Uncle Jean-Marie and Uncle Louis usually arrive at 6:30 AM to help Grandpa through the hay season," stated Edouard informatively.

"Does your father also work on the farm?" asked Jacques.

"No, my father works in a factory in Longueil," replied Edouard, avoiding Jacques' gaze.

"What's his name?" queried Jacques.

"Frederic," replied Edouard, annoyed at Jacques' personal questions.

Jacques sensed that Edouard did not want to talk about his parents, thus avoided further questioning.

"Does anyone go swimming in the river?" asked Jacques.

"Oh! Sure. Did you bring a swimsuit?

"Yeah! I sure did. I love swimming," replied Jacques enthusiastically.

"The Richelieu River gets deep very fast and the water is pretty cold this time of year. It doesn't get warm until the beginning of August, but we have a row boat we can use to go fishing," said Edouard authoritatively.

"Really. When can we use it?" asked Jacques.

"It depends on what time we finish work in the evening. Usually not before Saturday evening when we finish a bit earlier and Sunday, our day off," replied Edouard.

"Well, what time do we usually get off work during the week?" asked Jacques

"We work from sun up till sundown, around 8:00 PM," replied Edouard. "Then you'll be too tired to do anything except sleep because you'll be up again at 5:30 AM," added Edouard.

"So you have worked here on this farm last year, hey?" asked Jacques.

"Oh! Yeah. I worked on this farm last summer too," replied Edouard.

Jacques then heard a loud voice call his name from downstairs, "Jacques, come on down, I need to talk to you," yelled Madame Antoinette Beaulieu.

As Jacques arrived at the bottom of the stairs, Madame Antoine asked him to come into the kitchen.

"Sit down Jacques. I want to tell you the rules of the house during your stay here. We all get up at 5:30 AM. We have only one bathroom, so I expect you to take no more than five minutes to brush your teeth and wash your face. After that we eat breakfast in the dining room. Sometimes my two sons come early to eat breakfast with us so we have a full house. Afterwards you and Edouard will go with my husband Armand…Mr. Beaulieu to you, who will show you what your duties are. This is the hay season, and we have only a short time to cut and load the hay and transport it to market, so we are up at first daylight and don't leave the field until sundown. Is that understood?" asked Madame Antoinette in a stern voice.

"Yes Madame," replied Jacques, who felt like a stranger begging for food at the back door.

"Now, I know that it's hard work for a boy of your age so I'll give you $5.00 each Sunday morning in addition to your free room and board. How does that sound?" asked Madame Antoinette with a slight smile.

"That's very generous of you Madame," replied Jacques, not aware of the fact that his mother Nora had given Madame Antoinette $60.00 to be dispensed to Jacques as his allowance of $5.00 per week.

"I understand that Sunday is our day off. Is that correct Madame?" asked Jacques politely.

"Yes, that's correct. You can use the row boat as long as you don't go out too far and you can also swim in the river, but you should be careful because the river bank gets deep very fast," said Madame Antoinette.

"Well, do we go to Sunday Mass?" asked Jacques.

Madame Antoinette looked at Jacques, annoyed that he had brought up the subject of Sunday Mass. "The closest church is at least five miles from here and we only have four horses who are worked very hard this time of year. Sunday is the only day they can rest, so we have no transportation during this season to attend Sunday Mass."

Jacques did not find Madame Antoinette's explanation for not attending Sunday Mass persuasive, but since he was only a guest there, he felt compelled to accept it.

"You can now go out and play with Edouard. Supper will be ready at 6:00 PM. Be back on time, otherwise the kitchen will be closed," said Madame Antoinette sternly.

During the next week, Jacques learned that the farm was totally unmechanized. All equipment was horse-drawn and shoveling horse manure became one of Jacques' duties. Jacques enjoyed the hard work required in the gathering of hay, especially the way in which the two Uncles taught him to pick up large stacks of hay with a pitchfork and load it onto the horse-drawn wagon. Those hay stacks were quite heavy and Jacques could feel his back and shoulder muscles getting stronger as the weeks went by. However, that turned out to be the only experience on the farm that he truly enjoyed.

Three weeks after his arrival at the farm, Jacques had saved his weekly allowance now totaling $15.00, which he had nowhere to spend. He kept the money under his mattress. When he received his next $5.00, he went to place it with the rest of his money under the mattress at which time he discovered it missing. He looked under the entire mattress and under the bed to no avail. He thought of Edouard, and hesitated to look at his belongings, but soon overcame his reluctance and searched the entire room without finding any money. He wondered whether he should confront Edouard or report the loss to Madame Antoinette. He decided to confront Edouard.

It was Sunday and lunch time. After lunch, Edouard asked Jacques if he wanted to go boating. Jacques saw an opportunity to be alone with Edouard at which time he could ask him about the missing money.

"Sure," replied Jacques. "I'll put on my bathing suit so that I can dive off the boat."

Jacques arrived at the wooden dock in back of the farm house where the wooden row boat was tied. He was wearing only a bathing suit and carried a towel which he had obtained from the linen closet in his bedroom. He climbed down into the boat and sat on the planked seat reserved for the person who pulls the oars. Jacques had experience with row boats from his trips to the Lac Castor with his mother and the Lake of the Fourteen Islands where Roland had taken him the previous summer at St. Emile, about sixty miles north of Montreal.

Edouard showed up in a one piece bathing suit that covered his upper and lower torso. Jacques thought how funny he looked in that old-fashioned bathing suit, but said nothing about it inasmuch as he had a more serious topic to discuss with him.

"Before we start, I have something very important to ask you," said Jacques, looking directly into Edouard's eyes.

"What's that?" replied Edouard with a frown.

"I had saved three $5.00 bills given to me by Madame Antoinette which I hid under my mattress, and this morning I discovered that all of my money was gone. Now I need a straight answer…did you take that money?" asked Jacques staring deeply into Edouard's eyes for any evidence of mendacity.

"No, I don't know what you're talking about. I didn't even know that you had any money," replied Edouard, his face turning pale.

"You didn't know that Madame Antoinette was giving me $5.00 each week?" asked Jacques.

"No, I didn't, I swear," answered Edouard, who now seemed quite agitated.

"Alright. I'll take your word for it. Maybe Madame Antoine found it when she cleaned the room and didn't have a chance to tell me about it yet," replied Jacques, who doubted it, but felt that he had to give Edouard reasonable doubt.

"OK! Let's go boating," said Jacques, who grabbed the oars. "Untie the dock line, Edouard, and jump in."

Jacques rowed out onto the lake with Edouard sitting in the back of the row boat.

"I swear to you Jacques, I didn't take that money," said Edouard pleadingly.

"I believe you, now forget it. Let's have some fun. Listen, it's been about an hour since we ate lunch, so it's safe to go swimming. Why don't we take turns diving off the boat?" asked Jacques.

"I'm not a good swimmer and we're too far from shore," said Edouard, sounding a bit frightened.

"We're only about one hundred and fifty yards from shore and you want to make sure you don't hit bottom or a rock when you dive," replied Jacques.

"You go and dive and I'll row the boat if you don't mind," said Edouard.

"That sounds alright to me," said Jacques, changing places with Edouard, making sure they didn't tip the boat in the process.

"Make sure the boat stays close to me because I can't swim far and this is a deep lake, OK?" said Jacques.

Edouard nodded affirmatively.

Jacques dived off the back seat of the boat and disappeared under the smooth surface of the river, and after a few seconds reappeared about twenty yards facing the back of the row boat and Edouard's intent eyes.

Jacques started swimming towards the back of the row boat in an awkward overhand freestyle that lacked the use of his legs and knowledge of breathing, necessitating that he keep his head above the water. As Jacques came closer to the back of the boat, he saw to his disbelief that Edouard was rowing away from him all the while staring at Jacques who was quickly tiring and losing the race. As Jacques' arm stroke slowed to a crawl, he yelled a desperate plea.

"Stop the boat; I can't swim anymore. I'm too tired…..I'm sinking," said Jacques as he watched Edouard row away from him with a smirk on his face.

As Jacques' legs descended towards the bottom while he still had some strength left in his arms to keep his head above water, he suddenly felt sand underneath the bottoms of his feet. With great relief, he felt what appeared to be a sand bar underneath him that kept his chin at water level if he stood on the balls of his feet. He yelled at Edouard to come back for him, and then heard a voice from shore calling out to them. Edouard turned the boat around and came back to fetch Jacques who climbed into the back of the row boat tired, but also very angry at Edouard.

"What the hell is the matter with you? Couldn't you see that I was tired out and couldn't catch up to you? I could have drowned, you son of a bitch," yelled Jacques, ready to punch Edouard, but thought better of it when he realized that Madame Antoinette and her son Jean-Marie were at the dock waiting for them.

Edouard gave no verbal response. Instead he rowed furiously towards the dock for the protection of his Grandmother and his Uncle.

Jacques started wondering about what would have happened if there had been no sand bar which miraculously appeared in a lake that was known for its great depth. What if Madame Antoine and her son Jean-Marie had not appeared at the dock, would Edouard have returned to pick him up? *Why did he want to see me drown?* Jacques asked himself. *Probably because he suspects that I know he stole my money and he's afraid that I will report it to Madame Antoine, who will unintentionally reveal that Edouard did know about my allowance. Unbelievable,* thought Jacques, *that Edouard would want to murder me over fifteen dollars.* He was unaware that other forces such as envy and jealousy also played a part.

Jacques decided not to say anything to Madame Antoinette about this incident because he felt that she would side with her Grandson and make life miserable for Jacques. Besides, he had no place else to go. Now that he was forewarned, he was forearmed.

That night, Jacques awakened to the sound of water and without revealing his awakened state, observed Edouard urinating in one of his rubber boots. Once finished, he walked over to the opened window and dumped the urine out of his boot onto the side of the house and ground below. He returned to his bed after placing the boot under it and went back to sleep as if nothing had happened.

Jacques wondered how many times he had done this before when he was asleep. Perhaps he did this while sleep-walking. *It was a possibility,* he thought. He must give him the benefit of the doubt when he approaches him with this matter.

The next morning Jacques confronted Edouard with the urinating incident, mindful of the boat incident the day before which had a definite influence in his approach to this matter.

"Do you have a bladder problem, Edouard?" asked Jacques.

"Why do you ask?" replied Edouard nervously.

"Because I saw you urinate in your boot and dump the stuff out of the window last night," replied Jacques firmly.

"You saw that? I thought you were asleep," replied Edouard.

"I saw the whole thing. Why couldn't you use the bathroom downstairs?" asked Jacques.

"Because it's too far and I don't want to wake up my Grandmother," replied Edouard in justification.

"Well, you ought to clean that boot afterwards because it stinks up the room," said Jacques disapprovingly.

"You sure ain't from the country, are you?" replied Edouard sarcastically.

"No, and I don't think your Grandmother would approve either," replied Jacques confidently.

"You going to tell my Grandmother?" asked Edouard nervously.

"No I won't, if you promise to clean up that boot," replied Jacques.

"O,K.! I'll clean it up…alright?" replied Edouard.

Jacques did not reply, but walked out of the room shaking his head in disgust.

The hay season was at its peak and the horse-drawn wagons were being filled to the top with hay. One late afternoon, the wagon filled with hay was being pulled by two horses. The horse on the left was young, but the horse on the right was much older. The two horses pulling the wagon filled to the top with hay were attempting to climb the wooden ramp leading into the barn. Grandpa Armand Beaulieu was standing near the old horse cursing it for supposedly not pulling his load.

Jacques stood a few feet from Mr. Beaulieu who had a long leather strap in his right hand with a chain attached to it.

"You lazy ass old horse you, get up that ramp, come on get up there," yelled Mr. Beaulieu while he swung that leather strap and chain repeatedly hitting the side of the old horse, who was starting to foam at the mouth while struggling at pulling the wagon with the aid of the younger horse.

Jacques stood in horror at the sight of this poor horse being beaten with a chain.

"Stop, please stop beating him. He's foaming at the mouth," yelled Jacques in a pleading voice to Mr. Beaulieu.

"Mind your own business and go inside the house," replied Mr. Beaulieu angrily.

Jacques stood there while the old man struck the horse again with the chain and the two horses finally pulled the wagon up the rest of the ramp and into the barn.

The old man turned around with the strap and chain still in his hand facing Jacques, who noticed that there was a pitchfork leaning against the fence near him.

Jacques' anger and loathing for this brutal old man overcame any fear he might have had of him. Jacques stepped next to the pitchfork within arm's reach which did not go unnoticed by Mr. Beaulieu who had observed while working with that young man that he possessed unusual strength for a boy of his age and appeared quite capable of defending himself. Jacques was only going to use the pitchfork to fend off an assault with the chain, not to hurt the old man. But the old man decided not to test Jacques' resolve, especially with a pitchfork at his disposal.

"You don't know anything about horses, kid. Sometimes you have to motivate them," said the old man. "As you saw, it worked and now we can quit for the day," said Mr. Beaulieu, hanging the chain on a nail on the side of the barn.

Jacques walked past the old man with the gait of a boy who had suddenly grown into a young man. Jacques knew the futility of ever changing the attitude of this old man towards animals. He was simply a mean person. Jacques went down to the dock and sat on the edge of it overlooking the river. He didn't want to eat supper with the old man present at the table, so he spent the rest of the evening at the dock thinking about the past, the present and his longing to return to College St. Paul to be with his friends which included those wonderful books in the school library. Jacques rejoiced at the thought that tomorrow was Sunday and he would go fishing, hopefully alone without Edouard's company.

Meanwhile at the farmhouse, the old man sat at the dinner table with Edouard for supper,which was served by Madame Antoinette.

"Where's Jacques? Isn't he eating dinner?" asked Madame Antoinette, coming into the dining room from the kitchen.

"I guess not. I think he's angry at me for whipping the old mare. She wouldn't pull her load up the ramp into the barn," replied the old man. "For a minute there, I thought he was going to stick me with a pitchfork."

"Really. Well, I'll teach him some respect. Tomorrow I won't give him his allowance," said Madame Antoinette.

"Better yet, why don't you put him to work in the potato field tomorrow?" replied the old man. "And let him stay there till he drops from the heat," added the old man vindictively, to the delight of Edouard who had stopped eating to savor every word of the conversation between the old man and his wife.

"He probably won't last more than three hours out there by his lonesome," added Madame Antoinette. "And then he'll come crying, demanding to know why he has to work on Sunday. But crying ain't going to do him any good, cause he has no one to complain to," she said smugly.

Madame Antoinette knew that Jacques' mother was in New York City and the only way Jacques could communicate with her was by letter, but Madame Antoine had control over all incoming and outgoing mail. He couldn't effectively complain to his Grandmother in Montreal as she was old, frail and not in the best of health. *Challenge the old man did he...let's see him challenge me that arrogant, defiant brat,* her temper rising at the thought.

"Don't be fooled by that kid's curly hair and boyish face; he's a lot tougher than he looks," said the old man.

"We'll see about that," said Madame Antoinette defiantly.

It was a bright and cloudless Sunday, perfect for fishing. Jacques was planning on digging up some worms after breakfast, but as soon as he finished eating his rolled oats and toast, Madame Antoinette asked Jacques to follow her onto the porch. She handed him a hoe and told him to follow her as she walked across the road into the potato field.

"I want you to take this hoe and cut all of the weeds around the potatoes and loosen the earth. When you are finished with this row you can start on the next row and so on," said Madame Antoinette in a dictatorial voice. She looked at Jacques for any evidence of resistance or complaint, but did not get any. As she walked back to the house, Jacques realized that Edouard was not out there working on Sunday, their day off, hence this had to be punishment, but for what? Jacques looked at the rows of potatoes which seemed to never end and felt a sense of futility at such a large task with a measly hoe. Nevertheless, he commenced dutifully to hack away at the weeds for the rest of the morning completing three long rows. As he started a fourth row, he thought how he was wasting his mind on such a menial task. He was sure that he was destined for greater use of his brain, but he reasoned this experience would serve to strengthen his tenacity and resolve to complete whatever assignment may be required of him in the future when the stakes are more important. A voice from the house interrupted Jacques' reverie. It was Madame Antoine calling him to report for lunch, after which she walked back into the house with the door slamming behind her, annoyed that Jacques had not behaved as she had predicted.

Jacques brought the hoe back with him and laid it against the wall on the porch before he walked into the house where he went to wash his hands before sitting at the dining table.

"Here's a balogna sandwich and a glass of milk. We've already eaten lunch. When you're finished eating your lunch, you can go back to work in the potato field," announced Madame Antoinette, after which she left the dining room and into the kitchen where she told Edouard in a low voice to go out to the river and enjoy the afternoon.

Jacques did not utter a single word during the entire lunch. He ate his sandwich, drank his glass of milk, then exited the house and went back to the potato field to resume his hoeing.

At supper time, old man Beaulieu asked Madame Antoinette in the presence of Edouard if she was going to call Jacques in to eat his supper.

"The kid is still at it, I see. I don't think he's going to give up," said the old man.

"He's a stubborn kid; I'll say that, but he'll use supper time as an excuse to leave the field, you'll see," said Madame Antoinette.

It was now 8:30 PM and the potatoes and surrounding weeds were barely visible as the sun had almost vanished.

Jacques felt that he was working in a slave labor camp operated by unsympathetic despots and the sooner he left the Beaulieu farm the better. Thus, his days at the farm were numbered as he planned to leave as soon as possible. He had managed after the disappearance of his first fifteen dollars to save another twenty-five dollars which he kept on his person at all times to avoid being victimized a second time. As he worked in the potato field, he thought out a plan of escape which could only be executed when Edouard would be asleep, and that could be risky because of his nocturnal urination.

Meanwhile at the farm house, the old man and his wife came to the realization that it was getting dark outside and Jacques was still working in the potato field.

"I think you had better call the kid into the house. He can't work the field in the dark," said the old man to his wife.

"I guess I'd better," replied Madame Antoinette.

"He missed his supper. You gonna give him something to eat?" asked the old man.

"He knows what time we serve supper. He didn't bother to come in, therefore he can go without it," replied Madame Antoinette in a vindictive tone, knowing full well that Jacques would not leave the field until he was relieved by her or her husband.

Madame Antoinette stepped onto the porch and called out to Jacques to return to the house. Jacques was too far up the field to hear her calling him, but as he raised his eyes he could see her waving at him to come back to the house. He wiped his brow with his shirt sleeve, then placed the hoe handle over his right shoulder and started walking back towards the house. It had been a very long, hot day and Jacques was tired, but he also felt good at having resisted the temptation to quit before sundown. As he entered the house, Jacques could hear Madame Antoinette talking to her husband in an adjacent room and Edouard had apparently retired to his room upstairs. Jacques observed that the kitchen light was off and the dining table had been cleared of dishes and utensils, hence no dinner for him. At this point, Jacques didn't care as he had made other plans.

Jacques learned from Edouard that he was leaving the farm Friday evening to spend the weekend with his father who was visiting his brother Louis in Saint Luc. Jacques saw this as the opportunity he was looking for to make his escape.

That Friday evening, after Edouard left with his father, Jacques retired to his room and very quietly packed the few belongings he had in his suitcase. He had left his winter clothing including his one and only suit and black low quarter shoes in his school wall locker secured with a padlock. His brown beat-up suitcase had a belt at the center to hold it closed due to the poor locking mechanism. Jacques remembered from his journey with Uncle Roland and Aunt Pauline from Montreal to the farm, that there was a train station in the small village at Saint-Jean-Sur-Richelieu about five miles from the farm, and the road in front of the farm ran parallel to the river all the way into the village. He figured that if he left the farm at 4:00 AM, he would get to the village train station by foot at about 6:00 AM, and hopefully he could be on a train to Montreal before anyone at the farm knew of his departure. He didn't know what the train fare would be, but he figured it couldn't be more than the twenty-five dollars he had with him.

Jacques looked at his pocket watch given to him by his Grandmother Nancy when Grandpa was admitted to the hospital with a terminal illness. It was 3:45 AM. Jacques removed the bed sheets from his bed and Edouard's bed and tied them together to form a rope. He tied one end to the radiator underneath the window and tied the other end to his suitcase. Jacques then leaned out of the second story open window with his suitcase, which he slowly lowered to the ground. He then took his handbag and looped it over his left shoulder and grabbing the bed sheet, slowly climbed down to the ground where he untied the suitcase from the sheet, and with his two bags, swiftly walked around the house onto the road on his way to the village without ever looking back. Jacques at first felt a sense of anxiety, followed by relief, then the excitement of adventure. His five mile trek to the village was no different than other long distance marches he had participated in during heavy snow storms sponsored by the College Saint Paul. Jacques encountered no vehicle traffic during those early morning hours, for which he was thankful in case someone became curious about a boy carrying luggage along a deserted road and alerted the authorities.

Jacques arrived at the outskirts of the village and noticed a small wooden building across railroad tracks about one hundred yards from the road. As he approached the building, he observed that it was empty except for several wooden benches. A train schedule was posted on the wall which revealed that a train would be arriving at this station at 6:30 AM with Montreal as its final destination. Jacques decided to sit inside, but out of the line of sight of anyone driving by the station as a precaution. When the train finally arrived, Jacques was the only passenger to board the train, and he was immediately met by a ticket agent who asked him his destination, to which Jacques replied, "Montreal." As the train started moving again, the ticket agent told him the fare was $8.50 and Jacques gave him two five-dollar bills. Accepting the ticket and change, Jacques took a window seat feeling gratified that his plan had so far been a success and he was truly on his way to Montreal.

He wondered though how he would be received by his Grandmother whom he knew loved him, but was apparently not in a condition to look after him. But he rationalized, it would only be for a few weeks before he would be back at the College St. Paul.

The train arrived at the Gare de Montreal. Jacques left the train station and quickly found St. Catherine Street, a major thoroughfare which Jacques knew ran into St. Denis Street which had electric trolleys that traveled right up to his Grandmother's house, located at 5318 St. Denis Street. As Jacques descended the trolley on the corner of the street and walked with his suitcase and shoulder bag on the sidewalk leading up to his Grandmother's residence, he observed no one that he knew. He walked up to the front door to Grandmaman's lower apartment and rang the doorbell. After several seconds the door opened and Grandmaman stared at Jacques in complete surprise, but Jacques observed to his chagrin that there was no welcome smile on her face.

"Hi, Grandmaman," said Jacques in a soft voice.

"Hey! Bien. What are you doing here, Jacques?" asked Grandmaman, totally puzzled at his appearance there.

"Can I come in?" asked Jacques, rather disappointed in the poor reception.

"Of course, mon cher. Come on in," said Grandmaman, opening the door wide and regaining her composure. "Here, leave your bags in your old room and come in the kitchen where I will make you a cup of tea and you can tell your Grandmaman all about it."

Jacques now felt better at Grandmaman's acceptance of his arrival. He thought he would find a sympathetic ear, but now he was not so sure. He felt that Grandmaman was not prepared or perhaps even able to take him in as a boarder for the rest of the summer, although there certainly was enough room in the house. However, as he related to her his reason for leaving the farm to Grandmaman, but omitting his near drowning and the theft of his money, she became visibly upset at the treatment of her Grandson by the Beaulieus.

"For certain Jacques, you're not going back there. You'll stay here until you go back to St. Paul," said Grandmaman sympathetically. "Listen Jacot, I'm going to bake a cake and you can eat the chocolate frosting that's left over, OK?"

"That's sounds great," replied Jacques, happy that he was back with someone who loved him. He learned from Grandmaman that Roland and Pauline, now married, were living with Grandmaman to save money on housing, but both were out at the moment. When they returned to the house later that day to find Jacques residing with them at Grandmaman's home, they accepted him back with love as if he had never left them.

Soon thereafter, Jacques was back at the College St. Paul with his old friends.

"Did you see what's on the school curriculum for us this year? Typing, Bookkeeping and Accounting, and English," said Patrick to Jacques and Claude.

"I don't mind the Typing and English, but that Accounting I hear is tough. Do you know that we have to take the Provincial examinations which are six hours long?" said Claude.

"That's what I heard," said Jacques, who thought to himself that at least he had an advantage with learning English even though he had not spoken English since the age of four. Nevertheless, that was the first language he learned, it was in fact his native language.

"Hey! Jacques, you're going to have a leg up on us in English class, being an American," said Claude.

"I don't know about that. Patrick is Irish-Canadian and his father is fluent in English. That had to rub off on Pat," replied Jacques.

"Can you speak English, Patrick?" asked Claude.

"Not really. I never did speak it. I only listened to my father when he spoke English to other people and picked it up like that. My father tried to teach me some sentences, but I have forgotten whatever he did teach me," replied Patrick. "How about you, Jacques?"

"Whenever my mother spoke with my Grandmother and her sisters and they didn't want me to understand what they were saying, they would call out, 'Big ears..big ears' and switch to English. So after a while I picked up English, enough to understand a lot of what they were saying," replied Jacques.

"Big ears, hey!" laughed Patrick.

Jacques smiled nostalgically.

That afternoon, Jacques and his two friends reported to Typing class and what they saw astounded them. In this narrow room stood two rows of Underwood mechanical typewriters, twelve on each side. A wooden paper holder was fastened to the wall above each typewriter and a black cloth apron hooked to the wall separated the paper holder from the typewriter. The other end of the apron that was not fastened to the wall contained a loop large enough to fit over the head of the typist so that he could not see the typewriter nor the paper on which he was typing on. All that he could see was what was above the apron: the wooden paper holder with the text to be copied.

"Boy! There won't be any chance of cheating in this class," said Claude sarcastically.

"Why Claude…you mean that you cheat in other classes?" replied Patrick in amusement.

"I can see the reason for the apron. The keys are marked with letters. You couldn't avoid looking at the marked keys unless you had such an apron. I think it's a great idea. I wonder which Brother thought of this?" remarked Jacques.

"I don't know, but I'm not ready to pin a medal on him," replied Claude.

"Hey! Here comes Brother Samuel, let's pick a seat," said Claude.

"Alright everyone. Take a seat of your choosing. I am going to pass out to each one of you a booklet that reflects the Lasalle Typing Method. I want you to read this material. It's not very long. You will notice the position of your fingers on the typewriter. With the Lasalle Method, your ring and middle finger of the left hand are placed on the letter W and E while the middle and ring finger of the right hand are placed on the letters I and O. That permits those fingers to be closer to the numbers above. The remaining fingers of the left hand cover the letters A and F and the right hand cover the letter J and the colon/semi-colon. The thumbs are used to hit the space bar at the bottom of the keyboard. This typing method is unlike other methods that require all of your fingers to be placed on the same line of keys such as ASDF and JKL and colon/semi-colon. You will find that when typing numbers using the Lasalle method, your typing speed will not be affected. I want you all to practice on the typewriter without using the apron. When you have had sufficient time to master the keys, then you will use the apron and all of the tests will require that you use the apron. Just remember that speed is not everything, accuracy is what counts. In fact, when you are graded, I will take off five words for every typographical error you make. So you must attempt to make as few errors as possible, otherwise your final speed will suffer dramatically. Alright, take time to read the booklet," said Brother Samuel.

Through the fall until Christmas, Jacques, Patrick and Claude practiced on their typewriter until they were able to produce reasonably accurate typing papers with the use of the apron, in excess of fifty words per minute.

This Christmas season for Jacques was to be spent with his mother Nora at his Grandmother's residence in Montreal. Nora was returning to Montreal just for the Christmas holiday and was returning after New Year's day.

A day after his arrival in Montreal, Jacques got reacquainted with his neighborhood friends Jean-Guy, Pierrot, Bertrand and Marcel who had formed a neighborhood hockey team with other neighborhood teenagers whom Jacques had never met. They called themselves the 'Penguins.' Jacques was invited to join them in a hockey game against an English neighborhood team at the local school rink. Jacques would never be without his hockey skates, pads and stick in winter, thus gladly agreed to play Center for them.

It was just three days before Christmas on a sunny afternoon that Jacques found himself playing for the Penguins. As each team skated around the rink in their respective sectors, Jacques noticed that one of the members of the other team looked vaguely familiar to him.

"Hey! Jean-Guy," called out Jacques. "Come here a minute."

"Yeah! What is it?" replied Jean-Guy, approaching him in full hockey gear.

"That guy over there talking to the goalie. The one wearing the red and white beanie on his head. Isn't that Lapin, the red headed-kid that used to bully us?" asked Jacques.

"By God, it is him. I'll be damned," uttered Jean-Guy in amazement.

"Everything comes to he who waits," said Jacques, repeating one of Grandmaman's sayings.

The referee summoned both teams to take their positions on the ice and Jacques skated to the center of the rink with Jean-Guy on his right wing and Pierrot on his left wing. To Jacques' surprise, Lapin skated towards him and stopped in front of him as the Center player for the English team. He placed his hockey stick at the ready to seize the puck when dropped by the referee, and Jacques looked straight into Lapin's eyes and said, "Remember me, Lapin? I'm the kid you chased out of the school yard two years ago."

Lapin's body tensed as he recognized Jacques as the kid who dared punch him in the school yard, but never caught up with him afterwards. But before Lapin could reply, the referee threw the puck onto the ice between their sticks and with the swiftness of a cat, Jacques lifted Lapin's stick by sliding his own under it and simultaneously caught the puck with the blade of his stick, sending the puck to Jean-Guy who immediately advanced towards the two defensemen. Jacques skated forward blocking Lapin from intercepting Jean-Guy, who then sent the puck to Pierrot to his far left, who skated past the first defenseman. He sent the puck to Jean-Guy, who by now was to the side of the goalie. Jean-Guy quickly flipped the puck into the net for the first goal of the game.

As they faced off again, Jacques got control of the puck and sent it to Jean-Guy again and Pierrot took over Center position while Jacques went to the left. Jacques received the puck and as he gathered speed, Lapin came behind him and unable to overtake him, kept hitting his skate and right ankle causing Jacques excruciating pain. He tried to disregard it while he skated forward outdistancing Lapin, then sending the puck to Pierrot, who sent it to Jean-Guy, who drew the goalie out of his net then scored his second goal. Jacques skated to the side of the rink feeling like his right ankle had been shattered. The one place he thought that you don't have any padding for protection is at the ankles. Of course they didn't wear helmets either.

"Listen, Jean-Guy, my ankle is killing me right now, so why don't you take Center position and I'll take the right wing," said Jacques.

"Sure, no problem Jacques," replied Jean-Guy understandably.

After the face off, the puck went to Pierrot who skated forward, but the puck was taken away from him by an opposing team member, who now skated towards the Penguins' goalie, but was intercepted by Jacques as he got control of the puck and started skating forward in a burst of speed alongside the boards, but was tripped by Lapin who had come from the right side sticking his stick between Jacques' skates sending Jacques off balance but not off his feet. Jacques managed to regain control of the puck, but was being checked against the boards by Lapin who was attempting to get the puck. Unable to seize the puck from Jacques, Lapin whose hands were hidden from view by his body, held his stick firmly in his left hand while driving the top portion of his stick through the loop formed by his right hand, into Jacques' ribs. Jacques hit Lapin in the face with his padded left elbow then suddenly with the speed of a rocket, he skated away with the puck towards the two defensemen sidestepping the one to the left, then sending the puck to Pierrot,then sent back to Jacques, who slapped the puck hard between the goalie's legs into the net for a goal.

"That Lapin is playing dirty hockey," said Jacques to Pierrot and Jean-Guy. "He was punching my ribs with the end of his stick."

"Yeah! But we're scoring the goals and we're winning," said Jean-Guy.

"You know that the referee isn't going to call any penalties. It's just a neighborhood game," said Pierrot.

"Alright. Let's play hockey," yelled the referee.

As they lined up for the face off, Lapin had changed his position from Center to right wingman. Jacques immediately changed position with Jean-Guy and took his position as left wingman, opposite Lapin.

The face off went to the English team which immediately skated into the French sector of the ice rink, but another face off was called by the referee. This face off took place to the left of the Penguins' goalie, and Lapin was positioned facing the entrance/exit door to the rink which is slightly higher than a player's waist and held closed with a single bolt.

Jacques was positioned about ten feet away from Lapin. The referee dropped the puck which went from the stick of the English center to Lapin, who received a full body check by Jacques-the-rocket, driving him through the wooden door so hard that the bolt mechanism was ripped from the door jamb sending both players out of the rink. Lapin landed on his back with his stick flying past him, but Jacques who had gotten into a crouch, remained on his feet. He looked down at the dazed Lapin and said to him in a strong voice, "You want to play rough, you have to learn to take it as well as dish it out." Jacques turned around and stepped back onto the ice rink and skated away from the crowd that had started gathering. The referee was now talking to Jean-Guy about the incident and Jean-Guy explained to him that it was a legitimate body check because Lapin had control of the puck and the door had not been properly locked. When the referee saw Lapin coming back onto the ice, whose pride was bruised more than his body, he decided not to call a penalty and resumed the game. But Lapin's left shoulder was hurting him and he didn't know if he could continue to play. He asked one of his teammates to take his place temporarily.

"I think you put him out of the game," said Jean-Guy to Jacques.

"I didn't think that I hit him that hard," replied Jacques.

"You kidding?" replied Jean-Guy. "You came at him like a freight train."

Jacques felt guilt and remorse. He reacted to what his Grandmother told him, *If another kid hits you, I don't want you to come crying to me, I want you to hit him back.* But he also remembered what the Jesuit priests had preached to him during his yearly religious retreat, *Revenge is mine said the Lord* and *Vengeance is not cured by another vengeance, nor a wrong by another wrong.*

Jacques skated over to where Lapin was sitting on the long bench immediately outside the midsection of the rink where the extra players normally sat. Lapin became visibly nervous at Jacques' sudden appearance before him.

"I want you to know that I'm real sorry for that...body check. I shouldn't have let my temper get the better of me. But you gotta quit poking me with your stick."

"Yeah, alright," said Lapin meekly.

"You're OK...you're not hurt, right?" inquired Jacques.

"No, just a little bruised. But I'll be back in the game in a little while," said Lapin.

"Good. See you on the ice," said Jacques as he turned and skated back towards his comrades. The Penguins won the game 4 to 1.

Jacques was soon back at the College St. Paul for the remainder of the hockey season. But hockey was not the only winter activity in which Jacques and his friends were involved. The school's proximity to the St. Lawrence River, a major seaway for large ships servicing the major cities of Quebec and Montreal, provided the students with one of the world's largest skating rinks. Jacques and his friends would sometimes skate under the supervision of one of the Christian Brothers on the frozen river from the Village of Varennes to the Village of Vercheres and back, a round trip of about 24 kilometers.

Once in Vercheres, the Brother would lead the boys, usually no more than twenty, up a boat ramp to the ice-covered main street where they skated about one hundred and fifty yards to a small brick house that was the town bakery. The Brother would buy each student one hot loaf of bread right out of the oven, which they devoured with utter delight. Feeling rejuvenated, the students would then skate back to Varennes with warm stomachs on the frozen river. The trip back was always best because the wind would be at the boys' backs. These long skating treks developed strong legs and ankles not to mention tremendous endurance, but not many students felt motivated to skate under such frigid conditions for a mere loaf of bread, hot or cold.

When spring arrived, the ice still covered the St. Lawrence River and Jacques observed that there was a large ship plowing into the ice in the channel. Jacques alerted Patrick and Claude and the three boys put on their ice skates and went down to the river's edge. The temperature was just below freezing, but well above temperatures that required heavy winter clothing by these boys who were accustomed to 40-below-freezing weather. That day radiated with sunshine and the ice appeared in some areas to be melting.

"I think that is an ice breaker if I'm not mistaken," said Jacques, looking across the wide expanse of ice towards the deep channel where the ship's bow was surrounded by a huge pile of ice wedges, giving the impression that it was stuck in the ice.

"Let's skate over to the ship and see what's happening," said Jacques, and the others agreed.

While skating over the frozen river, they had to dodge occasional small mounds of snow and ice that had formed on the river. As Jacques lead the pack, one of his skates cut through the ice and into the water below. Jacques quickly reacted by shifting his balance on his skate still on firm ice, thus allowing him to pull his other skate out of the water and onto firm ice. Jacques cautioned Patrick and Claude and all three boys examined the hole in the ice and discovered that the surface ice was about two inches thick with about three inches of water underneath, but then underneath that water was more ice, the thickness of which was unknown to Jacques and his two friends.

"Let's continue skating to the ship. I can see some sailors walking on the ice next to the ship," said Jacques.

"Gee! I don't know Jacques. We don't know how thick this ice is and it looks as if it's melting. Maybe we shouldn't risk it," said Claude apprehensively.

"I tell you Jacques, if we fall through the ice we'll last only a few minutes, and especially with ice skates on, we'll sink like anchors," said Patrick, agreeing with Claude.

"C'mon guys, there's probably two feet of ice underneath those few inches of water. We're more than halfway to the ship. Might as well go the whole way," replied Jacques, who was intrigued by the sight of his first ice breaker. Jacques started to skate towards the ship without turning to see if his two friends were following him, but they did.

They tried to avoid those ice areas that had gathered water at their surfaces, indicating they were sagging and melting at a faster rate. Finally they arrived a few feet from the ice breaker. A ladder leaned against the forward side of the ship, which allowed sailors to climb down onto the ice. Two sailors were measuring the depth of the ice with a long round metal bar the size of a broom handle.

"Excuse me, Sir. How deep is the ice?" asked Jacques of one of the sailors.

The sailor looked at Jacques and his two friends wearing ice skates, and smiled at their adventurous naivety. "It measured 38 inches at this spot," answered the sailor.

"So you're plowing through the ice to clear the channel, hey?" said Claude.

"That's right young fellow," replied the sailor. "I'd advise you to skate back to shore because there's no telling where the ice has thinned out and could break off."

"Let's get out of here," said Claude, anxiously pulling at Jacques' sleeve.

"Alright," said Jacques reluctantly, as he was enjoying watching the sailors working.

"The last one to shore is a rotten egg," said Patrick in a competitive mood, and off they went with Patrick initially leading the pack as Jacques took a last look at the ship on ice. Patrick was well ahead of Claude, occasionally skating around snow-covered ice mounds. Jacques passed Claude and caught up with Patrick when they both noticed that the ice about fifty yards ahead was cracking open like an earthquake fissure. The ice breaking ship behind them had pulled back and then moved forward with its bow climbing atop of the ice causing a huge tear that quickly moved in a large, circular pattern, returning to the open water already cleared by the ship.

Assuming that Claude was right behind them, Jacques yelled, "We gotta move fast and jump over that crack before it gets any wider." Side by side, Jacques and Patrick, in a burst of speed leaped over the three foot gap, both landing on the other side and putting the brakes by turning the blades of their skates sideways sending a spray of powdered ice in the air. As they looked back, they saw Claude still on the other side of the widening gap.

"C'mon Claude," yelled Jacques. "Get yourself a good lead and jump over before the gap in the ice gets wider."

"I don't think I can make it," said Claude, fearful of falling in the frigid water.

"Mon Dieu," said Patrick. "He's frozen with fear. What are we going to do?"

"You stay here and be ready to catch him if he doesn't make a good landing. I'm going over to him," said Jacques.

Jacques turned around and skated back a few yards, turned and with a burst of speed that earned him the nickname of rocket, he leaped over the gap that had now widened to five feet, landing near Claude, who appeared in a state of panic.

"It's alright Claude, you can do it. You must make the jump now before the gap gets any bigger. Here," Jacques said to him, pulling out his Boy Scout knife and opening it to lock the blade in place.

"If you do miss the edge of the ice on the other side, punch a hole in the ice in front of you with this knife and hold on to the handle. It'll keep you from sliding down into the water. Patrick is there to help you and I'll follow right behind you to help you too."

"Jacques, I'm scared," said Claude.

"Here, take the knife and hold it with the blade down so you can drive it into the ice if you need to, OK! Now step back here and get yourself a good lead, Claude."

Claude skated back a few yards with Jacques at his side.

"Alright Claude, give it everything you've got. Go, go, go," yelled Jacques.

Claude took off with the knife in his right hand and leaped off the edge of the ice gap, but his skates missed the edge of the ice on the other side by a foot, causing him to land on the edge of the ice with his upper torso and outstretched arms. Claude started to slide back off the ice into the water when he drove the knife into the ice which stopped his descent. Claude's panic-stricken face stared at Patrick for help. Patrick approached Claude within a few feet, but was afraid to get any closer for fear that he would slip into the water because of the slight incline. Jacques hurriedly made the leap over the gap and assessed the situation.

"I can't hold onto the knife much longer," said Claude.

"Hang on Claude. Hang on. We're coming to get you right now," replied Jacques.

Jacques told Patrick that they would lie down on the ice and use the tip of the skates to keep from sliding into the water. Jacques laid down first and Patrick down behind Jacques and held onto Jacques' skates by the blades. Jacques moved forward with Patrick immediately behind him until he reached Claude. At first, Claude would not let go of the knife to grab Jacques' left hand. Jacques reassured him by grabbing his left hand with his right hand in a firm grip and started to move backwards by moving one skate back, digging its tip into the ice then moving the other skate back and digging that tip into the ice, both Jacques and Patrick repeating the process until Claude's feet were visibly out of the water. Claude then threw the knife aside and grabbed Jacques' other hand and they literally crawled their way back onto firm ice.

Patrick stood up and Jacques got onto his knees in an attempt to help Claude to his feet.

"I can't feel anything in my legs and feet. I think they're frozen," said Claude.

"It's just a temporary thing. C'mon Pat, give me a hand. We'll each hold onto one of his arms around our neck and skate back with him," said Jacques. "Claude, can you just stand on your skates while we carry you forward?"

"Yeah! I think so if you help me up," answered Claude.

"Could you get a hold of the knife that's sitting on the ice over there?" asked Claude.

"Sure," said Jacques, who quickly retrieved the knife, closed the blade and gave it to Claude. "Keep it as a souvenir."

"Hey! It saved my life," replied Claude.

On shore, Brothers Samuel and Antoine, dressed in their usual black habits covered with dark coats and wearing their leather and fur hats, observed the three boys moving towards them in military unison, two of them carrying the wounded one back to the academy.

"Mon Dieu! Look who's waiting for us on shore," said Jacques.

"It looks like Brother Samuel and Brother Antoine," replied Patrick. Claude didn't seem to care at this point. He just wanted to get into a warm place.

"Qu'est sera, sera," said Jacques. "No use worrying about it now, hey!"

As the three boys approached the shore, Brother Antoine spoke to the boys first.

"What were you boys doing on the lake this time of year? Didn't you know it's dangerous to skate on the lake when the ice is melting?" said Brother Antoine.

Before the boys could answer Brother Antoine's questions, Brother Samuel added, "What's wrong with Claude?"

"He fell into the water when the ice broke," replied Jacques.

"How are you feeling, Claude?" asked Brother Samuel.

"My legs are frozen," answered Claude meekly.

"OK! Get him to the infirmary right away. Afterwards, I want to see you, Jacques and Patrick, in the Principal's office. Is that understood?" said Brother Antoine.

"Yes, Sir!" replied Jacques and Claude in chorus.

Jacques and Patrick first brought Claude to the recreation room where they took off his ice skates and retrieved his boots from his locker, but Claude's socks and trousers were all wet. Claude could now stand up and feeling was coming back into his legs and feet, but with great pain. They helped him get to the infirmary where he was attended to by Brother Michel. As Jacques and Patrick walked out of the infirmary towards the Principal's office, they wondered about their fate.

"What do you think they're going to do to us?" asked Patrick.

"I think the best thing to do is to tell the truth and let the chips fall where they may. After all, what did we do wrong except perhaps use poor judgment, but that's not a crime is it?" replied Jacques.

"I suppose you're right," answered Patrick. "We did save Claude's life. That should be worth something towards lessening our punishment, right?" exclaimed Patrick.

"Well we're now here," Jacques said, pointing to the door to the Principal's office.

Jacques knocked on the door and heard the voice of Brother Denis say, "Come in."

After entering and closing the door behind them, Jacques and Patrick stood side by side before

Brother Denis, who was sitting behind his large, imposing desk. Standing to his right stood Brother Samuel.

"Brother Antoine is interviewing Claude as we speak. So I want the complete truth as to what happened out there on the river. We'll start with you Jacques," said Brother Denis in a firm, no nonsense voice.

Jacques related the entire incident exactly as it happened.

"Patrick. Do you agree with Jacques' version of the incident?" asked Brother Denis.

"Yes Sir, I do. It's exactly what happened Sir," replied Patrick.

After knocking on the door, Brother Michel entered and asked to speak to Brothers Denis and Samuel out of earshot of the two boys who remained standing at attention.

Shortly thereafter, Brothers Denis and Samuel re-entered the Principal's office.

"You can both stand at ease," said Brother Denis.

"I think all three of you boys used very poor judgment in going out onto the river at this time of year. You should have known better and I ought to punish all three of you most severely. However, I must applaud your courage and ingenuity in saving your classmate's life, for I have no doubt he would have perished without your help. And for that reason, I am not going to impose any punishment. But I must warn you not to go skating onto that river again, at least not until next winter. Is that understood?" said Brother Denis.

"Yes Sir and thank you," said Jacques, with Patrick echoing his thanks.

After exiting the Principal's office, Patrick expressed his relief to Jacques.

"Boy! We sure lucked out this time," said Patrick.

"Yeah! And an experience we won't soon forget," replied Jacques philosophically.

As Jacques' athletic abilities improved, so did his typing speed and English studies as limited as they were. By now Jacques was competing with Emile and Patrick for the typing championship. Emile had already established the lead with 75 words per minute after errors were subtracted, with Jacques at 73 WPM and Patrick at 71 WPM. The final contest was scheduled on the forthcoming Thursday where they had to type five minutes in French and five minutes in English and the scores for both would be tallied for an average speed. Emile was so sure that he would win the contest that he openly bragged to his classmates that he was the 'King' of all typists and no one could beat him.

"What do you think of the King's claim that he's the best typist in school?" said Patrick to Jacques, with Claude listening in.

"He wants to be King, let him. Employers don't want Kings, they want workers who can type. And by the way, the accounting exams are coming soon, and that's going to be the toughest challenge of them all. Are you ready for that?" asked Jacques.

"God! Don't remind me. I'm not so good at numbers," said Claude to Jacques and Patrick.

Friday arrived and the typing test results were posted on the bulletin board. Jacques had won with the score of 84 words per minutes followed by Patrick at 81 WPM and Emile the King at 77 WPM.

"Hey! Jacques, let's go over to the King and rub it in about his typing score," said Patrick.

"Naw! I think he got the message about the virtue of humility. And frankly, who cares anyway?" replied Jacques, dismissing the idea as childish even though he himself was still a juvenile.

The rest of the school year went without unusual incidents. During the warm spring weather, Jacques learned to play softball where the pitcher delivers the ball to the batter with an underhand pitch, which Jacques found to be an awkward way to throw a ball. He found it more natural to throw a ball with an overhand pitch as they do in baseball, a sport not available at the College St. Paul, which was unfortunate as Jacques later discovered.

On June fifteenth, the end of the school year approached, Jacques received a letter from his mother who was still in New York City, informing him that he would be spending the summer at a Boy Scout Camp in the Lake of Fourteen Islands, near St. Emile about 60 miles northwest of Montreal. Again, Uncle Roland and Aunt Pauline transported Jacques from the College to the Boy Scout Camp. Jacques was told that even though this was arranged through the Catholic Church in Montreal, parents had to pay a substantial fee for their children to spend the summer at camp. Due to his mother's limited finances, the Church agreed to accept Jacques' labor at the camp as payment. Jacques was therefore expected to assist in cleaning the kitchen and dining hall among other duties at the discretion of the Chief Camp Counselor who turned out to be an arrogant, egotistical young man who enjoyed wielding his authority over the youngsters under his control in camp.

Jacques, now fifteen years old, had already developed the physique of a young man with unusually developed shoulders on a broad back and thick powerful thighs which reflected his formative years of aggressive athletic activity. Jacques appreciated his physical prowess, but also knew that he would not reach his full potential unless he continued his participation in sports. The Boy Scouts had a swimming and canoeing program at this camp on the Lake of Fourteen Islands, and Jacques decided to take full advantage of it in spite of his work schedule.

On his first day at Camp, Jacques reported to the Chief Counselor, Mr. Vincent Beaujolais, a tall, slim, dark-haired young man of twenty-five years who sported a wide mustache. He greeted Jacques and another boy named Matthieu without any friendliness. Instead he got right down to business.

"You boys have been assigned to me to earn your keep. The cook, Mr. LaPorte, will give you your duties which include cleaning all of the pots and pans, clearing all of the tables in the dining room, gathering all of the dishes which all have to be washed and stacked in their proper place for the next meal. Also after supper, you will have to mop all of the floors. I will inspect your work daily and if you have performed your duties to my satisfaction, you will then be permitted to participate in Scout activities. Do you have any questions?" said Mr. Beaujolais in an authoritarian tone.

"Do we eat here in the kitchen or with the other Boy Scouts in the dining room?" asked Jacques.

"You will eat here in the kitchen," replied Mr. Beaujolais. "Any other questions?"

Neither boy responded.

"Alright then, you stay here. Mr. LaPorte will be here shortly to get you to work," said Mr. Beaujolais.

After Mr. Beaujolais left the kitchen, Matthieu walked over to Jacques and offered his hand as a gesture of friendship.

Jacques shook Matthieu's hand and said, "Welcome to Camp Beaujolais."

Matthieu smiled and replied, "You think he owns the camp?"

"No, he doesn't. But he acts like it. How old are you Matthieu?" Jacques asked, because he was small in stature.

"I'm 13 going on 14 years," replied Matthieu, "and you?"

"Just turned 15 a few months ago," replied Jacques.

At that moment an older, balding but otherwise hairy man in his late thirties walked into the kitchen and greeted the boys with a "hello." After introducing himself as Mr. LaPorte, without revealing his first name so that they would address him only as Mr. LaPorte, he instructed both boys as to their respective duties and then got them to work.

Two weeks went by without incident and both boys got into the work routine which allowed them to participate in many of the camp activities. Jacques perceived Matthieu as timid in nature, who loved sports, but did not possess a natural ability to excel in them. Jacques liked him because of his honest effort to be nice to everyone he met. He was just a nice kid who would never think of hurting anyone.

Then one day, the milk delivery man appeared at the kitchen door asking for Mr. LaPorte, and Jacques informed him that he had just left and would not return until 3PM.

The deliveryman told Jacques that the refrigerator had only one five-gallon can of milk left, hence he needed three more cans of milk instead of one, and asked if he could find someone to authorize the extra delivery. Jacques told the delivery man to wait while he sought the Chief Camp Counselor, Mr. Beaujolais.

There sat Mr. Beaujolais in a folding chair of wood and cloth with four other counselors sitting around him talking in a jovial manner. Jacques quietly approached them, careful not to interrupt their conversation when Mr. Beaujolais looked straight at Jacques in a condescending manner and asked, "What do you want?"

"The milk delivery man sent me to find you because he said that we need an additional two five-gallon cans of milk and he needs your authorization," said Jacques.

"How dare you interrupt me with kitchen matters? That's Mr. LaPorte's responsibility, not mine, now get out of here," replied Mr. Beaujolais tersely.

"But Sir. Mr. LaPorte is gone and won't be back until 3 PM, and the delivery man can't wait that long. That's why I came to you," replied Jacques, annoyed at Mr. Beaujolais' demeanor towards him.

Embarrassed in front of the other counselors who secretly despised his treatment of this young boy, Mr. Beaujolais attempted to regain his command.

"You've got my authorization, now run along like a good little boy and deliver your message to the milkman," replied Mr. Beaujolais with a sardonic laugh.

Jacques felt unduly humiliated and as he left he uttered, "And shoot the messenger, why don't you?" which was overheard by Mr. Beaujolais and the two counselors sitting to his left. Mr. Beaujolais sat there for a moment trying to decide what to do regarding that last remark made by Jacques. *How dare this young wipper-snapper talk back to me,* he thought. With that, he got up from his chair and walked back to the kitchen to find Jacques, who by that time had delivered the message to the milkman, who had since departed.

Mr. Beaujolais quickly entered the kitchen to find Jacques near the sink drinking a glass of water.

"How dare you talk back to me, and in front of my colleagues? I'll have you know that you are here at my pleasure and I can send you back to Montreal at anytime I so desire," threatened Mr. Beaujolais.

Jacques realized that he could not afford to be dismissed and sent back to Montreal. His Grandmother was in ill health and he simply could not return to the city, not a second time. He knew he was in trouble, nevertheless…

"I was merely doing my job of relaying a message and didn't deserve to be treated like a dog, especially in front of the other counselors. I'm sure that Father Clement who sponsored me on behalf of my mother would agree that I came here to work, not to be abused, Sir. So you do what you have to do…and so will I…Sir," said Jacques firmly, with a gaze that spelled determination and unbending will.

Mr. Beaujolais knew that Father Clement was in charge of funding the camp for the church and wielded enormous power. He also knew that he could be summarily fired for abusing any of the boys at camp, and there were at least four witnesses who heard the entire conversation. Mr. Beaujolais decided to drop this matter, but there would be other opportunities to redress this insolent young man.

"Alright Mr. Markham, I'll treat this matter as a misunderstanding and leave it at that," said Mr. Beaujolais, and walked out of the kitchen and the matter was never raised again. However, Mr. Beaujolais was still steaming over this impertinent boy getting the best of him.

It was Friday at 7:30 PM. The dining room had been cleared by Jacques, who also had washed the pots and pans. Matthieu had just stacked the dishes, glasses and cups. He had cleaned and gone to the bathroom to get ready to meet his mother who had come up to see him from Quebec City. They were to spend the evening and part of Saturday before she went back to Quebec City. Mr. LaPorte the cook had left a few minutes earlier. Jacques noticed a number of clean cups that had been left by Matthieu on the kitchen counter that should have been placed on the shelf against the kitchen wall. He placed the cups on a tray and brought them over to place them on the shelf ,when he heard someone walk into the kitchen. It was Mr. Beaujolais, wearing britches and carrying a swagger stick in his right hand. Apparently he had been riding a horse.

"Well Markham, are you enjoying your work?" he said sarcastically.

"Yes, Sir," replied Jacques, continuing to place the cups on the shelf without turning his head.

Mr. Beaujolais walked over and grabbed one of the cups remaining on the tray, examined it and said, "That cup is dirty. Needs washing again," and placed the cup on the counter. Mr. Beaujolais grabbed another cup and examined it. "That cup is dirty too, damn it," and threw the cup to the cement floor, shattering it. Jacques picked up the first cup from the counter and looked at it and failed to see any dirt in it.

"I'm sorry Sir, but I don't see any dirt in this cup," said Jacques, observing Mr. Beaujolais hitting his swagger stick against his right leg while staring at Jacques intently.

"Are you questioning me, boy?" asked Mr. Beaujolais.

"No, Sir. I am merely making an observation," replied Jacques, who did not want to reveal to Mr. Beaujolais that it was Matthieu who had washed the dishes and cups for fear that he would punish him in some way that would prevent him from seeing his mother that evening.

"I want you to rewash every cup in that cupboard and on the shelf right now, and I don't care how long it takes. Is that clear, boy?"

Jacques felt like stepping up to this arrogant man and punching him in the face so hard that he would drive his nose into his feeble brain, but he knew that the consequences would be too grave, hence swallowed his pride and answered, "Yes Sir," and walked over to where the broom and dustpan were kept and started to sweep up the pieces of the broken cup, after which Mr. Beaujolais left the kitchen feeling very pleased with himself. Jacques asked himself why God permitted people like Mr. Beaujolais to go unpunished, then remembered the retreat priest's description of Purgatory in all its horror, which satisfied his desire for justice.

Jacques never told Matthieu of the incident with the cups because he didn't want him to feel guilty about Jacques having to rewash them. The lesson he learned was not to linger in the kitchen after the work is done.

It was a bright, sunny afternoon at the camp and Jacques had just returned from canoeing, which required that they wear their bathing suits in case the canoe overturned. As Jacques neared the cabin where he slept and kept his clothes, counselor Bernard approached him and asked him to go down to the lake where the boys swam and fetch Paul Germain to call his father back from the office immediately on an urgent matter.

Jacques ran down to the lake shore and perused the small beach area to no avail. He then looked out at the raft floating about 150 yards from shore and observed several boys jumping and diving off the wooden raft supported by four pontoons. Jacques yelled out Paul's name several times and a middle-aged man dressed in beige trousers and a dark brown shirt walked up to him.

"You've got a powerful voice young man. Ever thought of becoming an opera singer?" he said to Jacques, who looked surprised at the man's compliment.

"No, I never thought about it, but thank you," he replied. Jacques then focused his attention on the raft and decided to swim out to it and see if Paul was there.

Counselor Lance appeared on the beach as Jacques began swimming to the raft and observed with interest Jacques' style of swimming. As Jacques was swimming back with Paul behind him, Lance again observed Jacques and Paul swimming with their heads out of the water, struggling with each arm stroke without the benefit of leg strokes and thought to himself, *These kids needed a lot of help with their swimming style.*

As Jacques and Paul exited the water, both breathing heavily, Counselor Lance walked up to them.

"I've been watching the two of you swimming, and I'd like to give you some tips that would improve your swimming. For sure you wouldn't be out of breath after only a 150 yard swim."

"Yes Sir. We'd appreciate any help you can give us," replied Jacques for the two of them.

"First of all you must learn how to breathe. You breathe the same way when you're swimming as when you're on land. You inhale and then exhale, right?" said Lance.

"Now let me show you the position you must take when swimming," added Lance, who then bent over at the waist so that his upper body was parallel to the ground.

"Your head should be resting in the water with your eyes in the water looking straight ahead. The water should be at your forehead. Think of yourself as lying in bed in a prone position, totally relaxed. Now, as you're looking straight ahead, you begin your arm stroke like this," said Lance, stretching his right arm and hand forward.

"Your hand with closed fingers, catches the water, you then bring the hand and forearm down pulling at the water, then as your right arm passes your head, you turn your head to the right without raising it, and you then open your mouth wide to catch a breath of air, all the time your right arm is moving back and now it is pushing the water until it is then out of the water with your elbow high out of the water. When your right arm is about to end its pushing, the left arm begins its cycle of catching, pulling and pushing the water, thus moving you forward. But the only time you turn your head to take a breath is when your right arm passes your head. As soon as you have taken a breath of air, you turn your head back to its forward position and you start exhaling the air slowly through your nose," explained Lance, demonstrating the arm strokes while inhaling and exhaling.

"OK, guys, let me see you do it on land like I just showed you," said Lance.

Jacques and Paul each took their bent position and started copying Lance, who again was demonstrating the stroke.

"No, no, don't lock your arms straight down. Bend your arms at the elbow near the end of the pulling cycle and through the pushing cycle. At the end of the pushing cycle, it is your elbow that should come out of the water first and it should be higher than the hand. That way your hand and forearm are resting while you are bringing it forward for the next cycle. Your shoulder is then doing all of the work," Lance explained.

"Now you must learn to use your legs and feet to give you extra propulsion and better position in the water. While you are swimming using your arms, you must also be using a flutter kick. Let me show you from this bench," said Lance, sitting at the edge of a wooden bench and stretching out his legs.

"You kick from the hip or upper thighs, not from the knees, and you leave your ankles loose so that they flip-flop like flippers on a fish. Bend your feet slightly towards each other as if you were pigeon toed, that will give your feet a larger surface to push against the water, and as you kick up and down, bend your knees only slightly. Most of the kicking effort should come from the hip and thighs. By the way, don't kick your feet above the water, you get no power from the air, only from the water. OK, let's see you guys practice on this bench."

Jacques and Paul each took their sitting position on the wooden bench and practiced their leg kick while Counselor Lance watched with a feeling of satisfaction at having helped these two boys who would probably remember this event all of their lives.

"Alright, guys, I've got a meeting to attend, so you go and practice what I've taught you in waist-deep water first and after you've mastered it, you'll be able to swim anywhere," said Counselor Lance.

"Thanks a lot. That was great advice, Mr. Lance," said Jacques, with Paul shaking his head affirmatively.

"I've got to go now, so take care," said Counselor Lance, leaving the beach.

"Paul, have you forgotten that you're supposed to call your father right away?" said Jacques.

"Oh! Yeah. I'll see you later Jacques," said Paul, leaving the beach in a run.

Jacques went back into the water to practice what he had learned from Counselor Lance and within a week of practicing every day, he had become a very proficient swimmer. One day, Lance came down to the beach and observed Jacques swimming back from the raft and couldn't believe how smooth a swimmer Jacques had become in such a short time. He thought that this boy was a natural athlete who with good coaching could become a world class swimmer. Too bad that he probably would never see this boy again in four weeks when the camp closed for the season. As Jacques walked out of the shallow water onto the beach, he spotted Counselor Lance and went over to him.

"Hi, Mr. Lance. I've been following your swimming instructions and what a great difference it made in my swimming," said Jacques gratefully.

"Yes, I noticed your progress. Listen Jacques, you've got great potential as a swimmer. You should join a swim team the first chance you get," said Lance encouragingly.

"I will, first chance I get Mr. Lance," replied Jacques, and subsequently reflected on his chances at joining a swimming team which he knew were nil. College St. Paul at Varennes did not have a swimming pool. Perhaps later on when he moved to another school he might get such an opportunity. *Oh well,* he thought, *qu'est sera, sera.*

As Jacques was returning to his cabin to change clothes so that he could go to work in the dining room, he came across Paul who was also returning to his cabin from the camp office where he had been in consultation with his counselor after talking to his father on the telephone.

"Hey, Paul. Everything OK?" asked Jacques, noticing that Paul had apparently been crying.

"I just found out that my Grandmother died," Paul said, holding back tears.

"Gee! I am so sorry to hear that. Listen, is there anything I can do for you?" asked Jacques with great empathy.

"No, thank you. She was my favorite human being in the whole world since my Mom died when I was small," replied Paul.

Paul's remark reminded Jacques of his closeness to his own Grandmaman Nancy, whom he adored, and a feeling of great sadness came over him at the thought of losing his Grandmother.

"I understand what you're saying Paul, believe me. Tonight we have apple pie for desert. If you want, I'll get you an extra piece from the kitchen, how's that?" said Jacques in an attempt to cheer up his friend.

"I don't feel much like eating, but I'll see," replied Paul thankfully.

"Alright, see you at dinner. I've got to get ready now," said Jacques, who then went to his cabin.

At dinner time, Jacques looked for Paul, who failed to appear at the dining room.

Having been quite busy at his job, Jacques thought that perhaps Paul had come to dinner and left before Jacques had a chance to see him. Jacques and Matthieu worked in the kitchen and dining room longer than usual after the Scouts had been served dinner due to a breakdown of the metal tray washing clipper, which necessitated that all trays be washed by hand. Tired after a long day of activity and work, Jacques walked back to his cabin shared by five other boys and retired for the night.

Daylight made its way through the east window to the cabin, and Jacques awakened simultaneously with two of the other boys sleeping in the same cabin to a commotion of loud voices somewhere outside their cabin. Jacques got up from his bunk and opened the door to see what the fuss was about and saw several counselors going around each cabin telling them to stay in there. Then Counselor Bernard came over to Jacques, who was standing in the cabin doorway, and told him to step inside the cabin. Once inside the cabin, Mr. Bernard instructed all of the occupants of the cabin to remain inside until further notice.

"Can you tell us what is happening, Sir?" asked Jacques.

"No, I cannot at this time. You'll know soon enough. Now please remain in your cabin," said Mr. Bernard, leaving and closing the door behind him.

Jacques immediately went to the cabin window that faced the wooded area. Several of the other cabin occupants crammed next to Jacques to see what was happening. From the cabin window Jacques observed two uniformed policemen and two stretcher-bearers walking into the woods behind the row of cabins, followed by a Priest dressed in the usual black robe and white collar, plus another man of medium-build wearing a three-piece suit and a hat and two of the counselors, all walking in Indian file.

"Mon Dieu! What is going on?" asked the boy next to Jacques rhetorically.

"I don't know, but it must be something serious that happened in the woods," responded another boy.

After some time had elapsed, Jacques observed from the window that two men were carrying a stretcher with a black cloth completely covering the person they were carrying. One of the uniformed policemen was walking in front of the stretcher-bearers and the other uniformed policeman was walking behind them while talking to the man in the three-piece suit. They were followed by the Priest who was carrying a small Bible, and then several counselors. Jacques speculated that someone was found seriously hurt or possibly dead. He quickly rejected that latter possibility, not in this camp.

Soon after, Counselor Lance came into Jacques' cabin and asked Jacques to come with him to the office. Jacques looked puzzled, but followed Lance to the bewilderment of the other cabin occupants.

As Jacques entered the camp office with Counselor Lance behind him, Jacques was greeted by the gentleman dressed in the three-piece suit who asked him to have a seat. Jacques could now identify the two policemen standing behind the gentleman as Royal Canadian Mounted Policemen from their distinct uniforms. The Priest was not present nor were the two stretcher bearers. The Chief Camp Counselor Vincent Beaujolais and Counselor Lance were also present in the background.

"I'm inspector Larue. I'm told that your name is Jacques Markham, is that correct?" asked the gentleman in the three-piece suit, now smoking a curved pipe that dispensed an aroma of honey and burnt wood.

"Yes Sir, that's correct," answered Jacques, finding the pipe's aroma quite pleasant.

"I understand that you knew Paul Germain quite well," said Mr. Larue.

"Well, I only got to know him well today, Sir," answered Jacques politely.

"When was the last time you saw Paul Germain?" asked Mr. Larue.

"After he had just learned from his father that his Grandmother had died," replied Jacques thoughtfully.

"What did he say to you? Try to think of his exact words. Don't leave out anything," said Mr. Larue.

"Well, he told me that his Grandmother was his favorite human being after his mother died. He was very upset over her passing, Sir. I told him that I would see him at dinner time and offered to give him an extra piece of pie in an effort to console him, but I never saw him at dinner time. I don't know if he ever showed up at the dining hall," replied Jacques.

"Was that the last time you saw him?" asked Mr. Larue.

"Yes Sir. That was the last time. Was that him that they carried out on a stretcher?" asked Jacques inquisitively.

"I'm afraid so, young man," replied Mr. Larue.

Jacques hesitated, afraid to ask the crucial question.

"What is Paul's condition, Sir?" asked Jacques as delicately as possible.

"I'm very sorry. Your friend was discovered hanging from a tree branch in the woods behind his cabin. We believe it was a suicide," answered Mr. Larue in a low and somber voice.

Jacques left the camp office in disbelief at what he had been told by Mr. Larue, and wondered if there had been anything he could have done to prevent it. Were there any signs that he had missed? Jacques never found the answer.

That was to be the first and last summer that Jacques would spend at the Boy Scout Camp at the Lake of Fourteen Islands.

Jacques was glad to be back in the familiar surroundings of the College St. Paul at Varennes in the Quebec Province where he could socialize with his student friends.

During the fall season, the students played rugby in addition to the game of drapeau, both of which were impromptu games that solicited interested players available at the playground. It was during one of those games of rugby that Jacques was tripped by another student, which sent Jacques flying into one of the wire-covered posts of the softball backstop which happened to be located within the area where the students play rugby. Jacques hit the wire-covered post with the right cheek of his face. He rolled on the ground, stunned by the impact. As he stood up Claude and another student Alain ran up to Jacques, while the boy who tripped Jacques was backing away fearful of what he had done. Claude and Alain noticed bloody gouges and shredded skin on Jacques' left cheek. Claude noticed that Jacques appeared groggy so he placed Jacques' left arm around his neck while Alain did the same with Jacques' right arm and they walked him to the school dispensary. There was no doubt in Claude's mind that Jacques would be permanently scarred and possibly disfigured from this injury, and Brother Gaston who attended to Jacques' injury thought the same due to the depth of the gouges caused by the wire. However, to everyone's surprise, after six weeks of careful nurturing of the wound, there was hardly any evidence of the injury, and a month later, there was not even a visible scar on Jacques' normally perfect skin. Brother Gaston remarked to Brother Samuel that this boy's healing power was extraordinary, not only in this instance, but in other instances where he had sustained injuries. Jacques' physical appearance did not betray the slightest evidence of having been involved in any fist fights, hockey or rugby injuries, although he had experienced many of them. This blessing could indeed have a negative impact on Jacques' welfare in those instances where bullies seeking soft victims might mistake Jacques for one of them due to his lack of battle scars and rough edges, but for one exception, his hands, which because of the cold weather were mostly covered. Not only did Jacques have large, well-padded hands, but his knuckles and especially the joints at the first phalange of his index and middle fingers contained protruding calluses that over time had become part of the bone as a result of constant pounding of the punching bag. Fortunately, at the College St. Paul, Jacques was well known for his physical prowess and lack of timidity, thus not vulnerable to those who preyed on the weak.

Christmas arrived with plenty of snow as expected at that global latitude, and two-thirds of the students went home for the holidays. Jacques was one of the unfortunate few that remained at the college this Christmas. What made it worse for him was the absence of his close friends Patrick and Claude, who both went home for the holidays. On Christmas Eve, Jacques and the other remaining students attended Midnight Mass at the Village Church where the church choir composed of young boys from the village school and an adult female vocalist sang like angels from heaven. To Jacques, Midnight Mass was the most impressive and enjoyable religious worship in the annals of the Catholic Church. As Jacques exited the church, he noticed that some of the adults with their children were leaving by sled pulled by one or two horses. A large blanket was strewn over their legs as they sat in their well-padded seat facing the pulling horses. Some of them had a bell or two tied to the horse's harness which rang in concert with the horse's gait. Large snow flakes floated down over the entire scene imprinted forever in Jacques' memory. All that was missing was the 'Reveillon' with the family gathering. A sudden sadness came over Jacques, who soon dismissed it as a luxurious sentiment he could not afford.

On the 10th of March 1947, Jacques' birthday, his mother Nora surprised him by her arrival at the College. She brought him a heavy turtleneck sweater for his birthday, plus a gift of ten dollars. Then she made him a proposition.

"Jacques, you know that your birthplace is Brooklyn, New York?" Nora asked him.

"Yes, I know," he answered questioningly.

"How would you like to move to New York City?" Nora asked him.

"Well, I don't know. It is my birthplace…and I am an American," he answered pensively.

"It's your choice Jacques. You decide, mon cher," said Nora.

"I've got one more year to go here you know, Maman," Jacques stated.

"You can enter an American high school in New York and finish your schooling there," answered Nora.

"Where would that be…the school I mean?" asked Jacques.

"Actually we would live with Mrs. Robb, in Rego Park, Long Island, New York and you would go to high school there on Long Island. It's a nice neighborhood," said Nora encouragingly.

"Where's Rego Park, Long Island, Maman?" asked Jacques.

"It's about a half hour subway ride from Manhattan, New York. You've heard of Manhattan, haven't you?" said Nora.

"Yeah! I've heard of it," answered Jacques, who was much in thought about his mother's proposition. "Well, I am an American and I should see my birthplace and my native country."

"That's right, mon cher. Do you want to come live with your mother in New York?" asked Nora anxiously.

"Yes I do. I'm looking forward to it," answered Jacques, with an adventurous mind.

After his mother's departure, Jacques informed Patrick and Claude of his imminent move to New York at the end of the school year in June. Neither of them was happy about his declaration, which made Jacques a bit uneasy about his decision. However, the thought of seeing and living in his native country overcame any doubts he may have had about his decision. The fact that he still had one year of schooling to complete before graduation at the College St. Paul was overcome by his mother's insistence that the high school in Long Island, New York that he would be entering was more progressive and he would be residing with her in Mrs. Robb's house where he would have his own bedroom. In addition, he would have access to several wonderful beaches and to the most exciting city in the world. *I'm sixteen,* he reflected, *and ready to trade the provincial lifestyle for the big city life and all of its opportunities. New York here I come!* he yelled in silence.

CHAPTER II
REPATRIATION

Jacques left Montreal with his mother Nora aboard a train that transported them to Grand Central Station in the middle of Manhattan, New York. From there Nora, accompanied by Jacques carrying two large suitcases, boarded a subway train which took them to Forest Hills, Long Island, New York. A short taxi ride later, Jacques and his mother arrived at Mrs. Robb's house on Austin Street in Rego Park. Her house consisted of a two-story wood frame Colonial with a gable roof, much like all of the other houses on that street. Mrs. Robb, a retired elderly widow and long-time friend of Nora, received Jacques with mixed emotions. She never had boarders before, and the sudden although expected appearance of Nora with a fully grown son, awakened her to the realization that her privacy would now be limited. She wondered whether the monthly rent from Nora would truly compensate her for the required sacrifice of her peace and tranquility even though her primary motivation for inviting them was to help her friend Nora and son Jacques establish roots in the United States.

Mrs. Robb liked Jacques' good manners and kindness towards her. She observed that he was a quiet and well disciplined teenager who appeared in a hurry to become a capable and independent adult. As the summer neared its end, Jacques expressed his eagerness to matriculate at Forest Hills High School, well known for its modern facilities and sports activities.

It was September, the day after Labor Day that Jacques enrolled at Forest Hills High School under the name of James Markham as reflected on the birth certificate that he had to bring to the school administration office. Markham was impressed by the enormous size of the school and its grounds. Markham was also surprised by the fact that there were approximately four thousand students of both genders enrolled there, a far cry from the College St. Paul with an enrollment of only one hundred and fifty boys, but Forest Hills High School was not a boarding school.

Markham explored the school grounds including the outdoor sports facilities located in back of the school which included a quarter mile cinder track. From the rear campus which extended about one hundred feet from the school building to a ledge that dropped thirty feet lower to the athletic grounds occupied mainly by the cinder track, Markham observed that several tennis courts surrounded by a high wire fence occupied the land in back of the track. The soccer field with its two goals was situated within the track. The baseball backstop faced the east end of the track. As Markham leaned against the wrought iron fence situated at the top of the thirty foot cement ledge that ran the width of the athletic field, a lanky, dark haired teenager wearing sneakers and carrying a shoulder bag full of school books strolled up to the fence near Markham.

"Looks like they're going to have to do some work on that track," remarked the teenager. "I don't think I've ever seen you on the athletic field…are you new here?" asked the teenager, who was sure he would have remembered a student with Markham's unique physique and appearance.

"Yeah! I'm new here," replied Markham cautiously.

"My name is David…David Shlackter," turning his body towards Markham and extending his hand.

"I'm Jim Markham," he said, shaking David's hand firmly.

"Where are you from, Jim?" asked David.

"I just moved here from Montreal, Canada," answered Markham.

"Montreal…really. Boy, it gets cold up there. I guess you played a lot of hockey, huh?" said David with a keen interest in his new acquaintance.

"Yeah! It gets pretty cold, but we get used to it," said Markham.

"Did you ever do any competitive running like on a track team?" asked David.

"No. This is the first time I ever laid eyes on a track for runners," said Markham.

"Well, I am a member of the school track team and I'm also on the cross-country team. You know, they have try-outs for the cross-country team tomorrow afternoon after school at 4:00 PM. Would you be interested?" asked David.

"I don't know…how far do you have to run in a cross-country race?" asked Markham.

"The race itself is two and a half miles, but in practice we run three miles," answered David.

"Oh! Yeah! Where do you practice?" said Markham.

"In the large open field over there," he said, pointing to the west side of the school campus. "Past the school yard. That's where we will meet tomorrow for the try-outs. Just wear your gym shorts, T-shirt and sneakers and you'll be all set," David added, hopeful that Markham would show up.

"I'll think about it. Maybe I will try out for the team," said Markham.

"You've got nothing to lose, Jim. Hope to see you there tomorrow," said David as he started to leave the athletic grounds. Markham followed David with his eyes, observing him being joined by two other students walking off the campus.

The next afternoon, Markham had a student-faculty conference wherein he learned that due to his limited English language skills he was being set back academically at the sophomore level which meant that he probably would not graduate until he turned nineteen. While Markham was disappointed with the news, he was not discouraged as this would give him more time to assimilate into this new environment and participate in the available sports which he did on that same afternoon by reporting for the cross-country try-outs.

There were about thirty male students dressed in shorts, sleeveless shirts and sneakers gathered around the coach, Mr. Hovett, a middle aged portly man and veteran of the Second World War. Several of the boys were already members of the cross-country team such as Charlie Goldberg who had been appointed Team Captain the previous year by the Coach because of his devotion to the sport and his best performance in cross-country and also in the half-mile run in Track and Field. He was definitely the man to watch. Markham stood there amongst the other runners listening to Coach Hovett giving instructions.

"You new boys who are not familiar with the course will have to follow veteran runners. This is the starting point and you'll be running straight down to Flushing Meadow and around the field, then back up the other side of the field to the starting point again and then you'll continue and run that same course a second time. That's a total of three miles. Now this is not a race. I want you to pace yourself so that you can go the distance. Those of you who make the team will be expected to run this course five days a week. Actual competitive races usually occur on Saturdays at Van Cortland Park in the Bronx. In those instances, you will not practice on that Friday before the race. You'll use that day to rest. Anyone have any questions?" asked Coach Hovett.

"Yes Sir, Mr. Hovett. Can we wear spike shoes or is there any particular type of running shoe that we should get?" asked one of the new boys.

"No spike shoes in cross-country. Your feet will come in contact with dirt, rocks, asphalt and hard surfaces. You're not running on a cinder track like in a Track and Field competition. I recommend that you wear a light but sturdy type of running shoe. Stay away from basketball sneakers; they're too heavy," said Coach Hovett.

"OK! Boys, lineup six abreast with the rest of you behind them. Charlie will lead," said the Coach.

"OK! Get Set. Go," yelled the Coach. And the group of runners trotted off, lead by Charlie Goldberg down the sloping terrain towards Flushing Meadows. A half mile into the practice run, Charlie was leading the group which had thinned out to only five runners immediately behind Charlie; the rest of them dispersed one hundred yards or more behind the leaders. Markham was running at Charlie's heels which made Charlie feel uncomfortable so he kept increasing the pace to test this newcomer's endurance which only succeeded in shaking off the other four runners, but not Markham, who kept right on his heels.

As Charlie, followed by Markham, ran past Coach Hovett and a few onlookers at the half-way mark, Hovett could see that Charlie's pace was much too fast for the new recruits and indeed for a practice run at the beginning of the season. Charlie and Markham were several hundred yards ahead of the nearest runner and the distance between them was increasing as Charlie attempted to lose Markham. On the other hand, Markham felt that he could pass Charlie at any time he desired, but was not familiar with the course, and in any event, it was purely a practice and try-out run, hence he was satisfied at finishing second this time around, which he did.

As Markham crossed the finish line immediately after Charlie, he walked around a few minutes to loosen up and recoup his wind. Coach Hovett walked over to him.

"What's your name son?" asked Coach Hovett.

"Jim. . .Jim Markham," he replied.

"That was a nice bit of running you did. Did you ever run cross-country before?" asked Hovett.

"No. This is my first time," answered Markham.

Coach Hovett noticed that Markham spoke with a strong accent, but couldn't place the country of origin.

"Where are you from, Jim?"

"I'm from Montreal," answered Markham.

"Oh! So you're Canadian, huh?" replied Hovett.

"Well, no. I was born in Brooklyn, but I lived most of my life in Montreal until this past summer when I returned to the United States," answered Markham.

"Well, son, from what I have observed today, you have the makings of a great cross-country runner. I hope you'll join our team, 'cause we can sure use you," said Coach Hovett.

"I'll do my best Mr. Hovett," replied Markham.

As Markham walked away from the field, David Shlackter and another veteran runner caught up to him .

"Hey Jim. That's the first time anyone from the team gave Charlie a run for his money," said David. "I want you to meet Simon Silverstein who's our best 220 man on the track team."

"Pleased to meet you Simon," said Markham, extending his right hand for a handshake.

"I hope you beat Charlie next time we run," said David, obviously not a fan of Charlie Goldberg. "The guy is too full of himself."

"Yeah! Since he was made Captain of the team, he thinks his shit don't stink," said Simon in support of David.

Markham made no comment, but the rivalry between team members amused him. At the next practice run, Coach Hovett instructed Markham not to go all out, but to reserve that for competitive races. As a result, Markham stayed behind Charlie during practice runs with Charlie ever increasing the pace until he was utterly exhausted at the finish line while Markham finishing right behind him appearing composed and ready for another run.

Coach Hovett made the announcement to his cross-country team that they would be entering the Queens Borough cross-country race at Van Cortland Park in two weeks, and they could only enter the ten best runners on the team to represent Forest Hills High School. Finally, Markham was going to get his chance to find out if he was a better cross-country runner than Charlie Goldberg, and the scuttlebutt among team members was equally divided as to the winner.

The subway ride from Forest Hills, Long Island to the Bronx in New York City was tediously long and not made any easier by the crowded trains, but the FH cross-country team consisting of Coach Hovett, Captain Goldberg and the other nine members were undaunted and looking forward to the first major race of the season. There were approximately seventy schools represented. The Forest Hills team arrived at Van Cortland Park at 0930 hours and found that all of the other competing teams were already there with their runners warming up by jogging or performing calisthenics. Coach Hovett immediately acquired the numbers printed on individual sheets that had to be pinned on each of his runners for accountability during the race. In the meantime, Charlie Goldberg, Markham and the other runners already dressed in their sweat suits, put on their soft-soled running shoes and started jogging to warm up their muscles in preparation for the impending Queens Borough Race.

Jim Markham, who had ceased jogging approached Charlie Goldberg as he was retying his running shoes.

"Charlie. You've run this course before. There must be about five hundred runners in this race. How are they going to line them up?" asked Markham.

"They're going to have each school line up their runners in single file and side by side with the runners of the other schools," said Charlie.

"That means that there will be fifty runners at the starting line with four hundred and fifty behind them," said Markham.

"That's right. So each school will put their best runners up front, and I have to tell you that it's about a quarter of a mile from the starting line to those hills you see over there and at that point you enter a path that can accommodate no more than two to three runners abreast, which means that you have to sprint at top speed for that first quarter of a mile to get into a good position when you enter the path, which by the way goes uphill with twists and turns for about a mile. Then it levels off, but quickly goes down in a serpentine fashion for another mile ending at the bottom with a quarter of a mile stretch to the finish line."

"Sounds grueling," replied Markham.

"It's the toughest cross-country course I've ever encountered," said Charlie. "By the way Jim… practice is over so don't hold back," he said with a knowing smile, "cause you're competing against the best that Queens Borough schools have to offer."

"I won't Charlie, and good luck to you too," replied Markham.

David Shlackter stood behind Markham, who stood behind Charlie at the starting line. Markham thought about having to sprint for the first quarter of a mile amongst so many other runners; that would most certainly drain his energy for the remaining two and a quarter miles. Suddenly the starting gun cracked and off the runners went from a wide group to the shape of a human arrow with the fastest runners at the point of the arrow moving forward towards the dirt path at the bottom of the large hills.

Markham had to dodge a few runners in his quest to move to the head of the pack and in the process lost sight of Charlie and his teammates. Markham entered the path amongst the first twenty runners and commenced the arduous ascent for the next mile. After a while his thighs started to ache from the constant uphill run without relief. A few runners ahead of him had spent all of their reserves and were slowing down rapidly, allowing Markham and a few others to pass them by. At the top of the hill Markham had no idea how many runners were ahead of him because of the serpentine course with its many trees and boulders, but guessed it to be approximately seven, yet only four were within view. Running down the serpentine path at times was so steep that Markham's legs involuntarily moved faster than he would have thought possible to prevent him from falling forward on his face. *One slip on a rock or smooth stone surface or a twisted ankle from an unexpected hole and this race will be over,* Markham thought. But he kept on running at full speed until finally he reached the bottom of the hill where the path led into an open field with the finish line a quarter of a mile away and Markham could see only three runners ahead of him. Markham suddenly felt a sharp pain in the right side of his abdomen just below the ribcage. He jabbed his straightened right fingers into his right abdomen to push out any gas that may be the source of the pain, to no avail. Markham disregarded the pain and attempted to overtake the runners ahead of him, and in sheer agony managed to pass one of them, finally finishing third in the race. Passing the finish line, Markham doubled up in pain but refused to lie down, as he had been told prior to the race by Coach Hovett that it was the worse thing to do; he must keep walking, which is what Markham did. Coach Hovett caught up with Markham with elation over his placement ahead of more than four hundred and forty-seven runners.

"Your time, Jim, is twelve minutes and ten seconds. That's fantastic my boy," said Hovett enthusiastically.

Markham did not react to his race time as he had no previous record for himself or the course with which to compare. All he knew was that two other runners finished ahead of him and next time he would try to change that. He subsequently learned that Charlie Goldberg finished 48 and David Schlackter 97 in a field of over 500 runners. One Forest Hills harrier failed to finish the race and the FH harrier with the slowest time crossed the finish line as the 276th runner.

During the daily forty-five minute gym period, students were free to play whatever sport was available in the indoor gymnasium including basketball, or working on the parallel bars, horse or high horizontal bar. Most played basketball, but Markham didn't care for that sport and favored gymnastics, especially the parallel bars. He soon was able to perform handstands with the shoulder roll on the parallel bars and eventually the one-hand handstand. However, the high bar interested Markham the most and he soon mastered the full over-the-bar swing and dismount during his gym period. While he did not consider himself a gymnast nor would he be able to devote the time necessary to join the gymnastic team, some of its members who practiced during the gym period recognized his potential and encouraged him to join their team which would require him to quit the cross-country and track team. Markham found gymnastics more fun but he felt a loyalty to Coach Hovett and his team which he could not betray, thus he declined the offer.

The following spring, the track and field season opened and Coach Hovett assigned Markham to run the mile in part because none of his other harriers had expressed an interest in running that distance coveted by some of the best high school milers in the Northeast United States. The competition in the mile run was fierce and quite embarrassing to those of mediocre talent left so far behind to the ridicule of the spectators and opposing team members. Charlie Goldberg had found a niche in the half-mile run. David Schlackter was comfortable in the 440 yard run, which required both speed and endurance.

The first track meet of the season took place on a sunny afternoon at the home track against the Sunnyside High School track team. In practice, Markham had clocked at 4 minutes and 45 seconds for the mile run, but that was without competition. At that time the outdoor world record was 4 minutes and 1 second. The Northeast High School record was 4 minutes and 30 seconds established by Charlie Mendoza of Stuyvesant High School in Queens, NY.

The track meet started with the 100 yard dash followed by the 220 yard run, both of which were won by Sunnyside with Forest Hills taking second place. However, David Schlackter won the 440 by three yards and Charlie Goldberg lost the 880 by only a few yards. Now the final race was about to begin and Jim Markham was Coach Hovett's last hope for a win in the mile run.

Five milers from Sunnyside High School lined up at the starting line with four milers from Forest Hills High School. Markham was at the front next to Sunnyside's best miler, Sam Washington, positioned on the inside. As the gun went off, Markham immediately took the lead followed by Washington. Markham was not sure if he would have enough energy left at the last 200 yards to sprint to the finish line, known as a "kick," so he decided to run as fast a pace as possible to distance himself from the other runners, thus avoiding the necessity to kick during the last hundred yards to the finish line. As Markham completed the first of four laps, Coach Hovett yelled out his time of 59 seconds, and told him to slow the pace, but Markham ignored him and continued running at the same pace. At the completion of the second lap, Washington had fallen behind Markham by 30 yards, but Markham continued to run at a fast pace to further the distance between them. By the third lap, Markham could feel himself getting tired, but had succeeded in getting ahead of his nearest competitor by a good 75 yards. Now if only he could maintain that distance between them without wearing himself out before the end of the race, he would win. As the bell sounded for the last lap, Markham attempted to increase the pace, but his legs were starting to get heavy and to his chagrin he noticed that Washington was shortening the large gap between them. With less than 300 yards before the finish line, Washington had begun his kick and now was moving up rapidly. Markham needed to increase his speed or he would soon be overtaken, but his knees were becoming more difficult to lift and his breathing had become much heavier. *Whatever happened to the second wind I've heard other runners talk about, why doesn't it kick in?* he wondered. *God knows I need it now.* As he looked back he could see Washington only about fifteen yards behind him coming on strong. Markham summoned all of the strength he could muster, practically foaming at the mouth in desperation to keep his lead to the finish line which was now only 10 yards away when Washington appeared within his peripheral vision to his right, and a struggle ensued between them, with Markham crossing the finish line one second before Washington.

Coach Hovett came over to Markham, threw a towel around his neck and announced the winning time of 4 minutes and 39 seconds. While Coach Hovett was pleased with Markham's performance, Markham was disappointed by his lack of energy at that crucial moment in the last three hundred yards of the race. Maybe he should have eaten a better lunch or something more nutritious. *Whatever happened to that second wind that is supposed to refresh you after you have exhausted your first wind. That certainly didn't happen to me in this race,* he thought. *Well, maybe I'll experience it in my next race and maybe it's just a myth.*

During the cross-country season, Markham had wondered during each race why he was going through all of the pain and punishment he had to endure for the sake of a possible medal and his name in the local newspaper, neither of which he cared about. He much preferred swimming, which he felt more naturally suited to his powerful shoulders, trim hairless body and strong legs. During his off time Markham would swim at the Jamaica High School pool where the Forest Hills High School swimming team would practice because Forest Hill H.S. did not have a swimming pool. Forest Hills had elected to have a music tower rather than a pool. One afternoon, the swimming coach for the Forest Hills team approached Markham and invited him to join his team after watching him swim.

"Where did you learn to swim the American crawl?" asked Coach Murphy.

"I learned the freestyle in Boy Scout Camp in Montreal," replied Markham, "but then I read a book in the library which showed the Olympic champion Johnny Weissmuller swimming the American crawl." Markham didn't want to tell Coach Murphy that what really generated his interest in the American crawl was seeing Weissmuller swimming in several Tarzan movies. Markham enjoyed swimming more than any other sport and diligently practiced the Japanese crawl and the Australian crawl before he settled on the American crawl as his favorite style of swimming.

"I'm afraid that I can't join the swimming team, because I'm already on the cross-country team and the track team," said Markham disappointedly.

"I know Coach Hovett. He would be the first to tell you that you shouldn't be mixing running and swimming; they each require differently developed muscles. You should stick with one or the other, but not both," advised Coach Murphy.

"Yeah, but I enjoy swimming a lot. In fact, this summer I'll be swimming every day at the Aquacade in Flushing Meadow," answered Markham.

"Well son, let me know if you decide to switch sports," said Coach Murphy.

Markham left the pool pondering Coach Murphy's offer, but quickly dismissed it for the time being. *There is always next year,* he thought.

Spring was also the soccer season at Forest Hills High School and one of the most popular sports on and off campus. The soccer team practiced within the confines of the cinder track, thus came into contact with the track team members who ran around the track during their practice sessions. The soccer team Coach was always on the lookout for long-distance runners because of the stamina required in soccer, and Markham was always a recruiting target, however he was never seriously considered due to his obvious loyalty to Coach Hovett.

Coach Hovett noticed that Markham had missed a few practice sessions after school and soon learned from Coach Murphy that Markham had been swimming at the Jamaica pool. Murphy reassured Hovett that he was not attempting to recruit Markham for his swimming team. Coach Hovett decided to have a personal conference with Markham about his athletic future and the sooner the better, in view of the forthcoming race with Stuyvesant High School which had the fastest high school miler in the Northeast United States. The opportunity offered itself when Markham reported for practice and was changing into his running clothes in the school locker room.

"Markham. When you've changed clothes, I'd like to talk to you outside if you don't mind," said Coach Hovett in a personal tone of voice.

"OK Coach," replied Markham casually.

Markham stepped outside of the locker room and found Coach Hovett standing in the hallway talking to one of his harriers. As soon as he saw Markham, he excused himself and walked over to Markham and they both started walking towards the building exit leading onto the track field.

"I heard that you have been doing a lot of swimming lately," said Hovett.

"Yeah, I've been practicing at the Jamaica High swimming pool," replied Markham, immediately realizing that Coach Murphy must have reported that information to Hovett.

"You know Jim, you're developing two different kinds of muscles, and frequent swimming is not advisable if you want to become a top ranking runner. Because you're swimming in cold water, your body naturally develops a layer of fat to insulate it from the cold. That's the last thing you want as a runner, especially a long-distance runner. Furthermore, the time you spend swimming is depriving you of time you should be spending at the track practicing. You're going to wear yourself out Jim, and you won't have any energy left when the time comes for you to deliver your best in competition," said Coach Hovett.

"I know that you're right Coach, but I love swimming and I was curious about my ability to swim the American crawl. Now that I know I can do it, I can put it on hold 'till summer and concentrate on my running," replied Markham in an attempt to appease Coach Hovett who appeared distressed.

"You know Jim, if you're a jack of all trades, you're a master of none, as the old saying goes. At this point in time, your only hope for an athletic scholarship to a university is by being noticed and picked up by one of their scouts, and in that regard, I am planning on making you Captain of the Track and Cross-Country team next season, if you apply yourself exclusively to this sport," said Coach Hovett with a sincerity that deeply touched Markham.

He was pleased by this surprise announcement and thanked Coach Hovett.

"Don't worry Coach. I won't participate in any other sports, except during the summer. I'll concentrate on my running and I'll do my best to live up to your expectations," replied Markham.

"Jim, I'm going to ask you to keep the fact that you will be appointed Captain of the team next season a secret between you and me until I make the official announcement at the beginning of the season next September. I think that Charlie will be more receptive to this change in leadership by next September. OK?" said Coach Hovett.

"Sure thing, Mr. Hovett. I won't say a word until you make it official," replied Markham reassuringly.

"Now, you know that you're facing the biggest challenge you've had so far in the mile run only two days from now, and that's at Stuyvesant High School. You'll be running against Charlie Mendoza, who holds the Northeast Regional record of 4 minutes and 30 seconds for the mile run. He has already been offered several scholarships by Ivy League universities, and you can be sure that the scouts will be there," said Coach Hovett encouragingly.

"That's Friday afternoon," replied Markham, worried that he would not be ready for such competition in such short notice.

"When was the last time you practiced, Jim? According to my recollection, you haven't been to practice in the past four days. I guess you were at the Jamaica pool," said Mr. Hovett reproachingly.

"Last Thursday I think, Coach," replied Markham apologetically.

"Well, Jim, concentrate on your calisthenics today, and then do four laps at medium speed. Don't over exert yourself today. Tomorrow I want you to do the same thing, only I want you to jog the four laps after your calisthenics, no strain. I want you to save your strength and energy for the next day, Friday. In addition, I want you to get as much sleep as possible for the next two nights until the race Friday. On Friday, eat a good breakfast and a solid lunch of meat and potatoes. You need protein, but also carbohydrates. You got that?" asked Coach Hovett.

"Yes Sir, Mr. Hovett. I'll be ready," replied Markham firmly.

"OK, Jim. Go to it and I'll see you later," concluded Hovett as they parted company.

Early Friday morning, Markham was awakened by his mother.

"Jim, wake up. It's Mrs. Robb; I think she's had a heart attack. She's passed out on the kitchen floor. Hurry!" said Nora excitedly.

Markham put on his pants and ran down the stairs into the kitchen to find Mrs. Robb lying face up on the kitchen floor. She was still breathing, but had apparently vomited.

"Did you call the ambulance, Mom?" asked Markham.

"Yes I did. I called the police because their number is pasted on the telephone and they said they'd call an ambulance," replied Nora, who by now was frantic.

"I think you should call them again to make sure an ambulance is on the way," said Markham with urgency in his voice.

"Alright," replied Nora, and she dialed the police again and learned that an ambulance was on its way there.

About 10 minutes later, an ambulance arrived and the medics entered the premises and after evaluating Mrs. Robb's condition, they carried her out on a stretcher into the ambulance with Nora insisting on riding by her side to the hospital. The medics opined to Jim and Nora that Mrs. Robb had apparently suffered a heart attack, but it was not fatal and she would probably recover.

Markham had a deep affection for Mrs. Robb, who had opened her house to him and his mother when no one else would. He owed her a deep debt of gratitude and now felt that he may lose her which created anxiety to the extent that he couldn't eat breakfast. He reported to school and at lunch time, forced himself to eat the meatloaf and mashed potatoes served in the school dining hall, knowing that he would be participating in the most important race of the season that same afternoon. He had to get Mrs. Robb off his mind, he told himself, and concentrate on the race, but he couldn't shake the anxiety that prevailed throughout the day. During breaks between classes, Markham telephoned the hospital where Mrs. Robb had been transported by ambulance, and only learned that she was in the Intensive Care Unit.

It was 2:00 PM Friday when Markham boarded the school bus with the other track team members and Coach Hovett for the trip to Stuyvesant High School. Coach Hovett noticed that Markham was unusually quiet and talked to no one during the entire trip. He suspected that something serious was bothering Markham and that it most probably was a family matter. When the team exited the bus, Coach Hovett approached Markham as they walked to the school locker room.

"You don't look your usual self, Jim. I don't mean to pry into your personal affairs, but you look like you're down in the dumps. Is there anything I can do…?" said Coach Hovett.

"It's a long story Mr. Hovett. There's nothing anybody can do about the situation. I'd better start thinking about the race," replied Markham solemnly.

"You're not just facing runners from Stuyvesant. You're also facing runners from Sunnyside High School, Bayside High School and Jamaica High School. This is an important event and I hope that you're mentally as well as physically prepared for it. Try to compartmentalize whatever it is that is bothering you and concentrate on this event, because you also need the will to win," said Coach Hovett encouragingly.

"I'll give it everything I've got, Coach. Thanks for the pep talk," replied Markham, who then opened his wall locker to suit up.

Markham suddenly felt very thirsty and he knew that he hadn't had enough to eat that day which would impact his energy level. He found a water fountain and drank like a camel at an oasis. He looked around the locker room and the adjacent hallway for a candy machine for quick energy, but found none. He changed into his running attire and sweat-suit then went out to the track to join the rest of the team.

Markham observed many runners working out and wondered if Charlie Mendoza was one of them, when Coach Hovett walked over to Markham.

"See that guy over there in the maroon sweatshirt and pants talking to the two middle-aged gentlemen near the starting line? Well that's your real competition…that's Charlie Mendoza. Don't try to pass him, just stay close behind him and let him set the pace until the middle of the last lap. That's when you make your move. OK Jim?" advised Coach Hovett.

"Yeah Coach, I got it," replied Markham, feeling a slight nausea which he would not reveal to the Coach. Markham knew instinctively that he was not physically or mentally prepared for this race and there couldn't have been a worse time for him to engage in competition, but he knew that he had a responsibility to the team and Coach Hovett to do his best regardless of how he felt. Besides, he reasoned, opportunity never knocks at your convenience, and this was a singular opportunity if not a timely one.

The call for all runners to report to the starting line was announced and as expected, Charlie Mendoza was afforded the front inside position, flanked by the best runners from the competing schools. Markham placed himself directly behind Mendoza from the start as planned by Coach Hovett. The sound of the starting gun sounded louder than usual for Markham who immediately leaped forward almost running into Mendoza, who quickly took the lead followed by Markham, Miller from Bayside, Garfield from Jamaica, Washington from Sunnyside and several aspiring milers from those same schools. Mendoza immediately set down a very fast pace that only three other milers were able to maintain to stay with him. After the second of four laps was completed, the leading four runners grouped together at least 75 yards ahead of the rest of the pack of runners, which apparently worried Mendoza who looked behind to see who and how many runners were still at his heels. Mendoza increased the pace to separate the wheat from the chaff and determine who was the real threat. Only Miller fell behind as Mendoza, Markham, Garfield and Washington ran immediately behind each other single-file until the middle of the last lap when Mendoza burst ahead in a sprint that left the other three runners behind to fight for second and third place. Markham had exhausted all of his strength and was unable to increase his speed during that last 100 yards when challenged by Garfield and Washington who passed him only a few yards to the finish line. Markham continued past the finish line into a walk on the track away from everyone. Markham was not surprised at the outcome and his only disappointment was the effect this would have on Coach Hovett and his teammates. He felt that he had let them down and he promised himself that he would get his act together and do much better next time. Markham learned that Mendoza had broken his own track record, finishing first in 4 minutes and 24 seconds. Having finished in fourth place, Markham was only interested in his best time, which he knew was sometime ahead.

Mrs. Robb's medical condition improved enough for her to return to her home in Rego Park, but she appeared very weak. School ended and Jim Markham spent the summer swimming every day at the Aquacade in Flushing Meadow where the old World's Fair had taken place in the 1930s. It was a huge pool with a high diving platform and boards at each end of the pool that had a depth of 20 feet. From his daily swimming, Markham had made several friends who would dive in the deep end of the pool that was so deep that they had to swim down to reach the bottom and pick up loose change as proof of their feat. By the end of that summer, Markham swam like a fish, having mastered not only the American Crawl but the breaststroke, sidestroke and backstroke. However, Markham's summer holiday was to end with very sad news.

Markham had just returned from an afternoon of swimming at the Aquacade, which was closing for the season the following week, when Nora told her son Jim that she wanted to have a talk with him in the living room.

"Jim, Mrs. Robb is very ill and she is moving in with her sister in Boston, Massachusetts next week. She has put up the house for sale with a realtor and we have to find another place to live," said Nora with trepidation at his reaction to this awful news.

"When did you find out about all of this, Mom?" asked Markham.

"About one month ago. I didn't want to tell you until I had found a place for us. I didn't want to worry you and ruin your summer vacation, mon cher," Nora said kindly.

"Well, where is this new place we're going to live in?" asked Markham.

"I couldn't find anything affordable in this area, Jim. The only affordable place I could find was in lower Manhattan," said Nora apprehensively.

"In lower Manhattan?" replied Markham with alarm and astonishment.

"It's not as bad as it sounds, Jim. It's an apartment on 10th Street and Bleeker. I've talked to the principal of the school at Forest Hills and with the help of Mr. Hovett, your track coach, the school agreed to let you continue to attend Forest Hills High School until you graduate. It will only take you half an hour to travel from 10th street to Forest Hills by subway. So you see, nothing's really changed except your residence, and there's lots to do in New York City, mon cher. You'll see," said Nora reassuringly.

Markham sat silently, digesting all of this information. Once he realized that this was the only course of action his mother could have taken, he accepted the change and felt a sense of gratitude towards Nora for preserving the impending bad news until his summer vacation was over.

"OK Mom. When can we move to our new location?" said Markham enthusiastically.

Relieved at her son's enthusiasm, Nora replied, "Next weekend, mon cher. I have to work during the week as you know. This new location means that I won't have to travel far to get to and from work, since I work in mid-Manhattan on 33rd Street. So that will be a welcomed convenience."

Mrs. Robb's sister Thelma and her husband arrived by automobile to take Mrs. Robb to Boston. They were going to stay there for a couple of days then drive back to Boston with Mrs. Robb after closing the house for the realtor. Nora and her son Jim were scheduled to leave that same day for their new lodging in Manhattan.

Markham waited for his mother to bid Mrs. Robb farewell, then he hugged her for the longest time for fear that if he pulled away too soon, she would see the tears that he had been fighting back. He then kissed her on both cheeks as is the French custom, and abruptly turned around, picked up the two large suitcases and walked out of the house where a taxi cab was waiting. As the taxi driver loaded the two suitcases into the trunk of the automobile, Markham looked back at the house that had been his home for such a short time and wondered if his neighborhood friends realized how fortunate they were to have a permanent home with two parents to care of them. *No,* he thought, *they probably take it for granted.*

The taxi transported Nora and her son Jim to the Independent Subway station where they embarked on their subway trip to lower Manhattan where they got off at the IRT Sheridan exit. It was only a short walk to the three-story Brownstone mansion which had been transformed into an apartment building on the corner of 10th Street and Bleeker Street.

Nora took out her key and opened the door to the first floor apartment which led directly into a large living room. Markham followed his mother into the living room and deposited the two large suitcases next to a large couch that he subsequently learned converted into a bed for his mother. The living room led into a wide hallway where a single bed rested against the wall, which was assigned to Jim. As Markham continued his exploration of the apartment, he stepped into the small kitchen and finally he found the bathroom which had a toilet, sink and bathtub, but no shower.

"Well, what do you think of your new home, Jim?" asked Nora.

"Well, it does need repainting, but that's no problem. I could paint the entire apartment in one day or two at the most," replied Markham.

"Well, you've got to admit, it's a bargain for only $22.00 per month, but that's all I could afford," said Nora. "I'll get some nice curtains for the living room window. You'll see, it will be real cozy here, and you'll make new friends sooner than you think."

Markham nodded affirmatively and picked up his suitcase which he placed on his bed, opened it and emptied its contents into the various drawers of the bureau resting against the opposite wall.

"Jim, I'm going to the store for some groceries. Do you want anything in particular for supper?" she asked.

"Anything will do, Mom. I'm going out for a while to look over the neighborhood, but I'll be back in time for supper," said Markham, and he left the apartment.

Markham stepped down the five cement steps to the sidewalk and turned left to the corner of the street. Markham crossed Bleeker Street and on its corner stood a small diner which he did not enter. He then crossed 10th Street which was crowded with people picking vegetables from the display carts standing outside the grocery store. A burly, blond-haired guy about 20 years of age, wearing an apron, was serving customers when he noticed Markham standing in front of the apple cart trying to decide whether to buy an apple, inasmuch as his mother was going to shop for groceries anyway.

"Those are Macintosh apples. They're the greatest. Hey! You must be new here," said the groceryman.

"How do you know that?" asked Markham.

"'Cause I know everybody in the neighborhood and I've never seen you before," answered the groceryman.

"You're right. I just moved here and I'm scouting the neighborhood," replied Markham.

"I'm Boris. Welcome to our neighborhood, and here's an apple on the house," said Boris, smiling.

"Thanks. I'm Jim. Jim Markham," he said, accepting the apple with obvious gratitude at Boris' act of friendship.

"Listen, Jim. Me and some of the guys usually meet after dinner in front of Ryker's diner across the street. Why don't you come over and make their acquaintance?" said Boris.

"I'll try. We just moved in today and I have to help my mother get settled in," replied Markham.

"Hey! I understand. We're usually at the corner on most evenings. Got to get back to work," said Boris, turning his attention to other customers.

Markham left the grocery store biting into the apple of friendship while walking down the street to parts unknown.

Markham had just finished eating a spaghetti dinner with his mother and decided to go down to the corner and meet the 10th street boys at Boris' invitation. As Markham stepped from the bottom stoop step onto the sidewalk and turned left towards the corner, he immediately observed a group of young men gathered around the stoop of a brownstone apartment building next to Ryker's diner. Markham crossed Bleeker Street and as he neared the entrance to the diner, Boris noticed him and called him over.

"Hey! Jim, come on over," then turning his head back towards the group Boris said, "That's the new guy I was telling you about. Maybe he plays baseball."

Markham approached the group in a casual manner and extended his right hand to Boris who shook it with a pronounced grin that exuded an air of camaraderie.

"I want you to meet the nucleus of our baseball team," said Boris with his outstretched arm towards the group of young men sitting on the stoop or standing at the side of the stoop.

"Nucleus! Where did you get that fancy word, Boris?" said Frankie Biondilini, a short, dirty-blond-haired teenager with a fair complexion and a hook nose that shared a few freckles with the surrounding cheeks. He had a pleasant manner in spite of the teasing he got from his friends about his having an Italian family name with such light colored hair, eyes and complexion. Frankie was never without his baseball glove which he claimed he was breaking in with the constant pounding he gave it with a baseball he caught at Ebbets Field during a Dodgers game.

"Yeah! Boris, who you trying to impress, man?" said Bernie McHenry, adjusting his baseball cap. Bernie was a tall, lanky guy of obvious Irish descent who walked with an awkward gait and also sported a hooked nose. It was believed that Bernie slept with his baseball cap on his head. Bernie was the encyclopedia of baseball, able to rattle off the names of every player on every professional baseball team with their batting averages and other facts reduced to baseball cards available for sale at the local retail stores.

"So we are the NUCLEUS, hey? Can you spell it for us Boris?" said Don Domingo amusedly. Don was normally a quiet, pleasant guy of Spanish heritage who loved a good, friendly argument. At six feet in height and 175 pounds, Don had the physique of a strong baseball outfielder and batter and a very respectful demeanor towards elderly people and members of the opposite sex.

"You see all the abuse I have to put up with from these guys, Jim," said Boris shaking his head and both of his hands in unison for emphasis. "We just started a baseball team and so far we lost the first three games. Not a very good start."

"Hey! Man, those were just practice games. What do you want?" said Tony Tucci, a small, dark haired Italian teenager who spoke with an accent that suggested that his parents were directly from Italy.

"I want a win. That's what I want," replied Boris.

"Hey! Jim, you play baseball?" asked Frankie, who had been sizing up his physique.

"I've only played softball," replied Markham apologetically.

"Oh! Yeah! Where?" asked Bernie inquisitively.

"At the school I went to in Montreal," answered Markham, who did not want to go through the trouble of explaining that Varennes was off the St. Lawrence River not far from Montreal, and that College St. Paul was actually a high school.

"It's not much different than baseball, except that the ball is smaller and we use bigger bats," said Boris.

"Yeah, but don't forget that the pitcher throws the ball overhand, not underhand, and even though the pitcher is much farther from the batter, the ball comes in a lot faster," said Bernie, who pitched for the team.

"Hey! Here comes Brewer," said Frankie as Brewer Franklin, the only black person on the team came strolling in. At six feet in height and about 180 pounds, Brewer was also a member of the outfield who had much potential as a heavy hitter.

"Hey, Brew. Where've you been? We haven't seen you in a couple of days?" asked Boris.

"I've been busy with school work," answered Brewer with a contagious smile that reflected an innate kindness towards all who met him. Markham sensed that Brewer would never hurt a fly even if it landed in his food.

"Listen Jim," said Boris. "Why don't you join us Saturday afternoon for baseball practice at the local ball park? Some of us meet right here at this corner and walk over to the park. We'll meet here at one o'clock."

"You got a glove, Jim?" asked Frankie.

"A baseball glove...no I don't," replied Markham.

"I've got an extra glove I can loan you," replied Frankie, who was impressed by Markham's refined features on such wide, well-developed shoulders and athletic build. To Frankie, Markham looked like the classic clean-cut, all-American teenager who didn't drink alcohol nor smoked tobacco and whose sole interest was sports.

"You must've played a lot of hockey up there in Montreal, huh?" asked Boris.

"Yeah! That's about all we can play in those long winters," replied Markham.

"What about skiing, did you do any of that?" asked Bernie.

"No, I didn't get an opportunity to do that," answered Markham.

"Well you're not going to do either of them here I tell you," replied Bernie, chuckling.

"So where do you go to school?" asked Frankie.

"At Forest Hills High School, in Long Island," replied Markham.

"Man, you're going to travel all the way to Long Island each and every day to go to high school… you're a better man than I am, Gunga Din," said Frankie jokingly.

"It's not so bad by subway. It only takes a half hour each way, and besides, I've paid my dues so to speak, so it's easier to just stay there, finish up and graduate," replied Markham.

"Well listen you guys, it's getting late so if I don't see youse before Saturday, we meet here at 1 PM, alright?" said Boris to all of them. "And pass the word to Phil, Ray, Vic and Nye, and Johnny Sexton, OK? And I hope to see you too, Jim on Saturday," said Boris as he started to cross the street on his way home.

With Boris' final comment, the group dispersed and they all went home including Markham who was happy to have met these pleasant, easy-going and sports-oriented young men.

That Saturday, Jim Markham, dressed in white low-quarter sneakers, navy blue trousers and a white short-sleeve undershirt, walked to the corner of 10th street and Bleeker where he was met by Boris and his younger brother Adolf, Frankie, Bernie, Tommy, Al Albee, Johnny Sexton and Ray Balantine. Boris introduced his brother Adolf, Albee, Sexton and Ray to Markham. At this time, Frankie gave Markham a left hand baseball glove for his use during that day's practice.

"I suppose you know how to use a baseball glove since it's basically the same as softball," said Frankie, not sure about Markham's experience.

"At the school I went to, softball was not that popular and the season was short. Only the catcher and the first baseman used a glove; the rest of us used our bare hands and frankly, because the ball was so big, we preferred using our hands to catch it," said Markham with his listeners looking at him in disbelief.

Boris looked at Markham's beefy hands. "No wonder you didn't use a glove, those hands are natural mitts. How did you get those calluses on your knuckles?"

"Punching a leather air bag at school," replied Markham softly, while putting both of his hands in his trouser side pockets in an attempt to avoid further conversation about his hands.

Boris surmised that Markham must have some experience boxing, but he would have expected Markham's face and especially his nose to show some disfigurement, however, there was no apparent evidence that Markham had ever been in a fight of any kind.

"What are we waiting for? Let's get going to the ball park," yelled Bernie..

"Wait a minute. Brewer, Vic, Nye and Don are not here yet," answered Boris.

"Brewer is always late and Don can't make it today. I talked to him early this morning…he can't come," said Frankie.

"What about Vic and Nye?" said Boris to Bernie and Frankie.

"They know where the ball park is…they can join the practice when they get there. No sense holding us up," replied Frankie.

"Yeah, let's get going. We're wasting time," said Bernie.

"OK guys, let's go," said Boris and they all started walking towards the ballpark.

The school ball park was not very big, Markham thought. Heck, he could bat a softball out of that park. But there was a backstop made of thick wire wrapped onto a wooden frame. There was a home plate within the confines of the backstop where the batter stood to one side of it or the other depending on whether he was a right or left-handed hitter. Facing the home plate some 60 feet away was the pitcher's mound with a rectangular rubber plate two feet long and six inches wide for the pitcher to step on as he made his pitch of the baseball to the catcher crouched behind the home plate. Of course, baseball being the national pastime, everyone knows that there is a first base to the pitcher's left, a second base directly behind the pitcher and a third base to the pitcher's right, and a batter who, when he strikes the baseball, must run over all of the aforementioned bases before he can step onto home plate and score a point for his team. Markham knew the basics of baseball and not much more than that, but he was willing to learn.

Nye stationed himself at home plate with a baseball bat and several baseballs which he started hitting into the infield where Frankie, Tommy, Albee and Tony had picked their usual positions. As Boris was putting on his catcher's gear consisting of shin and knee pads, chest protector and face mask, Markham observed with great interest Bernie going into a long stretch before releasing the baseball to Albee who was playing the role of catcher armed only with a catcher's mitt. Markham walked closer to Bernie, studying his every move.

"You always stretch before throwing the ball?" asked Markham.

"Yeah! You should stretch, and the farther you lean back before throwing the ball, the faster the ball will travel. But you also have to follow through if you want to control where the ball will land," said Bernie with an air of authority. "The only time you can't stretch before a pitch is when there is a man on base, then you have to do a short version, like this." Bernie stood with his left side facing the catcher. He raised his gloved hand and the hand that held the ball together over his head then brought both hands down over his chest, and threw the ball to the catcher. "That's how you do it when there's a man on base. Here, you want to try it?" He handed the ball to Markham. "You haven't warmed up yet, so don't throw the ball hard or you'll pull a muscle. You first have to throw the ball easy for about 15 to 20 minutes before you can show your stuff, otherwise you'll throw out your arm, possibly for the season."

"OK, I understand," said Markham, who then placed his foot on the imaginary pitcher's plate, stretched both his left-gloved hand and his right hand holding the ball in front of him at eye level, then brought both hands down and in back of him while bending his head and upper torso forward. Markham then leaned backwards with his left-gloved hand straight up in the air and his right hand with the ball nearly touching the ground, and he catapulted forward with his right hand coming down towards the catcher, releasing the ball which traveled directly into the catcher's mitt without the catcher having to move it, for a perfect strike.

"Man, you didn't hear what I said about first warming up. You're throwing the ball too hard. Take it easy," said Bernie, sounding a bit annoyed.

"But I didn't throw it hard Bernie. I was just practicing the stretch and delivery," answered Markham to Bernie's surprise.

"Well, your stretch is fine. Just alternate throwing the ball to Albee with me," said Bernie, feeling a bit threatened by this surprising display of pitching talent by Markham on his very first throw.

As Bernie and Markham pitched to Albee, Boris walked over to them in full catcher's gear, wearing his mask over his head and carrying his catcher's mitt in his left hand.

"You guys are warmed up. Let's see you throw a fastball Jim," said Boris, anxious to see what control as well as speed Markham had.

Albee threw the ball to Markham, who then went into his newly developed stretch, leaning back as far as he could then catapulting forward and releasing the ball with such swiftness and force that had Albee moved his glove from his targeted position, he may well have missed it, but the ball exploded into Albee's glove exactly where he had held it.

Albee, who was the alternate catcher, immediately asked Boris to lend him his catcher's mask, sensing the danger of Markham's fastball.

Bernie was speechless, but Boris wanted to assure himself that this was not just a fluke pitch, hence asked Markham to throw several more fastballs and asked Albee to offer different targets to see if Markham could hit them with equal accuracy. After several pitches, Albee asked for time out while he took out his thickly folded handkerchief which he placed inside the catcher's mitt.

"Hey Boris. You need a new catcher's mitt," yelled Albee.

"Why's that?" retorted Boris.

"Because my hand is swelling from Jim's fastballs," answered Albee.

"Give your hand a rest. We'll go onto the field where I'll do the catching," replied Boris.

Boris called Bernie over to talk to him. "Listen, I want to see what Jim's really got, so why don't you stay on the side-line to observe him while I try him out? I'm going to get a few batters up here to test him," said Boris quietly.

"OK Coach," replied Bernie, who now looked upon Markham as an intruder.

Nye got up at bat and Boris used his catcher's mitt as a target for Markham, placing it where he felt the batter would miss the ball due to the particular weakness of that batter. Catchers are expected to know the weaknesses of each and every batter that comes before them, remembering their previous batting successes and failures. It is the catcher who signals the pitcher as to what type of pitch he should throw based on his previous experience with that batter, but the pitcher has the discretion of rejecting the catcher's request.

Boris walked up to the pitcher's mound to talk to Markham.

"Jim, I know that you're new at this and the only pitch you've got is a fastball. But you can throw the batter off with a slow pitch once in a while. So I'm going to use my right hand and when I point one finger down, that means you throw a fastball exactly where I put the mitt. If I point two fingers down, that means you throw a slow ball as a change of pace. You got it?" said Boris.

"Yeah, that's easy enough," replied Markham.

Boris walked back behind the home plate. Phil D'Amato appeared and took his usual position as short-stop. Ray positioned himself at first base. Frankie took second base and Tommy took third base. Nye ran out to right field, Sexton center field, and Brewer who had arrived late, took left field thus filling all of the positions.

Nye kept swinging his bat over the home plate in anticipation of hitting the ball. Boris threw down his index finger signaling for a fastball right down the middle of the plate. Markham reared up and threw a sizzling fastball that made a loud noise as it hit the catcher's mitt without Nye taking a swing at it.

"Hey Bernie," yelled Boris, "why don't you stand behind me and empire the pitches?"

"No way am I getting behind you without the same protection you got, are you kidding?" replied Bernie.

"OK then. Go up to the pitcher's mound and stand behind Jim. You can call the pitches from there," ordered Boris.

Bernie yelled time out while he walked up to the mound and stood behind Markham as the empire.

"OK let's play ball," yelled Bernie.

Markham saw that Boris signaled for another fastball to the inside near Nye's waist. Markham placed his right foot on the mound's rubber plate situated at a level that is 15 inches higher than home plate, and made a full high stretch of both arms then leaned back until his right arm almost touched the ground, then swung his body and right arm forward leaping off the mound sending the ball too fast for Nye's eyes to follow it.

"Strike two," yelled Bernie.

This time Boris wanted Nye to get a chance at hitting the ball because it was supposed to be batting practice, so he signaled Markham to throw a fastball right down the middle of the plate.

Markham again wound up and threw his fastball right into the catcher's mitt with Nye swinging too late to hit the ball.

"Strike three, you're out," yelled Bernie with delight.

Boris knew right then that he had himself a new pitcher for his team and with time and practice, Markham could develop other pitches to augment his fastball thus saving his arm so that he could last the customary nine innings of play.

Incredibly, Markham threw against two other batters, namely Frankie and Phil, striking both of them out without a single hit. Markham felt that he had finally found his niche in the realm of sports. He loved the challenge that pitching demanded and he was elated over his newly discovered skill as a baseball pitcher, although he knew that he would have to develop other pitches in order to master the game.

Boris announced to his team members that he had arranged for them to play a Harlem baseball team in Central Park where there are several baseball fields always in use by sandlot teams from all over the city of New York with minor league scouts actively searching for new talent.

The Harlem Tigers, as they called themselves, had professional looking uniforms with the name of their team on the front of their shirts and individual numbers on the back of each uniform. All Tigers were black except for two players who were Puerto Rican, which was not surprising as Puerto Ricans were deservedly known in New York City as outstanding baseball players who lived and breathed baseball. The Tigers' manager, known only as Bill, flipped a coin and asked Boris to pick heads or tails as to which team would go up to bat first. The Tigers won the flip and the Planets with Bernie as the starting pitcher went out into the field. Boris wanted to appease Bernie and elevate his self-esteem by giving him the starting position with Markham as the relief pitcher which Boris thought was fair in view of Bernie's longevity with the team. Markham was only too glad to watch the Planets performance against an apparently seasoned baseball team so that he could learn from the experience.

Bernie did not have a fastball. He relied on a well-placed straight ball that cut the corners of the home plate or else his curve ball which unfortunately was slow enough for the batters to follow into the wood of their bats for base hits. By the third inning, the Tigers had hit two home runs and the score was five to nothing in favor of the Tigers. Frankie and Nye had managed to score base hits, but never got to cross the home plate, hence no one scored for the Planets. Boris decided that it was time to replace Bernie with Markham. Markham had been watching Bernie intently and felt that without a fastball he needed to develop a better curve ball and other pitches as well. Markham also realized that he needed to develop other pitches and thus decided to not only talk to pitchers from other teams, but to read books on the subject.

Markham stepped up to the mound, this time wearing a baseball cap, and looked around at each of the players on his team. Nye was on first base, Frankie on second base, Phil as shortstop and Tony on third base. Ray played right field, Brewer at center field, and Tommy at left field. Boris, with his mask over his head, walked up to Markham.

"Jim, you just place your fastball where I tell you and they'll never hit it," said Boris confidently.

"You got it," replied Markham.

"O.K. Jimbo, strike him out. He's only the pitcher and he can't hit," yelled Frankie from second base. These were called pep talks from players in the field to their pitcher.

Boris signaled for a fastball on the inside to dust the player away from the plate.

Markham leaned back into his usual stretch and fired the ball directly into Boris' mitt with the sound of thunder for a call of strike one from the umpire stationed directly behind the catcher. The batter's astonishment at the speed of Markham's fastball turned into fear of being struck by the next pitch from a pitcher whose accuracy or wildness was as yet unknown.

The batter was careful not to hog the plate so that he could quickly step away from the strike zone should the pitch be a wild one. This worked to the pitcher's advantage because now Boris signaled Markham to throw a fastball on the outside corner of the plate and just below the strike zone so that even if the batter hit the ball, he would only get a glancing blow or a hit in the direction of first base and be easily thrown out.

Markham stretched back and then catapulted off the mound into a crouch that seemed to extend his pitching arm so far forward that the batter felt he had only a short distance in which to measure the speed and direction of the ball before it passed him into the catcher's mitt. The ball came at the batter so fast that he could not see its threads and he could only guess as to when and where it would pass him. He swung his bat into thin air and the umpire yelled, "Strike two."

"You got him, Jimbo. He's running scared," yelled Frankie.

"One more strike and he's out my man," yelled Tony.

"Take the bum out Jamie Boy," yelled Phil.

Markham was not used to this pep talk and encouragement, especially not the pet names they were coming up with, but he was getting accustomed to it and he liked the team spirit.

Markham threw another fastball right down the middle at which the batter failed to swing.

"Strike three. You're out," yelled the umpire, and the batter walked away towards his teammates with a sad look of disappointment.

To the amazement of Markham, his teammates and the other team as well, Markham struck out 16 batters using only his fastball, thus preventing the Tigers from scoring another point, however the Planets failed to score but two runs, thus losing the game to the Tigers five to two. As the players from the Planets and Tigers were gathering their baseball equipment, Bill, the coach of the Tigers, walked over to Markham to congratulate him on his pitching.

"You know you've got one hell of a fastball my man. You wouldn't care to pitch for us would you?" he asked with a sincerity that astonished Markham. *After all,* Markham thought, *I would be the only white player on their team and in Harlem at that.* But then he thought, *hell, we have only one black player on our team amongst an all-white team, so what's the difference?* Markham was flattered by Bill's offer.

"I really appreciate your offer, believe me. That's quite a compliment coming from you because you've got some great players on your team. But I can't accept your offer because these are my friends and I wouldn't be playing baseball if it weren't for them. It's a matter of loyalty, Bill. I'm sure you understand."

"Yeah! I do understand. But if you ever change your mind, you know where to find me," replied Bill who then shook Markham's hand with both of his hands. Markham couldn't remember when he had a better time.

Markham spent time at the local library reading books on baseball and pitching in particular and learned that the secret to making the ball curve or drop was in the placement of certain fingers on the stitches that held the skin covering the ball together and the manner in which the pitcher released the ball. Markham spent the rest of the summer practicing various spins on the ball until he developed a curve ball by placing his index and middle finger against two stitches that ran parallel to each other and then snapping his wrist at a 135 degree angle just before releasing the ball which would travel towards the batter then make a long curve downward towards the catcher crossing home plate within the strike zone. Unfortunately, the trajectory of the curve was long enough for a good batter to adjust his eye and swing for a hit. However, one day Markham threw what was to be his curve ball in the same manner he normally threw his fastball; completely overhead at a 180 degree angle with a strong downward snap of the wrist as he released the ball towards the batter's left shoulder. What he saw amazed him. The ball traveled towards the batter like a fastball and within a few feet of hitting the batter, the ball slid sideways to the left and over the home plate without falling an inch. Boris rose up with the ball in astonishment and asked Markham to throw that pitch again. The ball had moved over at least two feet in such a short distance from its breaking point that it made it extremely difficult for a batter to recover in time to hit the ball. Markham repeated the pitching process again and again, each time realizing the same effect of the ball sliding over the plate at the last minute, thus he named the pitch a 'slider,' not realizing that the term had already been coined by professional pitchers.

However, baseball season was coming to an end for Markham who was preparing to re-enter Forest Hills High School. Markham cherished this past summer playing baseball as the best ever, and he was looking forward to the next summer where he would resume playing with the possibility of being discovered by a major league scout.

As the school year began, Markham attended his regularly scheduled gym class and was asked by his friend Dave Shlackter to join him in a game of basketball with other students and although Markham didn't care for basketball, he accepted to please Dave. During the game, Markham came in possession of the basketball and moved rapidly towards the basket while dribbling the basketball when he collided with a tall player of the opposing team. No one was hurt, but the other player approached Markham.

"I'll see you after school on the back terrace," said the tall basketball player in an unfriendly tone, then he turned around and got back into the game.

Markham didn't quite understand what the individual meant, but he was quickly informed by Dave that he was being challenged to a fight after school in the terrace overlooking the track.

"I can't believe that he would want to fight me over an accidental bump in a basketball game. What's this guy's problem?" asked Markham of Dave who had observed the incident.

"He's the basketball team's star player and his name is Leonard Lowenstein. He's a member of the biggest fraternity on campus. He doesn't know you and he likes to throw his weight around. You going to meet him?"

"I guess so. I've never backed down from a fight yet. I just don't understand what all the fuss is about," answered Markham.

"You think you can handle him, Jim? He's six-four and easily 220 pounds," said Dave.

"Size has nothing to do with it. To me he's just a tall drink of water with a head that is just as vulnerable as anyone else's," answered Markham with calm confidence.

The students spilled out of their classrooms at 3:30 PM and Markham, joined by Dave, walked to the back of the school and onto the terrace to meet the challenger who had not yet arrived at the scene of the duel.

Two members of the track team walked by and started talking to Dave, who quickly informed them of the impending duel with their newly appointed captain. A moment later Leonard the challenger appeared with a group of his fraternity brothers and started walking towards Markham who stood facing them as they approached. Dave and the two track team members were careful not to stay too close to Markham as they wanted to be seen as observers only.

Leonard, flanked by several fraternity members on both sides, advanced within five feet of Markham then stopped.

"Well, I'm here. What do you want?" asked Markham in a calm, fearless voice.

One of the fraternity brothers standing next to Leonard, apparently a fraternity leader, stepped forward to answer Markham's question.

"We're here to see a fair fight between you and Leonard," said the fraternity brother.

"What'sa matter with him? Somebody cut out his tongue?" asked Markham. "You challenged me to a fight, then let's get on with it," he added, raising his fists into a boxer's stance.

Several of the fraternity brothers immediately jumped in between Leonard who looked petrified and Markham who had the appearance of a professional pugilist.

"No, no, no," yelled one of the fraternity brothers. "No punching is allowed…only wrestling… those are the rules."

"Rules," exclaimed Markham in astonishment. "What rules? I fight with my fists and my feet if I have to. There ain't no rules. Now get out of my way and let's get this over with," growled Markham, who had worked himself up into a raging lion ready to do battle with the lot of them if he had to. It was evident to all those present that Leonard welcomed the protection of his fraternity brothers who apparently had never seen or been exposed to such an aggressive Neanderthal. The frat brothers were now joined by Dave and some of the members of the track team who by now had been joined by others due to the commotion. The frat leader held out his right hand towards Markham in an act of friendship.

"Leonard wants to apologize. It was just a big misunderstanding. Let's just shake hands and forget this ever happened. OK?" said the frat leader.

Markham looked at Leonard and his entourage with bewilderment and contempt at their fear of brutal combat that he expected in a country that celebrated pugilism and honored its war heroes. *These are poor excuses for men,* he thought, *but I guess that's the way they're raised here in Forest Hills.* Markham felt that he had been wronged by being challenged to a fight which he didn't want in the first place, hence was justified in his anger, but now that the matter was resolved, it was time for conciliation, hence he agreed to shake Leonard's hand with no comment. As Markham was walking away from the crowd that had gathered, Dave came over to him and told him that the president of the fraternity would consider it an honor to have Markham join their fraternity.

"You've got to be kidding. Me, joining their fraternity. What for?" exclaimed Markham in total surprise.

"He said that you wouldn't have to pledge like other new members do," said Dave encouragingly.

"First of all, I find that pledging is sadistic and humiliating, and I'm not interested in joining any such group, Dave. I'm going to run a couple of miles around the track and let some steam off. I'll see you later," said Markham.

It was the fall season and the numerous trees and well-maintained lawns surrounding Forest Hills High School lent an air of affluence and serenity disturbed only by the exodus of its students. The fall session had just begun and Markham, now officially the Captain of the Track Team and Cross-Country Team, was informed by Coach Hovett to assemble all of the members of the Cross-Country team at the usual practice field behind the school. At the meeting, all were informed that they had four weeks to get into shape for the City-Wide cross-country meet at Van Cortland Park in the Bronx where more than 1200 runners would be participating in the largest cross-country event in the state of New York. Only five runners would be allowed to represent each school, hence the five Forest Hills runners with the best running times would be entered in this City-Wide race. As the weeks progressed, it became evident to Coach Hovett that Markham, Goldberg and Schlackter would be contestants and the other two positions were still up for grabs.

Three days before the City-Wide race scheduled for that Saturday morning, Markham ran his last practice session on the rough terrain in the fields at Flushing Meadows and on his last lap, he had the misfortune of stepping down hard with his right heel on a stone that sent a shooting pain up his right leg. Markham continued to run, mostly on the ball of his foot to avoid further pain and aggravation of his bruised heel, until he reached the top of the hill where Coach Hovett was waiting at the imaginary finish line. Mr. Hovett noticed Markham walking with a slight limp and approached him.

"What happened out there Jim? Did you hurt your foot?" asked Hovett.

"It's just a bruised heel. It'll be alright by Saturday," answered Markham.

"Maybe you should go to the dispensary and have it looked at," suggested Hovett.

"No, that won't be necessary. I'll just put an extra cushion underneath my heel inside my sneaker until Saturday," replied Markham. "I'll be alright Mr. Hovett."

Twelve hundred runners from every high school in the city of New York were lined up five deep and ready to go the two-and-a-half-mile distance over rocky and hilly terrain, and only the first 15 runners would be officially recognized with an honorable mention. Markham's bruised heel had gotten worse to the extent that he suffered pain even when only the ball of his foot touched the ground. Markham walked far enough away from Coach Hovett and his teammates so that they would not observe him while he took a handkerchief out of his pocket which he folded so that it would fit under his heel inside his spikeless track shoe which he laced tightly so that the padding would not slip forward. He hoped that this would minimize the pain to a tolerable level.

The race began with the loud bang from a starter's gun and twelve hundred runners sprinted towards the narrow gorge for the long uphill struggle that separated the winners from the losers. Markham was within the first pack of about 30 runners and as he struggled uphill, he noticed that the folded handkerchief had slipped forward inside his right track shoe and now was offering no protection to his bruised heel. In fact, the weight and bulk of the handkerchief had become a hindrance. Markham quickly stepped to the side, almost getting run over by the other runners, unlaced his shoe, removed the handkerchief which he threw away, then after re-lacing his track shoe, got back into the race. He knew that he had to disregard the pain and make up for lost time. As he reached the peak of the hill, he estimated that he faced approximately 50 runners ahead of him, and the downhill run might be easier on his bruised heel. As Markham continued to pass runners who appeared completely exhausted, he realized that he would have to make a Herculean effort to place within the first fifteen runners, but the continued pounding of his injured heel might well cause damage serious enough to keep him from running for the rest of the season. Markham remembered Coach Hovett's remark at one of the practice sessions, *A person's conduct in a cross-country race will reflect his conduct in life. A quitter in a race is a quitter in life.*

Markham pushed himself to the limit, grimacing in pain as he passed one runner after another, finally reaching the half-mile stretch leading to the finish line. Sweat was covering his body and his eyes were half-closed from the exertion and pain wracking his body and mind as he neared the finish line only about 70 yards away, when the runner in front of him fell face-down, forcing Markham to step over him as he lay there apparently unconscious. As Markham ran past the finish-line, he heard a voice call out, "Number 11," but Markham just wanted to lay down and collapse where he stood. However, he knew that was the worse thing he could do under the circumstances, so he started walking and to his surprise, the pain in his right heel had diminished into a numbness. Coach Hovett and a couple of team-members who had not entered the race due to their slower time, but were there to support the team, walked over to where Markham had stopped walking and was now stretching.

"You placed eleventh Jim, out of twelve hundred runners. You did a great job," said Coach

Hovett, gently grabbing Markham's left bicep. "I noticed during the last stretch that you were favoring your left foot and you appeared to be in pain. Did you injure your right foot?"

"Not really. I bruised my right heel, but it'll get better soon," answered Markham reluctantly, for fear that the Coach would ground him if he knew that he ran this grueling course with a known injury to his heel. However, as things turned out, Markham was not to run again in either Cross-Country or Track. Three weeks later, the teachers went on strike and all extra-curricular activities including sports were suspended until the strike was resolved. Unfortunately for athletes, especially those who hoped to obtain college scholarships, the teachers' strike appeared to have no ending in sight.

Markham's injured heel did not prevent him from swimming at the various school pools and he discovered the salt-water indoor pool at the King George Hotel in Brooklyn, which afforded him more buoyancy. Markham heard that the New York City Municipal Lifeguard training course was open to those who could qualify and a job as a pool or beach lifeguard would follow upon graduation. After taking a written examination, Markham reported to the indoor city pool where he had to swim 50 yards in a minimum of 35 seconds to qualify for training. There were approximately 60 young men at the pool awaiting their turn to qualify, and most of them were shivering from the cold water in the pool which didn't appear to be heated, although it was January.

Markham stepped up to the edge of the pool with five other swimmers lined up with him. The instructor called out, "On your mark...get set...go," and the swimmers leaped forward and started swimming the two laps that would complete the 50 yard swim. Markham had deliberately dived with his head and feet equidistant to the water so that his stretched out body and arms hit the water flat like a pancake hitting the pan, thus preventing the body from sinking and allowing Markham to immediately start his arm stroke and flutter kick. On the return and final lap, Markham and another swimmer were yards ahead of the other swimmers, but Markham finished first with a time of 26 seconds, followed by Pete Storm who finished second at 28 seconds. Markham and Pete became fast friends as they met five days a week in the evening at the Municipal Lifeguard Training pool for the next three months. Each evening, the lifeguard trainees had to swim two laps more then the previous day's practice, so that by the time two weeks had elapsed, Markham, Pete and the other trainees had to swim 20 laps of the pool before the training would start that day. The training included the basic swimming approaches to a drowning person, i.e. the surface approach, the underwater approach, the side carry, the back carry, and if working at the beach, the use of rope and reel involving two lifeguards. There were also instructions in methods of untangling oneself from the grip or choke hold of a drowning man while underwater. All in all, Markham was quite impressed with the training he received which he felt would serve him well in the future. Upon graduation, Markham and Pete accepted positions as lifeguards at Coney Island for the summer for the sum of $42.00 per week.

However, Markham's days in attendance at Forest Hills High School without the glamour of sports and athletics became dull and tedious, especially in those courses requiring in-depth knowledge of the English language as Markham was still translating and calculating English composition and mathematical problems in French, oftentimes creating great confusion. In one particular instance, while sitting in the back of the class in geometry, Markham raised his hand for clarification of a statement by the teacher Ms. Meyerson, when Markham overheard her muttering to the student in front of her, "Those dumb Canadians." Markham was appalled by her remark and deliberated whether to challenge her or report the matter to the school principal. Markham decided to do neither, reasoning that she wasn't worth the effort. However, her remark reminded Markham that he now lived in a multi-racial and cultural society that often breeds discrimination and intolerance of those of a different background.

Back in Manhattan, the Planets were already talking about the forthcoming baseball season, and resorted to the game of stickball in the streets to hone their batting skills. It was on a sunny Saturday afternoon that some of the Planets were playing stickball on Bleeker Street with the use of a Spalding rubber ball and a broomstick for a bat, using the sewer cover in the middle of Bleeker near 10th Street as the home plate. They would stop cars and buses in order to permit the pitcher to throw the ball to the batter and oftentimes stalled the traffic in the process, but this was New York City, where pedestrians and autos dodged each other with the skill of matadors.

It was Markham's turn at bat. Bernie threw the ball so that it would bounce once, a few feet in front of Markham, who then had to hit the ball after it bounced off the ground, but as Markham swung the stick, it just sliced the bottom part of the ball, sending it upward towards the sidewalk. Frankie, who was playing catcher, started to run over to the sidewalk when a tall, dark haired man dressed in a white opened neck shirt and dark jacket caught the ball, but held onto it. Frankie waited for the man to throw him the ball, but the man just stood there slowly bouncing the ball off the sidewalk back into his hand. Markham wondered why Frankie did not ask the man for the ball as he was holding up the game, but Frankie appeared reluctant and even fearful of demanding the ball. Markham became impatient.

"Hey! Mister, how about giving us the ball back?" demanded Markham.

The man simply looked at Markham as if to say, *Come and get it if you can.*

Markham, with the broomstick in his right hand, started walking towards the man with the ball.

"Hey! Whatsa matter with you? You're holding up the game. Now give me the ball, goddamnit," demanded Markham as he continued his walk towards the man, who realized that Markham meant business, thus threw the ball to Frankie and the game resumed without further confrontation.

"Hey! Jim, you know who that was that you challenged?" asked Frankie. "That was Tony, the numbers runner for the Don's bookmaker. Man, you got some nerve I tell you. One word from him and you've got major trouble."

"I don't give a damn who he is. He was holding up the game and he knew it. He was just being cute, that's all," replied Markham, not particularly concerned about the incident.

A few days later, Markham decided to have lunch at Ryker's diner at the corner of 10th and Bleeker where he always sat at the counter. On this particular day, all of the counter seats were taken except one which Markham took. The man to his left, who appeared to be in his mid-twenties with dark hair, wearing an open white shirt with dark trousers, glanced at Markham and recognized him as the teenager that had challenged him when he failed to return the Spalding ball that had ricocheted off Markham's stick while playing stickball on Bleeker Street.

"I hear you're quite a pitcher," said the dark haired man turning to Markham.

Markham turned his head towards the man at the same time that Mr. Ryker placed his American cheese, lettuce and tomato sandwich in front of him on the counter.

"Thank you," he said, turning his head back quickly towards Mr. Ryker, then turning his head back towards the dark-haired man who he immediately recognized as the individual with whom he had a confrontation.

"Thanks, but I think that's a bit of an exaggeration. I just started playing baseball. Who told you that?" asked Markham.

"Boris across the street. I've known him for years and he says you've got the makings of a pro. By the way, I'm Tony," he said, extending his right hand to Markham.

"And I'm Jim," replied Markham, shaking Tony's hand. "I heard about you and they told me that you pack quite a punch."

"That didn't seem to bother you the other day when I held on to your ball. You looked ready to fight me," replied Tony.

"I wasn't looking for a fight, just the return of my ball, that's all," replied Markham.

"I note an accent. Boris tells me you're from Montreal, Canada," said Tony.

"Yeah! That's right."

"You know, Jim. You don't mind if I call you Jim?" then he immediately continued, "You're in New York City now, and things are a lot different than in Montreal. You seem like a nice guy, so let me give you some friendly advice. You challenge someone to a fight here in the Big City, and you're liable to end up dead."

"You know, Tony. You don't mind if I call you Tony? If I'm going to be righteous then I should be willing to pay the ultimate price and I don't have any problems with that," replied Markham with a tone of confidence that convinced Tony that he had made the right decision when he failed to return Markham's challenge.

"Boy, the Army loves guys like you. What's your standing with the draft?" asked Tony.

"I just registered for the draft. I expect they'll eventually notify me to report for the physical exam," replied Markham nonchalantly.

"What about you Tony?" asked Markham with curiosity.

"Naw! I'm just over the age and besides, I've got flat feet," replied Tony with half a laugh.

"Flat feet, huh! How come you ain't a cop?" asked Markham jokingly, having been told by Boris of his work for a mafia don.

"Cops with flat feet also have flat wallets," replied Tony, showing his disdain for cops. "You know there are ways of getting deferred from the draft, but I don't think you're going to fail the physical."

"I'm not looking for a deferment. In fact, since it's inevitable that I'll be drafted into the Army, I'll probably volunteer for the Navy's UDT," replied Markham.

Tony didn't know that the term UDT meant Underwater Demolition Team and he didn't want to reveal his ignorance of the term, hence didn't ask Markham for an explanation; he simply accepted his remark. Tony couldn't help admiring Markham's spirit and courage, but thought he was a sucker and hopefully there would be a lot of them so that he wouldn't have to be drafted.

Tony stepped off the stool he'd been sitting on and extending his hand again he said, "Well it was nice meeting you Jim. Maybe I'll catch one of your ball games."

"I hope it's one of the games we win," replied Markham, shaking his hand in return.

When it came time for Markham to pay the bill for his sandwich and milkshake, he was advised by Mr. Ryker that his tab had been paid by Tony.

The following week Markham was returning home one evening from swimming practice and as he approached the corner of Bleeker and 10th Street, he noticed several police cars with red lights flashing. Boris and several of the Planets were converged on the stoop next to Ryker's diner watching the commotion. Markham walked up to them and asked Boris what had happened.

"A guy just got shot while walking with his girl right on the corner across the street next to my vegetable stand," said Boris somberly.

"Do they know who did it?" asked Markham.

"The girl went into hysterics. They had to take her away. But I heard Johnny Sexton's brother, who was one of the cops on the scene, tell one of the other cops that an old lady upstairs saw the shooter, but couldn't identify him 'cause it was too dark but she thought he was in his mid-twenties with dark hair and he wore a white shirt and jacket, no tie," said Boris, who was proud of the fact that he was privy to such inside information.

Markham immediately thought of Tony the bookmaker's runner, but then surmised that the cops on the beat knew everyone in the neighborhood, thus would put the pieces together and interview the likely suspects.

"Sounds to me like the work of a jealous suitor. What do you think, Boris?" asked Markham.

"You never know in this neighborhood. We're right next to Little Italy and there's no love lost between the micks and the dagos, you know," said Boris, referring to his own neighborhood composed mostly of Irishmen with some Italians and Poles in the mix.

"You wanna see a tough neighborhood, just go down to the Red Hook district in Brooklyn where the Irish rule. Even a gun won't help you if you go there alone," said Frankie.

As the crowd started to disperse at the cops' insistence, Markham excused himself as he had to attend school early the next morning, but the violence of that evening brought home the reality of the various types of people that inhabit such a large city as New York. *Don't trust anyone* was the mantra heard throughout the neighborhood. *No one does something for nothing. In any offer of a gift, always look for the hook.* That was the ingrained mentality of most New Yorkers who are automatically suspicious of anyone who wants to do them a favor.

As it turned out, Frankie's words were eerily prophetic. A few nights later, Domingo traveled by subway to Brooklyn to visit a girl he had met at his part-time job in Manhattan. After dropping her off at her house at the end of his date with her, Domingo made his way to the subway station for his trip back to Manhattan when several guys started chasing him. As Domingo entered the subway station, he saw that the train had arrived and the doors were still open, so he jumped over the turnstile and entered the nearest train, but one of his pursuers managed to get inside the train before the doors closed. There stood Domingo, nearly alone in the car occupied only by two women, and an old man, probably due to the late hour. His pursuer, a young man of about twenty with reddish hair, wearing a red and blue waist-jacket, Levis and sneakers, advanced slowly towards Domingo in a stalking fashion, then suddenly a shiny six-inch blade sprung out from the handle of a knife which he now held in his extended right hand. Domingo's blood turned cold at the sight of this man's sadistic facial expression as he waved the knife's blade in front of him. His uncontrollable fear caused butterflies in his stomach and a weakness in his legs. He backed up to the end of the car and saw that the train door guard was standing in between his car and the next one and he could open the car door at anytime. He banged on the door and asked for help, but the door guard did not want to get involved and did not respond. At this moment, the assailant swung his knife and cut Domingo's left hand as the train arrived at the next station. The train doors opened and Domingo quickly stepped out of the train where a policeman was standing on the platform. Upon seeing the policeman, the Brooklyn assailant remained inside the train and the door guard closed the doors before the policeman could enter the train and make an arrest, and the train continued on its journey without justice being served. Domingo was taken to a hospital where his hand was sutured. Domingo later recalled the event to the Planets with the promise that he would never again venture into the Red Hook section of Brooklyn.

The Planets spent many an evening in the club-house consisting of a large upstairs room over Elie's Butcher Shop around the corner of Bleeker and 10th Street. Boris had made Elie, a bachelor who was a balding man in his late thirties, an honorary member of the Planets, hence Elie reciprocated by providing its club members with the upstairs room where they shot pool and played cards, including poker when the weather was lousy. One of the conditions of membership was the lack of any criminal record, and all sixteen members prided themselves on that fact notwithstanding the influence of their environment. It is there that Markham learned the intricacies of playing poker and blackjack with some of the older members, including Phil D'Amato, Nye's older brother Carmine, Sexton's older brother Michael the policeman, and Elie. Markham learned how to spot a card cheat and the various methods used by them, including crap games where the dice is altered by side slicing or weighing. Markham was warned that his impending entry into the military service would inadvertently expose him to a variety of shysters, hucksters and con-artists. Markham learned that judges sometimes offered defendants a choice of jail or joining the U.S. Army resulting in the military absorbing many undesirables. Furthermore, draftee eligibility was minimal, thus allowing a wide spectrum of society's misfits into the military service.

Swimming practice at the Municipal Lifeguard Training was over and Markham graduated from the course with the offer of a lifeguard job at Coney Island which Markham accepted commencing on the first of June, 1950. In the meantime, Markham took a part-time job after school as a stockclerk at Gimbels Department Store on 33rd Street in Manhattan to pay for his expenses and assist his mother. It is there that he met Rosalee, his first encounter with a seductress.

Gimbels and Macys occupied opposite sides of 33rd Street, but they did not quite face each other. They were undoubtedly the two biggest department stores in Manhattan and fierce competitors. At lunch time, several employees from both stores would converge at a small delicatessen across the street from Gimbels which would place it next door to Macys, and it was there that Markham met Rosalee, a strawberry blonde about 26 years old with a voluptuous figure on a slim frame that conveyed party girl on a fast track. Markham always went to lunch on Saturdays with two other men of older vintage who also worked in the stock section of the store. Rosalee, a buyer for Gimbels who was acquainted with Markham's co-workers, took an immediate interest in Markham and invited herself to their table. Markham managed to evade Rosalee's rather personal questions and correctly concluded that she was interested in dating him, although he believed that she was too old for him, having just turned eighteen. As Rosalee got up to leave the deli, she grabbed Markham's bill and disregarding his protests, paid his bill along with her own, and left. Markham's two companions started kidding him about his newly found paramour expressing their envy at such opportunity. Markham's inexperience with women was betrayed by his shyness around them, a quality that did not escape Rosalee, eight years his senior. Two lunches later, Rosalee felt that she was sufficiently acquainted with Markham to invite him to attend a Broadway show with her on a Saturday evening. At first, Markham politely declined the offer, but Rosalee visited the lower floor at Gimbels where Markham worked and with some persistence, managed to extract an affirmative answer from him. She told Markham that a friend had given her the two tickets and they should not go to waste. That Saturday evening, they met under the marquee of Radio City Music Hall. Markham was wearing gray slacks and a midnight-blue blazer with a white shirt open at the top, but no tie. He had arrived on time, but Rosalee was already there to meet him. She wore a black one-piece dress with a generous cleavage that flattered her well-developed breasts, and her small waistline accentuated the roundness of her buttocks on a pair of long legs that promised heaven on earth. Her long blonde hair which at work was always tied at the back, was now loosely combed and flowed over her shoulders. Markham felt like he was the target of seduction and he was not sure she should be the one to initiate him. After all, he thought, he was a devout Catholic who should reserve sex for the one he would marry whenever that situation materialized, and besides, what if he got her pregnant, then he would be stuck with her for the rest of his life, and with that last thought, Rosalee lost her sex appeal. In any event, since he was old enough to admire a woman's beauty, Markham's focus had always been the face. To him a woman's face, through which her eyes reveal her very soul, is what makes a man fall in love and the rest is mere window dressing. Markham saw in Rosalee a carefully camouflaged tigress in lamb's clothing who had devoured many a prey. Her oval green eyes adorned a perfectly chiseled face that lacked the warmth of a tender heart. *She may be a fun date,* Markham thought, *but not someone to take home to my mother.*

Radio City Music Hall was the largest theatre in New York City and possibly in the United States, if not the world. The show was impressive with the Rockettes doing their Folie Bergere dance kick. After the lights had dimmed for the main feature presentation, Rosalee, who had wrapped her right arm around Markham's left arm, slowly lowered her hand onto his left thigh. With the slyness of an experienced seductress, she maneuvered her hand over his crotch and circled her learned fingers around his large penis which was struggling against the confines of his jockey shorts. Embarrassed at the location in which he found himself being aroused, Markham pulled her hand away and held it over the armrest while he attempted to cool off. Rosalee leaned over and whispered to Markham "That's alright big boy, we'll save it for later," and then squeezed his hand with a desire that moistened her vagina. As they left the theatre, Rosalee suggested that they take a leisurely walk through Central Park. After about ten minutes of walking on a wide path, they came upon a park bench right next to a lit lamp post and Rosalee immediately pulled at Markham's arm to sit down next to her on the wooden bench at which time she slipped out of her high heel shoes, declaring relief. She then pulled her feet up onto the bench and leaning onto Markham, she wrapped both of her arms around his neck pulling his head towards her lips and gave him a French kiss that at first stunned Markham, who felt her firm breasts against his chest. Markham suddenly found her sitting on his lap facing him with both her knees on either side of him. She quickly reached down and unzipped his fly, pulled out his rising penis and inserted it into her naked vagina before Markham could protest.

Rosalie could feel every inch of this beautifully long, thick and stiff penis filling her entire vagina. With each upward and downward stroke of her ass, Markham felt a growing surge of semen building up to an ejaculation and he realized that he wasn't wearing a condom and he could get her pregnant.

"Rosalie, stop, I'm not wearing a condom," as he tried to move her off of him.

But she quickly replied, "It's OK, I'm wearing a diaphragm," and continued to fornicate him with great delight, and then it came…the climax that lasted several seconds which didn't slow her down as she had already attained her climax and was working on a second one, seeing that his penis was still stiff, big and strong. But as Markham recovered from his climax, he realized that they were having sex under a street light and he was amazed that no one had walked by them in all this time, their luck was bound to run out soon which made it hard for him to fully enjoy this sexual experience. At that moment, Rosalee's head rolled up towards the moonlit sky in ecstasy as she reached the peak of her climax, then threw herself forward embracing Markham with both of her arms wrapped around him while resting her ass on his crotch with his penis still fully inside her vagina.

"We've got to get out of this position before someone discovers us," said Markham anxiously. Reaching into his back pocket, Markham pulled out his folded handkerchief and handed it to Rosalee.

"Thanks," she said, putting the handkerchief against her vagina as she pulled out his penis to keep the love juice from spilling onto Markham's pants, but it was too late as much of the semen had already stained the fly area. She stood up and went behind a tree where she repaired herself while Markham quickly zipped up his wet fly which failed to hide his penis which was still too erect to insert inside his jockey shorts. Markham was never so embarrassed and buttoned the front of his jacket in an attempt to hide the big lump pushing against his pants' leg.

As Rosalee re-entered the bright light of the lamp post where Markham was standing, she wore a satisfied smile and wide eyes that spelled passionate love and gratitude for the most sensual experience. She wrapped her left arm around his waist as they started walking back in the direction of 59th street where they had first entered the park. Markham was disappointed that his first sexual experience with a woman should have been under such rough circumstances. He was also worried about the matter of pregnancy. *Did she lie to me about wearing a diaphragm, and how safe were they?* he asked himself. Rosalee must have read Markham's mind by his silence during the walk out of the park, as she reassured him that she was in fact wearing a diaphragm and they were completely safe, hence he had nothing to worry about. Markham, however, promised himself that he would never again date her as she was too aggressive and he didn't trust her motives.

It was just before lunch-time on Wednesday following that exciting Saturday evening in Central Park that Betty, an older buyer for Gimbels approached Markham, who was hanging up some clothes on a rack.

"Jim, I hear that you are engaged to Rosalee," she stated in an inquiring voice.

"What did you say?" exclaimed Markham in astonishment.

"I have to tell you; she's been going around the store saying that you and her are engaged. Is that true?"

"Hell no, that's not true. I dated her once," he said nervously. "I can't believe her saying that."

"You'd better be careful Jim. She's dangerous," she warned.

"Yeah! I guess she is at that," Markham replied and thanked her for the warning. Markham walked back to the stock room where old Tom was sitting at a card table eating his usual sandwich with a mug of coffee.

"Whatsa matter Jim? You look agitated. Something wrong?" Tom asked.

"I'll say. I just found out that Rosalee is going around the store saying that we're engaged. Can you believe that?" he asked rhetorically.

"I told you she was hot to trot after you. Man, you'd better watch out. At this rate you'll be at the altar before summer's over," said Tom jokingly.

"This is all happening too fast. I'm not ready for this," Markham said worryingly.

"My advice to you, Jim, is to get the hell out of here, permanently."

"You mean quit the job?"

"Yeah! Quit the job now. Leave and don't look back my friend. Chalk this up to experience and be leery of experienced women," Tom said with the voice of authority that one acquires with age and travel.

Markham took off his Gimbels jacket and put on his own.

"Take care Tom, and thanks for the advice," Markham said, shaking Tom's hand warmly. Markham left Gimbels Department store, never to return.

The summer weather arrived early that year to the delight of the Planets who looked forward to baseball practice before the hot summer games. Markham was torn between playing baseball and working as a lifeguard for the Municipal Lifeguard Authority at Coney Island. He decided to try to do both and reported for duty as a lifeguard. Markham was assigned to Bay Three with another lifeguard named Steve Bentley who was his senior by four years. It didn't take long for them to get their feet wet. Within the first hour of being on duty, Markham spotted a man struggling to stay afloat through his binoculars. He was beyond the rock jetty where the ocean current was strong and treacherous. Markham immediately alerted Steve and volunteered to do the first rescue of the day by putting his long rubber fins on his feet. He then grabbed with his right hand the lasso end of the rope from the reel cylinder containing 200 yards of quarter-inch rope, which he placed over his left shoulder allowing the rope to dangle over his right hip. Markham trotted towards the water with Steve following him holding the reel with a round stick at the center of the cylinder that would allow it to release the rope as Markham swam out into the ocean towards the drowning man. The beach was not as crowded as expected due to the early morning hour and the expected rain that day.

Markham plunged into the crashing waves and surfaced past them with the rope still attached to his left shoulder. As he neared the victim, Markham raised his eyes above the water level to see where the victim was located. He was a balding man of about 50 years of age who appeared to be exhausted and on the verge of sinking. Markham decided to use the surface approach and as he swam towards him, he grabbed the man's right wrist with his right hand, simultaneously bringing his own legs downward, thus putting on the brakes causing the man to turn on his back. Then Markham placed his left arm across the man's chest grabbing him firmly with Markham's left hip against the man's lower back. With his right hand, Markham grabbed the lassoed rope and extending his right hand forward, started to swim towards shore using his scissor kick while Steve pulled steadily on the rope to help Markham fight the strong ocean current. As Markham reached shallow water, Steve released the reel and ran towards Markham to assist him in carrying the man onto the beach. The man appeared to have lost consciousness. Markham checked his mouth and rolled him over onto his stomach and Steve started to apply artificial respiration. Beach people started to surround them, but Markham managed to keep them from interfering with their rescue work. Finally the man started coughing and the first aid crew arrived with a stretcher and whisked him away for further medical treatment.

"Hey! You did good my man," said Steve.

"All in a day's work," replied Markham. "Thanks for your help. That current is murder. I can now see why they issued us with that reeled rope. Without it I don't know if anyone could manage those currents while carrying someone."

"This is the ocean, man. It's not like in the pool. This current can take you out to sea. It's one thing to swim on your own, but when you have to tug a 200 pound man with only your feet for propulsion, you'd better have some shore help or else you're a goner," replied Steve, who was on his second season as a lifeguard.

That same day, Markham and Steve pulled out three other males and one female from the ocean and all of them survived.

Back in Manhattan, Markham was pressured by his teammates to attend baseball practice during the week in preparation for the forthcoming weekend games, but Markham explained to Boris that his work as a lifeguard prevented him from attending those practice sessions, and he would be available on weekends in time for the games. Boris was not too happy about Markham's absence from practice, but also understood that Markham had to earn money to help his mother support them while he was still in school.

"You know we have a game this Saturday with the Manhattan Indians," asked Boris.

"That's what Bernie said," replied Markham.

"How's your pitching arm, Jim? You think you're ready for this Saturday?" asked Boris.

"Yeah! I'm ready. I do get a lot of strenuous exercise as a lifeguard you know, Boris."

"That's not the same as baseball practice, Jim. You develop different kinds of muscles swimming, and moreover, you've got to practice your slider and curve pitches. You know that."

"Yeah! I know Boris. But don't worry, I'll be ready."

That Saturday afternoon, the ballpark at Staten Island had a surprisingly large non-paying crowd, mostly fans of the Manhattan Indians versus the unknown Planets. Boris had been grooming Johnny Sexton as a relief pitcher in case Markham suffered an injury or had to be relieved before the last inning. Boris decided to give Sexton an ego boost by having him as the starting pitcher in this game, thus giving Markham a lengthy warm-up and fewer pitching innings to reduce the stress on his arm, which did not go unnoticed by an appreciative Markham.

Johnny Sexton was primarily a side-arm pitcher who had trouble controlling the ball, which scared a lot of batters because the ball would be released at a point directly in line with the batter who hoped that the ball would eventually move over the home plate and not hit him. Johnny threw a good fastball and a decent curve ball, that with enough practice, he could learn to control. But that was not the case in this game.

It was the third inning and the Indians were now up at bat. The score was three to one in favor of the Indians whose players were older and more experienced than the Planets. The sole point for the Planets was scored by Boris who hit a home run, unfortunately with all of the bases empty. Johnny Sexton's first pitch was wild for Ball One. His second pitch was a curve ball that crossed the home plate for a Strike One. His third pitch was a fastball that traveled directly towards the batter who hoped it would curve, but it didn't and the ball hit the batter squarely on the hip. The batter dropped the bat in agony and then in a fit of anger ran towards the pitcher ready to cause mayhem. Boris and each of the basemen ran towards the pitcher to protect him but the batter got there first. Sexton had his arms and hands raised in front of him in an attempt to block punches thrown by the batter when several of the infield players managed to subdue the batter. The Indians manager took Boris aside and suggested that in order to pacify the rest of his team he should remove Sexton and replace him with another pitcher. Boris told him he would think about it. After explaining the situation to Johnny, Boris left the decision to Johnny as to whether he should leave the game. In view of the animosity of the Indians towards him at this juncture, Johnny was only too happy to relinquish the reigns to Markham.

Markham stepped up to the mound and after a long windup threw a sizzling fastball right down the middle of the home plate for a Strike One call. Markham then threw another fastball on the inside, close to the batter's chest for a Ball One call. Now he thought, the batter is ready for a slider that will also be directed at his chest, but this time it will slide over the plate and it did just that to the batter's surprise for Strike Two. Markham then threw another slider just above knee high which the batter expected to drop below the strike zone even if it did move over the plate, but the slider maintained its height and slid over the plate for Strike Three and the batter was called OUT. Markham pitched a no hitter and the Planets won by a score of 4 to 3. The Planets retired to Tony's Pizzeria on 10th Street for a well-deserved celebration. As usual, several large cheese and pepperoni pizzas were served along with beer to the team members and Tony did not discriminate as to who would be served beer. After all, Johnny Sexton's brother was a well-known cop in the neighborhood who didn't hassle anyone. They were joined by Ely the Butcher and some of the elder brothers of the team members. At one point during the joyful reunion, Boris spoke to Markham about his turning professional.

"You know, Jim. You've got to be seen by scouts from the big leagues, 'cause you've got what it takes to make it. But so far, we've played at locations that don't seem to attract scouts," said Boris. At that point, Vic Racci, by far the best short-stop and infielder Boris had ever seen, who was sitting on the other side of Markham, interrupted them.

"We've got to actually go over to one of the training camps and talk one of the managers to give us a try-out. I think that's the only way we're going to get our foot in the door if you ask me," said Vic.

"You may have a point," said Boris while Markham listened attentively, still eating his pizza.

"I think the Brooklyn Dodgers use Ebbets Field for their training and try-outs too," said Boris.

"Well, it certainly is worth a try," replied Vic, directing his comment to Markham.

"Yeah! I guess so. But the Army might have something to say about that," replied Markham.

"Screw the Army," said Boris. "Maybe by the time the draft gets around to you two, the war may be over…a truce maybe. You never know."

"We'll see. In the meantime, we'll keep playing ball," said Markham.

That summer was best remembered by Markham for the baseball games in which he pitched no hitters, a thrill which easily surpassed his experiences as a lifeguard at Coney Island.

As fall arrived, Markham faced his last semester at Forest Hills High School with graduation scheduled for January 1951. He had no illusions about entering college after graduation. His grade point average was only 85 percent, mostly due to his limited command of the English language which he tried to improve, he would say jokingly, by going to see a lot of movies, which he did. Markham was especially impressed by English actors which he believed were the masters of the English language. But he also despised the pretense and arrogance that often hid behind the lavish prose. He admired principled men of action and women of substance and beauty. Since he never had a father as a role model, he conjured his own model after the heroes he met in his favorite books and movies. War had been declared between the United States and North Korea and Markham knew that any plans for college or a career would have to be put on hold until he served his time in the military. The military draft left him and his peers with no options.

During his last semester at Forest Hills High School, Markham's teacher in Wrought Metal entered Markham's work in the form of a silver soldered copper lamp which Markham himself designed and made from scratch, in the Henry Ford Foundation's National Contest. Markham won an Honorary Mention Award from the Foundation, but just before graduation, his teacher told him privately that Markham deserved the school's achievement award, but he had to give it to another student because he needed it to bolster his academic credentials in his application for a scholarship to an ivy league college, and he knew that Markham would not be going to college. Markham felt betrayed, but remained silent as he knew that nothing could be done about it. He simply turned away from the teacher in disgust and disbelief at the lack of fairness displayed by people who are supposed to serve as role models.

Markham graduated from Forest Hills High School without fanfare, but his class yearbook bore this comment "May He Wing His Way to Fame," referring to his running exploits as Captain of the Track and Cross-Country Team.

Markham now needed to find a steady job while he waited to be drafted into the Army. Dressed in his dark blue sports jacket and gray pants with white shirt and tie, Markham appeared before the receptionist on the first floor of a tall building on Wall Street seeking directions to the Human Resources Office that was listed in the employment section of the local newspaper. Markham was informed by the lady that he was in the wrong building, that this was the National Insurance Company building, but since he was there, she was certain that a job would be available for him if he reported to the Personnel Office on the third floor and asked for Mrs. Peachman; she would be expecting him. Markham was elated and thanked her for her kindness. As he walked towards the elevator, the receptionist called her aunt Mrs. Peachman and told her that a very nice young man was coming up to see her for a job and that she would be pleased if she hired him.

Markham was well-received by Mrs. Peachman, who hired him as a mail clerk with the possibility of training and advancement. Part of his duties consisted of wheeling a cart full of mail collected from the different offices to the Mail Center in the basement of the building where it was to be sorted and weighed for postage by the clerks assigned there. One of those clerks was a young tough named John who always gave Markham a look of displeasure each time Markham delivered his cart full of mail. Markham ignored him until one day at lunchtime in the company cafeteria while sitting at a table, he was joined by the receptionist who had recommended him to Mrs. Peachman for the job. She identified herself as Joyce Shapely and asked him how he liked his new job. Markham noticed that she was much prettier than his first encounter with her. Her dark hair parted in the middle framed her pale skin which accentuated her cheery blue eyes. She was so busy asking Markham personal questions that she hardly touched her lunch. Markham could barely get a word in edgewise, when he noticed that John the basement clerk had entered the cafeteria and was staring at Joyce.

"Oh! No, not him again," muttered Joyce.

"You mean John standing over there?" said Markham.

"Yeah! I made the mistake of dating him once and he keeps calling me even though I told him I'm not interested in going with him…ever. He simply won't take no for an answer."

"Is he bothering you at work, here?" asked Markham.

"He hasn't approached me physically, but he calls me on the telephone and he has my home number, which I think I'm going to change to an unlisted number."

"You can always report him to management and as far as your home telephone, as you said, you can have that number changed to an unlisted number."

"He has a violent side to him, Jim. I don't want you to get into trouble with him over me."

Markham shrugged his wide shoulders, "C'mon, I'm just an acquaintance to you. Why should that bother him?"

"He's the type that can't stand rejection and I think he's the type who'll become violent against anyone that he considers a rival."

Markham looked up to where John had been standing and noticed that he had left the cafeteria. No doubt Markham thought that John now probably considered him his rival for Joyce's affections which could develop into a nasty confrontation regardless of the fact that Markham wasn't really interested at this point in getting involved in any romantic relationship. Markham sensed that somehow he was involuntarily appointed as the savior of a lady in distress. That premonition was realized sooner than expected.

The very next day, Markham went on his routine round of collecting the mail in his cart on wheels. Upon arrival in the basement, Markham wheeled his cart full of mail down the aisle towards the desk occupied by the head mail clerk, Mrs. Tamborin, when John stepped directly in front of Markham's cart, grabbing the edge of the cart with both hands. Markham looked John in the eyes and saw raw anger.

Markham tried to diffuse his anger by politely asking him to step aside so that he could finish his route delivery, but John just stood there staring at him while holding onto the mail cart.

"I'm going to ask you one more time. Please move out of the way," said Markham in a firm tone of voice.

"And what if I don't? What are you going to do about it?" John challenged and let go of the cart tightening both hands into fists that Markham recognized as those of a boxer; thumbs tucked over the index and middle phalanges with the top of the hands rigidly in line with the forearm. Markham noticed John tensing his whole body ready to spring into action. John had now stepped to the side of the cart to gain access to Markham, who by now realized that there simply was no honorable escape from this bully. As John took a step closer with both clenched fists down at his side, Markham saw an opportunity to end the conflict quickly and with blinding speed threw a left and a right punch to both cheekbones dropping John to the floor unconscious. Mrs. Tamborin went frantic.

"Oh, my God. What have you done? You killed him," she said throwing both hands up to her face in disbelief.

Markham looked at Mrs Tamborin with impatience and told her to calm down.

"He's not dead, Madam. He's just unconscious," he said. Markham walked over to her desk and picked up the half-empty glass of water and threw the water over John's face. John started moaning as he raised his head, not knowing what had hit him.

"You see, he's alright. But you're the boss down here, you could have prevented this from happening," said Markham, somewhat perturbed at her favorism towards John. Markham left the cart there and walked over to the elevator which took him upstairs where he met Mrs. Peachman. He told her of the incident and advised her that he was resigning his position there. Even though John's assault on Markham was eminent and he therefore felt justified in striking the first blow, Markham knew that John could file charges of assault and his boss Mrs. Tamborin would probably support his allegation. Hence he knew that the best course of action was to resign from the firm immediately, which he did. Markham had no regrets over his actions which he felt were fully justified. His only regret was that John would probably continue to harass Joyce and he would not be there to protect her.

Back on 10th Street after dinner time, some of the Planets had gathered on Tommy Bernadi's stoop next to Ryker's Diner, talking about the baseball game of the previous Saturday, when a big, fat young man was spotted by Bernie walking towards them.

"Here comes Fat White," said Bernie to the rest of the guys on the stoop which included Boris, Tony, Al, Tommy, Frankie, Brewer and Jim Markham. Bruce 'Fat' White resided on the opposite end of the block on 10th Street from Markham, and seldom mixed company with the Planets, who never invited him to join their baseball team because of his obesity and also his crassness and bullying attitude towards those smaller than him. But that said, the guys would converse with him whenever he came on the scene. Markham had seen him around the neighborhood on several occasions, but never had a conversation with him.

"Hey! Fats. What have you been doing with yourself?" asked Boris, who could get away with the pejorative name because of his bulky build that left no doubt as to who would win in a fight and his maturity over White, who had just turned 19.

"I've been working on the docks," replied Fats.

"How'd you get that job?" asked Bernie.

"My uncle works there and he's knows some people," answered Fats.

"I hear they pay those longshoremen pretty good money," said Bernie.

"Yeah! You start at $10.00 an hour, but I tell you, it's back-breaking work," said Fats proudly.

"At $10.00 an hour it might be worth it," said Frankie.

"Yeah! But you gotta be big enough to handle the heavy lifting," said Fats, implying that Frankie was too small to be a longshoremen.

"I guess if you can lift your stomach Fats, you can lift anything," said Bernie laughingly, but Fats was not laughing at all and if Bernie had not been surrounded by his teammates, Fats might have assaulted him for that remark.

"So how long have you been working on the docks?" asked Boris.

"A month now," replied Fats, who now turned his attention to Markham.

"Hey! I hear that Amy is sweet on you, Jim Boy. Yeah! I heard her and her older sister Stacy talking on our stoop the other day," Fats said, smiling at Markham in a way that made him feel uneasy. No one said anything to Fats' comment.

"Yeah, man. I'll bet she'd make a good piece of ass. You shouldn't pass that up Jim Boy," said Fats sarcastically.

"I don't know what you're talking about. I've never talked to either of those girls," said Markham defensively.

"Well, Amy sure has a crush on you Jim Boy," replied Fats.

Markham knew of the two girls who resided in the same apartment building as Fats, and they didn't have a good reputation, hence Markham had remained aloof.

Boris interrupted the conversation, knowing that Markham was embarrassed by it and he didn't care for Fats in the first place. "Hey! Jim, lets go down to the Sheridan diner and get the late evening paper."

"Hey! I'll go with you," said Frankie.

"Me too," said Bernie.

The rest of the group dispersed for their respective residences.

At the diner, Boris, who was in his mid-twenties thus more experienced about New York City life than Markham, felt obliged to warn him about risks that might endanger the welfare of his star pitcher.

"I know you're looking for another job, Jim, but don't even think of working as a longshoreman. It's run by the mob and these longshoremen are much older than you and mostly toughs with a criminal record. 'Accidents' occasionally happen on the docks to people they don't like or who they think can cause them trouble," said Boris warningly.

Markham listened attentively as he respected Boris' experience and contacts, but he also suffered from youth's mistaken belief in immortality, thus felt capable of handling himself in any unforeseen situation. But the newspaper headlines quickly gained their attention announcing that due to the polio epidemic, all New York City pools were being closed for the summer.

"There goes any possibility of my getting a job as a lifeguard this summer," exclaimed Markham to Boris, Frankie and Bernie.

"There's always the beaches," said Bernie.

"Yeah, but they go by seniority, and those lifeguards who worked at the pools will now apply for beach duty and I'm a newcomer so I'll be near the end of the employment line for a job at one of the city beaches," replied Markham.

"At least now you'll have plenty of time to play baseball," said Frankie optimistically.

"Yeah! But that don't bring in any dough," replied Boris, looking at Markham for a reaction.

"Who knows. I could get my draft notice anytime this summer," replied Markham.

"You've got to get your notice to take a physical examination first," said Boris. "Don and Nye got theirs already."

"Not to change the subject, but the King George Hotel in Brooklyn has a large indoor saltwater pool that gets its water from artesian wells. I'll bet you they won't be closed," said Bernie to Markham.

"Well, that's encouraging, but it's a long way to travel just to go swimming," replied Markham.

"By subway it doesn't take that long, maybe twenty minutes," replied Boris.

"We can always go swimming in the Hudson River off the docks on 10th avenue," said Frankie. "Hell, we did that a couple of times last summer with Brewer, Ray, Don, and Nye."

"Yeah! That's when Brewer almost drowned," said Bernie, laughing.

"Naw! He didn't almost drown. He was just clowning around," said Frankie.

"Let me know when you guys do go swimming off the docks, 'cause I'd like to join you," replied Markham.

"Yeah! You can be our lifeguard," said Bernie with a friendly laugh.

Markham had started going to the YMCA on the corner of 23rd Street and Seventh Avenue three evenings a week to work out in the weight room when one evening he learned that classes in the martial art of Jujitsu were going to be held on the evenings of Monday, Wednesday and Friday which coincided with the same evenings Markham worked out in the weight room. Markham became fascinated by this oriental method of self-defense, which seemed to use the opponent's strength and momentum against himself and he welcomed the discipline involved in this art form of combat. However, in spite of this training, Markham still preferred the art of boxing. Nevertheless, to his friends, he only admitted attending the YMCA to lift weights.

One late afternoon, Markham was coming home from school carrying some books when he saw Fat White teasing Amy who was straddling her bicycle on the curb in front of Markham's residence. Fats kept poking her with his open hand in the ribs and then he grabbed her to prevent her from paddling away.

"Leave me alone you fat pig," yelled Amy at Fat White. She then looked at Markham. "Hi Jim," she said.

"Hi Jim," Fats mimicked her in ridicule, then he grabbed her by the waist and pulled her off her bike, all the time laughing. Amy struggled to get free of Fats to no avail, and looked at Markham with eyes that pleaded for help.

Markham had no feelings for Amy, but he couldn't refuse to help a woman in distress. So he turned towards Fats with his books still in his left hand.

"Let her go Fatso," Markham said in a stern voice that unmistakably conveyed a threat of physical action. When Fats failed to immediately respond, Markham placed his books down on the stoop and started walking towards Fats, who was still holding Amy. Fats realized he had misjudged Markham's willingness to aid Amy and now he faced a very real possibility of losing this fight and being humiliated in front of Amy and the neighbors. He released his grip on Amy, who then climbed back on her bike and rode away. Fats stood still with hands at his side facing Markham, who now was within five feet of him deliberating whether to teach this son-of-a-bitching bully a lesson, but decided that he wasn't worth the effort, thus turned around, picked up his school books and went inside his residence without a word being said between them. But Fats would not forget this humiliating event and wondered if he shouldn't have accepted Markham's challenge.

A week went by without any remarkable incident when at last the letter from the Selective Service Department that Markham was expecting finally arrived, which directed him to report to Whitehall Street in New York City for a physical examination. While waiting for his turn to be examined by a doctor, Markham made the acquaintance of two young men also scheduled for an examination. One was Gene LaConti of Italian origin and the other was Johnny McCoughlin, obviously of Irish descent. Both of them resided with their parents on the east side of Manhattan. All of them agreed that being drafted into the Army was a guaranteed shipment to the fox-holes of South Korea, hence they discussed the advantage of joining the Navy or Air Force in lieu of being drafted into the Army, but that would mean a four-year commitment rather than the Army's two-year draft. Markham expressed his desire to join the Navy's Underwater Demolition Team because of its stringent swimming requirements and life at sea. Gene and Johnny preferred the Air Force because of its technical schools. As they parted company, none of them expected to meet again, considering the thousands of young men being drafted into the military service. Markham was not surprised when he learned that he had passed his physical examination, having been an athlete for most of his young life.

The summer of 1951 was a hot summer indeed in New York City, and Markham yearned to go swimming, thus convinced some of his friends to join him at the 10th Avenue pier which was a short walk from the 10th Street neighborhood. Boris was working at the vegetable stand on that Saturday afternoon, but promised that he would join Markham, Bernie, Frankie, Brewer, Adolph, Vic and Nye at the docks after work.

Some of the boys wore their bathing suits under their pants while others wore shorts that would serve as their bathing suits. Upon arrival at the 10th Avenue docks, they saw several piers jutting out from the main dock into the Hudson River. These piers, about 60 yards wide, were like fingers extending some 100 yards into the river, and each of those piers held large warehouses, most of them two to three stories high. Each pier was separated by about 150 yards of open water that allowed ships to dock and load or unload their cargo. Markham and his friends decided to use the first body of water between the two piers across from 10th Street primarily because of a wooden ladder nailed to the dock that permitted them to descend the approximate 12 feet to the water below, thus avoiding the otherwise necessity of jumping or diving 12 feet in uncharted waters where unseen pylons could be present just a few inches below the water's surface. Having slipped out of his loafers and taken off his white T-shirt, Markham, wearing only his tan shorts, descended the wooden ladder located at the beginning of the pier into the water below and started swimming the length of the dock that separated the two piers for any underwater obstructions that might injure someone who dived from the dock above. Markham noticed that there were some submerged pylons at the north and south end of the dock near each pier, but none in the center of the dock where the depth was at least 20 feet and clear of any debris or other obstacles.

"This area here is OK for jumping or diving guys," yelled Markham to his friends, whereupon Frankie who was standing on the dock above yelled "Bombs away!" and jumped into the water below creating a big splash next to Markham, who had managed to swim out of his way. For the next hour, Markham and his friends enjoyed their private swim-hole, that is, until Fat White and five of his friends appeared at the dock and they were not wearing swim-suits. Markham, who had just dived from the dock and was now treading water, looked up towards the dock and saw Fat White and some of his friends talking to Brewer while Bernie and Nye looked on with apparent concern at the tone of the conversation between Fat White and Brewer.

"We don't want niggers on any of these docks. So you'd better get your ass on out of here before we cut off your balls and feed them to the fishes," said Fat White to Brewer, who by now was surrounded by Fat White's five friends who had formed a tight circle around Brewer to prevent Bernie and Nye from coming to his aid.

Markham called out to Frankie, Adolph and Vic that Brewer was in trouble and they should get onto the dock at once. With that said, Markham swam speedily to the ladder and once on the dock walked immediately towards Fat White and his circle of friends. Upon seeing him advance towards them followed by Frankie,Vic and Adolph, they widened their circle to allow Markham to confront Fat White. It appeared that Fat White's friends were not anxious to have an altercation with so many adversaries and would rather watch their leader Fat White represent them in a singular fight with Brewer or his appointed leader.

"What are you doing bringing this nigger swimming on our docks, Jimmy Boy?" asked Fat White.

"His name is Brewer, Fatso," said Markham with his anger building up, "and he has every right to be here."

This was Fats' first chance to observe Markham with his shirt off, standing only in his wet shorts, and he couldn't help observing Markham's exceptionally well-developed physique. *But does he know how to street fight?* he asked himself.

"What are you, a nigger lover?" asked Fats.

With that remark, Markham stepped in between Fats and Brewer, and facing Fats with only a few feet between them, Markham asked him to repeat that remark.

"You're a fucking nigger lover, aren't you?" said Fats, reaching into his left front pocket, which caused Markham to instinctively step back a couple of feet, placing him on the alert. Fats pulled out a ring which he inserted onto the ring finger of his right hand and he closed it into a fist. Markham immediately noticed that the ring had a curved blade welded onto it that protruded about half-an-inch above the ring.

"Hey! Jim," yelled Frankie. "That's a longshoremen's box cutter he's wearing."

Markham had never seen one of those box or line cutters before, but he had heard that you could rip a man's face to shreds with it.

At that moment Nye had opened up his penknife and threw it at Markham's feet.

"Here's an equalizer, Jim. Use it," said Nye.

Fats suddenly got worried that Markham would now be armed with a knife and his advantage would be gone. But Markham kicked the knife back towards Nye, thinking that if he picked up the knife, he would then have to use it and would probably end up killing Fats, which would most certainly mean a prison sentence for him. Better to fight Fats without any weapon and win than risk the alternative.

Fats stood tall and moved both of his fists in a rotating motion at chest level with his feet firmly planted on the dock a few feet from the edge of the pier while Markham slightly crouched like a tiger sizing up his prey, moved in a semi-circle to Fats' left, thus causing Fats to have his back to the edge of the dock and the water below. Without hesitation, Markham threw two sharp left jabs to Fats' face, bloodying his nose. Fats instinctively moved his fists up to cover his face, leaving his stomach open for Markham to throw a hard left jab to his solar plexus, instantly paralyzing Fats into catching his breath with both of his arms immobilized for a couple of seconds, enough time for Markham to hit him on the chin with a hard right punch that sent Fats over the edge of the dock, falling all 12 feet into the water below. Markham had hit Fats with the same momentum he used to throw his fastball, and judging from the roll of Fats' eyes, Markham was sure that he was unconscious before his feet left the dock. Fats' huge carcass hit the water with the splash of an elephant. Everyone but Markham ran to the edge of the dock to observe Fats' defeat, expecting that big tub of lard to return to the surface where he could float indefinitely, but to everyone's amazement, Fats remained under the surface and Markham heard one of the spectators utter the comment, "Where the hell is he? Man, he's going to drown for sure."

Markham walked over to the edge of the dock to see for himself and worried that Fats may indeed die from drowning as a result of his devastating punch. Markham, still in his bare feet and shorts, dived off the dock into the water below, making sure that he did so several feet from the spot where Fats fell, so that he wouldn't collide with him. As he entered the water, he saw Fats in a vertical position with his head about a foot from the surface with no visible movement. Markham immediately swam to him while still under the surface and grabbing him from behind, brought him to the surface where he then placed his left arm over his chest and swam a side-stroke towards the ladder at the end of the dock. *It's like pulling a barge,* Markham thought. Fats required a major swimming effort on Markham's part to pull him to safety. As Markham approached the ladder, he thought he heard a whizzing sound coming from Fats' throat, which was reassuring to Markham who was worried that Fats may not regain consciousness, but alas no movement from Fats. Markham then remembered that Fats was still wearing that longshoremen's ring blade on his right ring finger and for his own safety he should remove it at his first opportunity, but he couldn't reach his hand in this position. He couldn't let go of Fats for a second, less he slip under the surface again. By this time, several of the guys above had moved over to the top of the ladder. Markham yelled up that he needed a rope to lift Fats onto the dock. More than a minute expired before Brewer found a rope from the pier, which he threw one end down to Markham.

"Would someone tie a lasso at the end of it so I can wrap it around Fats' chest?" yelled Markham.

The rope was pulled back up and Brewer grabbed the end and tied a knot then slipped the end of the rope through the knot-hole, making a wide lasso big enough to accommodate Fats, which he then lowered to Markham who then called out for someone to come down the ladder to assist him. Vic descended the ladder and got into the water with Markham.

"Grab his right hand and remove that ring from his finger, and watch out you don't cut yourself, Vic," said Markham.

Vic grabbed Fats' limp right arm and then his hand and with some effort, removed the ring which he threw into the water. Markham grabbed the loop of the lasso and placed it over Fats' head and down under his hands bringing up the lasso over his chest and under his armpits with the knot at Fats' upper back.

"OK guys, you can pull him up now," yelled Markham and several guys, led by Brewer, grabbed onto the rope and started pulling him up onto the dock, surely leaving rope marks on his chest and armpits while they were pulling him up. Once on the dock and the rope removed from Fats, Markham, who had climbed up the ladder while Fats was being pulled up onto the dock, turned Fats over on his stomach, raised his hands at head level and checked his tongue to insure he was not choking on it. Markham then straddled his thighs and placed both of his hands over his lower rib cage and with elbows locked, leaned over pushing down on his rib cage while mentally saying "Push the bad air out," and then releasing the pressure by sitting back up, saying "Let the good air in." After about two minutes of applying artificial respiration, Markham asked Brewer and Bernie who were kneeling near Fats' head for any evidence of resurrection to again check his tongue when suddenly Fats let out two short coughs followed by some vomit, then started moaning. Markham ceased artificial respiration and let Fats remain in the same position a little longer to allow further expectoration. Fats started moving his arms and attempted to turn over at which time Markham asked some of the guys to help him sit Fats up against a nearby wooden crate, which they did by dragging his heavy carcass.

Fats sat on the floor of the dock leaning against the crate like a drunken bum with his disheveled hair, wet clothes and glassy eyes. "What happened?" uttered Fats, now aware of his condition.

"You took a swim," said Bernie with half a laugh.

"I can't swim," lamented Fats in a weak voice.

"You don't float either," said Vic.

Fatso looked up at Markham who was standing directly in front of him with his legs planted firmly apart and his hands on his hips staring at him. Fats now remembered his last moments of the fight before he blacked out and surmised he got knocked off the dock into the river below.

"You're lucky you're not dead Fats. I just want you to know that it was Brewer, a black man, that found and looped the rope that pulled you up out of the water and onto this dock. So now you're indebted to a black man," said Markham, who then turned around and walked off the dock accompanied by his friends, leaving Fats and his companions in subdued silence.

While walking back to the 10th Street neighborhood, Brewer approached Markham and thanked him for coming to his aid.

"Brew, he's what we call white trash, and unfortunately, you gonna come across scum like that occasionally, but most white folks are not like that believe me," said Markham apologetically. However, Markham's remark reflected the naivety of having been raised in Montreal, Canada where the social struggle between the southern and northern states of the United States was foreign to him.

As they neared Bleeker Street, Bernie suggested they go to Tony's Pizzeria and they all agreed.

"I thought Boris was joining us for a swim after work," said Frankie.

"I can see him still working at the vegetable stand," said Bernie as they reached the corner of Bleeker and 10th Street.

"Hey Boris, come join us at Tony's for a pizza," yelled Frankie.

"I'll be off in about 10 minutes. I'll see you then," replied Boris, then went back inside the grocery store.

The Planets gathered around two rectangular tables placed together to accommodate their crowd, and pitchers of beer were ordered along with large pizzas. Soon Boris walked in and joined his baseball team.

"Hey, we've got a game on Saturday afternoon at Central Park. I hope you're all going to be able to make it," said Boris.

"Who with?" asked Frankie.

"A team from the East Side called the Broncos. I hear they're pretty good," said Boris.

"Yeah! I heard of them. They're Puerto Rican. These guys eat, sleep and breathe baseball. You're going to have your work cut out Jimbo," said Frankie.

"You haven't pitched for a while Jim, so you shouldn't pitch the whole nine innings; you might damage your arm. I'm going to have you pitch the first three innings, followed by Bernie three innings, and then Johnny Sexton the last three innings, that way you'll all get a good workout without anyone getting hurt," said Boris.

"It's alright with me," said Markham nonchalantly, which made Bernie happy. Johnny Sexton wasn't there, so he could hardly object, nor would he.

"Listen guys. It doesn't do us any good if the pitching staff allow no runs, if we ourselves don't score any runs, so let's get some runs on Saturday, alright!" said Boris, trying to generate some enthusiasm.

"Yeah! Yeah! Boris. The last game we hit the ball plenty of times; they just went foul, that's all. We'll do better this time. Here come the pizzas...let's eat," said Frankie with delight.

It was indeed a beautiful, sunny afternoon in Central Park. The Broncos were already in the field practicing their baseball skills when the Planets arrived. The Broncos infielders were good, thought Markham. Their motions were fluid, fast and accurate. Their batters appeared confident and fearless.

After looking the Broncos over, Boris confided to Markham and Frankie standing next to him. "They work well as a team...they're not going to be a push over...that's for sure. I think we've got our work cut out for us."

"It's only a game Boris; don't worry so much," said Frankie.

"He's right Boris, it's only a game, so let's have some fun," replied Markham, who had his glove and a baseball ready to throw to Al the substitute catcher. "I've got to warm up. I'm the starting pitcher remember?" said Markham to Boris in a matter of fact tone.

Markham felt unusually good that day and he noticed during warm-up that his slider was working exceptionally well. He was anxious to get started, but since they just got there, the Broncos had to relinquish the field to the Planets for their warm-up before the game could get started. Boris started batting balls to the infield and also to the outfield to get them loosened up. Vic played short-stop like a professional and when at bat he had the ability to 'place' a ball anywhere in the infield or between the infield and the outfield to the extent that you could always depend on him to get on base. Ray played first base, Frankie second base and Phil third base. Nye took the center-field position while Brewer played right-field and Don left-field. Bernie and Johnny rounded up the pitching staff and of course Boris was the primary catcher and team manager. A coin was flipped by the Manager of the Broncos while Boris and Bernie looked on to see if their choice of 'heads' came up, but unfortunately the Broncos won the first time at bat.

Markham walked up to the pitcher's mound and waited for Boris to get his catcher's mask on, then he threw several medium speed straight balls to Boris, who then signaled him to throw a slider which Markham did with ease. Boris did not signal him to throw a fast-ball as he wanted to reserve it as a surprise to the Broncos when they came up at bat.

"OK!" yelled the umpire standing behind Boris with full protective gear. "Let's play ball."

There was a lot of chatter from the members of both teams encouraging their batter and pitcher, respectively. The first Broncos batter stepped up to the plate. He was a six-footer whom Markham had noticed playing first base for the Broncos during practice. Boris signaled to dust him off the plate with a fast-ball on the inside waist-high. Markham went through his stretch and then catapulted off the pitcher's mound descending from the high foot plate down towards the batter with a fast-ball that landed in the catcher's mitt before the batter had a chance to move back, which had an unnerving effect on the batter who wondered about this pitcher's control of the ball. The batter stepped back a few inches farther from the plate exactly as Boris intended. Boris now signaled Markham to throw a slider, which came in fast towards the batter's left shoulder causing him to lean back to avoid being hit, but to his late surprise, the ball slid over the middle of the home plate for a Strike One call. Now the call was One Ball and One Strike. Boris signaled for a fast-ball right down the middle and Markham obliged with a perfect Strike Two. Markham finished off the first batter with another slider which cut the inside corner of the plate for a final count of Strike Three and the batter was OUT.

"One down and two to go," yelled Boris, smiling. Markham struck out the next two batters using only his slider pitch. A crowd started to gather, at first behind the backstop, which then extended to both the first and third base lines. At bat Vic managed a hit between second and third base, which allowed him to make it safely to first base. Johnny then struck out, but Vic then stole second base. Boris then came to the plate with his big bat and after a count of two balls and one strike, hit the ball to center-field, which allowed Vic to run to third base and then slide into home plate for the first run of the game, but Boris' hit was caught by the Broncos' outfielder, making it two outs. Markham then came to bat and twice hit foul balls for a count of two strikes. Markham saw a curve ball coming and knew that if he didn't hit it, the umpire would certainly call it a Strike Three and he would be out and the inning over, hence he swung his bat and hit the ball high into the air towards the left field, but alas it was caught by a very able outfielder, ending that inning.

Markham again struck out all three batters without a single hit, and without having to throw his fastball, only sliders to the amazement of Boris who at one point after catching the ball turned around towards onlookers behind the backstop yelling, "Did you see this; did you see this?" shaking the ball in his right hand excitedly. The ball's trajectory had moved at least 30 inches to find the home plate. The third and last inning for Markham that day ended with the striking out of all three batters again to the amazement of the Broncos batters who simply could not follow or predict the path of the ball, since Markham started mixing some fastballs with his sliders during the third inning.

At the fourth inning, Bernie walked up to the mound to pitch for the next three innings as planned by the manager Boris. at that instant, several of the Broncos players started yelling at Boris to bring Markham back so that they could get a chance at hitting him, but Boris was steadfast in his decision. Markham sat on the bench for the remainder of the game, content and pleased at his performance, when a middle aged man, dressed in a suit, and white shirt open at the neck with loosened tie, carrying his coat jacket over his left arm, approached Markham.

"You've got a darn good fastball young man."

"I was pitching mostly sliders," replied Markham.

"Yeah! I noticed that too, but your fastball is amazingly fast and you've got great control. How long have you been pitching?" asked the suited man.

"Two seasons," replied Markham, wondering who he was.

"What's the name of your short-stop?" the man asked.

"That's Vic Racci," replied Markham.

"My name is Mike Bradley. I work for the Brooklyn Dodgers Farm Team. Can we talk over here where it's more private?"

Markham stood up and followed the suited man towards the first base where they both stopped walking.

"You two boys have a lot of talent and great major league potential. How would you like to try out for our farm team? We're holding try-outs right now at Ebbets Field."

"Are you a scout for the Brooklyn Dodgers?" asked Markham.

"I guess you could call me that. Here's my calling card. I'm going to write something on the back of the card. You call this number and ask for Stan Monroe and he'll tell you when to report for the try-out. Here's a card for your teammate Victor; the offer is good for the both of you."

"Well, I sure appreciate this opportunity mister," he said, accepting the annotated cards.

"Good luck young man," he said, shaking Markham's hand, and then he left the park without talking to Vic who was still in the field.

When Vic returned to the bench, Markham told him about the meeting with Mike the scout and then gave him the card to call Stan Monroe. Boris and some of the other teammates listened to Markham with envy and also happiness that two of the Planets were going to become major-league players. The very next day, Vic called Stan Monroe and got one of his assistants who made the appointment for him to report to Ebbets Field that Saturday at noon for his try-out. But out of pride, Vic never told Markham about his appointment because if he didn't make the team, he didn't want anyone to know that he had been rejected.

On the same day that Vic made his try-out appointment, Markham received his draft call from the Department of the Army. Markham knew that he had to enlist in the United States Navy or the Air Force right away or else end up in the Army. With a sad heart of disappointment at not being able to try-out for the Brooklyn Dodgers, Markham went to Whitehall Street in Manhattan where the recruitment offices were located and observed that there were three desks in the same large room, one for each service.

Markham walked up to the Navy recruiter and asked if he could join the Underwater Demolition Team also known as the UDT. The recruiter told him that he would first have to sign up for four years, then the Navy would determine whether he was qualified to join the UDT.

"You've got to be kidding. You want me to sign up for four years and then I end up mopping decks? No thanks," replied Markham, who then walked over to the Air Force Recruiter.

"What've you got to offer me if I sign up for four years?" asked Markham.

"You sign up for four years and after basic training you'll go to either a technical school or even to a university for at least one semester, depending on what your aptitude test reveals as to what field you are best suited," replied the recruiter.

"You mean that I'll attend a school of some type, perhaps a university?" asked Markham.

"Yes, that's correct. I guess you received your draft notice, didn't you?" asked the recruiter knowingly.

"Yeah! That's right."

"Well, you're making a smart move by joining the Air Force," replied the recruiter.

"Let's do it. Where do I sign up?" asked Markham who had resigned himself to the fact that his potential career as a professional baseball player would have to be put on hold. The only choice he had was to be drafted into the US Army or enlistment in the US Air Force. Markham had learned early in life not to fret over things he could not change and to concentrate on those matters over which he had some control.

"Just fill out these forms and I'll do the rest," replied the recruiter, only too willing to oblige to meet his quota. Markham had now joined the United States Air Force and he was looking forward to the excitement that he was sure would ensue from joining such an elite organization whose combat history he'd seen in numerous war movies starring his favorite actors such as Clark Gable, Alan Ladd, Jimmy Stewart, Spencer Tracy, Tyrone Power and Van Johnson. Yes, he was going to wear that uniform with pride and make something of himself in the process of serving his country.

When Markham returned home at 10th Street and Bleeker, he waited until he and his mother had finished eating supper, then he announced his enlistment to her. At first Nora said nothing. She got up and picked up the dirty dishes from the table and brought them to the kitchen, then she started crying quietly so that Jim didn't hear her, but his wolf-like hearing picked up the near silent lament. He debated whether to go to her to comfort her or let her grieve in privacy, and elected to do the former. He approached her gently from behind and placed both of his strong hands on the side of her small shoulders holding her so gently and in the softest voice reassured her.

"The Army was going to take me anyway, and the Air Force offers me better opportunities, Mom. I'll be alright."

"You might get killed and I'll never see you again," said Nora, still in tears.

"There's much less chance of that in the Air Force, Mom. And besides, I'm a man now; I can take care of myself," said Markham reassuringly.

Nora turned around towards her son James and gave him a big hug. "Your Grandma would be proud of you, Jim."

"Look at it this way, Mom. It's fate. I have no choice. It's either the Army or the Air Force. As you used to say 'Quest sera, sera.'"

A couple of days later, Markham met up with Boris and the rest of the Planets at which time he told them of his enlistment in the Air Force. He was to report to Whitehall on the 31st of August 1951 for transportation to Samson Air Force Base in upstate New York.

"Well, at least you don't have to leave until the end of the baseball season. But we're sure going to miss you, Jim," said Boris sadly.

"I wonder if Vic will be affected by the draft. He's got a good chance to make the Dodgers' farm team," said Markham.

"I guess you didn't hear. Vic went to Ebbets Field and they tested his fielding and batting ability. Guess who pitched to him at his try-out? None other than Hugh Casey, would you believe it?" said Frankie.

"Hugh Casey? Why he must be in his late thirties," said Bernie.

"Yeah, but according to Vic, he's still got it," said Frankie.

"Did he make the team?" asked Markham.

"Apparently he did 'cause they told him to report on Monday morning to sign a contract and then receive his assignment with their farm team," said Frankie.

"Well I hope that the draft board somehow forgets about him because that's a chance of a lifetime," said Boris.

"Man, that's got to make you feel bad, huh, Jim," said Bernie.

"Naw! Not at all. At least one of us has a chance to make it and I'm glad for him. It just wasn't in the cards for me. I guess that the man upstairs has something else in mind for me as he has for the rest of you guys," said Markham philosophically.

Boris knew that all of the Planets would miss Markham because he brought excitement and laughter to the group and never displayed arrogance or pretentiousness in spite of his exceptional athletic ability and handsomeness, which he didn't seem to acknowledge. After Markham left the group to go home, some of the guys remained on Albee's stoop.

"What a rotten break for Jim. Man, I would've loved to see him pitch in the majors," said Frankie.

"Yeah! He would've made it too. A talent like that only comes around once in a lifetime," said Boris. "I can't believe how calmly he's taking it."

"Man, that guy is something," said Bernie. "I wonder if we'll ever see him again after he goes into the Air Force?"

"Why not? This is where he lives," said Boris.

"Hey! When you leave New York, you're not going anywhere. He'll be back; don't worry," said Frankie.

"Hey! Brew, you've been real quiet all evening," said Bernie to Brew who had been sitting on the top step of the stoop listening to the other guys talking.

"You know what I think. I think the Air Force is going to broaden Jim's horizons to an extent that we can't even envision, and I doubt that he'll come back here except maybe for an occasional visit," said Brew. "Man, on that mound, he was sure something to behold."

"He sure was something," said Boris pensively.

There was a moment of silence as each person's private thoughts emerged. Boris reflected on the sheer joy and experience of catching for such a superb pitcher in baseball games that he would cherish and relive the rest of his life. Bernie admired Markham for treating him as an equal, never lording his superior talent as a pitcher and his constant encouragement when he felt depressed over his performance. Frankie knew he would greatly miss the camaraderie and sincere friendship he'd developed with Markham, but most of all, he would miss his remarkable presence. Brewer felt that Markham was the only white man who never saw him as a Blackman. Brewer loved him for re-instating his faith in humanity. It was people like him, he reflected, who would make a better world and he was the saddest at learning of his impending departure. *Oh, God,* he thought, *please protect this man whose destiny is as yet unfulfilled.*

CHAPTER III
The Korean War

Having said all of his goodbyes, Markham left home on August 31st dressed in light civilian clothes and carrying a small overnight bag containing only underwear and shaving gear as recommended in the reporting orders and instructions given him, explaining that he would only be permitted to wear military clothing during his entire basic training. Upon arrival at Whitehall Street, he boarded a bus with other recruits destined for Samson Air Force Base, Geneva, New York about an eight-hour drive from Manhattan. Markham learned that two other buses loaded with recruits had already departed for Samson Air Force Base earlier that morning.

The recruits were from all five boroughs of New York, but the greater percentage of them came from Manhattan and Brooklyn, and many of them were toughs from street gangs that had seen much violence. Others were in the military service to avoid a prison term, an offer they couldn't refuse by a judge who felt that the military would take them off the city streets and teach them discipline and possibly a trade that would be useful upon discharge. The mingling of recruits from such diverse and challenged backgrounds with young men of privilege who usually hailed from Queens, Long Island and Richmond, created a unique situation which produced events and results that would have surprised most sociologists. In the course of just eight weeks, which is the duration of basic training in the U. S. Air Force, the Drill Sergeant is able to take these raw recruits from all walks of life, with some exceptions of course, and create a cohesive military unit that would work and if necessary fight together, and even sacrifice their lives for the other members of their unit and their country. That is no accident but the result of an evolutionary training process spanning two centuries. But not all drill sergeants are equal to the task.

As the bus carrying Markham and his fellow recruits entered Samson Air Force Base, Markham observed that most of the buildings were constructed of wood and appeared to be of Second World War vintage and perhaps older. After ten minutes of driving through the base, the bus stopped in front of a wooden two-story barracks, which at one time had been painted white, but now was weather-beaten. The recruits disembarked and were met by a Sergeant and a Corporal. They were ordered by the Sergeant to fall out into a formation shoulder to shoulder, forming three lines with their bags on the ground to their right. The Sergeant identified himself as Sergeant Greenberg and introduced his assistant as Corporal Bailey. After a short and curt welcome, they were informed that they formed the first half of Flight 748. The second half was due to arrive shortly from Kentucky and they would occupy the bunks on the right side of the barracks, thus 54 New Yorkers and 54 Kentuckians would occupy the lower floor of the barracks. They were instructed to enter the barracks on the first floor and pick any bunk located to the left of the middle isle and place their underclothing and toilet articles inside the footlocker at the head of each bunk. The upper bunk footlocker would be located under the lower bunk. As they entered the barracks, Markham observed that some bunks had already been taken by recruits from a previous busload. Markham selected the bottom bunk two thirds of the way in back of the barracks. They were told that in 15 minutes they had to fall out into formation to be marched to the supply warehouse where they would be issued their military clothing.

The march was a joke. Many of these recruits didn't know their right from their left foot and were catching the butt of the Drill Sergeant's abusive language.

Upon arrival at the Supply warehouse, the recruits formed a single line that moved along a long wooden counter served by several Army Supply personnel who would ask each recruit their shirt size, waist size, shoe size, etc., and then were issued clothing and shoes that most approximated their given size. While their dress blues were closely fitted to the individual's size, the one-piece fatigues were always too big, leaving it to the recruit to use a pair of scissors or a razor blade to cut the length of the fatigues down to size. The boots were made of rough cowhide that had to be polished black to a mirror shine, which was accomplished by using a rag dampened with alcohol and water to apply black shoe shine until the boot glistened like a mirror.

Upon their arrival back at the barracks, they were met by recruits from the previous bus who had already acquired their military clothing, and to Markham's surprise, two of them recognized him from their previous meeting at Whitehall Street.

"Hey! James. Fancy meeting you here," said Johnny McCoughlin.

"Yeah! This sure is a small world ain't it?" said Gene LaConti.

"Well, I'll be darn. Where are you guys bunked?" replied Markham.

"Over there," said Gene, pointing to the far end of the barracks about two bunks further down than Markham's.

"That's good; I'm bunked in the same vicinity," replied Markham.

"Say, let's go over to the snack bar. I saw one on the way over here," said Johnny.

"It's chow time in an hour and the Flight Sergeant told us to be here for formation at 5 o'clock," said Gene, who did not want to spend money on food unnecessarily.

"Yeah! Gene's right. It's not smart to miss a formation on the first day here and be labeled as a screw-up," said Markham. "How come your fatigues fit you so well, Gene?"

"I cut them with scissors and used my sewing kit to give it a cuff. Man, you gotta learn to be your own tailor here," said Gene.

"How about lending me your needle and thread, and your scissors too, 'cause my fatigue pants are about a foot too long, no exaggeration," replied Markham.

"Gene did mine. If you hadn't told him you could sew, he would have done yours too. He's a real obliging guy," said Johnny with a laugh.

"Hey! Don't laugh so hard, there may come a time when I'll ask you to do me a favor and you then won't be able to refuse," replied Gene smartly.

Markham appreciated Gene's logic and his sense of humor. He observed that Gene was built like a gymnast, with well-developed shoulders and upper body with slim, muscular legs. He was only about 5 feet 9 inches tall, but Markham believed that Gene would make a formidable opponent with much street savvy. Johnny, on the other hand, had a tall, lanky non-athletic body that had apparently been exposed to very little sun, probably due to the vulnerability of his light Irish complexion to the sun's damaging rays. Gene was the more reserved of the two, while Johnny possessed the Irish gift of the gab. Markham liked them each for their own individual personality which he found intriguing and amusing. They became fast friends and dubbed themselves the three musketeers.

At 2 PM, two busloads of Kentuckian recruits arrived and disembarked at the barracks occupied by Flight 748. They were a quiet bunch, not disposed to being friendly to Yankees, with only the middle aisle separating the Northerners from the Southerners. Someone at Headquarters was displaying a perverse sense of humor when he assembled these two factions into one barracks. This was the military's attempt to integrate not only minority groups, but also dissolve historical and philosophical differences between the Northerners and Southerners in order to have a unified and cohesive military unit.

The Kentuckians marched to the Supply Warehouse where they were issued their uniforms, boots and low quarter shoes. Upon their return, they were ordered to change into their fatigues and be ready to join the New Yorkers for a march to the Mess Hall. Markham heard the Kentuckians speak to each other in a drawl he'd never heard before.

"Hey! Gene, do southerners all talk like that with a drawl?" asked Markham.

"Where've you been, man? All southerners talk with a drawl. Oh! That's right, you come from Canada so you wouldn't know," answered Gene.

"You see this middle aisle," said Johnny, "that's the Mason-Dixon line dividing the North from the South. Make sure you don't cross it or else you're liable to get slugged."

"You're kidding?" replied Markham.

"No, I'm not kidding. Wait till the lights go out tonight. There'll be skirmishes between north and south…you'll see," said Johnny. "Did you notice, there are only two colored guys in the entire flight and they're both from New York. They'll be a target."

"John, I think you're way off-base. You're an alarmist," replied Markham.

Markham took what Johnny said with a grain of salt. He didn't feel any animosity from them nor did he have any reason to dislike them. As far as he was concerned, they were all Americans from different parts of the country with expected differences in dialectal accents.

At 5 PM they were all marched in military formation to one of the three chow halls where they each picked up a metal tray, then walked in single-file along a food dispensing line. They were not allowed to touch the food, but were served a portion from each food receptacle by Mess Hall attendants all referred to as cooks, although that title was mostly undeserved. That day they were served beans, frankfurters, boiled potatoes and bread, and the coffee urns and milk were located at the end of the line.

Markham joined Gene and Johnny at a table and Markham could hear Johnny voice his dissatisfaction over the food.

"Man, I traveled eight hours on a bus and this is the crap they serve us. Man, where's the snack bar?" complained Johnny.

"You'd better get used to it 'cause this may be your only source of food for the next eight weeks," said Gene.

"The snack bar is probably for the permanent party and the casuals who have completed basic training and are awaiting further orders," replied Markham. "At least that's what I heard from someone in the barracks."

"Hey! They can't watch me 24 hours a day. I'll find a way 'cause I can't eat that shit," said Johnny with disgust.

"Oh! You get that too. You ever hear of SOS? It stands for Shit-on-a-Shingle. It's made of ground beef in a white sauce spread over a slice of toast," said Gene, laughing.

"You're kidding me, right?" asked Johnny.

"I wish I was. You'll see," replied Gene.

"That's it. I quit. Where do I get my discharge?" said Johnny half-jokingly.

"The Chaplain's office is right down the street," replied Markham in amusement over the whole conversation.

Of course Markham loved beans, reminiscent of his boarding school days, hence ate them to his heart's content to the amazement of his two friends.

Upon return to the barracks, Markham met the recruit that occupied the upper bunk above him. His name was David Lopat. He couldn't have been more than 5 feet 4 inches in height and 100 pounds soaking wet. He appeared to be an amiable young man, but Markham wondered whether he would be able to sustain the rigors of basic training, although it was not supposed to be as arduous as that of the Army. Lopat was attempting to cut the length of the legs of his fatigue pants and succeeded with the left leg, but before he could cut the other leg to the same length, the Flight Chief announced in a loud voice that it was 9 o'clock and turned all of the lights off.

"Hell, what do I do now? We only get three minutes in the morning to fall out in formation for roll call and I need to cut the other pants leg," muttered Lopat to Markham.

"Give me your fatigues. I'll lay them on your foot locker and line up the pants leg already cut with the other pants leg and then cut along the edge of the finished one," said Markham.

"Yeah! That should work," replied Lopat.

Markham pulled out Lopat's footlocker from underneath his bunk and laid down Lopat's fatigues on the footlocker top. He felt along the leg that had already been shortened and then with a razor blade, cut through the other pants leg, then told Lopat the job was done.

At wake-up call the next morning, everyone in the barracks jumped into their fatigues and ran outside the barracks to stand at attention in flight formation. But Lopat called out to Markham.

"Jim, you cut my pants leg about a foot too short," said Lopat standing incredulously in his fatigues with his right pants leg cut at the knee while his left pants leg was properly cut at ankle length.

Markham and several of the other recruits still in the barracks all started to laugh at the amusing sight. Although Markham felt bad about his mistake, he couldn't help laughing at Lopat standing there like a clown.

"Listen, we can't correct it now. Just stand in the last row of the formation, and maybe the Chief won't notice it," said Markham. "We'll think of something when you get back into the barracks, OK?"

"Alright," said Lopat, who then exited the barracks and stood in formation, luckily without being observed by the Flight Chief who quickly dismissed them to get ready for their march to the Mess Hall.

Back in the barracks, Markham borrowed some thread and needle from Gene and sewed the cut portion of the fatigue pants back on, then under the light, cut the pants leg to the correct length.

"OK! Dave, right after breakfast we get an hour's break. I suggest that you then go over to the Supply Warehouse and trade these fatigues for a new pair. Shouldn't be any problem," said Markham. "Listen, I'm really sorry about that. It was dark."

"Hey! No problem Jim," replied Lopat.

During the ensuing week, Markham had occasion to meet at least one Kentuckian who used the sink next to him to shave. Markham struck up a conversation with this blond-haired, muscular middle-weight prize fighter, who claimed to have won first place in the state's amateur boxing championship. He, like many others, joined the Air Force to avoid the Army draft. He identified himself as Charles Applegate and after exchanging some personal information, Markham found him pleasant and non-prejudiced towards northerners. Markham made himself his first southern friend and found the other Kentuckians he met were amiable and seemed to lack the bravado that many New Yorkers displayed.

Several days passed without incident, when one night, shortly after lights went out, someone surreptitiously entered the cubicle where airman Lopat was sleeping in the top bunk above Markham's lower bunk and shoved Lopat off his bunk causing him to fall a distance of five feet to the floor, hitting his head on the corner of his footlocker which was sticking out from Markham's lower bunk. Lopat let out a yell of pain as he lay on the floor. Markham jumped out of his bunk and lifted Lopat to his feet.

"You alright?" asked Markham.

"I hit my head against the edge of my footlocker," replied Lopat, who was still hurting from the fall.

"Does someone have a flashlight?" asked Markham to those bunked around him.

"Yeah, Jim. I've got a pocket flashlight," said Johnny, who slept two bunks away.

"OK! Thanks," replied Markham.

Markham turned on the flashlight and looked at Lopat's face and head. "Well, you're not bleeding, but you've got a lump on the side of your forehead and some skin abrasion. You should go into the latrine and run some cold water on it to get the swelling down. Who could have done this? Do you have any enemies here?" asked Markham.

"No, I don't know anyone here except for you, Gene and Johnny. I don't know why anyone would do such a thing," said Lopat, himself puzzled.

"Hey! Markham," said the occupant of the top bunk to his right. "I saw somebody run back towards the front of the barracks on our side," indicating that it was someone from New York, not a Kentuckian.

Markham was getting visibly angry over such a dastardly deed and could no longer contain his anger.

"Whoever shoved Lopat out of his bunk is a godamn coward, and I dare you to come back to this cubicle and try on someone your own size, you son-of-a-bitch," yelled Markham so that the entire barracks could hear him. Sergeant Greenberg and Corporal Bailey, who shared the same room at the entrance to the barracks, also heard Markham's loud invitation and decided to let them fight it out amongst themselves and they would later pick up the pieces.

Markham didn't expect anyone to respond to his invitation, but to his surprise three individuals started to enter his cubicle. Markham who was standing with both his arms and hands resting on both sides of the two upper metal bunks quickly observed that the threesome was led by a burly young man, followed by two smaller individuals. As the burly guy entered the cubicle, Markham raised his whole body with both arms straight up as he would on parallel bars in gymnastics and then swung his whole body with feet forward hitting the burly fellow on his chest, driving him back against the other two trespassers. Markham fell to his feet at the entrance to his cubicle and didn't wait for them to recover from their fall. Markham quickly hit one on the forehead with his right elbow as he was getting on his feet. The burly one came charging at Markham, who extended his left leg and foot outward hitting him in the groin, which caused him to bend over in agony and ended when Markham struck him with a hard right punch to the side of his head knocking him out flat on the floor of the middle aisle. The third trespasser ran back to the front of the barracks where he disappeared in his own cubicle. Markham, with chest heaving and fists still clenched, looked over the scene where two bodies lay on the floor in the middle aisle. Then he heard a voice calling out to him.

"Hey! Jim. You need any help?" asked Johnny chuckling.

"Talk about a Johnny-come-lately," replied Markham sarcastically.

"Hey! Man. We didn't think you needed any help, and from the looks of things, we were right," said Gene approvingly.

Markham then noticed that Charlie Applegate had been standing at the head of his cubicle in the Kentuckian zone observing the entire incident. As their eyes met each other, Charlie gave

Markham a wave of his hand and a smile, then retired to his bunk. Markham had a feeling that had the going got rough, Charlie would have come to his aid.

Gene and Johnny stepped into the middle aisle to assess the situation.

"Hey! That's Eric Bachmann," said Johnny, pointing to the burly one. "I think he's coming to."

"Who's the other one?" asked Gene while Markham looked on.

"That's Van Gorden," yelled someone from the front of the barracks who apparently had seen him leave his cubicle.

"Let them sleep it off on the floor till they come to," said Johnny.

At this point Bachmann had regained consciousness and was attempting to get back on his feet. Markham grabbed him with his left hand around his throat and his right hand holding his left wrist and slammed him against the railing of the upper bunk.

"You son-of-a-bitch. You ever bother Lopat or come into our cubicle again, I'll do you some serious damage. You understand me?" said Markham in a low but threatening voice. When Markham didn't get a response from Bachmann, he repeated his question, "You understand me?"

Bachmann answered with a weak, "Yes," due to Markham's hold of his neck with his powerful left hand. Markham released his hold on Bachmann, who walked back to his cubicle and bunk. By this time Van Gorden had regained his consciousness and groggily walked back to his bunk.

"Hey! Jim," said Gene. "If I were you, I'd move my pillow to the wall side of the bunk so that your head is not near the aisle and you can see any incoming traffic. Just a precaution. I'll keep my eyes open for a while, but I'll eventually fall asleep."

"Thanks but I don't think any of them will come back tonight. I think they've had enough," replied Markham, who then did move his pillow to the other side of his bed and as usual, slept on his back facing the upper bunk and the entrance to the cubicle.

The next morning Sergeant Greenberg called Lopat into his room as Lopat was entering the latrine.

"Close the door Lopat," said Greenberg."You got a nasty bruise on your forehead." commented Greenberg.

"Yeah, but it's alright now," replied Lopat, who felt uncomfortable.

"Do you know why Bachmann and his cronies attacked you last night?" asked Greenberg.

"No, I don't," replied Lopat.

"Because you're a Jew, that's why," replied Greenberg.

"How do you know that?" asked Lopat.

"Because I've been a Drill Sergeant for four years now, and I've seen these German anti-Semitics come and go. Have you forgotten that only six years ago the allies discovered all of those German concentration camps that killed more than six million Jews? Like you Lopat, I happen to be a Jew, but don't advertise that to anyone because you won't always have people like Markham around to protect you. Look, I know that you and one other New York recruit in this flight have college degrees. That qualifies you to apply for Officers Training School after which you'll become a Second Lieutenant and then you won't have to put up with the harassment so prevalent amongst the enlisted population."

"Yeah, it does make sense, but when can I apply?" asked Lopat.

"You can put in your application at any time during basic training and upon graduation, you'll be sent to OTS. It's as simple as that," replied Sergeant Greenberg.

"Thanks for the advice, Sarge, I mean Sir," said Lopat to a smiling Greenberg.

"OK! You'd better get ready for formation," concluded Greenberg, and Lopat left the room with mixed emotions.

Later that day, Lopat told Markham of his conversation with Greenberg and his recommendation to apply for OTS.

"That's good advice. You ought to seriously consider it," replied Markham, who then thought about his own experience at Forest Hills High School where the majority of students were of Jewish origin and their focus was primarily on academic achievement which brought scholarships at ivy league universities and positions of leadership and power. Versus sports, celebrated by gentiles, which after graduation from high school, with few exceptions, brought you a trophy or two to garnish the mantle piece of a proletariat's house and the chagrin of lost opportunities. *Yes,* he thought, *education was the ticket to a better and more productive life.*

Several days later, Flight 748 marched up to the Mess Hall and stood at parade rest while they waited for their turn to enter the mess hall. Another Flight commanded by a Drill Sergeant with an unmistakable southern accent arrived next to Flight 748.

"What's your flight number Sarge?" said Sergeant Greenberg to the southern flight sergeant.

"734, the best flight on Samson," said the southern flight sergeant.

"What part of the south you from, Sarge?" asked Sergaent Greenberg.

"Alabama," he replied proudly.

Markham noticed that 'Alabama' had all of his recruits standing at attention.

"Well, Alabama, why don't you give your guys a rest while waiting for their chow?" said Sergeant Greenberg.

"You take care of your flight, Yank, and I'll take care of mine," replied Alabama.

"For Pete's sake, why don't you give the guys a break?" said Sergeant Greenberg.

The conversation between Sergeant Greenberg and the Drill Sergeant from Alabama could be overheard by at least the first three rows of men in each flight. Alabama did not reply to Sergeant Greenberg's last remark and ignored him for the remainder of his stay in the chow line.

Several days later, while Flight 748 waited at parade rest in front of the Mess Hall, Flight 734 marched into position next to Flight 748 with an apparently new Drill Sergeant. Sergeant Greenberg recognized the Flight from some of its members in the first row, and in particular the tallest man he'd seen in any flight who must have been six feet six inches in height.

"This is Flight 734 isn't it?" asked Sergeant Greenberg.

"You got it right Sarge; what's your Flight number?" asked the new Flight Sergeant.

"I'm Sergeant Greenberg and this is Flight 748. What happened to the Flight Sergeant from Alabama?" asked Greenberg.

"He got into an accident and is no longer the Flight Chief. By the way, I'm Sergeant Mark Cleveland."

"Accident? What kind of accident?" asked Sergeant Greenberg.

"Apparently some of the men in this flight threw him a blanket party that resulted in injuries that required hospitalization," answered Sergeant Cleveland.

"Did they ever find out who did it?" asked Sergeant Greenberg.

"Nope," answered Sergeant Cleveland.

"I'm not surprised. They're probably considered heroes by the rest of the men," replied Sergeant Greenberg. Greenberg had heard of a previous 'blanket party' conducted in the past where a bunch of recruits in the middle of the night, entered the Flight Chief's unlocked room in the barracks, threw a blanket over his head and beat him with fists and broke one of his legs with a metal bed adapter, because he had been abusing his troops. Apparently, Alabama had suffered the same fate.

After several weeks into basic training, members of Flight 748 were administered aptitude tests to determine where they would be sent for training. Markham was informed by the examiner that his highest score was in Electronics and his second highest score was in Administration. Markham told the examiner he knew nothing about electronics, but his typing skill was exceptional and as a clerk typist he would vastly improve his command of the English language, hence he chose Personnel Administration as his first choice. In his last week at Basic Training, Markham was given his written orders assigning him to attend a Personnel Course at Arizona State College in Tempe, Arizona. As it turned out, McCoughlin and LaConti also received orders to attend the Personnel Course. Lopat applied and was accepted as a candidate at OTS.

With his military orders, Markham received an advance payment voucher for travel to Arizona State College. After landing at Tempe, Arizona, Markham boarded a bus to the college and once there, he was directed to the Administration Office. He was told by an administrative clerk that he would not be staying or attending classes at the college, but someone from the Thunderbird campus outside of Scottsdale, Arizona, about 20 miles from Tempe, would be picking him up to drive him back to Thunderbird where he would be residing with the other students attending the Personnel Administration Course. About forty-five minutes later, Markham's ride arrived and he was driven through Scottsdale, which had a bar, a few houses and not much else in the middle of a desert spotted with occasional cactuses and the Camelback Mountains appearing, as its name implied, in the distance.

Thunderbird campus was an oasis in the middle of the desert. Several one-story stucco buildings that served as billets for the students were strewed around the inside perimeter of the compound. There was also a dining hall, a large classroom with adjoining office and an Orderly Room where the First Sergeant tended to the daily business of running a school and a detachment of Air Force students. Teachers from the main campus in Tempe traveled to the Thunderbird campus each day to conduct their classes in personnel administration and typing lessons. The students attended class until 3:30 PM, then were free the rest of the day. A bus made the round trip from Thunderbird to the Tempe campus once a day, departing at 5 PM and returning from Tempe at 11 PM, weekdays. But on Saturday night, the bus returned to the Thunderbird Campus at midnight. Students could take a taxi if they missed the return bus trip, but it was costly unless several of them pooled their money together for a united return. Two days transpired without incident, when a newcomer arrived on the Thunderbird campus.

Markham was walking on the sidewalk between the dining room and his one-story stucco barracks when he noticed Johnny McCoughlin standing next to a big, barrel-chested student with short hair and a pudgy face that Markham had not seen before, staring at Markham as he walked to his barracks. Even though Johnny was talking to this new student of obviously larger physical stature, the new student never once turned his head towards Johnny, but kept staring at Markham. He got the impression that Johnny was aligning himself with someone whom he feared, thus the subservient behavior observed by Markham. There was something about that new student's deportment which gave Markham the feeling that the school bully had arrived.

After chow that evening, Johnny came up to Markham who was talking to Gene in the barracks.

"Hey, guys. How you doing?" asked Johnny.

"Alright," replied Gene with Markham looking on.

"I met this new guy who arrived here three days late for school. He's from Missouri," said Johnny. "You saw me talking to him in the parade ground this afternoon, Jim."

"Yeah, I saw you, John. What did you say to him that made him stare at me?" asked Markham.

"Oh! I just told him that you were not someone he'd want to pick a fight with, that's all," replied Johnny.

Gene and Markham were both astonished at Johnny's last remark.

"Why would you tell him that to begin with?" asked Markham incredulously.

"He looks like a big bad dude and I didn't want him to bother my friends," replied Johnny.

"Hey! Man, you don't have to intervene on my behalf," said Gene. "He messes with me and I'll nail his ass."

Markham looked at Gene and then Johnny, and smiled at both of them, remembering his initial impression of that dude and the accuracy of his instincts.

"What's that guy's name anyway?" asked Markham.

"Bill Chucklock," replied Johnny.

"You know John, my Grandmother once told me that 'you tell me who you hang around with and I'll tell you who you are.' Choose your friends carefully, John."

"Hey! He's not my friend. I just met the guy," replied Johnny apologetically.

"A word to the wise, that's all John," replied Markham.

"Hey! Did I tell you, I met these two guys at the bar in Scottsdale and they're transplanted New Yorkers. Their folks moved from New York City and bought a horse ranch outside of Scottsdale. They invited me to the ranch and they'll teach me how to ride horses. You guys want to come?" asked Johnny.

"Naw, not me, I don't like horses. I'm a city guy," replied Gene.

"How about you Jim?" asked Johnny.

"Yeah, that sounds interesting. I like horses and I wouldn't mind learning how to ride one," replied Markham.

"Alright! I'll call them, Mike and Jeff, they're brothers, at the ranch and make arrangements," replied Johnny excitedly.

Johnny left the barracks to return to his own barracks and Markham grabbed his soap dish and toothbrush and went into the latrine to prepare to retire for the night.

At the sink, Gene took the sink next to Markham and engaged in conversation.

"You really going to visit that dude ranch, huh?" said Gene.

"Why not? Not much else to do, and anyway it's a new experience for me," replied Markham.

"That new guy, what's his name, Bill; he sounds like trouble waiting to happen," said Gene.

"Yeah! I know it. But he won't pick on you or me, he'll pick a fight with someone he knows for sure he can win to make himself feel powerful. Guys like that are really cowards," said Markham knowingly.

"I think you're right Jim. Sounds like you're speaking from experience," said Gene.

"It's deja vu and having to deal with it gets mighty tiresome, so I try to avoid it," replied Markham.

"Yeah! I know what you mean," replied Gene, who liked and admired Markham for his humility and fortitude.

The next afternoon, while on break in typing class, Johnny came up to Markham with news.

"Hey! Jim. Mike and Jeff are going to leave two Palomino horses tied up to the hitch outside the compound for us so we can ride them and they will pick them up later this evening. How's that for service, huh?" said Johnny excitedly.

"That sounds great. But why didn't they simply invite us to their ranch where we could have gotten on the horses from there and they wouldn't have to bring the horses all the way over here and then pick them up again? I don't understand." said Markham inquisitively.

"That's because they're busy during that time of day and for them it was simpler to do it this way. They're just nice guys," said Johnny.

"They're real generous. Nice people like that I'd like to meet and thank," replied Markham.

"You'll get your chance," said Johnny.

After class ended that afternoon, Markham got into his jeans, T-shirt and army boots that had heels for the stirrups and walked out of the barracks to meet Johnny who was already waiting for him with the two horses still tied to the railing. Both horses were gold with white mane and tail and each carried a western saddle with the customary horn at the front of the saddle near the horse's mane. Markham had seen enough western movies to know how to mount a horse and he felt that he knew the basic rudiments to navigate one.

"You ever rode a horse before?" asked Johnny.

"No but I'm about to," replied Markham as he mounted the horse nearest him after he grabbed the reins from the post. Markham turned the horse around towards open country and started into a slow trot. Johnny had mounted his horse, which instinctively followed Markham's horse. Markham was trying to master the rhythm of the horse's up and down motion with his own body to eliminate the impact of his derriere with the saddle and soon learned to squeeze his legs against the sides of the horse, thus raising his derriere away from the seat of the saddle with much success. Johnny had claimed to have ridden horses before in upstate New York, but from appearances, he was not managing his horse very well and he still bounced against the saddle, but Markham's horse was leading, hence he couldn't see Johnny except on occasional glances. Markham decided to put his horse to a full gallop in the open desert and pressed his heels against the horse's sides and loosened the reins and yelled, "Giddyup, c'mon giddyup," and his horse went into a full gallop. Markham felt he was riding into a western movie as he felt the power of the horse's stride, which exhilarated him. Johnny's horse automatically followed Markham's horse into a full gallop in spite of Johnny's efforts to stop him to no avail. Johnny started yelling at Markham to stop as he was deathly afraid he might fall or get thrown off his horse, but Markham had gained a significant lead thus was not aware of Johnny's howling. Markham noticed that there was a barbed-wire fence about 100 meters ahead so he slowed down his horse which allowed Johnny's horse to catch up to him. Johnny was in a state of hysteria.

"You crazy son-of-a-bitch. What are you doing, racing the horse? You don't know how to ride a horse. You could have gotten us killed. You're crazy I swear," said Johnny, visibly shaken from the ride. But Johnny's verbal assault stopped abruptly when he realized from Markham's unruffled demeanor that he had just revealed his fear of danger and low panic threshold to a man whose past demonstrated courage that he admired and envied. Markham did not utter a single word. Instead, he turned his horse around and slowly galloped back towards the Thunderbird compound. When they arrived at the school compound, Markham tied the reins of his horse to the post and walked over to the maintenance shed where he found a bucket which he filled with clean water. Markham then brought the bucket of water to his horse where he placed it on the ground and his horse immediately drank to his heart's content.

"Thanks for the ride John. I'll see you around," said Markham as he started to walk back to his barracks. Johnny was too embarrassed to reply.

At the barracks Markham met up with Gene who had obviously just taken a shower and was now putting on his dress civilian clothes.

"Hey! Jim, where've you been? I've been looking for you," said Gene.

"I was out riding a horse with Johnny and I just got back," replied Markham.

"Well, listen. There's a dance at the main university campus in Tempe. There'll be lots of girls from the university there. Why don't you put your duds on and come along?" said Gene.

"I don't know how to dance," replied Markham.

"Hey! I don't do so well either, but you gotta start someplace, and this is as good as any," said Gene. "C'mon man. You'll get a chance to meet a nice girl. What have you got to lose?"

"I guess you're right. I've got to take a quick shower first though, and then I'll be ready in a few minutes. OK?"

"Yeah, but hurry up. The bus leaves in half an hour," replied Gene.

There must have been at least 400 students at the dance, the gender equally divided. The university band played all of the latest songs, many of them modern westerns which Markham particularly liked as it lent the proper atmosphere to that area of the country. Markham loved the hot but dry weather with near cloudless skies that produced the starriest nights he'd ever seen. He stood there with Gene on the fringe of the circle of people that stood around those who had the nerve to dance. Gene and several of the young men around Markham asked girls to dance and none of them were refused. Markham had not attended any of the few dances held at Forest Hills High School and now wished he had. He felt a bit intimidated and just stood there watching the dancers at work trying to remember the steps they were taking, when an attractive red headed, green eyed, female student of slender build and medium height who had been standing a few feet behind him sizing him up, decided to approach him. What first attracted her was his dark curly hair and smooth skinned face on a pair of the widest shoulders she had ever seen on such a lithe body. She wanted to see what it felt like to be held in his arms, so she decided to ask him for a dance.

"Hi! My name is Cynthia. You must be a new student here," she said.

"Yes I am. My name is Jim," Markham replied shyly.

"Would you like to dance?" she asked.

Markham looked at her and hesitated due to his lack of expertise in that area, but answered in the affirmative.

"Yes, I would really like that," he answered, and they walked to the dance floor a few feet away where he carefully placed his right hand lightly against her upper back while she grasped his left hand with her right hand at shoulder level and they started to walk to the beat of the music.

"This is a fox trot," she said. "Just follow me. One, two, three-four, one, two, three-four, that's it, you've got it. Just keep doing that and you'll have the hang of it," she complimented him. "You're a quick study," she added. They danced several slow dances after that to their apparent complete enjoyment. Markham made a date with Cynthia to go to a movie that forthcoming Saturday night. Markham had lost contact with Gene inasmuch as he had agreed to walk Cynthia back to the sorority house where she resided. As he approached the bus rendezvous for a ride back to Thunderbird, he realized that the bus had already left only a few minutes earlier and the only way for him to return to his barracks was by taxi. He really couldn't afford to pay full fare for a taxi, but to his surprise another airman arrived at the bus stop too late. He had never met this Air Force student before, even though he was also from Thunderbird, but they agreed to split the fare and got a taxi back to the Air Force school compound. Upon arrival, the airman asked Markham if he would turn in his off-base pass for him to the Charge of Quarters inasmuch as Markham had to go there to turn in his own pass, and Markham agreed.

As Markham was walking towards the Orderly Room he kept humming in his mind one of the western songs he'd danced to with Cynthia. It came to an abrupt halt when he opened the door to the Orderly Room and saw this big, burly guy whom he instantly recognized as Bill Chucklock, standing over a puny airman laying on his back with both his hands up to protect himself against Chucklock, who was attempting to punch him in the face. Chucklock appeared intoxicated. Markham observed that there were six airmen standing in line to turn in their passes to the Charge of Quarters (CQ) and no one including the CQ made any attempt to stop the assault. Chucklock raised his head to see who had entered the Orderly Room and after he saw that it was Markham, he turned his head back towards his victim and attempted to punch him again. Markham walked over to the CQ.

"Aren't you going to stop this?" Markham asked the CQ, who was himself no bigger than the victim, and he didn't bother to look up from the sign-in ledger, nor did he respond to Markham's question, obviously afraid to interfere with Chucklock.

Markham walked over to face Chucklock, who now had delivered a punch that glazed the airman's face. He started crying in fear and looked at Markham for help.

"Leave the kid alone, Bill," Markham said in a strong, low voice.

Chucklock ignored him and got ready to throw another punch at his victim when Markham realized that to try to wrestle with this 250 pound drunk would take more effort than he was willing to expend, and a punch to the head would be much more expedient and effective. With that thought, Markham planted both of his feet firmly and delivered a right punch to the side of Chucklock's head that was felt by everyone in the room as Chucklock dropped like a huge bear to the floor for the count. The kid stood up and ran out of the Orderly Room. Markham walked directly to the CQ and dropped both passes on his open ledger when Johnny accosted him.

"Hey! Man. I was going to stop him when you came in and beat me to it," said Johnny.

Markham ignored Johnny's remark and addressed the CQ.

"You're the CQ. It was your responsibility to stop this guy from beating that airman, and if you couldn't do it, you had six airmen here at your disposal that you could have ordered to do it," said Markham in an admonishing tone.

As Markham was walking out of the Orderly Room, he turned momentarily towards the six airmen and admonished them also.

"Six of you and you couldn't stop one bully. You had a moral obligation to protect that kid from this bully, but you were more concerned about saving your own skin. You should be ashamed of yourselves." No one replied and Markham walked out of the Orderly Room utterly disgusted with the human race and Johnny in particular.

The next day, Markham was ordered to report to the First Sergeant at the Orderly Room.

"Markham, I read the CQ's report of last night and it indicates that you were involved in a brawl in the Orderly Room last night," said the First Sergeant.

"It wasn't a brawl, Sir. I stopped an airman from beating up on a smaller airman when the CQ failed to act," replied Markham.

"I heard all about it and in the process, you knocked Chucklock unconscious. I'm restricting both you and Chucklock to the school compound until further notice; that means no pass off-base until I decide your fate. Is that understood, Airman Markham?"

"Yes Sir," replied Markham.

"That's all, dismissed," replied the First Sergeant.

That evening, Markham asked Gene, who was going to Tempe to see his newly found girlfriend who resided at the same sorority house as Cynthia, to deliver a message to Cynthia that he was restricted to the base, therefore would not be able to keep his date with her for that Saturday.

"Man, you got a raw deal," said Gene to Markham.

"Tell me about it. I didn't want to hit Chucklock, but nobody would do anything to stop him; I had no choice Gene," replied Markham.

"Hey! Man, you did the right thing and that's what counts. I heard Johnny was there and he joined the rest of the sheep," said Gene.

"Do me a favor Gene. Don't tell Cynthia that I got involved in a fight, OK?" said Markham.

"Why not, you had a damn good reason. I'm sure she doesn't want a wimp."

"Women are sensitive to violence; you'd better not mention it, Gene."

"OK! My man. I'll see you later," said Gene as he departed the barracks for Tempe.

Markham's restriction to the school compound was not lifted until December 24th, which was too late for him to make any plans for the Christmas holidays. He also learned from Gene that Cynthia was now dating another university student not associated with Air Force personnel at Thunderbird. He couldn't blame her. Neither he nor she had any idea when his restriction to the base would be lifted, if at all, hence he expected her to accept other offers. Markham rationalized that this relationship was not meant to be and he had no regrets regarding his actions in that Orderly Room incident. Many of the students at Thunderbird had gone home for the Christmas Holidays by airplane, train or bus. Markham was one of those who remained at the Thunderbird compound during Christmas and New Year's. The school put on a Christmas dinner for the remaining students and New Year's Eve was modestly celebrated in the student lounge.

Graduation certificates were issued to each student in mid-February 1952 and military orders were issued to each student designating their new military assignment.

There were four black students in the class and the only assignments to South Korea where the war was taking place were given to the four black students. All of the other students were assigned to either the United States, England, Germany or Japan. Markham conveyed this obvious discriminatory action to Gene, who agreed that it wasn't fair, but those assignments were written in stone by Army Headquarters. Markham and Gene were both assigned to Fairford Air Force Base, England and were to report to Camp Kilmer, New Jersey for embarkation on a troop ship to Southampton, England. Johnny received orders for assignment to Germany, and Chucklock was reassigned to Fort Sill, Oklahoma for training in artillery.

Markham and Gene arrived at Camp Kilmer, New Jersey at the end of February 1952 and were placed on 'casual' status pending surface transportation to England. During that 'casual' time they were subject to work details such as Kitchen Police or Garbage Detail, neither of which was envied by any of the casuals who made every effort to avoid being selected for such undesirable duty. Unfortunately for Markham and Gene, they were standing near the front of the daily morning formation when a Sergeant selected the first two front lines for Kitchen Police and the next two lines for Garbage Detail. Markham and Gene worked from sunup to sundown cleaning pots, pans and metal trays in the Mess Hall that fed more than 18,000 troops. They had KP pushers whose duty was to make sure that the KPs were not slacking off and working at full capacity during their 12 to 14 hour tour of duty. Markham and Gene returned to the barracks with their fatigues stained with grease, which they had to drop into one of the washing machines in an adjacent building for cleaning prior to dropping onto their bunks for a well-deserved rest. The next day, Markham and Gene made sure they would stand in the last line of formation to avoid being called again for KP duty.

Finally, after a few days of attending morning formation without anyone taking roll call, Markham and Gene realized that they had no accountability for the men standing in formation, hence they would not be missed if they did not attend formation. After all, they reasoned, they were at Camp Kilmer to embark on a ship to England, therefore each morning Markham and Gene left the barracks through the back door and spent the rest of the day in the huge snack bar frequented by hundreds of airmen and soldiers awaiting transport to Europe. The juke box was in constant play with popular numbers such as 'Wheel of Fortune' by Kay Starr, that gave the men a temporary aura of civilian freedom.

Then came the official Notice of Embarkation to England which included Markham and Gene. The Notice stipulated that only military clothes stuffed in one duffel bag could be brought aboard ship. All civilian attire was prohibited. Markham had brought a large suitcase containing all of his civilian clothes including two suits tailored in Brooklyn, New York. Everything he owned was contained in that suitcase. He had no forwarding address, hence he had to leave the suitcase with someone whom he trusted to forward to him upon his arrival at his permanent base of assignment. Gene had mailed the few civilian clothes he had at Thunderbird to his mother in New York City. Markham went to the Orderly Room to see if he could make arrangements with the Officer or Non-Commissioned Officer in Charge to leave his suitcase in their custody with a sum of money that would cover the shipping costs when they received his permanent mailing address in England. Markham was informed by the Staff Sergeant there that the Lieutenant was not available, but that if he left his suitcase with him, he would make sure that it would be forwarded to Markham when notified of his new address. The Sergeant who identified himself as S/Sgt. Anthony Pucelli gave Markham the address of his unit and agreed that $50.00 was sufficient to ship a parcel at an APO address overseas, which Markham gladly gave him.

CHAPTER IV
Voyage to England

Markham, Gene and three thousand other men in uniform stood with their duffel bags on their shoulders in a long line on the dock alongside a Liberty Troop Ship, the USS Patch, waiting to step onto and climb a long wooden plank that extended from the dock to the first deck of the ship. A Sergeant with a manifest on a clipboard checked the name and orders of each man before he stepped onto the gang-plank. Eventually, Markham and Gene found themselves inside the ship in the hole where the men slept in bunks that were stacked four high with only 20 inches above each other.

Markham selected the top bunk and Gene selected the bunk directly beneath him, leaving two empty bunks below them. Markham's thought was that by being in the top bunk, no seasick airman would vomit on him. Each man was issued a few paper bags medically coated on the inside to be used in the event of seasickness. Markham loved water and the sea and did not expect to get seasick at any point during this long voyage. For him, this was an adventure of a lifetime.

Having only one stripe on their sleeve indicating their rank as Airman Third Class, one step above Private, Markham and Gene were vulnerable to being selected for any work detail that was required on the ship. Gene was assigned to the Kitchen Police and Markham to cleaning the toilets and urinals. Markham and two other airmen were given mops, buckets and other toilet cleaning material and shown the large toilet room which must have had 20 toilets lined up in a row against the hull of the ship and another 20 urinals lined up against the opposite wall. As the ship rolled, the water in the toilet bowls flowed out of them onto the floor and luckily into center drains. When they got through cleaning that toilet room, they were taken to another toilet room in another section of the ship for the same cleaning procedure. They were able to perform all of those duties before dinner time and thus were released, whereas Gene's duties as KP did not finish until two hours after dinner time. Markham saw Gene as he went through the chow line in the ship's mess hall. As Markham left the chow line, Gene accosted him and slipped him a paper bag containing two oranges and an apple which he had acquired from the mess hall.

Later, Markham met up with Gene and he offered him the apple, but Gene showed him a bag he had brought with him that also had fruit. "One of the perks of pulling KP on a ship," Gene said to him. However, the stench of so many people vomiting in the sleeping area and even in the hallways was getting to Markham, who felt that even though he did not expect to get seasick, surely the smell of vomit might make him sick. Therefore, he decided to go onto the deck outside of the ship, even though it was strictly prohibited for anyone except guards on duty to be on deck at night.

Markham put on his heavy blue Air Force overcoat and flight cap and exited the foul smelling ship's hole onto the dimly lit deck where he situated himself next to one of the large vents that expelled hot air. Markham sat next to the vent and wrapped his right arm around a chain tied to a post and watched the ship's bow plunge into the cold sea sending a spray of salt water high into the air that hit the right side of Markham's face as he sat waiting for the bow to rise up and plunge again into the frigid waters of the North Atlantic.

It was the fifth of March, his Grandmother's birthday, and here he was crossing the North

Atlantic aboard a troop ship bound for England, the land of constant fog that hid the mysteries of Sherlock Holmes as Markham had so often seen in the movies. *I must see London,* he thought, *and all that it has to offer.* Markham sat through the night on deck and fell asleep with his right arm gripped firmly around the chain as a precaution against being swept overboard.

When he woke up at sunlight, he found that the right side of his face was covered with a thick coating of salt from the salt spray. He went below and found Gene was still asleep. Markham went into the shower room, which was hardly occupied due to the early morning hour, and took a refreshing shower and shave. He then went upstairs to the Mess Hall where breakfast was now being served and feasted himself on eggs, bacon, toast, cereal, and milk.

As he went past the bulletin board in the hallway after exiting the Mess Hall, Markham noticed that they were seeking volunteers for guard duty. Markham decided that guard duty was a lot better than cleaning toilets, consequently he signed up for duty as a guard and was assigned to 4-hour shifts in the open tower amidship with instructions to look for anyone who happened to come on deck and fell overboard to sound the alarm. That was the extent of his instructions and duties. However, standing guard in that tower amidship in the freezing March weather in the North Atlantic was more than Markham had bargained for, or so one would think. But Markham had been issued the proper outerwear for that duty and eventually became accustomed to the frigid weather. He enjoyed the feel of the ship's motion in the heavy seas and the ship's ability to withstand the power of those huge waves. At no time did he see any other ship within his view which gave him a sense of awe at the immensity of the ocean. He felt that perhaps he should have joined the Navy instead of the Air Force because of his affinity for life at sea.

The USS Patch took seven days to cross the Atlantic Ocean from New Jersey to Southampton, England. Upon arrival the troops were loaded into buses which took them to various Air Bases throughout England. Markham and Gene boarded the same bus destined to Brize Norton Air Force Base, and on the way there, the bus stopped at a pub on the outskirts of a small village for lunch. Markham and Gene were amongst the last to descend the bus, and as they were walking towards the entrance to the pub, they saw the First Sergeant exiting the pub followed by several airmen.

"Let's all get back in the bus," the Sergeant ordered the airmen.

"What happened?" asked Gene of one of the airmen that exited the pub.

"Apparently the lady who owns the pub refused to serve one of the airmen named Altman because he was German. I guess his blonde hair and blue eyes betrayed his nationality, although the First Shirt tried to explain to the lady that he was American of German descent, but that didn't make any difference to her. She said she lost her son to the Germans and 'No Kraut was going to be served in her pub.' So the First Shirt told her that, 'What goes for one American goes for all of us' and he ordered all of us to leave the pub."

"Man, I don't believe it. Are the Brits that narrow minded?" asked Gene.

"Naw! I can't believe that all of the British are like that. This must be an isolated case of one woman's tragic loss and unfulfilled desire for revenge against a general enemy, the Germans," said Markham philosophically. "Her frustration blinds her to the fact that Altman is an American German who had nothing to do with the war."

Back on the bus, Altman felt a sense of pride at being an American and the total support he received from the First Sergeant and his comrades. Onward they went to the next village where they were received with open arms, and no indication of prejudice against any of them. In fact, several English customers expressed their gratitude to the Americans for their support of England in its hour of need in a World War that ended only seven years ago.

At Brize Norton, Markham and Gene were directed to another bus that was to take them to their final destination, Fairford Air Force Base, about 120 Kilometers or a two-hour train ride to the big city of London, known to G.I.'s as the Big L. Upon arrival at Fairford AFB, Markham and Gene were directed to their billets in a Quonset hut that housed 16 airmen, all below the grade of Sergeant. They were to report for roll call each morning until they received their permanent assignment orders. They had arrived on a Thursday. Friday they were instructed to turn in all of their United States currency referred to as greenbacks in exchange for military Script which could only be spent on United States Military Bases. They could also exchange some of their Script and greenbacks for English currency to be spent on the English economy. At that time in 1952, one English pound was worth $2.80 in U.S. funds. Markham and Gene each exchanged $50.00 for English currency, which netted them each 17 pounds plus some change in the form of shillings and pence.

"Hey! Jim. How many shillings to a pound?" asked Gene, looking at the English currency he had just received in exchange for his U.S. currency.

"According to the sheet posted on the bulletin board over there, there are 20 shillings to a pound," replied Markham. "Why don't we take a bus and go to town after dinner?"

"That sounds like a good idea. But which town were you thinking of?" asked Gene.

"I hear that Swindon is a fairly big town and it's only about 20 kilometers from here," said Markham.

"How many miles is that?" asked Gene.

"I'd guess about 15 miles, that's all," said Markham.

"Hey! I've got to go to the BX to buy some toilet articles and stuff. I'll meet you back here at the hut by chow time," said Markham.

"OK! Jim. See you later," replied Gene.

About a half-hour later, two Sergeants walked into the Quonset hut.

"Alright you men," addressing Gene and three other airmen still in the hut. "Give your names to Sergeant Butts here. You're all detailed for guard duty. Get into your fatigues and report immediately to the Provost Marshall's office."

"Haw! Hell! I just got here yesterday and I haven't even had a chance to unpack, Sarge. Give me a break," said Gene in disgust.

"My heart bleeds for you. Get your ass in gear and report for duty. That's an order," said the Sergeant sternly.

When Markham returned to the hut at 5 PM, he found no one in the hut, but he did find a written note on his bunk from Gene, stating that he'd been shanghaied into guard duty for that evening, thus could not go to town with him. *Shit,* he thought, *you can't plan on anything in this goddamn Air Force.*

Markham decided he would go to Swindon alone and reconnoiter the area for the both of them. Markham put on his dress blue uniform bearing one lonely stripe on each sleeve below the shoulder, and his garrison hat. He filled that uniform perfectly and looked like someone pictured on a recruitment poster. There was no precipitation that evening, therefore he didn't bother wearing his Air Force trench coat, although the general advice was to never leave the base without it. While riding the bus to town, Markham was told by some of the airmen riding the bus with him the names of some of the most popular pubs frequented by American Servicemen in Swindon.

Upon arrival in Swindon, Markham went off on his own walking through the main street of town until he found a pub that resounded with laughter and the pounding of a piano to the tunes of World War II music. Markham entered the crowded pub and as he walked along the bar towards the piano, an old man left his bar seat. Markham asked the young woman sitting next to the empty seat if the man was returning and as she looked Markham up and down, replied "I don't think so. Why don't you take it love? If he should come back, you can always relinquish it."

"Thank you," replied Markham, who found her to be quite an attractive brunette with a face that probably had never seen a blemish.

"What will you have, Yank?" said the bartender.

"I don't really know. I just got into country and I'm not familiar with your brew.What kinds of beer do you have?" asked Markham politely.

"Well, we have Guinness which is quite heavy, and then we have Pale Ale which is the opposite, very light, and then we have…"

"Try the Pale Ale, Yank," interrupted the brunette sitting to his left. "I'm sure you'll love it."

" OK! I'll have a Pale Ale," said Markham. "And get whatever the lady is drinking."

"Another gin and tonic, Barry," said the brunette. "Thank you for the drink. My name is Brenda and my girlfriend's name is Mary. What's your name?" she asked.

"Jim's my name," he replied.

As they were conversing, two top sergeants sitting at a table near the wall several feet behind Markham had been observing Markham interacting with the two women at the bar since his arrival. They were not too happy about his success with the ladies, since they themselves had been rejected by them earlier that evening when they attempted to converse with them with immoral intentions rather obvious to the two young women.

Master Sergeant Joe Buckley, Non-Commissioned Officer in Charge of Personnel, and Master Sergeant Miguel Esperanza, NCO in Charge of the Mess Hall, were getting inebriated with the mixing of Irish whiskey and warm English beer, especially Sergeant Buckley who was now feeling combative towards Markham the intruder. Sergeant Buckley stood up. Sergeant Esperanza knew Buckley's intent and tried to dissuade him, but Buckley ignored his friend and walked towards the bar where he stuck his arm and shoulder between Markham and Brenda, placing his hand against the edge of the bar as he faced her with his back to Markham.

"Hiya Babe. What are you doing with this Peon?" referring to Markham with only one stripe on his sleeve. "Why don't you and your girlfriend join us Sergeants over at our table? If you're nice we may just take you to the NCO Club at Fairford," Sergeant Buckley said, trying to impress her with his rank and the allure of entertainment at the NCO Club, not accessible to lower grade airmen such as Markham.

"Why don't you be a good boy and go back to your table? You're interrupting my conversation with this gentleman," said the brunette sarcastically.

"Listen bitch, nobody calls me boy and that's no gentleman," said Sergeant Buckley, lifting his right hand from the bar to point at Markham.

"Watch your language, Sarge," said Markham.

Sergeant Buckley turned towards Markham and grabbing Markham's left arm, attempted to pull him off the bar stool. Markham remembered his Jujitsu training and rather than resist the Sergeant's pull, went along with his effort, in fact speeding up the momentum which caused the Sergeant to fall backwards, losing his grip on Markham in an attempt to break his fall against the table. The table tilted under his weight, sending the beer bottles and glasses in the direction of Sergeant Esperanza, who ended up with wet trousers and Sergeant Buckley on his rear end on the floor. Both Sergeants looked up in the direction of Markham, who was now standing facing them with both feet planted for action. Brenda got off her bar stool and gently placed both of her hands on Markham's right bicep "Let it go love; they're not worth it," she said softly.

"What's your name, airman?" asked Sergeant Esperanza, who had helped Buckley to his chair behind the table.

"Markham, Jim Markham," replied Markham, knowing full well that revealing his identity would surely result in retribution back at the base.

"What unit are you in?" he asked.

"I'm a casual at Fairford, Sergeant," replied Markham.

"You'll be hearing from us you can be sure of that," replied Sergeant Buckley, who knew that he was in no shape to tackle this young bull.

"C'mon James. Let's go elsewhere to another pub," said Brenda, with Mary grabbing his other arm guiding him towards the exit.

"Sounds like a good idea," replied Markham as he walked down the main street with an attractive girl on each arm to the envy of passersby including some American Servicemen.

"Let's go to the Lion's Head," said Mary to Brenda. "It's a little quieter there."

"You have a mate Jim, someone nice like you for Mary?" asked Brenda.

"Yeah! His name is Gene. He's a real nice guy from New York City. Next time I come to Swindon, I'll bring him with me," replied Markham.

"Is that where you're from, Jim?" asked Brenda.

"Yes, I'm from Manhattan, New York," replied Markham.

"Here we are, the Lion's Head. Let's have a good time tonight," said Brenda, and that they did.

Monday at Fairford Air Force Base went without incident, but Tuesday was different in that Markham was issued orders for permanent assignment to Stanstead Air Base, about 50 kilometers from London. Stanstead Royal Air Force Base was being re-opened by the United States Air Force for use as an American Air Base and thus needed to have its runways thickened and extended to accommodate the larger and heavier post-WWII bombers. A large unit of Army Engineers was working on the runways 24 hours per day in eight-hour shifts, thus a 24-hour Mess Hall was needed to feed these hungry men as well as the airmen assigned as support personnel to get the base into active status. Even though Markham's Air Force Specialty Code or AFSC was Administrative Typist, thanks to the influence of Sergeants Buckley and Esperanza, he was assigned as Permanent KP to the Stanstead Mess Hall. Kitchen Police referred to by military personnel as KP was the bane of the Air Force and considered the worse duty possible by those assigned to it, namely enlisted men below the rank of Sergeant with the lowest ranks most often called for such duty. Markham bid his friend Gene LaConti adieu and boarded the Army bus with other airmen assigned various posts at Stanstead AFB.

The first thing Markham observed upon arrival in the early evening at Stanstead was the sparse number of light posts which gave the base a dank and dark atmosphere. Except for some aircraft hangers and warehouses, all of the buildings at Stanstead were Quonset huts, some of which were connected together to form office buildings and the like. Quonset huts also served as barracks to house the airmen and Army engineers. They were all lined up in rows with an asphalt walkway running the length of the front and the back of these Quonset huts and another asphalt walkway connected each barracks to the main walkways. Interspersed with these Quonset hut barracks were a few Quonset huts converted into bathhouses containing open shower stalls, toilets, and sinks for the troops housed adjacent to these bathhouses. Markham was assigned to barracks number 18 which was situated directly in front of one of the bathhouses. The Quonset hut contained two pot bellied oil stoves each located in the center aisle, which turned cherry red when turned on high to the detriment of anyone who accidentally fell against it. Drunken airmen were particularly vulnerable to their central location. Markham selected the second bunk to the left of the entrance, which was only a few feet away from one of the stoves. One of the overhead lights hung directly between his bunk and the adjacent bunk, which could be turned on and off by pulling on a long string with a knot at the end.

The wooden footlocker at the foot of each bunk and the metal wall lockers situated between each bunk against the curved wall of the Quonset hut reminded Markham of boarding school at Varennes, Quebec. Markham soon became acquainted with the rest of the men in the barracks, some of whom stood out from the others. Ernest Hudlow stood six feet three inches tall and weighed about 280 pounds with a big head and ears that reminded Markham of an elephant. Hudlow was a slow talking fellow from Tennessee whose speech and size betrayed a sharp mind and a heart of gold. Then there was Lincoln Berryman, a slim, short-haired individual whose appearance and zany behavior reminded Markham of the famous comedian Jerry Lewis. Al Backus, a tall, heavyset young man from Louisiana loved to chew tobacco and then spit into a metal bowl he used as a spittoon to the disgust of those bunked near him. Then there was George Mayou, a studious and timid young man of slight build and sandy hair whose fastidiousness became a subject of mockery by many of the men in the barracks. Sean McLean fancied himself as a middleweight amateur boxer who would spar with anyone willing to oblige, but Markham did not visualize him as a bully, rather as a soldier in need of action who would have been better suited for the Marine Corps. Another airman who caught Markham's attention was Romero Montez from Mexico City, who joined the US Air Force to speed up his application for U.S. citizenship. Markham noticed that Montez was particularly fond of his stiletto knife, which had a retractable 4-inch blade considered illegal in the United States. Montez did not engage in much conversation with the rest of the airmen in the barracks, but instead associated with Mexican airmen located in other barracks. Elmer Harper became known as the 'Hillbilly' because of his Missouri traits and booze-driven behavior of howling at the moon. Ed Butler, a rugged six-footer, was from Wyoming and his deportment and personality was consistent with what Markham would expect of a family-oriented young man brought up on a ranch; a clean-cut no-nonsense type of guy. Steve Gorski, of average build, let everyone know the first day he entered the barracks that he was from Chicago, the city that produced the worst gangsters in the history of the United States. The airman bunked next to Markham was known to all as Fats Domino for the obvious reasons that he was fat and his last name was Domino. His joviality and great sense of humor was a constant morale booster to men who saw themselves as numbered slaves in a concentration camp.

Markham's KP duty required him to get up at 5 AM and report to the Mess Hall at 6 AM, where he would work until 6 PM, then he would eat dinner at the same Mess Hall, not arriving back at the barracks until about 7 PM, which left him little time for showering and arranging a change of clothes for the next morning. His only day off was Sunday, which he had to devote to doing his laundry and other personal matters that could not be accomplished during the week. The knowledge that this KP duty was a permanent assignment for Markham, whereas the other airmen on KP were only on Temporary Duty, made Markham resentful of the treatment he was receiving from the Air Force, that had promised him duty in the specialty of his choice and training.

Markham was surrounded by whiskey and beer consumed in the barracks and everyone smoked cigarettes, including Markham who soon succumbed to the habit. Markham liked the allure of smoking portrayed by male movie stars such as Humphrey Bogart, with a cigarette dangling from the side of his mouth, or another star who would hold his cigarette all the way between the third phalanges of the index and middle finger as he took long drags from it and exhaled the smoke through his nostrils.

Markham learned to drink whiskey straight from the bottle and chase it with a drag from his non-filtered Camel cigarette, but he didn't make a habit of it due in part to the fact that he didn't like the taste of whiskey. These were hard times at Stanstead, surrounded by Army Engineers billeted in adjacent barracks who disliked Air Force personnel and engaged in altercations with them whenever the opportunity offered itself, which was whenever they stepped outside their barracks. In one instance, a drunken Army engineer waited in the dark outside the exit to one of the airmen barracks, and when an airmen stepped out to go to the latrine in the adjacent bathhouse, he would hit the airmen with a broomstick in the face or the head, until a couple of airmen exiting the bathhouse caught him stalking his next victim and beat him senseless. Markham couldn't believe the wildness of these men whose only thoughts were drinking and fighting. *Does God have a reason,* he thought, *for subjecting me to this most unpleasant experience? If I am to understand it, I must experience it,* he thought, *hence I might as well embrace it,* and so he did.

Immediately after eating dinner at the Mess Hall that Saturday, Markham packed an AWOL bag with a few toilet articles and a change of underwear and went to London for the evening with the intent to return the following evening on Sunday. He got off the train at Charing Cross Station which is within a short walking distance to Piccadilly Circus, which he was told, was the center of activity in London.

As Markham was walking out of the station, he was accosted by a least two Englishmen wanting to know if he had any American cigarettes in his AWOL bag for sale. Markham replied that he had none to sell, but was curious at how much they were willing to pay for a carton and he was told two pounds, which Markham evaluated at $5.60, a profit of $4.50 inasmuch as it would cost him $1.10 per carton. It didn't take long for Markham to realize that if he brought 10 cartons of cigarettes to London, he could make a total profit of $45.00, which would defray all of his costs for a weekend in London with some money left over. The problem was getting enough ration tickets from airmen who did not smoke or smoked very little. However, there were risks because it was illegal for any American Serviceman to sell cigarettes to an English national. But a majority of servicemen sold small amounts of cigarettes on the black market to pay for their incidentals. Everywhere an American Serviceman went, he would be recognized as an American, especially if he was in uniform, and without fail someone would approach him to buy cigarettes. The American and English police were primarily interested in those involved in serious, large scale black marketing. However, at that time in 1952, the Status of Forces Agreement between the United States and Great Britain excluded American Servicemen from English Legal jurisdiction, hence all an English policeman or bobby, as they were called, could do if he apprehended an American G.I. was to hold him until the American Military Police arrived and took custody of the G.I. for possible arrest and prosecution by U.S. military authorities. This was a very frustrating arrangement for the British police, who would sometimes apprehend a drunken G.I. several times within the same evening, as the Military Police oftentimes released the G.I. some distance away from the initial site of apprehension with a warning only for the G.I. to return and cause more trouble and be apprehended again by the same British bobbies, who sometimes lost their patience and gave the G.I. a beating with their sticks on body parts covered by clothing before releasing him to the Military Police. All in all though, the British police demonstrated extraordinary tolerance towards the thousands of American Servicemen who invaded London and other large cities on weekends to release their rowdiness on the British populace.

Markham quickly referred to a small map of the West End of London he had purchased from a vendor in Charing Cross Station which confirmed that he was in fact only a few blocks away from Piccadilly Circus. He'd been told that there were several inexpensive bed and breakfast hotels in the West End which were in fact three and four story houses with rooms for rent on a nightly, weekly or monthly basis that usually advertised with a small sign or simply word of mouth. Markham decided to find a place to stay for the night before exploring Piccadilly Circus and the West End; therefore he walked nonchalantly, wearing his dress blue uniform, garrison cap and blue-gray trench coat and carrying his blue AWOL bag. Markham's leisurely walk permitted him to observe all of the buildings, vehicles and pedestrians within his view in a detail only surpassed by camera. His confident gait and powerful body in the glorious uniform of the United States Air Force gave Markham a presence that could not be ignored. But his extraordinary confidence was sometimes mistaken for arrogance, which Markham himself despised.

Markham finally found a bed and breakfast place at the Aaland hotel on Coram Street in Russell Square which rented him a small room for 30 shillings a night or $4.20. The room contained a double bed, a stuffed chair, a dresser with mirror, and a gas heater that looked like a small fireplace against the wall which was coin-operated. The bathroom which had a sink and a tub, but no shower, was down the hallway. Markham placed his AWOL bag on the floor next to the dresser and left the room, which he locked with an old-fashioned key reminiscent of western jail cells.

It now was nightfall and the city was lit up like a Christmas tree. He grabbed a double-decker bus going towards Piccadilly Circus and got off near the large circle that centered Piccadilly Circus. In the center of the paved circle stood a winged statue of Eros the Greek God of Love where pedestrians and pigeons alike gathered around to admire the center of entertainment in the West End of London. As Markham stood still on the sidewalk gazing at the scene, a young, attractive woman accosted him.

"Hello Yank! You look lost. You want me to show you around?" she asked with an inviting smile.

Markham looked at her in surprise at her boldness, then looked behind her and realized that there were several 'ladies' of the night gathered in doorways and walking the street. "No thanks. I'll find my way," he replied politely.

"Well, if you change your mind, you know where to find me," she said disappointedly.

Suddenly a man in his mid-twenties, dressed in a tweed suit, white shirt and dark tie appeared at his side and introduced himself as Jeffrey. He claimed to be a Welshman who worked for the American Officer's Club in London. He invited Markham to walk with him away from the center of the call-girl district and as they strolled up a side street, Markham became suspicious of the Welshman's motives, thus kept tabs of his whereabouts at all times. It didn't take long before Jeffrey's motives surfaced.

"I work at the Officer's Club at night on weekends and I have a very good friend who is an Air Force Captain. I let him use my apartment while I'm working at the Club and I provide him with a girl and a few bottles of whiskey and he reimburses me for the whiskey later. Unfortunately, I got the girl waiting for him at the apartment with the liquor which I purchased, but when I called him a short while ago, he informed me that he had to report for duty and couldn't make it tonight. I've got to go to work, but if you want to use my apartment tonight, I can call the girl whose name is Joyce and tell her you're coming and she'll be glad to entertain a handsome man such as yourself," said Jeffrey.

Markham listened attentively and remembered what he had learned from residing in New York City. *No one gives something for nothing.* He wondered when Jeffrey was going to show the hook.

"Of course," Jeffrey continued. "I need to get the money I spent for the liquor."

Markham remained silent. At that moment they had reached a red telephone booth. Jeffrey said that he was going to call the girl to let her know he was coming, and he immediately entered the phone booth and closed the door, but Markham could see him through the glass panes, and suspected that while he took the phone off the hook and talked into it for a short while, there may not have been anyone listening at the other end. Jeffrey exited the phone booth.

"Here's the key to my apartment and on this piece of paper I have written my address," Jeffrey said, handing the key and piece of paper to Markham. "Now all I need is four pounds to pay for the liquor," he added.

Markham looked at him in disbelief. "Aren't you going to accompany me to your apartment before you leave for work?"

"Oh! No, I can't. I'm late for work as it is," he said nervously as he observed Markham's eyes narrow.

"You think I'm going to give you four pounds without seeing the goods?" Markham said with grave suspicion, which was immediately confirmed when Jeffrey suddenly took off running down the street, not to be seen again. Markham looked at the key which he knew one could buy for one shilling and that piece of paper surely contained a fictitious address. Markham couldn't believe the audacity of that con-man and realized that he was in the Big City of London where anything could happen.

As Markham was walking back towards Piccadilly Circus, he noticed a small neon sign on a side Street that spelled *New Yorker Club.* He decided to investigate it. As he approached the Club, he noticed that he had to step down a short flight of cement stairs to reach the entrance where a large, balding, middle-aged man dressed in a dark suit, white shirt and dark tie was stationed to screen customers.

"That'll be ten bob to get in, Mister," said the man.

Markham could hear a band inside the club playing American music with a male vocalist singing one of Frank Sinatra's songs. Markham handed the man a ten shilling note and entered the dimly lit club which consisted of a back room to his right where the drinks were prepared. To his left were small tables for two lined up on both sides of the wall, which widened into a larger room that had a dance floor at its center with tables for two around both sides with the four-piece band on a raised platform against the back wall. Each table had a low voltage colored lamp that enhanced the ambience and veiled a woman's imperfections. There were several men all dressed in suits sitting at separate tables in the company of a young, attractive woman, no doubt in the employ of the club. At the entrance, near the back room, sat several unattached young women. One of them, a dark-haired girl with pale skin and dark eyes raised her slim, taut body upright and facing Markham, held out both hands towards him.

"I'm Cherie. Would you like for me to join you?" she asked with a warm smile.

There was something about her that appealed to him, even though he realized that she was an employee of a night club that would normally attract women of ill repute. But Markham believed that there were always exceptions, and there was a freshness about her that impressed him. Besides, he was only going to talk to her, nothing else.

"Sure, why not," he replied, and she directed him to a table near the dance floor.

As they sat down, a waitress immediately came over to their table to ask Markham what he would like to drink.

"I'll have a Scotch and soda," he replied. "And what'll you have, Cherie?"

"I'll have a sherry," she said.

"I don't notice any other American Servicemen here tonight. Do many of them come in here?" asked Markham.

"We get a few of them, but they usually wear civilian clothes. Have you been in England long?" she asked.

"No, not long at all. My civilian clothes have not yet arrived from the States," he replied.

"So that's why you're in uniform," she said, smiling.

The waitress came over with the two drinks. "That'll be one pound sir," the waitress said.

Markham handed her a pound note, thinking he couldn't afford to order many more drinks at those prices.

Cherie liked Markham instantly. There was a warmth about him she thought was comforting and he was so handsome in that uniform with those broad shoulders. Although she had just met him, she knew that she had to see him again.

"Listen Jim, don't let on that I told you, but my drinks have no alcohol in them and your drink is watered down, so don't order any more of them. We'll make them last the evening by dancing," she said.

Markham was pleased with her honesty and grateful for saving him the money he had worked so hard to earn.

"Listen, what time do you quit?" he asked her.

"I can't leave until closing time at 2 o'clock," she replied. "And we're not allowed to leave with customers either," she added. "But since we're not busy, Ralph won't mind if I dance with you the rest of the evening."

"Who's Ralph? Is that the owner whom I met at the entrance?" he asked.

"Yes, Ralph is one of the owners. Marty is the other owner who was here earlier," replied Cherie.

At this time, the band was playing a slow number, a fox trot, and Cherie asked Markham if he would like to dance with her.

"I'm not much of a dancer; I have to warn you," he said half laughingly.

They both stood up and Markham danced to the steps he had learned at the dance in Tempe, Arizona. She followed him like a feather in his arms. She had the grace of a ballerina. She taught him the basic steps to the English version of the American Lindy or rock-and-roll, which they referred to as the London Bop, a combination of several very smooth movements that left both dancers unruffled, but the audience dazzled with the cleverness of the choreography.

Although Markham had little exposure to dancing, his innate musical talent for so long subdued, finally found an outlet in a country where dancing is a national pastime. Cherie was amazed at Markham's rhythm and speed of movement for a man of his large physique, but she recognized that while he had the upper body of a weight lifter, he had the waist and legs of a runner, a great combination for a dancer. *Yes,* she thought, *I'm going to see that man again.*

At closing time, Markham said goodnight to her, but before she joined her two girlfriends with whom she resided, she stepped up to Markham and kissed him on both cheeks, stating "That's a French custom, you know? Bonsoir, Jim."

As Markham exited the club, he noticed that a thick fog had settled over London and he could hardly see the light from the lamp post. *My God,* he thought. *This is just like I visualized London from the Sherlock Holmes movies.* He felt a sense of adventure and mystery. However, the fog wasn't so bad that night that he couldn't see where he was going. But the taxis and buses had slowed down their pace to a walk. Markham walked back to the hotel in his leisurely fashion, enjoying the night fog and its lurking danger.

The next day was a bright and sunny Sunday. Having eaten his breakfast at the Inn consisting of eggs, toast and tea, he checked out of the Inn, and started walking towards Piccadilly Circus dressed in his Air Force uniform. He intended to check his AWOL bag in one of the lockers at the Underground Station at Piccadilly Circus or else at the Charing Cross Station where he would eventually embark on a train back to Stanstead Air Base. However, on his way there he entered Leicester Square where a large crowd had gathered on both sides of the avenue to observe a massive gathering of people marching down the main street carrying banners with derisive slogans towards the United States Military based in England. One slogan in particular caught Markham's attention. A middle-aged woman flanked by a man most likely her husband and two young girls between eight and 11 years old, carried a sign which stated *Send the Yanks Home and Save our Young Girls.* When that same woman noticed Markham in full military uniform standing at the inner edge of the observing crowd, she whispered something into her young daughter's ear and she broke rank and walked up to Markham and said loudly, "Go home Yank; we don't want you here."

Markham's astonishment was interrupted by the voices of two Englishmen standing close to him.

"Don't pay attention to them, Yank. It's the Communist Party's yearly march in London," said one of the men.

"Yeah!" said the other Englishman reassuringly. "They're definitely in the minority in this country."

As Markham walked away from the crowd, he noticed several approving smiles by many people in the observing crowd which made him feel welcomed. He was also impressed by the civility of the British people and a warmth towards strangers that he had not seen in New York City.

That evening, Markham embarked on a train from Charing Cross Station with several local stops before reaching Stanstead. Markham felt as if he was boarding a series of stage coaches pulled by a locomotive. Each train had a door with a vertical moving window on each side separated by two long padded seats. Due to the short run between stations, no toilet accommodations were deemed necessary nor available.

As Markham boarded the train, he noticed that an elderly English couple was already seated on the left seat next to the far window. Markham took the seat opposite them, leaving room for one more occupant on their seat and two on Markham's side. The last call for boarding was heard from the locomotive's whistle when two drunken American Servicemen dressed in civilian clothes, each carrying a bottle of beer in their hands, entered their compartment, taking a seat opposite each other. As the train departed, one of the servicemen, a tall, blonde-haired skinny young man took a slug from his beer bottle which was near empty and said to his friend: a stocky, brown-haired man of the approximate same age, that English beer tasted like urine and not fit for animals, to which his friend agreed with much laughter.

Markham looked at the elderly English couple for their reaction to these two young American drunks and he could see that they were repulsed and also fearful of them. Markham remained silent, hoping that they would calm down and fall asleep as many drunks do. But to his disappointment, they became rowdier as the train ride progressed. Finally one of them pulled the strap that held the door window up, which brought the window down waist-high. They both threw their empty beer bottles out of the window, and the tall one unzipped his fly and standing towards the open window, urinated with the wind blowing some of it back towards him and his friend sitting next to the window.

"Hey man. You're pissing on me. Close the damn window, you asshole," said his friend.

"I couldn't help it. I drank too much of that English beer," replied the tall serviceman. He then zipped up his fly, closed the window and sat down looking at the elderly couple for their reaction, but they simply looked towards each other and down at his hands holding hers reassuringly. Markham felt that they were too afraid to say anything.

"Hey, man, pass me your flask. I know you've got some whiskey left," the tall one said to his stocky friend, who then pulled out his flask, took a swig, and gave it to his friend who took several gulps from it. "Man that's good stuff, better than that fucking warm English beer."

"Hey! Fish Head," he said loudly to the elderly Englishman. "You wanna taste of American whiskey?"

The Englishman did not reply and both he and his wife looked out the train window into the darkness, hoping that this nightmare would go away. At this time Markham had heard and seen enough and his temper was starting to rise, and at that moment the train pulled into the first local station. Markham stood up, took two steps toward the tall serviceman, opened the compartment door, pulled the tall one to his feet and pushed him out the door onto the station platform. He then grabbed the stocky, drunken serviceman by the lapels of his jacket and pulled him off the train onto the platform, at which time the tall one cocked his right fist to punch Markham. He beat him to the punch with a quick right blow to the tall serviceman's chin, dropping him to the ground like a wet noodle while his drunken pal looked on in disbelief. Without uttering a single word, Markham climbed back on board the train where he occupied the same seat opposite the English couple, mostly because the other end of the seats may have been sprayed with the drunken serviceman's urine.

Markham looked at the elderly couple and said in a soft voice, "I apologize for their behavior which was a disgrace to the uniform they were fortunately not wearing."

The elderly English couple did not reply, but the old man gave a slight nod in agreement and acceptance of Markham's apology. Markham then turned his head towards the window and gazed into the darkness of the night where his mind found solace in the belief that his actions had been necessary to rescue the image of the American Military Servicemen, even though he knew from his experience at Stanstead that this would not be an isolated incident.

Markham made several more trips to London on weekends and on each occasion he visited Cherie at the New Yorker Club, although the relationship remained platonic, at least on Markham's part.

Cherie resided with her two girlfriends, Kim and Dawn, in a small apartment. Markham learned that Cherie and Kim came to London from Nottingham to become professional dancers, and Dawn had been an aspiring actress from Liverpool. While they were all recognized talent in their respective home-towns, London rejected them mercilessly, compelling them to acquire regular employment: Cherie and Kim as secretaries in an insurance company, and Dawn at a travel agency. They worked at the New Yorker on weekends only to make extra money. Through Dawn's travel agency, the three of them had managed to spend a month in Paris the previous summer, residing in an inexpensive flat. It was during that period that Dawn became romantically involved in Paris with a young French student named Jean-Paul Beauchamp, who promised to visit Dawn in London the following summer. Indeed, he and several of his student friends rented an apartment in the French Quarter of London and spent many weekend evenings dancing at the New Yorker Club where the owners were receptive to the gaiety they brought to the club that enhanced its reputation in Soho as a fun place to be.

Markham was the only Yank frequenting the New Yorker Club who spoke fluent French which made him a near celebrity with the French crowd and at Les Enfants Terrible Café in the French Quarter. Markham danced for hours and reveled every night that he visited London, loving every minute of it. He learned to dance not only the traditional way, but jazz dancing and the French style, too. Unfortunately, his London visits were limited to weekends only and sometimes those were curtailed by unexpected additional military duties. However, after two months of KP duty, the Mess Hall Sergeant took pity on Markham and told him that he would give him Saturdays as well as Sundays off, hence he would pull KP duty only from Monday through Friday.

One Saturday afternoon, Markham and several other airmen occupants of the Quonset hut barracks were lounging around talking about their past excursions into the various neighboring

English towns, when Sean McLean started sparring with an unwilling Fats Domino, who told him to pick on someone with more aptitude like Markham.

Sean then turned his attention to Markham, who was folding his laundry.

"C'mon Jim, let's go a few rounds," Sean said, throwing a few punches into the air towards Markham, who smiled but did not physically respond.

"C'mon man, let's see what you've got," insisted Sean.

Markham dropped what he was doing and faced Sean with his hands loosely closed so as not to hurt Sean, who warned, "No head shots, OK Jim?"

"Yeah! OK," replied Markham, and they began sparring with Markham blocking several of Sean's punches and scoring some of his own to Sean's body, when one of them caught Sean in the solar plexus, momentarily knocking the wind out of him. Markham was genuinely surprised because his punches were very light in delivery.

"Sorry Sean, I didn't mean to hurt you," Markham said apologetically. Sean quickly recovered and wanted to go another round, but in light of what had just happened, Markham declined and returned to finishing his laundry chores and Sean left the barracks.

Early that evening, right after dinner at the Mess Hall, Markham and several other airmen had showered and were getting dressed to go to town, when Romero Montez, who bunked across the aisle from Markham and was also getting ready to go to town, became hostile towards Markham for no known reason.

"Hey! Markham. I saw you sparring with Sean this afternoon. You think you're hot shit, but I can take you," Montez said. However, Markham ignored his comment which made Montez more brave.

"Hey! Man. How about stepping outside for a real fight? Man, when I get you down, I'll kick you in the head," he said, slamming his thick-soled shoe hard on the floor for effect.

As Markham was putting on his tie, he looked around at Montez and smiled at the thought of this punk challenging him to a fist fight. Here he was all cleaned up in his dress blue uniform, which he wasn't about to get dirty fighting this inconsequential hoodlum, hence he again ignored his challenge.

"Hey! I think you're afraid to fight me. Yeah! I think you're yellow, Markham. I dare you right now to step outside and fight me," said Montez, which again elicited no response from Markham.

At this time all of the airmen in the barracks had stopped their activity and were awaiting Markham's response. Hudlow the elephant walked over to Markham to appraise the situation.

"Jim, it's now a matter of honor. You've got to fight him. He's thrown down the gauntlet," said Hudlow in a low, friendly voice.

"Goddamn it. I'm all dressed and ready to go to town and now I've got to deal with this punk. But you're right. I might as well get it over with," he told Hudlow.

Markham was now visibly angry as he turned towards Montez.

"OK! Buster. You wanna fight? Well, you've got it. I'll see you outside momentarily," said Markham as he began to undress so that he could put on his fatigues and boots.

At this time Hudlow walked over to Montez while other airmen stood by.

"This is going to be a fair fight, Montez. Pass over your knife. Don't worry; you'll get it back when this is over," said Hudlow with several other airmen agreeing with his request. Montez pulled his stiletto from his front pocket and handed it to Hudlow reluctantly, knowing that if he didn't relinquish it, Hudlow and the other airmen would take it forcibly. Montez misinterpreted Markham's reluctance to fight as an indication of fear of being defeated, hence this gave Montez a false sense of confidence to the extent that he didn't feel it necessary to change his clothes. By this time the word spread to the other barracks, including the Corps of Engineers, that a fight was about to take place outside the barracks and a crowd of about 75 servicemen gathered in a large circle between Markham's Quonset hut barracks and the Quonset hut bathhouse, which were separated by a cement walkway that formed a cross between the barracks. It was dark outside except for a full moon assisted only by the small light fixture above the doorway of each barracks. There was a slight drizzle, which dampened the already muddy ground surrounding the cement crosswalk.

Markham stepped outside the barracks onto the cement crosswalk and observed Montez standing on the other side of the crosswalk anxiously waiting for him and playing to the large crowd. Markham decided to stay on the cement crosswalk which offered better footing and as he focused his attention on Montez, he adopted his fighting stance and watched Montez dancing back and forth in front of him throwing jabs that never made contact. Markham stalked Montez in a slow advance that caused Montez to occasionally leave the firmness of the walkway for the muddy ground. So far Montez had not touched Markham and Markham had not thrown any punches. Suddenly, Montez crouched and rushed into Markham, who instinctively threw two punches at his oncoming head. Markham's left fist hit Montez on the forehead, driving him back and down on his back in the mud. Stunned, Montez rolled over onto his hands and knees trying to recover from the blow, but couldn't get up. Markham knew he had damaged his left hand from the sudden pain he felt when moving his thumb, but he ignored it in order to finish the business at hand. He walked over to Montez, who was now slowly standing up. Markham delivered a powerful right punch to his stomach that moved Montez off the ground flat on his back into the mud, to a loud exclamation from the crowd watching the fight. Montez started coughing and rolled over onto his hands and knees again, but couldn't get up. Markham was walking around him like a crazed lion getting ready for the kill. Markham remembered the words uttered by Montez in the barracks, that when he got Markham down, he would kick him in the head. The thought occurred to him that he was in a position to do just that to Montez, who was on all fours staring at the ground. One kick in the face with his G.I. boot would most certainly disfigure and possibly kill him, but Markham quickly dismissed the idea as too cruel to even contemplate. When Montez failed to get up, Markham grabbed him with both hands by the front of his shirt in an attempt to raise him up and upon feeling a sharp pain in his left hand and thumb, immediately dropped his left hand, while still holding him with his right hand, but the shirt tore under Montez's weight.

"C'mon Montez, get up. You wanted this fight. Now get up and fight, you bastard," yelled Markham in anger. At that moment, Montez got up on one knee, then stood up long enough for Markham to hit him with a hard right punch to the side of the head that knocked Montez's face down in the mud, unconscious, to the approving roar of the engineers to his left. As Markham stood there, Hudlow walked over to Markham and placed his hand gently on Markham's right forearm.

"Jim, you're going to kill him if you don't turn him over. Hell, he's had enough," said Hudlow.

Without saying a word, Markham grabbed one of Montez's outstretched arms and pulled him onto his back. Montez appeared alive, but still unconscious. Markham then walked back into his barracks and into the light to examine his left hand which had now swollen around the base of his left thumb.

Suddenly three Air Policemen walked into the barracks looking for Markham, who was sitting on his bed examining his left hand.

"I want you to leave Montez alone, you hear," said one of the Air Policeman, addressing Markham in a loud voice.

"Hey! I didn't start this fight. He did, so don't tell me to leave him alone. Get your facts straight," replied Markham, angry at the wrongful implication.

"I'm going to tell you one more time. You let Montez alone, you hear me?" said the same Air Policeman.

"And I told you that I didn't start this fight, so I don't need your warning," replied Markham, who was getting tired of this policeman's unjustified warning.

At this point, Hudlow and two other airmen who had witnessed the entire incident confronted the three Air Policemen and related to them what had actually happened. Nevertheless, that same Air Policeman refused to admit he'd been warning the wrong person and reiterated his warning again to Markham, who now stood up in frustration and started to advance towards the Air Policeman, in total disregard of the condition of his left hand, when Hudlow intervened by placing his large body between the Air Policeman and Markham, with whom he pleaded to return to his bunk before he landed in the stockade. Markham returned to his bunk and the three Air Policemen left the barracks with no further ado.

"Can you move your fingers?" asked Hudlow, now that the Air Policemen had gone.

"Yeah, but I can't move my left thumb without pain. I may have broken it," replied Markham.

"You'd better get to the hospital and have someone look at it tonight before the swelling gets worse," said Hudlow.

"Yeah! I guess you're right. Now my whole weekend is screwed because that son-of-a-bitch wanted a fight, and for what?" Markham said in disgust.

At the hospital, X-rays were taken of Markham's left hand and the diagnosis was that he had a greenstick fracture of the metacarpal or bone that connects the wrist to the phalanges of the thumb. Without warning the doctor, under the pretense of examining his thumb further, grabbed Markham's thumb and pulled back hard thus straightening the bone to its original shape, to the consternation of Markham who thought the doctor had gone mad.

"You're lucky. Your bone bent, but did not break. So I just straightened it out. Now I'm going to put it into a cast from hand to elbow and you're going to have to live with it for six weeks. Now, for the record, how did you say you got this injury?" said the doctor inquisitively.

"Someone accidentally slammed the barracks door on my hand," replied Markham.

"Huh! Huh! And how does the other guy look?" asked the doctor, smiling.

That following Monday morning Markham, with left hand and forearm in a plaster cast, was summoned before the First Sergeant.

"Airman Markham. How did you hurt your hand?" Sergeant O'Brien asked knowingly.

"I got my thumb caught between a door and a doorjamb," replied Markham, knowing full well that the First Sergeant knew all of the details of the fight from his informants.

"Oh! Yeah. Well, I'm pulling your pass until the cast is off your hand and you're ready to go back to work. That means you're restricted to the base until I give you back your pass. Is that understood?" asked Sergeant O'Brien.

"Yes Sir. Is that all?" replied Markham, who felt unjustly punished simply because he was the victor in an unprovoked fight generated by the loser now perceived as the victim.

"Yeah! That's all. Now get out of here," replied Sergeant O'Brien with finality.

Markham's medical condition prevented him from working in the Mess Hall or anywhere else for that matter over the next six weeks, but he was restricted to the base, hence could not use the time off to visit London. A few days after the fistfight, Markham found himself in the Base Snack

Bar passing the time away when a couple of Army Engineers came over and mentioned that they were present at the fight, then they noticed that his white plaster cast contained several signatures.

"I'm Joe and this is Marty. Hey! You mind if we sign your cast?" asked Joe.

"No, go ahead," replied Markham, and they both signed their names on the cast.

"Man, after you went into your barracks, they had to carry him into the next barracks. He looked like he was in bad shape," said Joe.

"Yeah! I heard the APs then transported him to the hospital," said Marty.

Markham remained silent as he wanted to forget the incident, but his cast was a constant reminder of it. He tried to change the conversation to another topic.

"You guys must live in one of the barracks next to mine, then," he asked.

"Yeah, right next to the bathhouse across from your hut, but I just moved there a week ago from the Corps of Engineers barracks at the other end of the base near the flight line," said Joe "We've got a bunch of guys living in Quonset huts not far from the runway. We call it Tiger Town and for good reason. If you think you got a lot of action near your barracks, you should come to Tiger Town where heavy gambling and fighting is a daily occurrence."

Markham just sat there listening to Joe and Marty's informative chatter.

"Hey! Jim. You play poker?" Joe asked.

"Yeah! I know how to play poker," Markham replied.

"Well, there's a game of poker at Hut C-7 in Tiger Town. If you're interested, you're welcome to join us. It usually starts at about seven o'clock till the winners clean out the losers," said Joe amicably.

"I'll think about it. Thanks for the offer," replied Markham, and they left the snack bar.

After having dinner at the Mess Hall, Markham returned to his barracks, and unlike the rest of the airmen there who had worked all day, he still felt energized and decided to accept Joe's invitation to play poker in Tiger Town. It was a long walk from his barracks to Quonset hut number C-7, but it was easy to find. The Tiger Town barracks were near the chain link fence that surrounded the base and runways. Markham entered the barracks and saw several Army Engineers sitting around a homemade card table in the middle of the barracks. Joe immediately recognized Markham and invited him over to join them. Joe pulled out a footlocker from under a nearby bed for Markham to sit on.

"Have a drink Jim, and join the party," said Joe who then introduced Markham to the four other men sitting around the table playing poker. One of the players had an open footlocker converted to a portable bar with various size glasses.

"Tonight we've got gin, plenty of it," said Marty as he passed a full glass of gin to Markham who accepted it. Markham was not familiar with gin, hence decided to try it.

"You want me to deal you in, Jim?" asked Joe who was now dealing.

"Yeah, count me in," replied Markham.

"A dollar minimum to get in and the maximum raise is $50.00," said Joe who then added, "It's five-card stud."

Markham had only $25.00 on his person and didn't feel that he could afford to lose it, but he felt lucky in that the Quonset hut number was seven. Markham was the type of person who knew when to cut his losses and certainly was not prone to addiction of any kind, including gambling. Markham drank several glasses of gin without a chaser throughout the evening while playing poker with the four working fingers fully exposed from the plaster cast on his left hand and his uninjured right hand. The topic of his restriction to the base came up and Joe informed him that they had cut a five foot high doorway in the chain link fence directly behind their barracks, which was on wire hinges, that permitted them to leave the base perimeter whenever they wanted, and Markham was welcome to use it, but not to mention it to any of his airmen friends.

The next morning, Markham awakened to find all of his clothes hanging neatly in his wall locker, but couldn't remember most of the poker game, nor his returning to the barracks. Markham asked the airmen on both sides of his bunk if they had hung up his clothes for him and they both stated that he himself had hung up his clothes and gone to bed,but he didn't appear to be inebriated. Markham checked his clothes and to his amazement found more than $145.00 in small bills stuffed in the pockets of his jacket. He realized that the gin must have had a blackout effect on his brain and he promised himself that he would never again drink gin.

The next day, Markham encountered Joe and Marty in the Snack Bar and they related that he was one lucky son-of-a-gun at cards and that they had played until one o'clock in the morning trying to get back their money, to no avail. Furthermore, they knew that he didn't feel any pain when he left the game, but he did not appear to be drunk. Markham didn't tell them about his blackout, but their testimony reaffirmed his pledge to completely abstain from the consumption of gin.

More than three months had transpired since Markham had written to Sergeant Anthony Pucelli at Camp Kilmer, New Jersey to inform him of his address in England where his suitcase containing his civilian clothes should be shipped, and he had so far not received his clothes nor any word from him, which started to worry him, especially since he had mailed him a second letter a month ago with no reply. Markham was not on good terms with the First Sergeant, hence could not expect any assistance from him regarding this matter. Markham decided to put the money he'd won gambling to good use by purchasing a suit from Alexander Taylors which had a small shop on Stanstead Air Base that catered to American Servicemen at very reasonable prices. However, due to the plaster cast on his left hand, he would have to wait until it was removed before he could be fitted for a suit.

That Friday evening, Markham used the camouflaged wire door in the fence perimeter in Tiger Town to escape his restriction to the base and walked about half a mile to the nearby village train station where he boarded the train to London. Markham was getting tired of wearing his uniform into town because the plaster cast would not fit through the sleeve of his uniform jacket, but it did fit through the sleeve of his trench coat, therefore he folded his jacket neatly into his AWOL bag and wore the trench coat over his shirt with tie, whose left sleeve had been cut to accommodate the cast, without anyone being the wiser that he wore a cast.

That Sunday afternoon, Markham was walking up Shaftsbury Avenue in the Soho section of London to a coffee house when he spotted Hudlow lumbering alone towards him.

"Hey! Ernest. What are you doing in London?" asked Markham.

"I was going to ask you the same thing, Jim," replied Hudlow. "You know that Sergeant O'Brien has been looking for you and he suspects that you broke restriction."

"Really? But he doesn't know for sure does he?" asked Markham.

"No, but he had his flunky Scarborough check the base Snack Bar and all of the airmen barracks and came to the conclusion that you flew the coop, so he's got the Air Police staking out the train station at Stanstead this evening so they can arrest you when you get off the train," said Hudlow. "That's one of the reasons I came to London to warn you. I figured I'd run into you at the Charing Cross Station because you always take the last train."

"Thanks, Ernest. I owe you one. I'll just get off the train at the station before Stanstead and take a taxi the rest of the way."

"Yeah, but they'll be waiting for you at the main gate too," replied Hudlow.

"But I won't go through any of the gates Ernest," said Markham, who wanted to keep his promise to the Army Engineers that he would safeguard the location of the secret exit.

"Oh! Yeah? How you going to get into the base, then?" asked Hudlow.

"I made a promise that I wouldn't tell anyone, and it's better if you don't know, Ernest," replied Markham apologetically.

"OK! I understand," said Hudlow.

"Hey! If you're not doing anything, I know of a great Chinese restaurant nearby that's reasonably priced too. How about joining me for an early dinner?" asked Markham.

"Sounds like a good idea to me," replied Hudlow, and they walked to a Chinese restaurant located on Shaftsbury Avenue near Piccadilly Circus where Markham ordered Chicken Chow Mein with soft noodles, sweet and sour pork and a tall glass of English ale, which Hudlow copied due to his unfamiliarity with Chinese food.

That evening, Markham and Hudlow boarded the train from Charing Cross Station to Stanstead, but when the train stopped at Sudbury Station, Markham bid his farewell to Hudlow and exited the train to hire a taxi for his remaining journey to the base.

The following morning, Lincoln came into the barracks and told Markham that Sergeant O'Brien wanted to see him in the Orderly Room immediately. As he walked towards the Orderly Room accompanied by Lincoln, he was informed by Lincoln that Sergeant O'Brien knew everything about his trip to London, and it would be best if he told the First Sergeant the truth. Markham couldn't believe that Lincoln was betraying him, but his instincts told him that he was being set up by Lincoln who was either collaborating with the First Sergeant to ingratiate himself with him or he desired to see Markham's downfall for personal reasons, or both. Markham decided not to trust Lincoln and to follow his own instincts. As they entered the Orderly Room, Markham noticed several people standing around the First Sergeant who was sitting behind his massive desk. Wearing his fatigues and boots, he walked up within a few feet of Sergeant O'Brien's desk and stood before him.

"You wanted to see me Sergeant O'Brien?" said Markham.

"Yes I do. I know you went to London and broke restriction. Do you deny it?" asked Sergeant O'Brien.

"Yes, I do deny it," replied Markham.

"We looked high and low for you Saturday and Sunday and you were nowhere to be found. Can you tell me where you were?" asked Sergeant O'Brien.

"Sure I can. I was in Tiger Town playing cards," Markham replied firmly.

"You mean with the Army Engineers?" Sergeant O'Brien asked in surprise.

"Yeah! They're friends of mine," replied Markham.

Sergeant O'Brien looked at Markham with frustration. "If I could prove that you were off-base and broke restriction, I would have the APs here right now to take you to the stockade. You're dismissed."

Markham turned and as he walked out of the Orderly Room, he gave Lincoln a severe look that conveyed his disrespect and disappointment which Lincoln misinterpreted as a promise of retribution. After Markham exited the Orderly Room, Lincoln asked Sergeant O'Brien if he could talk to him privately out of earshot of the other people in the Orderly Room, but Sergeant O'Brien wouldn't grant his request and insisted he speak openly.

"Sarge. I think that under the circumstances, I would like to move out of Barracks 18 to another barracks," said Lincoln.

"What's a matter, you afraid that Markham might break his other hand on you?" replied Sergeant O'Brien sarcastically.

"No, it's not that Sarge. It's just that I'm trying to avoid any unpleasantness. You know what I mean Sarge," said Lincoln imploringly.

Sergeant O'Brien looked at Lincoln with loathing, but he did on occasion find him useful, thus agreed to his transfer to another barracks. Lincoln made sure that Markham had gone to the Mess Hall before he transferred all of his belongings from Barracks 18 to his newly assigned Barracks 24. That evening, most of the occupants of Barracks 18 were lounging around in the barracks chatting out loud about current events at Stanstead and their conquests and exploits during the past weekend.

"Hey! Markham, when's that cast coming off?" asked Fats Domino.

"In another three weeks and not too soon," replied Markham.

"I see Lincoln moved to another barracks. Does anybody know why?" asked Al Backus.

"Nope. You'll have to ask him," replied Hudlow.

"Hey! Jim. I heard you had a run in with the First Sergeant this morning. Did this have anything to do with Lincoln moving out?" asked Sean McLean.

"As Hudlow said, you'll have to ask Lincoln," replied Markham, who didn't want to discuss the matter, hence decided to change the subject of conversation.

"I heard that there's a dance every Saturday night in the town pavilion in Stanstead. Have any of you guys gone to one of those dances?" asked Markham.

"Yeah! Sean and I went last Saturday and there were lots of broads there, but many of them were chaperoned by their parents who also danced. It was a family affair for many of them," said Backus.

"If you had a young daughter, wouldn't you want to supervise who she socialized with? I know I would, and what better place than a town hall dance?" said Hudlow.

"Isn't that what they did in the olden days when the whole town turned out?" said Elmer Harper.

"Yeah! But the British take their dancing seriously with big orchestras and it's at regular intervals. You should see the way they dance, like professionals a lot of them," said George Mayou. "I went to Molesworth three weeks ago to visit a friend of mine and we went to a dance in town. Those girls were outstanding. No wonder so many G.I.s get married to these English girls."

"I read somewhere; I think it was the Stars and Stripes, that on an average, seven G.I.s get married every day to English girls; that translates to about 3000 marriages a year," said George Mayou.

"Yeah, but I wonder how many of those G.I.s got married because they got the girl pregnant?" said Fats Domino.

"If you get a girl pregnant, you should marry her," said George Mayou.

"I don't agree with you, George. Just because you get a girl pregnant doesn't mean you have to marry her," said Sean McLean.

"That's a choice you make when you don't use a rubber. Do you want your child to be fatherless, a bastard? I think it's your responsibility to make an honest woman of your child's mother," said Mayou.

"What do you think, Ernest?" said McLean.

"That's a tough question. It depends on the circumstances. If it was a one-time event that resulted in a pregnancy, then I suppose that the Father should at the very least enter into a contractual agreement to support the child. On the other hand, if the Father courted the girl for an extended period of time then gets her pregnant, the question of love and compatibility arises and whether the marriage would work. Morally, should he marry the girl? Probably." said Hudlow.

"You guys seem to have forgotten one important thing, and that is that many of these English girls deliberately get themselves pregnant in order to coerce the G.I.s into marrying them, and many of them don't give a shit about the G.I., they just want a ticket to the good old U.S.A.," said Sean.

"Not only that, but some of them don't even know who the Father is and blame it on the best prospect," said Al Backus.

"Yeah! But they can always tell if it's yours with a blood test," said Fats Domino.

"Not always. What if you have blood type 'O,' which 60 percent of the population has and the baby is also type 'O,' then you have a problem," said Al Backus.

"Hey! I heard that some guy brought in three of his friends into court and they testified that they all had sex with the girl and the judge had to dismiss the case," said Sean.

"I also heard recently that a British judge in a similar situation found all three G.I.s who had testified they had sex with the girl culpable and they all had to pay child support," said George Mayou.

"Hey! Jim, you're from the big city, what's your view of this?" asked Sean.

"Well, you have to do what your conscience tells you is the right thing to do. Otherwise you'll live with regrets the rest of your life," replied Markham.

"You going to the town dance this Saturday, Jim?" asked Sean.

"You know I can't. I'm still restricted to the base," answered Markham. "In any case, if I could get off-base, I wouldn't bother with a local dance when I can go to the Lyceum or the Hammersmith Palais in London. You have to see those two dance halls, they're palaces with revolving band stands and some of the best musicians and vocalists in the world. I tell you guys; you don't know what real dancing is until you've been to one of those two dance palaces," said Markham.

"Yeah! But don't you ever get tired of going to London?" asked Sean.

"When you're tired of London, you're tired of living," said Markham with finality.

"Hey! Sean. If you haven't been to London, you owe it to yourself to go there at least once, especially Piccadilly Circus," said Al Backus.

"Hey! I can get laid in Stanstead anytime I want. I don't have to go to London for that," answered Sean.

"Yeah! I saw who you went out with last Saturday, Sean. If that's the best you can do, you deserve a trip to London," said Al Backus.

"Hey! Man, I resent that," replied Sean.

"Alright you guys, let's not start a fight over women," said Hudlow, concerned about the direction of the conversation.

"You think these girls go with you because they're madly in love with you? Think again. They're attracted to you for your money buddy. That's the bottom line," said Al Backus.

"That's not true. Half the time I'm broke and they buy me beer," said Sean.

"For your information Sean, the average salary for an English secretary is the equivalent of $5.00 per week, which makes even the lowest ranking G.I. appear to be rich by comparison. That makes you and every G.I. a perfect target as a potential husband and a ticket to the United States. So don't let your ego get too inflated," replied Al Backus.

"There's not a man in this barracks above the grade of Airman Second Class, and most of us are Airmen Third Class with a monthly salary of $108.00. That may sound like a lot of money to an English girl, and you can live quite decently on that in England, but once you return to the United States with your bride and child, you'll be living on poverty row, eligible for welfare. When your wife and child are starving, love flies right out the window," said Markham, recalling his last sentence from the words of his Grandmother Nancy when he was a young boy in Montreal.

"You've got a point, Jim," said Mayou. "But have you forgotten that when you get married, you get a quarters allowance of about $120.00 on top of your monthly salary?"

"That's true, but that quarters allowance will be completely used up by the rent and utilities, and frankly, what kind of quarters are you going to get for that pittance?" replied Markham.

"That's why so many G.I.s who get married to English girls extend their tour of duty in England…because they can't afford state-side prices and they hope that by the time they do return to the States, they'll have been promoted to a higher grade," said Fats Domino.

"I read somewhere that there are seven girls for every man in England due to the Second World War," said George Mayou. "That means there's a lot of competition amongst the English girls for the American G.I."

"No wonder there're so many available women," said Fats Domino.

"You know Fats, these Englishmen died to save their country and their families, and the least we can do is treat their women as we treat our own," said Markham in an attempt to introduce some dignity into the conversation. "Furthermore, a lot of English women won't date American servicemen because of the poor reputation that precedes them. It's no different than in the States…some women are attracted by a man's wallet, others by his heart and soul."

At this moment, Ed Butler and Steve Gorski walked into the barracks.

"What's going on? You guys having a conference?" asked Gorski.

"We're discussing pregnancy," replied Fats Domino.

"What! One of you guys got pregnant?" asked Gorski kiddingly.

"Yeah! Fats Domino," yelled Sean McLean.

"Wish I was. I'd get discharged and make a million bucks," said Fats.

"So, who got pregnant?" asked Steve.

"Nobody, yet, but what would you do if you got someone pregnant?" asked Backus.

"Hell, I'd hope for an abortion, or else that I'd get shipped back to the States before the kid got born," replied Gorski.

"And if neither happened, then what, smart ass?" said Sean.

"I'd pray that she is beautiful," replied Gorski.

"Who, the girl or the child?" asked Sean.

"The girl of course. If I have to get married, it ought to be with someone I don't mind waking up to in the morning. Anyway, I don't have to worry about that. I always use a condom or else I get a blow job, that way I'm safe," replied Gorski with a laugh.

"You're a pig Steve, you know that?" said Mayou with disgust.

"Hey! What's the deal here anyway? Did someone here get a girl pregnant? Tell me the truth," said Gorski.

"No, nobody is pregnant," replied Hudlow, smiling at the lot of them whom he found most amusing.

"Hey! Ernest. What's your take on this subject?" asked Mayou.

"I think an audio tape of this conversation should be sent to your mother's," replied Hudlow with a wide smile, which was followed by laughter from the men in the barracks.

Six weeks had gone by and Markham went to the infirmary to have his cast removed. Markham then went directly from the infirmary to the Alexander Taylor Shop on base where he had a midnight-blue suit tailored in the Hollywood style of the one-button front with long lapels and no split in the back or sides that accentuated the broad shoulders and narrow hips. His black military, low-quarter shoes matched the suit. Markham also ordered a black camel hair, double-breasted overcoat for protection against the damp, cold weather that lasted nearly eight months of the year. He had noticed that the young Englishmen at the London dances wore dark suits and ties with white shirts which made them appear classy without having to don a tuxedo. Markham liked that conservative attire, but with an American style.

Markham was expecting a return to his Mess Hall duties, now that his cast had been removed, but to his surprise, he received transfer orders for permanent assignment as a clerk typist at Headquarters, Molesworth Air Base. He learned it was about 100 kilometers north of London, twice the distance he previously had to travel to reach London, not a happy prospect for Markham who found it the most exciting city he had ever visited. However, on the positive side, he was delighted over his new job assignment which he knew would have a major impact on his command of the English language. Markham knew that in order to advance his career, he had to master the English language and his assignment to England offered him a superb and lengthy opportunity to enrich his vocabulary and diction to university level and beyond.

At Molesworth Air Base, Markham was assigned to the Base Adjutant's office under Master Sergeant Tom Ripley whose boss was the Adjutant, Major George Duval who worked directly for the Wing Commander, Colonel Charles Whiteley. Markham had his own desk and manual Underwood typewriter, which he used to type Special Orders and also the Daily Bulletin distributed to all base personnel that informed them of the latest Air Force directive changes and base activities. Markham had immediate access to a library of Air Force Regulations and Directives written mostly by lawyers which he used in his daily duties, but he was most interested in the composition styles of Major Duval and Sergeant Ripley from whom he learned a great deal that improved his writing style. After several months, Markham was promoted to Airman Second Class, which meant a moderate increase in his monthly salary that enabled him to resume his travels to London.

The lodgings for the airmen at Molesworth were no different than Stanstead or any other Air Base in England for that matter. Markham was assigned to Quonset Hut number 12, not far from the Airmen's Club restricted to airmen below the rank of Sergeant. The Club served beer, hamburgers and hot dogs but no meals, and dances were held with a live band on Saturday evenings for the airmen and the busloads of English girls from local towns. During weekdays, the airmen had to be satisfied with the Club's jukebox of their American favorites. Markham was not impressed with the atmosphere of the Airmen's Club, which he found vulgar and the band mediocre, and much preferred the sophisticated environment of London, which he visited every weekend.

Markham's new lodgings at barracks number 12 housed a variety of distinct personalities including; Marc Dillinger, an experienced chess player and aspiring intellectual of rather large physical stature from Cleveland, Ohio; Robert Bruner, a non-athletic academic of slight build from Terre Haute, Indiana; Guy Gardner, known as GG from Philadelphia, Pennsylvania, who was very conscious of his shortness and early baldness; Seth Billings, a tall, slim Texan whose claim to fame was a stint as a rodeo bull rider; Frank Cummins, a reddish-blonde-haired Irishman of medium height with a weight lifter's build and a perpetual twinkle in his eye and smile on his face that charmed the ladies; Jack McFarland of light hair, complexion and medium build, who hailed from Los Angeles, California; Stan Williamson from Boston, Massachusetts, whose favorite pastime was spending each weekend in the company of a quart of vodka which never for an instant ever left his side; Andy Tripplet from Chicago, Illinois, who fancied himself as the best pool shark on base; and finally, Jason Walden, of American-Indian and German descent from San Diego, California, who stood at six feet five inches and 275 lbs of solid muscle with amateur boxing experience, yet the most well-mannered airman in barracks number 12. Unlike barracks number 18 at Stanstead Air Base, the men in barracks number 12 were a cohesive bunch of men who enjoyed each other's company and conversation. Markham became close friends with Jason Walden, Frank Cummins, Jack McFarland,

Marc Dillinger and Robert Bruner, oftentimes going to the local pub with them during weeknights, but Markham always reserved his weekends for London.

Markham loved to explore the side streets of the West End of London for their intriguing private night clubs which required an easily obtainable membership card for entry to comply with the after-hours liquor law. They reminded Markham of the roaring twenties speak-easys during the Prohibition Era in Chicago and New York as depicted in the movies he'd seen on Manhattan's 42nd Street. Some of the clubs were located on narrow side streets with poorly lit signs that oftentimes could not be discerned through the fog that overtook the darkness of the night.

It was on such a night that Markham found himself walking up an alleyway to a club he'd been told had a great jazz band. As he reached the alley's elbow, he saw through the fog what appeared to be three men dressed in dark suits beating up another man who was leaning against the wall of a building attempting to defend himself. As Markham got closer, he saw one man pull out a straight razor and slash the lone man across the forehead. At that instant one of the other assailants saw Markham approaching them and alerted his companions who momentarily turned their attention to Markham. He knew he had to act quickly and decisively. Markham did not want to attempt to disarm a man with a razor using his hands, when his feet were protected by heavy-soled military low quarter shoes. He leaped into the air towards the razor-brandishing man, landing one foot in his face and the other against his chest, driving him back against one of his companions. Markham landed on his feet and drove a right punch square into the face of the other assailant, feeling something crack against his knuckles, most likely his teeth. As the assailant with the razor attempted to rise from the pavement, Markham kicked him under the chin sending the razor flying into the darkness of the alley. The third assailant appeared to have run away. Markham immediately went to the victim, who had fallen on his knees holding his head. Markham grabbed one of his arms which he placed around his neck and picked up the still conscious man to his feet and they both walked through the short, poorly lit hallway into the club where the light revealed the extent of his injuries. The band was on its break which explained the lack of music in the club when Markham entered half-carrying the victim of the assault.

"My God! It's Chubby. He's bleeding all over. Hey! Judy. Come quickly," yelled one of the men in the club, which was half-empty.

Markham sat Chubby in a chair. His face and white shirt were covered with blood flowing from a long slash on his forehead. Judy attended to him with clean towels and water, trying to wash away the blood from his face and forehead, while several men ran out of the club in search of the assailants.

"Luckily it's not a deep cut," Judy said to the several men surrounding Chubby. "But I'll have to keep the pressure against the cut or he'll bleed to death. We've got to get him to a hospital. Joe, get the car ready to take him to the emergency room."

Chubby looked up at Markham. "You saved my life, mister. Another stroke of that razor and I'd have been a goner. What's your name, mate?"

"Jim Markham. I was just walking up to this club when I saw those three guys beating on you."

"By Golly, he's a Yank," said Judy. "Why don't you take off your coat and I'll see what I can do to get that blood off your sleeve?"

"Who was it, Chubby?" asked one of the men.

"It was Stevie and his Teddy boys," said Chubby.

"We'll take care of those bastards later. Right now we've got to get you to the emergency room to close up that wound."

Several men returned from the hunt for the assailants and one of them announced that he'd found the straight razor on the pavement in the alley, and surrendered it to Judy who soaked it in water, wiped it, then gave it to the bartender to hold for Chubby as a souvenir.

Two men helped Chubby to a car which then drove away, leaving Markham in the club where he was given a large drink of Scotch by the bartender.

"You know who that man you saved is, Yank?" asked the bartender.

"No, not really," replied Markham.

"He's one of the West End villains. He carries a lot of juice in these parts, you might say. We don't see any Yanks around this neighborhood. It could be a dangerous place for you. But after tonight, you'll be well known as the Untouchable Yank under Chubby's protection," said the bartender.

At this time two men approached Markham and introduced themselves as Harry and Rich.

"That was a brave thing you did, mate. I hear your name is Jim. Listen Jim, if you should need anything you let us know. And by the way, if you have any American cigarettes to sell, don't go anywhere else, we'll buy whatever you bring to London and we'll give you top price," said Harry with a wink. They then shook Markham's hand and went back to their table to join another man and his lady. Markham didn't respond to their invitation, but knew full well that he would never sell cigarettes to anyone who knew his identity. Furthermore, he no longer would entertain the idea of selling cigarettes to anyone, mostly due to the fact that non-smoking servicemen came to realize the value of their cigarette ration coupons and now sold them to other servicemen, who would then have to add that to the cost of the cigarettes, resulting in a profit too small to be worth the risk.

The owner of the club, a balding middle-aged man in his late forties, came over to the bar and gave Markham a club card with the inscription George Manley and his personal telephone number on the back. "I'm George, the owner of this club. You're welcome anytime. Glad to have you," he said, and left the bar.

About a half-hour transpired when Markham felt it was time for him to leave as the band was not what it was cracked up to be. As he left the club, two men from the club escorted Markham to the end of the alley, under Markham's protest, in case the Teddy Boys were lying in wait for him. Markham walked back to the Piccadilly Circus area and went up a side street named Denham to the Mazurka Club, situated on the second floor of a building adjacent to the Regent Hotel. He was greeted at the door by Peppie, the owner, who had issued Markham a membership card in a previous visit with a friend. Markham checked his black camel-hair coat, which Judy had managed to clean,and entered the small one-room club. Directly across from the entrance was the bar with a back mirror and plenty of liquor bottles. To its left in the corner stood a female vocalist backed by a pianist, drummer and bass player. The walls to the right and left of the corner band contained several seats for customers and a very few tables sat near the walls. A wooden circular dance floor accommodated no more than six couples to a slow dance. Markham walked up to the bar towards its center and managed to squeeze his right shoulder between customers to order and grab a Scotch and soda, all the while listening to the vocalist, who gave a good rendition of 'Lover' with surprising professionalism for such a small and mediocre night club. She didn't miss a thing, noticing every customer that entered the club as a possible date and potential ticket to a better life. She was in her mid-thirties, suave and confident, wearing a tight-fitted dress and high-heel shoes. Her dark brown hair was pulled back tightly into a bun, which emphasized her perfectly made up face that betrayed years of practice in show business, having entertained the British Troops with the USO during the Great World War.

Markham stood on the fringe of the dance floor against the bar crowd, with a glass of Scotch in his left hand while he puffed on a Camel cigarette, which he customarily held between the second or third phalanges of his index and middle finger, depending on whether or not he was holding a drink in the same hand.

The band took a break and the vocalist went to the corner of the bar nearest the band stand where the bartender had already poured her a gin and tonic. As she entered into conversation with a couple of men standing near her at the bar with whom she was acquainted, she took several glances in Markham's direction until Markham turned and caught her staring at him. She gave a slight smile that indicated to Markham that she was interested and eventually she worked her way through the bar crowd to Markham, when she introduced herself.

"I'm Elaine and if I'm not mistaken, you're an American serviceman stationed here in England."

"That's correct and my name is Jim," answered Markham, not immediately revealing his last name.

"I haven't seen you in here before. Is this your first time here?"

"No, I've been here twice before but you were not performing on those occasions," replied Markham. "You have a nice voice and you seem to be at ease when you're performing."

"Thank you. I've had a lot of practice. I don't work here, I just sing whenever I visit the club. Peppie and his wife are old friends. They own this club," said Elaine. "Are you stationed in London?"

"No, I wish I was. Unfortunately, I'm stationed at Molesworth which is a two-hour train ride from here, so I can only visit London on weekends, and not every weekend at that," replied Markham.

"That's too bad, because there is so much to see and do in London," she said.

"I couldn't agree with you more, but the gods didn't want me to have too much fun, lest I refuse to return to my birthplace," replied Markham humorously.

"Sounds like you've found a second home," she said.

"Right now this is my home...for the next two years," he replied.

"Well, perhaps I can help you enjoy it," she said with a twinkle in her eye, then she excused herself to return to the band stand to do another medley of songs.

Markham enjoyed talking to Elaine, but he instinctively knew that he would never date her as she appeared to be a calculating woman with too much experience in the ways of the world. Markham left the club before Elaine finished her medley of songs, and went to the New Yorker Club where he met with his friends Cherie, Kim and Dawn, who shared his love of dancing.

The following day, Sunday afternoon, Markham walked along the main street of Piccadilly Circus which was the meeting place for many American Servicemen to hang out before their departure by train to the Air Base. Markham ran into Andy Tripplet, Frank Cummins and Jack McFarland. As they stood there talking about the adventures of the previous evening, two men dressed in drab clothing slowly approached them and the taller of the two addressed Andy as if he knew him. Andy immediately recognized him as Herman Schmidt who had been busted from Airman First Class to Private and deserted the Air Force nearly one year ago. Herman took Andy aside for a private talk where Markham saw Andy reach into his AWOL bag and give Herman three packs of Lucky Strikes cigarettes, all that he had remaining in his bag. Herman then left with his English friend and Andy returned to tell Markham, Frank and Jack a tale of woe.

Apparently Herman and his English friend had been involved in several larcenies throughout Britain in order to support themselves and the last one resulted in being identified and sought by the British police. He attempted to extract some money from Andy, who told him he barely had train fare back to the base. The general consensus was that Herman was heading for a catastrophe, because even if the British police didn't apprehend him, the U.S. military would eventually find him and try him as a deserter with a stiff sentence at Leavenworth Federal Prison. It wasn't long before Andy received a letter from Algiers, North Africa. It was from Herman, who had joined the French Foreign Legion in order to escape the British police, having already arrested his English accomplice. Herman asked Andy to send him a few cartons of American cigarettes, and to give an English waitress he knew in a London pub his mailing address for her to write to him. Andy shared the contents of Herman's letter with the men in barracks number 12.

"I'll bet you that if Herman had known that he would end up in the French Foreign Legion, he never would have deserted the Air Force," said Frank Cummins.

"I agree with you. Only an idiot would ever knowingly do that," said Andy.

"Man, this guy not only deserted the Air Force, he also deserted the country of his birth," said Jack McFarland.

"Well, Herman's a Kraut so he should feel right at home with all the Krauts that joined the French Foreign Legion to avoid prosecution by the allies at the end of the Second World War," said Marc Dillinger.

"He's really an American you know, and I feel sorry for him, although he did make his bed, now he has to sleep in it, as the old saying goes," said Robert Bruner.

"I think Herman will probably end up as a citizen of France and live the rest of his life there. I don't see any workable alternatives," said Markham pensively.

"Yeah! I think you're right, Jim. No alternatives that would exclude prison time," said Jason Walden. Herman's story gave much food for thought to every man in barracks number 12.

On Markham's next trip to London, he visited the Douglas House located in the West End. The Douglas House was sponsored by the United States Air Force to provide American-style meals, alcoholic beverages and other services including monetary exchange of military script into English currency and the purchase of cigarettes with coupons, etc., to American Servicemen of all branches of the service. Servicemen frequented the Douglas House primarily for their very inexpensive meals and drinks. On this occasion, Markham ran into Jason Walden whose English date was introduced to him as Estelle Bentley, a very attractive and enthusiastic, gray-eyed, blonde-haired young lady. Jason and Estelle insisted that Markham join them for dinner, which he did. Markham ordered a T-Bone Steak with all of the accoutrements at the low cost of $1.50 and mixed drinks such as a whiskey-sour went for all of 25 cents. Estelle was simply amazed at the variety of food and its low cost to American Servicemen, as did all English women who were invited as guests of enlisted servicemen. Commissioned Officers had their own Officers' Club in another part of London.

Markham was happy for Jason, whom he admired as a real gentleman who knew how to treat a lady, a role that Estelle could fulfill just as easily as the tomboy she also liked to play. At dinner, Estelle mentioned to both Jason and Jim that the Coronation of Queen Elizabeth II was going to take place on June 2, 1953, the following weekend. The procession route would include Trafalgar Square and The Mall, not far from Piccadilly Circus and that people would be congregating and sleeping on the sidewalks along that route overnight so that they would have a good vantage point to see Queen Elizabeth early the next morning. Jason announced that he was unfortunately scheduled for Charge of Quarters duty that weekend and thus would be unable to accompany Estelle to the Coronation. Markham thought it inappropriate to offer his company at the Coronation to Estelle, especially since she was dating his friend Jason.

However, the following weekend, in the early evening of the first of June, Markham was walking from Trafalgar Square through The Mall amongst the vast crowd of people strung along the procession route, laughing, drinking and enjoying the early celebration of the coronation of Queen Elizabeth II. The sides of the streets along the procession route were crammed with people seeking positions on the sidewalks near the curbs where they sat on sheets, blankets, sleeping bags, raincoats and even sheets of newspapers to offset the cold dampness of the pavement. As Markham walked in the slight drizzle and chilling wind along that part of the sidewalk unoccupied by the festive crowd, he heard someone calling out his name. Markham continued walking, believing that it was someone other than himself who was being called, when this time he heard his full name being called.

"Jim, Jim Markham, over here," yelled Estelle.

Markham turned around and saw Estelle, wearing a baseball hat and dressed in a sweatshirt and Levis waving at him from the edge of the sidewalk. Markham walked over to her, smiling at seeing her again. Estelle asked people to move in order to make room for Markham to join her and her friend Sharon Conroy, whose great big blue eyes immediately captured Markham's attention. He noticed that unlike Estelle, whose hair was light-blonde, Sharon's hair had a golden tint to it which she also tied into a bun at the back and because of the drizzling rain, she wore a clear plastic hat designed for such occasions. She also wore a collarless sweatshirt over a shirt with collar and Levis.

Markham noticed as she stood up to greet him that she was shorter than Estelle, almost of petite size, but well-proportioned. They liked each other instantly to Estelle's pleasure at having found someone she liked to date her friend. Estelle's only sorrow was that Jason had been unable to join them for this once in a lifetime historical event.

"Fancy meeting you here," said Estelle with enthusiasm at seeing Markham. "I want you to meet my very dear friend, Sharon."

Sharon, who had stood up when Estelle called out to Markham, extended her right hand to greet Markham. "Please to meet you, Jim," she said, as she looked him over approvingly.

"The pleasure is all mine, Sharon," Markham replied with a genuine smile.

"Listen Jim, why don't you sit between us, that way you can keep us both warm," said Estelle with a contagious laugh. They made space for him to sit, but he had some difficulty crossing his legs. Sharon pulled out a small clear plastic package which unfolded into a large rain cover which she draped over the three of them. Both girls had each brought a bag of food, mostly sandwiches and soft drinks, but Sharon brought one additional beverage.

"Would you care for a bit a Scotch James?" said Sharon, pulling out a fifth of Scotch from her bag. She had that mischievous look on her face that promised joy but also tears. She pulled out two plastic cups and poured at least two jiggers of Scotch in each cup. "You want soda or Coke with it," she asked Markham.

He replied, "Soda, thank you."

Estelle didn't want any alcohol at this time. In fact, it wasn't long before Estelle fell asleep leaning against Markham who then used her bag as a pillow for himself while the two girls leaned on his broad shoulders and chest, with Estelle fast asleep and Sharon telling Markham about herself, her Father and the fact that her Father was part owner and general manager of one of the big hotels on Shaftsbury Avenue within walking distance of Piccadilly Circus, and that there was plenty more Scotch available from the bars in her Father's hotel. Markham listened attentively to Sharon as she related her life story which left him with the impression that she dearly loved her Father who was very much in love with her mother, but she resented her mother for leaving her Father to live by herself in a swanky apartment with her dog. Sharon was apparently used to high living and unchallenged behavior. Markham did not believe she would be tolerant of a man who could not accommodate her expensive wants. But he also realized that he could be wrong in his assessment of her and thus would let the matter take its course. Markham fell asleep, leaving Sharon still awake to imbibe another drink of Scotch before she also fell asleep with her head resting on Markham's right shoulder and chest with her right arm and Estelle's left arm both crossing each other across Markham's broad chest.

Estelle awakened first at a few minutes past 8 AM and after assessing the situation around her, shook Sharon awake which awoke Markham in the process.

"Sharon. Why don't we use the public restroom in the tubes at the corner while Jim saves our place here and watches our stuff? Then when we come back, Jim can go to the restroom," said Estelle.

"Sounds like a good plan, let's go," said Sharon. "God, I could use a cup of coffee right now."

"We've got a thermos full of tea," said Estelle. "That should do us fine."

"OK! Girls. I'll hold the fort while you're gone. Take your time, ladies," said Markham. The girls got up with their make-up bags and left for the restroom. A half-hour transpired before the girls returned refreshed and ready for the forthcoming procession.

"OK James. It's your turn, but don't be too long because the procession is supposed to start at ten o'clock," said Estelle. Markham's toilet articles were back at the hotel in Russell Square so when he did manage to find an occupied sink in the restroom crowded with people, he rinsed his mouth out with soap from the dispenser and after washing his face which he wiped with paper towels, he felt rejuvenated and returned to join his two female companions.

"Well, James," said Sharon, "you feel better now?" she asked.

"Oh, yes. Much better," he replied. "I see some British troops arriving," said Markham, still standing.

Both girls stood up and witnessed troops lining up along the route to set up a panoramic procession of rare grandeur and stateliness. After some forty minutes of anxious waiting, the procession appeared within view of Markham and his two companions and the golden state coach drawn by eight grey horses came into view.

"There's the Queen and the Duke of Edingburgh sitting in the carriage," said Estelle in a loud voice of excitement.

Markham looked on and enjoyed the pageant in silence while Sharon joined Estelle in voicing their wonderment of this real-life fantasy and their admiration for this most cherished Queen. Soon thereafter, the procession was over and Sharon suggested that they all go to her apartment near the top of her Father's hotel to refresh and eat a decent meal, and no one objected. As they arrived on foot in front of the hotel marquee, the uniformed doorman greeted Sharon, who asked if her Father was in the hotel and his courteous reply was that he had not been back since early that morning. Sharon, accompanied by Estelle and Markham, walked through the lobby to the elevator which took them to the Seventh floor where her private apartment was located. Once inside, Sharon showed her two guests the layout of her spacious apartment and then announced that she was going to shower and dress into some clean, dry clothes inasmuch as they had been subjected to a night of drizzle, and she invited Estelle to do the same, but Estelle declined, saying she would wait until later when she got home.

"I'm going to order us some food from the hotel restaurant downstairs. What would you like? You can order anything you want...steak, fish, whatever you like," said Sharon to Markham and Estelle.

"Steak? You're kidding!" said Markham.

"No, I'm not kidding. In fact that's what I'm going to order for you. How would you like your steak, Jim?"

"Medium is fine," he replied.

"And what kind of potatoes…baked, mashed, boiled…and what kind of dressing would you like on your salad?" asked Sharon, smiling at Markham's astonishment.

"Baked with butter only, and Italian dressing on the salad, please," he replied.

"And what would you like to drink with that? Would you like a glass of red wine?" asked Sharon.

"Red wine would be fine," he answered.

"And how about you Estelle? What would you like?" asked Sharon.

"I'll have some fish…haddock if you please," replied Estelle. "Oh! And I'll have either baked or mashed potatoes…makes no difference to me, and Italian dressing will do."

"What will you have to drink Estelle?"

"Like Jim, I'll have a glass of red wine, too," said Estelle.

Sharon dialed one number on the telephone and ordered Markham and Estelle's dinners.

"Oh, yes. And the red wine, just bring a whole bottle of your best Merlot. As for me, I'll have a filet mignon medium rare with a baked potato and sour cream…no salad. Thank you, Martin," said Sharon,then hung up the phone. Sharon then walked over to the phonograph and put on a record of mood music, then excused herself to go to the bathroom where she showered and groomed herself for the ensuing evening. During dinner, Markham and Estelle each drank one glass of Merlot, but Sharon finished what was left in the bottle, then ordered three Scotch and sodas, which she consumed before they left the hotel for a visit to one of the nearby piano bars for a few more drinks at Sharon's suggestion. Markham was surprised at Sharon's ability to consume so much alcohol and still remain coherent and standing. Eventually, Estelle begged Sharon's forgiveness for having to go home as she had a heavy schedule of things to do the next day. The pubs closed at 11 PM however, private clubs remained open until 2 AM, but Markham sensed that Sharon had met her maximum quota of alcohol consumption and felt responsible for getting her back to her hotel apartment in a safe and presentable condition, hence he suggested that they leave, and to his surprise, she offered no objection.

She at times staggered, but Markham was always there to steady her, and each time she just laughed, finding her inebriated condition amusing. The uniformed doorman greeted them and opened the hotel street door for them to enter, after which Markham guided Sharon to her apartment, which she had left unlocked. Once inside, she awkwardly took off her raincoat, then turned around and put her arms around Markham's neck and kissed him passionately on the lips, then slipped into a limp state that required Markham to lift her up and carry her to her bed. He removed her dress belt and her shoes, then pulled the comforter over her, kissed her on the forehead bidding her goodnight, then left the apartment and the hotel for a leisurely walk to his hotel in Russell Square. Markham thought that Sharon drank too much and she possibly might possibly have a drinking problem, but this could have been an isolated incident, thus time would eventually reveal the truth.

Neither private nor public telephones were available in or nearby Quonset huts inhabited by the airmen at Molesworth, hence the only method of communication was by letter unless the airmen went to a pay phone near the entrance gate or else into the nearest town. Markham had not bothered to write down Sharon's telephone number, nor did he know the address of the hotel other than it was located on Shaftsbury Avenue in the West End of London. However on Thursday, he did receive a letter from Sharon who had acquired his address from Estelle, who corresponded regularly with Jason. Sharon apologized profusely for her inebriation and asked him to call her at the telephone number she wrote in her letter to confirm his visiting her in London that weekend.

Markham had a conversation with Jason regarding the extent of his knowledge of her drinking habits and his fear that this condition could lead to promiscuity which would be totally unacceptable to him, but Jason assured Markham that while he had met her only a few times whilst dating Estelle, he never saw her drunk, and he should chance another date with her to which Markham agreed.

It was Friday evening when Markham arrived at the Shaftsbury Hotel. Markham took the elevator directly to the Seventh floor and was greeted by Sharon, and she was dressed in a black dress tres décolleté. Her face was radiant and her blue eyes shined with excitement at seeing Markham. She leaned forward and kissed him on the lips then took his AWOL bag and put it in her bedroom as she expected him to stay with her the night. She then took him by the hand and told him that she wanted to show him something.

"Have you ever been in a Masonic Temple?" she asked.

"No, I can't say that I have," Markham replied.

"My father is a Mason and we have a Masonic Temple on the top floor of this hotel. Let me show you," she said, and they walked to the elevator where it took them to the top floor. As they walked into the Temple, Markham was surprised at the existence of such a Temple on top of a hotel. He had heard that Masons were sworn to secrecy about their rituals and wondered if she wasn't violating her Father's trust by bringing him into the Temple.

"Are you a Mason, Sharon?" asked Markham.

"No, I'm Catholic and that's against the Catholic religion," she answered.

"Why is that?" he asked.

"I believe that it's because they're a secret society. My father joined because it was good for business. Since he's been a Mason, his business fortune has grown tremendously," she said.

Markham noticed a long wooden table at the front of the Temple that contained various objects including an open Bible upon which lay a square and a compass. Also on the table lay a level and a plumb which Sharon explained were symbolic of working tools.

"This is a strange place, nothing like I expected. I wonder what kind of ceremonies they have here?" asked Markham.

"Not being a Mason, I've never attended any ceremonies and my Father never talks to me about what goes on here," she replied.

"Well, I must say, it's an impressive Temple," said Markham as he started to walk towards the exit with Sharon following him.

"Tell me Sharon. Does your Father reside here at the hotel, too?"

"Yes he does, but my mother is separated from my Father and resides in her own apartment in the West End. My Dad really loves my mother, but she prefers to live alone with her dog," she answered.

"That's too bad. He must be very lonely," replied Markham sympathetically.

"He outwardly appears to have adjusted to the separation, but I don't think he really has and he never will…he loves her too much," she said in a sad tone of voice.

"Why don't we go to the Lyceum and dance to that great 18 piece band and George Sharing Quintet?" suggested Markham.

"No. I like to be entertained, not do the entertaining. Besides, you can't dance with a drink in your hand, now can you?" she said in a manner that left no doubt she wasn't interested in an evening of dancing and preferred going to a night club where she could sit with a drink and be entertained by the customers as well as the club entertainers. Thinking of his pocketbook, Markham suggested the Mazurka Club which was not far from the hotel and the price tag would be affordable.

"Well, Jim. I was hoping you wouldn't mind taking me to Eve's Club in Soho. It's really a posh place and they have some of the best live entertainment in London," said Sharon in an almost imploring voice. However, Markham had heard of Eve's Club as a very expensive night club, well beyond his means.

"I really wish I could afford to take you there Sharon, but you must realize that I'm only an Airman Second Class with a very limited budget, that's why I suggested the Mazurka which is a nice, intimate club with a splendid trio and vocalist that's much more affordable," said Markham, who felt embarrassed and perturbed at her lack of thoughtfulness as she knew his rank and limited income even though it was above the average Englishman's wage.

"Well, that's OK, Jim. We'll go to the Mazurka," she said disappointedly.

The Mazurka Club was crowded that Friday evening, but one seat became almost immediately available as a man left the bar and Markham made sure that Sharon got that seat, because there were no vacant tables or other seats in the Club. There did not appear to be any other American Servicemen in the club and Sharon was flanked by two Englishmen, both dressed in suits with shirts and ties, which is the usual dress code of Englishmen who frequent London night clubs.

Markham had difficulty getting the bartender's attention, therefore asked Sharon who was closer to order for the both of them, which she did. Markham observed that the man to her immediate right who was about 30 years of age and of average height and build, sporting a dark mustache, couldn't take his eyes off Sharon and was looking for an excuse to start a conversation with her, but her back was partially facing him as she was focused on Markham, who was making small talk with her as the band was on break. Markham spotted Elaine the vocalist talking to a middle-aged gentleman near the end of the bar adjacent to the band stand. A few moments later someone tapped Markham on the shoulder from the back as he was conversing with Sharon, and as he turned around, he faced Elaine smiling at him.

"Hello James. Haven't seen you in a while. Where've you been hanging out?"she said.

Markham turned to Sharon. "Sharon, I want you to meet Elaine. She's the band's vocalist and quite good."

"I'm very pleased to meet you Elaine," said Sharon, sizing her up as potential competition.

"I believe I've seen you before, but I can't remember where or when," said Elaine inquiringly.

"I've been here a couple of times before with friends," answered Sharon.

"That must be it then," replied Elaine.

"Well, there's my cue to get back to the bandstand. Nice meeting you, Sharon and you too, Jim," said Elaine, parting.

"Where did you meet her?" asked Sharon.

"Here. We talked briefly once a few weeks ago, that's all. C'mon Sharon. You have nothing to worry about. She's a nice person and just a friend, nothing more," said Markham, attempting to reassure her, as she was obviously concerned. Sharon ordered more gin and tonics for herself as Markham was nursing his own Scotch and soda. Markham asked Sharon to dance to a wonderful song 'When I Fall in Love' made famous by Doris Day which Elaine apparently found appropriate, but Sharon declined.

Markham excused himself to go to the restroom and upon his return, found Sharon talking to the man on her right. He had ordered another drink for Sharon and himself and continued talking to Sharon upon Markham's return as if he wasn't there. Markham thought that if he was a gentleman he would have introduced himself to Markham upon his return. Instead, he acted as if he now was Sharon's date and Markham was out of the picture, and Markham didn't like it. Markham could see that Sharon's eyes were glassy and she had consumed too much liquor too fast, which was now catching up to her.

"Excuse me for interrupting," Markham said to the man. Then turning to Sharon he said, "I think it's time for us to leave, sweetheart. Do you want to go to the restroom first?" he asked.

Before she could answer, the man to her right interrupted Markham.

"What's the rush? She doesn't want to leave yet, do you darling?" he said to her.

Before Sharon could answer, Markham grabbed the man's left wrist with his right hand and squeezed it hard. "Listen mister, you stick your nose in my business and I'll break it. You understand me?"

Impressed with Markham's strength and directness, the man acquiesced, "Alright, OK!"

Markham released the man's wrist and helped Sharon off her stool, but as she stepped onto the floor from the elevated stool, her knees gave way and Markham quickly grabbed her by the armpit to keep her from falling to the floor. She was more inebriated than he realized. Markham grabbed her purse and helped her slowly take small steps to the exit door and down the long stairway to the street, but half-way down the stairs, she went limp in Markham's arms. He grabbed her right arm and slung her over his right shoulder holding her purse in his right hand while his right arm kept her positioned over his shoulder as he walked down the rest of the stairway to the street below. It was pouring rain and Markham attempted to hail a taxi to no avail, most likely because the cabbies feared she would vomit all over their taxi, seeing as he was carrying her over his shoulder. Finally, Markham, desperate for a taxi, stepped right into the pathway of a cab compelling it to stop whereby he offered the cabbie a one pound note to take him just a few blocks to the Shaftsbury Hotel, which worked. In the cab, Sharon started to moan and it wasn't long before they arrived in front of the hotel whereupon Markham helped her to her feet out of the cab and with her left arm around his neck and his right arm around her waist, helped her walk past the doorman.

"Hi Harry. Is her Father inside the hotel?" asked Markham.

"I believe he is. Probably in his office. Shall I get him, Sir?" asked the doorman.

"No, please don't. I'll help her up to her apartment. She just had a bit too much to drink, that's all," said Markham.

Markham walked her into the elevator and as he waited with her for the elevator to take them to the Seventh floor, she slurred, "Where you taking me?"

"To your apartment, Sharon. You need to sleep it off," said Markham.

Sharon did not reply. Inside the apartment, Markham laid her fully-dressed on the bed, loosened her wide belt, took off her shoes, then covered her with the comforter, and left the apartment hopefully never to see her again.

A couple of weekends later, Markham visited the Mazurka Club in mid-evening and he wasn't two minutes at the bar when Elaine came over to him.

"How are you James?" she asked with a knowing smile.

"Fine, thank you," he responded. He noticed that the band was playing, but she wasn't singing. "Is this your night off?" asked Markham.

"I really don't work here; I just sing at my pleasure when I visit the Club and my drinks are on the house," Elaine replied nonchalantly.

"Nice arrangement," said Markham.

"Did your girlfriend have a little bit too much to drink the other night? Did she get home alright?" asked Elaine with a suggestive look.

"Yes, I made sure she got safely home," replied Markham, not willing to elaborate on that evening.

"I see she's not with you tonight. Does that mean she's history?" she asked.

"That's one way to put it. Our lifestyles are not compatible, that's all," replied Markham.

"Well, James, do ladies always have to ask *you* to dance?" she asked teasingly.

"No, would you give me the pleasure of this dance, Madam?" he asked her jokingly.

"Madam...Do I look that old to you?" she asked.

"No, I was just kidding you," he replied with a grin.

"Tell me James, do I look manly to you?" she asked with a serious look.

Markham didn't know how to respond to her most direct question. He didn't find her manly, but he did feel that she was jaded and too worldly for him, although most men would find her very attractive. Markham wanted someone near his own age of twenty-two.

"No, of course not," he responded.

"How come you never made a pass at me or asked me for a date?" she asked.

Markham felt trapped not knowing how to respond to her question without offending her.

"I doubt that a woman of your popularity would be interested in dating a guy who lives more than 100 kilometers from London and can barely afford to come to London two weekends a month," replied Markham, hoping that would dampen her interest in him.

"Really. I'm surprised you haven't found a woman near your air base, James. What is it about London that you find so exciting that you're willing to travel 100 kilometers?" she asked inquisitively.

"Dancing to the big dance bands and jazz clubs. The contagious energy of Londoners and the unparallelled night life is what excites me. New York has nothing over London," replied Markham.

Elaine looked at Markham, silently wondering what kind of a man he really was and whether she would be able to control him. He didn't seem the submissive type, which she much preferred. *No, she told herself, he's too young and not my type.*

"Well, James. Thank you for the dance. I think I'll go earn my drinks now. Have a wonderful evening dear," she said as she walked over to the bandstand. Markham left the Mazurka Club shortly thereafter and went to spend the rest of the evening with his friends at the New Yorker where he met Dawn's French boyfriend Jean-Paul Beauchamp, a dark-haired young man with a medium but athletic build, who had a 'joie de vivre' about him that appealed to everyone who met him, especially Dawn, who was madly in love with him. With Jean-Paul was another young Parisian named Victor Vincente, also a dark-haired mid-size Italian-French student who spent most of his time at Les Enfants Terrible Café in the French Quarter of London accompanying his French songs with his faithful guitar, which never left his side and probably brought to bed with the many girls that pursued him. Then there was Jean-Guy Giroux, another dark-haired French student from Paris who reminded Markham of the famous French comedian Fernandel, not only with his hilarious behavior, but his voice as well. While some of the French male students found their way to the New Yorker, the French female students did not frequent the New Yorker with its stable of English girls, preferring to hang out at the Café Les Enfants Terrible which relied on the entertainment provided by the students themselves, some of whom were very talented musicians, such as Victor.

One particular weekend, the Shriners invaded London at the same time that the United States' Seventh Fleet arrived and gave its sailors liberty leave for a weekend of R & R, Rest and Recuperation, which the sailors translated into Revel and Riot. There was not a hotel room to be found and Markham finally decided that he would most likely sleep that night at a Turkish Bath which had clean beds and bath-shower facilities. He found himself at Les Enfants Terrible Café where he hung around with Victor and the French student crowd. At the end of the evening when the Café was near closing, Victor invited Markham to stay at his small apartment for the night inasmuch as Markham had been unable to acquire a reasonably-priced hotel room that night, and Markham accepted, not caring where he slept. However, he wasn't prepared for Victor's newest girl friend, Roxanne Beaulieu, a petite blonde Parisian student, who was determined not to leave Victor's side even though Markham would be sharing that same one room apartment. Markham slept on the large couch while Victor and Roxanne slept in the only bed in the apartment. However, it was difficult for Markham to fall asleep because while Victor was apparently asleep lying on his back, Roxanne was propped up next to him stroking his hair and his face while she murmured the same refrain, "Oh! Mon petit choux, mon petit choux, come je t'adore, oui mon petit choux, tu es si beau, Oh! Come je t'aime, je t'adore mon petit choux."

Markham thought to himself, *why can't that be me? What a lucky guy that Victor, but he deserves it, he's a nice guy.* But it reminded Markham of his lot in the military service living with a bunch of men in a Quonset hut that lacked any privacy and certainly no opportunity to experience a loving relationship with an adoring female. Oh,Well, he thought, *la vie est come ca, un jour tu pleure, un jour tu ris. Life is like that, one day you cry, one day you laugh.*

The next day, Saturday, Markham decided that he would not impose on Victor for another night's entertainment by Roxanne, therefore bid him farewell for his kind hospitality and went to the Douglas House for dinner. Afterwards, he visited the Mazurka Club and it wasn't long before Elaine approached him.

"James, I wonder if you would do me a favor. My girlfriend Kate who is sitting at the bar wearing a red dress wants to go to the house party being given by a bunch of Navy men...one of them you know as Bob Draper. She has no transportation and she needs an escort. I'll be there later."

Markham observed that she was a skinny, petite blonde-haired woman in her late twenties. He really wasn't interested in her and didn't care to escort her anywhere, but Elaine was very persistent.

"Listen James, you don't have to stay with her if you don't want to. All I'm asking you to do is simply escort her there and then you can leave her to party, that's all...please darling," she implored. Then she gave Markham a small piece of paper containing the address where the party was taking place.

"Alright, but I'm only going to take her there, after that she's on her own until you get there," replied Markham.

"Thank you. She's a nice girl. You might get to like her," she added, then waved her friend over and introduced her to Markham, then left to perform on the bandstand.

"I hope you understand, Kate, that I may not stay at the party very long so I've agreed with Elaine to escort you there because you need a ride," said Markham.

"Yes I know and I appreciate that you're taking me there," said Elaine, who was sipping a gin and tonic, apparently a most popular drink amongst British women.

Markham left the Mazurka Club with Kate and he hailed a taxi which took them through a wide alley which had two-story houses on one side and garages and storage facilities on the other. The taxi stopped half-way down the alley and the driver announced that they were at the address. It had been a short cab ride, almost within walking distance of Piccadilly Circus. Music was blaring from both the upstairs and downstairs apartments which were teeming with people carrying beer bottles and glasses filled with liquor. Markham escorted Kate upstairs which was slightly less crowded and after getting a drink of vodka for Kate and a beer for himself, sat down on a wide, unoccupied couch. He expected Kate to sit beside him, but she took off for parts unknown, obviously to socialize with the crowd of mostly men with a few women present. Markham's attention became riveted on a particular young man whose dress and demeanor identified him as an Englishman. He was sitting on a stuffed chair facing an American Serviceman dressed in civilian clothes who wore glasses and appeared frightened of the Englishman. He was attempting to calm the serviceman's noticeable fear of imminent assault apparently because of Markham's presence and obvious interest in protecting a comrade in arms.

Markham suspected that this Englishman, who was sitting only a few feet from him, was in fact a Teddy Boy known for carrying a straight razor and a reputation for slashing people's faces, and it was quite clear to Markham that the poor serviceman was being threatened and couldn't control his fear. Markham made sure that the Englishman knew of his intense interest in him and any offensive movement on his part towards that serviceman would be met with swift force. Markham decided to reassure the serviceman that he was not alone.

"Hey! Buddy, you alright?" asked Markham of the serviceman.

"Yeah! I'm OK," he replied meekly, not turning his head.

Markham stood up and walked over to a couple of Navy guys and told them that they probably had a Teddy Boy in their midst who was apparently intimidating one of their own, and the best way to find out was to frisk him for a razor, and they quickly agreed. Markham walked back over to the where the Englishman was still sitting and he took his seat facing the side-front of the Englishman.

"Hey! Mister," said Markham to the Englishman. "I have the distinct feeling that you've been intimidating this Navyman with a straight razor you have in your breast pocket." Then turning to the Navyman, Markham asked him, "Has he been threatening you?"

The Navyman observed that two burly Navymen were standing right behind the Englishman ready to pounce on him which gave him the courage to admit that he had in fact been threatened. "Yeah! He threatened to cut me." And at that moment the Englishman pulled out his straight razor with its blade glistening in the light. One Navyman grabbed the Englishman's right wrist which held the razor while his left arm choked the Englishman at the neck. Simultaneously, the other Navyman grabbed the Englishman's other arm while Markham removed the razor from the Teddy Boy's hand. At this point, all hell broke loose as several Navymen joined the conflict which ended up by throwing the battered Englishman down the stairs and into the alley where he lay bleeding from the nose and mouth. The party continued in full swing and Markham sat on the same couch he initially occupied before the fight occurred. Markham was contently consuming one beer after another when Kate appeared from downstairs and sat next to him, complaining that some Navyman had attempted to get fresh with her.

"Look, Kate. If you stay here with me, no one will bother you. But if you go off on your own, then I'm not responsible for you," Markham said, and Kate left in a huff at Markham's lack of interest in her. Kate never returned to Markham, who eventually fell asleep on the couch he'd been sitting on, from the consumption of beer and the late hour. During the late evening, Elaine arrived at the party and after seeing Markham asleep on the couch, borrowed a blanket from one of the rooms which she placed over Markham, then she left with one of the Navymen for the night, leaving Kate to her own devices.

Markham was sound asleep on the couch when at about 6AM, he suddenly awakened to see Bob Draper sitting straddled over Kate who was lying on her back half-way through a doorway with her hands in the air attempting to fend off Draper's punches to her face. Markham couldn't believe his eyes. Here was this 225 lbs man punching the face of a 95 lbs woman. Markham immediately got up and threw both of his arms under Draper's biceps locking his hands behind Draper's neck and pulling him back off of Kate. She had dropped into unconsciousness, but then quickly regained consciousness as Markham placed his body between Draper and her. But as Kate regained consciousness, she recognized Markham and attempted to scratch his face while Markham blocked Draper's attempts to kick Kate. Markham turned his head towards Draper whose eyes were glassy and yelled at him to get away. Markham grabbed both of Kate's wrists to stop her from hitting him and asked her to stop struggling, that he was going to help her stand up. Draper again attempted to kick her, but Markham again blocked the kick with the left side of his back and warned Draper to stand back or else and Draper finally complied. Markham then pulled Kate up on her feet, but she attempted to break loose of Markham to strike him and in the process fell back down on her back while he held her by her wrists.

"Listen, Kate. I'm not going to hurt you and Draper isn't going to either," said Markham in a voice meant for both Kate and Draper.

Kate looked up at Draper. "He's afraid of you, why don't you hit him? Hit him," she said to Draper, hoping he would hit Markham.

"Draper, stand down or you're going to jail, you understand me?" yelled Markham. Draper stood there motionless.

"Kate, I'm going to help you down the stairs and get you a taxi to take you home, OK?" said Markham, who realized that he had only three pounds and it would probably cost one pound for the taxi, which left him with just enough money to get something to eat and the train fare back to the base. Kate stopped resisting and appeared silently thankful that Markham was helping her to a taxi, while Draper stayed upstairs. Markham flagged a taxi and after helping Kate into it, he asked her to give the driver her address. He asked the driver if a pound would cover the fare, and he answered in the affirmative. As the taxi departed with Kate, Markham recognized that the cabbie only saw Markham with this obviously injured woman, which could be used as evidence against him should the matter come to the attention of the police. But, he thought, she would certainly attest to the fact that it was Draper, not Markham, who assaulted her, hence nothing to worry about.

Markham returned to the upstairs flat where he found Draper not so drunk that he didn't know what had happened.

"What the hell possessed you to assault her so viciously?" asked Markham.

"Cause she's a fucking bitch, that's why," Draper answered.

"Yeah! Well, If I hadn't woken up when I did, you would have killed her, then where would you be Bob?" asked Markham, who wondered about Draper's emotional stability.

Draper didn't answer Markham's question. But Markham suddenly realized by his own question, that he could have awakened to find Kate's corpse with Draper gone and Markham the logical suspect of a homicide. Markham decided to get out of there and take Draper with him in an attempt to sober him up at a coffee shop somewhere in the Soho district. As they walked from the party flat to Piccadilly Circus, Markham observed that Draper's gait was steady and his faculties were normal, but there was subdued rage in his eyes, face and general deportment leftover from his still unsatisfied anger towards Kate. Markham wondered if Draper's anger was due to Kate's rejection of his sexual advances. Had Kate teased him into believing she would submit then refused, or was Draper basically a predator of women? Those were questions that Draper left unanswered as Markham attempted to draw information out of him during their walk to a coffee shop that would be open at this early hour of the morning. After morning coffee, Markham left Draper to return to his hotel room to freshen up and gather his AWOL bag for departure by train to Molesworth Air Base.

Three weeks later, Markham ran into Elaine as he was walking through Trafalgar Square.

"You know, James, Kate ended up in a hospital from her injuries and she said that you beat her up," Elaine said with the expectation of an admission from Markham.

"What? Are you kidding me? I never beat her up. She knows full well that it was Draper who beat her up and I rescued her from a severe beating and possibly death," said Markham, visibly upset at Kate's mendacity. Markham related to Elaine the events that transpired.

"You know, James, that Kate is a dipsomaniac," said Elaine.

"Great. Now you tell me. Why did you fix me up with her to begin with?"

"I didn't know her condition until she ended up in the hospital," replied Elaine.

"I'm not about to escort any more of your friends, Elaine, that's for sure," answered Markham with finality. They then parted company.

Several weeks later, Markham was having a drink at the bar in the Douglas House when he saw Elaine walk into the restaurant section accompanied by Draper, who saw Markham, but looked away as the two of them disappeared inside the restaurant. Markham deduced that Elaine believed Draper's version of the incident supported by Kate. This unfortunate incident had a profound effect on Markham's faith in the justice system which would have undoubtedly found him guilty by the faulty, but convincing evidence which made him wonder how many wrongfully convicted innocent people are suffering the daily horrors of prison life.

The following weekend Markham spent most of his time between Les Enfants Terrible Café and the New Yorker Club and on Sunday he went to the Douglas House where he met some friends with whom they shared their experiences over many alcoholic beverages. At dinner time Jason and Estelle arrived and whisked Markham away from his inebriated friends for a hearty meal before going to the train station for their return to Molesworth Air Base. After dinner, they decided to take a taxi to Piccadilly Circus and because of the nice weather, they would walk the rest of the way to Charing Cross Station. Jason and Estelle were walking ahead of Markham, who was carrying his Alexander Tailored suit covered in a plastic bag which he was holding by the coat hanger with his left hand over his left shoulder, and he carried his AWOL bag in his right hand. Markham was feeling no pain, although he was not drunk by any stretch of the imagination. He was wearing a sports jacket with a white shirt unbuttoned at the top with necktie. They had just passed the Eros monument when two Bobbies stopped Markham.

"Where'd you get that suit?" asked one Bobby.

"What do you mean? It's my suit," replied Markham indignantly.

The two Bobbies looked at each other. "Can you prove it?" one Bobby asked.

"Certainly. My name is sewed on the inside pocket of the jacket," said Markham as he unzipped the plastic bag and showed the Bobbies his embroidered name on the inside pocket. "Don't you guys have anything better to do?" He zipped up his bag. Suddenly both Bobbies grabbed Markham by his arms, while two more Bobbies who had arrived at the scene grabbed his AWOL bag and suit bag and they loaded him into a black van in the company of one Bobby. He stayed inside holding his hand with his wrist bent down, which Markham found comical because he knew that hold from his lessons in jujitsu and knew how to get out of it if he had wanted to. Estelle was frantic, demanding that the Bobbies release Markham, while Jason tried to calm her down for fear that they would arrest her for interfering with the duties of police officers. Jason and Estelle flagged down a taxi and followed the police van to its destination. While seated in the black van with the Bobby at his side, Markham commented to the Bobby.

"Why do you have to hold my hand? You think I'm going somewhere with the steel door closed and locked? Give me a break," said Markham, and the embarrassed Bobby released his hand. "I don't know what charge you Bobbies are going to cook up, but it had better be good," said Markham amusingly. Once inside the police station, they asked Markham to remove all articles from his pockets, which they laid on a large desk. Behind it sat a rotund Bobby, apparently the Sergeant in Charge, flanked by three other Bobbies who examined each and every document including his military identification card and several club cards. It was at this point that Markham asked the Sergeant in Charge what his rights were.

"You're in England now, you have no rights," answered the Sergeant brusquely.

When Markham heard the Sergeant's negative response, he decided that it was futile to argue with an ignorant man whose ego would not allow him to be challenged, especially by an American. He knew that it was best to remain silent and wait for the Military Police to arrive, then in the presence of the American Military Police he could vent his objections. After finding nothing incriminating, they walked him down a corridor to a cell block where he was locked up for at least three hours. Markham found the cell spacious, clean, with its own toilet and a bunk, but for the first time he felt like a caged animal and he experienced an overwhelming urge to break out at any cost. He still felt the effects of the liquor he had consumed earlier, but his faculties were still intact. He noticed that there was a thick-glassed window above the toilet which was held in a frame by several screws. Markham took out his dog-tags and with its edge attempted to turn the screws, to no avail. Defeated, he laid down on the bunk and tried to sleep it off, but couldn't fall asleep, so he waited impatiently until a Bobby finally came to his cell and unlocked it.

"Alright. You can leave now," said the Bobby. Markham stepped out of the cell and as he started walking down the long corridor, he noticed two Air Policemen standing at the end of the hall waiting for him. Markham believed they were watching for any signs of staggering and intoxication, hence he made every effort to walk a straight line, which he did. He picked up all of his belongings from the Sergeant in Charge and his suit and AWOL bag, and then Markham asked the Sergeant.

"Are there any charges against me?"

"No, there aren't any," the Sergeant replied, seeming relieved at Markham's custodial transfer to the American Air Police.

"I didn't think so," replied Markham as he left with the Air Policemen who took him in their jeep to Military Police Headquarters in London. Jason and Estelle followed the jeep in a taxi and stayed at MP Headquarters, waiting for Markham to be released from custody. The Military Policeman on duty as Charge of Quarters wrote up a report of the incident then released Markham in time for him and Jason to catch the last train that would arrive at Molesworth in time for duty. A couple of weeks later the Adjutant, Major Duvall, called Markham into his office and showed him a letter he had received from the Sergeant in Charge of the British Police stating that Markham had been picked up on the streets of Piccadilly Circus in a disheveled and inebriated condition and his aggressive behavior compelled the British police to detain him until the Air Police could take possession of him.

"Well Jim, is any of this true?" he asked.

"No sir. None of it is true," he answered candidly.

"Well, I was detained once by the Bobbies for allegedly driving while intoxicated and I thought it was a bunch of bullshit," he said. "And I think this is a bunch of bullshit too. So this is what I think of that letter." He tore it up in two and threw it in his garbage can. "Don't worry about it, Jim. Just go back to work."

But Markham was silently furious about the fact that this British policeman took the trouble to send this mendacious letter in an attempt to cause him further harm. This experience further eroded his faith in the justice system.

The following weekend, Markham heard that Ted Heath's big band was playing at the Lyceum at the Strand in the West End of London and thus he decided to go dancing that Saturday evening, wearing his midnight-blue suit, white shirt and black slim tie. Markham was always on the lookout for new moves by dancers doing the London Bop whose choreography was infinitely smoother than its American Swing version. Markham was quite impressed with one dancer who took his lady's right hand in his right hand and brought his right hand behind his head releasing her hand on his left front shoulder, which slid down his lapel falling into his left hand, which he then signaled for her to make a complete right turn by simply flipping his left wrist and hand in that direction and so forth. The moves were clever and smoothly executed as a class act and Markham was absorbing it all so that he could later practice those moves and style.

As he was watching the dancers, Markham became aware of a strikingly beautiful natural blonde with the biggest blue eyes he'd ever seen. She was voluptuous and feminine, but what captured Markham's attention was her broad face with the biggest almond-shaped eyes and full lips that all at once spelled love at first sight. She stood there talking with another girl with brown hair and a model's slim figure, when Markham walked up to the blonde and asked her if she would give him the pleasure of this waltz and she readily accepted.

As they danced, Markham was admiring her beautiful features when she interrupted his reverie.

"My name is Sylvia. What's your name?" she asked with a slight smile.

"My name is Jim, Jim Markham. I'm very pleased that you agreed to dance with me," he said.

"What branch of the service are you in Jim?" she asked.

"The Air Force," he replied.

"Are you stationed near London?" she asked inquisitively.

"Unfortunately, no. I'm stationed at Molesworth which is about 100 kilometers from here," he replied sadly.

"You must like London to come all this way," she said with her eyes looking into the windows of his soul.

"Yes, I do love London. It's an exciting city," he said.

"You dance quite well for an American."

"I learned from the British mostly."

"Well, that explains it," she said with a hearty laugh.

They danced together the rest of the evening. The brunette was none other than her younger sister Joan, who thought that Jim Markham and Sylvia Pillar made a great looking couple. Finally he had found a woman he could easily fall in love with and he started to date her every weekend he was free to leave the air base. Sylvia lived with her mother and sister in a small apartment in Tottenham, London. Markham would often accompany Sylvia who walked her small dog along a path in a field on a hill that overlooked the town below, and they would sit on the grass while the dog roamed around the field. Markham loved the way she would tuck her hands under her armpits and look up to him with a gaze that invited him to kiss her forever, which he did with his heart and soul, but it never went beyond the soul kiss. He knew that he loved her and on one of those intimate occasions he told her so, but she never reciprocated.

On one particular occasion, Markham escorted her back to her house late at night and they sat together on the couch necking while her mother and sister were upstairs asleep. Sylvia was almost asleep sitting in his arms after much kissing and petting when Markham's left hand slowly found itself moving under her skirt towards her vagina without a whimper or objection from Sylvia. But Markham suddenly felt guilt and removed his hand from her thighs because he felt that he was taking advantage of her while she was asleep, although he suspected that she may have been feigning sleep so as to allow Markham to have sex with her without jeopardizing her honor and reputation. He loved her too much to risk the loss of her respect for him, although his hormones were screaming for sexual intercourse with her.

It was near the end of summer but some cafes in the West End of London still had small tables and chairs sitting outside for customers to enjoy the hustle and bustle of pedestrians walking the streets of London. Markham and Sylvia were strolling the streets of Soho when they decided to occupy one of those small tables outside the Mayfair café for tea and biscuits. They had been sitting at the table for about a half hour when Markham noticed four young Englishmen standing directly across the street with one of them talking while the others' attention was directed towards Markham and Sylvia. As Markham focused his vision on them, he unexpectedly recognized the talking Englishman as the same individual who had pulled a razor at the Navy party which resulted in his suffering a beating. Markham realized that he was almost certainly facing four razor-wielding individuals and he had no means to protect Sylvia unless he could quickly acquire a weapon. One knife would not be enough against four razors, but two sharp knives, one in each hand, might do the trick if he could place himself in a confined position such as a doorway where only one or two of them at most could confront him. He quickly surveyed the tables nearest him and found no knives, but he did observe that there were two empty bottles of beer still sitting at a nearby table that had not yet been cleared, which he knew he could break and use as sharp weapons if the need arose. He immediately grabbed the two empty bottles and placed them on his table.

"What are you doing, darling…collecting beer bottles?" asked Sylvia, smiling.

"I wanted to read the label since I'm not familiar with English Ale and these are two different types of ale."

Markham kept observing the four Englishmen gathered across the street, expecting them at any moment to cross the street towards him, when he suddenly heard a voice calling him.

"Jim, fancy meeting you here mate," said Chubby. Markham looked up at him standing there with two other men, all dressed in conservative suits. Chubby immediately sized up Sylvia with an appreciative smile.

Markham stood up to shake his hand, and he introduced Sylvia to Chubby, and his two friends introduced themselves to Markham and Sylvia. Markham took Chubby aside out of Sylvia's hearing with his two friends following them.

"Chubby, do you know any of those four men standing across the street?" he asked.

Chubby and his two friends looked at the men and Chubby replied, "Yeah! Sure. The second one from the right. The one wearing the bright red tie, that's Teddy the Bear we call him, a real puff. Why?"

"Well, that one you referred to as Teddy the Bear is the guy who pulled a straight razor on me and a Navyman at the Navy party and he got the crap beat out of him," said Markham. "I think he's looking for revenge. Why do you call him Teddy the Bear?"

"His name is Ted and I've known him since he was a kid and he's a real puff so I nicknamed him Teddy the Bear. He acts brave when he has other Teddys around him, but he's actually a coward. But you don't want to tackle four razors Jim, that would be daft," said Chubby. "I'm going across the street to have a talk with Teddy and I guarantee you he'll never bother you or your lady, ever." Chubby and his two friends crossed the street with one hand in their pockets, probably holding a stiletto type of knife far more deadly than a razor. Markham could only observe them, but was too distant to hear what was being said.

Chubby stood facing Teddy, who appeared quite nervous.

"Hi Chubby. How's things going mate?" asked Teddy.

"Alright, how about you?" replied Chubby with his two friends flanking him."I hear you pulled your razor on the wrong people the other day and you got yourself messed up."

"Yeah! There were too many for me to handle, but one of them is sitting right across the street without his friends this time," said Teddy menacingly.

"Well that's where you're wrong Teddy Boy, his name is Jim and he's a personal friend of mine and he's the only Yank who has my personal protection. So I'm going to give you some *life saving advice*, Teddy, if either you or one of your boys so much as touch a hair on his head, they will find your mutilated body in the Thames River," said Chubby, stepping up real close to Teddy with his rugged visage within inches of his blanched face. "Do you understand me, mate?"

"Yeah! Yeah! Chubby, you've got my solemn word, I won't go near the Yank and neither will any of my boys," replied Teddy, who respected Chubby's reputation as the most feared villain in the West End of London.

"Alright then, get a move on. I don't want the Yank to feel uncomfortable by your presence," said Chubby, and did not turn his back on Teddy and his boys until they had departed the scene. Chubby and his two friends then returned to the café where Markham and Sylvia were still sitting and he leaned over to whisper something in Markham's ear.

"I put the fear of God in Teddy. You can be sure he won't ever both you. If he does, you know where to find me."

Chubby then stood up straight, and bid farewell to Sylvia and shook Markham's hand and left with his two friends.

"Jim, how'd you get to know such rough characters?" asked Sylvia.

"They're really nice guys, but you've got to be tough to survive in a big city like London, Sylvia."

"Yes, but how did you, an American, get to know these men?" she asked.

"It's a long story Sylvia, but in essence, I happened to be at the right place at the right time and was able to help him. That's all really."

"I see. That doesn't tell me a lot, but I suppose that's all you're willing to reveal," replied Sylvia, somewhat disappointed in Markham's secrecy.

"Would you like to go to a movie before I take the train back to the base?" asked Markham, changing the conversation.

"Yes, that sounds good. I believe we can make the next feature at the Odeon in Leicester Square if we hurry," said Sylvia, and so they did attend the theatre show and Markham made it safely back to Molesworth Air Base.

Four days later, on Thursday, Markham learned that he had Charge of Quarters duty that forthcoming Sunday, hence it was not feasible for him to go to London that weekend to see Sylvia. She did not have a telephone for him to notify her of his unavailability, which frustrated Markham to no end.

That Saturday, Markham's barracks friends including Jason, Frank, Bob, Guy, Seth and Marc all went to either London or the local town to see their respective girlfriends, while Markham stayed on base because he had the CQ duty early the next morning. Marc had been dating a local English girl Jeanne that Bob and Guy nicknamed 'The Bean' because of her tall and skinny figure which they said reminded them of Popeye the Sailorman's girlfriend 'Olive Oil.' Marc ignored their derisive comments regarding 'The Bean' for fear that if he defended her, they would then make fun of his choice of women, hence he would never mention her nor reveal to his barracks mates the fact that most of his time off-base was spent with her.

Frank Cummins was very conscious about his height of five feet nine inches. Although his looks undoubtedly rivaled any Hollywood star, it was not surprising that before he would ask a woman to dance he would first unobtrusively stand next to her to make sure she was not taller than him which would disqualify her as a dance partner. It was suggested that he purchase elevator shoes or that he comb his hair into a pompadour or perhaps don a Top Hat. The airmen in barracks number 18 had to develop thick skins from the constant ribbing that occurred between them, otherwise there would have been regular fistfights amongst them.

Markham decided to have a quick beer at the Airmen's Club which was packed with airmen and a few English females. As Markham stood near the crowded bar with a can of beer in his hand surrounded by several airmen, none of whom he regarded as his friend, he was unaware that Max Beasley, a football player for the base team who envied and resented Markham's popularity, was standing behind him edging a football teammate named Jose Riveras, to start a fight with Markham with the understanding that he would get help from Beasley. Riveras was obviously inebriated as he stood before Markham.

"I don't like you," slurred Riveras, then knocked the beer can out of Markham's hand to the floor. Markham was utterly surprised by Riveras' action as he had never had any meaningful contact with him before, thus figured that his offensive action was the result of his intoxication, hence he ignored him and walked over to an empty table where he sat down with another can of beer. Shortly thereafter, Riveras appeared in an unstable run across the dance floor and upon reaching Markham, threw a right punch which landed lightly on his chin as he instinctively backed off from his sitting position, thus minimizing the blow. Markham was now standing in close proximity to Riveras, who was visibly surprised at his apparent invulnerability to his running power punch. But Markham's patience had run its course.

"You wanna fight? Well, you've got it. Step outside," he said , pointing his index finger at him, and without waiting for Riveras, quickly walked outside the Airmen's Club and waited for Riveras to appear, but he didn't appear until he had an entourage of his friends with him. The sun had gone down and only the light from the Airmen's Club entrance and the occasional lamppost lit the street on that cloudy night. Markham could see that Riveras was now hesitant about fighting him and only the prodding from his friends encouraged him to fight Markham. Practically everyone in the Club fell outside and formed a large circle for the two men to battle. Markham could have punched him out at the beginning of the fight because Riveras was obviously too drunk to adequately defend himself, let alone initiate an effective assault on Markham who had consumed only two beers and would have outclassed him even when sober. Markham was now reluctant to hit him because he felt that it would be unfair of him to take advantage of a man in his defenseless condition. At one point Markham, while facing Riveras, quickly jumped to his left and noticed that Riveras was still staring straight ahead where he had been standing. Markham could have blindsided him with several punches that would have finished him off, but he couldn't bring himself to hit the poor man, who had obviously been used by Beasley as his proxy.

When Beasley realized that his proxy was not fulfilling his expectations, he stepped out of the inner crowd circle and threw a right punch to the side of Markham's head that stunned him. Before he could recover from the blow, Beasley threw another punch to his head that brought him down to his knees and Riveras joined in and punched him on the side of the head that was now unfelt by Markham, having blacked out from the second punch delivered by Beasley. Markham was unaware of what was happening to him and all of his movements were now controlled by his survival instinct. He instinctively stood up and was hit by Beasley and Riveras until he went down on his knees again only to stand up and be knocked down once more. It became obvious to the crowd that Markham was unable to defend himself, but no one dared interfere with Beasley and Riveras who were soon joined by Dan Wiesel, another member of the group who wanted to inflict injury on a helpless victim. But to their chagrin Big Sam, the cook, an enormous black airmen about six feet six inches tall and weighing around 320 lbs stepped into the human ring and confronted Beasley, Riveras and Wiesel as they were getting ready to hit Markham who was on his knees attempting to rise to his feet again.

"Hey! Man. This ain't a fair fight! What'sa matter with you people, you gonna just stand there and watch this man get beaten to death?" said an outraged Sam.

"Hey! Nigger, this ain't none of your business, so get your black ass out of here!" said Wiesel, the smaller of the three who was obviously letting his mouth overcome his intoxicated body.

If Sam's eyes could kill, all three of those white men would have been dead. Sam pulled out a knife and in complete silence, but rage enveloping his entire being, advanced towards the three of them who found safe haven by fleeing into the crowd. Markham was now on his feet having recovered from the blackout, but was unaware that he'd been down on his knees or that he'd been hit several times about the face and head. He clearly saw Big Sam holding a knife in his hand, but couldn't understand why he was there or where Riveras had gone. Nor was he aware that Beasley and Wiesel had entered the brawl.

"Hey, man. You alright?" asked Sam, now a bit more calm with his knife back in his pocket.

"Yeah! I guess so," replied Markham, not aware of his physical condition. The darkness of the area did not reveal the true extent of his injuries and loss of blood.

"Can you make it back to the barracks?" asked Sam. The crowd had dispersed and most of them had gone back inside the Airmen's Club.

"Yeah! I'm alright, thanks Sam," said Markham, not realizing that Sam was the only person in that whole crowd of people who had the courage to come to Markham's aid and stop this unfair fight.

He started walking on the narrow and poorly lit cement walkway between Quonset huts on his way to his own barracks when without warning, Dan Wiesel jumped on his back bringing Markham's weakened, battered body to its knees. Wiesel started punching Markham in the back and on the side of the head, then he got off of him and kicked him in the face, and jumped on his back again while he was still on his knees and started to apply a choke hold. Markham, still conscious, could see the blood dripping from his nose onto the cement walkway partially lit by one of the barracks lights when two airmen returning to their barracks from the Airmen's Club arrived on the scene and recognized Markham as the victim of the earlier brawl. They immediately pulled Wiesel off him and sent him on his way back to the Airmen's Club. Markham surprisingly got back on his feet and waved the two airmen off, stating he was capable of returning to his barracks unaided.

He opened the door and entered his barracks where he stood still for a moment assessing his condition under the only light that came from the cubicle on his right where Peter Tronolone was reading a book. Peter looked up in shock at the sight of Markham, whose shirt was in shreds and covered in blood still dripping from his nose and mouth. Markham's eyes were swollen and closing, but he seemed totally unaware of his condition and truthfully didn't feel any pain either.

He was apparently regaining his strength as he started walking through the length of the barracks and out the exit door onto the cement walkway and into the bathhouse where he turned on a shower and stepped into it fully-clothed while he peeled off his torn shirt from his body. While Markham was taking a shower, Peter Tronolone ran over to the Air Police Office at the main gate and alerted the Officer of the Day, Chief Warrant Officer Summerville, of the assault on Markham. Chief Summerville sent two Air Policemen to find Markham, whom they located in the bathhouse still taking a shower. The mere sight of him told the Air Policemen that it must have taken more than one person to do that much damage to a man of Markham's size and apparent muscular strength.

"Your name Markham?" asked one of the Air Policemen.

"Yeah! That's me," replied Markham.

"Who did this to you?" asked the other Air Policemen.

"I don't know; it was dark," replied Markham. He could only remember his confrontation with Riveras, who had not landed any punches until after Beasley entered the fight which caused his blackout and memory loss.

"Listen, Markham, we're going to take you to the hospital. You're pretty badly hurt," said one of the Air Policemen.

"What for? I'll be OK by morning. Thanks, but don't bother," replied Markham.

"Oh, yeah? Take a good look at yourself in the mirror," said one of the Air Policemen.

Markham stepped out of the shower wearing only his wet trousers and shoes, having taken off his shredded shirt. He looked into the mirror above the sink opposite the shower stall and to his amazement saw a face that had a swollen and bloody nose, puffed eyes, swollen and still bleeding lips from his two lower dog's teeth having punctured his lower lip and some marks and scratches on his neck. *Not a pretty sight,* he thought, *but the physical damage is not as bad as it looks.* Nevertheless, to satisfy the policemen, he got into some dry clothes and accompanied them to the hospital where he was examined, X-rayed and then released to the Air Policemen who took him back to his barracks to rest.

In the meantime, Chief Summerville sent a couple of the Provost Marshal investigators to the Airmen's Club to gather information regarding the assault on Markham which revealed that Riveras, Beasley and Wiesel were the airmen involved in the assault. Chief Summerville issued orders for all three men to be incarcerated in the base stockade until an Article 32 hearing could be held to determine whether courts-martial of these three men was warranted by the evidence.

Sunday evening saw the return of Jason Walden, Frank Cummins, Marc Dillinger and Robert Bruner. Upon seeing Markham's condition, they started blaming themselves for having left him alone on the base, knowing full well that had they been there, Beasley and his two friends would never have dared carry out such a cowardly act. Jason was absolutely furious and wanted to tear Beasley to pieces with his bare hands, but fortunately for Beasley, he was safely locked up in the base stockade. When Markham walked into the Mess Hall that Monday morning for breakfast, none of the people who had witnessed the fight dared look him in the eye or even in his direction due to their feelings of guilt and shame at their failure to come to the aid of another American airman. Some uninvolved airmen came over to Markham's breakfast table and expressed their outrage at what had happened and their wish for just punishment to Beasley and his crew.

Colonel Charles Whiteley, the Wing Commander at Molesworth, called the Base Hospital upon learning of the assault on his Adjutant's clerk to find out if Markham could have died from his injuries and was informed by the attending doctor that he certainly could have died and the doctor was surprised that Markham had suffered no broken bones or apparent concussion and was not hospitalized. Colonel Whiteley assigned Major George Saperston the task of holding an Article 32 Hearing to be held within 48 hours. Markham was ordered to appear at the Hearing which took place in a small office in the Headquarters building adjacent to the Adjutant's office.

As Markham entered the Hearing room, Major Saperston could not avoid noticing his severely bruised face with darkened eyes, swollen nose and bottom lip. To Markham's surprise, Beasley was sitting in one of the two chairs facing the desk occupied by Major Saperston. Markham was instructed by Major Saperston to sit in the only unoccupied seat next to Beasley. Major Saperston gave Markham the oath and asked him to relate all of the events surrounding his assault last Saturday night. Markham soon came to the realization that Major Saperston had been swayed by the testimony of Beasley and his two accomplices when he displayed his bias during his testimony about the events that led up to the initial assault in the Airmen's Club.

"Jack McFarland, who was working as a bartender at the Airmen's Club that evening, told me that he saw Max Beasley standing behind me urging Jose Riveras to punch me," testified Markham.

The Major abruptly admonished him. "You should know better than to introduce hearsay evidence at this Hearing, Airman Markham. I only want to hear what you have observed directly, not what someone else told you. Is that clear?" said Major Saperston.

"Sir, how would you get direct evidence from Jack McFarland if I didn't make you aware of what he observed directly, Sir?" answered Markham, astonished at Major Saperston's aggressive tone and unfair admonishment.

"That's not your concern, Airman Markham, and you will testify only as to what you yourself observed…that's an order," replied Major Saperston.

Upon completion of his testimony, Major Saperston had one question for Markham.

"Didn't you leave out the reason for the assault that night, Airman Markham?" asked Major Saperston.

"No, I don't know the reason for the assault, Sir," replied Markham, puzzled by the question.

"Didn't you try to date Riveras' girlfriend?" he asked.

"I don't even know who his girlfriend is, and I didn't talk to any girl in the Club that night," replied Markham with visible indignation over this false allegation which conveyed a truthtelling demeanor that Major Saperston could not ignore. Major Saperston concluded the Hearing and the witnesses were dismissed, but Markham was still upset and surprised at the revelation by Major Saperston that Beasley and his two accomplices had given false testimony in an attempt to justify their assault.

A Summary Court-Martial was finally held and all three airmen were convicted of aggravated assault. They were all reduced in rank to Airmen Third Class and each sentenced to five months confinement at hard labor and forfeiture of all pay and allowances for their period of incarceration, but they were not issued discharges from the service.

Markham wrote a letter to Sylvia explaining to her that he'd suffered some non-life-threatening injuries in an accident that prevented him from leaving the air base, but he would be able to see her in London in about three weeks. She replied that she was looking forward to seeing him at the earliest opportunity.

However, as fate would have it, the Adjutant Major Duval suddenly became ill and was immediately transferred back to the United States for medical treatment. His replacement, to Markham's consternation, was Major Saperston who issued swift orders for his permanent transfer to the Third Motor Transport Company located at Sealand Air Base, near Liverpool, England, some 290 kilometers from London. One of the Third Motor Transport Company's trucks was making a delivery to Molesworth the next day and Markham was ordered to embark on that truck which would transport him and his personal effects to Sealand Air Base, leaving Markham no time to contact Sylvia and little time to bid his barracks mates farewell.

Upon arrival at Sealand Air Base, Markham soon learned that the Third Motor Company of 209 men led by Captain Eric Holtzhoch was the only U.S. Air Force combat unit in England, which meant that in addition to their normal duties, they would be conducting field combat training maneuvers normally associated with Army and Marine Corps exercises. Markham wondered if he would not have been better off being drafted into the U.S. Army with only a two year commitment, but believed in providence and accepted his fate in good spirit and marched on to his new assignment, and march he did.

Captain Holtzhoch had all of his men sew a black button near the collar of their Air Force blue overcoats which would hold the left flap to cover their shirts and ties and thus appear more militaristic. Captain Holtzhoch had a framed photograph of Field Marshal Rommel whom he greatly admired and attempted to emulate by having his troops conduct field maneuvers in the marshland of Wales where the men fired 50 and 30 caliber machine guns from an elevated plateau at stationary Second World War tanks in a ravine below.

The men were also trained in the live firing of grease guns and carbines at staggered silhouettes of enemy soldiers down a steep hill that allowed live rounds to pass over the heads of the airmen at the lower end, which gave the men a real sensation of actual combat conditions. While this could be considered valuable training for Army and Marine Corps personnel, Air Force recruits expected less rigorous ground force training and more technical schooling, and Markham was no exception. But unlike many of his comrade-in-arms, he appreciated the value of that training which he felt might come to good use in an emergency. As part of their training, Captain Holtzhoch held target practice with carbines for all of the men in the company and it was at such target practice that Captain Holtzhoch noticed Markham's sharp-shooting ability.

"Captain Holtzhoch," said the firing range Sergeant carrying a target sheet. "You should take a look at this target which I just pulled from the range. A perfect score, all rounds within the bulls-eye."

Captain Holtzhoch looked at the target sheet with surprise and amazement. "Who did the shooting?" he asked the Sergeant.

"Airman Markham, Sir. He's the Airman Second Class sitting against the fence over there."

Captain Eric Holtzhoch walked over to where Markham was sitting, but Markham didn't stand up.

"That's some pretty fancy shooting Markham. Where'd you learn to shoot like that?"

"At the 42nd Street Penny Arcade in Manhattan, Sir."

"I didn't know you could fire weapons in Times Square," said the surprised Captain.

"They were air pellet guns, Sir. The objective was to shoot out the lighted candles," replied Markham with a slight smile.

Captain Holtzhoch looked at Markham in a new light of interest. "How would you like to join my rifle team?" he asked Markham.

Markham thought that acceptance might mean the forfeiture of some weekends that he reserved exclusively for time off-base, primarily in London to see Sylvia, whom he hadn't seen in quite some time.

"I don't think so, Sir," replied Markham.

"Well, think about it. Come promotion time, it might make a difference," said Captain Holtzhoch, disappointed and irked by Markham's daring refusal.

Upon return to Sealand Air Base, Markham looked forward to his travel to London to see Sylvia who hadn't heard from him for at least two months. However, when Markham went to the Orderly Room that late Friday afternoon to pick up his weekend pass, he was informed by the Charge of Quarters that his pass had been pulled by the First Sergeant Calvin Tidwell because Markham was to relieve him as CQ at 0800 hours Saturday.

"How can that be?" asked Markham. "I'm not scheduled for CQ duty for another three weeks."

"Hey! Jim, I'm just the CQ. I don't know what's going on other than what I was told to tell you. That's all, man."

"Where's the First Shirt? Do you know?" asked Markham.

"Everybody's gone for the weekend, Jim," replied the CQ.

"Great, now my whole weekend is screwed up," said Markham, knowing that if he didn't report for CQ duty the next morning, he could be court-martialed and sent to a military prison known as the Stockade. Markham suspected that the reason for the sudden change in the duty roster was his refusal to join the Commanding Officer's request that he join his rifle team. Markham didn't lack stubbornness, but he also didn't lack common sense which told him that he would never get his pass back until he cooperated with Captain Holtzhoch and joined his rifle team.

Monday morning, Markham was ordered to report to First Sergeant Tidwell at the Orderly Room.

"Airman Markham. As of today, you are assigned as the Morning Report Clerk under my direct supervision. You're to replace Mark Peddler who has been admitted to the base hospital for psychiatric evaluation. Apparently he couldn't handle the job and attempted to cut his wrist with the blade in his nail clipper and the MO bought the suicide attempt as bonafide and admitted him to the hospital for observation. I guess those head shrinkers are in dire need of patients," said Sergeant Tidwell. "Bonafide attempt my ass. You couldn't cut butter with that little nail clipper blade. All he had were a few scratches on his wrist. I hope you're made of sterner stuff, Markham, because that Morning Report has to be accurate and perfectly typed, otherwise Captain Holtzhoch will come down on you like a bulldozer."

Markham listened attentively, but didn't reply. He knew one thing for sure though. Nothing they could throw at him could ever get him to consider suicide, especially over a Morning Report. *That Mark Peddler,* he thought, *must really be mentally weak and not suitable for military service.* Then maybe there was another more plausible and pressing reason for Peddler's desperate effort to exit Captain Holtzhoch's company. Time would tell, he reasoned.

"By the way Markham, have you reconsidered joining the rifle team?" asked Sergeant Tidwell.

"I gave my answer the first time I was asked, Sergeant Tidwell, and it hasn't changed."

"Let me tell you something Markham. You're never going to see an English road until you transfer out of Sealand which is not until you go back to the States, if you don't cooperate with the Captain," said Sergeant Tidwell threateningly.

"Are you saying that I am restricted to the base until I join the rifle team, Sergeant Tidwell?"

"No, you're not being restricted to the base. We are short-handed and you're needed for various duty assignments which includes weekends. No one has ordered you to join the rifle team. That's purely voluntary," said Sergeant Tidwell, careful not to provide Markham with a valid complaint to the Inspector General's Office.

"That's a bunch of bullshit, Sarge, and you know it. My answer is still no," answered Markham, trying to contain his anger at the Sergeant's subterfuge.

"You're very young Markham, but you're going to quickly learn to put some water in your wine which is called compromise, or else it'll be your demise," said Sergeant Tidwell as a warning to him.

Thinking that he had nothing to lose, Markham spoke his mind to the Sergeant.

"Where I come from it would be considered blasphemy to dilute wine with water and a grave insult to make the offer," said Markham.

Sergeant Tidwell gave him a stern look of disapproval. He knew that he would not be easily intimidated. *Let Captain Holtzhoch deal with him,* he thought.

"Alright, Markham. I want you to pull the last weeks' morning reports from the filing cabinet and review them as a guide to your making Monday's report which must be on the Captain's desk by 0830 each morning for his review and submission to base headquarters. I must tell you that the report must be perfect. No typos, is that understood?" said Sergeant Tidwell.

"Understood Sarge," replied Markham matter-of-factly.

The following Monday morning, Markham submitted his typed three-page morning report to Sergeant Tidwell who placed it on Captain Holtzhoch's desk in the adjoining office. A short time later, Captain Holtzhoch entered his office and within fifteen minutes summoned Markham into his office.

"Airman Markham. I will not submit a less than perfect morning report to Headquarters and I see two corrections of typographical errors in your report. That is not acceptable," said Captain Holtzhoch.

"I don't understand what you mean by corrections of typos, Sir."

"You made two typographical errors which you erased then typed over," said Captain Holtzhoch, holding one of the pages of the morning report up to the light.

"But Sir, you can't tell there was a typographical error unless you hold the page up to the light, as the error was completely erased and typed over with the correct spelling."

"That is my point Airman Markham. There must not be any corrections whatsoever. You must submit a report that has been perfectly typed without any typographical errors, is that understood?" said Captain Holtzhoch, looking directly into his eyes for a response.

"Yes, Sir. I'll retype it. Is that all, Sir?" replied Markham.

"No, that's not all Airman Markham. I expect the men under my command to do their best to further the performance and image of this combat unit. I therefore expect you to do your duty by joining the Third Motor Company Rifle Team to demonstrate the combat readiness and excellence of this company to Air Force Headquarters," said Captain Holtzhoch, and waited for an affirmative reply from Markham.

But Markham was unmoved by Captain Holtzhoch's request, because he felt that Holtzhoch was using the Rifle Team for self-aggrandizement and promotion before his superiors at Headquarters and Markham was merely being used as a pawn. Furthermore, he didn't care for Holtzhoch's Hitleristic demeanor and treatment of the men in his company.

"I'm not interested in joining your Rifle Team, Sir. If you don't mind, Sir, due to the time constraint that we have in submitting the morning report to Headquarters, I must get back to my desk and retype the report."

Annoyed at Markham's rejection and unable to pursue the matter further at this time, Captain Holtzhoch dismissed him with the silent promise that he would make his life so miserable that he would have no choice but to yield to his demands.

As Markham was retyping the morning report, Captain Holtzhoch conferred with Sergeant Tidwell in his office.

"Sarge. I want you to conduct an inspection of the barracks where Markham resides and see to it that he gets enough demerits to warrant his restriction to the base, and keep up the pressure so that the restriction becomes indefinite. He'll soon get the message and comply with my demands," said Holtzhoch with a smug face.

"That should do it, Sir. The scuttlebutt is that he's got a girlfriend in London from his previous assignment and he's dying to see her. Restriction to the base is just the ticket," said Sergeant Tidwell with a smile.

"You know Sergeant, if Markham can put all ten shots in the bulls-eye with an ordinary carbine whose sights have not been adjusted like he did on maneuvers, think what he could do with a precision rifle with calibrated sights. That man's got Olympic potential, I tell you, and he's wasting it on a goddamn typewriter. Well, I ain't gonna let it happen," said Captain Holtzhoch with a determined look that spelled trouble for Sergeant Tidwell if he didn't deliver the goods.

"So go get him Sarge, and good luck," said Captain Holtzhoch confidently.

That Thursday morning at 10 AM sharp, an inspection of the barracks consisting of a two-story brick building was held by Master Sergeant Tidwell, assisted by Staff Sergeant Picket. Each airman stood at parade rest in front of his bunk with two per room. As the two Sergeants entered the room occupied by Markham, whose roommate Jake Bronski was absent that day because he was on temporary duty at Burtonwood to deliver fuel, Sergeant Tidwell called Markham who was standing at parade rest, to attention.

Markham was attired in his dress blue uniform with eyes fixed straight ahead. Sergeant Tidwell, wearing white gloves, stood directly in front of him while Sergeant Picket, also wearing white gloves, looked around the room, touching various areas for evidence of dust or dirt.

"What's that rope doing on your shoulder Airman Markham?" yelled Sergeant Tidwell, who then picked off a thin thread from Markham's left shoulder and held it in front of his face for him to observe.

"Answer me Markham, what was this rope doing on your shoulder?"

"Looks like a piece of thread to me Sergeant," answered Markham, rather amused.

"That will cost you five demerits, Airman Markham," said Sergeant Tidwell.

"Well, looka here," said Sergeant Picket, pointing to an inch long piece of the broom used to sweep the room.

"First a rope and now we've got a log on the floor of your room. Tell me Markham, were you always such a slob? Huh! Well, we've got no room for slobs in this outfit. That's going to cost you another five demerits," said Sergeant Tidwell, looking very pleased.

Sergeant Picket walked over to Markham's bed and with his steel tape measure determined that the cuff of the top blanket turned over with the top sheet which should have measured exactly six inches in width, only measured 5 and 15/16th of an inch. Picket grabbed the top sheet and blanket and tore it off the bed.

"Sergeant Tidwell, this airman needs some additional training on making a proper military bed. His bed cuff was short of the six inch requirement," said Sergeant Picket with self-satisfaction. "And his room has not been properly dusted as evidenced by the dirt on my white gloves which now have to be cleaned."

"When's the last time you cleaned this room, Markham?" asked Sergeant Tidwell.

"Last night and this morning."

"Make up your mind. Was it last night or this morning?" asked Sergeant Tidwell impatiently.

"I cleaned the room last night and finished up this morning."

"I guess you'll have all weekend to clean up this mess of a room, now that you have accumulated a total of eighteen demerits, what with the rope, the log, the bed cover and the dirty room. Since two demerits warrants one day's restriction, you'll be confined to the base for at least nine weekends. Now that should give you plenty of time to get your room in order, Airman Markham," said Sergeant Tidwell, satisfied that he had accomplished Captain Holtzhoch's mission. Without saying another word, Sergeant Tidwell followed by Sergeant Picket left Markham's room to inspect the next room.

Markham knew that their mission was to break his spirit so that he would submit to Captain Holtzhoch's desire for him to join the rifle team. However, this chicken-shit inspection made him more determined than ever to resist their harassment.

That same evening, Markham's roommate Jake Bronski returned from his fuel truck delivery run and found Markham lying on his bunk with both hands behind his head looking at the ceiling in deep thought.

"Hey, man. What's happening?" said Jake, wondering about Markham's apparent depressed state.

"They inspected the barracks this morning and managed to give me 18 demerits which means that I won't be able to leave the base for at least 9 weekends," answered Markham in a monotone voice.

"Jesus, you're kidding me. What the hell happened?" said Jake in amazement.

"They were looking for the slightest infraction that would justify their restricting me to the base. It was an obvious way to pressure me into joining the Rifle Team," said Markham.

"Who did the inspection?"

"Sergeant Tidwell and his assistant Sergeant Picket. They both wore white gloves and touched everything in sight, expecting to leave without them being soiled. I wonder if anyone else in the barracks got any demerits?" said Markham as an afterthought.

"I'll bet no one else did. Hell, I knew they'd do something like this to get you to see things their way. So what are you going to do, Jim? Nine weeks is a long time and you know they'll keep up the pressure until you cave in," said Jake with obvious empathy for his roommate.

"I'm never going to give in to them, Jake. No way. But I've got to find a way to get to London to see Sylvia or else I'll lose her, if I haven't already," said Markham, who felt that his situation was desperate.

"The whole base is surrounded by a high link fence with razor sharp wire at the top which makes it virtually impossible to climb over. On top of that, they have the canine patrol unit with attack dogs guarding the perimeter against intruders. The only way to get in and out of Sealand is through the main gate and you need a pass for that," said Jake to Markham's chagrin.

"Yeah! I know, Jake. I've been thinking about that. When are you going on your next trip?"

"As a matter of fact, I'm leaving tomorrow for South Ruislip to deliver commissary goods and returning Sunday night. Then I get two days compensatory time off," answered Jake.

"Who's going with you as shotgun?"

"Lenny. You know…Lenny Boswick, the last room down the hall. He's good company on those long trips," answered Jake.

"South Ruislip is on the outskirts of London, isn't it?" asked Markham.

"Yeah, it is. I know what you're thinking, Jim. You could hide in the truck as we drive off-base and we could drop you off at the nearest subway station in London and pick you up at the same subway entrance on our return to Sealand Sunday night. There's enough room in back of the tractor cab to hide two men," said Jake, "and I know we can trust Lenny."

"I couldn't ask you to take that risk, Jake. If you got caught driving me off-base in a government vehicle knowing I had no pass, you could get court-martialed."

"I know you'd never squeal on me if you got caught and if we play it smart, there's no way they'll ever catch us. Besides, that egotistical Holtzhoch restricted me to the base for two weeks when I first got assigned to this outfit because I failed to salute him. He just stood there in front of the Orderly Room with a swagger stick, watching everyone salute him as they walked by him. I was walking on the other side of the street and he yelled at me to salute him, would you believe it? According to regulations, I don't have to salute an officer who is on the other side of the street, so I kept on walking and he yelled at me to cross the street and stand before him at attention and give him a proper salute, which I did. Next thing you know, my pass was pulled for two weeks. So you see, I don't mind helping you, Jim, and besides, I'm sure you'd do the same for me," said Jake.

"We'll have to plan for every contingency. There's always an outside chance that they'll search the trailer, but not the tractor cab. That is…on the way out. But should they be looking for me during the weekend and not find me, they'll assume I broke restriction and they'll have people stationed at the main gate and at the barracks, too. They might put two and two together and figure out that you drove a tractor-trailer to London and, being my roommate, could have given me a lift, so they'll thoroughly search your truck when you return from London through the main gate," said Markham, concerned about Jake's safety.

"Even after you get back on base, they might have someone stationed at the barracks Sunday night waiting for you to appear in civilian clothes, which would indicate that you were in town and broke restriction," said Jake.

"Can you get a hold of a bolt cutter from the motor pool and a bayonet?" asked Markham.

"Yeah! Sure, why?"

"Well, as we approach the main gate, if I see anything suspicious, I'm going to leave the truck and make my way around the perimeter fence for a way to get in without being seen," said Markham. "I can't put you at risk, Jake. I'll put a pair of fatigues, field jacket, cap and brogans inside a bag which I'll take with me and hide in back of the truck cabin and when I return on base, I'll change into my fatigues before approaching the barracks, leaving my civilian clothes in the same bag with the bolt cutter and bayonet which I'll hide somewhere near the barracks and retrieve later when the coast is clear," said Markham.

"Sounds like a good plan...but why the bayonet?" remarked Jake, smiling.

"If I have to cut through the perimeter fence to get on base, there's always the possibility that I might encounter one of the attack dogs, so I'll need that bayonet to defend myself. I hate the idea of hurting one of those dogs and I'm going to do my best to avoid them."

"Hurt them, hell! What about them hurting you? Man, they have vicious Dobermans and German Shepherds that go for your throat. I'll tell you what. I have a Bowie hunting knife which I brought from home that I take with me when I drive those tractor-trailers, take that instead of a bayonet, you'll have a better grip and a better chance," said Jake.

"Thanks, Jake. I owe you a big one," replied Markham, his spirits lifted.

That Friday at lunch time, Markham took one of the pepper shakers from the table in the Mess Hall which he inserted in his field jacket pocket. He learned from either a movie or book that he could throw off his scent from pursuing dogs by spraying pepper behind him. Jake had managed to delay his departure until shortly after 4 PM by faking routine maintenance on his tractor-trailer. Markham was counting on everyone in the Orderly Room leaving early as they usually do on Fridays, so that he could get an early start.

A few minutes past 4 PM, he called the Motor Pool and informed Jake that he would be ready in 15 minutes. Markham left the barracks dressed in his fatigues and carrying a large AWOL bag containing his civilian clothes and shoes, so as not to alert anyone of his intentions to leave the base. He walked towards the motor pool, then turned right at a predetermined side street with warehouses on both sides that would offer him cover as he awaited for Jake and Lenny, who within a couple of minutes appeared driving a military tractor pulling a large trailer filled to capacity with goods for the base exchange at South Ruislip. Lenny opened the passenger side of the tractor and descended to let Markham climb aboard and lie down in the cabin behind the two seats for the driver and co-driver. The back of the cabin was used for one of the drivers to sleep if necessary and also for storage of personal items during the trip.

"Well, my man," said Jake. "Here we go. Keep your fingers crossed."

As they arrived at the main gate, the Military Policeman on duty checked Jake's orders, then waved him on through the gate.

"I hope it's that easy coming back," said Jake.

"Yeah! Me too," said Lenny, "but somehow I don't think it's going to be that easy."

The trip lasted four hours and upon arrival in London, Markham, who had changed into his civilian clothes and placed his military clothing inside the bag provided by Jake containing the bolt cutter and his hunting knife, was let out at an Underground Station not far from Tottenham where Sylvia resided with her mother and sister. Markham carried a small AWOL bag containing toilet articles and a change of underwear and a few packs of Camel cigarettes. He hailed a taxi to Sylvia's residence and upon arrival noticed that the lights were on and it was now 8:35 PM. Sylvia's sister Joan answered the door and expressed surprise at seeing Markham standing there with AWOL bag in hand.

"Hi! Joan. Is Sylvia home?" he asked anxiously.

Joan stared at Markham with a look of puzzlement and undecidedness that worried Markham. "Yes, she's in. Come on in, Jim," said Joan, who then went to fetch Sylvia from the next room. Sylvia appeared nervous as she entered the small living room wearing her favorite turquoise evening dress.

"I haven't heard from you in so long that I didn't think you were ever going to see me again," said Sylvia.

"But I did write you a letter explaining my circumstances, Sylvia."

"Yes, but that was some time ago. I have a commitment tonight with some friends, Jim."

"Well, that's alright, I can come with you to see your friends."

"One of those friends is my date for tonight," replied Sylvia apologetically.

"Can't you break it? I came all the way from Sealand to see you. This was my earliest opportunity," said Markham pleadingly.

"No, I can't break it. I'm sorry Jim, but I have to leave now or I'll be late," said Sylvia as she put on her coat, grabbed her purse and walked towards the door. Markham escorted her out of the apartment and they walked towards the Underground Station.

"Can I accompany you to the Underground Station at least?"

"Of course," she said feeling somewhat guilty.

"Where are you meeting your friends?"

"On the exit platform at Piccadilly Circus," she said nervously, hoping that Markham would not accompany her that far where her friends and especially her date would see her with him.

"I'm going to Piccadilly Circus too, but don't worry Sylvia, when we get there I'll blend in with the crowd," he said in an attempt to reassure her that he would not embarrass her.

As they both stood holding the vertical pole inside the crowded subway train, Markham felt his heart swell with love and agony over the impending loss of the only woman he had ever adored.

"I love you Sylvia, doesn't that mean anything to you?" he whispered to her, and she looked up at him with the biggest blue eyes he'd ever seen, but remained silent as she observed the tears welling up in his eyes which Markham attempted to control by not blinking and looking away.

The train stopped at the Piccadilly station and Sylvia said goodbye as she exited the train, then walked directly towards a group of three young English women and four American Servicemen, whom she quickly joined without looking back once at Markham. He kept looking at her through his teary eyes as he walked past them in the crowd of people exiting the station. He walked down the main street of Piccadilly Circus in a daze without any notice of a prostitute calling out to him from a doorway as he walked past her.

The image of her beautiful face and wide blue eyes staring at him in total silence as he whispered his love to her lingered in his agonized mind throughout the evening no matter how many drinks of Scotch he drank, first at the Great Bear Pub, then at the Queens' Pub and finally at the Mazurka Club where Peppie the Club owner who had always liked Markham as the all-American male, sensed that he was attempting to drown his sorrows. As the singer Elaine started to approach Markham, Peppie waved her away protectively, feeling that he needed to be alone to sort out his troubles whatever they may be.

Markham felt like a time bomb ready to explode and while his mind was steadily being affected by his consumption of alcohol, his body seemed to absorb it without much visible effect. His frustration at being angry at the woman he loved without hope could have driven a man of lesser character to the depths of despair, but Markham's survival instincts would only allow his state of depression a limited stay. Markham saw the Club lights flicker which indicated that closing time was near and no more drinks were going to be served. He got his trench coat which Peppie held for him to put on and wished him goodnight.

Markham descended the stairs of the Mazurka Club to the street below and entered one of the foggiest nights of the year. The fog was so thick that taxis were being guided by pedestrians walking in front of them. However, for a big city like London, few people were out on the street. Some people hugged the buildings while others walked along the sidewalk curb to guide them to their destinations. Markham walked in the middle of the sidewalk guided by the street lights which put out a soft glow in the gray darkness of the night, with some vague idea where his hotel was located as the alcohol was finally taking its toll. Strolling in the fog of the night, he felt as if he had been excluded from the world and a great sense of loneliness came over him that made him desperate for human contact. Markham suddenly heard the sound of heels on the pavement coming towards him, then the vague figure of a woman approaching him through the fog. As she got closer, Markham noticed she was wearing a raincoat and a floppy hat which did not hide her radiant face that stared at him invitingly as she raised her head to look at him. Her impish smile and alluring demeanor intrigued his curiosity, but not enough to venture a salutation.

"Hello," she said to Markham as she came abreast of him and slowed her walk, never taking her eyes off of him.

"Hello," replied Markham with his head turned towards her.

"It must be fate meeting like this in the fog," she said mysteriously.

"Right now I'm hoping you're the guardian angel I've been praying for," replied Markham in a solemn voice that conveyed a man in desperate need for love. The beauty of her face was only exceeded by the softness of her voice and there was a magnetism about her that Markham had never felt before.

"You come with me," she said, "and I'll guard you the rest of the night." As he turned to walk in her direction, she put her left arm inside his right arm and identified herself.

"I'm Lillian Roberts," she said, "and you're American aren't you?"

"Yes and my name is James Markham."

"I am so delighted to meet you on this very special night," she said enthusiastically.

"Me too. It's been a very rough day, in fact, it's been a very rough year," said Markham pensively.

Lillian squeezed Markham's arm gently with empathy and they walked the rest of the way in contemplative silence to the small inn where she had rented a room for the night. Her room on the second floor was chilly, so Markham put a shilling into the small gas fireplace that produced heat and a warm glow to that portion of the room immediately adjacent to the double bed. There was also a dresser with mirror and a closet. The bathroom was located down the hall. Lillian took off her raincoat and gave it to him to hang in the closet along with his own raincoat. She stood with her back to the gas lit fireplace staring at Markham with anticipation and he didn't disappoint her as he walked up to her and embraced her with the passion of a man who had sunk to the depths of despair and now was about to reach the heights of ecstasy.

Lillian removed his tie, then his jacket and shirt, but Markham continued undressing himself while she took off her blouse, skirt, stockings, brassiere and panties. She stood in the nude in front of the fireplace waiting for Markham who had now taken off all of his clothes and stood there astonished at her extraordinarily curvaceous body all the while hidden under her non-revealing raincoat. She was so ravishing that he didn't know where to touch her first and so they fell onto the bed in each other's arms in complete abandon and neither seemed to tire as they reached climax after climax from the various sexual position, some of which offered Markham a view of the contours of her curvaceous body with her firm and perfectly shaped breasts and his long and thick penis sliding in and out of her vagina with her beautifully rounded buttocks begging to be squeezed by Markham's powerfully tender hands. After more than two hours of passionate love making, Markham went to the bathroom and upon his return found that Lillian had left the room, so he kneeled in front of the fireplace to gather warmth. Lillian returned with a tray containing a plate with two eggs, toast and a cup of tea.

"I knew you'd be hungry darling, so I went downstairs into the kitchen and cooked you an early breakfast," she said with her seductive smile.

"How'd you manage that at this hour?" asked Markham.

"Hmm..I've been here before and I know my way around," replied Lillian with a knowing smile.

Markham savored the breakfast with total delight and afterwards kneeled in front of the fireplace while Lillian lay in bed watching him. She reached out with her left hand towards him.

"Come back to bed, darling," she said smiling.

"Oh! God, I need a rest," he said, thinking that he'd been making love for more than two hours and she wanted more. *She must think I'm Superman.* But it pleased him that she still wanted him to make love to her. After much imploring, Markham yielded to her reaching hand and climbed back into bed for more love-making until they both fell asleep in each other's arms.

Markham awaked that morning at 11AM and to his chagrin, found Lillian gone and a note from her rested on the dresser besides him. The note was short, but encouragingly inviting.

"My darling James," she wrote. "I had to catch a train back home early this morning, but I didn't want to wake you as you were sound asleep. Here's my address where you can write me. Please do. Love, Lillian."

Markham placed the note in his pocket with the intentions of writing to her immediately upon return to Sealand. However, he wished she had delayed her return home one more day as he wanted desperately to get to know her so much more. It was Saturday and Markham wanted to return to Sealand that very day, but could not on account of his dependence on Jake and Lenny to drive him back to the base Sunday evening. He didn't dare chance a visit to the Douglas House for an American meal for fear that someone would recognize him and report his presence to his unit at Sealand Air Base. He decided to spend the rest of the weekend with his friends at the Les Enfants Terrible Café in the French Quarter of London, which was an unlikely stopover for American Servicemen.

Late that Saturday afternoon, Captain Holtzhoch telephoned Sergeant Tidwell from his quarters.

"Sergeant Tidwell. I think that now's the time to call the Chief of Security to inform him of the anonymous call we received to the effect that someone is going to attempt to penetrate our perimeter security at area number three sometime Sunday night. That should cause them to double their canine patrol. Now, can we depend on Airman Boswick to steer Markham away from the main gate?" asked Captain Holtzhoch.

"I think so, Sir. Boswick wants to marry that British girl in the worst way and he knows he needs your written permission before he can wed her, and he also needs that promotion you promised him in order to support her. Yes Sir, he can't afford to screw this up," said Sergeant Tidwell reassuringly.

"Apply the stick and the carrot. It works every time," replied Captain Holtzhoch. "Call the Chief of Security now to give them ample time to schedule the additional canine patrols, and I'll see you and Sergeant Picket in the Orderly Room tomorrow at 1900 sharp."

"Yes sir," replied Sergeant Tidwell, pleased that he was part of a plan that would undoubtedly result in the demise of Airman Markham, whose attributes and confidence he secretly envied, but also despised because of his own feelings of inadequacy.

That Saturday night, Markham sat sipping a glass of red wine at a table near the small platform where volunteer entertainers played their preferred musical instruments to the mostly French student crowd at the Café Les Enfants Terrible. Victor Vincente was singing French songs while accompanying himself on his classical guitar as his girlfriend Roxanne Beaulieu sat at Markham's table.

"Tell me Jacques. Why do you not have a French girlfriend?" asked Roxanne.

"Oh! I don't know. I guess it's because I don't come to London and the French Quarter often enough."

"You should come more often. You need a nice French girlfriend and I have just the girl for you. Her name is Suzanne and she will be here later," said Roxanne excitedly.

"That's very nice of you Roxanne, but I have to tell you that I'm returning to Sealand Air Base tomorrow night and I don't know when I'll be able to visit London again."

"Oh! You poor man. I feel so sorry for you. Never mind. Suzanne will cheer you up."

Victor left the entertainment platform to allow another student to play slow jazz on his saxophone to the accompaniment of a pianist.

"Cherie. I told Jacques that Suzanne is coming later. Don't you think she would be just right for him?" she asked Victor.

"She could be Roxanne's sister. You'll like her I'm sure," said Victor, smiling at Jacques. Markham didn't show any enthusiasm at the prospect of meeting her, primarily due to the fact that he was enamored with Lillian and his restriction to the base could be forever.

Victor was glad that Roxanne had arranged a meeting between Markham and Suzanne, because Suzanne had her own rented room, thus could put Markham up for the night, therefore providing Victor privacy with Roxanne. By the same token, Markham didn't want a repeat performance of that night when he had to listen to Roxanne's romantic declarations to her sleeping Victor; hence he was already prepared to sleep somewhere else, either at a bed and breakfast inn or the Turkish Bath.

It was about 10 PM when Suzanne arrived at the Café and she immediately joined Roxanne and Victor, and introduced Markham to her. Suzanne had the same blonde, fair skinned coloring as Roxanne, but the resemblance stopped there. She had green eyes and her hair was swept straight back into a pony tail. She wore tennis sneakers, jeans and a striped short-sleeved blue and white shirt that accentuated a curvaceous figure on her five foot six inch small bone frame. Markham couldn't deny her beauty and he found her vivacious personality most uplifting and appropriate for the Café environment. However, with all that said and done, he longed to be with Lillian and as the evening ended, he excused himself with the utmost politeness and regret, then began the long, lonely walk in the night fog to the nearest bed and breakfast inn that had a vacancy.

That Sunday morning, Markham had a late breakfast at Mary's Bed and Breakfast Inn in Covent Garden consisting of two eggs with sliced fried tomatoes, link sausage and toast, which he washed down with two cups of tea au lait. He had much time to kill, but didn't want to hang around Piccadilly Circus which was the gathering place for American Servicemen prior to returning to their respective stations, due to his mistrust of their discretion. Markham, carrying his faithful AWOL bag containing his toilet articles and change of underwear, walked to the Charing Cross Station where he checked his bag. The weather was bleak with the promise of fog, which coincided with his mood that he was going to change by attending the afternoon dance at the Lyceum in the Strand.

Jazz and the London bop, which was the smooth equivalent of the American rock-and-roll, was the rage of London and Sunday afternoons drew all of the 'spivs' in their fancy dark suits to show their self-choreographed moves to impress the other dancers and the audience gathered in the balconies, as well as the main dance floor and long bar. For quite a while, Markham sat at a table near the dance floor with a Coke to watch the various dancers with their latest moves and listen to the Ted Heath Orchestra with its superb male and female vocalists. After an hour, the bandstand started to revolve with the orchestra still playing and one could hear the George Sharing Quintet located on the other half of the bandstand picking up the tune while the orchestra disappeared. The Quintet came into full view finishing the tune started by the orchestra, and now dancers began their favorite London bop dancing, which demanded speed and endurance on the part of the female partners who had to make so many more turns than their leading men. But it was marvelous to watch and Markham tried to remember those moves he found unusual so that he would include them in his own repertoire.

He did not notice any other American Servicemen at the dance in the Lyceum that Sunday afternoon and wasn't really surprised as most of them would be suffering from their debauchery's hangover. Markham finally danced with a young brunette who was really serious about dancing and didn't care for small talk, even with the strangeness of an American. After a couple of dances with Markham, she nonchalantly walked back to join her girlfriend with seeming indifference. Markham sensed that she was simply playing the role of being 'cool,' but deep down inside, she really was interested and wanted to be pursued. However, Markham wasn't in the mood for the hunt and merely wanted to pass the time away until his departure for Sealand Air Base.

He went upstairs in the balcony where he sat watching and listening to the quintet and then the return of the orchestra until 6 PM, knowing that he had to be at the exit to the underground station at South Ruislip at 7:30 PM to meet Jake and Lenny for his departure to Sealand. At exactly 7:35 PM, there appeared out of the encroaching smog the grayish tractor-trailer with Jake behind the wheel. Lenny jumped out to allow Markham to climb into the back of the tractor cab with his AWOL bag and off they went north to Sealand Air Base.

As they rode north towards the Midlands, the smog got significantly lighter, but as they approached Chester, the town nearest Sealand Air Base a few kilometers south of Liverpool, the smog got dangerously dense, which made navigation even with the tractor's fog lights perilous. However, they were now only three miles from Sealand Air Base and they had surprisingly made the journey in only four hours. Lenny suggested that Jake not approach the main gate until they first assessed the situation with his binoculars for any signs of suspicious activity. However, the smog compelled Jake to drive closer to the main gate than he felt comfortable, so he extinguished his headlights and with only his fog lights to guide him, slowly approached within a hundred yards of the main gate.

"You see anything, Lenny?" said Jake anxiously.

"Some APs. Wait a minute. I think that's Sergeant Tidwell. Yeah! That's him; that's Sergeant Tidwell talking to one of the APs at the main gate," said Lenny excitedly.

"Are you sure?" said Markham.

"Yeah! I'm sure. The main gate is lit up like a Christmas tree. They even got the flood lights on," replied Lenny.

"Here, give me the binoculars," said Jake, taking them from Lenny.

"Yeah! That's him alright, Jim. Shit. They must've figured it out that you'd be coming back tonight and they're probably waiting for us to drive in with you," said Jake disappointed.

"I kind of expected that. Thanks for the ride, guys. It's time for me to exit. Lenny, let me out," said Markham, now dressed in his military fatigues.

"Alright Jim. You got the bolt cutters and my knife, right?" asked Jake.

"Yeah! It's in the bag. I'm leaving my civilian clothes in the other bag hidden in the back of the cab, Jake. It's like pea soup out there. Take care you guys," said Markham as he stepped out of the tractor cab carrying his AWOL bag.

"Watch yourself, Jim," said Jake, worried that he might get caught or worse.

Markham quickly disappeared into the thick smog with only the occasional lamppost to guide him on the narrow side road circling the northeast perimeter fence surrounding the air base, even though there was a full moon.

As Jake approached the main gate with all of his head and fog lights beating the thick smog, he noticed that Sergeant Tidwell was now standing in the Air Police Guard shack observing several Air Policemen performing a close inspection of the tractor-trailer without finding anyone other than Jake and Lenny to Sergeant Tidwell's delight.

Now, thought Sergeant Tidwell, *let the dogs do their trained duty.*

Markham could just hear the sound of his own feet as he marched along the narrow paved road by the perimeter fence that he could only see when directly under one of the occasional lampposts scattered along the perimeter fence as a security measure.

As Markham approached the third lamppost, he noticed a gate that was locked with a heavy chain and padlock. *That must be gate number three,* he thought. As he started to approach the gate, he suddenly heard the growl of a dog nearby followed by a whistle, then the growl of another dog coming from a slightly different direction. *The canine patrol, no doubt,* he thought. The smog was so thick that visibility could not have been more than six feet. Markham decided to avoid this area and continue towards the next gate and as he distanced himself from gate number three, the night became eerily silent and dark. Finally, Markham arrived at gate number four with the lamppost immediately adjacent to the locked gate. He approached it with catlike quietness, searching for the slightest sound that would alert him of the presence of a security guard or dog, neither of whom he feared nor wanted to harm. Markham took the bolt cutter and the Bowie knife out of the AWOL bag, sticking the long, thick steel knife inside his belt. He carefully applied the jaws of the bolt cutter to one of the chain links that held the gate closed and pressed both handles of the bolt cutter together in one mighty effort that severed the link, but not enough to pass the other link through the thin opening. He thought he heard a noise nearby and immediately stepped back into the darkness of the night smog and waited impatiently.

When the coast appeared to be clear, Markham quickly returned to the gate and placed the jaws of the bolt cutter on the shank of the padlock. With one powerful exertion, he cut the lock open and with the gentleness of a maiden removed the chain from the broken padlock and quietly swung the gate open just enough for him to slip through, then closed the gate and reinstated the chain with the broken padlock for appearances. With AWOL bag containing the bolt cutter in his left hand, Markham started to walk gingerly on the wet grass between occasional trees away from the fence towards one of the access roads inside the base that would lead him to his barracks. All of a sudden, he heard movement directly ahead of him, but couldn't see anyone due to the thick smog. Then he heard the bark and the growl of a large attack dog that he couldn't see, but felt was near enough to smell him. Markham immediately took out his knife, which he held tightly in his right hand with his arm fully extended, pointing the knife like a spear directly in front of him. He stood silently in a slight crouch waiting and listening for any sign of the direction of the imminent attack. Abruptly he heard the steady growl of the beast directly in front of him. Then through the night smog appeared the head with gnashing teeth followed by the body of a large Doberman attack dog traveling in mid-air directly into the path of his Bowie knife, which penetrated deeply into its chest with the dog's inertia, forcing Markham to turn clockwise holding the knife in the dog's chest until the dog fell to the ground on its side. The big Doberman was still alive, body twitching, when Markham stabbed him behind the shoulder through the heart to end his suffering. He then ran the blade of the knife through the wet grass to wipe the blood off, and heard the high pitch whistle from the dog's handler calling to it. Markham quickly removed the pepper shaker from his field jacket pocket and spread pepper behind him to prevent other dogs from picking up his scent and trail, as he speedily walked away from the dead canine. He couldn't run for fear of hitting a tree, but he managed with his quick walking pace to distance himself from the howling of several dogs now at the scene of the attack. He eventually found a paved road which he knew would lead him to the barracks, but he first had to bury the evidence of his involvement in the death of the Doberman, hence he marked the nearby tree with two deep slash marks on its bark then plunged the knife deep into the ground, stomping on its handle until only the tip of it could be seen when the grass blades were parted.

Now carrying only his AWOL bag containing the bolt cutter, he came upon an empty World War II barracks where he hid his AWOL bag behind the wooden stairs to the entranceway. In the darkness of the night, even when under the occasional street light, Markham couldn't definitely determine whether there were any signs of blood on his right hand or sleeve and couldn't take a chance of going directly to the barracks where one of the Sergeants or even Captain Holtzhoch might be waiting for his potential arrival, hence he decided to go to the Mess Hall for midnight breakfast and while there, clean up in its latrine.

However, his march towards the Mess Hall was interrupted by the approach of a couple of jeeps and a weapons carrier heading towards gate number four. Markham quickly ducked to the side of a building with the smog completely hiding him from view as he watched the head and fog lights of the vehicles pass him by. Finally, he arrived at the Mess Hall and in the lit hallway that led to the Mess Hall I.D. checker, he noticed that his right hand did have some blood on it and his right sleeve also contained splotches of blood. He quickly left the front of the Mess Hall and went around the back entrance which led him into the kitchen area where the pots and pans and metal trays were washed. His experience as a Mess Hall Kitchen Police came in handy and the KPss working there paid no attention to him as he was dressed in fatigues like them. Markham went to the rest room and cleaned up the blood, then left through the back and entered the Mess Hall by way of the front entrance where he signed his name to the Mess Hall register as testimony that he was on base at that particular time and date.

Markham was famished and ate three eggs, bacon, ham, French toast, and a container of milk. While eating, he saw Jake come into the Mess Hall and after signing in, he walked directly over to Markham with a smile on his face.

"I see you made it, OK!" said Jake. "But man, you got some people really pissed off at you. Both Sergeant Tidwell and Sergeant Picket were at the barracks and the Captain came over looking for you. They asked me if I'd seen you and I told them no since I just got in from a trip. The Captain took Lenny aside for a private talk. I hope he doesn't spill the beans," said Jake.

"Listen Jake, I buried your hunting knife where I'll be able to retrieve it later. As for the bolt cutter, that's also in a safe place. But I might as well tell you, I had to kill one of the attack dogs. It was either him or me, Jake. I feel bad about killing that dog, but I had no choice, believe me," said Markham apologetically.

"You're kidding. Man, you're something else," said Jake, looking at Markham in amazement.

"Good thing you loaned me your hunting knife, otherwise I might not be here eating breakfast with you," replied Markham with a grin.

"You know, Jake. I've been thinking about this and it occurred to me that the Security Police don't know who penetrated their perimeter and they've got to assume the worst, that it might be a saboteur, so they're going to be relentless in their pursuit until they find him."

"Yeah! Well, good luck," said Jake sarcastically. "I'm going to get some chow while it's still hot. Wait for me and we'll walk back together Jim."

"Don't worry, I might go back for seconds," replied Markham hungrily.

Having replenished his strength, Markham, accompanied by Jake approached the entrance to their barracks and were immediately met by Master Sergeant Tidwell and Staff Sergeant Picket standing inside the hallway to the entrance door.

"Where've you been Markham?" asked Sergeant Tidwell in a commanding voice.

"Midnight chow, Sarge," answered Markham, who kept on walking towards the stairs followed by Jake.

Jake added, "And I was with him, Sarge."

There was no point in ordering Markham to be in his office at 0800 hours, inasmuch as he worked there as the Morning Report Clerk, hence he would be there anyway. Frustrated, Sergeant Tidwell retorted, "I'll see you first thing in the morning, Airman Markham."

Markham didn't reply, but continued walking up the stairs to his room.

In the meantime, a jeep pulled up in front of the Provost Marshall's office and a young Lieutenant accompanied by a Sergeant from the Security Police jumped out and quickly stepped into the Marshall's office.

"I'm Lieutenant Chambers. Is Colonel Price in?" he asked anxiously.

"He's in his office, Sir. I'll tell him you're here, Sir," said the Buck Sergeant sitting at the reception desk. "You can go on in, Sir. The Colonel will see you."

The Lieutenant and his Sergeant walked in and both saluted Lt. Colonel Price.

"I want to report that an intruder cut the padlock to gate number four and stabbed one of our patrol dogs to death and got away to parts unknown on base, Sir," said the Lieutenant.

"When did this happen, Lieutenant?" asked Colonel Price.

"About an hour and half ago, Sir. We've searched the entire area without success. It was pretty foggy, but we put on every available dog into the search, Sir."

"I'd better notify the OSI. Sabotage is within their jurisdiction," replied the Colonel, who grabbed the phone and asked the operator for the OSI Agent on Duty at Sealand.

"Frank. This is Colonel Price. I guess your boss is home asleep like he should be," said the Colonel. "Listen, Frank. Within the last 90 minutes an intruder penetrated our perimeter at gate number four and killed a patrol dog in the process and it's expected that he's still on base. I presume you'll want to assume investigative jurisdiction?"

"That's correct Colonel. I'll be at your office within the next 15 minutes," answered Agent Frank Connely.

The Colonel hung up the phone and looked at Lieutenant Chambers thoughtfully. "Agent Connely is coming over," said the Colonel.

"The strange thing is, Colonel, that we got a call Saturday near dinnertime from First Sergeant Tidwell to the effect that they got an anonymous telephone call that someone was going to break through the perimeter fence somewhere in area three. When I asked him if the anonymous caller was a man or a woman of English or American origin, he said it was an English male. But how would anyone know the area or gate number unless they themselves were somewhat involved? And they certainly wouldn't call to warn us unless it was just a prank call, but it turned out to be real, but at gate number four which is quite a ways from gate three. Nevertheless, Sir, we figured that the intruder may have initially planned to enter at gate number three and got scared off by the noise the dogs were making."

"Another thing, Sir. Sergeant Tidwell was at the main gate that night waiting for the arrival of one of his tractor-trailers which according to the manifest, was returning from London, and he had the Security Police at the gate thoroughly search both the tractor and the trailer for an intruder, which seemed strange to me as he had never done this before to any of his trucks," said the Lieutenant. "Shortly thereafter, an intruder breaks into gate four and stabs one of our patrol dogs to death."

"Sounds like they were expecting someone, most likely one of their own who saw them first and went for the perimeter fence. Is that what you think, Lieutenant?"

"That's exactly what I think, Sir," replied Lieutenant Chambers.

"Here comes our resident OSI agent," the Colonel said looking out of his office window. "You tell him exactly what you told me and let's see what his response is."

There was a knock on the Colonel's door. "Come on in, Frank," said the Colonel loudly so that he could hear him.

Frank walked in dressed in his usual dark-striped suit covered by a trench coat with his hat in his hand. He was introduced by the Colonel to Lieutenant Chambers, then they both sat facing the Colonel sitting behind his large wooden desk. Lieutenant Chambers related the same information he had given to the Colonel to Frank.

"Well, I'll start by interviewing the two truck drivers," said Agent Connely.

"How'd you know there were two drivers?" asked the Lieutenant.

"Because regulations require two drivers in all military vehicles in the U.K., due to the fact that the steering wheel is located on the left side and in England we have to drive on the left side of the road, which means that the driver can't see if the coast is clear to pass, so he has to rely on his 'shotgun' driver."

"Well said, Frank. How long have you been in-country Lieutenant?" asked the Colonel.

"Ten days, Sir," he replied with embarrassment at not having known of the Air Force regulation.

"Well, that explains it," replied the Colonel.

"Do you have the names of the drivers?" said Frank, posing the question to both the Colonel and the Lieutenant.

"No, but we'll find out quick enough," replied the Colonel, who picked up the phone and directed his Sergeant to get the information from the Main Gate's In and Out Log. A few minutes later the Colonel's phone rang and he wrote down two names.

"The senior driver's name is Jake Bronski and the driver riding shotgun was Lenny Boswick, both from the Third Motor Company," said Colonel Price, handing the slip with the names to Agent Connely.

"I think I'll find out a little more about these two men before I select which one to interview first, but it'll be done by the end of the day tomorrow, Colonel," said Agent Connely.

"Would you take me to the scene of the break-in Lieutenant? I need to process the crime scene and pick up any available physical evidence," said Agent Connely.

"Most certainly, Mr. Connely," replied Lieutenant Chambers, anxious to work with an OSI Agent for the first time in his career.

OSI Agent Connely, driving a gray Ford sedan, property of the government, followed the jeep driven slowly through the smog and darkness of the night by the Sergeant with Lieutenant Chambers sitting beside him, to gate number four where they had to park their vehicles in a gravel patch alongside the narrow gravel road about 75 yards from the gate. Agent Connely took out a flashlight from the trunk of his vehicle and then pulled out a large tool box by its top handle, which he set down near the Lieutenant's jeep.

Lieutenant Chambers and his Sergeant, each carrying powerful electric lanterns, led the way to the area where the dog had been slain, but had since been removed.

"This is where the security dog was found laying on his side," said Lieutenant Chambers.

"Were you able to determine how the dog was killed?" asked Agent Connely.

"Yes. His handler, Airman First Class Fielding, who happens to be an avid hunter, examined his dog and determined that he'd been stabbed twice, first through the chest and then through the heart, apparently as a coup-de-grace. He said that when he found his dog, there was the distinct smell of pepper and when two other security dogs arrived on the scene with their handlers, the dogs became confused by the pepper and lost the intruder's trail. This guy knew what he was doing," said the Lieutenant.

"What kind of a dog was it, Lieutenant?" asked Agent Connely.

"A Doberman. He was Airman Fielding's pride and joy. He was really devastated by the loss of his dog."

"Did you search the area for the weapon or knife?" asked Agent Connely.

"Yes, we did the best we could under these weather conditions and found nothing, not even footprints which would be difficult to make in this tall grass."

"Let me see the gate where he broke in," said Agent Connely.

The three men walked to the metal frame and wire gate built into the perimeter fence topped with barbed wire containing razor edges.

"We didn't touch anything, figuring that whoever investigated would want to check for fingerprints," said Lieutenant Chambers.

"Well, it's too wet for prints to be lifted, but we can identify the bolt cutter from the markings left on the metal that was cut," said Agent Connely.

Agent Connely observed that the chain which held the gate closed was wrapped around the gate post and held in place with a large padlock. But when he tried to examine the padlock, it came loose and one end of the chain fell off.

"He cut the shank of the padlock, but was clever enough to put the padlock on again to hide the fact that the gate had been penetrated," said Agent Connely, then took a plastic bag from his toolbox and placed the padlock in the bag to which he attached a label. He took the two-foot chain and placed it in another bag and carried the lot to his vehicle where he turned on the ceiling light so that he could write on the labels of each bag the contents and where he had found the items, with the time, date and his initials to preserve chain of custody. "No sense in trying to take pictures of the crime scene with this smog. I'll have to come back tomorrow during daylight for that, then we can do a more thorough search," said Agent Connely.

The following afternoon in the OSI office, Agent Connely reported the status of his case of sabotage to the Agent-in-Charge, Mr. Paul Savage. There were only two agents assigned to Sealand Air Base, and the Agent-in-Charge was a commissioned officer while the agent under him was a non-commissioned officer between the ranks of Staff Sergeant to Senior Master Sergeant. For job effectiveness and security reasons, their ranks were classified and protected by the wearing of civilian clothes and as such, they were addressed as Mister Savage and Mister Connely. However, in such a small detachment of only two agents who depended on each other, their ranks, known only to each other, and their headquarters seldom interfered with the camaraderie that develops in a first name basis.

"So far, Paul, we have an alleged telephone call to the First Sergeant Tidwell of the Third Motor Company on Saturday about a possible penetration of the base in the area of gate number three to take place on Sunday evening, then Sergeant Tidwell alerts the Security Police of the anonymous phone call and suggests doubling the canine patrol. Then on Sunday Evening the First Sergeant stations himself at the Main Gate and causes the Security Police to thoroughly search a Third Motor tractor-trailer returning from a trip to London for an unauthorized personnel entry, which turned up nothing. About half an hour later, the padlock at Gate number four is cut and a patrol dog attacks the intruder, who fatally stabs the dog and escapes inside the base, leaving no trace of the weapon or the bolt cutter. I found out that the primary driver of the tractor-trailer rooms with Airman James Markham who has been on base restrictions for nine weeks. The scuttlebutt around the barracks is that Markham got restricted to the base for undeserved inspection demerits, because he has steadfastly refused to join the Company Commander's Rifle Team. Furthermore, Markham was not seen by anyone during the entire weekend leading some to believe that he jumped restriction to see his girlfriend in London which was the tractor-trailer's destination."

"I get the picture. It looks like James Markham is our intruder. What's the Company Commander's name?" asked Agent Savage.

"Captain Eric Holtzhoch."

"Wait a minute. A complaint was filed against him by one of his airman who attempted suicide and since it was determined that it wasn't a bonafide attempt, I turned it over to the Inspector General for them to investigate. I should have a copy of the complaint in the file, Frank. Let me pull it out." Paul walked over to the filing cabinet and after a quick search pulled out a large brown envelope from which he retrieved a statement executed by Airman Mark Peddler of the Third Motor Company.

"The statement is from a Mark Peddler and he alleges that Captain Holtzhoch constantly made fun of his small stature, ridiculed his administrative skills and found fault in everything he did to the point that he felt he was having a nervous breakdown which drove him to attempt suicide. He suspected that it was because he was a Jew and Captain Holtzhoch made no secret of his admiration for the German military and in particular Field Marshal Rommel whose picture he apparently prominently displayed in his office," said Agent Savage.

"It looks like Airman Markham is another one of his victims," replied Agent Connely. "I also found out that the shotgun driver Lenny Boswick is an Airman Third Class who is engaged to be married to an English girl. I talked to his roommate, who told me that he's been waiting for Captain Holtzhoch's permission to get married for three months and is getting impatient because normally such permission only takes about three weeks. Sounds like he's being held hostage by the Captain, but for what?" said Agent Connely.

"You know, Frank. I think he's the weak link in this whole affair and you should interview him first."

"I think you're right, Paul. I'll arrange to interview him without anyone's knowledge at Third Motor."

The next morning, Agent Connely arrived in his sedan at the Motor Pool where all of the Third Motor vehicles were parked, some of which were being repaired or undergoing routine maintenance. Connely asked one of the Sergeants on duty if someone could look at his sedan which was running rough and could possibly use a tune-up inasmuch as it was a government vehicle. He was directed to the service and maintenance station about 100 yards northwest of the main office and upon arrival was met by a burly dark-haired mechanic dressed in fatigues who seemed overwhelmed with the number of vehicles awaiting service.

"What can I do for you, Sir?" asked the mechanic, curious about this man dressed in a civilian suit, driving an American sedan in a military motor pool.

"I'm Special Agent Connely of the OSI. My government sedan is running real rough and I think it might need a tune-up. Is it possible you could give it a quick look to see what the problem is?"

"Yes, Sir. I can do that," he said, and walked over to the sedan and popped open the hood of the car. "Would you start the engine for me, Sir?" he asked, and Connely got inside his sedan and started the engine.

"By the way, is Lenny Boswick around here anywhere? A friend asked me to look him up," said Connely.

"Lenny? Oh! Yeah! He's working on his tractor in that hanger over there," said the mechanic.

"If you don't need me right now, I'm going to pop over there and say hello to Lenny," said Connely.

"It'll take me a good half hour to check out your engine, Sir."

"OK! I'll be back shortly."

Connely walked over to the hangar and an airman dressed in fatigues was leaning over the exposed engine of a tractor.

"Are you Lenny Boswick?" asked Connely.

Boswick turned around and when he saw Connely, a worried look came over his face. "Yes, that's me," he said.

"I wonder if I could have a word with you?" asked Connely, trying not to alarm Boswick.

Boswick dropped his wrench, wiped his hands on a dirty rag and in a slow, inquisitive manner walked over to where Connely was standing with briefcase in hand.

Connely pulled out his credentials from his left shirt pocket consisting of a wallet-sized, black leather case folded in half, the top portion containing a photo of Agent Connely with his name and that of the OSI and its commanding General, with the badge clipped to the bottom half of the leather case. "I'm Special Agent Connely of the Office of Special Investigations, United States Air Force," said Connely, showing Boswick his badge with credentials. "I want to reassure you, Lenny. Can I call you Lenny?" asked Connely.

"Sure," answered Boswick.

"I want to reassure you, Lenny, that no one but you and me knows that I'm talking to you. Even the Sergeant in Maintenance only knows that I'm looking you up for an old friend. Now I must tell you that we're investigating the killing of a security dog on patrol last Sunday night at Gate number four by an intruder. But we know that this intruder is an airman from Third Motor and furthermore, we believe that he's the *victim* of unlawful coercion and punishment by an officer and that you have also been a victim of that same individual. Didn't you submit an application to marry an English girl over three months ago? Shouldn't that have been approved long ago?"

Boswick looked at Connely briefly, then down at the ground with a lump in his throat. Connely could see that Boswick was struggling with his emotions and needed the right prodding to motivate him to reveal the truth about the whole incident.

"I'm not out to hurt you, Lenny. I understand your predicament and you're a victim too, but you must tell me everything to set the record straight. That whatever your participation in this incident, it was the result of duress, you had no choice in the matter, anyone in your position would have complied the same as you did," said Connely in a soft tone of voice.

"Am I going to get into trouble with Captain Holtzhoch?" asked Boswick with a worried look.

"No, you're not. I can assure you of that," said Connely in an authoritative voice that convinced Boswick that this OSI Agent had far more power and authority than the Captain.

"I might as well tell you everything. Where do I start?" asked Boswick, seeming relieved at his decision to cooperate.

"At the beginning, Lenny...at the beginning," replied Connely.

That afternoon Agent Connely briefed his boss Agent Savage of his progress on the case.

"As you can see, Paul, from Boswick's statement, Captain Holtzhoch coerced Airman Boswick to discourage Airman Markham from reentering the base by truck, thus forcing him to seek entry through gate three or four of the perimeter fence. With the information I acquired from Boswick, I was able to convince Sergeant Picket of the futility of withholding any information and he executed a statement which I have here for your review, wherein he relates Sergeant Tidwell's role and the fact that he and Captain Holtzhoch knew that Markham would be facing a certain encounter with the patrol dogs, due to the fact that the Captain had Sergeant Tidwell alert the Security Police to a false telephone warning of an impending intrusion at gate number three with the recommendation that they double their canine patrol. They were sending Markham to his death for his refusal to join the Captain's Rifle Team, can you believe that?" said Connely to Savage.

"Yeah! I can believe it. Markham dared challenge the will of an egocentric fascist commander at his own peril and a lesser man would have most likely perished," replied Savage. "Did you interview Sergeant Tidwell yet?"

"No I haven't, but he's next and then I'm saving Captain Holtzhoch for last."

"With all of those statements from Boswick, Picket, and Tidwell, you'll have plenty of ammunition to go after the Captain," said Agent Savage.

"Yeah, but I'll bet he'll clam up and ask for a lawyer," said Connely with conviction.

"Probably right after you read him his rights under Article 31," said Savage.

"It won't matter, 'cause we have enough testimony for the Judge Advocate to initiate a General Court-Martial," said Connely.

"I would add to your report the testimony and complaint filed by Airman Peddler, which shows a pattern of abuse of the men under his command," said Agent Savage.

"I was planning on it, Paul. I should have this case wrapped up by tomorrow at the latest."

"Listen, Frank. Don't interview the Captain in his office. Have him report to us at this office where we have home court advantage, and I will assist you in the interrogation."

Agent Connely smiled at his boss for his cunning strategy and went back out to find Sergeant Tidwell, the closest and last link to the Captain.

The following morning, Captain Holtzhoch received a telephone call from Special Agent Paul Savage to report to the OSI office on an official matter at 1300 hours. That would give Agents Savage and Connely at least four hours of uninterrupted interview time in which to pry a confession from him that would close the case.

Captain Holtzhoch arrived at the OSI office promptly at 1300 hours in his dress blue uniform with three rows of decorations pinned to his left breast. He announced himself to the secretary, who told him to have a seat in the waiting room while she informed Captain Savage of his arrival, but Captain Holtzhoch chose to stand facing the window to observe the outside traffic while his mind raced for an answer to the gnawing question as to the reason for this urgent interview.

"You can go in now, Captain," said the secretary, pointing to the door to her left.

"Thank you," he said curtly, then opened the door and entered a large room that contained several four-drawer gray filing cabinets and a desk with a small side table holding a Royal mechanical typewriter. Agent Connely walked from behind his desk to greet Captain Holtzhoch and as he approached the Captain, Agent Savage's private office door opened and Savage started to walk towards them.

Pulling out his credentials, Agent Connely identified himself and waited for Agent Savage who had decided to lead this interview to introduce himself to the Captain.

"I'm Special Agent Paul Savage," he said, showing his credentials to the Captain, "and I believe you've met Agent Connely."

"Yes, I have. I hope this isn't going to take long, because I have a company to run."

"No, it shouldn't take too long, Captain. Let's all go into that room over there where we can talk privately," said Agent Savage, leading the way to the interrogation room, rigged with a covert audio recording system. The room contained one small table with a chair on each side of it and another chair situated in the corner of the room behind the chair to be occupied by the Captain. The Captain's chair had rubber tips on all four legs that prevented its occupant from sliding his chair back when the interrogator wished to move closer to him by sliding the small table to the side to invade his space, a practice not often used, but readily available when the need arose.

As Captain Holtzhoch sat on the rubber-tipped chair facing the small table, Agent Connely, carrying a clipboard with writing pad sat in the far corner of the room behind Holtzhoch. Agent Savage sat at the table facing Holtzhoch and pulling out a small card, read its contents out loud to Captain Holtzhoch.

"I am Special Agent Paul Savage. I am investigating the alleged offense of conspiracy to commit aggravated assault of which you are suspected. I advise you that under the provisions of Article 31, UCMJ, you have the right to remain silent, that is, to say nothing at all. Anything you do say may be used as evidence against you in a trial by court-martial or in other judicial or administrative proceedings. I advise you also that you have the right to consult with a lawyer, if you desire, and to have a lawyer of your own choosing at your own expense, or, if you wish, the Air Force will appoint a military lawyer for you free of charge. You may request a lawyer at any time during this interview and if you decide to answer questions without a lawyer present, you may stop the questioning at any time. Do you understand your rights, Captain Holtzhoch?"

"Yes I do," replied Holtzhoch, "and I do wish to consult with legal counsel."

"Very well. This interview is over and you may now leave," replied Agent Savage, rather disappointed in Holtzhoch's decision to seek legal counsel. At this point, Captain Holtzhoch got up from his chair and exited the interrogation room and the OSI office, no doubt on his way to the Staff Judge Advocate's office for legal representation.

A week later at Commanding General Wolfe's office, sat two field grade officers gathered in front of the General, who sat behind his large, empty desk except for his name plate. General Wolfe was a tall, lean man in his late forties with a full head of dark hair graying on the sides near the temple. His immaculate blue Air Force uniform bore four rows of ribbons depicting his extensive war record as a Command pilot. The two officers facing him were his adjutant Major Robert Seawood; a short, stocky man with a receding blonde hair line, and the Staff Judge Advocate Colonel David Silverstein, a man of medium height and build sporting a dark mustache and horn-rimmed glasses.

"Bob, do you have Captain Holtzhoch's resignation ready for his signature?" asked General Wolfe.

"Yes, Sir," said Major Seawood, removing the one-page document from his briefcase and placing it on the General's desk.

The General picked up the document, read it quickly then placed it face down on his desk to his right. "For the good of the service I'm going to ask for his resignation rather than go through the time and expense of a court-martial. If he's smart, he'll resign and collect his severance pay which will amount to several thousand dollars, otherwise a court-martial will mean a felony conviction, confinement at Leavenworth Federal Prison, and forfeiture of all pay and allowances."

"A man with his superego will undoubtedly resign rather than suffer the humiliation of a court-martial and its consequences," said Colonel Silverstein.

"I think we are all in agreement, but should he choose the court-martial route, Dave, then I presume you have in your possession the necessary papers to serve him?" said the General questioningly.

"Yes, Sir. I have the Accusatory Instrument ready to be served," replied Colonel Silverstein.

A female voice called for the General on the intercom. "Sir, Captain Holtzhoch is here," said the General's secretary.

"Send him on in," replied the General as the two field grade officers stood up and moved to the right of the General's desk.

Captain Holtzhoch marched in, his back straight as a ramrod, without his garrison hat which he left hanging on the coat rack in the secretary's office. He walked directly to the front of the General's desk and raised his right hand to his forehead in a salute which he held until the General returned it with an obvious lack of fervor and respect. The General stood up to his full six feet and four inch frame and looking down at Captain Holtzhoch, gave him the dressing down of his life.

"Captain Holtzhoch. It is my most unpleasant duty to advise you that as a result of an exhaustive investigation by the Office of Special Investigations, you are being charged with violation of Article 81 of the Uniform Code of Military Justice, to wit: Conspiracy to commit aggravated assault on a subordinate; Article 107: Making a false official statement; Article 108: Suffering the destruction of military property; Article 93: Cruelty and maltreatment of subordinates, and Article 133: Conduct unbecoming an officer and a gentleman. I know that your appointed legal counsel was provided with a copy of the OSI report of investigation and the pending charges. Has your legal counsel provided you with that information?" asked the General.

"Yes, Sir, he has. If I may, Sir, there's apparently been a gross misunderstanding, Sir," replied Captain Holtzhoch.

"I assure you Captain, there's been no misunderstanding. The evidence is abundantly clear that you have violated every principle by which a good officer conducts himself. You are a disgrace to the uniform you're wearing and the sooner you are out of that uniform, the better it will be for the men of the United States Air Force," said the General, then turned over the resignation document and laid it directly in front of Captain Holtzhoch.

"Captain Holtzhoch. I'm going to give you a chance to resign your commission effective immediately in lieu of a General Court-Martial for the good of the service. I'm sure that you appreciate the consequences of a General Court-Martial," said the General sternly.

Captain Holtzhoch's face blanched as he blurted out his answer, "Sir, could I have some time to think this over?"

"You have exactly ten seconds to make up your mind, Captain," answered the General crisply.

"Under the circumstances Sir, I wish to resign my commission."

"Then sign it and Colonel Silverstein will witness it," replied the General.

With a trembling hand, Captain Holtzhoch signed the document then took a step back and stood at attention.

"You're dismissed Mister Holtzhoch," said the General, not returning Holtzhoch's salute. The Captain did an about face and walked out of the General's office in disgrace.

"Who've you got in mind to replace him at the Third Motor Company?" asked the General to Major Seawood.

"Captain John O'Reilly, Sir. He arrived today from Burtonwood in anticipation of Holtzhoch's resignation or criminal charges. The first thing he was told to do was disband the Rifle Team and rescind all restrictions," replied Major Seawood.

"That's a good start. But what do we do with that Airman who broke restriction and killed that security dog, what's his name?" asked the General to either officer.

"That was Airman James Markham, Sir. I recommend that no action be taken against him due to the fact that he was the most abused by Holtzhoch and I might add, offered the most resistance which unfortunately for Airman Markham, drew Holtzhoch's anger which led to the conspiracy that resulted in the break-in at gate number four, leaving Airman Markham with no alternative but to defend himself against a charging attack dog that suddenly appeared through a thick fog," said Colonel Silverstein.

"I agree with Colonel Silverstein, Sir. This Airman displayed uncommon bravery and ingenuity in the face of severe adversity which certainly could have led to his death. It would be a shame to blemish that man's record. The Air Force can certainly use men like him, Sir," said Major Seawood.

"So would the Marines," said Colonel Silverstein.

"It would also not serve the cause of justice. So let's give that young man a clean slate and a new start. And I might add, Dave, send a letter to the OSI District in London complimenting the work of their two Agents here at Sealand," concluded the General.

"Now what about those two Sergeants that conspired with Holtzhoch? Have you made a decision, Dave, regarding the disposition of their case?" asked the General.

"Yes, Sir. I recommend that Master Sergeant Tidwell be demoted to Staff Sergeant and Sergeant Picket be demoted from Staff Sergeant to Airman Second Class with no confinement for either of them," answered Colonel Silverstein.

"I guess you're offering them punishment under Article 15 of the UCMJ in lieu of a court-martial, then," said the General.

"That's correct, Sir. I believe that the punishment fits the crime and it permits them to re-establish their military careers," answered Colonel Silverstein. "However, I think it would be advisable to have these two men transferred to another unit where they are not known so that they can get a fresh start."

"I agree Dave. Well, gentlemen, if there is no other business, I've got an appointment with my dentist," said the General, then he added, "Job well done."

In the meantime, Jake had brought Markham a bag containing his civilian clothes that he had left in the back of the cab of Jake's tractor. Markham spread all of his clothes onto his bunk and looked through all of his trouser pockets and his coat jacket as well for that slip of paper containing Lillian Roberts' address.

"Jake, have you by any chance seen a slip of paper containing a name and address?" asked Markham nervously.

"No I haven't, Jim. I just took your clothes out of my duffel bag and placed them in that plastic bag that's on your bed. Why? Is something missing?"

"Yeah! An important piece of paper with the name and address of a girl I met in London. Man! I've got to find that piece of paper or else I'll never be able to see her again," replied Markham, obviously distressed over the loss.

"I can go back and look inside the tractor cab. Maybe it's there. I'll check it," said Jake, empathizing with Markham's concern.

"I tell you, Jake. I'm not having much luck at holding on to women."

Jake went to the motor pool and thoroughly searched the cabin of the tractor he had driven on that particular night and found no trace of the note. Markham took the news with apparent calmness, but internally he was devastated over the loss as he had been thinking about Lillian and his midnight encounter on an almost nightly basis. He decided to go back to London and find the bed-and-breakfast inn where they had stayed in the hope that she had registered her name and address. In that night's excitement, he never paid attention to the address on the note, merely placed it in his coat pocket for subsequent retrieval, and he couldn't recall her ever mentioning the name of the town she lived in, as their focus was on the passion that consumed them until dawn when they fell asleep.

Markham returned to London the following weekend now that his restriction to the base had been lifted by the new company commander, and he retraced his steps that foggy night which had hampered his visibility to the extent that he wouldn't recognize the building even if it had a sign with the name of the inn on it. He checked several inns along the only routes he and Lillian could have taken that night without any success. Finally, he resigned himself to the fact that he would never see her again unless by a miracle of destiny she appeared in his life again, but he wasn't full of buoyant hope of that happening.

Markham got on the next train back to Sealand Air Base and stopped along the way in Liverpool at the Duck House Pub frequented mostly by American Servicemen and English girls seeking their company. It was there that he met another Airman named Mike Seagrave from Burtonwood Air Base located near Manchester. Mike was nearly Markham's height and had an athletic build and good looks that attracted women as evidenced by the two blonde girls teasing him at the bar next to where Markham was standing drinking a beer. Mike was gregarious, but not loud, and he believed in sharing the wealth by introducing himself to Markham in an attempt to make it a foursome. Markham had a pleasant evening, but with Lillian still in his thoughts he made no effort to gain the affections of the girl thrusted upon him by Mike.

Markham did run into Mike by accident on a number of occasions at the Duck House in Liverpool, at the Queens Pub and the Royal Dance Hall in Manchester. One late afternoon, Markham stood alone in the crowded Queens Pub in Manchester frequented mostly by American Servicemen, when a petite English girl started a conversation with Markham, who was quietly drinking his beer directly from the bottle, showing moderate interest in her discourse. She left his side for a few minutes then returned to ask Markham if he would not accompany her for a ride with her two girlfriends and two G.I.s, who had a car at their disposal. At first Markham declined, but after much persuasion, he agreed and they all left the pub and boarded an old black English four-door sedan. Markham sat crowded in the back seat with his female companion and one of her girlfriends who herself sat on one of the G.I.s' lap, while the other G.I. sat in the front as the driver with the third English girl at his side in the passenger seat. It was drizzling rain and Markham had been under the impression that they were driving to another pub, but as the ride progressed, the G.I. next to him in the back seat started making advances towards the English girl he had just met to the point that her protests became a frantic call for help as his intentions of fornication became quite clear. Markham told the driver to stop the car, but his request was ignored. Markham then jabbed him in the back with the tip of his hand to stop the car, but he still ignored him. Finally, Markham jabbed him hard and yelled at him to stop the car, which he did. All three girls immediately jumped out of the car followed by the G.I. in the back seat, leaving only Markham sitting in the back and the driver still seated in the front. He noticed that the aroused G.I. had walked around the car and was attempting to open the door to his side obviously to strike him, but Markham quickly locked the door and the G.I. walked around the other side of the car again at which time Markham unlocked the door and stepped out of the car, wearing his long black camel hair overcoat over his midnight-blue suit with white shirt and black tie.

The girls were running down the street to the bus stop, yelling for him to come with them, but Markham, while not looking for a fight, was not about to run away from one either. He stood there in the middle of the street in the drizzling rain waiting for the G.I. to attack him, when he noticed a little boy of about 10 years of age standing on the sidewalk watching the whole incident. Markham didn't feel that this was something for him to watch, so in a loud, commanding voice he told the boy to leave, but the boy just stood there frozen at the sight of a fight between two Americans.

The G.I. came at him yelling, "You son-of-a-bitch. You had to mess things up," and started throwing round-house punches that Markham easily blocked with his forearms. He could hear the girls in the background yelling for him to join them, but he couldn't leave while this man was fighting him. Then he realized that if he missed that bus, he would have no way to get back and he didn't even know what part of the city he was in, hence he would have to end this fight quickly and get to the bus stop. He threw a left jab to the G.I.'s face and a right punch to his chin, knocking him down. He then stepped over him and punched him on the nose, then stepped back to see where the other G.I. was situated and to his surprise, he was still sitting behind the wheel of the car. The G.I. got up, staggering a bit with blood running from his nose and challenged Markham again, but Markham felt he had been sufficiently punished and started to walk away while the G.I. yelled obscenities at him for quitting the fight. As he arrived at the bus stop, the girl who had accompanied him admonished Markham for fighting the G.I. The girl he had saved from being raped added further insult by stating, "You're bigger than he is. Why did you have to hit him?" The bus arrived and the three girls climbed aboard and sat in the lower deck.

Markham couldn't believe his ears and ascended the bus where he sat on the upper deck away from the three girls in total disgust. He promised himself that he would not talk to another female for the rest of the evening and returned to the Queens Pub where to his surprise, Mike was drinking a pint of Guinness stout, chatting with another serviceman at the end of the bar.

"Well look-a-here," said Mike, seeing Markham walking towards him. "You look like you've been out in the rain, Jim. Did you just get into town?"

"Hi, Mike. I got in this afternoon and accepted an unfortunate car ride with two G.I.s and three girls that turned into a fiasco, so I think I'm going to have a few drinks then go back to Sealand tonight."

Mike walked over and stood on the other side of Markham at the bar where they could talk in confidence. "Hey, man. What happened?" he asked Markham.

"Oh, nothing much. This one guy tried to molest one of the girls inside the car and I didn't want to be a witness to it, so I had them stop the car and the girls all ran out to the bus stop leaving me to contend with the disappointed G.I. who started a fight with me and I had to slug him before I left, and would you believe it, the girls chastised me for hitting him. I tell you Mike, I'll never figure those women out," said Markham, taking a slug from his beer bottle.

"You've been a busy man, Jim. Can't say I blame you for being sore at them."

"I've got some leave coming and I may just spend it in London," said Markham.

"Hey! I've got leave coming too. Would you mind if I joined you in London? We could have a hell of a time there. I certainly don't know the city like you do, but I hear the women are plentiful, beautiful and available," said Mike with a gleam in his eyes. To Mike, Markham was a man's man who deserved the attraction of quality women and by his association, he hoped to meet some of them.

"Well, there's a lot of action in that town and the possibilities are limitless," replied Markham.

"When were you planning on going?" asked Mike.

"A week from this coming Monday for five days in combination with the two weekends, so that

I'll be charged with five days leave. But in effect, I'll be in London for nine days if you count both weekends at each end of the leave," said Markham.

"That makes sense. Listen, I'll put in for a leave at the same time and we can meet in London. Where'll you be staying?"

"At the Aaland Hotel on Coram Street in Russell Square. It's very reasonably priced and within walking distance of Piccadilly Circus, if you like to walk. I'll be arriving late Friday evening. If I get there first, I'll ask them to save a room for you if you want," said Markham.

Mike wrote down the name and address of the hotel on the back of a matchbook.

"Yeah! If you don't mind. If I can't make it Friday, for sure I'll make it Saturday," replied Mike enthusiastically.

"Well, that's settled then. There's a train going back to Liverpool in about half an hour. I think I'll take it. See you in London Mike," he said as he shook his hand, then walked out of the pub for the train station. Right then a voluptuous brunette walked over to Mike from the other end of the bar with a glass of gin and tonic in one hand and a cigarette in the other.

"That Yank that just left a friend of yours?" she asked.

Mike looked her up and down and figured she might be one of the prostitutes that hang around the pubs on that strip of Manchester. "Yeah! He is. What about it?" replied Mike.

"Is he coming back?" she asked, taking a puff from her cigarette.

"No, he's gone for the night," replied Mike, turning his gaze towards the mirror behind the bar where he could see her reflection.

"That's too bad, 'cause I kind of liked his looks. I'd a gone with *him* for nothing," she said in a throaty voice.

"Lady," Mike said, using the term loosely, "you wouldn't get to first base with him. I guarantee it."

"Well bolex to you mate," she said angrily and walked back to her end of the bar, while Mike finished his drink and exited the pub.

The following Friday evening, Markham, dressed in his customary attire of dark midnight-blue suit, white shirt and slim black tie covered with his black camel hair overcoat and carrying his AWOL bag, arrived in London by train at Charing Cross Station where he was met by the usual bunch of black marketers seeking to purchase American cigarettes from arriving G.I.s who were easily recognized by their rich style of civilian dress, but Markham avoided them as he had just enough cigarettes to last for the duration of his leave. It was drizzling rain, so he decided to take a taxi to the Aaland Hotel and as he booked a room he learned that Mike had not yet arrived, so he informed the Hotelier to save a room for him. Mike, who was stationed at Burtonwood, was coming from Manchester, thus would be arriving from a different train and time.

Markham emptied the contents of his AWOL bag into a dresser drawer, then took off his coat, jacket, tie and shirt and went to the bathroom in the hallway to wash his face. As he was returning to his room, he heard the distinct rumbling of the London taxi's diesel engine and the closing of its door. Markham looked out the window and saw Mike paying the taxi driver then enter the hotel. He met Mike in the hallway and welcomed him to London.

Markham smoked a Camel unfiltered cigarette in Mike's room while Mike freshened up.

"Where do we go from here Jim?"

"Let's go to Piccadilly Circus and stop at Wimpy's for an English-style hamburger. It's quick, nourishing and I'm famished," said Markham.

"Good idea. Let's go. I'm starved," said Mike as he finished freshening up and putting on his shirt, tie, jacket and raincoat.

They hailed a taxi to Piccadilly Circus and stopped at Wimpy's where Markham ate two hamburgers and a Coke while Mike ate one hamburger and a cup of tea.

"Let's go to that new bar and grill around the corner on Old Bond Street. I forgot the name, but the last time I was in London, it had just opened and there's apparently a lot of action there," said Markham to Mike, who agreed. They took a leisurely walk to the bar, passing a multitude of people, many of them young women traveling in pairs looking to party with American Servicemen. But Jim and Mike paid no attention to them and walked into the Brass Rail as the neon sign displayed. The place was packed with mostly American Servicemen and lots of English women to keep them company.

"Let's get a drink at the bar," said Markham to Mike, and they found an opening at the far end of the bar where the two of them stood next to an empty stool. Mike was getting ready to sit on it, although Markham had noticed that there was a full glass of liquor on the bar directly in front of the stool indicating that it was probably taken, but Mike was quickly informed by the petite brunette sitting next to the empty stool that it was occupied by her girlfriend who had gone to the restroom. Mike engaged himself in conversation with her and quickly became enamored with her charming personality without realizing that he was now sitting on the empty stool, when suddenly a slim but well-developed short-haired blonde appeared and interrupted his conversation.

"Pardon me, but you're sitting on my stool, mate," she said to Mike.

"Oh! Michael, this is my girlfriend Maureen," said Jeanne, who had been talking to Mike.

Mike quickly got off the stool, begging her pardon while Markham looked on in amusement and curiosity at this elegant blonde young woman named Maureen.

"Let me introduce you to my good friend, Jim," said Mike first to Maureen, then Jeanne. Both women turned their attention to Markham, who moved forward and shook their hands and quietly continued listening to their chatter. He sized up Maureen, who stood at five feet six inches, weighing 115 pounds, with blue almond-shaped eyes that looked out of a pale face with classic Roman features, an ensemble that could easily have been used to model anything from clothes to facial make-up. But Markham was most impressed by her playful personality and unpretentious attitude. He liked her and she sent subtle signals that she found him attractive, too. But just as important to Markham was his observation that Mike appeared smitten with her friend Jeanne, so he decided that the four of them could have a wonderful time together investigating the night spots of London.

Maureen was a better dancer than her friend Jeanne and she certainly looked more elegant on the dance floor of the Lyceum, knowing just when to tilt her head or cock her leg as she spinned to fast music, posing for the audience she knew was watching her every move. Markham loved her ability to anticipate his every move and follow through with style and panache. But her pronounced cockney accent betrayed her poor education and humble status of hairdresser in the East End of London where she was born, not that it mattered to Markham, who loved her generous heart and buoyant personality. Mike and Jeanne seemed comfortable with each other and content in following Markham's and Maureen's lead in the selection of activities in the West End of London.

The foursome ended each night of activity at about one or two in the morning, getting up around 11 AM, at which time Maureen and Jeanne would leave Markham and Mike to go to work at the Beauty Shop in the East End. They would meet each weekday at 7:30 PM at the Brass Rail for another night out on the town in the West End Soho District, repeating the same ritual the next day until the weekend arrived.

While the girls were earning their living at the Beauty Shop, Markham and Mike spent their afternoons visiting the sights of London then having an affordable dinner at a nearby restaurant before meeting their two ladies at the Brass Rail for drinks and partying. But time flies when you're having fun and Sunday, the day of departure, came too soon for all of them. Markham definitely had to return to Sealand Air Base that dreary Sunday. However, Mike stated that he had taken three weeks leave of absence, hence he was going to stay with Jeanne until his money ran out, which made Jeanne ecstatically happy. Maureen became morose at the prospect of being without Markham after such a wonderful week in which she had never felt happier. She wondered when she would see him again, if ever, knowing the reputation of American Servicemen's motto of 'Love 'em and leave 'em.' But then she reassured herself that Jim Markham was different than other Americans and that he would return to her as soon as the military permitted him. With that thought in mind, she cheered up and put on her usual happy face so that Markham would have a pleasant and joyful memory of her until his return. The three of them went to Charing Cross Station to send Markham off. Markham waited until the very last minute to board the train and at that moment Maureen threw both arms around his neck and kissed him on the lips then stepping back while holding both of his hands in hers, she wished him safe passage.

"Darling, you won't forget me will you? You have my address. Please write me."

"I won't forget you, sweetheart. I'll be back soon, don't worry," said Markham tenderly. He shook hands with Mike and Jeanne then boarded the train, and as he stood on the train's steps facing them, he waved a tearful Maureen goodbye and went inside the train to find an empty seat for the long ride north.

Mike Seagrave walked out of the train station escorted by Jeanne and Maureen, each holding his arm for the pleasure of his security and memory of the past week.

"How long have you known Jim, Mike?" asked Maureen.

"Not long, maybe a couple of months. We're stationed at different bases," replied Mike.

"Has he got a girl up there at Sealand?" she asked Mike.

"Not that I know of. From what he told me, he was restricted to the base for quite a long time."

Maureen seemed reassured. "He's quite a man," she said musingly.

"Yes he is," replied Mike as they walked in thoughtful silence.

Monday morning, Markham reported to the Orderly Room for work and was immediately informed by the new commander Captain John O'Reilly that he had to report to the OSI office on an urgent matter.

"Do you know what this is about, Sir?" asked Markham.

"No I don't, but you'd better get over there right away as they are expecting you."

Markham, wearing his dress blue uniform, walked into the OSI office and observed three men in civilian clothes waiting anxiously for his arrival. Two of them were obviously American, but the third man, in his mid-fifties and smoking a pipe, was dressed in a tweed suit usually worn by Englishmen.

"Airman Markham. This is Mister Seagrave," said Special Agent Paul Savage, pointing to the tweed-suited Englishman. "Michael Seagrave's Father, who has been trying to locate his son whom I understand went to London with you?"

"I don't understand, Sir," replied Markham, puzzled by the revelation that Mike's Father was an Englishman apparently residing in England.

"Mike is not American as you can see from this photograph of him in a British Air Force uniform with his flight group," said Mr. Seagrave, showing the group photograph to Markham and pointing Mike out in the first row. "He's a professional English soccer player who's been offered a contract with Norwich and I must find him before the offer expires. So you see, I really would appreciate your help in finding him. It is very important."

Markham was nearly in shock at the disclosure. "But your son represented himself as an American serviceman stationed at Burtonwood Air Force Base, and he had a perfect American accent. He sure had me fooled. But I'll help you all I can, Sir."

"Is he staying at any particular hotel?" asked Agent Savage.

"Yes, at the Aaland Hotel on Coram Street in Russell Square, and he's been dating a girl named Jeanne. At night they hang around the Brass Rail, Sir," said Markham.

"Do you know Jeanne's last name?" asked Agent Savage.

"I don't know it, Sir. But I'm willing to go back to London and help you find him," said Markham, wanting to return to London.

"That won't be necessary. If you think of anything else that might help us find Michael, I'd appreciate it if you would contact us immediately," said Agent Savage.

"Yes Sir, I will, but that's all I know," replied Markham.

"That's all for now, Airman Markham. You can leave," said Agent Savage.

Markham shook Mr. Seagrave's hand, then left the OSI office, still bewildered by Mike's deceit. He'd heard of some Englishmen that posed as American Servicemen in order to mingle with them and enjoy their lifestyle and the women that it attracted. He couldn't blame Mike for wanting to pass for an American, and after all, imitation is a most flattering compliment. However, the deceit left him with a bad taste in his mouth which he found difficult to ignore. Back in his room at the barracks, Markham told his roommate Jake about the incident.

"Man, you can get into more trouble than anyone I've ever known. The OSI is going to have a thick file on you before you leave this country," said Jake jokingly.

"I wonder if I will ever hear from him again," said Markham pensively.

"I doubt it, Jim. He'll be too embarrassed," replied Jake.

"You're probably right. I know I would be."

"Man, he really had you fooled, huh?" said Jake.

"Yeah! He had an American accent and he wore American-style clothes," replied Markham.

Markham wondered what Jeanne would do if and when she found out that Mike was not an American. With his Father and the OSI looking for him, it's very probable that Jeanne and Maureen would learn his true identity and possibly they may also believe that Markham was also an Englishman posing as an American Serviceman. *Good God!* he thought, *how do I manage to get into such situations?*

Two weeks later, Markham received a letter from Mike Seagrave postmarked from Liverpool, England. In his letter, Mike apologized profusely for his deceit and offered to meet with Markham at the Duck House Pub in Liverpool on the forthcoming Saturday evening at 8 PM to further explain his actions and salvage his friendship. Markham decided to attend the meeting out of curiosity and also because he had developed a strong camaraderie that transcended nationality.

The bus to Liverpool was a bit late causing Markham to arrive at the Duck House a few minutes past eight o'clock. The pub was crowded with American Servicemen surrounded by at least as many English women. Markham spotted Mike standing at the bar with a bottle of beer in his hand and upon seeing Markham, raised his beer to acknowledge he'd seen him come in. Markham walked over and shook his free hand, looking into his eyes for some emotional sign that would reveal his thoughts, and noticed only subdued embarrassment and perhaps a plea for understanding from the tone of his voice.

"I'm really sorry, Jim, that you had to find out this way. I meant to tell you, but didn't know how and before you know it, you were gone, back to Sealand. I've always admired Americans and wanted to be just like them," explained Mike apologetically.

"I understand Mike. At first the shock of being deceived was kind of overwhelming, but after some deep thought I realized that you weren't trying to hurt anyone, you just wanted to associate with us Americans. What better compliment? You're still my friend Mike. So don't worry about it. Now tell me, how's Jeanne and Maureen?" asked Markham.

Mike looked at Markham with a worried look on his face that did not go unnoticed by Markham.

"What is it, Mike?" asked Markham.

"I hate to be the bearer of bad news Jim, but I guess it's confession time."

"What do you mean?"

"After you left London, I found out that Jeanne and Maureen were not hairdressers and they didn't work at any beauty shop. They were prostitutes who worked the Hyde Park and Soho district during the afternoons and played with us at night," said Mike with a look of disappointment.

Markham looked at Mike in disbelief. "How the hell could this have happened?How come neither one of us discovered it? I don't believe it. You have proof of that, Mike?"

"Yes, I sure do. It was three days after you left. I was walking along Hyde Park wanting to hear some of the speakers on their soap boxes when I noticed Maureen coming out of a luxurious hotel across the street holding the arm of a middle-aged man and getting into a cab with him. She should have been working that afternoon at the beauty shop. Later that evening, I confronted both Jeannie and Maureen with what I saw and they both admitted that they had been turning tricks for the past two years to support themselves and save enough money to open their own beauty shop. They really are hairdressers, but they haven't worked at it lately."

"Jesus, Mike. Any more good news? Let's have it all while I can still swallow. Hell! I need a drink," said Markham with a look of disgust. "Hey! Bartender, give me a Scotch and soda."

"If it'll make you feel any better Jim, Maureen is genuinely in love with you. That night of the revelation, she went into a gin and tonic binge and cried most of the evening over the thought of losing you because of her illicit profession."

"That doesn't change my opinion that she is a kind-hearted person, but the thought of her having sex with other men leaves me cold and certainly eliminates her as a serious contender for matrimony."

Mike laughed at Markham's oratory. "I feel the same way about Jeanne and she knows it."

"So you're going to play professional soccer at Norwich, huh?" said Markham, attempting to change the conversation.

"Yeah! I signed the contract and I'll be going to Norwich in a couple of weeks to start training. Here's my home address where I can be reached. Let's keep in touch, Jim."

"Thanks," said Markham as he placed the small piece of paper with Mike's address on it in his wallet so that he would not lose it. "Yes, let's drink to lasting friendship," and he lifted his glass of Scotch to his lips.

As the months went by without incident, Markham settled into the routine and doldrums of military duty at Sealand Air Base, until the warmth of the summer sun awakened his desire for the pursuit of life's rewards for the young at heart. This was the time when the French Quarter of London came alive with visiting French students and the West End teemed with sightseeing tourists and people seeking entertainment. After a long absence, Markham made plans to return to London, alone, with no intentions of resuming his past relationship with Maureen for whom he now had only feelings of sorrow for the lifestyle she had chosen. The year was 1954, when the classic, award-winning film 'On the Waterfront' starring Marlon Brando made its debut, and the war between the communist/nationalist guerrillas of the Viet Minh and the French Colonial Army entered its terminal phase in the longest and most violent battle of the French Expeditionary Corps in the Orient at Dien Bien Phu, Vietnam.

Markham had gotten off work that Friday a bit later than anticipated which caused him to board a late train to London. Upon arrival in the Big L at about midnight, Markham checked his AWOL bag at the Charing Cross Station figuring that it was too late to book a room at the few inexpensive hotels he knew would either have no vacancies or else would be closed for the night. Hence he planned on eventually finding a clean bed and shower at the all-night Turkish bath, after visiting long lost friends at the New Yorker.

Upon entering the New Yorker Club, Markham was met by Ralph, one of the Club owners.

"Well, James, we thought you'd gone back to the States, seeing you hadn't visited us for so long. I'm sure the girls will be glad to see you," said Ralph meaning Cherie, Dawn and Kim.

"The Air Force reassigned me to Sealand near Liverpool which is a long haul from here," replied Markham.

"My partner Marty's from Liverpool. He ain't here now, but he could tell you the ins and outs of that place."

"I'll bet," replied Markham, examining the crowd of people in the Club for Cherie and her girlfriends, when Kim spotted Markham and signaled Cherie that he was in the Club entranceway. Cherie, who had been dancing with a male customer, excused herself and quickly walked up to Markham and kissed him on both cheeks in the French custom she had learned from Dawn's Parisian boyfriend Jean-Paul Beauchamp and some of his Parisian friends who hung out with him at the New Yorker as a change of pace from the French Quarter's Café Les Enfants Terrible.

"James, where have you been? We missed you, and I most of all." Cherie looked up at Ralph then grabbed Markham's hand and guided him to a small table at the other end of the Club not far from the small bandstand where a trio of musicians were playing to a male vocalist imitation of Perry Como.

"You know Dawn and Kim," she said to Markham.

"Of course, how can I forget your two closest friends?" replied Markham, smiling.

"Hi, James. Fancy seeing you here after such a long absence," said Kim.

"Yes. Too long," replied Markham, who noticed that Dawn was not in her usual happy mood. Throughout the evening, Markham remarked to Cherie that Dawn appeared to be depressed as if in mourning.

"That's right. You wouldn't have known since you've been away. Remember the young French student from Paris you met last summer? His name was Jean-Paul Beauchamp and was madly in love with Dawn, who was planning on marrying him?"

"Oh! Yes, I remember. He was a nice guy and Dawn was crazy about him," replied Markham.

"When he returned to France last summer, he was drafted into the French Army and sent to Vietnam," said Cherie.

"Man, that's a bummer," replied Markham.

"Well last week she learned that Jean-Paul was killed in action in Dien Bien Phu and it was a horrible massacre. She's been mourning ever since. That's why she's not her cheerful self, Jim."

"I don't suppose that now's the time to offer my condolences," said Markham.

"No, now is not the proper time, Jim. I'm trying to call you Jim instead of James, 'cause I think you like that better."

"No, I like the way you say my name no matter which one you use, Cherie," said Markham in a soft tone of voice.

They danced most of the night until closing time when the band broke up and the lead singer who had adapted the stage name of Perry Galanto came up to Kim's and Dawn's table in an attempt to make out by inviting himself and the members of the band to their flat for a party in which they would bring some Scotch and beer. After much coercion, the girls agreed and of course Markham was invited to join them by Cherie and her two girlfriends, especially since Cherie knew that Markham had no place to stay the night other than the Turkish bath. Louie the piano player was still toying with the piano keys when Dawn stepped up to the microphone and began singing the song she and Jean-Paul had adopted as their love song, and Louie quickly began playing the piano to accompany her. Some of the indoor Club lights had already been extinguished and most of the customers had already left leaving only the working girls, the remaining three members of the band and Ralph the owner, who all stood still as Dawn gave her heart's rendition of 'Charmaine.'

"I can't forget, that night we met, how bright were stars above

That precious mem'ry lingers yet, when you declared your love..."

Markham was certain that everyone in the Club felt the agonizing pain conveyed in that song by Dawn's soft, tender voice that sometimes cracked with the emotion of his memory. At that moment, Markham would have given her anything to ease her pain, but alas he was completely helpless. When Dawn stepped off the stage, she was met by Kim and Cherie who hugged her and left the Club together with Markham and the four band members piling into two taxis to the girls' apartment in the Islington section of metropolitan London. The apartment located on the first elevated floor was small with one bedroom, a living room, small kitchen and bathroom, but it was home to the three girls who all slept in the same bedroom: two in a double bed and one in a single bed. One had to climb several cement steps of the stoop that led from the sidewalk to the double-door front entrance to the apartments on the first floor. The party quickly got started with two bottles of Scotch, which were largely consumed by the four band members, as none of the girls were heavy drinkers. Markham sensed some uneasiness at the aggressive behavior of Perry the vocalist and Terry the drummer towards the three girls who were gracefully attempting to avoid their sexual advances and requests to stay with them at the apartment for the rest of the night. Finally, Kim announced that the party was over and the band members would have to leave. However, there was no mention of Markham having to vacate the premises which was quickly picked up by Perry who insisted that if Markham was staying the night, then he should be allowed to stay the night also.

"If the Yank can stay, then why can't I? He's no better than I am," said Perry in a loud voice to Kim within earshot of Markham and the other two girls.

"He's got no place to go," explained Kim to Perry. "You've got your own apartment, Perry," said Kim.

"I don't see why he should stay here," he said, looking directly at Markham with angry, envious eyes, "and I can't."

Markham looked at Perry with disdain and wondered how far Perry would push his demands and whether Kim and her two girlfriends would be able to handle him and the other band members. Markham didn't want to get involved in a fight with these Englishmen, but he would not tolerate any abuse of these women either, and hoped that the matter would be settled without any altercation. Cherie and Dawn joined Kim in gently but firmly pushing Perry towards the entrance door where the other three men were gathered. Markham stood a distance behind ready to intercede on the girls' behalf, but they managed to get all of them out the door, which Kim promptly locked with a deep sigh of relief.

"That Perry is so angry for having you here. He's really jealous of you, Jim," said Kim, and Cherie agreed.

"When men are liquored up, some of them become very aggressive," said Markham.

"He doesn't like Americans in general. Yet he earns a living imitating Perry Como. How's that for a paradox?" said Cherie.

"I hope you understand, James, that the apartment is small and we only have one bedroom and we're not accustomed to putting up guests for the night, but you're the welcomed exception," said Cherie, who guided him into the bedroom where Kim and Dawn had already changed into their pajamas and were getting into the double bed.

Dawn laid down a thick comforter on the floor broadside to the double and single beds. She then placed a pillow at one end of the comforter and placed a blanket over the comforter.

"There James. I'm sure you've had rougher surfaces to sleep on as a soldier. I'm so sorry we don't have another bed for you," said Cherie.

"That's quite alright, Cherie. This is more than adequate. I'm just thankful to you all for your kind hospitality," replied Markham.

Cherie went into the bathroom and returned wearing a light nightgown and promptly got into the single bed. Markham had taken off his suit, tie and shirt, and wearing only his jockey shorts and T-shirt, slipped under the blanket lying flat on his back with his head on the small pillow where he quickly fell asleep within a few minutes due to the long day of work, travel, dancing, partying and the early morning hour of retirement. About ten minutes passed, then Cherie's whispering voice directed at Markham could be heard only by Kim and Dawn, as Markham's hearing was now asleep with the rest of his body.

"James…James…you don't have to sleep on the floor. You can sleep in my bed.James…are you awake? Come to bed with me, darling," said Cherie in a whisper that grew louder, until Kim interrupted her.

"I think he's passed out," said Kim to Cherie. Cherie had been looking forward to this union and now didn't know when she would ever get another opportunity to have Markham make love to her. Cherie climbed out of her bed and guided by the morning light coming through the bedroom window, kneeled next to Markham's upper body looking at his haunting face which she caressed with her hand, first on his forehead, his left cheek, then she kissed him lightly on the other cheek at which time Markham moved his right leg and sighed, then resumed his deep breathing again. Cherie went back to bed wondering what it would be like to have sex with James Markham.

It was eleven before anyone awakened. Dawn got up and went into the kitchen to turn on the tea kettle. Kim then woke up and called out to Cherie, who responded by ducking her head under her pillow. Markham was still asleep on his back, dead to the world. Eventually, Cherie and Kim got up and joined Dawn in the kitchen where they cooked eggs and toast to go with their cups of tea. Cherie went into the bedroom and awakened Markham with the announcement that breakfast was ready. Markham rubbed his left eye and looked at Cherie, now attired in a gypsy dress and leather sandals, and asked her the time."It's now eleven o'clock sleepy head. We've got eggs and toast and tea awaiting you in the kitchen. I'm sure you're famished," she said with a disarming smile.

"Wow! What service. I must be at the Ritz," replied Markham.

"Indeed you are Sir James," said Cherie.

Markham sensed that Cherie's affection for him went beyond mere friendship and he knew that his feelings for her would never be anything other than platonic, hence he felt compelled to limit his visits to discourage the growth of her interest in him, thus preventing a broken heart. After the late breakfast, Markham said his farewell to the three girls, explaining he had made a previous rendez-vous with friends at the Douglas House.

Markham avoided the Brass Rail where Maureen and Jeanne might still hang out, and decided to walk around London sightseeing which took him to the British Museum. As he started walking up the steps to the entrance, he heard the beep of a car horn behind him, which he at first ignored until the beeping continued, compelling him to turn around to see who was being so annoying and that's when he saw a young, blond-haired woman sitting behind the steering wheel of an MG convertible waving at him. At first Markham didn't recognize the woman, but as he descended the steps towards her she called out to him, "James!" waving her gloved hand in the air. To Markham's amazement, it was none other than Sharon Conroy, the gal he last saw and delivered drunk to her Father's hotel on Shaftesbury Avenue. She looked healthy, radiant and sober.

"James. How do you like my little toy? Isn't it cute?"

"It suits you Sharon. You look very debonair," replied Markham.

"C'mon, get in. I'll take you for a ride."

Markham hesitated, remembering his last experience with her.

"Don't worry James; I haven't had a drink in the past six months. C'mon, be a sport and come with me for a ride."

"Alright, but you've got precious cargo in your trust, so please drive carefully," said Markham jokingly while he got into the passenger seat of the two-seater sports car. It was a sunny day as they sped away towards the outskirts of London.

"How did you happen to find me?" asked Markham.

`   "I saw that familiar physique of yours with your unique gait strolling down the street, but by the time I could turn around, you'd already started to walk up the steps to the Museum, that's when I beeped the horn at you," replied Sharon, smiling.

"Where are you taking me?" asked Markham.

"To the Epsom Derby, my dear. This is the horse race of the year and we'll just make it if we hurry. Estelle, you remember Estelle, well she was going to go with me, but fell ill and cancelled at the last minute, so I've got two tickets that my Father gave me and they're in the Grandstand too."

"I heard of the Epsom Derby, but I don't know much of anything about it," replied Markham.

"The story goes that Lord Derby and Sir Charles Bunbury tossed a coin to decide the name of the new one-and-a-half mile race and Lord Derby won resulting in the name of Derby at Epsom which is where we are headed just outside of London."

"Interesting. You apparently like horse racing."

"Not particularly, but I like the carnival atmosphere and the mingling with the rich and famous and even the Queen of England attends the Derby," said Sharon as she drove with the air of a debutante.

"And what do you like about the rich and famous that you've met?"

"Well, I disagree with F. Scott Fitzgerald's comment that they are different than the rest of us. Certainly they can afford more expensive toys, but they require food and toilets like the rest of us," said Sharon.

"I suppose that it also depends on how they acquired their fortunes," said Markham. "You can lose your fortune as quickly as you gained it, that's when you find out what you're made of."

"And the track at the Epsom Derby is a good place to gain or lose it," replied Sharon.

Shortly thereafter they arrived at Epsom Downs and Sharon parked her car and pulled up the top in the event of rain. She grabbed Markham's arm and they walked to the entrance where a crowd of people were still waiting in line to get in. Sharon grabbed a schedule of races then quickly hustled Markham to the Grandstand section where four seats were still vacant. After settling down in the two far seats, she quickly examined the race schedule of horses entered into the Derby.

"Are there any American horses in this race?" asked Markham curiously.

"As a matter of fact, James, there is a colt named Never Say Die from Kentucky, owned by two Americans that is entered. You want to bet on him?"

"Heck! Why not. But I have only a couple of pounds to bet."

"Do you feel lucky?" she asked.

"Yeah! I do," replied Markham.

"Well, the odds on Never Say Die are 33 to one and the jockey is Lester Piggott. Ever heard of him?" asked Sharon.

"No, I have never bet on a horse, let alone know the names of jockeys," replied Markham.

"Well darling, I haven't either, but you stand to win 66 pounds and I will bet 10 pounds which should bring me 330 pounds."

"OK! Let's do it before the race starts," said Markham. Sharon took Markham's two pounds and went downstairs to the betting cage and placed the bets then returned with two tickets.

"Here's your betting ticket," she said to Markham. She then pulled a small pair of binoculars from her purse and perused the course and the crowd. "Oh! My God. There's Lord Pomeroy and the Prime Minister and so many politicians."

"Here, James. You want to take a look," she said, offering him the binoculars.

"No thanks. I wouldn't recognize any of them, but when the horses come out, that's when I would want the binoculars, but since they're yours, I'll trust you'll keep me apprised of the progress of the race," said Markham.

"Oh! James. You are so thoughtful. You're such a gentleman."

"Thank you my dear. I'm at your service, your Majesty," he replied jokingly, and she gave a hearty laugh.

The excitement at the track could be felt as the main event grew near. To Markham's amazement, many people were eating fish and chips as Americans in the states would be eating hot dogs. There were several food stands and a restaurant as well. Finally the thoroughbreds were brought onto the track apparently for their warm-up. Then the competing horses with jockeys mounted on their backs lined up at the gate for the start.

"What's the number of our horse Sharon? Do you know?" asked Markham.

"According to the schedule, it's number 22. I see him now. Here they go!" she yelled excitedly as she continued to follow the race through the binoculars while Markham looked directly at the trail of horses running their fastest around the track with the spectators all around him shouting encouragement for the horse of their choice to move up and win. With 33 to one odds, Markham didn't believe that he had any hope of winning this race of thoroughbreds, but as the race progressed, Sharon mentioned that Never Say Die was running with the head of the pack and stood a good chance of placing. As they turned around the bend for the home stretch, Sharon started shouting as she stood on her seat to better see the finish, "C'mon Never, C'mon Never Say Die. You can do it. Don't Say Die. C'mon baby. C'mon baby, Never Say Die. YOU DID IT, YOU DID IT!" Sharon then put down the binoculars and looked at Markham nearly in shock.

"He did it, James. He won. Never Say Die won the Derby," she said in total disbelief.

Markham was going to say that he didn't believe it, when he heard several other spectators confirm that Never Say Die had won the Derby against all odds.

Sharon stepped off the seat and threw her arms around Markham's neck. "We did it James. We did it," she said happily. "Let's celebrate our win."

"Yes. But first let's collect our winnings," remarked Markham.

With their winnings secured, Markham and Sharon got back into her sports car and Sharon told Markham that she had to run a quick errand for her Father who had asked her to pick up an envelope from a bookmaker at a house on top of a hill overlooking the Epsom Derby race track. Sharon retrieved the thick envelope from the bookmaker which she placed in her purse along with her own winnings and drove off back to London where she stopped off at the Shaftesbury Hotel for a few minutes while Markham remained in the car waiting for her. Markham figured that the envelope contained money her Father had won betting on horses which she didn't want to carry around and probably secured her own winnings at her hotel apartment, especially since it amounted to the equivalent of $924.00 at the exchange rate of $2.80 per pound, no small sum of money for an English person in 1954's economy. By the same token, Markham's take of 66 pounds translated into $184.00, more than he earned in a month.

Sharon returned and jumped into the driver's seat. "James, let's celebrate with a delicious dinner at the Dorchester Hotel. They have a fabulous restaurant and live entertainment."

"That's an expensive place. Do we want to spend it all in one place?" asked Markham.

"Since I'm the big winner, I'm picking up the bill, so don't worry about the expense, James," said Sharon cheerfully.

"Oh! No. At the very least we'll split the bill in half. I must insist on that," said Markham.

"Alright then, we'll go half and half; it's a deal," she said happily. "Even though Dad's hotel has a great chef and all that, I didn't want the help to stare at us throughout the evening."

"We could have gone to the Douglas House. They have great food there too," said Markham.

"I've been there and frankly it's not in the same league as the Dorchester, James, trust me darling, you'll see and you'll be pleased at my choice."

"It's your town and you're the driver, Sharon. I'm just a passenger," said Markham.

"That's right darling. You leave the driving to me."

As they pulled up under the marquis of the Dorchester Hotel, Sharon stepped out of her sportscar and handed her car keys to the uniformed doorman, afterwards grabbing Markham's left arm as they waltzed into the luxurious entrance leading to the formal restaurant where they were immediately seated at an intimate table for two lit by an electric candle. A man dressed in a tuxedo played Chopin on a grand piano which gave an air of elegance to the large, well appointed dining room. The male waiter came over to their table and asked them if they wished to order a drink before examining the menu. Markham suggested a bottle of red wine to go with the dinner and Sharon agreed and ordered her favorite French wine she often ordered at the Shaftesbury Hotel. They didn't have Markham's favorite New York Strip Steak, hence he had to settle for a Filet Mignon, which Sharon copied, along with a baked potato and vegetable which was preceded by a substantial salad.

"You know James, I can't remember when I've had so much fun. I wish we could go on a vacation, just the two of us somewhere very private and warm. We've got the money to do it. You think you could take a leave of absence for a couple of weeks?"

Markham looked at Sharon thoughtfully. He knew that she received a generous allowance from her Father plus today's winnings which enabled her to vacation whenever she so desired. On the other hand, he did not earn enough money as an Airman Second Class to even maintain a savings account, and today's winnings would last him no more than a few weeks. Furthermore, his pride would not allow him to be supported by a woman even on a mere vacation. In any event, he had some reservations about her control over her penchant for alcoholic beverages which remained to be seen and confirmed.

"A vacation, especially with you, sounds great. Unfortunately, I don't have enough leave time accumulated; at least not for another six months, so just put that thought on hold sweetheart, OK?" said Markham with a disarming smile.

"Oh! Alright. But don't forget I asked you first. And don't pretend you don't have presence with other women, darling. I've seen how they undress you with their alluring eyes, but I have the secret potion to keep you forever happy."

"Really? And did you get that potion from Transylvania?" asked Markham kiddingly.

"From Ireland, darling, my parents' ancestry," she replied with a broad smile followed by a long sip of her red wine while she stared into his eyes seductively.

"Tell me James, when are you due to transfer back to the States?"

"Next March," replied Markham.

"That's only nine months from now. Are you leaving the Air Force then?" she asked.

"No, I'm not due for discharge until the 31st of August 1955," replied Markham.

"What are your plans after you leave the service, James?"

"I don't know. It depends on job availability and whether I can afford to go to college under the G.I. bill which only pays for the tuition and possibly the books. According to English standards, we G.I.s make a lot of money, but back home, a lower grade enlisted man's pay is at the poverty level. Did you know that an average of seven American Servicemen get married to English girls each and every day of the year, and they're mostly enlisted men? Some of these girls who think that the streets of America are paved with gold are in for a rude awakening," said Markham.

"I don't plan on moving to America, my dear. I'm perfectly content with my current situation and lifestyle. But America is a land of opportunity, n'est ce pas?" replied Sharon, injecting a bit of French for effect.

"I didn't know you knew French," said a surprised Markham.

"I really don't speak French. I only know a few words and sayings."

"True, America is indeed a land of opportunity, but opportunity usually doesn't knock at your convenience and that is why many people miss the boat. But for some unfortunate people, opportunity never knocks at their door, so they must create their own," said Markham philosophically.

"Would you ever consider residing in England, if you were married to an English girl?" asked Sharon with an ulterior motive in mind.

"I don't know. I love the English culture and its people and of course if I was married to an English woman, then I would have to seriously consider her wants and desires as well as mine, and of course the means by which I would earn a living," said Markham who cautiously added, "but that's not an issue that has yet arisen."

Sharon had by now consumed two full glasses of wine and was working on her third glass, which was slowly dampening her inhibitions. For the first time in her young life, Sharon found a man who aroused her passion to the extent that she was willing to relinquish her dictatorial personality for a submissive role. However, she realized that she may not get another chance to express her love and plead her case for matrimony in view of Markham's distant Air Base which limited his visits to London.

Sharon extended her hand across the table and placed it on Markham's left hand. "Do you know how much I love you, James?" she said, looking imploringly into his eyes for some positive response.

Markham was surprised by Sharon's declaration of love, especially since she hardly knew him, although he'd heard of 'love at first sight' and believed that such a phenomenon could and did occur. However, his own feelings for Sharon had certainly not developed that far and his reservations had not dissipated. He understood Sharon's urgency in view of his infrequent visits to London and his imminent departure to the States, but he also remembered the old saying that 'fools rush in where angels fear to tread' as sound advice.

"I'm deeply touched Sharon, but perhaps you're mistaking infatuation for love. After all, you've only met me a few times, hardly enough to really know me," replied Markham in a voice as tender as he could muster.

"Please don't treat me as a child, darling. I know the difference and I do love you, James. The question that I'm afraid to ask, but I must, is whether you love me too?"

"It's essential that I get to know you before I can fall in love with you Sharon, and that takes time."

Sharon looked at Markham in silence, then waved the waiter over and ordered her favorite drink, a gin and tonic. "Well, James, you've got nine months in which you can get to know me, and when you can't come to London, I will come and visit you at your air base. You know James, my Father is buying another hotel in Blackpool right on the seashore, and he could train you to manage it and you wouldn't have to worry about finances and we could have a wonderful life together."

"That's certainly something to think about later Sharon, but right now let's celebrate our winning at the Derby, shall we?" replied Markham in an attempt to lighten the mood.

The waiter arrived with Sharon's gin and tonic which she held up to Markham's glass of wine and he made a toast, "To Never Say Die who will live forever in the annals of horse racing."

As the evening wore on, Sharon managed to drink seven more gin and tonics to Markham's consternation. It became obvious to Markham that Sharon was in no condition to drive and he possessed only a military driver's license valid only for United States military vehicles. Markham called the waiter for the bill and paid it with his own winnings, then escorted Sharon, who offered no resistance, out of the hotel. Her car was brought around under the marquee by the valet who handed the car keys to Markham, who decided to drive and sat Sharon down in the passenger seat where she quietly fell asleep. It was drizzling rain again so the top remained fastened. The fact that the steering wheel was located on the right side of the car helped Markham's bearings to maintain the car on the left side of the road. Luckily, the Dorchester hotel was only a short distance from the Shaftesbury Hotel. Markham pulled up to the front of the marquis and the Shaftesbury hotel doorman walked over to the car and recognized Sharon sitting there apparently asleep. He stepped out of the car and handed the car keys to the doorman, then awakened Sharon and helped her walk inside the hotel and up to her apartment. To Markham, this was 'déjà vu' all over again. He exited the hotel and took a taxi to the Turkish Bath where he checked in for the night at a cost of only ten shillings, the equivalent of $1.40, but it was not without its problems.

Markham checked his valuables, including his watch, with the attendant who issued him a large bath towel plus a smaller towel. Markham then went inside a large room which contained several military style cots along the wall with lockers for hanging clothes. He stripped naked and wrapped the large towel around his waist and walked over to the adjoining area where several shower cubicles without doors were located. There didn't appear to be anyone else in the area so Markham took off the towel and stepped into one of the shower cubicles when he noticed that there was no soap. Suddenly two young Englishmen appeared out of nowhere wearing only towels around their waists, standing within a few feet of Markham while staring at his naked body.

"Hey! You guys know where there's some soap around here?" asked Markham.

"That's our job…to soap you down," said one of the Englishmen.

"What do you mean?" exclaimed Markham in disbelief.

"That's what these marble tables are for. You lie down on the slab and we soap you down," said the other Englishman.

Markham then observed that there were several marble tables with a few soap bricks lying on them apparently for use in soaping down customers. Markham deducted from their overall behavior that they were homosexuals looking for a playmate.

"Listen guys. I've been soaping myself all of my life and I ain't about to change, so pass me the soap," said Markham in a commanding voice. But the two Englishmen didn't budge, so he put his towel back around his waist, then walked over to a marble table and grabbed a soap brick, at which point one of the Englishmen attempted to grab Markham's wrist, but was not quick enough to avoid a shove from Markham's other hand which caused the Englishman to slide on the wet stone floor and fall against the base of another marble table. The other Englishman took one look at Markham's powerful physique and decided that he didn't want to suffer the same fate as his friend who now was whimpering like a girl who'd been physically rejected. Markham took the soap brick in his two hands and slammed the middle of it against the edge of the marble top, thus breaking the brick in half to make it more manageable to use in the shower. As he returned to the shower, he noticed that the two Englishmen were back staring at him again, so he made a quick gesture towards them and they suddenly vanished as quickly as they had appeared. After showering, Markham retired to a cot nearest the wall as a precaution against intruders.

The next day turned out to be a sunny Sunday and Markham went to the Douglas House for a substantial lunch, knowing that he would probably be skipping dinner on the long train ride back to Sealand Air Base. While eating lunch, Markham reviewed in his mind the events of the previous evening with Sharon and came to the conclusion that a marital union with her would be a serious mistake and it would be best if he didn't have any further contact with her.

After a couple of weekends spent on the base at Sealand, Markham became restless and decided to visit Manchester's dance hall and the King George Pub nearby. It took about 45 minutes by train to arrive there from Liverpool, which is the nearest major city from Sealand Air Base located about one half hour south by bus. The train stopped at every local station to pick up and discharge passengers, mostly English. When the train stopped at Warrington, several G.I.s dressed in civilian clothes boarded the train, and Markham recognized three of them as members of the Burtonwood Air Base football team. Big Al, short for Alvarez, weighing in at 325 pounds took up half the train bench, and Garcia who weighed 245 pounds took up the other half. Markham who at that time weighed 198 pounds sat on the other padded bench facing them and for some reason, never felt threatened by either of them, even though Garcia had a reputation of picking fights when drinking with people who made him feel inferior or unaccepted. The third football player who entered the compartment was the team quarterback Tim Bolanski, a relative lightweight. Other team members boarded the adjacent train compartment.

"I heard that you injured your left knee in the last game Al, but you don't seem to be limping," said Markham.

"Yeah! Well it's bandaged up pretty good and tight, but it still hurts like hell! I'll be out for another four weeks so the coach tells me."

"That's too bad. When are you rotating back to the States?" asked Markham.

"Not for another 15 months, but Garcia here is a short-timer. He's got only three months left. Ain't that right Pudgy?" said Big Al, teasing Garcia who had gained a slight beer belly.

"Hey! Man, don't call me that, OK!" replied Garcia, annoyed at the derogatory remark.

"You don't lose that gut, the coach is going to bench you," said Big Al, smiling.

"Just don't worry about it Al," said Garcia who looked at Markham to see if he was amused by Al's remarks, which would give him reason to take his frustration out on someone smaller than Big Al. But Markham, who was indeed amused, just looked at the two of them as if watching two overgrown boys in a comedic play.

"You ever play football, Jim?" asked Big Al.

"Nothing serious. I prefer baseball; that's my niche. Unfortunately, there are no sports at Sealand," replied Markham.

"Hell! Baseball's for sissies," said Garcia in an attempt to goad Markham who instinctively knew Garcia's game, but would not respond to it.

"Baseball's a game of skill and speed, Garcia, and with your beer belly, you'd never make it to first base," said Big Al, laughing.

Markham and Tim both chuckled at Al's remark, and Garcia was trying to decide which one of these two men, Tim or Markham, would bear the brunt of his anger and animosity since Al was too big to ever be considered as an opponent. Garcia observed Markham's large, well-padded hands, big, wide shoulders and muscular neck, which all conveyed a strong, athletic adversary who would be no easy mark in a fight. Garcia turned his attention to Tim who was smaller than Markham, but was known as a feisty individual and was also a member of the same football team whose members would not take too kindly to his physical abuse. Garcia decided to swallow his pride and keep quiet, at least until he'd had a few more drinks at the King George Pub where they were headed to meet their English girlfriends. Al and Garcia dated two English girls, Pam and Sheila respectively, who worked part-time as prostitutes in Manchester and spent their weekends partying with them.

It was still too early to go to the dancehall so Markham went to the King George Pub where most G.I.s congregated for a few beers. There were very few Englishmen in the pub, but the place was crowded with American enlisted men all dressed in civilian clothes, making out with an equal number of English women, some of them looking for Mr. Right, and others just looking for a good time which is what most G.I.s were looking for, except for Markham who hoped each time he went off-base that he would meet that special woman with whom he could have a serious relationship. This was more likely at one of the dance halls than the pub, although English pubs were frequented oftentimes by entire adult families, and it was considered a respectable place to visit for a few drinks. However, those pubs taken over by American Servicemen also attracted women of ill repute and camp followers.

Markham stood at the far end of the long bar sipping a pale ale while observing the patrons nearby when he noticed that the two English girls accompanying Big Al and Garcia at the other end of the bar were having a loud argument with another English girl and the bartender told them to take their problem outside which they did, while Al and Garcia remained at the bar drinking their beer. A few minutes later, the girl dating Garcia came back into the bar all excited yelling at Garcia and Big Al to come outside immediately because the British police had arrested Big Al's girlfriend along with the other woman for causing a disturbance. Big Al and Garcia, followed by several other patrons, went outside and observed several Bobbies place the two women inside a black paddy wagon and drive off. Markham also exited the pub to see what was going on.

"Where are they taking them?" asked Big Al of anyone who would listen.

"To the police station about half a mile from here," said one Englishman.

"How do I get there?" responded Big Al.

"I would take a taxi. He'll know where to go," the Englishman replied.

There were a line of taxis on the corner. Big Al, Garcia, Tim and several others piled into two taxis and directed the drivers to take them to the police station where the paddy wagon would have taken the two girls. Big Al was visibly upset over the arrest of his girlfriend, whom he cared for in spite of her illicit activities and had every intention of bailing her out of this mess. The two taxis eventually pulled up in a darkened street where they parked across the street from the dimly lit entrance to the police station. As the airmen climbed out of the taxis, they were shocked to see the two women, each being dragged unconscious on the sidewalk by two Bobbies, each holding an ankle while the women's arms trailed behind their heads which bobbed against the pavement as they were dragged up the stairs into the police station.

Big Al, Garcia and several other airmen ran across the street and into the police station where they were met by several Bobbies armed with nightsticks who blocked their intrusion into the station, but were finding it difficult to hold the line against such heavy men who were screaming for justice and police abuse.

Markham knew that if Al and his friends didn't calm down and act rationally they could be arrested for interfering with the police who would be more than happy to add assault to the charge. He made his way to the front of the crowd and grabbed Big Al's left arm and pulled on it to get his attention.

"Al, listen to me. Calm down a minute and listen to me," said Markham to the nearest Bobby's delight. "We're gonna pass the hat around and collect fifteen pounds and hire a British lawyer to represent your girlfriend and put these Bobbies on notice that their abusive behavior has been witnessed and will be reported to higher authorities and the court," said Markham.

Big Al looked at Markham. "You know of a good lawyer?"

"They're in the phone book, and the JAG office usually has an English lawyer on staff also, who can recommend one. That's no problem. Let me address this if you don't mind, Al," said Markham. "By the way, what is your girlfriend's name for the record?"

"Her name is Pauline Parker," said Big Al, calming down a bit.

Markham looked at the Sergeant behind the raised desk. "Sergeant. We're putting you on notice that Mr. Alvarez here is hiring an English lawyer to represent Pauline Parker whom you brought into this station unconscious in front of several witnesses and Mr. Alvarez insists that Miss Parker and the other woman receive immediate medical attention. Mr. Alvarez also wants to know the charge that is being levied against her in order to relay this to the solicitor," said Markham in the best officious voice he could muster.

The Police Sergeant gave Markham a severe look of disdain. "Is that big fellow standing next to you Mr. Alvarez?"

"Yeah! I'm Mr. Alvarez," replied Big Al.

"Your girlfriend and the other woman are being cared for by the female officers on duty. They're both being charged with disorderly conduct and resisting arrest," said the Sergeant.

"I want to see Pam right now and make sure she's alright," said Big Al.

"You can't see her tonight, Mr. Alvarez. I suggest that you return with your solicitor. In the meantime, I want you all to leave the premises or else I will charge all of you with interfering with police administration," said the Sergeant.

"C'mon Al," said Markham with Garcia, Tim and others agreeing. "We can't do anymore here. Let's go back to the pub and collect some money from the guys there and first thing Monday morning, go to the JAG office and get the name of a good attorney," said Markham, and they all started to leave the station to the relief of the Bobbies who for a time thought they were facing a riot within the police station.

"Hell, that means Pam will rot in that police station all of Sunday and probably Monday too," said Big Al.

"You can't do anything else right now," said Markham, "unless you want to end up in jail too."

"Yeah! I guess you're right. Man, I can't believe how these Bobbies treat their women. They're fucking animals, I swear," said Big Al who was having a hard time controlling his anger and frustration. Garcia, who had been relatively silent until now, started to voice his disgust at the barbaric scene he'd just witnessed, but Markham had witnessed a similar scene in Piccadilly Circus several months before when three women, apparently prostitutes, were being held one evening by several Bobbies within a recessed entrance way to a closed store while awaiting the police van. The public watched as the Bobbies punched two of the three women into unconsciousness for their profane objection to the Bobbies' molestful behavior towards them. Markham was surprised then as he was now at the apparent dichotomy between police brutality which he detested and British justice which he admired and wondered why the British people didn't protest the barbaric behavior of some of their police officers. These experiences started to generate an interest for him in the workings of the justice system in various countries such as Great Britain, Europe and the United States with frequent visits to available libraries. Markham did not return to Manchester after that eventful weekend as he felt it a waste of time better spent exploring the various historical sites in the area surrounding Sealand Air Base including Liverpool. However, Markham made one last trip to London before his scheduled return from England to the United States.

It was a rare sunny afternoon on that Saturday when Markham ventured up a side street from Piccadilly Circus to the Windmill Theatre reputed to have wonderful live musical shows when he suddenly got caught up in a hoard of people that surrounded a parked black car where two Bobbies were holding a man over the trunk of the car while apparently awaiting the usual black police van. The crowd that had grown to over 200 people formed a large circle around the two Bobbies and the man they had apprehended. Within that circle stood one man dressed in work clothes who was pleading with the Bobbies to release his friend being held off balance against the back of the parked car with both his arms behind his back by the Bobbies. Frustrated at the lack of response by the Bobbies, the man walked around the inner circle of the crowd begging anyone to come to his aid in forcing the release of his crippled friend.

"My friend is a crippled man who never hurt anyone. Those coppers have no right to hold him. Look at the bastards; they're hurting him. I need your help. Please, can anyone help him?" said the man as he walked around looking for anyone in the crowd to whom he could appeal directly. No one moved, but a couple of voices could be heard from the crowd asking the Bobbies to release the poor man. Then more voices joined the chorus to release the crippled man which apparently motivated two men to break from the crowd and enter the inner circle where they joined the suspect's friend in wrestling the two Bobbies from the crippled man and in the process, one Bobby lost his domed hat and stood there facing one of the men for no more than two seconds before the man hit the Bobby with a right punch to the jaw, knocking him unconscious onto the sidewalk while the other two men had beaten the other Bobby who was now lying unconscious on the street behind the parked car. The three men grabbed the crippled man and together they ran with the crippled man limping towards the crowd's inner circle which quickly opened up then swallowed them into obscurity never to be seen again. Within a minute, the unique clinging of the bell on the Police van could be heard approaching the crowd which had now begun to disperse, allowing several Bobbies to come to the aid of the two downed policemen. But no one until their arrival attempted to help the two Bobbies in distress, which conveyed to Markham that the Bobbies in the West End of London at least were not liked nor respected. As Markham walked away from the scene, he pondered that perhaps this was the public's reaction to their brutal treatment of women so overtly displayed in the West End, and covertly in other cities like Manchester where he witnessed it first hand. Markham felt that a major change in attitude and training of police officers in Great Britain needed to be implemented, but for certain this would not happen while he was there.

As Markham walked down Piccadilly towards Hyde Park his eyes caught sight of a blonde woman in the distance walking towards him with her arm linked with that of a black man which was not that unusual in London or other large cities in England. However, as the black and white couple got closer, Markham recognized the blonde woman as none other than Maureen whom he had previously dated while on leave with Mike Seagrave. But no sooner had he recognized her that the black man had suddenly disappeared from view and Maureen was now walking alone towards him until they came face to face.

"How are you Maureen?"

"Very well. Thank you for asking," said Maureen nervously. "I suppose you saw my friend?"

"Yes I did," replied Markham, not wanting to elaborate on the matter.

"I told him to let me talk to you alone and to meet me later. That's why he's not with me now," said Maureen a bit embarrassed.

"I noticed and I understand Maureen," said Markham.

"Jeannie hasn't heard from Mike since he left London and frankly I didn't expect to hear from you either James, under the circumstances. You know what I mean."

"How's the world treating you now Mo?"

"Not bad. I'll be honest with you James. The black man you saw is my boyfriend, and he treats me better than any white man has ever treated me, excluding you of course, and I've never been happier James...honestly. To him I'm the Queen."

"I'm so very glad that you are finally happy with your life, Maureen."

Maureen leaned forward and hugged Markham tightly for a moment, then kissed him on the cheek and stepped back with teary eyes looking at him for the last time.

"Take care of yourself, James," she said as she started to walk away down Piccadilly while Markham watched her departure with mixed emotions.

Markham took a taxi to the Douglas House where he ate a steak dinner then he decided to go to the Lyceum to dance one last time. The dance hall was crowded with mostly young English people. Markham was standing a few feet from the edge of the dance floor with the bar some thirty feet directly in back of him when he heard a voice calling him.

"Hello James," said the blonde young woman whom Markham immediately recognized as Joan, Sylvia's younger sister. She wore a long silver dress, very décolleté, and her hairdo was reminiscent of the roaring twenties which was very becoming on her oblong face.

"Hello Joan. It's been such a long time since I last saw you. Are you here alone?" asked Markham.

"No, I'm with my girlfriend Sara," said Joan, turning her head towards Sara who was standing alone near the bar facing them.

"How've you been James? I haven't seen you around London at all," said Joan.

"I'm stationed up north near Liverpool which makes it difficult to visit London," he replied. "How's Sylvia? Have you heard from her lately?"

"As a matter of fact, that's what I want to talk to you about. Sylvia got married to an American Sergeant and he now says that she was promiscuous with other men before he married her and he's beaten her up. She's very unhappy, Jim and she asked me if I ever saw you to get your address so that she can contact you and maybe you can vouch for her chastity."

"He beat her up? Tell her to leave him," said Markham, becoming visibly upset and angry at the thought of someone hurting Sylvia. "Why don't you give me her address?" asked Markham.

"No, I can't. She made me promise not to. But she does want your address, then she can contact you," said Joan.

"Alright. Do you have a pen and a piece of paper that I can use?" asked Markham.

"Yes I do," she said, pulling out a pen and a blank card from her purse which she handed to Markham who then wrote his name, rank, serial number, and postal address at Sealand Air Base. "I don't have a phone number of course, but she can reach me at this address, and if I should be reassigned, the mail will be forwarded to me," said Markham.

"Thank you James. I'll make sure Sylvia gets this, and it was nice seeing you again." Joan then walked back towards the bar to join her friend Sara, and Markham overheard Joan saying to Sara, "He's really in love with my sister Sylvia."

Markham walked away from them towards the exit with Joan's words still ringing in his ears, and left the Lyceum for the Charing Cross Station where he waited, in deep thought, for the next train back to Sealand Air Base.

Markham was due to be discharged from the United States Air Force on 31 August 1955 and was scheduled to rotate back to the United States on March 2nd 1955 which meant that he would be assigned to an Air Base in the United States until his date of discharge. Markham had indicated on his preference sheet to the Air Force that he wished to be assigned to an Air Base located in Florida where his mother Nora had recently moved and where he would then be discharged. Unfortunately, his Special Orders reflected his assignment to Loring Air Force Base located at Presque Isle, Maine, as far north on the East Coast of the United States as one could get without crossing the border into Canada.

"Hey, Jim," said Jake. "I see you got your orders for stateside assignment. Where are they sending you?"

"Loring Air Base at Presque Isle, Maine. Would you believe it? I asked for Florida. You'd think that inasmuch as I'm getting discharged, they'd give me an assignment to a place where I want to live, but hell no, that would make too much sense," said Markham, visibly perturbed and disappointed.

"The Air Force is not interested in helping its enlisted men. The exigencies of the service come first. That's what they'll tell you. Bull-shit. And they wonder why so many of us want to serve our time and get out," said Jake in sympathy to Markham's plight.

"For sure if I had any thoughts of re-enlisting, they're gone for certain now," replied Markham. "The only good thing about this is that I'll be arriving in northern Maine near the end of the winter season."

"Listen, Jim. Humphrey and I are going to the Long Bar in Liverpool tonight. Why don't you come with us? Apparently you're not going to London anymore, right?"
said Jake.

"Oh! Why not? OK! When are you leaving?" replied Markham.

"We'll grab the eight o'clock bus outside the main gate," said Jake. "In the meantime, let's get some chow at the Mess Hall. It's nearly six o'clock. The Mess Hall is going to close soon." Markham and Jake stopped at Humphrey's room on the way out of the barracks and the three of them went to the Mess Hall for their final meal of the day.

The Long Bar was right off of Lime Street, possibly the coldest street in the world, where the damp, cold wind swept down the wide main street of Liverpool, chilling the bones of any pedestrian daring to walk on Lime Street during the winter season. In spite of Markham's heavy camel hair overcoat, he felt the cold penetrating deep inside the marrow of his bones to the point of having to drink three straight shots of Irish whiskey in succession at the Long Bar to get rid of the 'Lime Street Chill' as he called it to Jake and Humphrey who followed his lead. The Long Bar was known to be frequented by longshoremen and mariners from various foreign ships docking at Liverpool. They were a tough bunch of men who often quarreled between themselves and on one memorable occasion with American Servicemen which resulted in the smashing of the longest mirror of any bar in the city. On this particular Saturday night, the bar was crowded with a variety of customers including several American Servicemen. As Markham, Jake and Humphrey stood at the far corner of the long bar consuming warm beer after the whiskey took its effect, they were engaged in conversation by two English females who had worked their way through the standing crowd to meet them.

"You come here often, Love?" asked the brunette to Jake and Humphrey while Markham was facing the bartender.

"No, not really," answered Jake, sizing her up as of average looks; passable.

"You're a Yank, right?" asked the red-headed female companion directing her question at Humphrey.

"That depends on who's asking?" replied Humphrey.

"What do you mean? Either you are or you aren't," answered the red-head.

"Not really. If a European asked me that question, then yes I'm a Yank, but if an American from the North asked me that question, then my answer is that I am definitely not a Yank, but a Rebel from the South; Georgia to be exact," replied Humphrey with pride, whose answer gained the attention of both Jake and Markham. Markham had now turned around to eavesdrop on the conversation between his two friends and their newly found female acquaintances.

"Do you have a name Mr. Rebel?" asked the red-head.

"Yeah! I'm Humphrey, and these are my friends Jake and Jim."

"Please to meet you," replied the red-head, "I'm Joyce and this is my friend Elaine." After shaking hands they all decided to sit at a table nearby and Markham ordered a round of drinks for all of them. A little more than a half an hour went by when two black American Servicemen entered the Long Bar accompanied by two attractive white English girls. They took the only vacant table available which was located next to the entrance to the bar. The obvious reason for its being vacant was that every time the bar door opened, it allowed the drastically cold air to envelop the customers seated nearby. While the two big American black men didn't seem to mind the cold draft, one of the English girls was actually shivering and her American companion took off his heavy coat and placed it on her shoulders to warm her up and then they ordered alcoholic beverages.

"Jesus. Will you look at that," said Humphrey with a look of disgust.

"What'sa matter Humphrey?" said Jake.

"Those two niggers over there with those two white girls. What'sa matter with those girls anyway?" asked Humphrey, directing his question as much to Joyce and Elaine as to Jake and Markham.

Joyce and Elaine looked at Humphrey in embarrassed silence, while Jake looked for an adequate response, but Markham decided to wait for all of their responses before he added his two cents.

"C'mon Humphrey," said Jake, "you see that a lot in England. It should be of no surprise to you. You're still thinking like a Southerner," replied Jake.

"Hey! Man. You're never going to convert me to your way of thinking. You Northerners gave them their freedom and I accept that, but I draw the line when it comes to interracial intercourse," replied Humphrey.

"Pardon me Humphrey, or is it Mr. Rebel, but I don't understand your objection. I dated an American black man for a short time and he told me that he was actually an American Indian, and there are no truer Americans in America," replied Joyce.

"American Indians are not black; they're brown in color, and he probably lied to you about his origin. So how come you're not with him now?" asked Humphrey.

"Because he went back to the United States," replied Joyce, "and it wouldn't have made any difference to me whether he was of African or American origin, he was a very decent man and he was an officer. I'll bet you're an enlisted man," answered Joyce.

"Rank doesn't make the man, Joyce. My friends here will attest to that. I know of some black Americans who have told gullible English girls that they are in fact white, but the United States Government has put them on special assignment as 'night fighters' and injected them with a chemical that made them temporarily black to avoid detection," replied Humphrey who felt himself on the defensive.

Jake and Markham started laughing at Humphrey's preposterous remark and the two English girls were looking at Humphrey with incredulity.

"Is that true?" asked Joyce, looking at Jake and Markham for verification.

"It's not true, but it makes a good story," replied Jake still laughing.

"Hey! I heard it from a reliable source," said Humphrey to Jake.

"C'mon Humphrey. It's just a story that's been passed around so many times that it eventually rings true, but it's not. You know that," replied Jake. "What do you think Jim?"

"What it comes down to is freedom. That's why we're here, blacks and whites, to fight for freedom, and that includes freedom of choice. If a white girl wants to date a black man, then it's nobody's business but her own. Sure there'll be hardships for them and their children if they get married and return to the States because of the continued lack of acceptance and discrimination, but eventually we will all come together as one people. It's inevitable, Humphrey," replied Markham.

"Markham's right, Humphrey. You Southerners are behind the times man, but we'll convert you yet. Let's have another round of drinks," said Jake and the conversation quickly turned to less serious topics including the lousy weather in England.

But Elaine, who had remained quiet throughout the conversation, thought that Markham was a man of unusual depth and vision without the flaw of academic pretentiousness she had experienced at the University of Liverpool where she was presently matriculated. In her view, this man was going somewhere and she wanted to go with him, but she didn't feel that she would meet his standards, whatever they may be, hence she would make no attempt to indicate her interest in him. Besides, she rationalized, he'll be returning to the States soon and some American girl will be waiting for him. At the end of the evening, they all parted company without exchanging addresses, leaving it to the next time they met by chance.

There were only six weeks left before Markham's date of departure for the United States, therefore he mailed all of his civilian clothes to his new military address at Loring AFB. He had not forgotten the fact that Staff Sergeant Anthony Pucelli never shipped his civilian clothes to England and also kept the $50.00 he paid him as well. Markham mused that somehow, somewhere, he would eventually encounter Sergeant Pucelli and he could not predict his reaction to that event.

The day before he was to board a military bus for transportation to Southampton for embarkation on a troop ship, Markham checked the mailroom one last time hoping that there would be a letter for him from Sylvia, but to his dismay there was nothing but disappointment. Markham was ordered to report to hanger number two for a medical inspection at 0900 hours. The hangar door was wide open and as Markham, dressed in fatigues, entered the hangar he observed a long line of airmen also dressed in fatigues numbering several hundred who were waiting to have their penises inspected by medics situated at a wooden table containing various medical items.

As each airman approached the medical inspector, he was instructed to expose his penis to determine if there was any evidence of venereal disease and further to milk the penis by squeezing it with his hand all the time moving his hand towards the head of the penis to see if any pus emanated from it. Any airman who displayed evidence of venereal disease was instructed to step into a second line leading to another desk manned by medics who performed a closer inspection and depending on the diagnosis, would either order the airman to report to the base hospital or if the diagnosis was gonorrhea, the most common affliction, then the airman would be given an immediate shot of penicillin with a prescription for another two shots to be administered on board the ship by navy medical technicians. These afflicted airmen would not be permitted to perform any ship duties connected with food handling including Kitchen Police (KP).

Markham noticed that the line of diseased airmen already numbered more than a dozen and the fact that everyone in the hanger could see and identify the diseased airmen had to be most embarrassing for them and the medical privacy issue obviously never came to the mind of the military commanders. Markham recognized one of the medics as George Gershon who also operated a private loan shark business to airmen who were always broke a week or two before the monthly payday.

Larry Barnes, the airman standing in front of Markham, also knew Gershon and in fact still owed him money. When his turn came up, he unzipped his fly and whipped out his penis and milked it without emanating any fluid.

"OK! Larry. Where's my fifty bucks?" asked Gershon.

"I'll tell you what George. I'll let you pull my dick for fifty bucks and then we'll be even," replied Larry.

"Get out of here, you sick motherfucker. I'll be on the ship where lots of things can happen to welchers," replied Gershon.

Larry walked away feeling uneasy at the thought of having Gershon as a shipmate. Markham couldn't help overhearing the conversation and wondered if Gershon would actually take some action against Larry or was it simply an empty threat to impress others within hearing distance? Markham passed the medical inspection and returned to his barracks to pack his military clothes in the provided duffel bag.

The next day Markham, along with three busloads of troops rode all day long until they arrived at Southampton, stopping twice along the way for food and use of the restrooms. Upon arrival at the docks, Markham noticed the name 'USS Patch' painted on the bow of the troop ship, the same ship that had brought him to England in the first place. They all boarded the ship in the same manner they had previously boarded it, in single file.

Markham found a bunk, the top one in the rear of the compartment. He was surprised that he hadn't met anyone of the men he came over with on his initial voyage, but then, he knew that many things can happen to a man in three years, especially in the military service. He decided that in order to preempt any attempt by the Noncoms to assign him to unwanted duties, he would seek out and volunteer for any desirable job that did not involve the kitchen or the latrines, hence he went up to the main deck and checked out the bulletin board for any job postings, and sure enough, there was a demand for someone who could type to report to the Merchant Marine in Charge of Ship Supplies.

Markham wasted no time and reported for the job, which he got on the spot. The Merchant Marine was a man in his late forties from New York City, who took a liking to Markham immediately. He asked Markham to address him simply as Sammy. He pointed to a mechanical Royal typewriter sitting on top of a small desk located in the middle of the ship for a very good reason, as he later found out, and told him that his primary duty was to type requisition orders and other forms as needed. But to Markham's chagrin, he could only type when the ship was on an even keel. As soon as the ship rolled to port or starboard, the typewriter carriage would slide to the end of its track, therefore, as the ship rolled, Markham would hold the carriage with his hand until the ship leveled again, then speedily typed until the ship tilted again to the other side. Actually, Markham found it rather amusing and something to tell his friends later.

He was given a ring of keys to various parts of the ship in order to acquire supplies as needed by Sammy. To Markham's surprise, as he ventured into the bow of the ship, there was enough water inside the ship's bow to swim or even dive without hitting bottom. Apparently a pump was in constant use to keep the water in the bow at a reasonable level. One of the perks of working for the Merchant Marine on board the ship was the privilege of eating with the Merchant Marine staff whom he thought ate like kings.

Markham had it made, he thought, until a Sergeant came into the sleeping quarters and commandeered several airmen for latrine duty. Markham's objections fell on deaf ears and he was corralled with the others and brought to the main latrine where they were issued mops, pans and brushes and ordered to work until the job was done under the supervision of two Sergeants who seemed to relish their position.

The next morning, Markham reported to his job and told Sammy what had occurred and Sammy issued him a card that stated that he was employed by the Ship's Supply Chief for the duration of the voyage and thus was absolved from any other duties which Sammy dated and signed, which relieved Markham from any similar incidents. However, as fate would have it, Markham had the unfortunate luck of being in the wrong place at the wrong time. As he was returning from the latrine that evening after washing his face and brushing his teeth, he found himself face to face with George Gershon in the narrow aisle between bunks, four high on each side with many of them empty due to shift duty. Markham immediately noticed a knife in Gershon's right hand and wondered if he had already used it, as he remembered, on Larry who owed him money.

"What's with the knife George?" asked Markham, holding his toilet articles in his left hand and his right hand holding the end of his towel laying on his right shoulder.

"Get out of my way Jim," said George menacingly.

"You know I can't let you get in close quarters with me while you're holding a knife George," said Markham, who now became aware that a couple of other airmen were now in the area observing the confrontation.

"Did you find Larry, George?" asked Markham.

"No I didn't. But what's it to you?" replied George.

"Just asked. Now just drop the knife, George, and we'll each go our separate ways," said Markham coolly.

"Fuck you. You back up to the end of the aisle," replied George.

Markham threw his toilet articles in George's face and kicked him in the testicles and as George bent over moaning, Markham grabbed his right forearm and wrist with both of his hands and slammed his wrist repeatedly against the bunk railing until he dropped the knife, then he hit him in the forehead with his right elbow, knocking him unconscious to the floor. At this point Larry arrived on the scene with several other airmen and upon looking at Gershon lying on the floor, expressed his disdain for him.

"The son-of-a-bitch ain't such a big shot now, huh?" said Larry.

"Here Larry," said Markham, handing Larry the knife. "Go up on deck and dump the knife in the ocean, will you?"

"With pleasure. This could be sticking in my back," said Larry as he left with the knife.

By this time, Gershon was regaining consciousness and after a few seconds got up on his feet to find Markham standing next to his upper bunk looking at him without comment.

"Where's my knife?" asked Gershon to anyone who would listen.

"It was thrown overboard," he heard someone yell to him.

Gershon looked at Markham. "I ain't going to forget this, Jim."

"Thanks for the warning, George. Just don't come back here unless you want more of the same," said Markham.

The lights went out at 2200 hours as usual, leaving only the red emergency lights illuminating the exits. Markham was in the twilight of his sleep when he was awakened by voices which got louder when someone yelled for the lights to be turned on. He jumped out of his upper bunk onto the floor in his shorts and T-shirt and walked over to the end of the cubicle where three men were standing over Gershon, who was lying on the floor, his T-shirt covered in blood. Gershon was gasping for air and trying to say something then became real quiet, his eyes fluttering.

"What happened?" asked Markham of the three airmen.

"Someone stabbed him and ran," said one of the men.

"Did he recognize the man who stabbed him?" asked Markham.

"He didn't say, but then it was dark. Who knows?" said another.

"Did somebody call for the doctor or medic?" asked Markham.

"Yeah! Kurt ran upstairs to get some help. Here he comes now."

The Officer of the Day (OD) along with the ship's doctor, a medical assistant and two unidentified Navymen carrying a stretcher arrived at the scene and the compartment lights were finally turned on. The doctor examined Gershon and announced matter-of-factly that he'd been stabbed twice and needed to be transported to the ship's medical facility immediately. As Gershon was transported on the stretcher out of the compartment, the OD aided by two other officers, who had since arrived on the scene, started examining Gershon's bed and the surrounding area when one of the officers found a knife under one of the nearby bunks.

"Lieutenant Arden, look what I found under this bunk," he said, showing a knife with traces of blood on its blade.

"Looks like you found the weapon used to stab the victim. Try to handle it so that fingerprints can be lifted from it by the investigators. It's evidence, so find a plastic bag and bag it and put a tag or label on it showing where you found it. OK?" said the OD.

Markham recognized it as possibly the knife he took from Gershon which Larry was supposed to throw into the ocean. He looked around to see if Larry was around, but couldn't see him. He stepped back from the small crowd and walked back past his own bunk to the end of the cubicle where he found Larry apparently sleeping in his bunk. Markham thought that Larry could very well have slipped back into his bunk without ever being seen by Markham, who was asleep. He didn't awaken until Gershon was discovered on the floor where he must have fallen in an attempt to get help after being stabbed, otherwise he could have bled to death in his bunk without anyone ever discovering he'd been stabbed until the next morning. The OD was apprised by some of the airmen about the earlier confrontation between Gershon and Markham, which prompted the OD and the other two officers to question Markham about the earlier confrontation in detail which is when they learned of the knife disposal by Larry Barnes. The OD decided that before he would question Larry Barnes, he would first determine if the knife with traces of blood was indeed George Gershon's knife which if positive, would narrow the list of suspects to Larry Barnes. Unfortunately, Gershon was being attended to by the ship's doctor trying to save his life and was not in a position to be interviewed, hence the OD postponed Barnes' interview until the next morning.

It was now 0100 hours, two hours after the stabbing and Doctor Wilkins had just stepped out of the makeshift operating room.

"How's the patient doing, Doctor?" asked the OD.

"Luckily for him, there were no vital organs or major arteries severed that would have required major surgery, but he did loose quite a bit of blood. He's resting comfortably and he should recover from his wounds absent a serious infection. You'll be able to talk to him later this morning."

"Would you say, Doctor, that judging from the wounds his assailant was trying to kill him?" asked the OD.

"Yes, it looks that way. Those were deep wounds and he did stab him twice," replied the Doctor.

"Thank you doctor," said the OD who then turned to the other two officers who had assisted him in his investigation. "The charge will be assault with intent to commit voluntary manslaughter. I'll inform the Captain who I'm sure will alert the ONI, who will undoubtedly take over the investigation once we land in New York."

The following morning at 0800 hours, the OD and his two aides reported promptly to the infirmary where Gershon was bedded.

"I see that you are awake," said the OD to Gershon.

"The medic just woke me up to give me some medicine," replied Gershon in a raspy voice.

"We found the knife that was used to stab you under a bunk not far from your bunk and we were wondering if you'd ever seen that knife before," said the OD, who then produced the knife contained in a clear plastic bag with a tag attached to it.

Gershon examined the knife and immediately identified it as his knife. "Yes, that's my knife. The last time I saw it was when Jim Markham knocked it out of my hand yesterday."

"Thank you. That's all we needed to know," said the OD, who then exited the room with his two aides. "Let's go find Larry Barnes. I believe we have enough evidence to successfully confront him."

"Lieutenant Arden, shouldn't we read Barnes his rights under Article 31?" asked one of the junior officers.

"Yes, I guess you're right. Is there a UCMJ on board?" asked the OD.

"I doubt it Lieutenant. But as I recall, we just have to inform him that under Article 31 of the UCMJ, anything he says can be used against him in a court-martial and that he has the right to consult an attorney and if he can't afford one, an attorney will be appointed free of charge," said the junior officer, "and then he's asked if he'll waive his right to an attorney."

"Sounds good to me. You can assist me in the interview by giving him his rights and I'll then conduct the interview while you take notes," said the OD.

"I think you also have to advise him of the charge," stated the other junior officer.

"He's not being charged at this time, only investigated as a suspect, and since he is a suspect, we have to advise him of his rights under the UCMJ, and of course the matter under investigation, that's all," replied the OD.

All of the airmen were gathered on the deck of the ship in order for the clean-up crews to clean the various compartments. The OD and his aides went topside and the Sergeant at Arms located Larry Barnes, who was asked to accompany them to an office on the upper deck. Barnes was recited his rights under Article 31 of the UCMJ and waived his rights to counsel, after which he was confronted with the knife and its identification by Gershon who, he was informed, was alive and recovering from his wounds. Convinced of the futility of denying his culpability in view of the evidence, he readily confessed to his crime and was immediately placed under arrest for assault with intent to commit voluntary manslaughter and confined to the brig located near the bow of the ship for the duration of the voyage to New York. When asked by the OD the reason for stabbing Gershon, Larry Barnes explained that he feared that Gershon would make another attempt to stab him and he couldn't bear to go to sleep each night in fear of his life waiting for Gershon to knife him, so he decided to stab him first and end the nightmare. He further explained that after he stabbed Gershon, in his haste to escape he bumped into one of the bunks in the dark and dropped the knife to the floor which slid out of sight and he simply didn't have time to look for it and had to return to his bunk before anyone could notice that he had left it. The chance confrontation with Markham and the accidental loss of the knife caused his downfall.

It didn't take long for the rumors to get around the ship and the fact that Larry Barnes had been locked up in the brig confirmed those rumors. Markham related the incident to Sammy who offered him a bunk in the Merchant Marine's quarters, but Markham declined, explaining that there was no danger and the matter was now resolved. However, Markham was moved by the kindness shown to him by Sammy. *There are many nice people in this world which makes the struggle worthwhile,* he thought.

The USS Patch docked in the New York Harbor and the troops were transported to Manhattan Beach Air Station for further processing. Markham had only five days travel time to report to his new duty station at Loring Air Force Base in Maine. He stood in his dress uniform outside the main gate waiting for a taxi that would take him to Grand Central Station in Manhattan. As he waited at the street curb, two young, uniformed airmen, who by their conversational accent were from the south, stood next to Markham also awaiting a taxi. As they stood at the street corner, a short, swarthy, pimpled face man approached the two southerners.

"Hey! You guys like to have a good time with a girl? I've got a real nice girl for you," said the swarthy man to the two young southern airmen, while Markham listened to the conversation. The two young men were puzzled by the directness of this intrusive man and they were hesitant in responding.

"Hey! Man. I tell you, no strings attached. I fix you up with a sexy woman who loves soldiers," he said.

"Yeah? How much it cost for this woman?" said one of the young airman, more out of curiosity than a willingness to accept the offer.

"No, no. It won't cost you anything," replied the swarthy man with a smile.

At this point, Markham felt it a duty to protect these two young airmen from this sleazy pervert.

"Don't tell me you're giving these guys something for nothing. What's in it for you?" said Markham in his distinctive New York accent.

The swarthy man who had avoided Markham's presence, now felt compelled to provide an answer clearly awaited by all three airmen.

The swarthy man looked at Markham and then at the two southerners, then back at Markham with a sheepish smile, "Well, you know. One night they sleep with the girl and one night they sleep with me," he said to the astonishment of the two southern airmen.

"Yeah! And I'll bet the first night will be with you, you sleaze-bag. Get the hell out of here before I knock your teeth in," said Markham, and the swarthy man quickly left the area.

"Listen guys. You're in New York now, so be extra careful. Just remember that nobody gives you something for nothing. I lived here. I know," said Markham who felt empathy for his fellow airmen.

Markham, carrying his large duffel bag, flagged down a taxi which took him to Grand Central

Station where he embarked on a train that took him as far as Bangor, Maine, then a bus the rest of the way to Loring Air Force Base.

As Markham walked up to the main gate of Loring Air Force Base after getting off the bus from Bangor, Maine, he noticed a sign arched over the security guard shack that proudly stated 'Strategic Air Command' (SAC). Markham showed his Special Orders and Identification Card to the Security Guard who then directed him to the 96th Air Refueling Squadron Orderly Room where he was to report for duty. A Sergeant drove up to the gate and upon seeing Markham with his large suitcase and shoulder bag, offered him a lift which he gladly accepted. At the Orderly Room, Markham was given a key with a room and barracks number that was to be his quarters during his assignment at Loring AFB. This was a time when he wished he had a car because the base was enormous and buses were far and few between. When he finally arrived at the assigned barracks, a two-story cement-block building, he found his room on the second floor was already occupied by two other airmen who identified themselves as Joe Portland and Steve Slagle. As it turned out, both of them were former Captains, one a pilot and the other a navigator, who were involuntarily discharged from the Air Force for being passed over for promotion twice. The term 'RIF' for Reduction In Force was used to describe commissioned officers who lost their commission and were offered the choice of rejoining the Air Force as enlisted servicemen usually in the grade of Airman First Class as in the case of Joe and Steve, until they had served a total of 20 years at which time they could retire in the highest held grade which in their case would be Captain.

It was always a severe blow to their morale as well as paycheck and they were invariably reassigned to another air base where they would not have to face previous subordinates and contemporaries. Only those officers with 18 years or more of active duty service were immune to the Reduction in Force threat that hung over any commissioned officer who was unfortunate enough to be passed over *twice* for promotion usually due to a less than excellent annual performance report issued by his immediate supervising officer. Unfortunately, even an excellent performance report may not be enough to compete against other officers with outstanding performance reports and the former does not have to be justified, hence good and even outstanding officers have found themselves RIF'd due to personality conflicts or politics.

There were two double bunks in the room and Markham was informed by Joe Portland that both the lower and upper bunks on the east wall were unoccupied, therefore Markham selected the lower bunk and started to unpack his clothes. Joe and Steve invited Markham to the snack bar which he accepted and it became obvious to Markham that Joe and Steve loved their beer as they each ordered a large pitcher for themselves. After a week of bunking with these two RIF'd airmen, Markham concluded that these two men had resolved to drown their failed careers and family life into an alcoholic escape. They admittedly were just marking time until their date of retirement. Markham felt sorry for these two older airmen who eventually shared their sad stories of hopes and disappointments. Markham, with his youthful optimism, reminded them of the professional qualifications that brought them to officer status which certainly could be used as a basis for starting a new career in the private sector after retirement from the Air Force.

Apparently Markham was just the light and message of hope they needed because both airmen significantly reduced their drinking and started attending classes at the Base Education Center to advance their chances at a new career. The three men became good friends and Markham learned a great deal about aeronautics from these two veteran aircrews.

Markham was not prepared for the experience he gained from his assignment at the 96th Air Refueling Squadron's Flight Operations, located in a two-story cement building with the first story partially underground and immediately adjacent to the flight line and control tower. The noise from the airplanes was sometimes deafening, especially when the huge B-36 bombers revved up their six propeller engines and then their four jet engines. Markham had been given a rundown by Joe and Steve about the B-36 which Loring AFB seemed to have in great numbers. At one point, Markham decided to step outside the Flight Operations building and see a B-36 bomber getting ready to taxi out to the main runway up close. This 162 foot aircraft with its 230 foot wingspan and 47 foot height had propellers that were 19 feet in diameter and the wings were seven feet thick at its root, large enough to allow a crewmember to crawl inside and reach the engines. In fact, a B-29 Superfortress could fit under one of the wings of the B-36. Markham was told that a crew member could travel or even send a meal from the forward cabin to the aft cabin by lying down on a wheeled cart and pull himself along an overhead cable through a two foot wide tunnel 85 feet in length. As Markham observed this magnificent airship, he noticed that there were six machine gun turrets and two 20 millimeter guns to defend it and the engine noise produced an entrancing drone that resonated down to the soles of his feet and rattled windows several buildings away. Markham learned that the B-36 could carry a bomb load of 70,000 lbs and in fact could carry the 43,000 pound hydrogen bomb, and fly at altitudes of more than 50,000 feet with a 10,000 mile range at a top speed of 435 miles per hour, making it accessible to any target on the globe and inaccessible to most fighter planes.

The Commander of SAC, General Curtis LeMay, relied heavily on the B-36 bomber as a deterrent against enemy aggression and in that regard instituted *Operation Chrome Dome* which required that twelve B-36 bombers armed with nuclear weapons be in the air 24 hours per day, 365 days a year so that in the event of a nuclear attack on the United States, SAC would still have a viable nuclear force in the air at all times capable of annihilating any country guilty of aggression against the United States. From his work as an administrative clerk in Flight Operations, which required a Top Secret Clearance, Markham knew about the alternate SAC command center with the code name *Looking Glass* that was aboard a SAC Aircraft continuously in the air in case of war and in the event that the primary SAC command center at Omaha, Nebraska got knocked out. Of course there was a safety feature in place before a nuclear attack could be launched from one of these B-36 bombers in that the GO Codes had to be authenticated by both the B-36 pilot and the Positive Control Member, usually the co-pilot or engineer on board before the order could be carried out. But Markham translated all of this information into one huge fuel bill for the United States Government and the fact that the 96th Air Refueling Squadron to which he was assigned provided the fuel to these monstrous aircraft really brought that fact home.

Markham's suitcase containing his civilian clothes finally arrived at Loring AFB, but there were no social events that required the wearing of a civilian suit. Loring AFB, located at Limestone, in the northern tip of Maine was nothing but country surrounded by lots of forest and not much to do other than camping and fishing. Luckily he didn't arrive at the heart of the winter season as he would have realized the purpose of all those underground passages to all of the buildings on the base.

Markham found himself a daily routine that was of necessity rather passive, then one day he received a letter from his mother Nora announcing that her long-time colleague and friend Freddie from New York City proposed to her on the telephone to Florida in those eloquent words that she would never forget, 'Come to New York and be my Queen.' And after giving an enthusiastically positive answer, Nora went to New York and married Freddie and now they were residing in an apartment in Queens, New York. Markham had previously met Freddie and liked his deportment as a gentleman of good nature with the values of a clergyman. Not only was Markham certain that Freddie would make Nora a good husband, but he was the type of man he could trust implicitly. In a brief letter Markham congratulated them on their impromptu marriage, but what was unsaid was his concern that his former home in New York City was no longer available to him while he sought employment and possibly attendance at a university under the G.I. bill. But Markham figured that he would cross that bridge when he got there.

Markham's discharge date was only two months away and the Squadron Commander was putting pressure and offering incentives to Markham for him to re-enlist in the Air Force, but Markham didn't like his assignment at Loring AFB. He knew that if he re-enlisted at Loring, he would be stuck there, perhaps for years to come, hence he resisted the offerings, including a promotion to Airman First Class. Markham was told by the First Sergeant that if he didn't re-enlist, the Airman First Class stripe would go to another administrative clerk who agreed to re-enlist. Markham believed that promotions should be based on merit, not on condition of re-enlistment, and that this unfairness was another reason for his wanting to leave the military service. On 31 August 1955, Markham received his discharge papers plus $300.00 mustering out pay, plus 30 days unused leave of absence which translated into another $150.00 which when added to the $350.00 he'd managed to save, amounted to a total of $800.00 to his name, not much to start a new life.

CHAPTER V
The Homeless Period

Markham had given his mother's new address to the taxi driver outside the Forest Hills subway station and to his surprise she and Freddie lived only a few blocks away in a four-story building that contained efficiency apartments. Markham was greeted by Nora at the door to her second floor apartment with a big hug and kiss and Freddie shook his hand vigorously as they invited him inside. Markham wore his dark blue blazer with gray slacks and open white shirt, carrying his one large suitcase which he set down next to the entranceway wall. The apartment consisted of one large room with a sofa bed, a love seat and a small table with four chairs near the small efficiency kitchen adjacent to the bathroom. There obviously was only room for two people in that apartment and Markham didn't expect to be invited to stay the night, however he would have liked to have known of this lack of accommodation prior to his arrival because now he would have to find a hotel room which he could hardly afford on his limited financial resources.

After dinner was served in the apartment, Freddie went to the bathroom which gave Nora an opportunity to speak to her son alone.

"You know, Jim, that I would love for you to stay here, but you can see dear that the apartment is simply too small. We just got married and you staying here in these cramped quarters would put a terrible strain on us. You understand dear, don't you?" said Nora apologetically.

"Of course I understand, Mom. I didn't intend to stay the night. In fact I must be going before it gets too late," said Markham, not wanting to be a burden.

Freddie came out of the bathroom and Nora told him that Jim was leaving in order to find a hotel room.

"Nonsense, at this time of the night? Naw! Would you mind sleeping on the couch Jim? I know it's kind of small for you, but it's only for one night. In the morning Nora can fix you a nice breakfast and then you can have an early start," said Freddie.

"That sounds like a good plan. Thanks Freddie," replied Markham.

"Are you planning on going into the old neighborhood in Manhattan?" asked Freddie.

"Yeah! It's a good start," said Markham.

"In that case, you can ride with me to the Long Island Railroad Station where I park my car then ride the train into New York City's Grand Central Station. We can ride together, then you can take the subway from Grand Central to the Sheridan Station," said Freddie.

"Yeah! I know the route Freddie," said Markham, who felt very much alone. He realized that his mother deserved a life too and finally she found a wonderful husband and he had no right to impose on her and disturb their privacy at such a critical time in their marriage. He felt that her right to a happy marriage superseded any expectation that he might have had of a home upon his return from military service. He was a man now and must learn to fend for himself.

The next day he said farewell to his mother at the apartment and then goodbye to Freddie at Grand Central Station. He then checked his suitcase in a locker at the station then made his way to the old neighborhood on 10th and Bleeker.

It was near noontime and Markham fully expected Boris Baranowski to be working at the vegetable stand outside the grocery store on the corner of 10th Street and Bleeker as he did in August 1951 when Markham joined the Air Force. As he walked up to the stand, sure enough, there was Boris, wearing a full white apron soiled from the vegetables he handled for the customers, standing talking to a middle-aged woman who had been shopping there for years. He spotted Markham from the corner of his eye and turned around to confirm that it was in fact his old pitching friend from the glorious baseball days. Boris excused himself and walked over and with both of his arms outstretched gave Markham a big welcoming hug.

"Good grief. When did you get back?" asked Boris, surprised.

"Last night actually," replied Markham.

"You son-of-a-gun. You didn't send us a letter, not even a postcard. We thought you were dead. Your mother moved to Florida so we had absolutely no news of you," said Boris.

"Well Boris, I was in England for three years, and writing is not one of my strong points, and they kept us pretty busy," said Markham.

"So, are you out now?" asked Boris.

"Yeah! I got discharged on the 31st of August and now I've got to figure out what I'm going to do with the rest of my life," said Markham.

"Listen Jim. I've got to work till 6, but I'm sure I can get out at 5:30 and then we can go for a pizza and beer across the street with Bernie and Tony and maybe Nye if we can get a hold of him. You've got the entire afternoon, so why don't you pay Bernie a visit and together you can round up whoever's left, which is not many," said Boris.

"Who is left?" asked Markham.

"Everybody's gone into the service and most have moved away afterwards. Hell there's only me, my brother Adolph, Bernie, Tony, Phil, who's now a pharmacist and never comes around anymore, Elie of course still manages his butcher shop, and Ray who I see occasionally. That's it my friend. It's not the same neighborhood Jim. Those days are gone forever, I'm sad to say," said Boris.

Markham was also saddened by the departure of his friends. "I wish those days would never have ended," said Markham pensively. "I'll pay Bernie a visit and pick you up later when you've finished work."

"Hey! By the way. Bernie is getting married in three weeks. I thought you should know," said Boris.

"To anybody I know?" replied Markham.

"Yeah! His old girlfriend Sally, you remember her, the gawky looking kid?" said Boris.

"I'll bet she's not gawky looking anymore," replied Markham with a knowing smile. "See you later Boris."

Markham walked up Bleeker Street until he reached the apartment building where Bernie resided on the fourth floor. When Bernie answered the door, Markham's first impression was that Bernie had aged 10 years, yet it had been only four years since he'd last seen him. Maybe he should hurry up and get married, Markham thought, because at this rate the poor guy will be an old man before he's 40. However, Markham was too much of a gentleman and considerate of other people's feelings to ever reveal negative thoughts that might enter his mind. They talked for quite a while and Markham learned that Vic Racci was drafted into the Army and was sent to Korea where he suffered frostbite of his hands and feet which had a definite negative impact on his potential baseball career. Frankie Biondilini was also drafted and he contracted hepatitis which resulted in a medical discharge. He and his parents subsequently moved to Arizona. Tommy Bernadi is making the Air Force a career as an officer and the rest of the guys moved away with their parents, some out of state. Bernie was saddened most of all by Frankie's departure as he never expected him to ever leave the neighborhood, although he did expect Markham to leave as he and the rest of the boys all felt that he was destined to leave the city for bigger and better things.

"You are coming to our wedding aren't you, Jim?" asked Bernie, a bit anxious.

"I wouldn't miss it for the world Bernie," answered Markham. "So where's your Mom, Bernie?"

"She's out shopping. She should be back in a little while. She'll be surprised to see you. You've changed some Jim," said Bernie.

"How's that?" inquired Markham.

"You've put on a few pounds in the right places; you look seasoned," he replied.

"Well, I'll tell you Bernie. It hasn't been a picnic in the service. But the experience was well worth the trouble, though," said Markham.

"I guess you've got lots of stories to tell, huh?" said Bernie.

"A few, but now's not the time to reminisce," replied Markham, who felt like taking a walk around the old neighborhood in the hope of encountering familiar faces. That evening, after eating pizza with his friends, Markham bought a toothbrush and toothpaste to save himself a trip to Grand Central Station where he had checked his suitcase, and went to the 23rd Street YMCA where he slept the night there. The next day he decided to look in the newspapers for employment opportunities as he knew that he could not support himself and go to college on the G.I. Bill and he wasn't sure that he could get into college with the mediocre grades he acquired in High School. As he pored over the newspapers for job offers, he realized that he had little skill to offer except his military training and experience as an administrative clerk. He pounded the pavement throughout the city seeking meaningful employment that offered an opportunity for advancement to an acceptable level that would permit him to marry, own a home and raise children to realize the all-American dream. However, nothing panned out. The old neighborhood was gone, his home had vanished and the city of New York offered him no hope. He missed London. At least he was happy there, even though he didn't get to visit it as much as he wished. The thought occurred to him that if he re-enlisted at Manhattan Beach they might offer him a direct assignment to England as a condition of re-enlistment inasmuch as they needed personnel in his Air Force Specialty (AFSC). If he could get them to make that offer plus the monetary bonus that comes with re-enlistment, he would have enough money to visit his Grandmother in Montreal before he left for overseas again. Once in England, he could devote most of his spare time taking college courses through the University of Maryland Overseas Program so that when he got discharged next time, he would have a degree or a good head start towards one. *Yes,* he thought, *that plan is the only one that makes sense.* Markham visited the recruiting office at Manhattan Beach Air Force Station, and was told that Strategic Air Command had a definite need for airmen with his AFSC and that if he re-enlisted for six years, he would be guaranteed a three-year tour of duty in England plus a bonus of $1500.00 and if he wished, a 30-days advance leave of absence before shipment to England. Markham signed his re-enlistment papers, collected his bonus money and 30-days leave and got on an airplane to Montreal, Canada to visit his Grandmother Nancy before she died.

After landing at the airport in Montreal, Markham hailed a taxi to his Grandmother's house on Saint Denis Street without having notified her or his Aunt Pauline and Uncle Roland who lived with her of his forthcoming arrival. Pauline answered the door and upon seeing Markham, exclaimed her surprise and hugged him.

"Guess who's here?" shouted Pauline to Roland and Grandmaman, and Roland came to the vestibule where Markham was now standing with his suitcase next to him.

"Well, I'll be dog-gone," said Roland, shaking his hand. "Why didn't you let us know you were coming?"

"I'm leaving for England soon and on the spur of the moment I thought I'd visit you and Grandmaman before I left because I'm going to be gone for a long time," said Markham.

"England? Is that right?" exclaimed Roland, grabbing Markham's suitcase and bringing it into the spare bedroom off the hallway. Pauline brought Markham into the living room where Grandmaman was sitting quietly in a large rocking chair, seemingly asleep.

Pauline called out to her, "Maman," gently touching her hand, "Maman. Your Grandson Jimmy is here." Grandmaman opened her eyes and looked up, but didn't seem to recognize Markham who was bending over to bring his face closer to hers. "Maman, c'est Jacques, he came here to see you from New York," said Pauline.

Grandmaman Nancy stared into her grandson James Markham's face and upon recognition, tears started streaming down her cheeks as she raised her left hand in an attempt to touch him. Markham held her hand in his, then bent down further and kissed her forehead. Markham looked up at Pauline and she explained, "Her memory is not so good anymore. I'm sure she recognized you, but she can barely talk, Jim."

"Hi! Grandma, I thought a lot about you while I've been away, and I've missed you," said Markham in a most gentle voice.

Pauline used a soft tissue to wipe the tears from Grandmaman's cheeks. "I think she needs to rest, Jim. This is the most excitement she's had in years," said Pauline, and Markham released Grandmaman's hand and stepped back to allow Pauline to attend to his Grandmother's needs. He wished people didn't get old, especially the ones he loved. It was so sad to see her reduced to such a degenerative state, waiting to die. Markham was glad that he had decided to visit her at this time because she would most likely be gone from this earth upon his return from England.

The next day, Markham visited Saint Joseph's Oratory located on the northern slope of Mount Royal in Montreal. He remembered that as a boy he had often visited the Basilica which was known to have the second largest dome of its kind after Saint Peter's Basilica in Rome, and could hold a crowd of ten thousand worshippers.

He also remembered seeing the heart of Brother Andre the founder of the shrine preserved and displayed in a glass container. However on this visit, Markham found that Brother Andre's heart was now stored in a closed container protected by steel bars as a result of an earlier incident when Brother Andre's heart was stolen for ransom and when the Church refused to pay the ransom, it was returned unharmed. He had attended many a Midnight Mass on Christmas Eve at many different churches, but none of them compared to the majesty and grandness of Midnight Mass at Saint Joseph's Basilica with a choir consisting of 180 boys supported by musicians and an organ comparable to Rome's Basilica. Upon entering the Basilica, Markham felt an overpowering need to kneel and pray, first to Jesus, then St. Joseph and finally to Brother Andre for spiritual guidance and assistance in a life that appeared to be rudderless. Alone, in a secluded corner of the huge church, Markham suddenly began crying uncontrollably and had to put his hands up to his face, then pulled out his handkerchief from his back pocket to absorb his tears and blow his nose to justify the use of the handkerchief in case someone was watching him. Finally, he felt relief and absolution for which he thanked God, then got off his knees and sat in the pew's seat to recover from the emotional experience of this spiritual event. Markham made a promise to God that he would henceforth practice goodness and kindness to all, and as he walked out of the Basilica he noticed the 99 wooden steps that climbed the steep slope leading to the entrance to the Basilica and decided to climb each of these steps on his knees reciting a prayer on each step as atonement for his sins.

However, Markham was unprepared for the pain he would suffer from knees that had not kneeled against hard wood in many years. By the fiftieth step, Markham's knees were so bruised that he doubted if he could climb another step, but he did and after a while his knees became numb until he reached the 99th and final step. Here he tried to stand up, but was unable to straighten his legs at the knee and had to grab the railing for support until the circulation partially returned at which time he felt excruciating pain in both knees. He noticed that a few people were staring at him, but he didn't care because he was gratified that he was able to finish his self-imposed penitence. Markham felt that he was back to his roots where spiritual guidance predominated his life and its pursuits. *I don't know what God has in store for me,* he thought, *but whatever it is, I'm ready for it.*

Markham spent another week in Montreal visiting relatives then elected to return to Manhattan in time to attend Bernie's wedding, hence bid farewell to his relatives and flew into LaGuardia Airport where he took a limousine to New York City and a subway ride to the 23rd Street YMCA where he reserved a bed for the next several nights.

As usual, Markham stopped by Boris' vegetable stand where the boys always met and Boris informed him that the wedding was going to be held at St Mark's church and the reception would be held on the second floor of the local fire hall where Fat White now worked as a fireman.

"Fat White is now a fireman?" asked Markham in astonishment.

"Yeah! Would you believe it?" said Boris.

"They must have a special ladder for him to climb aboard," said Markham jokingly.

Boris laughed at the suggestion. "Apparently he's trimmed down a bit, otherwise he wouldn't have been able to pass the physical," said Boris.

"Boy! Things really have changed around here," replied Markham.

"You got that right Jim, and not all for the better," said Boris.

"Well, I'm glad for Fats that he got himself a good job with security," said Markham, remembering his oath of 'goodness and kindness' to all.

"You got yourself a suit and a white shirt and tie?" asked Boris.

"Yes I have," replied Markham.

"Hey! Nye and Phil are having dinner with me at Luigi's tonight, so join us, OK? I mean, you don't have anything else planned, do you?"

"No, nothing planned. Sounds great. I'm looking forward to seeing Nye and Phil," replied Markham, pleased that he would see them before leaving for Europe.

"Bernie is too busy getting ready for the big day which is only two days away," said Boris.

That evening, Tony managed to find time to join Boris, Nye, Phil and Jim Markham for a reunion filled with spaghetti, wine and lots of laughs. Markham silently suffered from mixed emotions in that he didn't want to leave his friends nor the memories they brought with them, but the only place he could now call home was the United States Air Force and for the next six years his home would be where they sent him.

On the day of the wedding, Markham was surprised by the significant number of people that attended at Saint Mark's church. Sally apparently came from a very large Irish family and Bernie's family, who also had its roots in Ireland, filled many church pews. The wedding also drew a few people who had moved out of town that Markham now had the privilege of meeting for the last time, such as Ray Balantine, Brewer Franklin and Don Domingo. The groom was dressed in a black tuxedo and the bride in a traditional white gown and the car used for the getaway was a black, four-door Buick owned by Phil D'Amato which took them from the church to the Firehall for the reception. At the reception, Bernie and Sally now husband and wife, sat at the head of a long table where the best man, Boris, sat alongside with the parents of both newlyweds. Markham sat a table directly in front of the head table flanked by Phil, Elie, Tony, Nye, Brewer, Don and Ray. Markham observed that Fat White, accompanied by a petite brunette, sat at a table in the rear of the firehall with several other people whom he was told were firefighters. All of the tables in the firehall were occupied with mostly relatives of the two newlyweds, but care was taken to leave ample room at the center of the hall for dancing to a local four-piece band where the pianist wore a second hat as the vocalist.

Bernie and Sally fulfilled the customary first dance of the evening, although Bernie was not enthusiastic about being the focus of attention at a skill he had not developed, but they had chosen 'That's Amore' by Dean Martin as their musical number of choice. They sort of walked close together in a tight circle in the center of the dance floor talking to each other to cover their embarrassment at being all alone on the dance floor and when several other couples got onto the dance floor at the end of the song, Bernie and Sally maneuvered their way off the dance floor and back onto the elevated head table where they each sipped on their champagne, relieved that their performance was over. The band's music was obviously outdated in that no 1955 songs were played, however several songs that were popular in 1953 and 1954 such as 'Stranger in Paradise', 'Secret Love', and 'Hey, There' were played and sung rather well which brought nostalgic times to many in the audience. People were clinging their glasses with a spoon or other utensils demanding a speech by the groom or bride during the band's break, and at one point, Fat White stood up at the rear of the hall and in a loud voice called out to Markham who was sitting at the front table with several of his friends.

"Hey! Jim. If you don't have a home to go to, you can always stay with me," said Fat White in a deliberate attempt to humiliate him. Markham looked at him for a moment, then remembering his oath, remained silent, but truly felt hurt and debased by White's unkind remark which did not go unnoticed by Markham's friends, who themselves remained silent and made out as if they hadn't heard the remark. *No doubt,* Markham thought, *Fat White saw an opportunity to get even with me for the time I humiliated him by knocking him into the Hudson River.* As the evening wore on, people left the reception to go home and in Markham's case, the YMCA.

The World Series between the Yankees and the Brooklyn Dodgers was in its sixth game and the bets were against the Dodgers who had never won a World Series, whereas the Yankees had won several and were thought to have a better team. As the seventh and last game was being played at the Stadium, almost everything in New York City and Brooklyn came to a standstill until the ninth and last inning ended with the score of two to zero for the Brooklyn Dodgers who were pronounced the winners of the World Series. The cheers from Brooklyn could be heard clear across the river on the shores of Manhattan where the shock of their loss was still numbing their sense of comprehension. Many of the bars in Brooklyn were serving free drinks to the public and throngs of Brooklyn fans from New York streamed across the bridge to Brooklyn to celebrate the event.

Boris, Markham, Adolph, and Nye were all listening to the radio in Tony's Pizzeria when the final score was announced.

"The Brooklyn Bums won the World Series," exclaimed Boris. "What do you think about that?"

"Hey! They have some outstanding players and a good pitching staff," said Markham. "That Johnny Podres pitched a no-hitter and that was his second shutout of the Yankees in the Series. That's some pitching."

"Yeah! But so do the Yankees," said Nye. "Frankly, I'm surprised."

"What do you think Adolph?" said Markham.

"They played seven games so it's not a fluke, huh! I take my hat off to those bums, they played some outstanding baseball," said Adolph.

"Anyone interested in going to Brooklyn to help them celebrate the event?" asked Adolph, who got no positive response. "Hey! I've got the car gassed up and ready. What do you say guys?"

"Naw, I don't feel like going all the way over there now," said his brother Boris.

"The place is probably a mad house," said Nye.

"How about you Jim. You interested?" asked Adolph.

"I don't think so, but thanks for the offer Adolph," replied Markham, who was thinking that it now was time for him to leave New York City and begin his new life and career with England as his first stop.

CHAPTER VI
Return to England

This was Markham's third ocean voyage aboard a troop ship, but this time it was on the USS Geiger and the ship struggled through three violent storms that delayed the voyage by three days. When it finally docked at Southampton, England, the duration and roughness of the passage convinced many of the troops that they had mistakenly joined the Navy. At least that was the joke circulating aboard the ship. There were several Air Force buses waiting at the dock for their transportation to various American Air Bases throughout England and Markham boarded the bus whose header indicated Upper Heyford and Chelveston, the latter Air Base was Markham's destination located some 93 kilometers North of London.

Upon his arrival at Chelveston Air Force Base, Markham noticed that the Air Base was architecturally no different than Molesworth Air Base where he was stationed on his previous tour of duty in England. Most buildings were Quonset huts, some of them connected together giving the illusion of a large single story building such as the Headquarters of the 305th Bomb Wing where he was assigned as an administrative clerk for the Adjutant Major Edward Halpin and his assistant Master Sergeant Gunther. Major Halpin was a slim and trim man of average height with a receding hair line who wore glasses and appeared to be the quintessential bureaucrat, whereas Sergeant Gunther was the typical Army grunt who transferred to the Air Force for easier duty in his later years and found himself pushing paper as a desk jockey. However, regardless of the type of duty assigned to him, Sergeant Gunther was a disciplined perfectionist who demanded maximum performance from his subordinates which made the Adjutant very happy.

Markham was assigned to barracks number 24, a Quonset hut five rows back from the main street and a convenient one row from the shower and latrine hut. There were 12 airmen residing in hut #24 including Markham, and the only empty available bunk for him was located between the bunks occupied by Roger Hall and William Hicks. As it turned out, all of the airmen in hut #24 were friendly individuals and Markham learned that four of them were attending the University of Maryland Overseas Program through the Base Education Office, which elated him. Markham subsequently visited the Education Office and learned that he could challenge four tests offered by the University of Maryland and if successful, would be awarded six college credits for each test passed for a total of 24 credits, equivalent to nearly one year of college. Markham took all four tests and passed three of them, but failed the English test by two points; however, he was informed that in six months he could take the test again.

Markham went to the Base Library and checked out books on English composition and such notables as *The Elements of Style* to strengthen his command of the English language. Six months later, Markham took UM's English test and passed it with flying colors. Now that he was armed with 24 college credits, he felt encouraged to pursue his bachelor's degree with full speed ahead and enrolled in two courses at a time requiring four evening classes per week at the Education Center, leaving him only with weekends to study and complete homework assignments. This was a full schedule for anyone, considering that he had to work at the Orderly Room office a minimum of eight hours per day plus additional military duties such as Charge of Quarters, etc.

In September the Adjutant informed Markham that there was a course on International Relations in the Middle East offered at Cambridge University for American Servicemen during the Christmas Holidays. The students selected on a merit basis would be housed at the University's Madingley Hall campus for the duration of the course which would be funded by the United States Air Force. Markham would have to compete against officers and airmen applying for the course as the number of students selected was limited. He was subsequently notified that he had been selected to attend the course and on December 1st, he was driven by jeep to Madingley Hall in Cambridge, England.

Markham found Madingley Hall absolutely delightful and the staff of English Professors and instructors intellectually accessible and helpful. The topic regarded primarily the Middle East and the focus was on the Suez Canal and the history that preceded the current conflict and the possible solutions available to the participating governments. The rooms for the students were located on the top or fourth floor of the Hall and there were two students assigned to every room. Markham roomed with an Airman First Class named Brian McDougal whose wife resided off-base in an English village outside of Upper Heyford Air Base near Oxford University, Cambridge University's arch-rival.

On the first floor of Madingley Hall there was a small, narrow room which served as the official distributor of alcoholic beverages, primarily English brew, for a period of one hour per day in the late afternoon between 5 and 6 PM. The meals were delicious, but of small portions which left Markham and McDougal famished. Unfortunately, neither of them had a vehicle and Cambridge proper was a good 5 kilometers away.

Undeterred, they hitchhiked into town and purchased cheese, balogna, packaged ham and other sundry items, plus a keg of English beer. The problem was getting all of that food and keg of beer back to Madingley Hall without a vehicle. There they were, standing alongside the road leading to Madingley Hall, with Markham sitting on the keg of beer while McDougal stood by a large cardboard box full of food items, waiting for a vehicle to give them a ride. As luck would have it, an old Englishman driving a vintage pick-up truck stopped and asked them their destination and upon learning that they were American students at Madingley Hall, he offered them a lift right to the Hall. The old man was amused at the sight of the keg of beer and could imagine the students' revelry in such a Hall of austerity. Markham loaded the keg in the back of the pick-up truck with the box of groceries jammed against it to keep it from rolling about, then climbed in the cab of the truck with McDougal and the old man, who never identified himself. It was late in the evening and the Hall was quiet with no one in sight.

Markham carried the keg of beer on his shoulder while McDougal carried the box of groceries and they entered the side entrance that led to the stairs which took them to the top floor and into their room unhampered. McDougal set up the keg for a quick beer before retiring for the night. The next day after class, Markham came into the room to find McDougal and three friends drinking beer, so he joined them before they consumed the entire keg without him. But it didn't last even one more day as word got around Madingley Hall that a second pub was giving the brew away. One of the professors jokingly told Markham that this was the first time that a keg of beer had been introduced by students into Madingley Hall and as one would expect it, it had to be an American.

Markham and McDougal fully expected that one of the students, a full Colonel and Commanding Officer of an Air Base, upon getting wind of their beer escapade, would reprimand them and possibly have them dismissed from the program, but he reasoned that if the faculty wasn't bothered by it, then there was no need for disciplinary action. After all, students will be students regardless of age or rank.

Markham was accruing college credits at a prodigious rate and within 18 months had reached a total of 60 college credits including the 24 credits he acquired from the four tests he successfully completed. However, junior and senior level courses were much harder to acquire because the number of students applying for them were significantly fewer and a minimum number of students was required before a class could be formed, although the English teachers who were paid American wages truly needed only a few students to make it economically worthwhile. In one instance, Markham took a class in Sociology taught by England's leading Sociologist with only six students in the class. *Where else,* Markham thought, *can I receive such individual attention by such a leading authority on the subject?* But even six students were sometimes tough to get because not many airmen at Chelveston were pursuing a college degree.

It was now 1957 with only a year left in his tour of duty in England, when Markham was promoted to Airman First Class and sent to the Records Disposition School at South Ruislip on the outskirts of the city of London for one month. This gave him an opportunity during the weekends to visit his old haunts in the big city.

On such a weekend, Markham was walking up the stairs to the Mazurka Club when three young English women exited the Club at the top of the stairs and were attempting to squeeze past Markham, who noticed that the last one was unusually attractive. When he said hello to her, she replied likewise with a smile that indicated to Markham that she was interested, so he stopped his ascent and started talking to her. Apparently the three of them had been to a wedding reception and were now continuing their celebration at the Mazurka. They were now going home, but not before Markham obtained her name and address with the promise of a future meeting. Her name was Audrey Maclin and she resided in the East End of London with her parents and younger sister. Her long curly hair was jet black and her skin was white as a sheet with big dark eyes and high cheekbones suggesting that her ancestry was from a mixture of Spanish and Irish blood inasmuch as she was born in Belfast, Ireland.

After a few dates with Audrey, Markham learned that although at five feet 4 inches, weighing 110 pounds, she had an outstanding figure, she was a photographer's model primarily for her exceptional facial features. She also worked as a cosmetic consultant. Although she indicated to Markham that she wanted to date him exclusively and she wanted a commitment from him, he felt that she lacked a most important ingredient which was a tender passion that evokes affection and love. She looked great and she had a winning personality that attracted men from afar, but when in an intimate situation she would turn cold as if she feared that it might lead to sexual intercourse, an act reserved only after marriage in the Catholic Church.

Markham felt that here was a chaste woman worth pursuing, but he was still concerned about her failure to arouse his passion inasmuch as he envisioned a wife who like Sylvia made his heart swell, and like Lillian made his genitals throb with desire. Unsure about Audrey's feelings for him and his own for her, Markham made no promises or commitment and when it came time for him to rotate back to the United States, he said goodbye and as far as they both were concerned, the relationship had ended with his departure.

Markham had received orders to report to MacDill Air Force Base, at Tampa, Florida where he was to be assigned to a Wing commanded by Colonel Paul Tibbets, known as the pilot who dropped the atomic bomb on Hiroshima. The year was 1958 and Markham's arrival at MacDill AFB coincided with the Fourth of July festivities.

It was hot and humid and while Markham loved the tropical climate, he wasn't used to the extreme heat. After checking into the Orderly Room for his barracks assignment, he was told to report to barracks 108, second floor, and take whatever empty bunk was available. The barracks painted white were of World War II vintage and maybe even the First World War as they looked ready for demolition. Markham found an empty bed and wall locker which he made his own by putting a padlock on the locker. He met some of the occupants and one of them, Gary Outshout, a redheaded Irishman, invited him to join him and Tom Sloan for a walk to the Base Snack Bar and Markham accepted. At the snack bar Markham ordered a hamburger and milk shake and sat at a table near the juke box with Gary and Tom. Markham was nearly finished eating his hamburger when he felt a hand on his left shoulder which didn't alarm him because he saw smiles on the faces of Tom and Gary who sat opposite him.

"Jimbo. What are you doing in Florida?" asked the reddish-blond-haired Irishman with the perpetual twinkle in his eye and smile on his face.

Markham turned around in his chair and saw that it was none other than his old pal Frank Cummins whom he had known at Molesworth, England. "Well, I'll be darn. How long have you been at MacDill?" asked Markham, now standing and shaking Frank's hand.

"Hell, about a year I'd say," replied Frank. "Did you just get here?" he asked.

"As a matter of fact I got here today and just moved into barracks 108. Oh! Pardon my manners. This is Gary and Tom, my new barracks mates," said Markham.

"Listen, when you get through eating and unpacking, drop over to my barracks number 114 which must be one row past your barracks. I'm upstairs," said Frank. "See you later Jim, and nice meeting you guys," said Frank, gesturing to Gary and Tom.

"I can't believe it," said Markham to Gary and Tom. "This sure is a small world."

"Yeah! Especially in the Air Force," said Gary.

Markham didn't have much to unpack. Afterwards he walked over to barracks 114 where he found Frank Cummins sitting on a footlocker playing Poker with three other airmen. They were using a portable chess board over a bed with one guy sitting with his legs crossed at its head with a pillow behind him while the other three sat on footlockers around the bed. They were playing for dollars which is all they could afford on their small paychecks. Upon seeing Markham, Frank took his money and stepped out of the game to join him.

"Hey! Let's go off-base Jim. You haven't seen my convertible. It's a beauty," said Frank in his usual carefree manner.

"How'd you manage to afford that?" asked Markham.

"With the bonus I got when I re-enlisted," replied Frank. "Well, I still owe money on it. I'm on the 'Never, Never Plan.' Payments every month like clockwork. But I don't know what I'd do without it. Staying on base would drive me nuts."

"What year and car is it?" asked Markham.

"A 1957 Plymouth Fury," replied Frank.

As they exited the barracks, Frank led Markham to the side of the barracks where several cars owned by airmen were parked on a strip of blacktop. As they approached Frank's convertible, Markham was impressed by the huge tailfins and the metallic gold stripe on each side of the bright red car that ran its full length, spreading its gold color onto the tailfins, giving the impression that it was jet propelled. Both rear wheels were covered with a hardcover skirt and the tires had white sidewalls. Two chrome ornaments were fastened to the front fenders and outside rearview mirrors were fastened near the front side windows. Enormous chrome bumpers adorned the front and rear of this two-door behemoth.

"Man isn't she a beauty?" exclaimed Frank.

"Yeah! She sure is," replied Markham.

"She's got a 318 cubic-inch engine giving it 290 horsepower. She's also got two four-barrel carburetors with dual exhaust. Man, can she burn rubber," said Frank in awe of his own car.

"I see that you maintain it well. Looks like you just waxed it," said Markham admiringly.

"She's all I got, man," said Frank as they got in the car. Frank pulled out a pint size bottle of vodka from under the driver's seat and took a swig out of it. "You want a taste?" he asked Markham.

"No thanks. You forgot…I'm not a vodka drinker Frank," said Markham.

"That's OK!" said Frank as he started the car. He placed his left elbow and hand on the top of the windowless door and drove with his right hand only, never taking his left hand off the window even when making turns. He would simply place pressure with the heel of his hand on the steering wheel as he turned it in one direction or the other, which power steering made easy.

Once out of the Main Gate, they rode on a two-way road divided by a medium with palm trees spaced about every 50 feet until they reached an opening in the dividing medium. Frank turned left across the road and into a drive-in food and beverage joint where Frank parked his car in one of the parking spots surrounding the fast food restaurant that was designated for customers who desired curb service, which was most of them. A waitress came out with a tray which she attached to Frank's open window and asked them to place their orders. To Markham's amazement, Frank ordered a beer with his hamburger and the waitress didn't bat an eye.

"What kind of beer would you like?" she asked, smiling at Frank.

"Budweiser will do, honey!" he replied.

"And you, sir. What'll you have?" she asked Markham.

"I'll have a hamburger with everything on it and a Coke," he replied.

"That will be $7.58," said the waitress, and Markham forked over a ten dollar bill over Frank's objections, which she took stating she would be back with the change.

"I don't believe it. They serve beer to drivers…is that legal? Hell it must be, or else they wouldn't be doing it," said Markham.

"Yeah! It's legal alright," replied Frank. "Man if you think that's something, you should see the wild beer parties they have on the beaches around here. I'm going to get you acclimated to Florida's social scene my friend."

Markham digested Frank's words with great interest, but remained silent.

"This Saturday there's a dance in Tampa. You wanna go?" asked Frank.

"Sure. Why not?" replied Markham, who always loved dancing.

"Oh! Jesus!" said Frank as a Volkswagen pulled into the drive-in. "It's my ex-wife looking for me."

"Your ex-wife? I didn't know you'd been married. She lives here in Florida?" asked Markham.

"She found out I was stationed at MacDill so she came from Cleveland to Tampa trying to convince me to get back together with her," said Frank in a sour tone.

"Are you going to?" asked Markham.

Frank thought for a minute then said, "Naw! It wouldn't work. It didn't work then and it won't work now," said Frank. "She spotted me, but she can't find an empty parking space next to my car. Listen Jim. I don't want her to come over here and make a scene, so I'm going to go to her and see what she wants. I'll be back shortly," and Frank stepped out of his car and walked over to where his ex-wife was parked.

"You following me?" asked Frank of his ex-wife, a short woman with short dark hair and a pretty face with an upturned nose who had put on a few extra pounds over her previously petite body.

"What if I am Frank? You know how I miss you. I know I was a real bitch before, but I've changed now. I'll be real good to you. You know if we were married, you would then collect quarters allowance and we would be able to live off-base. What could be better?" she asked imploringly.

Frank thought about the continuous fighting that went on in Cleveland when they were married for a year before he joined the Air Force in lieu of the Army draft and simultaneously filed for divorce. Since then he gained quite a bit of experience with women in England and in Florida from which he could make a comparison with his ex-wife, and he realized that he was too young and inexperienced when he got married, and what he thought was love was in fact merely infatuation and lust. *No,* he thought, *we are both better off not being married to each other, only she doesn't know it yet.*

"Listen, Betty. It didn't work then and it won't work now. Why can't you realize and accept that? You're a nice girl and I like you as a friend, but that's all, Betty," said Frank in a soft tone of voice, noticing tears welling up in Betty's eyes. "I'm sorry, Betty, but I've got to go now. You should go back to Cleveland. There's nothing here for you."

With those final words, Frank walked back to his car and sat in the driver's seat without saying a word and just stared straight ahead, thinking about what he had said to his ex-wife Betty, wondering if he had done the right thing by chasing her away.

Markham observed Frank's solemn mood and knew instinctively to remain quiet until Frank broke the silence when he thanked the waitress for delivering the food which they quickly consumed and after several minutes passed, Frank started the car and drove out of the parking lot towards MacDill AFB. "Listen Jim, if you still want to go to the dance, drop by the barracks at 8 o'clock and we'll go from there, OK?"

"Sure Frank. I'll see you Saturday evening," replied Markham as they returned to MacDill and each retired to their own barracks.

That Saturday night, Frank and Markham attended the dance in Tampa to the music of The Teddy Bears. The place was packed with people, mostly in their twenties and there was standing room only. As Frank and Markham stood amongst the crowd of onlookers at the people dancing, Markham was unintentionally making a comparison between the English dancers and the American dancers at the Tampa dance hall and he came to the conclusion that when it came to dancing, the English were generally better dancers, but then he reasoned, that was their national pastime.

A blonde young woman who recognized Frank came up to him.

"Frankie. How are you? I haven't heard from you in weeks. Why haven't you called me?" she said.

Frank looked at her, disappointed that she was at the dance and had recognized him. "I've been busy at the base, Cindy," replied Frank.

"Aren't you going to introduce me to your friend?" she asked.

"Oh! Yeah! This is Jim. He just arrived from overseas. We were in England together at one time," said Frank.

"In England, huh? Well how do you compare those English girls with us American girls?" said Cindy.

"I just got here and haven't had a chance to make a comparison," answered Markham.

"Well, I know that those English girls will throw themselves at our boys so they can get a passport to the US. They obviously don't value themselves very much, but we Americans do," said Cindy.

Markham found her behavior somewhat aggressive and certainly not conducive to an agreeable meeting of the minds.

"Well, Jim, how did you find those English girls?" she asked.

"I found them to be generally very attractive, kind hearted and uncritical of others," replied Markham, who then excused himself to Frank, stating that he was going to the bar for a drink. Soon afterwards, Frank joined him at the bar.

"Don't mind Cindy. She lost her boyfriend to an English girl whom he married, and so she has an ax to grind," said Frank.

"Well, let her grind it somewhere else," replied Markham.

"Correct me if I'm wrong Jim, but I think your mind is still in England. Am I right?" said Frank.

"You're right it is, and I'm having a hard time dealing with it Frank," said Markham.

"That was then and this is now Jim. There's plenty of other fish in the sea, my friend. So let's reconnoiter the place," said Frank looking over the crowd. Two young ladies who had been standing a few feet from Frank and Jim made their presence known by staring at them and then talking to each other about them. Finally, Frank stepped forward and asked the shorter one for a dance and she accepted, leaving her girlfriend awkwardly alone. Markham, feeling her uneasiness, asked her the pleasure of a dance and she graciously accepted.

During the foxtrot, she displayed a smoothness of movement that surprised and pleased Markham.

"My name is Gloria. What's yours?" she asked.

"Jim Markham," he replied.

"I presume that you're stationed at MacDill?" she said in a rich voice.

"You presume correctly," replied Markham.

"And this is your first time at this dance hall?" said Gloria.

"Correct again. You've won the door prize," replied Markham with amusement.

"And what is the prize may I ask?" said Gloria, smiling.

"I could say 'ME' but that would be an exercise in arrogance, so I will say that your prize is in the knowledge that you did your patriotic duty in dancing with a lonely overseas returnee," said Markham.

"No one admits that they're lonely unless they really are," she said. "Are you really that lonely Jim?" she asked, looking into his eyes for a truthful answer.

"You're right about that, but that is something I will have to work on," said Markham, not looking into her eyes.

Gloria sensed that Markham was an unusually sensitive man and sufficiently intelligent enough to guard his privacy against intruders such as herself. She liked him and wanted to see him again after this dance, thus thought it wise not to pry further into his life at this moment in time and keep the conversation light.

Frank got on very well with his dancing partner, whom he introduced to Markham as Connie. After the dance the two girls got into their car and followed Frank and Markham to a nearby bar called Bailey's Tavern for a nightcap before going to their respective quarters. As they were going into the bar from the parking lot, Markham and Frank observed three young men facing a third man across the street on the grass. Of the three men, the one in the middle was talking to the lone man facing him when he suddenly punched him in the jaw knocking him unconscious on the grass. When the man failed to get up, the three men turned around and crossed the street towards Frank and Markham. The girls had already entered the bar. A couple of young men who had also witnessed the fight crossed the street to assist the still unconscious man. Markham got a good look at the man who did the punching, then turned and entered the bar with Frank to join the girls who had wondered what had happened to them.

They had a couple of drinks, with Connie and Frank doing most of the talking, after which they all exchanged telephone numbers and then left the bar. The only telephone number Frank and

Markham could give was the pay phone in each of the barracks. Markham didn't mind going on a double date with Gloria, Frank and Connie, but he didn't think he was ready for a serious relationship with Gloria or anyone else for that matter. He thought that there might be an outside chance that a letter from Sylvia might yet be forwarded to him from England and that she might need his help and the thought haunted him.

A week later Frank asked Markham if he wanted to go to a beach party that forthcoming Saturday and Markham accepted the invitation. That Saturday afternoon, Frank and Markham rode in the Plymouth Fury with the top down, even though the weather threatened showers and the road to the beach took them through some swamps which Frank commented were inhabited by alligators and poisonous snakes. They finally arrived at a heavily foliaged area which led them to a clearing onto a deep sandy beach. Frank parked his car next to a dozen other cars on a packed sand surface. Frank opened the trunk of his car and asked Markham to help him carry two cases of beer to the gang of people gathered on the beach. Frank seemed to know several of the men and two of the women there. A metal barrel full of ice and clams was at the center of the gathering and several coolers containing cans of beer mixed in with ice were sitting nearby for the taking. One man wearing a steel-meshed glove was opening the clams with a special curved knife. As the paper plates filled up with clams, they were passed around for consumption to those who had the stomach for it and Markham noticed that the women in the crowd avoided the raw clams. Frank and Markham both indulged themselves with a stomach full of raw clams and beer until they could hardly walk; they just sat there laughing at everything and nothing. It was just one of those times when everyone in the crowd was in a good mood and happy to be alive with no thought beyond the present.

By 1:30 AM the clams and beer had been exhausted and several people had already left. Frank had thoughts of sleeping on the beach, but the weather promised rain. Therefore, Frank and Markham bid farewell to the two couples still remaining and got back into the Plymouth Fury with the top still down. Frank started the car and being an auto mechanic, noticed that the starter hesitated. He looked at the instrument panel and to his surprise the generator needle had not moved. He left the engine running, lifted up the hood and after some examination, closed the hood, turned off the lights, and announced to Markham that the generator was malfunctioning and not generating any electricity, therefore they would have to depend solely on the battery for electricity to the engine.

"Can we make it back to the base on the battery?" asked Markham.

"Yes, I think so, if we turn off all other electrical equipment such as the lights and radio," answered Frank. "Well, we'd better get going 'cause we're wasting precious battery power."

Frank drove off without lights into the darkness, barely able to see the road ahead of him, with cloudy skies and no street or road lights, which was an invitation for another car to slam into them. Frank had consumed a lot of alcohol, more than Markham, who was not exactly sober.

"Frank. I see headlights in the rearview mirror. I think it would be wise for us to move over onto the shoulder of the road and wait for the car to pass us and then we can follow its taillights," said Markham.

"Good thinking, Jim," said Frank as he pulled over with engine running. As soon as the car passed him, Frank gunned the car forward and stayed right behind the other car for at least three miles when suddenly the car ahead stopped, apparently to make a left turn onto a side road, causing Frank to veer to the right to avoid a rear-end collision. But before he could straighten his course, the road curved left causing the car to leave the country road landing into the swamp. As the car sank with the water running over the doors of the convertible, Markham and Frank both realized that they had better swim quickly to the edge of the swamp before the alligators and snakes got to them. Fortunately, they didn't have far to swim. After climbing out of the swamp, they both sat down on the grass staring silently at the tip of the tailfins still faintly visible as the only sign that a car was submerged there.

"Cheer up Frank, your insurance will cover it," said Markham, trying to buoy his spirits.

"No it won't. I could only afford liability insurance," replied Frank.

Markham couldn't think of anything else to say after that revelation, so he stood up to see if his wallet was still in his back pocket and felt relieved to find that it was still intact.

"Hey! Frank. You might want to check to see if you still got your wallet," said Markham.

Frank checked his back pocket. "Yeah, I still got it, but what pisses me off is that I left my flask of vodka under the seat. I could sure use a drink right now," said Frank.

"There's nothing we can do here now," said Markham. "So let's get going. We can hitchhike back to the base and get out of these wet clothes."

Frank stood up and Markham noticed that Frank was barefoot. "What happened to your loafers Frank?" asked Markham.

"I lost them swimming out of the swamp," replied Frank.

"I hope we don't have to walk too far. Let's hope we get a ride soon," said Markham as they started walking down the road. Two cars passed them going in their direction, but neither of them stopped. After twenty minutes of walking, Frank suggested they stop as he had stepped on something in the dark that hurt the sole of his right foot. Frank sat on the shoulder of the road while Markham stood looking for signs of an oncoming vehicle when two headlights appeared from afar and Markham, seeing his friend unable to continue walking, was determined to stop this vehicle for help. As the vehicle approached them, Markham could see that it was an old pick-up truck moving at a very moderate speed. Markham stood in the middle of the road waving both of his arms over his head. The truck slowed down and then stopped within a few feet of Markham, who then stepped off to the side to talk to the driver who appeared to be a tough, old, seasoned man. By this time Frank had stood up and walked over to join Markham.

"You guys look like you've been out for a swim. Forgot your swim suits?" asked the old man.

"No. We missed a turn up ahead and drove the car into the swamp," replied Markham.

"The swamp, hey?" said the old man, "Well where you headed?"

"MacDill Air Force Base," replied Markham.

"So you're both airmen, hey? OK, get in the back. I don't want you to get my seats wet," said the old man.

"Thanks Pops," said Frank.

"My name is not Pops, son. I'm a retired Colonel so you can call me Sir, but Bob will do nicely."

"Yes Sir, Colonel," replied Frank, a bit embarrassed.

The colonel drove Frank and Jim right up to the main gate of MacDill AFB where he himself had been retired. The next day, Frank met Markham and they went to the Mess Hall where Frank told him that his car would be declared a total loss and he owed a substantial amount of money on the car, hence his credit would be worthless. They were now without transportation and Markham was the only one with a clean credit record necessary to purchase a vehicle on the never-never plan. They decided to visit various car dealers in Tampa for the purpose of purchasing a car for Markham, preferably a convertible, used but not too old. After looking at several used cars they came upon a one-year old 1957 Ford Fairlane 500 black convertible with dual spot lights, Hollywood skirts covering the rear wheels and the radio antennae sticking out of the middle of the trunk. This was a two-ton car with a V-8 Interceptor engine fueled by dual four-barrel carburetors. Markham didn't have to look any further. This was the nicest car he'd ever seen including the Plymouth Fury. The cost was

$1900.00 and with only a $300.00 down payment, he could have the car with payments for the next three years.

"I'll buy the car Frank, but you're going to have to drive it because I don't have a States driver's license, only a military license," said Markham.

"You'd better learn the civilian rules of the road before you take the driver's test, Jim. Tomorrow when they're open, we'll pick up their booklet for you to study then you can take the test," said Frank.

"Sounds like a plan. Let's do it," said Markham, who became the proud owner of a black 1957 Ford convertible, his very first automobile. However, like the best plans of mice and men, their elation was cut short soon thereafter when they learned that the Group to which Markham was assigned was moving lock, stock and barrel to Bunker Hill Air Force Base, Indiana and Frank was being reassigned to Keflavik Air Base (NATO), Iceland. When Connie, whom Frank had been dating since he met her at the dance, found out about his reassignment to Iceland she lamented to Markham while waiting for Frank that it was simply criminal to send such a handsome man like Frank to a place like Iceland.

"Maybe I should write a letter to the Base Commander and tell him that putting a man like Frank on Ice or Iceland is unfair to all American women and downright unpatriotic. You think he would listen, Jim?" asked Connie.

"I don't think so Connie. Make good use of the time you two have before he leaves," said Markham sympathetically.

"I hear from Frank that you're leaving in two weeks for Bunker Hill in Indiana," said Connie. "Have you ever been to Indiana before?"

"No I haven't, but frankly Connie, this place is too wild. All everybody thinks about is boozing, sex and fighting. You know how many palm trees have been knocked down by drunken drivers along the MacDill route? Too many. I'd hate to bring up a family in this area of Florida," said Markham.

"I know you're right Jim, but once you move a distance away from the Base, life is more normal and stable. It's the military influence," said Connie.

"Maybe I'm just getting older and ready to settle down to a normal life," replied Markham pensively. "There's more to life than this I'm sure, and maybe Indiana will provide the normalcy that I need to pursue my studies and do something with my life."

"You're really a nice guy, Jim, and Frank is lucky to have a friend like you because you're a good influence on him. What can he possibly do in Iceland except take college courses? I'm certainly going to encourage him to do that and I'm going to write to him often. It's only an 18 month tour of duty, you know."

"I'll do what I can to encourage him in that direction Connie. Here he comes now," said Markham as Frank walked out of the barracks doorway and strolled towards them.

"Hey Jimbo, what's happening?" said Frank in his gregarious manner.

"Not much, just chatting with Connie," replied Markham.

"You know you could come with us to the drive-in movie 'cause I'm sure Gloria would love to come and her house is on the way, Jim," said Connie, hoping Markham would agree.

"No, that's alright. With our transfers pending, you two should spend time alone," said Markham smiling at the two of them.

"OK! Jim," said Frank as he got into Connie's car in the driver's seat while she sat in the passenger side. "See you later," and he sped out of the parking area and out of sight.

Markham went to the barracks and wrote a letter to his Mother and her husband Freddie informing them of his transfer to Bunker Hill AFB. He seldom wrote to Nora, but when it came to his whereabouts he felt that it was important that she be notified of any change of address in the event of his demise.

Markham drove his 1957 Ford Fairlane 500 black convertible from MacDill AFB, Florida to Bunker Hill AFB, Indiana alone as he so often found himself throughout his young life, facing the unknown with only a map to guide his inexperienced mental compass. Driving his two-ton automobile at high speed on some of those lonesome highways gave Markham a feeling of exhilaration and also time to ponder the past, the present and his future.

About 15 miles west of Kokomo, Indiana, Markham came upon a wide, flat expanse of land surrounded by a high fence topped with barbed wire and the road led directly past the main gate of Bunker Hill AFB where he made a left turn up to the Guard Shack that had a sign requiring him to stop his vehicle for inspection, which he did. As expected, Markham noticed the Strategic Air Command (SAC) sign above the Guard Shack. He showed the Air Policeman his assignment orders and his Military Identification Card and the AP directed him to his unit of assignment. It was 3:30 PM as Markham reported to the Squadron Commander, Captain Thomas Lambert, a very slim man who appeared to be a heavy smoker judging from his ashtray full of cigarette butts and his chain smoking.

"Good to have you on board Airman Markham. I see that you're assigned to Combat Operations. You'll be reporting to Colonel Rockford tomorrow morning at 8:00 AM sharp. Combat Operations is located in a windowless building with only one entrance and the building number is 1050 near the flight line on Aero Drive. Did you fly or did you drive here?" asked Captain Lambert.

"I drove Sir," replied Markham.

"Good, then I won't have to worry about your transportation," said Captain Lambert.

"You're assigned to room 108 and your roommate is Airman Don Colby. He'll clue you in on what's expected of you. Sergeant Feebles is in charge of the barracks and he holds weekly inspections. If you have any problems, take them to Sergeant Feebles. Do you have any questions?" asked the Captain.

"No Sir. Everything's clear Sir," replied Markham.

"That's all Markham. You're dismissed," said Captain Lambert.

Markham unloaded his clothes into his room, which showed evidence of an occupant whose low quarter shoes and boots were neatly lined up under the edge of his single metal spring bed. Hence Markham took possession of the other bed on the opposite side of the room with its wall locker and footlocker. Don Colby was still at work and wasn't expected back into his room until sometime after 5PM when the various facilities close for the day, unless his job required shift duty, which it didn't inasmuch as Don Colby worked as a clerk in the Base Finance Office that had regular hours. After Markham had put away all of his clothes, he looked at his watch which showed 4:55PM, hence he decided to wait for his roommate and go to the Mess Hall with him unless he had other plans.

Markham laid down on his bed with both of his hands behind his head looking at the ceiling, thinking of things he must do after he settled down into the routine of daily military life such as registering at the Education Office for evening courses in pursuit of his college degree. Suddenly his thoughts were interrupted by the door being opened by a short, ruddy-faced airman who couldn't hide his surprise at seeing another airman in his room. Thinking he had entered the wrong room, he immediately closed the door then reentered it again after checking the room number, and looking at Markham, identified himself.

"Hi! I'm Don Colby. I guess you're my new roommate, hey?"

"Yes I am," said Markham as he sat, then stood up to shake his hand. "I'm Jim Markham."

"Is that your Ford Convertible parked out front?" asked Colby.

"Yes that's my car," answered Markham, who stood a foot taller than Colby and twice as wide.

"It's a beauty. Must have been fun driving it up here, hey?"

"Listen, why don't we drive to the Mess Hall in my car? I haven't eaten anything since noon today and I'm famished," said Markham.

"Sounds good to me. Just let me get out of this monkey suit and into some civvies and we'll go," said Colby, who quickly changed clothes and they both left in Markham's car to the Mess Hall. As they stood in line with their metal trays, Colby and Markham approached the food servers and one of them scooped up a bunch of smooth meatballs which he placed on Colby's tray.

"What's that?" asked Markham looking at the golf-ball-size meatballs.

"They're mountain oysters," replied Colby, smiling with the food server.

"Mountain oysters...never heard of it," replied Markham. "What the hell are they?" he asked seriously.

"Hog's nuts, man. Try 'em, they're delicious and nutritious," said the server, with Colby agreeing.

"OK! You can't say I'm not adventurous," said Markham as the food server placed a large spoonful of mountain oysters on Markham's tray. As they moved along the food line, they were also served with mashed potatoes, string beans, a roll of bread and a choice of beverage.

While Markham was eating and actually enjoying the mountain oysters, he was briefed by Colby about Bunker Hill AFB.

"Tell me Don, do you have any more dietary surprises in store for me that I should be prepared for?" asked Markham.

"Well, as a matter of fact, they also serve rattle snake meat and chocolate covered grasshoppers for dessert," replied Don Colby in a serious tone which slowly turned into a large smile. "No, I'm just kidding Jim. Nothing that exotic.

"I have to tell you Jim, this is a unique SAC base. It's the home of the Hustler, the Air Force's fastest light bomber aircraft, which exceeds speeds of 1500 miles per hour, but it has a lot of down time due to even minor malfunctions such as a malfunctioning $10.00 transducer, and the runway has to be constantly swept because its tires are prone to puncture by the smallest debris. We have frequent alerts sometimes lasting a week to 10 days where all military personnel are restricted to the base including those who reside off-base, and the flight crews and their support teams are on alert the whole time. I heard that SAC has the highest divorce rate of all the other commands combined and you can see why," said Colby.

"I'm surprised that there aren't more people putting in for transfer to other commands," replied Markham.

"You can apply for transfer all you want, but SAC won't release you unless you're a screw-up and then you're out of the Air Force altogether. So you're in SAC, you're here to stay my friend," said Colby.

"Gee! You make it sound so ominous," replied Markham.

"I'll tell you Jim. The Base Commander is so strict that he has people drive around the base with a ruler measuring the length of the grass in base housing and if the grass is longer than two inches, the occupant is issued a letter of reprimand which is entered into his file which may affect his annual performance report which you must know is critical to an officer's career. With non-commissioned officers, three of those letters can cause the resident to lose his base housing then he has to go outside the base to find housing for his family."

"I'm beginning to believe that stateside duty is nothing but chicken shit and overseas duty is the best kept secret in the service. I tell you from my experience Don, that discipline overseas is a lot more relaxed than stateside. Tomorrow I'm going to check out the Education Office. You know anything about courses they might offer?" said Markham.

"Naw! I've never visited their office, although I know that it's located way out in the boondocks," replied Colby.

The next morning, Markham reported to Combat Operations at 7:45 AM and as he had been told, there was only one entrance into the building with no exits except that same entrance way. The guard asked for his orders and his Identification Card and Markham explained the reason he did not have a SAC Security Photo I.D. Card was because he was newly assigned to Combat Operations. He was asked to remain there while the guard called someone on the intercom to come to the entrance, whereupon a Captain Brevard appeared and upon checking Markham's ID card and Special Orders, welcomed him and asked him to follow him inside the building.

"You'll be issued a Security ID Card, but that alone won't let you into the building. You must be personally recognized by one of the occupants in the building, and there's always someone here, 24 hours a day," said Captain Brevard. "They're not many of us working in this building, so everyone knows everybody like one big family. Everyone here has a Top Secret Clearance as you have, and no documents leave this building."

Markham was given a tour of the building which he found fascinating. The first large room to his left contained a long L shape desk that ran the length and width of the far wall behind which sat five officers ranging in grade from Captain to Lieutenant Colonel. Facing these officers was a desk with a side extension containing a typewriter, occupied by a senior clerk who typed all sorts of documents including flight plans at the behest of these officers who formed the nucleus of the War Room. That desk was unoccupied for a reason; Markham was to fill that vacancy. In the next room, which was significantly larger, Markham observed that two walls contained floor to ceiling maps of the world with metal backings that permitted the placement of small magnetized symbols for aircraft, missile sites, radar sites and various other military hardware which were constantly readjusted by two Sergeants with the use of rolling ladders according to the latest intelligence information.

In front of those maps were several desk chairs for SAC aircrews to sit and study their latest target assignments which they obtained from the third room in the building where the war plans were maintained and updated by the members of the War Room who formulated individual war plan books for crew members to study within the building. Markham was introduced to the only two non-commissioned officers in the building, Staff Sergeant Robert Woodland, a mild mannered man of average height and weight with a very pleasant personality who hailed from Tennessee, and Staff Sergeant Jack Batiste, a French Creole from Louisiana also of average height and weight who walked around with his chest out and his chin up like a peacock in constant search for approval by the officers he served. Markham was instructed to take the rest of the day off to get his personal affairs in order and then to report the following day at 0800 hours to begin work in the War Room.

Markham got into his car and drove immediately to the Education Office where he met a Technical Sergeant Laugenour in charge of the office. To his dismay, Markham was informed that the only courses available through the Education Office at Bunker Hill AFB were correspondence courses through USAFE which were not accredited by traditional universities. Sergeant Laugenour advised Markham that there simply had not been sufficient enrollment in college courses to warrant classes to be held at Bunker Hill, and the fact that Markham now needed junior and senior level courses would make that even less likely. Markham departed the Education Office with a heavy heart filled with discouraging news that left no hope for advancement while he was assigned at Bunker Hill AFB. He went back to his barracks room and laid on his bed in his usual thinking posture of having both of his hands behind his head, but no solution came to mind other than having to leave his fate in the hands of providence.

The next morning, Markham reported to Combat Operations where he met the Officer in Charge, Lt. Colonel William Rockford, Major Francis Randall, Major Ronald Casper, Captain Robert Brevard and Captain John Tinsley. They soon realized that Markham was the fastest and most efficient typist who had ever worked for them and as a self-starter, needed no supervision other than learning the special job requirements unique to that unit's mission. Markham developed a distinctive respect for Colonel Rockford who lived by a self-imposed code of ethics and principles that should have been the envy of his contemporaries and subordinates, but unfortunately was specifically despised by one of his subordinate officers, Major Francis Randall, who made fun of him to the other subordinate officers in Markham's presence when Colonel Rockford was absent. Markham learned that Colonel Rockford in his younger days had been a lumberjack amongst other occupations and had served as a navigator on bombing missions over Germany in the Second World War. Colonel Rockford kept a card under the Plexiglas on his desk that listed 12 ethical rules that served as his Commandments.

One day at the weekly Wing Commander meeting, the Wing Commander Colonel George Bragg demanded that all of his Group and Squadron Commanders obtain a 100% return on their United Fund Drive and they were to use whatever means at their disposal to acquire nothing less than one hundred percent contributions from their airmen. Lt. Colonel Rockford voiced his objection to Colonel Bragg's demand in front of the group of commanders stating that the airmen's contributions to the United Fund Drive were supposed to be voluntary with no coercion applied, hence a 100% return should not be expected nor was it fair for any commander to be penalized for not attaining that goal.

Colonel Bragg admonished Lt. Colonel Rockford for not being a team player and told him that inasmuch as he seemed to know so much about the United Fund, he was placing him in charge of administering the drive collection.

During the following week, several of the Squadron commanders usually accompanied by their Sergeant reported to Combat Operations to deposit their monetary collection from the airmen of their units to Captain Brevard or Sergeant Woodland. On one particular occasion, a Captain accompanied by a Warrant Officer brought in a bag holding more than 80 small brown envelopes containing money. The envelopes were marked only with a number, but no name as required by Lt. Colonel Rockford. However, as the Warrant Officer opened each envelope to determine the amount of contribution, he would call out the envelope number to the Captain who related the number to the name on his list of contributors, hence was able to determine how much each airman contributed to the United Fund.

In one particular instance, Markham and Sergeant Woodland both heard the Warrant Officer tell his Captain that Airman Jones contributed only $2.00 and the Captain answered that he was going to take him off the promotion list. This was exactly the type of coercion that Lt. Colonel Rockford wanted to avoid, and when Markham and Woodland reported the matter to Lt. Colonel Rockford, he immediately called the Captain and the Warrant Officer to his office where he read them the riot act.

The United Fund Drive did not reach the Wing Commander's goal of 100%, but it did attain a respectable 92%. Instead of hurting Lt. Colonel Rockford's career, his exemplary character earned him the respect of the Wing Commander who recommended him for attendance at the United States Air Force War College, which is usually reserved for Colonels with Command Pilot status, not navigators.

A couple of months went by when Markham noticed that he had been consistently losing weight and his energy level had significantly diminished. After he weighed himself on a scale and realized that he had lost nearly 25 pounds, he decided to visit the base hospital in an attempt to determine the cause of his weight loss which resulted in his being admitted into the hospital for one week, wherein they monitored his metabolic status and concluded that he was a healthy, muscular male with no evidence of disease or other explanation for his sudden weight loss. Markham left the hospital not totally disappointed inasmuch as he had at least eliminated those possibilities which left him with only one other explanation, which he concluded was his avid cigarette smoking and he felt that his immune system was sending him a serious message. He elected to quit smoking cold turkey by emptying a pack of Camel cigarettes which he threw in the trash can and filled the empty pack with toothpicks, so that each time he instinctively reached for a cigarette he would pull out a toothpick instead of a cigarette, thus satisfying the behavior part of his habit; the rest would be sheer will power. He also decided to simultaneously start a workout regimen lifting free weights at the base gymnasium which would solidify his weight gain and relieve the smoking withdrawal anxiety and also the frustration of not being able to pursue his educational goals.

At the weight room in the Base Gymnasium, Markham met Bob Petrovich who was in charge of the gymnasium which gave Bob all-day access to the weight room where he worked out five to six hours a day in his attempt to win the Junior Mr. America contest after which he intended to open his own gymnasium in Chicago, Illinois. Bob would ingest 30 animal protein tablets per day and consume special dietary drinks to enhance his physique, which was chiseled like a Greek God. He was 5'11' and only weighed 170 pounds which didn't appear extraordinary when dressed in street clothes, but when he appeared in his workout outfit, the result of his painfully long workouts became evident by his large and exceptionally well defined muscles on a small bone frame that exaggerated the size of his chest and shoulder muscles on his extremely small waist that produced the V shape desired by all body builders.

At any given time, there were several body builders and weight lifters working out in the gym each evening and Markham received a lot of good advice from these serious athletes. However Markham's interest was focused in weight lifting, not body building, and to that end he didn't care about the size of his waist or gaining weight in that area; he was interested in gaining maximum strength, hence he ate four big meals per day and worked out three hours per session at least three times per week. He mostly worked the upper body using Weider's progressive method of weight lifting, wherein he would start off with an Olympic bar loaded with enough weight at each end that prevented him from bench pressing it more than six or seven times, then with each set that followed that initial lift, Markham would add ten pounds at each end of the bar until he was able to lift it only one time. Within eight months, Markham had regained the 25 lbs he had lost plus another 25 lbs of muscle weighing in at 220 lbs on a six foot frame that allowed him to warm up with bench presses starting at 280 lbs, which ended with a bench press of 400 lbs, not to mention other routine exercises such as pull downs which developed powerfully large back muscles. Bob Petrovich had never seen anyone gain so much solid weight and strength in such a short period of time and encouraged Markham to enter competition at the forthcoming Chicago athletic meet, but Markham was only interested in personal achievement.

However, he was particularly interested in the techniques used by weightlifters to bring extraordinary weights above their heads in movements that required great skill as well as strength. Unfortunately, Markham's considerable increase in size required that he purchase new clothes, but as he continued to work out at the gym his body continued to increase in size until he could no longer afford it, hence he decided to change his workouts to high repetition sets which developed endurance and muscle definition instead of bulk. At a stable 225 lbs of solid muscle, Markham felt the most powerful he'd ever been in his life and he found through practicing Judo that he hadn't lost any of his speed of movement. Markham's dramatic physical change did not go unnoticed by his comrades in arms including the squadron commander Captain Thomas Lambert, who one day approached him in the hallway outside his office.

"Markham. You got a minute?" asked Captain Lambert.

"Yes Sir," replied Markham, who stopped to talk to the Captain.

"Do you mind if I went to the gym to work out with you? The change in your physique is simply amazing. Maybe you can teach me how to improve my physique. Heaven knows I could use it," said Captain Lambert in a joking manner.

"You're welcome to accompany me at the gym at any time, Sir," replied a surprised Markham.

"You don't have to call me Sir, Jim. Captain will do just fine."

"Yes Sir…Captain I mean," replied Markham. "But I must tell you Captain, that the first thing you ought to do is quit smoking. You can't expect to make any progress in the weight room if you're smoking two packs a day," said Markham.

"That's easier said than done Jim. I've tried several times to quit and I haven't been able to yet."

"Maybe if you try the method I used, by replacing all of the cigarettes in the pack with toothpicks, then whenever you reach for a cigarette you'll find a toothpick instead to put in your mouth. It worked for me. I haven't smoked a cigarette since I quit about eight or nine months ago," said Markham.

"Heck! I'll try that and maybe it'll work," said the Captain.

Captain Lambert went to the gymnasium weight room with Markham a total of six times then announced to Markham that his body couldn't take the regimen and he couldn't quit smoking either, but he thanked him for the experience.

One afternoon, Markham received a telephone call at work from the Air Policeman on guard duty at the Base's main gate informing him that he had a visitor who would be waiting for him in the restaurant across the street from the main gate. With great curiosity, Markham drove to the restaurant and as he entered it he immediately recognized Robert Bruner sitting in a nearby booth with a lovely lady catering to a small baby in a portable crib next to her.

"My God. What a nice surprise," said Markham, shaking Robert's hand.

"Oh! Jim, let me introduce you to my wife Elizabeth and that's my sevenmonth old son Jeffrey," said Robert proudly.

"I'm so pleased to meet you," said Markham, who sat down next to Robert facing Elizabeth and the baby.

"So what brings you here to Bunker Hill?" asked Markham.

"We were driving back from Indianapolis to Ball State University and this is enroute, and I found out that you were assigned to Bunker Hill Air Force Base from the Military Personnel Locator, and here we are," said Robert.

"Listen, I've got to tell you something that will blow your mind, Jim. After we all got transferred out of Molesworth Air Base and rotated back to the states, I got discharged from the Air Force and so did Guy Gardner and Marc Dillinger, remember them? About a year later I had to go to Cleveland, Ohio and so I decided to visit Marc Dillinger since he'd given me his address. When I got there and rang the doorbell, guess who answered the door? The Bean…Jeanne the Bean. You can imagine my surprise and embarrassment. He was the last one amongst us to rotate back to the states and so he married her. Man, when I think back to all those times when Guy and I would make fun of her skinniness comparing her to Popeye's Olive. All that time Marc had to hide his affection for her in our presence," said Robert.

"I can imagine how he must have felt. Marc's a sensitive guy. Have you told Guy Gardner about this yet?" asked Markham.

"Yeah! As soon as I got back home, I called Guy and at first he thought I was joking, but when I convinced him it was true, he blamed me as the instigator of course," said Robert.

"That's Guy. I'll never forget the time when Marc and I had to tie Guy down to his bunk so that he wouldn't attack you during the night. He was blind drunk and hell bent on beating you for some unknown reason that he himself the next day couldn't figure out," said Markham while Robert's wife Elizabeth was listening with all ears as she had not heard that story before from Robert.

"So, have you graduated from Ball State yet?" asked Markham.

"I'm graduating this year, then I'm going to do some substitute teaching while I get my Masters. I'm majoring in History. How about you, Jim, staying in for the duration?"

"I've been trying to get my degree but it's tough going here at Bunker Hill because there aren't enough people interested in higher education to form a class, especially at the junior and senior levels. I'll just have to wait for a transfer to a bigger base or one that's academically oriented. I'm not ready to give up the ship yet," said Markham.

"I know you'll make it," said Robert. "Well, Jim. It sure was nice seeing you again. Here's our telephone number. Keep in touch."

"It certainly was nice meeting you Elizabeth," said Markham as he shook both Robert's and Elizabeth's hand. Markham then immediately exited the restaurant and drove back inside Bunker Hill Air Force Base to return to work, happy that Robert had found his significant other and was well on his way to a satisfyingly productive career and joyful, stable home life. It also brought home the painful realization that he had not attained that all-American goal and he was not getting any younger.

Markham had on occasion driven from the base into the nearest town called Peru with his roommate Don Colby and some of the other airmen in his barracks, usually stopping at Jerry's fast food drive-in where the small town girls would park their cars next to the boys from the base and engage in conversations that often led to hot dates. There was another fast food drive-in down the street from Jerry's that wasn't as popular, but that particular evening, Jerry's parking spaces were full. Therefore Markham, accompanied by Don Colby seated next to him and Colby's girlfriend Marge and two of her girlfriends all seated in the back seat, drove over to the other drive-in and got in line behind other cars apparently waiting to find a parking spot, but in many instances cars driven by teenagers never parked but rode around the drive-in searching for friends in other cars. On this particular evening, the owner-manager of the drive-in got fed up with the sight-seeing drivers and decided to force them to park their car in the spaces reserved for service by stepping in front of the cars and directing them to the nearby parking space. Markham had full intentions of parking for service as he and his companions were hungry, but as his car following the other cars in single file approached an unwanted spot next to the dumpster, the owner stepped in front of Markham's car forcing him to come to a complete stop in order to avoid hitting him. The owner pointed to the parking spot with his outstretched hand ordering him to park there. Markham told him he didn't want to park there, but the owner insisted that he park there to which Markham refused, and the man just stood in front of his car with his arms crossed, stating that he was going to remain there until Markham parked his car. It was bad enough that Markham had to take orders from his military superiors, but he was certainly not going to take orders from some civilian trying to force him to buy food from his restaurant. It now became a matter of principle and Markham wasn't about to give in to that dictator who reminded him of Mussolini with his arms crossed against his chest. The thought occurred to Markham that he could step out of his car and forcibly remove the man from the path of his car, but in the process he could be charged with assault which would devastate his military career, thus dismissed the idea as unrealistic fantasy. However, the driver behind Markham got impatient and attempted to go around his car, compelling the owner to leave the front of Markham's car to step in front of the other car coming around it. Markham saw the opening and gunned the throttle of his interceptor engine past the owner, who was too late to stop it from driving out of the drive-in parking lot. Apparently the owner had taken down Markham's license plate number because the next day, he was called into Captain Lambert's office stating the owner had tracked him down by his license plate number and he reported that Markham had threatened to bring several airmen with him to beat the man up.

"Captain Lambert. Do you really believe that I need the help of anyone to beat up that middle-aged man? I never threatened him and I have four witnesses that will attest to that, Sir. He's just a bitter old man who's a sore loser in a contest of his own making," said Markham.

Captain Lambert shook his head affirmatively. "I agree with you Jim. Just forget it ever happened. That's all," said the Captain.

Markham walked into his room at the barracks to find his roommate Don Colby changing into civilian clothes.

"Hey Jim. My girlfriend's friend, Janie, the blonde riding in the back with her two girlfriends told her she likes you and wants to go out with you, but she's too afraid to ask.What do you think? You interested?" said Don.

"No, not really," replied Markham.

"Why not? She's got a great figure," said Don.

"She's also an airhead. She's got the body of a 20 year old with the mind of a ten year old. Not for me Don. Thanks," said Markham.

"Hey! You've got the best of both worlds. Old enough to screw and young enough to control," said Don, laughing.

"And smart enough to get pregnant and lock you in for life," replied Markham. "No thanks buddy."

"You don't know what you're missing Jim," said Don amusingly.

"What you don't know won't hurt you either," replied Markham, ending the conversation on that topic.

A few days later, Markham was sitting in the barracks' recreation room watching television when Al Budkins came into the room.

"How come you're not at the gym working out Jim?" asked Budkins.

"Because I don't work out on Tuesdays and Thursdays and today is Thursday," replied Markham.

"Then why don't we drive into town?" said Budkins.

"I'm watching this interesting program, Al, and I'm not in the mood to go to town."

"Listen, I'll put in a full tank of gas in your car. How about it Jim?" said Budkins.

"I'm still not interested. Now will you be quiet so I can listen to this?" said Markham, a bit annoyed at Budkins' insistence.

"OK! Jim. I'll wait until the program is ended then can we go into town?"

"Man you're a pain in the ass, you know that! I'll think about it when the time comes, alright?" said Markham.

"Good enough. I'll be back at 8PM," replied Budkins who then went back to his room.

The T.V. program ended and Budkins entered the recreation room at exactly 8PM. "Can we go now Jim?" asked Budkins.

"Jesus, you don't let up do you Al? What is so urgent that you have to go to town?" asked Markham.

"I've got to visit someone. I won't be long, no more than a half hour then you can bring me back to the base on a full tank of gas. You can't beat that for a deal, now can you?" said Budkins.

"Alright. Where is this place anyway?" asked Markham.

"It's just outside Peru. It ain't far," replied Budkins.

Markham got into his convertible with Al Budkins, and since the weather was dry, he kept the top down. They rode half-way through Peru when Budkins told Markham to take a side road that led them to the outskirts of town where Budkins directed him to a dirt road which brought him into an open field that faced a lonely, large, two-story, dilapidated wooden house that had grayed from the worn off paint. All of the windows were boarded up and there was no light coming from the inside of the house. To all appearances, the house was vacant.

"What did you bring me here for?" asked Markham.

"I'm going into that house. You wait here for me," said Budkins.

"There's nobody there. What the hell is going on here?" asked Markham.

"Yeah! There is. It's a whore house," replied Budkins.

"You're kidding me. You had me drive you all the way over here to go to a whore house?" said Markham in astonishment.

"Yeah! What's wrong with that? I'm horny. You got a better idea?" replied Budkins. "Listen Jim. Why don't you come on in with me? I'll pay for it."

"No thanks Al. I'll wait here for you," replied Markham, who watched Budkins walk at least 50 yards before he reached the wooden stoop and the front door. Markham observed him knock on the door and a big black man opened the door and looked around for any sign of cops then let Budkins inside. About half an hour later as he had predicted, Budkins exited the house and returned to the car with a grin of satisfaction on his face.

"Man, you should have come with me. Those black girls are great pieces of ass," said Budkins.

Markham remained silent as he started the car and drove back to the base, thinking that Budkins must be a desperate man with no pride to frequent a whore house.

"Listen Al. Next time you want to get your rocks off you'd better find someone else to drive you there, OK?" said Markham.

"Yeah! OK I'm sorry. I guess I should have told you, but I knew you wouldn't drive me there if I told you," said Budkins.

"You're darn right I wouldn't have," replied Markham, who wondered what would have happened if the police had raided the house while he was the only car parked in front of the house with his partner inside. Markham chalked that one up to yet another experience.

Lt. Colonel Rockford took a distinct liking to Markham whom he referred to as a young bull because of his strong build. The Colonel knew that Markham had limited funds and tried to help him by giving him odd jobs on his base housing grounds which required constant maintenance. The Colonel had no children and his wife was a southern belle who didn't have a green thumb, hence gardening was not one of her pastimes. Markham had been to the house on a number of occasions to help the Colonel with various chores, but never got to know his wife other than the usual polite greetings when one arrives and leaves the premises. However, on one particular occasion, the Colonel asked Markham to help his wife put up curtain rods inside the house while he was gone on Temporary

Duty for a few days. Markham was standing on a ladder putting up a curtain rod in the living room when Mrs. Rockford, a tall, slim and very attractive brunette walked into the living room and stood a few feet behind Markham whose back was facing her.

"Jim. Do you think that a woman's breasts are only to feed infants or do they also serve another purpose?" she asked in a suggestive voice.

Markham froze, not believing what he had heard nor knowing how to reply. She was the wife of his commander, for whom he had absolute respect and there was no way that he could violate his trust in him. Could he be mistaken as to the purpose of her question, he asked himself.

Markham turned his head around to look at Mrs. Rockford while still holding the curtain rod and he detected a slight smile of amusement at his obvious embarrassment.

"I wouldn't know the answer to that Mrs. Rockford," answered Markham as he turned his attention back to his work, and he heard her leave the living room. After that incident, Markham made plausible excuses to the Colonel whenever he requested work that would place Markham in close proximity to his wife. The gnawing question after this incident for Markham was whether any husband could trust his wife. But then he remembered his Mother and her three sisters whom he knew would never dream of cheating on their husbands, and were pillars of moral strength. It could also be Mrs. Rockford's first and only attempt at tasting the apple of sin, an understandable frailty of the human condition.

CHAPTER VII
The Last Yankee Stronghold in Africa

It was the first week of December when Lt. Colonel Rockford informed Markham that the Christmas holidays were approaching and the work load would be minimal and a unique opportunity offered itself for him to go to England for ten days aboard a KC-135 air refueling tanker. There was, however, one catch. The plane's primary destination was Wheelus Air Force Base in Tripoli, Libya where it would remain for approximately three weeks. Markham figured that visiting Libya would be an otherwise unknown experience and he didn't know when he would ever get another chance to visit England again, therefore he accepted Lt. Colonel Rockford's offer and was told he would be leaving in three days.

Markham was told to dress in his fatigues and he could bring a change of civilian clothes to wear off-base in England and Libya. He met the crew of the KC-135, a jet engine aircraft that carried a huge amount of fuel in its belly for transfer to bombers while in the air to increase their flight range. The flooring in the aircraft above the fuel reservoir served to carry cargo so that the aircraft served two functions. The crew consisted of the pilot Captain Tom Avery, the navigator Captain Stan Mahoney, the Flight Engineer Lieutenant Mark Sibley, Sergeant John Quigley the crew chief, Airman Dick Pritchard the boom operator, and crew members, Airmen Charles Becket, Fred Ruff and Larry Sabota. Markham was listed on the orders as a crew member and thus helped the loading and unloading of cargo that was delivered by the KC-135 to Upper Heyford Air Force Base, England on its way to Libya and back again to England before returning to Bunker Hill AFB, Indiana. Some of the cargo consisted of large steel fly-away kits on steel rollers that weighed nearly one thousand pounds each and were tied securely to the floor of the aircraft with the use of long belts with metal fasteners at each end that were hooked to metal rings on the floor of the aircraft at various intervals. Becket, Ruff and Sabota enlisted Markham's assistance in strapping down the cargo to the floor rings, then each man sat on a long wooden bench against the wall of the aircraft, two men on each side, while the aircraft engines whined to a high pitch, then the aircraft took off down the runway for a brief moment andsuddenly rose at such a deep incline that Markham worried that the cargo would somehow tear loose and take out the entire rear end of the aircraft. But the straps held the cargo in place and eventually the aircraft leveled off for the trip to England. Markham had flown on civilian and military aircraft before, but never in his entire life had he ever experienced such a steep climb and wondered if this was normal for that type of aircraft or perhaps he was in the company of air cowboys.

Markham learned from the boom operator that their primary mission to Libya was to air refuel a B-47 bomber that would have no bombs, but instead would be loaded with electronic eavesdropping equipment and its mission would be to fly along the perimeter of iron curtain countries and intercept communications for intelligence data, hence the B-47 needed extra fuel to complete its mission and thus would rendezvous in the air at predetermined coordinates with the KC-135 to receive 40,000 pounds of fuel. Upon landing at Upper Heyford Air Base, Markham and the crew were told that they would be there for five days and to be sure to report back a 0800 hours on that fifth day, sober and ready to go to Libya.

Upper Heyford Air Force Base, located right outside of Oxford, England, was well known for its Ivy League University of Oxford, the arch rival of Cambridge University that Markham had attended for a very brief period. It was approaching Christmas and he was anxious to visit Oxford and join the merriment of the pubs with his newly found friends in arms: Chuck Becket, Fred Ruff and Larry Sabota. The four of them took a taxi into Oxford and stopped at the Kings Head for some action and before long, entered into conversation with three young English women who invited the four of them to their flat nearby. Markham felt that if things developed, one of them would be left out, and he didn't want any of his friends to miss an opportunity, thus excused himself from the invitation, telling his friends he would catch up with them at the base quarters later. Markham sat at the bar drinking his usual lager and simply enjoyed hearing the British accent being spoken by the various people in the pub. He felt at home in England, but the memory of Sylvia returned to haunt him again and no amount of alcohol would blur that remembrance.

At the end of the evening when pubs closed at 11PM, Markham left the pub intoxicated, but not without consciousness of events around him and as he stepped into the vestibule leading to the front door, a dark-haired woman in her late twenties who had been observing Markham sitting at the bar all evening, accosted him within the small confines of the vestibule and asked him if he would like to accompany her to a Christmas party that would be going on into the early morning hours. Not feeling any pain, Markham could still discern that she had a very attractive face with a pleasant smile that promised good company at a time when he was alone in a strange town at Christmas time.

"Thank you for the invitation, but what is your name?" asked Markham.

"My name is Ann, what's yours?" she asked.

"My friends call me Jim. Where's this party?" said Markham.

"Not far from here. Don't worry, you're safe with me," she said with a chuckle, as if this big man had to worry about his safety.

"OK! Lady. Lead the way," replied Markham.

As they stepped outside the pub, a taxi pulled up at Ann's signal and they boarded the cab which took them to a big stone house set back from an iron fence with an open gate that had allowed several cars to be parked along the long driveway and in the street. Markham could hear the sound of a piano accompanying amateur vocalists singing Christmas carols and as they approached the door, many voices could also be heard above the singing indicating that there was a substantial crowd of Christmas revelers at this party. As they entered, Markham helped Ann remove her coat then removed his own trench coat and she took them into a small side room. She then returned and placed her left hand inside Markham's right arm at the elbow and guided him into the large living room crowd where she was greeted by everyone in their path. Then an elderly man with gray hair and mustache walked up to them.

"Well my dear, I wondered where you'd gone to," he said as she kissed him on both cheeks.

"Father, I want you to meet my American friend Jim," said Ann.

The elderly man looked into Markham's eyes trying to read his mind and intentions. "Merry Christmas young man; I'm Alistair Fleming. Welcome to our home."

Markham realized that this large, beautiful house was indeed her residence and her Father was apparently one of Oxford's leading citizens. It occurred to him that it was safer for Ann to bring an American of unknown background than an Englishman whose background her Father would most likely not approve. But that was entirely speculation. During the evening, Mr. Fleming managed to find a moment alone with Markham while his daughter excused herself briefly, and in the process acquired enough information from Markham to know that he was not the right man for his daughter. He knew that time was of the essence because one night of passion could change her life and his forever, thus he had to take immediate action to intervene before his daughter's impulsive nature took over. Mr. Fleming found his daughter in the kitchen and asked to see her in his library immediately. Appearing visibly alarmed, Ann followed her Father into his study and he closed the door for privacy.

"You know, darling, that I've seldom ever interfered with your choice of men," said Mr. Fleming, but before he could continue, his daughter interrupted him.

"Yes you have Father, and I'm assuming that you've brought me here to object to my new relationship with Jim, an American Serviceman," said Ann.

"You just met him tonight. You know absolutely nothing about him. I've had a long chat with him and probably know more about him than you do," replied Mr. Fleming.

"Oh! So now you've gone behind my back to interrogate him. How could you Father?" said Ann angrily.

"Let's be calm about this my dear. He's leaving England in four days and he may never return to England again. He's married to the United States Air Force and he's stationed in Indiana where he's likely to remain for several years. How can you possibly have an adequate and proper courting period to get acquainted before you can even contemplate marriage?" said Mr. Fleming.

"Aren't you jumping to conclusions Father? I just met him tonight. He's a nice man whom I'd like to know better and if something does develop from it than it's my life, I'll make the choice," said Ann.

"Have you considered that if you end up marrying this young man that you would have to live in the United States, away from your family and lifelong friends and I would hardly ever get to see you or my grandchildren? Have you thought of that my dear?" said Mr. Fleming. "Before you get involved with a foreigner and I'm sure he's a very nice man, you should consider the fact that this is your birthplace and your best chance of happiness is to reside in the country of your birth with a husband of the same culture."

Ann remained silent as she listened to her father, whom she respected and loved.

"Think about what I've just said darling. I'm only concerned about your happiness. Now let's go back to the party before people wonder what's happened to us," said Mr. Fleming.

Ann appeared from the crowd and found Markham indulged in conversation with an Englishman who was a former student of Mr. Fleming whom Markham learned was a professor of Literature at Oxford University. Ann knew that her Father was correct in his assessment, but she had such a strong attraction to Markham that transcended all reason. She had an unabashed desire to soul kiss him and nakedly ravish his body until dawn. She knew that a few more drinks and she would succumb to the temptation, never contemplating any serious resistance from Markham and so confident of her seductiveness. She knew that she needed time to think, thus would delay any thought of having sex with Markham, but she desperately wanted to see him during his stay in England, if only for a few days that she could memorialize.

Ann had an MG sports car that she did not drive on the night of the party because she knew that she would be consuming alcohol and she was very much against drunken drivers ever since one of her girlfriends got killed in a car accident because of her intoxication. For the next four days until Markham's departure from Upper Heyford Air Base to Libya, Ann picked up and returned Markham each day with her sports car, and those four days convinced Ann that she was in love with him and would definitely marry him if only he resided in England, but alas the United States was his home and the twain shall not meet. Markham promised that he would call her the moment he returned to Upper Heyford from Libya and as they embraced on the night before his early morning departure, she felt like going with him to Libya and wherever else he went in spite of her Father's warning and her brain's pragmatic reasoning.

"Come back to me soon, darling, and have a safe trip," said Ann tearfully.

At the sight of her tears and trembling voice, Markham's heart swelled with the emotional need to console her. "Don't worry sweetheart; I'll be back before you know it and I'll call you as soon as we hit the ground," he said in his baritone voice that made her weak in the knees. She got back into her sports car, started the engine, but did not drive away until he had walked out of sight into the dimly lit barracks area.

Aboard the KC-135 air bound for Tripoli, Libya, the cargo consisting of four fly-away kits in rows of two each were tied with straps on both sides of the aircraft. Chuck Becket and Larry Sabota sat on the opposite side of the aircraft while Markham and Fred Ruff sat next to each other on the port side of the aircraft facing one of the two fly-away kits nearest the rear end of the aircraft. On take off, the straps held the cargo in place, however as the plane slowly turned to port the two side-by-side fly-away kits which were only a foot away from the knees of Markham and Ruff started to roll in their direction as a result of one of the straps, designed to keep the cargo from shifting to port or starboard, having come loose on Becket's and Sabota's side. Markham immediately raised both of his feet above the seat which he instinctively placed against the side of the metal fly-away kit that had now moved to within an inch of Ruff's knees who had unfortunately dozed off. Markham shoved him awake but it was too late for Ruff to pull up his feet as he was wearing the bulky military boots, which he couldn't pull off or pull through the now small opening between the fly-away kit and the edge of the wooden bench. Markham marshaled all of his strength to keep the fly-away kit from getting any closer, knowing full well that the sheer weight of the cargo against Ruff's knees could cripple him for life, if not sever his legs at the knee. Markham kept taking deep breaths as if weight lifting and pushed his feet against the wall of the fly-away kit while Ruff yelled for Becket and Sabota to help from the other side and tell the pilot to level the aircraft. Slowly, Markham succeeded in moving the heavy cargo away from Ruff's knees, first half an inch, then one inch, two inches, then three inches, at which point Ruff pulled both of his feet up and onto the bench in near terror and shock. The plane had now leveled off and Becket, aided by Sabota, reclamped the failed strap and added another strap for additional safety. Only Ruff witnessed and knew of the tremendous display of strength expanded by Markham who just sat there recovering from the physical exertion.

"Thanks Jim," said Ruff, still in awe of Markham's feat of strength.

"Don't mention it," replied Markham without turning his head.

Upon arrival at Wheelus Air Force Base in Tripoli, Libya, the aircraft taxied to a nearby hangar on the other side of the runway known as Tiger Town where Quonset huts were located for visiting crews which is where they were billeted. After the crew disembarked from the air refueling aircraft, they were directed to one of the Quonset huts where they were met by a briefing officer who informed them briefly about the political and security reasons for avoiding the city of Tripoli to the consternation of Markham, who had been given a note from one of the airmen at Bunker Hill AFB which contained the name and address of a Libyan uncle who lived in Tripoli and owned a night club called the Black Cat, whom he wanted Markham to visit with a message about the condition of his family in the states. Furthermore, his friend wanted him to go to the center of the city where vendors are strewn around the large square and purchase a special Zippo lighter which had a miniature emblem of the American dollar imprinted on it.

The briefing officer told the crew that Tripoli was located along the Mediterranean Sea in northwestern Libya and is its capital. The city was split in two parts; the modern city built by Mussolini prior to the Second World War situated in the southwestern part of Tripoli and the old city inhabited by the poor. He informed them that in 1801 through 1805 the United States Navy bombarded Tripoli which at the time was a haven for Corsair pirates that demanded ransom from American ships. In 1911, Italy colonized Libya which brought a mass emigration of Italians to Libya, many of whom settled in Tripoli which still numbered about 30,000 Italians. He remarked that Mussolini's auto race track was still intact as evidence of Libya's association with Mussolini's fascist government. The briefing officer, a young First Lieutenant who took his job seriously, stated that in spite of the Unites States giving a total of 24 million dollars worth of aid per year, plus 50,000 tons of flour to counteract the effects of a drought, not to mention the millions of dollars we were paying in rent for the use of Wheelus Air Base which was the last air base that the United States possessed in North Africa, the United States was unsure whether the Libyan government would renew the lease on the air base which was expiring in one year. Hence the United States government could not afford any incident that would incite the already anti-American feelings of the Libyan population.

"I can't stop you from leaving the base and going into Tripoli, but if you do and you get yourself involved in an incident or altercation with a Libyan national, we don't care who's responsible; you will be court-martialed and that comes from the Base Commander himself. So consider yourselves on notice. That's all," said the briefing officer and then left the Quonset hut.

Markham looked at Ruff, Becket and Sabota and said, "The hell with that; I didn't come all the way to Libya to look at Quonset huts. I'm going to Tripoli at the first opportunity and I don't see how any harm can come to us if we go in the middle of the afternoon when it's bright and sunny."

"I don't know about that Jim. You heard the Lieutenant. It's pretty risky," said Becket.

"Hell, I've got a note from Omar Sulaiman at Bunker Hill to contact his Uncle in Tripoli. Apparently his Uncle owns the Black Cat Café. Anyone want to come with me?" asked Markham.

"Yeah I'll go with you," said Fred Ruff who felt very safe with Markham at his side. "Hell, what can happen in broad daylight in the middle of the city square anyway?"

The next day right after lunch in the Mess Hall, Markham and Ruff took a taxi to Tripoli and got off in the town square which divided the old city from the new. The Square was quite large with nothing at its center and it was almost completely empty except for a series of kiosks covered with tent like material to protect the vendors from the sun. The weather was sunny, but chilly, and Markham wore a thick sweater as did Ruff. They both started walking across the square towards the kiosks on the other side when an Arab of about 25 years of age dressed in western clothes accosted Markham and attempted to intimidate him into buying a straight razor by holding half a dozen of them in his right hand with the blades uncovered only a few inches from Markham's face. Markham looked him straight in the eye and holding his right hand in his pocket told the Arab who spoke broken English that he had a stiletto knife and didn't need to buy one of his razors, at which point the Arab withdrew the razors and grudgingly left as Markham and Ruff continued their march towards the kiosks only to be accosted by a more aggressive young Arab man who reminded Markham of a city tough.

The Arab walked alongside Markham on his right, occasionally feeling the muscle of his right bicep covered by his thick sweater, and each time Markham would shove him away. Finally as they approached the Arab vendors, the Arab tough attempted to intercede between Markham and the vendors in order to get his cut of any sale, and at this point Markham told the Arab tough to go away and told the vendor he wasn't going to do any business with any of them until they got rid of this Arab tough who now became extremely agitated towards Markham. He suddenly became surrounded by a crowd of Arab men that encircled him with the Arab tough facing him while other Arabs encircled Fred Ruff to prevent him from aiding Markham. Markham was surprised at the number of Arabs which he estimated at about fifty that had so quickly surrounded him and noticed that some of them were businessmen who wore robes over their suits. They were all silent, waiting for Markham to fight this Arab tough who stood facing him waiting for him to make the first move. Markham did not experience fear, only anger and frustration at the knowledge that if he assaulted this Arab tough he would probably receive a dozen puncture wounds from the knives of the Arabs surrounding him. However, he did not want to give the appearance that he feared them either, so he looked into the Arab tough's eyes conveying deep contempt, spit at his feet and while taking a deep breath to enlarge his stature, slowly turned his back on him and started to walk with a show of power and decisiveness to the back section of the crowd, which to his surprise and elation, immediately opened up to let him pass. As he walked out of the crowd he could see Fred Ruff still encircled by a bunch of Arabs. Markham called out to him, "C'mon Fred, let's go," and the crowd opened up and allowed him to walk away and join Markham.

"Don't look back Fred. Just keep walking alongside me as if nothing happened." Finally after a few minutes, Markham looked behind him and observed that the crowd of Arabs had completely dispersed, but he also noticed that ahead of him was a Libyan policeman standing on the corner who must have witnessed the entire incident and never came to their aid. Markham walked up to the policeman and asked him if he spoke English and the policeman avoided his gaze and acted as if he didn't understand him and couldn't be bothered with his inquiry. Just in case he did understand English, Markham made it a point of telling the policeman that from the way the Libyan police protected visitors, it was no wonder that there were no tourists in that town, and then he left the square to find a taxi which was not easily available.

"Man, I thought we'd had it. I've never been so scared in my life Jim. How'd you manage to walk out of that without a scratch?" asked Ruff, still a bit shaken up by the ordeal.

"I don't know Fred. Somebody up there likes me. I guess it just wasn't my time yet," said Markham philosophically.

"Man, let's get back to the base before we encounter more of those Arabs," said Ruff.

"Listen Fred. If anything was going to happen to us, it would already have happened. Relax. I want to find a cab and ask him to take us to the address on this note Omar gave me," said Markham.

Eventually a taxi appeared in the square and Markham got his attention causing him to stop. He pulled out the note and showed it to the taxi driver who spoke broken English. He said that the address was incomplete and besides there were dozens of cafés named Black Cat. Markham dismissed him and decided to explore the old city of Tripoli on foot. As they walked through the narrow dirt streets of the old city, he pointed out to Ruff that only a blanket or tapestry covered the doorway of the cement houses in that district and he doubted that they had any running water. Living conditions were obviously very primitive and many of those Arabs they did see appeared to suffer from diseases which Markham found troubling when the country was receiving so much aid from the United States and other countries. At Ruff's urging, Markham finally agreed to return to the base which was no small task as taxis were rare that afternoon. The crew members decided to have dinner at the NCO Club on base and while at the Club, Ruff told the other crew members of the incident in Tripoli. An Italian national who worked on the base and had Club privileges overheard the story while sitting at the next table and chimed in that Markham and Ruff were very fortunate indeed to have escaped unarmed and that it must surely have been Markham's show of strength and lack of fear that caused their inaction because there had been similar incidents where the Americans were stabbed to death. The man related how the British citizens were not treated with the same disrespect and cited a particular case when a British Army Corp woman was raped by a Libyan soldier and reported it to her commanding officer who gathered several weapons carriers and jeeps with mounted machine guns which they drove into the Libyan compound. The British soldiers rounded up the Libyan soldiers at gunpoint and after the British WAC identified her assailant, the British hung him in full view of the Libyans. "That," he said, "is why the Libyans don't mess with the British. But Americans are fair game because they know of your extraordinary sensitivity to world opinion."

"That must have been some time ago though," said Becket to the Italian man.

"Yes, but it doesn't alter the point that I was making," replied the Italian man.

"Your English is quite good," said Markham.

"Yes, I completed my graduate studies in London, England," replied the Italian man.

At this point, Sergeant John Quigley the Crew Chief and Airman Dick Pritchard the Boom Operator walked in and came over to Markham and his companions to inform them that they were going to be at Wheelus Air Base until the day after New Year's, hence they were going to spend Christmas and New Year's Eve at Wheelus Air Base.

"Man, you mean I've got to drink this reconstituted milk for the next three weeks?" said Becket.

"After a while you won't notice the difference," said Sergeant Quigley. "Cheer up, at least you don't have to spend 18 months in this hell hole like the airmen who are assigned here."

"If I had to spend 18 months here I'd go out of my gourd," said Sabota.

"Well, I can't wait to get back to England," said Markham.

"Amen, brother," said Ruff, Becket and Sabota in unison.

Christmas Eve arrived without fanfare and Markham felt that he could redeem himself for not observing weekly Sunday Mass as a Catholic by at least attending Midnight Mass on Christmas Eve which is held at many American Air Bases, usually in the Base Chapel. Markham was surprised to find a large compliment of Italian nationals employed on the base attending Christmas Mass along with American Servicemen that completely filled the small chapel.

Markham thanked the Lord for protecting him and Fred Ruff and further asked for guidance in his future pursuits and wondered if Ann Fleming was destined to be his significant other. He knew that there were many factors that argued against such a union and he resigned himself to the fact that the ball was really in her court and the only thing he could do at this point was wait and see.

New Year's Eve arrived and the entire crew spent that most reveled evening at the NCO Club where a bottle of champagne cost only one dollar. Markham drank so much champagne that his tongue literally turned black.

The Boom Operator Dick Pritchard held up his glass of champagne and suggested another toast. "I propose that we name this Club the 'Gay Palace' cause there ain't ever any women in it."

"I second the motion," said Chuck Becket who'd been holding his own, drinking champagne.

"And I third the motion. Hey! Is there any such thing as a third motion?" asked Larry Sabota obviously intoxicated.

"I don't think so," said Markham. "But in this case it's most appropriate. You know, I could certainly use some breakfast, but I guess the kitchen is closed, huh?"

"Yep, it sure is James. It sure is. And I ain't getting up in the morning for breakfast either," said Chuck Becket slurring his speech.

"I think the management wants us to leave guys," said Quigley.

"What time is it anyway?" asked Pritchard.

"3 AM," answered Sabota.

"Yep! It's time to get back to base, but who's driving?" asked Pritchard.

"I am," said the Club Manager. "Compliments of the Club."

The next day, Markham couldn't drink enough water to quench his thirst and his head throbbed incessantly from the excessive drinking of champagne. Luckily he wasn't returning to England until the following day.

Upon arrival in Upper Heyford Air Force Base, England, Markham descended onto the runway, got on his knees and kissed the ground, uttering out loud "It's great to be back in England." Markham and the rest of the enlisted crew members then went directly to their barracks in Tiger Town. Larry Sabota, the first man to enter the barracks, noticed a note tacked to the inside of the door.

"Hey! Jim. There's a note here for you. You've got mail," said Sabota.

Markham took the note off the door. The note read that he had mail waiting for him at the mail room in the Headquarters building. Anxious to find out who would mail him a letter in England, Markham departed immediately for the mail room and upon arrival was given an envelope addressed to him without a return address or postage.

"How'd the letter get here? There's no postage," asked Markham of the mail clerk.

"A lady brought it here saying that you were part of a KC-135 crew residing in Tiger Town and were due to return to this base in a couple of weeks, so I figured correctly that you would get the note and her letter," answered the clerk.

"Thank you," replied Markham gratefully and left the building afraid to open the letter, knowing that it could only have been written by Ann Fleming. Markham went back to the barracks and sat on his bunk where he opened the handwritten letter which read:

My dear James:

Writing this letter to you has been the most difficult task I have ever undertaken and it truly breaks my heart to tell you that I will be unable to see you again, ever. I do owe you an explanation, therefore I will begin by telling you that I do love you, but I also love my family and they are located here in England, whereas you reside in America and for me to consummate our relationship would mean deserting the people I have loved and cherished all of my life. My meeting you was a serious mistake which I must correct now before it's too late, hence by the time you read this letter I will be gone on holiday where you will not find me. If not now then eventually you will realize that I am doing the right thing for the both of us. I wish you all the happiness that the future can bring and perhaps in the next life if there is one, we will meet again under different circumstances.

Love, Ann.

As Markham finished reading the letter, his whole upper body became almost limp with emotional fatigue and the letter fell out of his hands onto the floor. Markham just sat there with his head bent forward then he raised both of his hands to his face to cradle his head. Larry Sabota and Chuck Becket walked into the barracks from the restrooms and upon seeing Markham sitting on his bed with his head in his hands, looked at each other and decided to leave him alone in his apparent grief.

"He probably got a 'Dear John' letter," whispered Larry to Chuck.

"Probably. Hey! It hurts. I know from experience," replied Chuck in a low voice.

Larry and Chuck got dressed and left the barracks, leaving Markham alone in his grief. Markham never left the base after receiving the letter from Ann and when he finally boarded the KC-135 for the trip back to Indiana, he had resigned himself to the fact that Ann was not destined to be a permanent part of his life. The trip back to Bunker Hill AFB from England was uneventful and upon his return to the base Markham got back into the daily mundane work routine.

Then one Saturday afternoon, Markham went to the barracks laundry room located on the ground floor of the barracks just down the hall from Markham and Colby's room. Colby had already done his wash and went back to the laundry room to remove his wash from the washing machine and place it in one of the two dryers. Markham was bringing his basket full of clothes to be washed and as he entered the laundry room he observed his roommate Colby removing dried clothes from one of the dryers and placing the clothes on top of the dryer so that he could insert his own washed laundry in the dryer.

"Do you know who these dried clothes belong to?" asked Colby.

"Not a clue Don," replied Markham as he loaded his clothes into the washing machine.

"Hell, I can't wait all day for whoever owns these dried clothes to remove them from the dryer," said Colby.

"I don't blame you. Anyhow, it can't hurt the clothes to put them on top of the dryer. Everybody does it," replied Markham.

At that moment, Tony Boloni, whom Markham recognized as the guy who punched out another man outside a bar in Florida and now resided in the upstairs barracks, entered the laundry room. Boloni of Sicilian heritage was a six feet, two hundred pound wannabe Mafioso who walked around with a swagger that intimidated other airmen of smaller physical stature. Markham had never had occasion to meet or enter into conversation with him as he resided upstairs and was hardly ever in the barracks, spending most of his time off-base with his girlfriend in Kokomo.

Boloni recognized his dried laundry lying on top of the dryer and immediately adopted a hostile attitude, demanding to know who had taken his laundry out of the dryer.

"I did," replied Colby. "The laundry was dry and I needed to use the dryer."

"You touched my laundry? Who the fuck you think you are?" said Boloni, shoving Colby backwards with his right hand on his chest.

"Hey! Tony. That's my roommate. Leave him alone," said Markham who was wearing a pair of khaki trousers and a sleeveless undershirt which accented his overdeveloped upper torso and powerful arms which did not go unnoticed by Boloni.

"Mind your own business. I'm talking to this little fart," replied Boloni.

Markham took a step forward, knowing full well Boloni's reputation for fighting. "When I see bullies like you picking fights with little guys that don't have a chance to win, then I make it my business, so why don't you take your laundry and leave?" replied Markham, now watching Boloni's every move.

Boloni's Sicilian pride and super ego was now at stake and he knew that he couldn't afford to back away from a fight with Markham even if he wanted to, as the word would get around that he was only a paper tiger, but Markham had not offered him a challenge hence he was given an opportunity to save face and leave the room with his laundry and pride intact. However, Colby made the fatal mistake of laughing and repeating Markham's last remark to Boloni, "Yeah! Why don't you take your laundry and leave?" Markham thought it was a stupid and mocking comment by Colby.

Boloni's face turned beet red with anger and without thinking, threw a right punch which landed on Colby's jaw knocking him against the second dryer, but Colby saw the punch coming and had time to withdraw his head back a bit thus reducing the effect of the blow. Nevertheless, Colby was sitting up against the dryer afraid to get up and be hit again. As Boloni moved towards Colby, Markham grabbed Boloni's right wrist with his left hand and simultaneously grabbed Boloni by the throat with his powerful right hand and slammed him against the wall of the laundry room and held him there pinned against the wall.

"Listen you Dago son-of-a-bitch. You're not in Little Italy now. You're in the Armed Forces of the United States and you just assaulted another airman which could land you in a Federal prison," said Markham while holding Boloni by the throat just tight enough to control him, yet not cut off the circulation. Boloni felt powerless and realized that even though Markham had a very muscular physique, he had vastly underestimated his strength and quickly abandoned any thought of engaging him in a fist fight.

"I'm now going to let you go Boloni, but if I hear of you picking on Don again, I'll nail your ass. You understand me?" said Markham, but Boloni did not respond "I said, do you understand me?" repeated Markham, tightening his grip on his throat then loosening it enough for him to respond.

"Yeah! I understand," said Boloni hoarsely and Markham released his grip on him, but watched his every move while he picked up his laundry from the top of the dryer and left the room with his tail between his legs.

Markham looked at Colby who now stood up. "You know Don. If you hadn't laughed at him, none of this would have happened." Markham thought to himself that little guys invariably cause or instigate the fights between the big guys as some form of entertainment.

"I think that if you hadn't been here, he would have beat the shit out of me. He's that type of guy; I just know it," said Colby.

"Maybe you're right, but the fact remains that I was here and it could have been avoided. I hate conflict. It gets my adrenaline going for hours afterwards," said Markham.

"I'm sorry about that Jim, but I'm glad you were here to help me out. I owe you one," said Colby. "What the hell makes a guy like that tick? I mean, why does he feel a need to beat up on people at the slightest provocation or for the slimmest reason? I don't get it."

"Don't you know, Don? A guy like that has a super narcissistic ego that constantly needs nurturing to reaffirm his feelings of superiority which cannot afford to be undermined by a single defeat, hence he chooses victims that will guarantee him victory thus confirming his supremacy and dominance," explained Markham.

"He's probably a control freak," said Colby.

"Probably. He'll require a submissive wife, no doubt," said Markham.

"And I hear he's getting engaged to that girl from Kokomo he's been dating. Marge told me that she's a real nice girl. Man, what she doesn't know *will* hurt her," said Colby.

"That's life. By the time you have gained enough experience to make intelligent decisions, you're too old to make use of it," said Markham.

Back in his room folding his laundry, Markham wondered why some men felt the need to challenge him when he considered himself a pacifist and his demeanor non-threatening. Don Colby suddenly entered the room disrupting Markham's reverie.

"Hey Jim. How about going on a picnic with us?" said Colby.

"With us? Who's us?" asked Markham with obvious curiosity.

"Me, Marge, and Dorothy," said Colby.

"Dorothy? Who's Dorothy?" asked Markham.

"She's another one of Marge's girlfriends. She's divorced with no kids and she's seen you several times at drive-ins and at the lake. She's got a gorgeous figure and if I wasn't dating Marge, I'd date her in a minute. How about it Jim? Hell, you're not doing anything this evening. We'll take a drive out to the Woodlands and the girls will bring the food and we'll bring the beer and a radio."

"You said Woodlands? Where's that?" said Markham.

"It's about five miles outside of Peru. It's got a large pond for swimming and there's a large wooded area overlooking the pond. There'll be no one there but us Indians," said Colby.

"So you want me to go on a blind date? Is that it?" said Markham.

"Not really. You've seen her a couple of times. She's got short brown hair, nice face and she's stacked like a brick shit house. Listen, what have you got to lose? Nothing," said Colby imploringly.

"Oh! Alright. Hell, as you say, I've nothing to lose except time, and I've got plenty of that," said Markham resignedly.

They all went in Markham's convertible with the top down as the early evening sun glowed like a huge orange on the horizon. At Colby's direction, they drove to the Woodlands and parked near the pond. Colby and Markham stretched out an army blanket and the two girls placed a large basket full of sandwiches and a few apples. Markham unloaded a case of beer from the trunk of the car and they all made themselves comfortable on the blanket eating and drinking beer. Eventually Colby and Marge moved several feet away so as to engage in a personal conversation and allow Markham some privacy with Dorothy who by now had consumed several cans of beer. Her eyes were glassy while she just stared at Markham, then for some unknown reason, Dorothy suddenly exclaimed to Markham, "You don't love me; I know you don't," then she stood up and walked away from the car onto a narrow dirt road in the direction of the woods. Markham was completely surprised and puzzled by Dorothy's statement and behavior. He walked over to Colby and Marge who were only a few feet away talking with apparently no idea of what had just transpired.

"Hey! Marge. Your girlfriend Dorothy just took off for no apparent reason towards the woods. You wanna go get her?" asked Markham.

Marge just looked at Markham and shrugged her shoulders as if she didn't care and that it was Markham's problem. Colby remained silent.

"Well aren't you guys concerned about her safety? For no reason she's gone into the woods. She's been drinking and anything can happen to her. It's getting dark," said Markham.

"She's a big girl. She can take care of herself," responded Marge.

"Well, I'm gonna go find her and bring her back before she gets lost or worse," replied Markham who started walking towards the wooded area along the narrow path.

The sun was down and the glow of the full moon and starry skies gave sufficient light for Markham to see Dorothy's figure a couple of hundred yards ahead of him. As he caught up to her, he called her name, but she continued walking rapidly forward until Markham grabbed her arm and turned her around.

"Dorothy, where are you going?" asked Markham.

"Leave me alone Wayne," she said struggling. "Leave me alone you bastard."

Markham realized that she was mistaking him for her ex-husband Wayne. The effects of alcohol, he thought.

"It's me Jim, Jim Markham. Don't you recognize me?" said Markham while she violently struggled to free herself from Markham's grip on her arm. She started to strike him with her free hand and Markham knew that if he allowed her to go forth, she could possibly end up being assaulted and killed by any stranger who happened to come along, and since he brought her to this picnic, he felt responsible for getting her safely back home. She was acting like a wild cat and he was losing patience with her strong resistance. Markham had never struck a woman before, but he felt that under the circumstances the only way to bring her to her senses was to slap her across the face which he did and to his surprise, she went limp like a wet noodle. He grabbed her left arm and swung it over the back of his neck and carried her body over his right shoulder. She was out like a light. Markham started the walk back to the car through the narrow path flanked by heavy foliage and as he came within a hundred yards of the car, Dorothy regained consciousness and stood up on her own two feet wondering what had happened. She felt the left side of her face with her hand.

"Did you hit me?" asked Dorothy.

"Yes I did. You went wild. You thought I was your ex-husband Wayne and you ran into the woods and I brought you back," said Markham. "I didn't mean to hurt you, Dorothy, but you were uncontrollable. I was trying to wake you up to the reality of the situation and I guess I don't know my own strength."

"That's alright, Jim. I sometimes get like that when I drink," said Dorothy.

Marge watched Markham and Dorothy as they approached the car and wondered what had happened.

Marge took Dorothy aside as Colby stood next to Markham quite intoxicated and not cognizant of much of his surroundings, especially since he didn't have to drive. Markham overheard Marge talking to Dorothy.

"What happened out there, Dot? Did he rape you? Hey! Tell me the truth, did Jim rape you out there in the woods?" asked Marge in an accusing tone that presumed the worse, which made Markham angry.

"No, he didn't Marge. Nothing happened. I just got drunk and confused. I'm glad he brought me back to my senses. Who knows what could have happened to me out there?" said Dorothy.

"You shouldn't drink so much Dot. You know these guys will take advantage of you when you get drunk," said Marge.

"Jim's not like that Marge. I really like him," said Dorothy.

Seeing Dorothy holding her hand against her jaw prompted Marge to ask her, "Does your jaw hurt? Let me see," said Marge. "Well, it doesn't seem swollen."

"It's a bit sore, that's all. I'll be alright. Would you talk to Jim on my behalf? I think he's mad at me and he probably won't want to see me anymore after this," said Dorothy.

"OK! I will Dorothy," replied Marge.

"Is she alright now?" said Markham to Marge.

"Yes she's alright. She really likes you Jim and she's really sorry about what happened. She wants to see you again," said Marge.

"Well, I don't know about you people, but I've had enough excitement for one night. Let's pack up and call it a night," said Markham, avoiding Marge's question.

As they drove back to Kokomo, Markham remained silent leaving the chatter to the rest of them. He dropped Dorothy off at her house first and Marge stepped out of the car for a few minutes to talk to Dorothy privately before Dorothy went into her Father's house. Upon Marge's return to the car, she told Markham that Dorothy wanted him to call her the following day. However, Markham had already decided that Dorothy had too much emotional baggage for him to bear through an as yet uncertain future. Furthermore, Marge's ready assumption of felonious assault by Markham gave him reason to be cautious about any association with either one of these women. He thanked his lucky stars that this incident didn't turn into a tragedy and gladly relinquished both women to his roommate Colby.

Since Markham's assignment in the War Room, there had been rumors circulating amongst airmen on the base that Major Francis Randall was a homosexual primarily due to his mannerisms and the way he walked 'with a swish' as someone described it. Major Randall was a Command Pilot and a graduate of West Point hence above reproach, especially since there was no evidence to support the rumor. However, one day, Markham reported to work at the War Room and learned that Major Randall was being discharged from the US Air Force after 15 years of service for having been caught in a homosexual act with a civilian in the back of a parked car in Washington, D.C. Markham then reflected on past comments and criticisms of Lt. Colonel Rockford by Major Randall and began to understand the underlying reason for his animosity and disdain. It was a fact that sodomy was a violation of the Uniform Code of Military Justice and homosexuality in the military service was grounds for dismissal due in part to the loss of the individual's security clearance because his homosexuality made him vulnerable to blackmail. Captain Brevard who for years sat next to Major Randall in the War Room was emptying Major Randall's desk of personal items which he was placing in a cardboard box.

"Jim," said Captain Brevard, "Major Randall needs some help in carrying some of the heavy boxes from his base housing to the trailer he's got hitched to his car. Would you be willing to help him? He'll pay you $10.00 an hour."

"Sure, why not?" replied Markham who could always use the money.

"You can take tomorrow morning off and be at his house at 0800 hours. The house is located at 69 Somerset Street, right around the corner from Lt. Colonel Rockford's house," said Captain Brevard.

The next morning, Markham, dressed in his usual military fatigues, reported to Major Randall's house and was politely received and instructed as to which boxes were to be loaded first into the trailer. Markham was certain that Major Randall knew that he had been apprised of his involuntary discharge from the US Air Force, but Major Randall made no mention of it. However, Markham felt as if the Major was evaluating him all of the time he was there. Finally, the loading job completed after 90 minutes of work, Major Randall gave Markham $20.00, telling him to keep the change. He then looked at Markham in the strangest way as if he was having a debate within himself.

"Jim," he said. "How would you like to make a quick $50.00?"

Markham looked at him perplexed, waiting for the other shoe to fall.

"Well," he said with a semi-embarrassed smile. "The cat's out of the bag now, so I don't have to pretend. I'll give you $50.00 if you will let me perform oral sex on you."

Markham couldn't believe the nerve of this disgraced officer, a West Point graduate and Command Pilot. The thought that Major Randall would think that Markham would ever consider participating in an act of sodomy arose his anger.

"When I first heard of your involuntary discharge after 15 years of honorable service I felt sorry for you Major, but your attempt to corrupt me, a subordinate, convinces me that the Air Force was right in getting rid of a degenerate like you," said Markham who then threw the $20.00 at his feet and walked out to his car and returned to Combat Operations where he thought of informing Captain Brevard of the solicitation, but then decided that since Randall was leaving the Air Force permanently, there was no point in blemishing his reputation further.

Major Randall was replaced by a newly appointed officer to the War Room, Major Glenn Sostak who appeared to be a likable, but no-nonsense type of man. It didn't take long for the War Room to resume its normalcy.

Lt. Colonel Rockford's recommendation for the promotion of Markham to the rank of Staff Sergeant was endorsed and he officially became a non-commissioned officer which pleased Markham because it indicated that his work was being appreciated by his superiors, but it also increased his salary and benefits. That same week Jack Batiste got promoted to Technical Sergeant, one rank above Markham and Bob Woodland. In the past, S/Sgt Woodland and S/Sgt Batiste worked in the aircrew study room where the large world maps were located while Markham worked with the War Room officers as their clerk. However, with T/Sgt Batiste's promotion, all of that suddenly changed. Lt. Colonel Rockford and the two majors were on Temporary Duty elsewhere for a week leaving the two Captains in charge, but Captain Tinsley had taken the afternoon off to attend to a personal matter, leaving only Captain Brevard on duty in the War Room with Markham who was typing a memorandum. Sergeant Batiste, now a Technical Sergeant, felt a need to exercise his newly acquired rank by marching through the rooms of Combat Operations as if on an inspection and as he wandered into the War Room, he witnessed Markham pull out the memorandum from his typewriter, obviously dissatisfied with its contents and crumbled it into a ball which he threw into the wastebasket. Sergeant Batiste immediately ran to the waste basket next to Markham's desk and pulled out the crumpled memorandum which he unraveled and smoothed out while standing in front of Markham.

"We don't waste paper in this organization Sergeant Markham. Yanking that memo out of the typewriter is not conduct that I will tolerate in this office," said Sergeant Batiste in an officious voice.

Markham couldn't believe his ears. Had this man gone insane? How dare he tell him when he can and cannot remove a paper out of his typewriter in whatever manner he chooses? This was nothing but harassment and he wasn't going to stand for it. Markham stood up with clenched fists, his anger mounting by the second and his powerful muscles surging with blood as his blood pressure was climbing. Markham wanted to climb over the desk and pulverize this peacock and Batiste realized that he had just poked an angry bull who was getting ready to stick a horn up his ass, and so took a couple of steps back with visible fear in his eyes. Captain Brevard was well aware that in the next few seconds all hell could break loose and he needed to calm the situation immediately.

"Jim, cool down, don't do anything rash," said Captain Brevard as Markham stood facing Batiste with clenched fists and utterly speechless from suppressed anger.

"You'd better get this son-of-a-bitch away from me, Captain before I do something to him that we'll all regret," said Markham.

"Now Jim, he's the NCO in charge now, so you'll have to learn to get along with him," said Captain Brevard.

"You mean I've got to put up with this clown?" said Markham, still visibly angry. "No way Captain. Request permission to leave the War Room, Sir, in order to consult with my Squadron Commander about a possible reassignment," said Markham.

Captain Brevard knew that Batiste had overstepped his boundaries and he also knew that if Markham stayed in the War Room, there literally might be a war between these two men and there was no doubt as to who would be the victor, hence he thought it best to allow Markham to leave the room and visit his Squadron Commander, giving him time to calm down.

Captain Lambert and Sergeant Feebles were discussing the forthcoming barracks inspection when the door to the Orderly Room opened and Markham walked in still upset over the prior incident.

"Captain Lambert. I just came from the War Room and I have a major problem, Sir," said Markham who had been asked to sit down in one of the chairs facing the Captain's desk. Markham related the event as he recalled it and stated that he was afraid that if he returned to that office, he might not be able to contain his rage against future harassment by Sergeant Batiste, hence he wanted a transfer to another unit.

"Tell me Jim, did this harassment by Batiste start right after you got promoted to Staff Sergeant?" asked Captain Lambert.

Markham looked up at the Captain and Sergeant Feebles standing next to him. "Why yes, as a matter of fact it did," replied Markham who then saw Captain Lambert and Sergeant Feebles look at each other with a knowing smile.

"We thought so," said the Captain. "You definitely won't have to go back there Jim. I'll take care of that. I'm going to enroll you into the NCO Academy which is an 8-week course starting Monday.

While you're attending the Academy, we'll get you another unit of assignment. Of course, Colonel Rockford is not due to return until a week from Monday and he may decide to remove Batiste from Combat Operations in order to retain you. We'll see. In any event, attendance at the NCO Academy certainly can't hurt you. Right?"

"You're right Sir. I really appreciate your help," replied Markham.

"Alright then Jim. It's Friday so have a nice weekend," said Captain Lambert, dismissing Markham.

Attendance at the NCO Academy was no picnic, with white glove inspections and the ultimate in chicken shit discipline being the rule of the day. But to Markham, anything was better than having to work for Mr. Peacock. As the weeks went by, Markham knew that Lt. Colonel Rockford had returned from his trip and now was aware of the situation between Batiste and him and half expected that Batiste might get transferred to another unit. However, fate stepped into Markham's life again in a most unusual way. It was the latter part of November 1961 when several American Air Bases were opened throughout France in response to the Berlin crisis and each base required the services of the US Air Force Office of Special Investigations known as the OSI. The OSI agents assigned to these air bases needed American-born French Interpreter-Translators and past attempts to fulfill those duties by College graduates who had majored in French failed miserably as they did not possess the fluency required for the job which included the collection of strategic information from various French sources. What made matters more difficult was the requirement that these Interpreter-Translators be born in the United States to insure their loyalty, especially in view of the fact that their job title was 'Intelligence Specialist' and they were to use their language skills to gather intelligence information for the OSI. A computer search of the personnel files in Washington revealed that James Markham was born in Brooklyn, New York, but was raised from childhood as a French-Canadian with complete fluency in French, a perfect candidate for the job.

Special Orders from the OSI Directorate in Washington, D.C., arrived at Bunker Hill Air Force Base, Indiana, ordering James Markham to report to Dreux Air Base, France via McGuire Air Force Base, New Jersey by 10 January 1962. Inasmuch as the OSI needed his service in France immediately, Directorate did not want to waste time bringing him to Washington, D.C. for intelligence training when the task could be performed on the job at an OSI Detachment in France. Upon receiving his Special Orders assigning him to the OSI in France, Markham's waning faith in providence and divine intervention was joyfully restored. As a Staff Sergeant, Markham was entitled to have his privately-owned automobile shipped to France at government expense. All he had to do was deliver his car to the Brooklyn Navy Yard and they would ship it to France.

Two days after graduating from the NCO Academy, Markham drove out of Bunker Hill Air Force Base's main gate on that bright sunny day for the last time, with the top down even though it was December, and waved goodbye to a drudgeful past, looking forward at great speed to a bright and adventurous future in the OSI.

CHAPTER VIII
The French Experience

By the time Markham had left the state of Indiana, the mid-December cold weather compelled him to raise the soft top of his convertible and turn on the heat, although it was not unusual for him to turn on the heat and still leave the top down as he loved to ride in the open air, but snow flakes were starting to appear and by the time he reached the state of Pennsylvania, the weather required the use of his windshield wipers and headlights. Markham hoped to reach his mother's new house in Long Island before Christmas so that he could spend his three weeks leave with them before boarding a military aircraft to France.

As he drove through several long tunnels in the mountains of Pennsylvania, Markham noticed that the temperature gauge on the dash indicated that his radiator was overheating so he pulled over to the side of the road, stopped the car, lifted the hood and observed steam pouring out of the radiator cap. Markham allowed the engine to cool down before he removed the radiator cap. It was obvious that he'd lost a significant amount of coolant from the overheating and he suspected that a malfunctioning thermostat was the culprit. He needed a tool to remove the thermostat, which he didn't have, but a trucker driving an 18 wheeler must have taken pity on this young man broken down between mountains on a wintry road, because he stopped his rig in front of Markham's car and walked over to offer his assistance.

"What happened? Did it overheat?" asked the trucker, a big man sporting a dark beard.

"Yeah! It did. Thanks for stopping Mister," Markham replied."Looks like I need a new thermostat."

"Well, I can take the old one out, but I don't have a replacement. But you won't need one. We'll generate heat by putting a piece of cardboard in front of the radiator. Just an old trucker's trick," said the bearded man jovially. The trucker went back to his truck and brought back a box of tools which he quickly used to remove the thermostat, thus allowing the coolant to flow freely without obstruction. He then cut up a large piece of cardboard from a box he had on his truck which he placed between the grill and the radiator. "Well that should take care of it. You're all set. I noticed that you have an Air Force sticker on your windshield," said the trucker.

"Yes I'm in the Air Force and I'm heading home for Christmas," replied Markham.

"Glad to be of help to a serviceman and Merry Christmas to you," said the trucker as he walked back to his truck.

"Thanks again and Merry Christmas to you too," replied Markham gratefully.

Markham started his car and watched the temperature needle climb a quarter of the way up then stop, and to his relief the needle remained there which meant that he could continue his drive to Long Island, but now the question of heat came to mind and sure enough the cardboard protected the radiator from the oncoming cold air, thus permitting the engine to heat the coolant to a temperature warm enough to keep Markham comfortable throughout the remainder of the trip.

Nora's husband Freddie had given him great directions to the house in Oceanside, Long Island which Markham found without any deviation. It was a three-bedroom ranch style house with finished basement and a nicely groomed front and back yard. The next day after his arrival, Freddie took Markham to the local garage where they replaced the thermostat and gave the car a complete examination before its scheduled shipment overseas where the servicing of an American car would be hard to find and auto parts even harder. The holidays for Markham were uneventful except for meeting Freddie's relatives. Finally, the holidays over, Freddie volunteered to follow Markham in his car to the Brooklyn Navy Yard where he had to deliver his automobile for shipment to the Port of Saint Nazaire, France.

After delivery of the car, Markham got into Freddie's Buick and they drove to McGuire Air Force Base, New Jersey which shared Federal land with Fort Dix, New Jersey, a large Army basic-training facility. Freddie was a prince of a man with a great sense of humor and Markham was pleased that his Mother had married such a gentle, kind man. Wearing his dress blue uniform, Markham had been instructed to bring with him at least one dress set of civilian clothes and that he would be given a clothing allowance to purchase additional civilian clothes which would be the required dress during his assignment with the OSI in France. Two days later, Markham boarded a MATS aircraft with destination Paris-le-Bourget airfield, France.

During the flight to France, Markham remembered the French books he had read while growing up in Montreal that described life in Paris and its rich history and he looked forward to meeting with the French people who spoke what he still considered his native language inasmuch as he still did his mental arithmetic in French and when lost for words reverted to French. *After all,* he thought, *my mother's ancestry is from France.*

Apart from his reverie, the flight for him was monotonous. Upon arrival at Paris-le-Bourget, Markham, still wearing his dress blue uniform, was met by a slim man wearing a brimmed hat and a trench coat who identified himself as Mister Keith Heller of the OSI. He had a pleasant manner, yet Markham noticed that his left eye was not synchronized with his right eye and Markham wondered if that eye was functional, but dared not ask. They got into a Ford four-door gray sedan and Mr. Heller started driving out of the airport towards Dreux Air Base.

"You can call me Keith, but Mr. Moss is the officer in charge of the detachment so you'd better call him Mister Moss, just so you know the rules. There's just the three of us, Mr. Moss, me and you and our ranks are classified. As soon as you get to Dreux you'll put on your civilian clothes and you can put your uniform away for the duration of your assignment in France. You don't reveal your rank to anyone. By the same token, don't pass yourself off as a Special Agent either. You're Mister Markham, the official Interpreter-Translator for the OSI Detachment at Dreux and you'll be given an identification card to that effect by Mr. Moss. For your information and your information only, my rank is Technical Sergeant and Mr. Moss is a Captain, but that is classified info," said Mr. Heller matter-of-factly.

"What's Mr. Moss' first name? You didn't mention it," said Markham.

"His first name is Milton and he hates it, so don't mention it, just call him Mr. Moss," replied Heller. "By the way, how's your French Jim? Good I hope, because the last interpreter we had couldn't cut the mustard and had to be sent back to the States," said Heller.

"It's been at least 10 years since I've had an opportunity to have a conversation in French. I also understand that Parisian French is a lot different than Canadian French. At least that's what I've been told," said Markham hesitantly.

"We'll find out soon enough. Mr. Moss has already scheduled you to take a French test at Evreux Air Base in a couple of days," said Heller.

"What will my duties involve?" asked Markham.

"Well, for one, you'll accompany us to any meetings with our French counterparts which includes the French National and Local Police, the French Military Security to name a few. You'll also be expected to read several of the French newspapers for intelligence information, that is, information that should be of interest to the OSI and the United States Air Force. The French Communist Party is the second largest Communist organization in Europe after Italy and its legal and they have their own newspaper which is called 'L'humanite Dimanche.' We need to know if and when they're planning demonstrations or strikes against any of our bases, things like that. When you find something worthwhile to report you put that information into an EEI report for Mr. Moss' signature which he sends to District Headquarters in Paris."

"What's an EEI report?" asked Markham.

"That stands for Essential Elements of Information Report," replied Heller.

"I presume that the report is in English," said Markham.

"Of course, none of us read French except Mr. Belanger, the Chief of G.I. Division at District Headquarters," said Heller.

"How far is Dreux from Paris, Keith?"

"About 75 Kilometers west of Paris. It's about a one-hour drive," replied Heller.

"You mentioned that I will have to take a French test at Evreux. How far is that from Dreux?" asked Markham.

"Evreux Air Base is only about 35 kilometers northwest of Dreux," said Heller.

"I heard that these new bases we opened up are manned by National Guard Units that were recently activated, is that true?" asked Markham.

"You heard right. Dreux is manned entirely by the Alabama National Guard, mostly from Montgomery, Alabama and they all know each other and they're having a ball over here away from their wives," said Heller. "You'll meet them. In fact, you'll be staying in one of their barracks composed of NCOs and airmen, temporarily until we can find you other more suitable quarters."

"Won't that reveal my rank?" asked Markham, a bit puzzled.

"Well, not really. They'll know that you're an enlisted man, but they won't know your rank," replied Heller. "The important thing is that the French don't know that you're not a commissioned officer, because they like to think that they're dealing with officers, you know, the upper crust. It flatters their egoes and you're more respected, hence more productive in acquiring information from them."

"But you're not billeted in the barracks, right?" asked Markham.

"No, I'm billeted in the Bachelor Officer's Quarters, and that's because as a Special Agent, it's important that my rank be classified otherwise I would not be effective in conducting investigations involving American military personnel as well as foreign nationals in counterintelligence investigations."

"That makes sense. I hope you don't mind me asking all of these questions, but no one has briefed me about the OSI and my duties here," explained Markham.

"Hey! I'm glad you asked. How else are you going to know these things?" replied Heller.

After a while they arrived at Dreux Air Base and Heller flashed his OSI credentials and was waved past the Guard shack. Heller drove down a few streets then pulled up to a small wooden building where there was one other car parked near the front door to the building. "That's Mr. Moss' car," said Heller as they stepped out of the vehicle and walked into the OSI office where Mr. Moss was sitting behind his desk smoking a cigar. Mister Moss was a middle-aged man of small stature, no more than five feet five inches in height with a small pot belly that was natural for a man of his age. He appeared to be an easy-going person, but Markham sensed that he could be very assertive when the occasion demanded it. Upon entering the office, Moss stood up and walked around his desk and shook Markham's hand with a welcoming smile that he felt was genuine.

"I gave Jim a cursory briefing of his assignment while driving him over here from the airport," said Heller to Moss.

"Well, that's good. Why don't you take him to the barracks where he'll be staying so that he can unload his gear, then when he's finished, you both can join me for dinner in the Village?" said Moss.

"Sounds good to me," said Heller with a smile. "Anything's better than that Mess Hall."

Mister Heller drove Markham to his barracks and it didn't take long for Markham to change from his military uniform into a pair of slacks and a sports jacket. After placing his gear in his wall locker, Markham left the barracks with Mister Heller and returned to the OSI office where Mister Moss was waiting for them. They all went into Moss' vehicle to a French restaurant named Chez Madeleine in a village a few kilometers from Dreux Air Base. It was a quaint restaurant with red table-cloths, probably to hide traces of wine. They were seated at a table for four next to a window that overlooked the countryside road. The menu entirely in French included 'escargot' known to Americans as snails, which Markham had previously tasted in Montreal and found them to be absolutely scrumptious, but he had also seen them prepared in an Italian restaurant in New York City where they covered the little animals with cheese which Markham did not favor the flavor, hence he was curious as to how they prepared them in France. As they were reading the menu and Heller was making small talk with Moss, he noticed a crystal platter on the table to his right that contained a pile of chocolate-covered things that looked like some sort of insect.

"Are these what I think they are?" asked Markham to his two companions.

"What, those chocolate covered insects?" said Heller. "I've never tried them, but Mr. Moss has and he can tell you all about them."

"Actually Jim they're quite delicious. Keith is not the adventurous type, but if you are, I'm sure you'll like them. I believe they're grasshoppers. I never asked; I just ate a few of them," said Mr. Moss.

Markham tasted one then several of the insects while waiting for the waiter often referred to as 'Garcon,' literally meaning 'boy,' although these waiters were men in their twenties and even thirties. "Order whatever you want Jim, it's on the OSI expense account," said Moss.

Markham ordered one dozen escargots and frog's legs as an entrée followed by French pastry for dessert. A bottle of Beaujolais wine was ordered for the three of them with dinner.

"The escargots were excellent. I could eat another dozen, and next time I come here, I'll make them the entrée," said Markham with a smile of contentment. Moss loved a man who enjoyed good food and Markham didn't disappoint him. "However the frog's legs were very bland. If it wasn't for the sauce, there'd hardly be any taste to them," said Markham.

Moss briefed Markham on the details of his work and explained to him that the successful completion of the French test he would be taking in two days at Evreux would add another Air Force Specialty Code, to wit: Intelligence Specialist, to his Air Force credentials at the Third level and to reach the Seventh level which is the highest level in that Specialty. He would need to take another test later on, but only one person in the OSI in France possessed a seven level in that field and he had been stationed at District Headquarters in Paris for several years.

The following day, Markham accompanied Moss and Heller in their routine visits to the local gendarmerie and the Renseignment Generaux also known as the RG which was connected to the Surete Nationale. He noticed that the French officials were always eager to receive Moss and Heller and ready to ingratiate themselves in order to ply favors from the Americans in the form of refrigerators and other appliances from the Base Exchange where the cost was significantly less than on the French economy, and oftentimes they were provided as gifts from Uncle Sam in return for cooperation in the acquisition of intelligence information useful to the United States. Not all French officials had to be bribed. A few of them genuinely liked Americans and a long-lasting relationship developed between them well beyond their years of service, but those were mostly from the generation that fought in the Second World War and remembered the major role the Americans played in the liberation of Paris and France. As time went on, Markham noticed that the youth of France resented the presence of American Servicemen in France.

The OSI issued gasoline coupons in booklet form to its agents and interpreters that could be redeemed at any ESSO station in France for the low cost of .15 cents per gallon of gas. These gasoline coupons were enormously beneficial to Markham, whose eight cylinder gas-guzzling automobile got only 18 miles per gallon on the highway. Markham carried a five gallon Gerry can full of gas which he kept in the trunk of his car for emergencies. On a number of occasions, Markham stopped to help a Frenchman who'd run out of gas by pouring a couple of gallons of gas into the Frenchman's car from his Gerry can, and never asked for money in return, and sometimes he got a 'thank you' and at other times he did not, as if it was expected from a 'rich' American.

One evening, he drove to Paris to experience their night life and wandered into a place that had dancing. As he stood in line to pay the entrance fee he saw that the patrons were being charged 1000 francs, but when it came Markham's turn, the cashier asked him for 2000 francs. In perfect French, he asked the cashier why he was charging him 2000 francs when he had charged the other French customers only 1000 francs. The cashier responded, "You're an American; you can afford it; take it or leave it."

Markham gave him a few choice French words and left the dance with a feeling of great disappointment with the French people. He decided to better spend his time in Paris by visiting historical places he'd heard and read about including the cafés frequented by the 'Lost Generation' of famous writers such as Ernest Hemingway, F. Scott Fitzgerald, Sherwood Anderson, Ezra Pound, John Dos Passos, who frequented and made famous the Closerie des Lilas, the Rotonde and the Select café, and the dean of Existentialism, Jean-Paul Sartre who made 'Les Deux Magots' café legendary. Markham also remembered the famous Moulin Rouge immortalized by Henri de Toulouse-Lautrec, a crippled painter of Paris night life, and Picasso who spent much of his social time at Toklas and Stein. These were the places that Markham wished to visit and somehow feel the ambience of those days gone with the storms of war.

Paris at noontime radiated with sunshine as Markham arrived in his Ford convertible with the top down which drew the attention of most people who could not avoid the largesse of the automobile with its dual spotlights, trunk antennae and Hollywood skirts. He had studied a map of Paris and knew the location of those places that were of historical interest to him, but finding a parking place was not easy, especially for such a large automobile. He finally found a parking place in the Montmartre area at the Parvis du Sacre Coeur located on a hill overlooking all of Paris. It was easier for him to take a taxi from there to those places too far to walk than attempt to park in the city. Markham then hailed a taxi to the Gothic Cathedral of Notre Dame, considered the spiritual and geographic center of Paris, located in the eastern part of the Ile de la Cite. Markham was in awe at this architectural masterpiece and he noticed a marking on the square of the cathedral that marked Point Zero from which all distances to Paris are calculated. As he ventured further east of the island, he came upon a shrine dedicated to the thousands of Parisians deported to German concentration camps during World War II.

As he stood there reading the plaque, he heard a bystander telling a friend that the French Police rounded up more than 13,000 Jews and sent them to their deaths in German concentration camps. Markham hoped that the world learned a lesson from this tragedy. To lift his spirits Markham hailed a taxi that took him to the famous Closerie des Lilac for a late lunch and managed to get a table not far from the sidewalk so that he could watch the people walking by. The tables and chairs were small and close together to allow for more customers. A waiter came over and Markham ordered in French a cup of French onion soup, a ham and cheese sandwich and a glass of red wine. As the waiter left, one of the two young French women sitting no more than a few inches from Markham turned towards him and in perceptible Parisian French asked Markham if he was Canadian.

Surprised but pleased at her boldness, Markham responded in French, "No I'm not Canadian, but I was schooled in the Quebec province."

"You must be an American then, but your French is excellent if not for your obvious Canadian accent," said the attractive, violet-eyed brunette sitting nearest him.

"Yes, I'm a New Yorker," said Markham continuing the conversation in French, "and my name is Jacques when I speak French, otherwise it's Jim."

"Well, Jacques, I'm Yvonne Gautier and my friend's name is Charlotte Ledoux, and what did you say your last name was?"

"I didn't, but it's Markham, James Markham."

"Would you like to join us at our petite table, Jacques?"

"Thank you; I'd love to," replied Markham who moved his chair around facing their table, sitting between the two ladies.

"Do either of you young ladies speak English?" asked Markham.

"No, not really. We understand it somewhat, but we can only speak a few words. We prefer to converse in French if you don't mind. It's so much easier, and besides, your French is fluent," said Yvonne.

"Are you here on vacation or business?" asked Yvonne.

"Neither actually. I'm in the United States Air Force stationed near Paris and in my off-duty time I like to visit those historical sites I've read about," said Markham.

"So you're an American in Paris. Have you been to the Louvres yet?" asked Charlotte.

"No. I'm reserving that for some other time when I have several days to spare, as I understand that one could spend a couple of weeks in there and still not see everything," said Markham.

"You're right about that," said Yvonne. "It's a huge place. But I was born and raised in Paris and I know all the places worth visiting. Did you know for instance that your famous writer Hemingway used to come here often with other American writers?"

"Yes I did. As a matter of fact, that's why I'm here at this restaurant. This is my starting place, and from here I will go to other places that were made famous by great artists," said Markham.

"Aren't you interested in famous French artists too?" asked Charlotte.

"Of course. I plan on visiting Les Deux Magots which Jean-Paul Sartre celebrated. I read his book several years ago on Existentialism," said Markham.

"I'm impressed that you know the works of Jean-Paul Sartre," said Yvonne who now wished to test Markham's knowledge further. "What other places frequented by French artists do you plan on visiting?"

"The Moulin Rouge, immortalized by Toulouse-Lautrec and let's not forget Picasso at the Toklas," replied Markham.

He's such a handsome man, thought Yvonne, *and he speaks French, and he's from America, a place where I have never been. I should like to spend the rest of the day with him.*

"You know Jacques. You should have a tour guide and I do know all of those places and a lot more," said Yvonne.

"Are you volunteering for the job?" asked Markham with a smile.

"Yes, but on one condition," replied Yvonne.

"What's that?" asked Markham.

"That afterwards you take me out to dinner at the restaurant of my choice," said Yvonne.

Markham weighed her answer for a moment, wondering if he could afford this lady's taste, when Yvonne interrupted his thoughts.

"I won't break your wallet, I promise you," she added laughingly.

"O.K,! It's a deal," replied Markham.

"Charlotte has to go meet her husband so this works out perfectly," said Yvonne, nudging her girlfriend to excuse herself so that she could be alone with Markham.

Charlotte looked at her watch and said that she had overstayed her lunch time and must trot along to meet her husband Etienne. As she stood up, Markham stood up also and shook her hand with the usual verbal pleasantries associated with new acquaintances and goodbyes.

Now that Markham was alone with Yvonne, he suggested that they visit the Rotonde next and then Les Deux Magots leaving the rest of the tour in Yvonne's able hands. The waiter had now just arrived with Markham's lunch so while he ate she told him about Jean-Paul Sartre's lifelong partner Simone de Beauvoir, and all of the artists that flock the Parvis du Sacre Coeur at the Montmartre, the highest hill in Paris where one can purchase a painting for a pittance in the winter time when tourism is low and artists are starving. She told Markham that the Moulin Rouge was very commercialized and one visit is enough and she wasn't too keen on going in there again. She explained that the Latin Quarter was named not because there were Latins living there, but because the University of Paris which was the oldest in Europe and located in that Quarter, used Latin as the official language of learning until 1789. Furthermore, the Left Bank of Paris was located on the south side of the River Seine and the Right Bank was located on the north side of the Seine.

"Of course Jacques, we must go to the top of the Eiffel Tower," she said while watchingMarkham eat his sandwich. She thought, *this man is built like an American pioneer, but I'll bet he's got the passion of an Italian and the sensitivity of a Frenchman,* and she planned to find out.

That afternoon, they walked, took taxis, visited several places of interest and rode the elevator up the Eiffel Tower and finally found themselves walking along a tree-line path in the Jardin du Luxembourg filled with formal gardens and a large fountain where children sailed their model boats, which immediately brought back memories to Markham of those days when he sailed his model sailboat in the Lac du Castor at the backside of Mount Royal in Montreal.

"It's getting late, where do you plan for us to eat dinner?" asked Markham.

"It's only 7:30, Cherie, we eat late in Paris. It's a surprise. We'll take a taxi there and I guarantee that the food will exceed your expectations and at a very reasonable price. Leave it to me Cherie," said Yvonne as she guided him out of the park.

While riding in the taxi, Markham became curious regarding their destination.

"What part of Paris are we headed for?" asked Markham.

"Saint-Germain-des-Pres," replied Yvonne, holding on to Markham's left arm. "It's one of the more elegant neighborhoods of Paris."

The taxi pulled up to a well-lit façade of an obvious restaurant. "We are here Jacques, at La Maison Saint-Germain." Markham paid the taxi driver and they entered the restaurant and the Maitre D gave Yvonne the usual two-cheek embrace of recognition as a frequent customer and after looking at the seating arrangement, led them to a small candle-lit table for two against the wall which had just the right atmosphere of intimacy.

The restaurant was crowded and Markham surmised that Yvonne must have called ahead to make reservations, otherwise she couldn't have possibly gotten a choice table this quickly. He looked over the menu which was expensive, but not outrageous, thus felt more comfortable knowing that he wouldn't have to wash the dishes after they ate dinner. Markham wasn't a connoisseur of wines, yet, but he did learn one thing about ordering French wines from Mr. Moss. Always look for the words 'Appelation Controller' on the bottle label. Those two words, he told Markham, insured that the wine was at least palatable as its distribution was controlled. Markham inquired of Yvonne as to her menu preference and she asked him to order for her a steak Chateaubrian with baked potato and a salad as well. They both agreed on red wine to accompany their dinner and Markham, an avid steak eater, ordered the same as Yvonne.

Markham enjoyed Yvonne's company and from her conversation gathered that she was a night person who seemed quite familiar with the boite-de-nuit and restaurants of Paris for a woman of such tender age. She never once told him whether she was employed and how she supported herself, and each time he neared the subject, she would adroitly move the conversation into another direction. He decided to enjoy the evening with a good meal, plenty of wine and a very attractive woman in intimate surroundings which would be the envy of any red-blooded American. As the meal progressed to dessert, a man and a woman both dressed for the theatre appeared at their table.

"Bonjour Cherie," said the goateed man leaning over to kiss her on the cheeks. "You know Marianne of course," he said to Yvonne. Markham stood up to shake the man's hand, but due to space constraint couldn't get past the man for the obligatory cheek-kissing.

"Jacques," said Yvonne. "I would like you to meet Henri and Marianne."

"A pleasure to meet you," said Markham.

"Had we known you were here we would have had you join us at a larger table," said Henri. "Oh! Well, perhaps next time, Oui!"

At this moment the Maitre D approached Henri. "Monsieur Gautier, your taxi has arrived and is waiting," he said in a low voice that nevertheless was clearly heard by Markham.

"Ah! We must go to the theatre my dear. Nice meeting you Sir," said Henri with Charlotte remaining silent as they departed the restaurant.

Markham wondered what relationship she had with Henri whose last name was the same as hers. *Perhaps she is a relative, in any case why not ask her?* he thought.

"I overheard the Maitre D addressing Henri as Monsieur Gautier. May I ask what your relationship is to him?" said Markham.

Yvonne knew that Markham had overheard the Maitre D and thought that if there was to be any relationship with Markham, he would eventually find out the truth anyway and besides, Paris has no secrets.

"Henri is my husband and Charlotte is his mistress," said Yvonne, looking into his eyes for his reaction.

Markham swallowed hard. "I see," he said, obviously lost for words to the amusement of Yvonne who knew that now that Henri and Charlotte had met Yvonne's beau for the night and he was satisfied that his wife would be safe and happy, they could excuse themselves and go to the theatre sans ennui. Markham sat at the table staring at the half-full glass of wine resting on the table with his right hand holding the stem while Yvonne looked at him for any sign of acceptance.

"Is there something wrong, Cherie?" asked Yvonne.

"Something wrong?" he asked. "I wish you had told me you were married, that's all," replied Markham.

"I didn't think it would make any difference to you. After all, my husband and I have an arrangement that pleases us both," said Yvonne.

"Tell me Yvonne. Do you love your husband?" asked Markham.

"Of course I love Henri, and I'm sure that he loves me too," said Yvonne. "However, we see no reason why we can't enjoy the variety of people who stimulate our fancy as long as neither of us brings any of them into our home. Variety is the spice of life and that freedom is what keeps Henri and I together."

"I'm afraid that I'm a traditionalist where marriage is a sacred bond between two people who agree to be faithful to each other for life and that's why it's so important to select the right person to begin with. Doesn't it bother you, Yvonne, that your husband is intimately involved with another woman?"

"No, not at all. I know that he loves me, not that other woman and he only goes with her to satisfy his lust for a different woman, but he always comes back to me," said Yvonne.

"But how do you know that he doesn't love the other woman, or that he loves any woman including you, Yvonne?" said Markham.

"That's a silly question, Jacques. A woman knows. A woman always knows when a man loves her," she responded.

"Do you really want to know what I think about all this?" asked Markham.

"Of course. This is most interesting," answered Yvonne.

"I believe that there are degrees of love, and not everyone is capable of the deepest kind of love where if one dies the other soon follows from a broken heart. The thought of a woman with whom I was deeply in love with being unfaithful to me especially if she was my wife would be so devastating that I would probably lose the will to live. On the other hand, people who lack empathy and sensitivity cannot fathom such faithfulness and seek only to please themselves thus need constant stimulation from outside sources," said Markham in his deep baritone voice that found its mark in Yvonne's psyche.

"I think you puritan Americans live in a fantasy world. Most men of means in Paris have a mistress and allow their wives the same privileges."

"Well, Yvonne, I happen to like that fantasy world," replied Markham.

"I guess that means you won't be seeing me again," said Yvonne, looking disappointed.

"I've thoroughly enjoyed your company and I'm very appreciative of the time you've spent with me today. However, I don't date married women. It's against my religion. Speaking of religion, Yvonne, what would Notre Dame think of your philosophy about marriage?"

"I don't know and I really don't care," answered Yvonne, sounding a bit annoyed.

"Well, Yvonne, I don't want to overstay my welcome, so I'd best be on my way back to the base. Is there any place that I can drop you off?" asked Markham.

"Yes, you could drop me off at the Select Café, the taxi driver will know where it is," said Yvonne. Markham signaled the waiter for the check which he paid with the customary tip after which he hailed a taxi. During the ride to the Select Café, Yvonne placed her right hand inside Markham's left arm at the elbow and occasionally squeezed his arm. "You sure you want to go back to the base tonight? I've got this cute little place reserved for us where I could make you forget all of your inhibitions," said Yvonne seductively.

"Thanks for the offer and don't think it's not tempting, but a man has to live by his convictions. Sorry sweetheart. No can do," said Markham, and the taxi pulled up in front of the Select Café. Yvonne kissed Markham directly on the lips before he could resist then she stepped out of the taxi and walked into the Select without looking back.

Markham instructed the driver to take him to the Parvis du Sacre Coeur in Montmartre where his car was parked. Paris was lit up in an assortment of colors that justified its name as the 'City of Lights' with hues of red, gold, blue and yellow reflecting on the buildings accosting the narrow cobblestone streets. Markham felt that he was seeing the exact replica of the images of Paris as seen by the famous personages who walked those streets of Paris half a century ago. He didn't want to leave Paris at such an early hour and elected to walk the streets of Montmartre to enjoy the gaiety spilling out of its cafés and nightclubs. As Markham wandered south he came upon La Place Pigalle which made London's Piccadilly Circus mild by comparison regarding the sheer number of prostitutes plying their trade. As Markham walked through the crowd, he was bombarded with overt offers of sex in every conceivable manner imaginable and he found that the prostitutes employed the rich French language in ways that were so vile and debasing that Markham felt he was walking through a hellish snake pit.

Markham left the area and returned to his car which he drove back to Dreux Air Base and he took a long hot shower before going to bed.

One evening a few days later, Markham, wearing only a sleeveless undershirt and shorts, was tidying up around his bunk area while all of the other airmen in that barracks were tending to their personal effects and talking to each other, when Daniel Abney, a blond-haired Reservist with a slight, unathletic build got into an argument with Mike Redmond, a large man weighing in at about 260 pounds, but much of it fat. There was no doubt that Redmond would have pulverized Abney in a fight and Abney knew it, but he was an instigator who loved to get other people to fight for him.

"Why don't you pick on someone your own size Mike. Someone like Jim Markham," said Abney, pointing to Markham who was busy arranging the articles in his footlocker.

Markham turned around and looked at Mike who was sitting up on his upper bunk looking at Abney and now at Markham to see if he would take the bait. Markham became annoyed at Abney for involving him in his personal problems and looked directly at Abney as he told him, "Listen buster, don't get me involved in your problems. If you ain't got the stomach to fight your own fights, then you shouldn't let your mouth overload your body." Markham then turned around, grabbed his toilet articles and walked over to the restroom to wash up for the night, leaving Abney to lick his wounded pride in silence. Markham knew Mike Redmond as an easy-going man who was a professional cook or chef as they called them in France, and he suspected that Abney was a trouble maker.

A week later, while Markham was lying on his back on his bunk, a Reservist from the adjacent barracks approached him wanting directions to a café that supposedly had a scantily clad entertainer as he and his friends wanted to go there that evening. Markham told him he wasn't familiar with that place and asked him why he would want to go there anyway. The Reservist, a muscular middleweight man of Italian origin and slightly shorter than Markham took offense to his comment.

"Hey! It's my business. You know where it is or not?" he asked sullenly.

"I told you I didn't know the place, alright!" replied Markham and the Reservist left.

That evening, Markham stopped off at the Bistro bar popular to the Dreux reservists because it was located on the main road between Dreux and the nearest town. There must have been at least 50 American reservists from Dreux Air Base in the Bistro drinking and having a good time. The flooring on the left side of the bar was raised about 12 inches and near the end corner lay a wooden game of soccer resting on four legs which could be played by two or four live players moving wooden soccer players across the field with metal rods that traversed the width of the box surrounding the soccer field.

Markham walked over to it after getting himself a bottle of French beer and out of curiosity started working the rods when Pete Reiner, a short, puny Reservist and Daniel Abney came over and asked if the both of them could play against him to which Markham agreed. While Markham was playing against the two Reservists, he heard a voice calling out to him from his left and when he turned to look in that direction, he noticed the middleweight Italian man whom he had encountered earlier in the barracks was holding a bottle of beer in his hand while leaning against the wooden railing that separated that section of the bar.

"Hey! You still got the rag on?" asked the Middleweight in a challenging tone.

Markham ignored him and started playing again, but Abney and Reiner would not continue playing as they sensed a fight brewing and they wanted to watch the action.

"I heard you talking about me," said the Middleweight man as he slowly started walking towards Markham who was attempting to avoid a fight by continuing to play the soccer game, but Abney and Reiner refused to play.

"C'mon guys, let's play," asked Markham, but they both just looked at him with a smile on their faces which told him that they were delighted that someone would challenge Markham to a fight which promised to be memorable in view of his powerful physique. Markham knew that he couldn't afford to get involved in a public fight which would most certainly cost him his job with the OSI and possibly his career in the Air Force, whereas these Reservists were returning to Alabama in a few months to resume their civilian lives, hence had nothing to lose if they got into trouble. He had no choice but to turn around and face his opponent who by now had gotten rid of his beer bottle and was facing Markham toe to toe with every Reservist in the bar standing in back and to the side of the Middleweight man, waiting to see the fight.

Markham stood a few inches taller than the Middleweight and outweighed him by at least 50 pounds. He knew that one quick punch would probably drop this arrogant bastard to the ground. He looked over the crowd of Reservists and observed that Master Sergeant Richter, the Non-Commissioned Officer in Charge of the Air Police Reservists was in the back of the crowd and when their eyes met, Richter walked out of the bar's back door to the restroom rather than break up the imminent fist fight as was his duty.

Markham was in total frustration inasmuch as he dearly wanted to knock this punk out and if he had to, slug it out with his friends which he didn't mind, but he knew that none of them were worth his newly-acquired position in the OSI, so he waited for his opponent to throw the first punch which would then enable him to punch him back in self-defense, but his opponent just stood there with his friends behind him waiting for Markham to make the first move. He looked his opponent in the eye. "You're not worth it," said Markham, and he turned his back on him and slowly walked away. As Markham was walking away from the fight, a fairly large Reservist came alongside him.

"A man of your size. You could have pulverized him. That was a smart move not to get involved in a fight with this bum," said the man. Markham nodded affirmatively and walked out of the bar, still frustrated at not being able to answer the challenge. He was also perturbed at Abney and Reiner for facilitating the fight. Shortly thereafter, all Non-Commissioned Officers residing in the barracks were moved out of the barracks and into newly acquired trailers with two men to each trailer. Markham ended up rooming with the professional chef Mike Redmond who would get recipes from various French restaurants and cook up all kinds of dishes for Markham to taste, and before he knew it, he had gained 10 pounds. Redmond was definitely a great chef.

One day, Redmond told Markham that the internationally famous Le Mans car race was due to take place the forthcoming weekend and he suggested that they drive down there in Markham's car. Since the race lasted 24 hours, they could sleep on and off in the car on the grounds as he heard from some Frenchmen that most people did that. Markham asked Agent Heller if he wanted to join them and he agreed, thus the three of them drove 32 kilometers south to Chartres to see the renowned 11th Century Cathedral, then they drove another 70 kilometers southwest to Le Mans. The outdoor race track was surrounded by a wooded area that had a circus atmosphere with kiosks and large tents housing various attractions including a kangaroo that would box any human contender for a nominal fee and of course the kangaroo always won.

The cars in the race included Ferraris, Maseratis, Jaguars and a Chevrolet Corvette which proved to be a huge embarrassment to American observers. You could hear the Ferraris, Maseratis and Jaguars going by with a fast 'zoom..zoom..zoom' sound followed by the slow intermittent 'thump… thump…thump' sound of the Corvette lagging way behind. It was a joke having a Corvette in the same race with these high-powered European race cars. Redmond spoke for Markham and Heller when he voiced his great disappointment in the outcome of the race which was only too predictable with the Ferrari winning the race followed by the Maserati. At least they saw a real live Le Mans car race.

However, Markham was more impressed with the Chartres Cathedral and its nearly thousand year history including its role in hiding downed allied pilots from the Germans during the Second World War. But Chartres had another distinctive feature that amused him. Around the corner from the Cathedral was a bistro that Markham had frequented a few times before inasmuch as it was only some 30 kilometers from Dreux. The owner would never charge Markham for his Pernod, one of his favorite French drinks and he wondered why, until on his third and last trip, one of the customers who befriended him told him that he was the entertainment during his visits there. It was explained to him that the French-Canadian language had not evolved much in the last 100 years and many of the words he used were 'old French' that had not been heard by these older Frenchmen since they were children, not to mention that the younger generation had not heard of them at all. It was like Shakespeare appearing in a Brooklyn bar, said the Frenchman who introduced Markham to the owner of the café, an older Frenchmen who had pleasant memories of the American Servicemen who liberated Chartres in the big war. However, Markham and his Le Mans companions did not return by way of Chartres as they were exhausted from lack of sleep in the car and wished to return directly to Dreux Air Base for a hot shower, a good meal and a restful sleep.

One morning, while Special Agents Moss, Heller and Interpreter-Translator Markham were sitting in the OSI office, a telephone call came through and Heller answered it. After a brief conversation, he hung up the phone and announced to Moss and Markham that they had a murder case on their hands and five National Guardsmen from Dreux were the suspects according to the Staff Judge Advocate's office which had just called Heller. The French prosecutor from Paris was due at the Staff Judge Advocate's Office at Dreux Air Base that afternoon at 3:30 PM to present his case, and the SJA Colonel James Myers wanted the OSI with its interpreter-translator to be present at the meeting.

"Heck! It's only 10 AM and it only takes an hour to drive here. Why are they coming here so late in the afternoon, Keith?" asked Mr. Moss.

"You know how the French are…they must have their two hour lunch with wine and add the one hour drive and that easily makes it three o'clock," replied Heller.

"Yeah! But the wine doesn't slow down their driving, I tell you," said Mr. Moss.

"Well James," said Heller, "here's your chance to practice French a la Parisian."

"Listen Jim," said Mr. Moss. "It's important that you interpret the Prosecutor's words exactly as spoken, but also note any nuances that may prove valuable later in evaluating their statements. Just remember that most of them understand English quite well so anything you relate to the Colonel or us in their presence will be understood by them."

"How come they don't speak to us in English then?" asked Markham with genuine curiosity.

"Because to speak to us in English would make them look less skilled than us in conversation thus give them a feeling of inferiority and place them at a significant disadvantage in negotiations.

Since this is their country, they can and do insist on speaking only in French, forcing us to use an interpreter hence placing us at a disadvantage," said Mr. Moss. "Vous comprenez?"

"Yes, I understand," replied Markham, smiling at Mr. Moss' attempt to speak the few words of French he had learned there.

"Where are we going to have lunch today?" asked Heller of Mr. Moss.

"If the French Prosecutor is going to have a long lunch, we might as well have one too. Let's go to the Maison de Pain. It's only a few Ks from here and it's reasonable," said Mr. Moss.

"Sounds good to me," replied Heller. "You'll like this place, Jim. Great food."

Mr. Moss, accompanied by Mr. Heller and Markham arrived at the Staff Judge Advocate's Office at three o'clock in case the Prosecutor arrived early. They were met by Colonel James Myers, his assistant Major Ronald Dunbar and the Provost Marshall Lt. Colonel Frank Copland.

After everyone greeted each other, Mr. Moss was curious as to what information had been furnished to the Staff Judge Advocate.

"Colonel Myers. Have the French authorities provided you with any information regarding the nature and site of the crime and the name of the victim and the names of the National Guardsmen that they have as suspects?" asked Mr. Moss.

"No, not a thing. That's what they're coming here for. To apprise us of the particulars of the incident and I'm sure they'll want access to the National Guardsmen for interrogation. This is a capital offense so they have primary jurisdiction. However, we must insist on having those boys represented by counsel before any interview process takes place," said Colonel Myers.

"I understand that they go by the Napoleonic Code which is quite different than our Code of Military or Civilian Justice," said Lt. Colonel Copland.

"You're quite right Frank," said Colonel Myers. "The legal presumption of innocence until proven guilty beyond a reasonable doubt is found in English-based legal systems such as in the United States and Great Britain. But in France under the Napoleonic Criminal Code, the law presumes guilt and the defendant must prove his innocence. While that might seem tyrannical, we are here as guests of France and as such must adhere to their laws."

"At what point does the presumption of guilt enter the picture," asked Lt. Colonel Copland, a question that everyone else in the room wanted to ask.

"Once they have enough evidence to charge you, the burden of proof shifts over to the defendant in proving his innocence."

"It's important to keep a case from going to trial in this country because once it's in the Court, the likelihood of a conviction is uncomfortably high," said Colonel Myers. "That's where you come in Mr. Moss. I want you to investigate every aspect of this case and leave no stone unturned, because the very lives of these five young men may be at stake. Whatever resources you need will be at your disposal."

"Colonel Myers Sir. As soon as we learn of the particulars of this case, I believe it would be a good idea to notify the Attorney General of the State of Alabama about the status of this case since these boys are National Guard Reservists from Alabama," said Lt. Colonel Copland.

"Yes. The Governor may want someone from the Attorney General's office to be present during these proceedings. Now you understand that none of the attorneys in this office are qualified to represent these boys in a French Court. The United States Air Force will have to hire a French attorney for each one of the defendants; that's five separate French attorneys," said Colonel Myers.

"I believe, Sir, that the French authorities will want to have these men released into their custody and I would most strenuously resist such a request, Sir," said Mr. Moss.

"Good point Mr. Moss. We have to be ready for any eventuality. We could guarantee their availability for interviews with their French counsel present, and their appearance in court if necessary, but they will remain incarcerated on this base," replied Colonel Myers.

"Even this base is in fact their air base. So if they really want these boys, there's not much we could do about it, except protest. But I think that if we handle this matter with tact and diplomacy, we should be able to satisfy all parties to a just and fair adjudication," said Major Dunbar.

"I think it's them that just arrived," said Mr. Heller, looking out the window at four Frenchmen carrying briefcases descending from a Citroen automobile. A portly gentleman wearing a three-piece striped suit led the other three suited men, all carrying briefcases up the three steps onto the porch to the main entrance to the building where the Staff Judge Advocate's office was located. The four men were greeted by a secretary who showed them into the conference room where Colonel Myers and his staff including the OSI agents were assembled to meet them. Markham stood alongside the Colonel ready to translate and interpret any verbal exchange.

"I'm Colonel Myers," he said, shaking the portly gentleman's hand, "and this is my Assistant Major Dunbar, and Lt. Colonel Copland the Provost Marshall, and this is Mr. Moss and Mr. Heller from the Office of Special Investigations."

"And I'm Mr. James Markham the Interpreter-Translator."

Markham then introduced to Colonel Myers and his staff the four Frenchmen.

"This is Monsieur Henri Richelieu the Prosecutor, Monsieur Pierre Beaudet his assistant Prosecutor, Capitaine Jean Desroches and Inspector Alain Giroux both of the Sureté Nationale," said Markham, interpreting Monsieur Richelieu's presentation of his staff.

They all sat around a long narrow conference table with the Americans on one side and the French facing them on the other side of the table.

"I'll come directly to the point," said Monsieur Richelieu. "Three weeks ago, a French soldier dressed in civilian clothes was found dead with his mangled bicycle along a road leading from a Bar frequented mostly by American Servicemen from Dreux Air Base. At first it appeared as a hit and run vehicle accident, but then a woman came forward and issued a statement to Capitaine Desroches to the effect that on the night when the French soldier's body was found, she witnessed five American Servicemen get into an argument with that soldier, Sergeant Claude Besoin, outside the bar whereupon he was hit several times with a round stick and thrown into a car with his bicycle in the trunk and driven away. Some time later this same French soldier was found dead on the road about a mile from the Café au Cheval Noir near Vernouillet with his bicycle mangled as if run over by a vehicle. These five soldiers were all known to this woman, a prostitute who works at that same bar, the Cheval Noir. The reason we did not report this to you sooner is because we had to insure correct identification of these five American Servicemen who visited the Cheval Noir frequently. We have here several photographs of the scene on the road where the French Soldier was found and photographs of the Cheval Noir where the fatal assault allegedly occurred. We also have an affidavit from Mademoiselle Giselle Bacardi setting forth the events of that evening which led to the fatal beating of Sergeant Claude Besoin."

Inspector Alain Giroux opened his briefcase and laid on the conference table several photographs and Mademoiselle Bacardi's statement for the Americans to review.

"Do you have an autopsy report?" asked Mr. Moss, with Markham interpreting.

"Indeed we do," said Prosecutor Henri Richelieu. "The injuries sustained by Claude Besoin could have been caused by blows with a stick to the head of the deceased."

"Were there two autopsy reports, Sir? The first one when it was believed to have been caused by a hit and run vehicle accident, then a second one after Mademoiselle Bacardi executed her statement?" asked Mr. Moss.

Monsieur Richelieu consulted with his assistant and then with the Capitaine.

"We only have one autopsy Sir, and that was performed shortly after Mademoiselle Bacardi reported her observations to Capitaine Desroches."

"We would like at this time to make a formal request for permission to have our investigators interview each of the suspects whose names we have listed here for you," said Monsieur Richelieu, giving the list to Colonel Myers.

"Hmm! I see you even have their ranks. Staff Sergeant John Mulhaney, Airman First Class Michael Stevens, Airman First Class Sylvester Marconi, Airman Second Class Carl Lingo and Airman Second Class Robert Hagler," said Colonel Myers, reading the list out loud to his staff. "We certainly have no objection to your investigators interviewing these airmen, but as you can appreciate, we have just now learned of these charges and we are obligated to provide each one of these servicemen with legal representation by attorneys licensed to practice law in France which will take a little time as we must immediately inform our headquarters in Paris and in Montgomery, Alabama of this most serious matter."

"Yes, of course we do understand and we will most certainly allow you a reasonable amount of time to acquire all that is necessary to prepare your airmen for the investigatory process required by French law. When do you feel you will have your airmen ready for interview by our investigators?"

"About two weeks I would say," said Colonel Myers, turning to his Assistant Major Dunbar who shook his head in agreement.

"Two weeks is a long time. Couldn't you expedite matters a little bit Colonel Myers?" asked Monsieur Richelieu.

"Perhaps we can get things in order in 10 days, but I can't guarantee it because this matter has to go through several channels and echelons, then there is the matter of finding and hiring French lawyers to represent these airmen. But I promise you our full cooperation and expeditious handling of this matter, I assure you Mr. Prosecutor," said Colonel Myers.

"Mr. Moss, do you or your assistant have any questions for Mr. Richelieu or his colleagues before they leave?" asked the Colonel.

"Just one, Sir. How long after Sergeant Besoin was fatally injured did Mademoiselle Bacardi come forward to report her witnessing of the alleged assault by the American Servicemen?" asked Mr. Moss.

The Prosecutor Richelieu again consulted with Inspector Giroux who looked at the date of the statement then conferred with Capitaine Desroches.

"Seven days after the incident," answered the Prosecutor.

"Do you know why she took so long in reporting this matter to the authorities?"asked Mr. Moss.

The Prosecutor Richelieu turned to Capitaine Desroches for that answer.

"Mademoiselle didn't know that Sergeant Besoin had died until she read in the papers of the reported road accident which is when she realized that it coincided with the beating she had witnessed that same night outside the Cheval Noir, then she was afraid to report it for fear that something might happen to her, but then developed the courage to report it," said the Capitaine.

"Who did she report the incident to, Sir?" asked Mr. Moss.

"To me personally," answered Capitaine Desroches.

"But I was under the impression that you were from the Paris district and this incident occurred near Dreux, one hour away from Paris," answered Mr. Moss in a soft tone.

"I was transferred three months ago from Paris to this area," answered the Capitaine, looking a bit uneasy.

The Colonel looked at his staff to see if anyone else had any questions and when no one raised any, he thanked the Prosecutor and his staff for bringing this important matter to his attention and reassuring them that this would indeed be handled most expeditiously. The French officials left the premises appearing quite satisfied and Colonel Myers requested that his staff including the OSI agents remain for a debriefing.

"Mr. Moss. As an experienced investigator, what was your general impression of this entire matter?"

"I got the distinct impression that there were two autopsy reports and that we must find the first one. Secondly, the only evidence they appear to have so far is the statement of a known prostitute who waits a full seven days before she reports it to the authorities. I believe that we should conduct our own interviews of these boys with legal counsel present, of course, before we let the French get to them, and we'll need to investigate that bar and Mademoiselle Bacardi," said Mr. Moss, who held back the fact that he felt very uncomfortable about Capitaine Desroches' demeanor and body language, as if he was withholding information.

"All good points Mr. Moss. I'm sure you've got your work cut out for you so I won't hold you any longer. Keep me abreast of your investigatory results," said Colonel Myers.

"I most certainly will Sir," said Mr. Moss, who along with Agent Heller and Markham excused themselves and went back to the OSI office with the photographs of the crime scene and a copy of Mademoiselle Bacardi's statement.

"Keith, I smell a rat. Something's not right with this case," said Mr. Moss.

"I agree with you. I think they were withholding the existence of a previous autopsy which most likely reflected that the injuries were consistent with a vehicular accident. I'd like to put that prostitute on the box to see if she's telling the truth," said Agent Heller.

"The French don't believe in the use of the polygraph and they wouldn't agree to have her submit to one from our examiner in Paris," said Mr. Moss.

"By the way, Jim. You did an excellent job in there. You handled yourself very professionally," said Mr. Moss.

"Thank you, Sir. It's surprising how fast my French is returning to me after so many years of abstinence," replied Markham. "And what surprises me the most, is that they spoke Parisian French which I've been told would be very difficult for a French-Canadian to understand, which turned out not to be true, luckily for me."

"Luck had nothing to do with it. You had a sound education and you have a good ear for languages, that's all. Don't be so modest," said Mr. Moss.

"OK! This is what we have to start with," said Mr. Moss. "Keith, you take Jim with you and pay a visit to the Cheval Noir tonight and see what information you can get on that Mademoiselle Bacardi and see if there were any other witnesses to that event outside the bar that night. Find out where she comes from, etc. You know the drill, Keith. Tomorrow morning I'm going to the OSI District Headquarters in Paris to visit Mr. Belanger, Chief of the Criminal Division. You can follow through and find out if there was another autopsy. Pay a visit to that doctor who signed the one they gave us, but possibly it could have been another doctor who performed the first autopsy. Any questions?"

"No questions, Chief," replied Heller.

"OK! Then let's get some nourishment because we're gonna need it," said Mr. Moss.

That evening, Agent Heller and Markham, both dressed in very casual clothes, drove to the Cheval Noir which was crowded with American Servicemen and a few Frenchmen. As they entered the bar, Heller walked to the rear and found a place to sit even though the place was loaded with people, mostly men and a few women. Markham managed to elbow his way to the bar and ordered a beer while Heller sat watching Markham's back and all of the activities taking place in the bar. Markham noticed that there was a stairway at the end of the bar to his right and he occasionally saw men escorted by women going up those stairs and sometime later returning downstairs and the same women going back upstairs again with different men. It didn't take long for him to realize that this was a bar inside a brothel. Markham wanted to talk to the bar owner who he learned was the man tending bar with two other female bartenders, one of whom was referred to by customers as Big Monique, a tall, shapely, dark-haired woman.

"Monique, come here a minute," said Markham in French.

Monique approached him thinking he wanted to order another drink, but instead he asked her if she could get the owner to come over, as he wanted to talk to him. She walked over to the owner, a middle-aged balding man and whispered something into his ear as he looked at Markham, then she returned to Markham.

"He says he's simply too busy right now. If it's something important, why don't you come over tomorrow at noontime? He'll be here," she said.

"Thanks Monique. You tell him that I will be here tomorrow at noon for sure."

Monique went back and relayed the message to the owner who nodded his head affirmatively while continuing to serve customers. Monique returned to Markham intrigued by his French fluency as an American.

"Tell me Monique. Were you acquainted with Giselle Bacardi?" asked Markham.

"Mais Oui! She worked here for about two to three months then quit last week and went back to Paris. Why do you ask? You wanna go with her?" said Monique.

"No, no. It's my friend sitting back there. He's kind of shy, you know," replied Markham.

"I like your French accent. Where'd you learn to speak French so well?"

"In Canada," replied Markham. "You said that Giselle went back to Paris. Is that where she's from...Paris?"

"Oh! Yes. She worked the Place Pigalle for a couple of years at least."

"Did you know that French soldier who was found dead on the road with his bicycle?"

"Sure I knew Claude, he was a regular...once a month to go upstairs with one of the girls," said Monique.

"Did you know him well?" asked Markham.

"No. He liked petite women. Me, I was too big for him," she said."Listen, Jacques. How about you and me going upstairs? I'll show you a good time."

"No, I don't have much money Monique," answered Markham.

"It'll only cost you seven US dollars, that's all," said Monique.

"Naw! I can't afford it," answered Markham, who heard a couple of other men at the bar trying to get Monique's attention, but she just ignored them.

"Jacques, I'll make it five dollars. How's that?"

"Naw, still too much," answered Markham. "Monique, how long have you been working here?"

"About 18 months," she replied. "Listen Jacques, three dollars, please come upstairs with me. You won't regret it."

"I'm sorry Monique, but I've never paid a woman to have sex with me, never," answered Markham.

"Alright, I'll go upstairs with you for free," she said anxiously.

"Monique, I really appreciate your offer. You're tres gentil. Since you've been here for a year and a half you must know all of the Americans that come in here, yes?"

said Markham.

"Oh! Yes, most certainly, and they all know me too," said Monique proudly.

"So you know Sergeant John Mulhaney, Mike Stevens and Sylvester Marconi, oui?" asked Markham.

"John Mulhaney I know well. He has an old black Citroen. John always hangs out with his friends Mike and Sylvester. Yes I know them, they come here often," said Monique.

"Did you also know Carl Lingo and Robert Hagler?"

"I know Carl and Bob who also hang out with John. They always come together in John's car, the five of them," said Monique.

"Do you remember the night when Claude Besoin got killed if he had been in here that night and who was with him?" asked Markham.

"I know that all the girls talked about it when we read of the accident in the newspaper. He did go upstairs with Antoinette for a little while and Antoinette mentioned that he had been drinking too much and she couldn't get him to reach a climax, then he left the bar."

"Well did you see John Mulhaney and any of his companions in the bar that night?"

"I believe that John, Mike and Sylvester were here that night," said Monique.

"Did you see them leave the bar at any time when Sergeant Claude Besoin left the bar?"

"No, I don't think they left the bar till much later," said Monique.

"Was Giselle Bacardi in the bar that night?" asked Markham.

"Yes she was here working and I know that she had something going with Sylvester, because when he'd spent all of his money, she then gave it to him for free. I think he loves her," said Monique.

"Really. What makes you think that Sylvester Marconi loves Giselle?"

"You can see that he visibly gets upset when she goes upstairs with another man, so he spends most of his paycheck on her to keep her from going with other men," said Monique.

"He's got it really bad, huh? So through him she must know all of his friends then?" said Markham.

"Oh! Sure. She's even gone with him in John's car with the guys several times," said Monique. "Please Jacques, come upstairs with me, enough talk. I'll do whatever you like."

"Monique," said the owner, "a customer wants you."

"In a minute," replied Monique. "Jacques, I don't understand why you won't come upstairs with me when it will cost you nothing. Don't you like me?" she asked.

"My dear Monique. You are a very attractive woman. But you must understand that I am of French heritage. I speak and think like a Frenchman. Now you know how a Frenchman makes love…How can I make love to you that way when I know that you have just had sex with another man not more than fifteen minutes before. I find the thought of that most repulsive. I could only consider making love to you when you are pure with no trace of any other man. Do you understand what I am saying Monique?"

She looked at Markham with an intense desire and reached for his hands resting on the bar. "Oh! Jacques. You come tomorrow then and I'll be pure as a virgin, just for you," she said.

"Well, I'm busy tomorrow, but I will be back. One last question Monique. Did you ever see any French policeman or investigator visit with Giselle Bacardi?" asked Markham.

"Come to think of it, I did see a French policeman come here a few times in the past few months to talk to Giselle and I can spot a policeman a mile away. Marcel the owner got worried about him being here until Giselle told him he was just a friend," said Monique.

"Do you recall his name, the policeman that is?" asked Markham.

"No, sorry I don't," replied Monique, who then went about serving other customers.

Markham left the bar with Heller at his heels and they drove back to the OSI office where Markham wrote down all of the information he'd gathered from Monique after relating everything to Heller.

"Jim, you sure got a lot of information from that gal, but I have to tell you, there were a few guys who were getting real mad at you for keeping Big Monique occupied."

"Oh! Yeah? Well, we have to go back to the Cheval Noir tomorrow at noontime to talk to the owner. It'll be quiet then, I hope," said Markham.

It was near noontime and the countryside foliage reflected the sun's rays in magnificent hues that made Markham feel that he was inside of one of those French paintings he'd seen in books and museums. Driving his Ford convertible with the top down listening to the radio playing 'Parler moi d'amour' in such surroundings made Markham feel that if there was ever a time for him to be with the love of his life, this was the moment, but alas providence could not hear his lament as he drove through the countryside on to the main gate to Dreux Air Base and then to the OSI office to pick up Agent Heller. They drove back off-base to the nearby Cheval Noir to pay a visit to its owner Marcel. Although Agent Heller was in charge, he recognized Markham's language capability and ability to acquire the essential information needed to prove or disprove the elements of the alleged crime, hence allowed him much latitude as long as Markham kept him apprised of the progress being made at each step of the investigative ladder.

They both entered the Cheval Noir and found no one inside the bar, not even the proprietor whom they assumed was somewhere in the back of the premises. Markham called out in French, but no one answered. As they stood at the bar, a Frenchman dressed in work clothes, apparently a laborer, entered the Cheval Noir and walked directly over to the bar where he stood only a few inches from Markham's right elbow. Heller was standing to the left of Markham and no one was talking, expecting the owner to appear at any moment, when the Frenchman spoke up.

"You know," said the Frenchman to Markham. "I waited most of the evening last night trying to go upstairs with Monique, but no, she wasted her time on you. I had the seven dollars, but she didn't want to go with a Frenchman; we're not good enough. She only goes with Americans. Yes, I heard her offering it to you for free. I was there at the bar." Hostility was in his voice. "You fucking Americans. I wish DeGaulle would boot you out of France."

Markham was surprised by his comments and decided that this was not the time to get into an argument with anyone, especially this hostile Frenchman who was apparently attempting to provoke him. He felt like smacking him in the face with his elbow, but resisted the urge in the name of professional conduct.

Markham turned his head to his left and muttered in a low voice in English to Heller, "This guy was here last night and overheard my conversation with Monique and he's pissed off because he'd saved seven bucks to go with her and she refused to go with him. So he's mad at me and all Americans."

Heller snickered, "Ignore him and maybe he'll go away."

After a minute or so, the Frenchman walked away from Markham to the other end of the bar sulking, then in a moment of quiet rage, slid the metal ashtray sitting on the bar in front of him sideways with sufficient force that it traveled the length of the bar, coming to rest against Markham's right forearm. Markham looked at the Frenchman trying to decide whether to go over there and pound the shit out of him or just ignore him and to Heller's relief, Markham decided on the latter. Unable to provoke Markham, the Frenchman exited the Cheval Noir.

A few minutes later, the owner appeared from the kitchen in the back excusing himself profusely for the delay. He did not speak English so the entire conversation between Markham and Marcel the owner was in French with occasional English interpretations for Heller's benefit. Marcel did not have much to offer except that the policeman who visited Giselle Bacardi was in fact Capitaine Jean Desroches who used to be stationed in Paris where he first got acquainted with Giselle. Curiously, Giselle moved up here from Paris about the same time that the Capitaine got transferred to this area and since the incident with the death of the French soldier, she has not returned to the Cheval Noir.

"You know, Jim. I wonder why the Capitaine got transferred out of Paris? Sounds to me like he may be Giselle's pimp, what do you think?" said Heller.

"I think you're right on the money Keith. I'm sure that Mr. Moss will pass this information on to the OSI in Paris and they'll check out the Capitaine and Mademoiselle Giselle Bacardi," said Markham.

Back at the OSI office, Mr. Moss expressed his pleasure with the progress made by Heller and Markham on the case. He advised Markham that in addition to his duties as the Detachment Interpreter-Translator, he would have to drive to Paris at the end of each day to deliver daily progress reports to the OSI district located on Rue Weber off the Place de l'Etoile, a very busy section of Paris. In fact the Champs-Elysees, the most spectacular thoroughfare of Paris, ran west from the Place de la Concorde to the Place de l'Etoile, and this broad avenue accommodated all major parades including the Bastille Day celebration.

"One of us will ride with you on those trips so you won't be lonely," said Mr. Moss in his dry sense of humor.

"Him, being lonely…surely you're kidding," said Heller with a laugh. "He's got to beat them off with a stick."

Markham wasn't too amused as he didn't consider himself a Romeo, but just the same he smiled at the comments being made in good fun. However, driving into the busy center of Paris with a big American car was a task fit only for drivers wearing white gloves. The driver to the right has the right-of-way, thus if you are driving in one of those wide circles in the center of the city around the Arc de Triomphe or Place de l'Etoile, and the car to your right doesn't wish to yield, you may be stuck inside that circle until you run out of gas. Fortunately, most of the French cars were very small and fragile in comparison to Markham's two-ton vehicle which would crush any of those cigarette rollers they call cars that got into its way, thus through sheer intimidation and audacity, Markham managed to navigate his way through Paris each day to deliver the latest reports of investigation to the OSI District Headquarters.

One early evening while driving back from Paris to Dreux with Mr. Moss, Markham learned that through OSI contacts with the French Government, the Capitaine Desroches had been denied promotion and disciplined by transfer out of Paris to the Dreux area for serious investigatory violations. Mr. Moss also learned from well-placed OSI informants that Mademoiselle Giselle Bacardi had been the Capitaine's mistress for some time and he turned her into a prostitute to finance his extravagant lifestyle. Mr. Moss suspected that the Capitaine fabricated the beating incident with the assistance of his mistress Giselle in order to turn an ordinary vehicular death into a celebrated homicide that would propel him into the limelight and the good graces of his superiors in Paris, thereby effecting a transfer back to Paris. The problem was proving it. So far they discovered that there had in fact been two autopsy reports and the first one indeed opined that the cause of death was by vehicular accident. Secondly, two of the five National Guardsmen had alibis for that night showing they were not in fact in the Cheval Noir that evening from affidavits obtained from at least two witnesses, albeit National Guardmen. As expected, the French authorities refused to consider the use of the polygraph on Giselle Bacardi stating that they did not consider the polygraph reliable and that it was inadmissible as evidence in French courts. It appeared that the entire case against the National Guardsmen rested on the testimony of a prostitute who owed her allegiance to a corrupt French Policeman seeking reinstatement in Paris.

"The United States Air Force has officially hired five separate French lawyers to represent each of the National Guardsmen. The Governor of Alabama has also sent his Attorney General to Paris as a sort of Ambassador for the Governor in an attempt to influence a fair and just outcome of this case. These boys are scheduled to appear before a magistrate the day after tomorrow and I want you, Jim, to accompany these boys to give them comfort and assurance that their Government is with them all the way and I also want you to be there as an observer and note anything that would be of interest to this case," said Mr. Moss.

"I noticed on the Paris newsstand that this case is even on the front page of tabloids and magazines. It's touted as the most celebrated homicide case in France in the past 50 years," said Markham. "This Capitaine sure got a lot of mileage out of this case."

Markham accompanied the five National Guardsmen escorted by several Air Policemen and two American lawyers from the Staff Judge Advocate's Office who had explained to them that they were only appearing before the Magistrate to officially notify them of the charges against them and that the presence of their French attorneys at this point in time was not required.

The large, brown, three story building was old and creaky due to its wooden construction. The wooden floors were uncovered and the winding staircase to each floor was narrow and confining. As each Guardsman's name was called, Markham would escort him up the stairs where they would both stand before a solid wooden door to the magistrate's office waiting to be invited to enter. The five National Guardsmen knew full well the severity of the charges and the solemnity of the proceedings enhanced their anxiety to the extent that when it came Sylvester Marconi's turn to stand with Markham outside the magistrate's door, Sylvester suddenly put his hand over his mouth, but wasn't quick enough to prevent his vomit from hitting Markham's left shoe as he tried to step away. Markham pulled out his handkerchief from his back pocket and gave it to Sylvester who didn't have one of his own so that he could wipe his mouth and part of his pants leg.

"C'mon Sylvester," said Markham. "Let's find a bathroom so you can clean up." Not to mention that Markham wanted to wipe the vomit off his shoe. They had to go back to the first floor where they found a restroom.

"Listen Sylvester. This is only a formality to officially make you aware of the charges pending against you and your rights under the French Criminal Code. The Air Force has hired top-notch French attorneys to represent you and the Governor of Alabama has even sent his Attorney General to intercede on your behalf. So if you're innocent of those charges and I expect that you are, you have nothing to worry about. So compose yourself and let's go back upstairs and show them that you have nothing to fear or hide. OK?" said Markham, trying to instill some confidence in Sylvester and allay his fears.

"Thanks Mr. Markham. I really appreciate your support. I think I'm alright now," replied Sylvester.

"You're ready to go back upstairs now?" asked Markham.

"Yeah! As ready as I'll ever be I guess," replied Sylvester as they exited the restroom and went back upstairs. They didn't have to wait but a minute before the magistrate's door opened and Sylvester alone was invited inside. With the magistrate was an interpreter who advised Sylvester of the charges and his right to legal counsel and his plea of not guilty was entered into the record. A few minutes later Sylvester exited the magistrate's office and returned downstairs to join the other guardsmen who then were escorted by the Air Police back to Dreux under house arrest until trial.

That evening, Mr. Heller got a call from Mr. Moss instructing him to drive immediately to the Base Hospital where Sylvester Marconi had been taken for attempted suicide. Even though Heller didn't need an interpreter, he invited Markham to go with him if he wished and Markham accepted, curious as to the reason for Sylvester's attempted suicide. Heller wondered whether his suicide attempt was the result of a guilty conscience about the death of the French soldier, and now was the time to interview him when he would be most vulnerable to uttering a confession. But in Markham's mind, things just didn't add up to murder.

Upon arrival at the Base hospital, Heller asked to interview the attending emergency room Doctor who treated Sylvester Marconi. After showing his OSI credentials to the physician, Heller asked him if this was a bonafide suicide attempt or merely a suicidal gesture.

"It was most certainly a bonafide suicide attempt Mr. Heller. We had to pump his stomach, apparently he had ingested nearly a full bottle of tranquilizers. He's lucky his roommate found him when he did and he was brought here before the drugs had a chance to take full effect, otherwise he'd be history," said the Doctor.

"Is he conscious right now, Doctor? Because if he is, it's important that I talk to him briefly," said Heller.

"I believe that he's conscious, but let me see if he's able to talk to you. That tube we put down his throat caused a lot of irritation," said the Doctor as he walked down the hall to one of several rooms occupied by patients until he stopped before one room and raised his hand to indicate that Heller and Markham should wait outside while he entered the room to examine Sylvester.

A minute later, the Doctor returned into the hall. "You may go in, but keep the interview short. He's a very depressed young man whose going to need some psychiatric help."

"Thank you, Doctor. I'll be careful not to upset him," replied Heller, who then entered the room followed by Markham.

Sylvester lay in bed, slightly propped up with an intravenous tube feeding dextrose into the antecubital vein of his left arm at the elbow. He immediately recognized Markham from his experience with him at the magistrate's office and welcomed a familiar face which Heller felt would be useful in establishing rapport with him, so he allowed Markham to introduce him.

"This is Special Agent Heller from the OSI office here at Dreux and of course you know who I am. Mr. Heller is here to help you resolve whatever problems you may have so I encourage you to be as truthful as you can with him, OK Sylvester?" said Markham in a most friendly tone of voice. He then stepped back a few paces to allow Heller to conduct his interview with apparent privacy although Markham's proximity allowed him to hear the entire conversation.

"As Mr. Markham told you, I'm Special Agent Keith Heller of the OSI and I'm conducting an official investigation into the reported homicide of a French soldier named Claude Besoin. As a formality, I have to read you your rights under Article 31 of the Uniform Code of Military Justice, you understand?"

"Yeah! I understand," replied Sylvester, and Heller recited from a small, clear, plastic-covered card the Rights under Article 31 of the UCMJ.

"Do you understand your rights Sylvester?" asked Agent Heller.

"Yes I do," replied Sylvester.

"Do you waive your right to have an attorney present while I interview you?" asked Heller.

"Yeah! I don't need a lawyer present for you to talk to me. It's the French police I don't trust," said Sylvester.

"Well, I can't say I blame you. But tell me Sylvester, why did you attempt to take your life tonight?" asked Heller.

"I couldn't take the anguish anymore. Death seemed the only way to end the pain," said Sylvester.

"Why were you in such pain Sylvester?" asked Heller.

"Because the only woman I ever loved abandoned me and I can't live without her," he replied with tears welling up in his eyes.

"What's her name?" asked Heller.

"Giselle," replied Sylvester.

"Do you mean Giselle Bacardi?" asked Heller.

"Yes, her last name is Bacardi," answered Sylvester.

"You're in love with her?" asked Heller, looking directly into Sylvester's eyes.

"I know that nobody will understand, but I can't help it, I love her that's all there is to it," he replied with his voice shaking with emotion.

"Why do you feel that she abandoned you?" asked Heller.

"She told me she loved me and then she falsely accused me and my friends of murder. How could she do this to me? She knows how much I love her...how could she?" asked Sylvester in bewilderment.

"Why do you think she did this to you Sylvester?" asked Heller.

"I don't know. But if you see her, will you tell her that I still love her and forgive her...please tell her that," said Sylvester.

"Do you by any chance have a picture of Giselle?" asked Heller.

"Yeah! I've got a photo of her in my wallet, why?" asked Sylvester.

"Well, I have to know what she looks like if I'm going to pass your message on to her," replied Heller.

"My personal effects are in the table drawer, but I can't reach it," said Sylvester.

"Do you mind if I get your wallet for you?" asked Heller.

"No, I don't mind," replied Sylvester at which time Heller reached into the drawer and pulled out his wallet which he gave to Sylvester. He used his right hand to flip it open and with his fingers went through the plastic sleeves containing various photos, including one of Giselle. "That's her in that picture," said Sylvester, holding the sleeve with the photo.

"Can I borrow that picture? I promise you that I'll bring it back intact," said Heller.

"Sure, I've got the same picture enlarged in a frame in my room at the base," replied Sylvester. "You can borrow it, but I'd appreciate it if you could give it back to me as soon as possible."

"Will do, I promise," replied Heller who passed the picture over to Markham for his examination.

"Sylvester...I know that you don't want to hear this...and I respect your choices, but I must tell you that she is not your friend...she used you. I strongly suggest that you confide with a minister of your faith for guidance and strength," said Heller in an attempt to help this poor soul. Heller thanked him for the interview and stepped away from the bed to allow Markham who had been standing in the background to move forward and say goodbye.

"How are you feeling Sylvester?" asked Markham.

"OK, I guess," replied Sylvester.

"Listen Sylvester. You have many friends here and a family back home who care for you. You only have to ask for their aid and support. OK?" said Markham. "You need anything; you just call me."

"Thanks Mr. Markham," replied Sylvester, whose spirits seemed to have been lifted a bit.

Heller and Markham walked out of the hospital and while driving back to the OSI office they discussed the interview with Sylvester Marconi.

"This guy's got it bad," said Heller. "Man, he's head over heels over that whore."

"I wonder what it is that she's got that pleases him so much that he's willing to sacrifice his life for her?" asked Markham rhetorically.

"She probably gives him the kind of kinky sex that Parisian prostitutes are known for that he's never experienced, being a young hick from Alabama," said Heller.

"I just don't think he's involved in the alleged murder of that French soldier," said Markham. "But then I'm not an investigator."

"I agree with you Jim. The evidence so far doesn't support the murder charge," replied Heller.

"You know, Keith. The thought just occurred to me that Giselle doesn't know yet that her lover attempted suicide. What if we went down right now to the Place Pigalle where she plies her trade and I told her that I was a friend of Sylvester and that I had just come from the hospital where he was admitted for attempted suicide and that he asked me to find her and tell her that he still loved her and forgave her for abandoning him? After all, it is the truth. Maybe in a moment of weakness or remorse she might make an admission that we can use. I'm not an Agent, so legally I don't have to identify myself as an Agent or Investigator," said Markham.

"That's a damn good idea, but we'll need to record the conversation in case she does admit to something useful in our case. Let's stop by the office and get the cassette recorder," said Heller. "But ain't it going to be kind of late by the time we get to Paris to find her?"

"Naw! We should be there by midnight and that's when things start in Paris. It's the city of lights; haven't you heard?" said Markham.

As they arrived at the OSI office, Heller called Mr. Moss at his Bachelor Officer's Quarters and informed him of the plan to have Markham record his conversation with Giselle Bacardi. Moss confirmed that it was an excellent idea, but that Markham should be covered by Heller at some distance away for security purposes.

"Mr. Moss. It's the other way around. He's not the one that needs protection," said Heller jokingly.

"Well, you did say that he had to beat them off with a stick, did you not? Well, he might just need your help after all," replied Moss with his distinct laugh.

"OK! Chief. We're on our way. If anything develops, I'll call you," said Heller and hung up the phone.

Markham and Heller drove to Paris in Markham's convertible to make a splash in Pigalle that would attract Giselle. As they neared the Place Pigalle, Markham let Heller out of the car with the pre-arranged meeting in front of the Moulin Rouge in exactly one hour, but in the event that Markham got somehow detained, Heller was to remain there until he did come back for him. It was important that neither Giselle nor any of the other girls at the Place Pigalle see Markham with Heller or anyone else. Markham placed the small cassette tape recorder inside an empty pack of cigarettes which he inserted in his shirt pocket. But in case someone asked for a cigarette, he also inserted a few loose ones in the same pocket alongside the pack. Markham drove his car with the top down along the streets of Pigalle very slowly with Giselle's photo in his mind and on several occasions, women attempted to get his attention, but since they didn't fit Giselle's description, he paid no mind. He slowly continued his journey through the streets of Montmartre and after several passes through

Pigalle, decided to stop at the curb in front of a group of street women. Two of them immediately walked up to his car.

"Whow! What a grand automobile," said one of the prostitutes in French. "You must be American, oui?" said the other prostitutes in broken English.

Markham replied in French, "Yes, I'm American and I'm looking for Giselle. You know Giselle?"

"Which Giselle? What does she look like?" asked the shorter prostitute.

"Giselle Bacardi," answered Markham.

"Giselle Bacardi…that Giselle. She was here a little while ago. How do you know her?You go with her?" asked the taller prostitute.

"Hey! My love life is personal. Tell me, where may I find her when she does return?" asked Markham.

"She usually hangs out either in front or sometimes inside the Bistro over there for coffee," said the tall one. "Hey! You gonna take us for a ride?"

"I can't right now. I've got to go somewhere, but I'll be back shortly, so if you see Giselle, tell her to wait for me. OK?" said Markham.

"Alright lover, but if she doesn't show up, you'll take us for a ride, oui?" said the tall one.

"We'll see," replied Markham as he took off and rode around Montmartre for a while to pass the time away. A half-hour later, Markham returned to the Place Pigalle and stopped in front of the Bistro and was gratified to see that Giselle, who looked very much like her photo, was standing at the entrance to the café talking to another woman. She couldn't have missed Markham's flashy convertible pull up to the curb and, having been told by the other two women of this French-speaking American driving a huge convertible automobile asking for her specifically, her curiosity was certainly piqued. She excused herself and walked over in a deliberate slinky fashion that translated into sex personified. She was no more than five feet five inches, with a slim, but well-developed body and her long red hair suggested an untamed wildness.

"I hear you've been asking for me," said Giselle in French.

"Yes. I have an important message for you from a very dear friend," said Markham in French.

"Oh! Yeah? Who's the friend?" she asked.

Markham reached over and opened the door to the passenger side of the car, "Why don't you make yourself comfortable because I have a lot to tell you?" said Markham with a winning smile that promised many good things.

Giselle looked around to see who was watching, then got into the car and closed the door. "Why don't we take a ride? Your car brings a lot of attention," said Giselle.

Markham drove off with Giselle sitting next to the door looking at Markham's allure, wondering who this friend was that brought this hunk of a man with this splendid automobile into her life. Things were looking up, she thought and she moved closer to Markham and placed her left elbow over the back of the seat with her hand resting on Markham's right shoulder.

"It's a beautiful car," said Giselle. "I've never seen one like it in all of Paris."

"And you won't either," replied Markham as he drove up to the Parvis du Sacre Coeur where he parked in a spot that overlooked all of Paris.

Markham then turned towards Giselle and pulled out the photograph of Giselle which he showed to her.

"Mon Dieu! Where did you get this?" she asked incredulously.

"From my good friend Sylvester Marconi who is presently in the hospital near death," said Markham.

"In a hospital…what happened?" asked Giselle.

"He tried to commit suicide and if his roommate hadn't found him when he did, Sylvester would have died, but luckily he's in the hospital in serious condition," said Markham, looking for signs of empathy.

"He must be crazy to do that…why would he want to do that?" asked Giselle.

"Because he loves you and he feels that you betrayed and abandoned him and now he has nothing to live for," said Markham.

Giselle remained silent, obviously thinking about what Markham had told her.

"Do you realize that when you accused him of murdering that French soldier you in effect took away his life too, and he's probably the only man who truly loves you. Do you know what he told me to tell you? He said that he still loves you and he forgives you. All he wants is to see you again," said Markham.

"He still wants to see me?" asked Giselle with a surprised look on her face.

"Yes he does. The man loves you Giselle. Don't you understand? I wish the hell I found a woman who loved me that much…I'd marry her in a minute," said Markham.

"I never accused him of murdering that French soldier. I saw the other Americans beat him and since they all hang out together, I assumed that he was already in the car," said Giselle.

"Did you see Sylvester at all that night?" asked Markham.

"He was in the Cheval Noir earlier that evening, but then he left. I don't know if he got a ride with one of the other Americans back to the base or if he got into John's car and waited for his friends," said Giselle.

"Well, who did you see beat up the French soldier?" asked Markham.

"John, Mike, Carl and I think Bob Hagler," said Giselle, unsure of herself.

"Well, I think that Sylvester will be relieved to know that you are not accusing him of being involved in the beating of that French soldier," said Markham. "That is correct isn't it…you didn't see him at all from the time you saw the beating of the French soldier until they took him away… right?"

"That's right…I didn't see him at all outside the Cheval Noir that night," said Giselle.

"Out of curiosity Giselle, who did actually beat that French soldier?" asked Markham.

"Sergeant John Mulhaney…he's the one that hit the French soldier on the head with the round stick," said Giselle.

"Did any of the other Americans you named in your statement to the police hit the French soldier?" asked Markham.

"Yes, I think they punched him and then they threw him in the car," said Giselle who now felt uncomfortable talking about the event.

"What did they do with his bicycle?" asked Markham.

She thought for a minute. "They put it in the trunk."

"Did they close the lid before they drove off?" asked Markham.

"I don't remember," said Giselle. "Listen, I've got to get back. I'm supposed to meet someone at the Bistro."

"Alright Giselle, I'm going to drive you back. But tell me Giselle, by your own admission, since Sylvester wasn't even there, why did you say in your statement to the police that he was involved in the beating of that French soldier?" asked Markham.

"I don't know; I made a mistake," she said, wringing her hands together nervously and now sitting nearer to the door. "You sound just like a policeman…take me back," said Giselle.

"Gladly. What shall I tell Sylvester. Mademoiselle Bacardi?" asked Markham.

"Tell him to find himself another woman, but don't trust any of them...that's my advice," said Giselle with a coldness that sent chills down Markham's spine. Markham made sure he had Giselle's photo back in his coat pocket before he let her off in front of the Bistro. She stepped out of the car, closed the door and with a look of disdain uttered words that Markham would never forget, "You can also tell Sylvester that a French woman needs more than juvenile love."

"I'm sorry to hear that, 'cause Romeo and Juliette exemplified the purest love of all," replied Markham.

"You Americans; you're such dreamers," said Giselle contemptuously. As she walked away in her slinky gait, her calloused demeanor reminded Markham of just how ugly even the sexiest female could appear to a man with a kind and romantic heart.

Markham drove over to the Moulin Rouge and as expected, saw Agent Heller standing in front of the pillar that separated the two main doorways waiting for him. Markham couldn't miss the large red letters that spelled out the name Moulin Rouge at the roof line just below the round gray tower with red roof that held a four-sided windmill. Heller got into the car and they drove off.

"Well, did you meet her?" asked Heller.

"Yes I did and I got the recording which I think will be very useful. I haven't had a chance to check it out yet. Why don't you do that? It has to be rewound first though." Markham handed the recorder to Heller who took it out of the empty cigarette pack. After rewinding it, he took his penknife out and removed the tab from the cassette tape to prevent accidental erasure. He then played it back, holding it to his ear while Markham drove to a place where he could stop and put up the convertible top.

"Man, this is great stuff. Wait till Mr. Moss hears this. Hell, wait till Mr. Belanger at Headquarters hears this. This tape shatters her credibility as a witness. This tape is so important that we must make at least one duplicate right away as soon as we get back to the office," said Heller. "I'm sure that Mr. Moss will want you to drive this tape in to Headquarters tomorrow...tomorrow hell...it's past midnight...today, I mean," said Heller, elated over this newly acquired evidence.

Upon arrival at the OSI office in Dreux, Heller immediately called Moss at his BOQ quarters and told him about the tape. Afterwards he connected a second recorder to the first one and made a copy of the original tape. He then marked both tapes and had Markham write his initials and the date on each tape. He then bagged the original with an evidence tag for transportation to OSI District 62 Headquarters in Paris later that day.

A week went by without any news at the OSI detachment in Dreux of any fresh legal activity in the case against the National Guardsmen, then Mr. Moss was notified by the Staff Judge Advocate's Office that the five guardsmen, each represented by their French attorney, were scheduled to appear in the French court the following day, but the OSI was not invited as expected. On the afternoon of the court appearance, one of the Staff Judge Advocate's legal representatives, Captain Coutts who had been invited as an observer with a French employee who was bilingual, came into the OSI office with the court verdict.

"Mr. Moss," said Captain Coutts. "All of the charges against the five National Guardsmen have been dismissed without prejudice. I have to tell you that the audio tape played a significant role in the court's decision, not to mention of course several other factors including the first autopsy report."

"Well, I'm sure glad to hear that, and I'm sure those boys are elated," said Mr. Moss.

"I believe that those boys are going to be rotated back to the States shortly," added Captain Coutts.

"I think that's a good idea," said Mr. Heller, with Markham listening attentively.

Three days later, all five National Guardsmen were flown out of France by military aircraft with

Montgomery, Alabama as their final destination. Three weeks later, the Base Commander announced that all National Guard personnel stationed at Dreux were going to be shipped back to Montgomery, Alabama by order of the Commanding General of the United States Armed Forces in Europe also known as USAFE and the base was being turned over to the French authorities. Mr. Moss and Mr. Heller were being reassigned to the United States and Markham was replacing the Interpreter-Translator at Chambley Air Base, France who fell ill with hepatitis and had to be shipped to a military hospital in the United States. Chambley Air Force Base, located some 300 kilometers east of Paris and about 25 kilometers southwest of the city of Metz in the Alsace-Lorraine area near the German border was another Air Base occupied by United States Air Force National Guardsmen who were from the State of Indiana.

Markham procured himself a map of France which he studied in preparation for his trip from Dreux Air Base to Chambley Air Base, his new assignment to the OSI Detachment there. The large trunk of his Ford Fairlane 500 automobile permitted him to put all of his belongings inside , thus permitting him to drive with the convertible top down during his trip without fear of having any exposed items stolen. He made certain that his five gallon Gerry can was filled with gasoline and that he started off with a full tank of gas and noted the various ESSO gas stations along the route that would accept his gasoline coupons. Having said his goodbyes to Mr. Moss and Mr. Heller, Sergeant Redmond and a few other airmen who had befriended him, Markham started his engine and drove east on his way to Chambley.

Markham was now about a half-hour east of Paris on route E-50, admiring the flat countryside consisting mostly of farm land when he entered the small town of Meaux. As he was exiting the town, he noticed a young man and a woman each with a suitcase hitchhiking. Markham stopped his car and asked them where they were going. The young, shapely brown-haired woman spoke up first, stating that they were headed for Reims which Markham knew from his previous study of the map was about 90 kilometers in the direction he was heading, so he invited them both for a ride to Reims which they happily accepted.

She immediately dumped her small suitcase on the back seat and her male companion placed his bag on the floor of the back seat behind the driver. She then held the back of the passenger seat forward indicating to him that he would be sitting in the back while she sat in the front with the driver and he complied.

"I'm Judy Weld," she said to Markham, holding out her right hand for him to shake, but she didn't introduce her male companion.

"I'm Daniel Herring," said the young man quietly, without offering his hand probably because he could see that Markham had started moving the car back onto the road and was occupied with the driving.

"Where're you from Judy?" asked Markham.

"I'm from London," she replied.

"And you Daniel. Where're you from?" asked Markham.

"I'm from London too," replied Daniel.

"Oh! So you're from the same city, huh? That explains why you're traveling together," said Markham.

"No. Not really. He's from East London and I'm from the Southend," she said. "I never knew Daniel in London. I just met him on the road here hitchhiking." She then moved away from the door to the center of the seat and looked at Markham. "We, that is Daniel and I, we're not really traveling together, you know."

Markham was astonished at Judy's declaration of freedom and apparent availability, and suddenly felt deeply sorry for Daniel who must have felt abandoned by her remark which he had to have overheard. It took about an hour to drive the 90 kilometers to Reims and Markham played music on the radio all of the way there to avoid any lengthily conversation with Judy, whom he felt was an opportunist with no empathy for others. By the time they reached Reims, Judy realized that Markham was not going to displace Daniel as a traveling companion and thus thanked him for the ride and descended the vehicle with Daniel who now had become a very silent partner, at least until Markham had driven off and was out of earshot.

"You were going to ditch me for that Yank, weren't you, you fucking cunt?" said Daniel in a vicious voice.

"No I wasn't, Dan. I was only trying to see if I could get him. That's all. I wouldn't have left you for him. Every woman wants to know if she's got what it takes to attract a rich and attractive man, but that doesn't mean that I would go with him. You should know me better than that Dan," said Judy imploringly.

Daniel looked at her wondering whether he should believe her, then looked at the ground before him, trying to decide whether to leave her or believe her, when Judy walked up close to him and put her arms around his waist. "Don't be mad at me Dan; I'll make it up to you later; you'll see; I promise," she said, lowering her right hand onto his buttocks which brought a slight grin to Daniel's face as he envisioned that night's forthcoming act of atonement.

As Markham approached Watronville, he knew that he was near the side route that would take him to Gorze which was located only a few kilometers from Noveant-sur-Moselle, which again was only a few kilometers from Chambley Air Base. As he entered and drove slowly through the small town of Gorze which was surrounded by hilly terrain, he observed an occasional male with deformed features walking the street which struck him as odd. Markham then drove up a hill and onto the road towards Noveant only a few kilometers away and upon entering Noveant, observed that the small village bordered the Moselle River. Markham parked his car in front of a local tavern to confirm his directions to Chambley Air Base.

He then continued on the same route and some 10 kilometers later arrived at the entrance to Chambley Air Base. He was directed to the base hospital where the OSI Detachment had its offices, but upon arrival there he learned that the OSI was closed for the evening, so he drove to the Provost Marshall's office to alert the OSI Agent on Duty that he had arrived. The Air Policeman on Duty made a telephone call to Special Agent Ernest Meehan, then informed Markham that Agent Meehan would be there in a few minutes.

About ten minutes later, a thinly built man in his early forties, wearing a tweed suit with a white shirt and maroon bow tie, appeared at the Provost Marshall's office and upon seeing Markham shook his hand with the welcoming remark, "If that's your convertible out there, you're going to have to get rid of it, 'cause it's too ostentatious for the OSI," said Meehan waiting for Markham's expression and reply. When he got none he added, "No, I'm only kidding. Hell, I'd like to borrow it for a few days to relive my youth, but my wife would kill me." He laughed. "I'm Special Agent Ernest Meehan," he said, extending his right hand for Markham to shake it, and he complied.

"Had a good trip?" asked Meehan.

"Yes, long but pleasant…no rain is always good when you drive a convertible," said Markham.

"I presume your gear is in your car, so why don't you follow me to the BOQ where you'll be staying, then we can go for something to eat or coffee and get you acquainted?" said Meehan.

"Sounds good Mr. Meehan," said Markham.

"Just call me Ernest. We're very informal up here," said Meehan.

"OK Ernest, I'll follow you," replied Markham.

At the Bachelor Officer's Quarters known as the BOQ, Markham was given a key to a second floor room which contained a single bed, a dresser with mirror, a bureau of drawers, and a closet to hang his clothes. A community restroom with showers, toilets and sinks was located downstairs. After unloading his suitcase in his room, Markham put up his convertible top and secured his vehicle for the night, then rode in the gray Simca driven by Meehan to the NCO Club on base for a bite to eat.

"That Simca. Is that your car or an OSI car?" asked Markham.

"It belongs to the OSI. It's a French car and would you believe it, it has an eight cylinder engine. Small cylinders mind you, but nevertheless it's an eight cylinder car, but it's a piece of crap. That thing'll fall apart in no time," said Meehan. "But your car is something else. Must be the only one of its kind in France, probably in all of Europe I'll bet."

"Probably. I never really thought about it until someone mentioned it," replied Markham. "Who's the OSI Detachment Commander?"

"That would be Mr. Alex Petrov," answered Meehan.

"What's his rank?" asked Markham.

"He's a Captain. A Fordham University graduate and an avid student of military history. He also speaks fluent German which is mighty handy in the Alsace-Lorraine area which is where we are located in case you didn't know. The Alsace-Lorraine is a ten-mile strip of land bordering the French-German border which had been changing hands once every generation so that one family's generation will be raised as Germans and the next will be raised as French, and the Alsatian language is a mixture of both German and French which I defy you to understand," said Meehan.

"Good grief Ernest. I presume there is a need for me as an Interpreter-Translator?" said Markham.

"Of course there is and let me tell you there's plenty of work to be done here because this is the industrial sector of France with a large labor force with unions infiltrated by the Communist Party which is a legal entity in France. There's more counterintelligence activity here than anywhere else in France. In fact, the Canadian Intelligence Service has only one office in Europe and guess where they located it? Yep, right here at Chateau Merci just outside of the city of Metz. That should tell you something," said Meehan.

"Tell me something Ernest. Any special reason for the bow tie?" asked Markham out of curiosity.

"No. That's my daily uniform. I like bow ties. On the other hand, your tie gives an opponent a strangle hold on you while he pounds the hell out of you, whereas my bow tie just clips on and pulls off. If I were you, I'd buy a clip-on tie so you don't become a victim," said Meehan.

"As a practical matter you're probably right, but those clip-on ties sure are ugly and they're usually too short," said Markham.

"Better to end up with an ugly tie than an ugly face," replied Meehan.

"OK! You've convinced me," said Markham, laughing at Ernest's humor. Markham liked Meehan and knew that he would get along with him just fine. After Markham finished eating a hamburger and Ernest drank his cup of coffee, they left the Club and Meehan drove Markham back to the BOQ with the understanding that he would be reporting to the OSI office at 0800 hours.

The next morning, Markham entered the one-story hospital consisting of several wings, one of which contained the OSI office. As he entered the office, Markham was met by a tall man who reminded him of a young General MacArthur at six feet three inches, weighing in at about 225 lbs with straight blonde hair parted to one side and a hook nose that separated two steel blue eyes. Markham's first impression was that this man was endowed with mental as well as physical strength, thus commanded respect. He received Markham with a hearty smile. "You must be Jim Markham. Been expecting you. Heard many good things about you from your former boss," said Mr. Petrov.

"Thank you sir," said Markham.

"I'm Alex Petrov, the CO of this Detachment. I guess you've already met Agent Ernest Meehan. He speaks French quite well, having been raised in Vermont you know, but we need someone who can read and write too, and that's where you come in Jim. As a matter of fact, you've arrived just in time. We're going to have lunch today with the DST Monsieur Antoine Lorain in Metz. He can be very helpful to us. He's one of only ten DSTs in all of France and this is the most active sector. Ernest will hold down the office while you and I meet with Monsieur Lorain."

At noontime Mr. Petrov accompanied by Markham met with Monsieur Lorain, a middle-aged, squarely built man of short but strong stature whose handshake was full and firm which conveyed to Markham a person with confidence and courage. This was confirmed by events that occurred during the Second World War, when as a young French Resistance fighter, Monsieur Lorain carried messages between the French Resistance and the British Intelligence Service via Spain and also risked his life in the rescue and clandestine transportation of downed allied pilots to the safety of the British Isles. Monsieur Lorain was the Director of Territorial Security for his District and as such acquired much intelligence information that was of interest and value to the United States Military Services. By the same token, the OSI acquired information, some of which was of value to France, hence during these luncheons Lorain and Petrov exchanged this information then each went back to his respective office to write an Intelligence Report citing the other as his confidential source which was then submitted to their respective Headquarters. And so the lunch went extremely well with many stories and pleasantries exchanged for their mutual benefit with the expectation of another meeting in about a month.

Towards the end of that day at the OSI office, Mr. Petrov invited Markham to have dinner at the Chateau de Berceau that evening. It was explained to him that Madame Elisabeth Andre, nee Pidancet, a cousin to President Charles DeGaulle, could no longer afford the maintenance and taxes of the Chateau de Berceau and thus was obliged to rent one half of the Chateau to the only people who could afford it, American Officers. At that time, American Servicemen, including officers, were not allowed to bring their wives to France at government expense, therefore those who elected to do so had to finance their dependents' transportation and also their lodging once in France. Both Meehan and Petrov elected to have their wives reside with them during their assignment in France. Meehan lived with his wife in a trailer on Chambley Air Base, while Petrov resided with his wife Anne and now one year old son Evan at the Chateau de Berceau which was situated on Rue de Berceau, the main street in Noveant-sur-Moselle.

As Petrov and Markham arrived in the Simca at the high iron gate, Petrov asked Markham to descend the vehicle and open the gate wide enough to allow him to drive the French car into the front yard of the Chateau, which Markham obliged.

The Chateau was of modest size with separate quarters for the servants which consisted of a married couple with a small male child. There was another car, a red Valiant, parked in the enclosed front yard which Petrov identified as his own POV primarily for his wife Anne's use. Markham noticed that there was a chicken coop to the side of the Chateau which promised fresh eggs. Markham was led inside the Chateau through the large front door by Petrov, who then opened another door to the left which finally brought them both inside that part of the Chateau that served as the Petrov residence.

Petrov's wife Anne appeared from another room to greet her husband and Markham. It was not her shapely figure at five feet seven inches and 120 lbs, nor the stunning features of her Irish and

Creek bloodline of dark-brown hair and pale, slightly freckled face that most impressed Markham, but the goodness and kindness that emanated from her hazel eyes and soft melodious voice that Markham had so seldom found in his social encounters. She softened her husband's rough edges as a military man and Markham found them well-suited to each other. What was remarkable was that Anne had been a First Lieutenant in the United States Air Force as a registered nurse when she met Alex Petrov and the rest of course was history. After meeting their now one-year old son Evan, he understood why they refused to be separated during Alex Petrov's two-year tour of duty in France.

"I hope you like chicken because that's what we're having for dinner this evening," said Anne with a smile. She wore no make-up except for a light touch of lipstick and her shoulder length page-boy haircut gave her the allure of the All-American girl next door, while wearing a simple light-colored blouse and dark pants with low-heeled shoes. Alex still wore his suit trousers and white shirt, but had removed his tie and suit jacket, hence Markham did the same.

"I like just about everything and I'm quite adventurous when it comes to food," replied Markham.

"Well that's good, but this is Madame Jurain's special recipe that Anne has been using, which I might add, with great success," said Alex jubilantly.

"Madame Jurain lives just down the street. Her daughter Mireille works at Chambley Air Base," said Anne.

Anne brought out a large salad bowl filled to the brim with lettuce, tomatoes, slices of cucumber, onion strips and sliced black olives already marinated in Madame Jurain's oil and vinegar recipe that tenderized the lettuce and enhanced the natural flavor of the various ingredients that made its consumer want to make a meal of it. A whole chicken cooked and seasoned a la Francaise was brought to the table in front of Alex who was appointed by Anne as the official carver. She then brought out a bowl of mashed potatoes and also French-cut string beans, and of course, a French baguette which is the traditional long and narrow loaf of bread that Frenchmen are often seen carrying like a large stick, which has a hard crust, but soft interior. The meal was accompanied by a bottle of Beaujolais red wine. It was a simple meal, but a memorably delicious one, thought Markham. The conversation during the meal served to inform all parties of their individual backgrounds, which was not without surprises.

"Tell me Jim...how long have you been in France?" asked Anne, now sitting at the table with Alex and Markham eating dinner.

"About six months," replied Markham.

"He has another 18 months to serve in France," said Alex to his wife Anne.

"How do you like it so far?" asked Anne.

"To me it's the people who make the country, not so much the architecture or its history, and I'm somewhat disappointed in the attitude of the French towards us Americans, particularly the young generation who do not wish to acknowledge our contribution to their freedom from fascism in the First and Second World Wars," said Markham.

"Well, you're right Jim. We've encountered that attitude too; but like you said, it's mostly from the French youth. The older generation who suffered under the Nazi regime is still very thankful to us and we've become good friends with some of them," said Anne.

"You have to understand, Jim, that the French defeat by the Germans who paraded up the Champs Elysees in Paris in 1940 was the most humiliating blow to French pride in the history of France and they haven't recovered from it yet," said Alex. "As an Army, they're a joke. General George Patton once said 'I would rather have a German division in front of me than a French one behind me' and for good reason. A few weeks ago, Anne's cousin Jeremy, who's an Army Captain and Commander of a tank unit stationed at an Army post near Nuremberg, Germany, visited us here at the Chateau and he told us of an incident that actually happened to him. Each year, the US Army, the German Army and French Army tank corps engage in maneuvers to test each others' tactics, and in this particular engagement, the French tank unit engaged the US Army tank unit commanded by Jeremy and the German tank Commander acted as the arbitrator. Jeremy's unit drew the French tank unit into a narrow ravine, then from the hillside above, Jeremy's unit knocked out the lead French tank and the last French tank, thus bottling up the entire French tank unit inside the ravine. The German arbitrator called a halt to the engagement and announced to the French Commander that his unit had been wiped out by the US Army unit. The French Commander protested, stating, 'With our esprit de Corps we would have overcome all odds and become victorious.' "You see," said the German arbitrator to Jeremy. 'The French are dreamers. That's why we beat the crap out of them in the last war."

"The French did capitulate rather quickly. I guess that's why they are known as lovers, not fighters," said Markham.

"Yes and 'Vive la difference,'" said Alex, lifting his glass of wine in a toasting gesture.

"I heard that American wives were not welcomed by the military authorities to travel with their military husbands to France. That must have been quite a problem for you, Mrs. Petrov," said Markham.

"It wasn't easy and if I had known what I had to go through, I doubt that I would have had the desire to make the trip in the first place. At our expense, I booked passage with my five-and-a-half month old son Evan on the Isle de France which was on her maiden voyage back to France and apparently the Captain wanted to set a record crossing in March when the seas were very rough which resulted in both me and Evan being seasick for the better part of the voyage. And when we docked in France at Le Havre, we were not allowed to disembark because there had been a terrorist threat of a bomb aboard the ship. I stood on deck with Evan for over two hours while Alex managed to finally get through customs and the port security using his OSI Carte Blanche to get us off the ship," said Anne, reliving the incident.

"France is having major problems with the Algerians ever since DeGaulle gave them independence which resulted in the formation of the OAS, the Organization Algerie Secret. Many of those Algerians referred to as 'Pied Noir' or Black Foot have settled here in Eastern France and Lieutenant General Massou's paratroopers stationed here in Metz are often seen walking the streets of Metz carrying sub-machine guns, primarily to keep those Pied Noir in line. I have to tell you Jim, that General Massou is not one of DeGaulle's favorite generals, but he must know that Massou could be a decisive factor in a General Coup d'Etat. So there's a lot of people in France walking on pins and needles right now," said Alex.

Anne got up to clear the empty dishes from the table and bring out the dessert for the evening, and once gone into the kitchen, Alex Petrov confided a secret to Markham.

"For your information Jim, Mireille Jurain is one of my best informants. She's a good source of information about what goes on with the foreign workers at Chambley," said Alex.

"Does your wife know this?" asked Markham.

"Yeah! She knows. Otherwise how would I explain our meetings?" replied Alex. "You'll get to meet her tomorrow. She works in the Base Housing Office, so she knows who comes in and who goes out. She's smart as a whip and a very attractive petite blonde, but remember Jim, don't mix business with pleasure," said Alex with a hearty laugh.

Markham made a mental note of Mr. Petrov's remark without comment.

"On the other hand Jim, it might not be a bad idea if you and Mireille appeared to be good friends so that she could pass on any information to us through you and not involve me directly," said Petrov.

"I'll work on it," replied Markham.

"From what I heard about you from Moss and Heller, I don't think you'll have to work at all," said Petrov with a laugh.

"I think those two guys like to exaggerate," replied Markham, a bit embarrassed.

As Markham was leaving the Petrov residence, Alex and his wife Anne both gave him a warm farewell as they liked his All-American appearance and conservative views.

The following day, Petrov and Markham visited the Base Housing Office where Mireille was introduced to Markham. Mireille wore her blonde hair in a bun and wore high heel shoes that elevated her five feet two inches to the height she wished nature had given her. Mireille's 100 pounds was extremely well distributed in all of the right places, to the chagrin of all the men she met and rejected. Her sky blue eyes never revealed her intimate thoughts, but her ready smile was ever present when she wanted to disarm you, and that she did when she was introduced to Markham.

"This is my new assistant and Interpreter, Jim Markham. He's your new direct contact in case you have anything for us. In the event he's not available, then you can contact me directly, otherwise you call Jim. OK?" said Petrov.

"I'm very pleased to meet you Mr. Markham," said Mireille in English, extending her right hand to Markham.

He gently held it with his right hand with the thought of bending forward to kiss it in a gallant gesture, but quickly rejected the idea in view of the business relationship and Petrov's presence. "Likewise Mireille," he said in French.

"You can speak to me in English if you wish. I don't mind," said Mireille.

"But I do need the practice," said Markham.

"In that case, I'll call you Jacques if you don't mind," said Mireille.

"No, I don't mind. In fact, that was my name for many years until I returned to the States," said Markham.

Mireille smiled at Markham, but her eyes were cautiously measuring him. *A handsome American who is fluent in French, a combination worth exploring,* she thought.

After they left the Housing office, Petrov wanted to know Markham's opinion of Mireille.

"Well, what do you think of her Jim?" asked Petrov.

"She is every bit as attractive as you said she would be, but you didn't mention her marital status. I didn't see a wedding or engagement ring on her finger," replied Markham.

"She's divorced from an American Sergeant who returned to the United States two years ago and she didn't have any children by him either," replied Petrov. "She's a very good source of information and Anne has become very good friends with her family who live right down the street from us. Her Mother has given Anne some great recipes."

"Don't worry Mr. Petrov, I'll keep the relationship platonically professional," said Markham, smiling.

"Since we're going to be working together on a daily basis, you can drop the 'Mister Petrov' and just call me by my first name, Alex."

"OK, Alex. If you don't mind my asking, where were you stationed before you came to France?" asked Markham.

"Keflavik, Iceland for a year then I entered the OSI and they assigned me to DO 2 in New York City. You know, I'm originally from New York. I was a New York State Trooper stationed in Suffolk

County, Long Island before I was commissioned in the Air Force. I still have the blackjack from those days as a State Trooper. You never know when it might come in handy, especially when you're not permitted to carry a gun," said Alex.

"How was it being assigned to District Headquarters in New York City?" said Markham.

"All they had us do is run leads in Personnel Security Investigations. They had a large bowl full of subway tokens. You took a bunch of tokens and PI leads with names and addresses of references to be interviewed and you spent all day running those leads all over the city of New York, including Harlem," said Alex.

"Harlem! That's a dangerous place to be, especially unarmed. You'd think they would send black agents into that area so as not to invite trouble," said Markham.

"As a matter of fact, on one occasion they had a new agent assigned to DO 2 that they wanted me to break in. He was a tall, blond-haired guy from Texas with a drawl that wouldn't quit. Some of the leads I had that day took us into Harlem, by subway of course. I did the two interviews without incident and as we went down the stairs of the subway station the train was getting ready to close its doors when the Texan yelled out 'Hey nigger, hold the door,' which immediately got the attention of every black man on the platform. As they started coming after us, I grabbed the Texan by the arm and yelled at him, 'Let's get out here before we get killed,' and we ran for our lives out of the subway station onto the street and as luck would have it, an empty taxi had just pulled up at the light. We got in the taxi and took off just in time and went back to District Headquarters. I told the PI Chief, 'Don't you ever assign that Texan to me again. He almost got us killed in Harlem.'"

"Sounds like the OSI should be giving an orientation course to all new agents assigned to New York City, especially the southern ones," said Markham.

"No kidding. Boy, that was an experience I won't soon forget," replied Alex.

Two days later, Markham received a telephone call at the OSI office from Mireille who informed him that she had information of possible importance that she could relay to him after work at the NCO Club to which he agreed.

Markham went into the NCO Club at 5:15 PM and sat at a vacant table against the wall of the restaurant portion of the Club where he could see and be seen by those entering the Club. About five minutes later, Mireille entered the club and upon seeing Markham, came over and sat at his table and he stood up to greet her. He invited her to dinner and she graciously accepted. After they ordered their dinner, Mireille informed him of the incident that generated the meeting.

"This Polish immigrant came into the Base Housing Office looking for a maintenance job. His English was not too good and when he asked the Air Policeman at the main gate for a housing job, they sent him to our office instead of the Personnel Office. He wanted a job cleaning buildings and I told him I didn't have any job openings at Base Housing and he then said that maybe he could clean offices at Headquarters building and where could he apply for the job. When he specifically asked for the Headquarters building, that's when I became suspicious about his reason for wanting to work on base," said Mireille.

"You did the right thing in calling me Mireille. It may be nothing, then again it could be a Communist or low-level agent seeking intelligence information from offices at Headquarters. You have his name?" asked Markham.

"Yes. I told him that I would inquire about work for him, but I needed to see his identity card and I made a copy of it on our office copying machine. Here it is," said Mireille, handing it over to Markham.

"I see that he entered France only one month ago. His name is Leon Krazinski and he lives in

Metz. I'll pass this on to Alex, but in the meantime, if Mister Krazinski comes back to your office for any reason, stall him. Tell him there may be an opening soon," said Markham.

The following morning Markham gave the information about Krazinski to Alex Petrov.

"I'm going to give this guy's name to Andre Lazzard of the Renseignment Generauz. The RG keeps track of all aliens that come into France from iron curtain countries. Andre will know if Krazinski belongs to the French Communist Party and possibly other relevant information. That will take a while so I'm going to arrange to have this man get a job as a janitor in the Headquarters building and put a surveillance on him. We'll pick up his trail when he leaves the base," said Alex Petrov.

"Yeah! But while he's working in the Headquarters building, he could steal documents. How are you going to prevent him from doing that?" asked Markham.

"By alerting the Provost Marshal and the Security Chief to insure that all classified material is locked up and the offices are all secure. He will only have access to certain offices that don't possess classified documents, but we're going to plant certain innocuous documents that will have Secret and Top Secret stamped on them inside designated desk drawers in those offices to which he will have a key and access. Then we'll see if he grabs the bait and to whom he delivers the loot," said Alex.

"Are you going to tell the RG what we're planning on doing with this man?" asked Markham.

"Not on your life. If you learn nothing else, Jim, you treat all foreign intelligence agencies with suspicion and adversarial objectives," said Alex.

"I'll remember that," replied Markham.

"You'd better meet with Mireille before the day is over to get this matter in motion as soon as possible, Jim," said Alex.

"I'll call her right now and set it up," said Markham, and went back to his own office next door and telephoned Mireille.

"Mireille, it's Jim Markham," said Markham in French. "Meet me for lunch at the Club."

"OK! I'll be there," replied Mireille.

At the NCO Club, Mireille was told by Markham to direct Leon Krazinski to the Personnel Office in building 208 and ask for Lieutenant James Parlance who has a janitorial job at the headquarters building waiting for him. "If you wonder why I didn't tell you this over the phone, it's because I don't trust the switchboard operators," said Markham.

"I understand, Mr. Markham, Mr. Petrov told me the same thing," replied Mireille.

"Mireille, just call me Jacques, remember?" said Markham.

"OK! Jacques," said Mireille with a great smile.

"Has Leon Krazinski been back to your office?" asked Markham.

"No, but I expect he'll be back tomorrow," replied Mireille.

"Be sure to call me or Alex right away if he does," said Markham.

"I will; don't worry," said Mireille.

"Let me give you a lift home," said Markham.

"Are you sure? I don't want you to go out of your way for me," said Mireille.

"It's only about 10 kilometers from here. That's no big deal and besides, you're working for us, let's not forget that," said Markham.

"Oh! OK. You talked me into it," said Mireille and they left the Club together and got into Markham's Ford Fairlane with the top up due to an expectation of foul weather. As Markham entered Noveant-sur-Moselle, he passed the Chateau de Berceau where Alex, Anne and their son Evan resided, then they approached a large house on Rue de Berceau which was recessed about 30 feet from the street. An open iron gate led onto a paved walkway to a three step cement stoop abutting the large entrance door to the two-story house. Markham parked his car on the street in front of the house and escorted Mireille to the door and bid her good afternoon, then returned to his car and drove back to Chambley Air Base.

That Friday, Agent Meehan informed Markham that there was a square dance at the base gymnasium and he ought to come.

"Hell, I've never square danced, and besides I need a partner, don't I?" said Markham.

"Why don't you ask Mireille? I'm sure she'd go square dancing with you. It's not the sort of dancing that promotes romance; it's safe," said Meehan.

"I suppose I could ask her, but I don't want to get romantically involved with a source if you know what I mean," replied Markham.

"I understand, but even if you did get romantically involved, it wouldn't be the first time that happened," said Meehan.

"Alright, I'll ask her," said Markham, not exactly enthusiastic about it.

Later that afternoon, Markham called Mireille and asked her if she would like to go with him to the square dance the following evening and she immediately accepted, so Markham made a date to pick her up at 7 PM that Saturday. As it turned out, there was a square dance scheduled each Wednesday and Saturday evening for the next four weeks at the Chambley Base Gymnasium as a preliminary to the European Square Dance to be held in Wiesbaden, Germany by the United States Armed Forces in Europe, to which Meehan and his wife were planning to attend. Markham, accompanied by Mireille, attended each of the square dance sessions for three weeks without Markham once making any overture towards Mireille. Then one Saturday evening, Markham went to pick up Mireille at her home in Noveant-sur-Moselle to go square dancing and found both her parents were gone for the evening and she was alone in the house dressed only in a negligee, obviously not dressed to go out dancing.

"Aren't you going to get dressed to go dancing?" asked Markham.

"No, I thought that since my parents aren't going to be home this evening that we would spend the evening here instead of going to the dance," she said with a look in her eyes that invited Markham to inspect her nude body under the near transparent negligee.

After three weeks of dating without any overture from Markham, Mireille decided to set the stage for an inevitable seduction, unless of course Markham was impotent. He most certainly was not, but a man of immense control when the situation demanded it. However, in this particular situation, Markham found Mireille irresistible and before either one knew it, they were making love, first against the wall of the dining room, then upstairs in her bedroom. Markham found her to be a woman who definitely needed a man in her life, and she knew how to please him. He thought it wise to leave the house before her parents returned home, even though Mireille didn't seem concerned about it.

A week later, Markham and Mireille were walking down the Rue de Berceau towards the Moselle River after eating dinner at her house when Mireille revealed a secret that astounded him.

"Jacques, I'm pregnant," she declared to Markham.

"What! We made love not more than a week ago, how can that be?" asked Markham incredulously.

"You're not the Father Jacques. I'm two-and-a half months pregnant and the Father is Major Bill Henderson who's since gone back to Indiana. He's married, so he doesn't want his wife to find out," said Mireille.

"Well, apparently your pregnancy is not yet showing," said Markham. "What are you going to do? Do your parents know?"

"No, my parents don't know. But Major Henderson sent Captain Hamilton, who's also from Indiana but is still here at Chambley, $600.00 with instructions to give the money to me so that I get an abortion," said Mireille.

"Is that what you want to do...get an abortion?" asked Markham.

"I don't know what to do," said Mireille. "What do you think I should do, Jacques?"

"The good Major is asking you to sell your soul for $600.00. You're a Catholic, Mireille. You know that abortion is against your religion. Major Henderson is asking you to relieve him of responsibility by killing your unborn child thus blackening your soul forever for the sum of $600.00. Ask yourself this question, Mireille. Would you accept an offer of one million dollars from Satan in exchange for your soul?"

"No I wouldn't," she replied.

"Then why would you even consider selling your soul for six hundred dollars and in the process murder your unborn child?" said Markham.

"You're right Jacques; I won't get an abortion. I'll have the baby, but will you still see me through this?" asked Mireille pleadingly.

"Of course I'll see you through this. I recommend that you inform your Mother at least of your pregnancy and she can diplomatically break the news to your Father. You'll need their assistance," said Markham.

"I will," said Mireille.

"If you need anything from the BX, just let me know. I think you should tell Captain Hamilton that you're not going to get an abortion and that you'll need some financial assistance from the Major to defray the cost of having his baby," said Markham who felt that the Major should meet his obligations in this matter.

Mireille nodded in agreement as they walked back to the house. In that short period of time, Markham had become quite fond of Mireille and suspected that he might easily fall in love with her if he continued to date her. As Markham lay in his bed in the BOQ that evening, he knew that if he did fall in love with Mireille, he would adopt the child without hesitation, and as the weeks went by, he realized that cupid's arrow had struck his big heart dead center and he was in it for the long ride.

In the meantime, Leon Krazinski did return to the Base Housing Office and was directed to the Personnel Office where he was instantly hired as a janitor to clean the offices located in the Headquarters building. In the first three weeks of his employment there, no bogus classified documents were removed from the targeted offices, but then one day, Mr. Petrov was notified by the Chief of Security that documents secreted in one of the targeted desk drawers had been moved and not placed back in their original order which suggested that they had been photographed, probably in haste.

"Jim," said Alex, "we're going to follow our Mr. Krazinski as he gets off work. We'll take the Simca. It's less noticeable than your Ford."

Markham was at the wheel and Alex Petrov sat in the passenger seat of the Simca which they parked just inside the main gate out of sight of cars exiting the base, waiting for Mr. Krazinski to drive himself off-base. After about 15 minutes of waiting, Mr. Krazinski appeared alone, driving an old Citroen referred to by Americans as a 'cigarette roller' due to its small, rudimentary structure. Markham and Petrov followed Krazinski at a good distance so as not to alert him that he was being followed. As Krazinski approached a small circle in the road, he stopped his car, stepped out and walked to the center of the circle where a white cement road marker stood planted in the ground. Krazinski pulled out a piece of blue chalk and drew a four inch vertical line on the stone marker then re-entered his car and drove off. As Markham started his car again to follow Krazinski while Petrov had been observing him through his binoculars, Petrov explained to him what had just happened.

"He's placed that mark on the stone to alert his contact that he's got something to place in their dead letter drop. He won't place anything in the dead letter drop until his contact confirms that he got the message and so will pick it up right away. They don't like to leave anything in the dead letter drop for long for fear that someone might stumble on it by accident," said Petrov. "Let's continue following Krazinski to see if and where he drops the item."

Krazinski drove directly to his apartment on the east side of Metz where he stayed for more than an hour, while Markham and Petrov sat in their Simca more than a hundred meters from the apartment building where they had a view of Krazinski's car. Finally, Krazinski exited his apartment and drove off in his Citroen back to where he had left his mark. Through his binoculars, Petrov could see that another chalk mark had been placed across the original mark forming an X, indicating that Krazinski's contact was now aware that a drop would be made by Krazinski. He rubbed off the chalked X from the stone road marker then drove off in a westerly direction followed by Markham and Petrov at a greater than usual distance because the road was rather straight and Petrov was making good use of his binoculars.

"Slow down Jim; he's turning onto a side road. He may have spotted us so we'll just drive by and double back," said Petrov.

As they passed the side road they observed that Krazinski had parked his car about 70 yards from the main road and he didn't appear to be in his car. Markham noticed that there was a country road about 50 yards further down and drove onto it and stopped the car which was now out of sight. They both exited the Simca and walked quickly to the side road and observed that the car was still empty. They hid behind the high hedges in case Krazinski suddenly returned and sure enough, he appeared and drove off back onto the main road in the direction from which he came.

"We're going to have to wait for the contact to appear. But I think we have time to search the area to see if we can find the dead letter drop before the contact gets here. If you hear any noise, hide in the bushes. When he picks up the item, we'll then follow him to his destination and attempt to identify him," said Petrov.

They walked around the area, which was farmland surrounded by trees. *Good place for a picnic*, thought Markham, when they both arrived at a brook that had a small wooden bridge for pedestrians to cross. Petrov looked underneath the bridge, first at one end and then at the other, when he found a small canvas pouch with a zipper. Petrov unzipped it in Markham's presence and found a silver cylinder which when opened, contained a roll of film. The pouch also contained a brown sealed envelope that apparently contained documents. Petrov returned all of the items back in the pouch and placed the pouch back in its hiding place under the edge of the wooden bridge. At that moment they heard the sound of a motor. They both looked at each other and quickly hid in the nearby brush. A moment later, a woman of perhaps 30 years of age dressed in slacks and a short woolen brown coat approached the bridge and stopped to look around, then went over the bridge and reached under its edge and pulled out the pouch, emptied its contents in a bag she had brought with her, then replaced the empty pouch back under the foot of the bridge and departed the area. Markham and Petrov ran back to their car after having observed that she had turned onto the main road in the direction of Metz driving a black four-door Audi, but unfortunately they were too far back to get the license plate number. Markham floored the gas pedal of the eight cylinder Simca, trying to catch up to the Audi which they now could see ahead of them. He slowed down enough so that their approachm to the Audi appeared natural and as the Audi came to a full stop at the sign in the road, Petrov was able to write down the license number and Markham was able to observe that the woman driving the

Audi was the same woman they had seen at the dead letter drop. They were now armed with enough information already to identify her, but they wanted to learn where she resided and in the event she was meeting another colleague, they desired his identity as well.

The Audi rode through the center of Metz where it parked on a street not far from the main train station. The woman walked across a grassy medium and entered a two-story apartment building. About one minute after entering the apartment building, Markham and Petrov observed that the lights were turned on in the second story window of the corner apartment and suddenly someone closed the curtain. It was surmised that the contact was a woman who resided in the second story apartment of the building, and its street address was noted by Petrov who then called it a night with excellent results.

"What's the plan now?" asked Markham.

"We do nothing yet, inasmuch as the information they got is worthless. I want to see if there are others involved in this intelligence gathering conspiracy. I'm not going to give this info to the French until I'm satisfied that we've got them all, as I don't trust that they'll give us all of the information they develop from this early lead," said Petrov. "We'll just keep an eye on Krazinski for the time being."

It was Friday afternoon about 5 PM at the Chateau de Berceau. Anne was preparing dinner for Alex and Markham, when there was a knock at the inner door to the Petrov residence. Apparently whoever was visiting them had entered past the street gate and the outer door to the Chateau, thus placing him inside the Chateau at the front door to the Petrov residence. Markham was standing in the living room watching Alex answer the door. As Alex opened the door, a man of equal height and weight as Alex, dressed in an old overcoat, and carrying a briefcase and an encyclopedia Britannica stared at Alex for a moment then started to excuse himself in German for having stopped at the wrong house and quickly backed away from Alex and walked speedily back to his black four-door sedan.

"This man looked at me as if he recognized me and panicked, stuttering in German," said Petrov, his mind working at warp speed.

Markham immediately ran outside past the gate and managed to read the license plate number of the black sedan before he had a chance to drive off. He kept repeating the license number to himself over and over again until he got inside the Chateau where he could write it down. He then gave the plate number to Petrov.

"I've seen this guy on base selling encyclopedias to the servicemen. He'll visit them at their off-base residence and try to develop a friendship that possibly can blossom into a paid source of information," said Petrov. "I think we've discovering a hornet's nest my friend."

"You sure have sharp instincts, Alex. You mean he recognized you from photographs they take surreptitiously of our OSI agents?" asked Markham.

"That's right Jim. The identity of OSI agents is readily available. We function as criminal investigators as well as counterintelligence agents, so everyone on base knows who we are, and I wouldn't be surprised if some of those foreign intelligence agents didn't position one of their agents with a camera with telephoto lens in a house facing the entrance to our headquarters in Paris or in a parked van for that matter and took pictures of everyone who entered and exited the building."

"So when he paid your residence a visit he didn't expect to come face to face with an OSI agent and the Commander no less. No wonder he stammered as he made his quick exit," said Markham.

Two days later, Markham was driving his Ford with the convertible top up, on a city road towards the center of Metz with several cars ahead and behind him, when all of a sudden he noticed that the license plate on the back of the car directly in front of him was the same license plate he had memorized from the black sedan outside the Chateau de Berceau. He looked up at the car which was the same black sedan and the driver appeared to be the same big man that had paid the Petrovs a visit at the Chateau two days ago. He immediately slowed down his car so as to allow two other cars to pass him and thus stand between him and the black sedan. Unfortunately, Markham's American car was so conspicuous that the man in the black sedan spotted it right away as the same car he'd seen in the courtyard at the Chateau two days earlier. Markham followed him into the city, past the train station and then into a dead end street where the man parked his car and sat there waiting and watching through his rearview mirror for any sign of Markham and his big American car. But Markham did not enter the dead end street. Instead, he drove past it and parked a block away, then ran back to the corner where he was able to look through the store window at the big man sitting in his car still waiting. However, the man couldn't see Markham who was hidden by two plate-glass windows at the corner.

The man finally exited his car and as he walked out of the dead end street towards a restaurant across the street, he kept looking right and left for Markham without success. As the man approached the corner, Markham eased himself inside the store still keeping his eye on the big man who then entered the restaurant. Markham crossed the street and looked through the large, plate-glass window of the restaurant where the big man sat at a table with his back to Markham who observed him ordering from the menu. Feeling that this would occupy the big man for a while, Markham left the area looking for a public telephone and after finding one, called Alex Petrov to inform him of this new development.

"Alex. I've got a 35mm camera, but no film in it. Should I take a chance and drive to the Army caserne to buy some film and get back here as quickly as possible? It sure would be nice to have a photograph of this man," said Markham.

"Yeah! Go ahead and get the film, but hurry back," said Alex.

Markham drove at speeds in excess of the speed limit and after going through the main gate to the Army Post, found the Post Exchange which was closing. He pleaded with the lady to sell him the film, but she had already closed her cash register. He called the manager and said it was an urgent matter, but inasmuch as Markham was not a Special Agent, he had no official credentials to present to them, hence he had to convince them of the importance of his request by his sheer expression of urgency, which yielded a roll of film that was immediately inserted into his camera ready for action as he drove past the restaurant where he parked his car on the street in the next block. He then returned on foot to the restaurant when he noticed that the big man was still sitting at the table eating his meal. Markham waited outside the restaurant and soon observed that after he paid his bill, he went to the public telephone inside the restaurant to make a telephone call. At this point Markham knew that he couldn't stay at that position, thus he crossed the street and sat at one of the outside tables occupied by several people. The big man's car was parked directly across the street from him, hence as the big man walked along the street towards his car, Markham, who was surrounded by a number of customers sitting at tables around him, was able to take several photographs of the big man approaching his vehicle then entering his car, with only a few customers being aware of his photography. Markham then walked quickly back towards his car and noticed that the big man had parked his car on the same street near the apartment of the woman who was the intelligence contact for Krazinski. The big man exited his car and walked away from the apartment in the direction of the train station. As Markham followed him, he noticed that the curtain of the window to the second floor corner apartment was drawn and the woman contact was staring down at Markham as he walked past the apartment building.

He realized that the phone call made by the big man in the restaurant was to alert this woman to take a photograph of the man following him. At this point, Markham knew that it didn't make any difference now whether they knew who he was, as he had enough information for the French Agents to apprehend them, but he had to follow the big man to his destination. The man, who now knew he was being tailed, brought him into the train station amongst a throng of people. The man stationed himself against a pillar with a newspaper in his hands which reminded Markham of one of those black and white spy movies of the Second World War. Markham decided to be bold and walked within a couple of feet of the big man, and took a quick look into his face, then walked past him where he stationed himself in a position to observe his every move. After a while, the big man went into the ticket sales room which had only one entrance and exit door. Markham waited for him to come out of that room, but he never did. Markham went to check the room to see where he could possibly have gone and found that the door was locked and the ticket office was now closed. This was an impossible situation, Markham thought. He never saw him come out of that room. He had to be inside, perhaps he was in cahoots with someone working inside the ticket office. Markham reported back to Alex at the Chateau de Berceau that evening with all of the acquired information and the film.

"I think we have enough now to contact Andre Lazzard of the French Renseignment Generaux. We'll pay them a visit tomorrow, but we won't tell them about the film, yet. We have to get that developed at the base lab and then you can drive it with our report to Paris right away," said Alex. "Hey! It'll give you a chance to get reacquainted with les Filles de Paris, huh! Huh!"

"I doubt that I will have time for that. But I'm curious about something Alex. Of those three people, who do you think is the ring leader?" asked Markham.

"That's hard to say at this point. I don't think it's Leon Krazinski, nor his female contact. My bet is that it's the German-speaking man whose photograph you took. We'll know more when the French authorities check these people out," said Petrov.

With the several photographs of the big man having been developed successfully which provided sufficient data for an identification, plus the written report of investigation by Petrov which he and Markham had worked on all evening now in his briefcase, Markham drove off in his Ford convertible for Paris.

While Markham was on his way to Paris, Petrov took Agent Meehan, who was fluent in conversational French, with him to meet with the RG Andre Lazzard for the purpose of providing him with all of the information accumulated so far in the investigation of Leon Krazinski, his female contact and their apparent accomplice who disappeared in the ticket office at the Metz train station.

Markham arrived at the OSI headquarters in Paris just after lunch time and delivered the investigation material to Mr. Belanger, Chief of Criminal Investigations, an American-born Parisian, who spoke to Markham in French to test his fluency and was pleasantly surprised by Markham's effortless dialogue.

"It's too bad that it's after lunch time, otherwise I'd have invited you to have lunch with me. I suppose you'll be heading right back to Chambley. Tell Alex that we're very pleased with the work he's doing up there and we'll be briefing the CIA regarding this matter," said Mr. Belanger, who then stood up and shook Markham's hand. "Have a safe trip back Jim."

Markham decided to have his late lunch in the Montmartre district and drove his car to the Parvis du Sacre Coeur. There were several parking spaces facing a low stone wall that overlooked Paris. To his surprise, two of them, side by side were empty, but a long windowed van pulled into one of the spaces so Markham quickly parked into the space next to the van. Several people exited the van, but one of them in particular gained Markham's immediate attention. She was a model in the flesh with her long blonde hair, blue eyes and a figure that belonged on a Christian Dior runway. She had gotten out of the van on the side facing Markham's Ford Fairlane with the convertible top down, which had obviously caught her attention and aroused her curiosity about its owner.

"Nice automobile you have," said the beautiful, young woman with a British accent.

"Thank you," replied Markham. "I noticed that the license plates on your van are from Germany. Is that where you're from?"

"That's very observant of you. Yes, I'm from Bad Godesberg, Germany, but the other people in the van are from other parts of Germany."

"Pardon me. My name is Jim Markham."

"And I'm Hildegard Hunslinger," she said, extending her right hand which Markham shook gently.

"So you're visiting Paris. Is this your first time?" asked Markham.

"Yes it is, and you?" asked Hildegard.

"No, I'm in the United States Air force stationed in France and I've been in Paris a number of times," replied Markham.

"I'm with the tour and I mustn't lose them, but if you wish you can accompany me since I don't know any of them, unless you have other plans," said Hildegard, who was confident of her beauty's magnetism on any man she desired.

"I have a few hours to kill before I head back to Metz, and I can't think of a better way to spend them. You've got yourself an American escort for the afternoon my lady," said Markham in a humorous tone.

"Did you say Metz?" asked Hildegard.

"Yes. I'm stationed at Chambley Air Base which is only about 20 kilometers west of Metz," replied Markham.

"I've been to Metz. It's only about 190 kilometers from Bad Godesberg where I live," said Hildegard, encouraged by the realistic possibility of meeting with Markham again.

"I guess we're neighbors, hey!" said Markham.

Markham and Hildegard caught up with the tour guide and his ten disciples who were close to entering the Museum of Art. Markham learned that Hildegard had been a college student in London which explained her English accent. Furthermore she worked as a secretary at the Nigerian Embassy in Bad Godesberg which hosted 32 embassies. Bad Godesberg was only a few kilometers from Bonn, a much bigger city. Markham wondered why a woman of Hildegard's beauty, who turned the heads of most men who saw her, would be on a common tour in a minibus, when there were plenty of wealthy men willing to drive her in a posh limousine to any destination she desired. Perhaps it was her independent demeanor that gave the impression of inapproachability which intimidated most men. But in Markham's case, he possessed the ingredients that attracted her which loosened her reservedness, although he wasn't sure exactly what they were. After visiting the Art Museum and the Musee de Montmartre, the tour group returned to the minibus to explore other areas of Paris.

"Well, we're back where we started," said Markham.

"Not quite James. Geographically perhaps, but I've found a new friend, and that made the trip to Paris very worthwhile," said Hildegard, opening her purse and pulling out a pen and a piece of paper on which she wrote her name and address, which she gave to Markham. "In case you should lose my address, would you write your address on this piece of paper for me please?" she said with a disarming smile.

"Of course," said Markham, who quickly wrote his Chambley Air Base address.

"Please write to me soon and I promise that I will write back. We must get together again. You'll love Bad Godesberg. It's a beautiful town," said Hildegard.

As Markham extended his right hand, Hildegard took his right hand in hers and then unexpectedly leaned forward and kissed Markham on the left cheek as she said goodbye to him. Markham watched Hildegard as she boarded the minibus and wondered if, with all of her beauty, she possessed the depth of passion that great lovemaking requires, but few women really possess. Markham's drive back to Chambley was uneventful, but it provided him time to quietly evaluate his relationship with Mireille and his new friend Hildegard. *Only time will tell,* he thought.

That evening, Markham was getting ready to retire for the night in his room in the Bachelor Officers Quarters where Alex Petrov had arranged for him to be billeted, when someone knocked on his door. Markham opened the door and an officer whom Markham recognized as Lieutenant Mark Sibley invited him to join the party in the room almost directly across from his own which was more like a suite reserved for field grade officers. Markham tried to excuse himself from the party as he was tired from the long drive from Paris and he had to be up early in the morning, but another officer joined Lt. Sibley and between the two of them they managed to get him to join the party which contained several American female teachers and nurses amongst several officers from Lt. Colonel down to Lieutenant.

Obviously, they all believed Markham to be a commissioned officer, although he wore civilian clothes and worked for the OSI, but in reality, Markham was a Staff Sergeant, a non-commissioned officer, who surely would not have been invited to their party had they known of his enlisted rank. Markham had been standing near the entrance to the door through which he came in, holding a drink of Scotch and soda, when he observed a burly officer standing nose to nose with a young, slim and academic-looking Lieutenant wearing thick glasses. The Lieutenant appeared frightened by the burly officer's aggressive behavior towards him. Markham asked one of the other officers who walked by him if he knew the burly officer, and he was told that it was Captain Stevens. When the Lieutenant attempted to leave the corner, Captain Stevens blocked his path. At this point Markham felt that he had to come to the poor fellow's aid.

"Hey! Captain. Why don't you leave him alone?" said Markham, who was standing about 10 feet away from them. The Captain looked at Markham, who by this time had put his glass of Scotch on a nearby lamp table. Captain Stevens' focus was now totally on Markham to the young Lieutenant's relief, and Stevens started walking towards Markham in a menacing manner, ready to punch him. Markham readied himself for the eminent assault knowing full well the dire consequences of striking a commissioned officer, but also his right to defend himself, officer or no officer. As Stevens approached him, Stevens attempted to grab Markham by the lapels of his shirt, at which time Markham with both hands grabbed both of Stevens' wrists and with sheer power, brought him down to a sitting position on the nearby couch where he held him there while several officers and female attendees looked on. Markham didn't want to strike an officer should it be discovered afterwards that he was only a Sergeant, so he decided to contain the Captain by holding him in a seated position until he cooled down. Captain Stevens struggled with all of his might to stand up and free himself from Markham's steel grip, but to no avail. When he realized that Markham was too strong for him and to resist would be futile, he started to relax.

"You promise you're going to behave yourself and I'll let you go?" said Markham.

The Captain didn't reply.

"It's kind of embarrassing, me standing over you like this. Now I'm going to release my grip on you, but if you fight me, I'll have no choice to knock you out in front of all these people. I'm sure you don't want that," said Markham.

"OK! I give up," said Captain Stevens at which time Markham let go of his wrists and sat down in a chair facing the him.

"Why did you want to fight me anyway?" asked Markham.

"Because you make me feel inferior," replied Captain Stevens to the amazement of Markham who thought that if he only knew his rank, he certainly wouldn't feel that way.

"Now that's absurd. You're a good looking man and with the rank of Captain that makes you a very eligible bachelor. You have no reason to feel inferior, believe me. But bullying people is not the way to make friends, and we all need friends," said Markham, who noticed an almost immediate smile in Captain Stevens' face when he complimented him on his looks and rank. *A little flattery can go a long way,* thought Markham, who then left the party and went to his room for a night's sleep.

The next day, Markham told Alex of the incident with the Captain at the BOQ party and Alex agreed that Markham should be billeted off-base and draw a quarters allowance inasmuch as he was a non-commissioned officer. Markham found an upstairs loft in a three-story house converted into an apartment building in Noveant-sur-Moselle, not far from the Chateau de Berceau. It was an inexpensive rental and there was a courtyard for him to park his Ford automobile. It also provided him the privacy he needed with Mireille who visited him often.

It was near Easter and Alex told Markham that he wanted to buy some baby land ducks for his son Evan. He heard from someone in the village that there was a farm near Pont-a—Mousson, some 20 kilometers south of Noveant-sur-Moselle, that raised domesticated ducks. Markham drove Alex in the Simca out into the country and after a couple of wrong turns finally arrived at the entrance to the farm which had a large iron gate that was padlocked with a chain. Alex and Markham, both dressed in suits as required by their jobs, stood in front of the iron gate trying to get the attention of an old man sitting on a wheel barrel in front of a two-story house about 50 yards from the main gate. Markham called out to the man in French, who stood up and started walking towards Alex and Markham. They were talking to each other in English about the non-functioning appearance of the farm with the locked entrance gate and the unlikelihood that they would have land ducks, when the tall, slim elderly man dressed in coveralls with straps over each shoulder spoke to them.

"What part of New York you guys from?" the old man asked in perfect English to the astonishment of Markham and Alex.

"We're both from Long Island," said Markham. "How'd you know we were from New York?"

"Because that's where I'm from, the lower east side of New York City," replied the old man, enjoying their surprise.

"When did you come over here?" asked Alex.

"During the first World War. I was a United States Navy gun crewman assigned to the Army and I deserted and met Rosine who hid me from capture by both sides through the war and I married her and have lived as a French farmer ever since."

"You mean you never returned to the United States?" said Markham.

"That's right, I never left France since I deserted in 1915," said the old man. "Tell me, is the Lackawanna Ferry that goes from New York to New Jersey still there?"

"Man, you have been away a long time," said Alex, laughing. "The Lackawanna Ferry went out of existence in about 1928 when the Goethels Bridge was erected."

"No kidding," said the old man. "I guess there've been a lot of changes, huh?"

"Hey! It's been almost half a century since you've been gone. By the way, my name is Alex Petrov and this is James Markham. We're looking for baby land ducks for my son Evan. I don't suppose you have any for sale?"

"No, I'm sorry, we don't have any land ducks and I wouldn't know where to send you. I forgot to introduce myself, I'm John Granville," replied the old man.

Markham could see the old man's mind reminiscing and he was anxious to ask him a very vital question.

"Tell me John, I'm sure you've had a long time to think about this…do you have any regrets about your desertion which caused you to remain in France all those years?" asked Markham.

The old man went into deep thought and finally responded. "Yes," said John Granville pensively. "I do have regrets about that."

Markham and Alex Petrov drove back to the Chateau de Berceau without the land ducks Alex wanted so much for his son Evan, so he purchased baby chickens instead.

A couple of days later, Alex Petrov learned from the RG that a Hungarian Bazaar had been erected in Metz and as they were a traveling troupe they would be there only two weeks.

"Jim, I'm sure that at least one of those booths is manned by agents from behind the Iron Curtain and they use the bazaar as a means of contact with their field agents. What I want you to do is go to the bazaar as an American tourist and take movie pictures of all of the people in each of the booths. I'll get the camera and film from District Headquarters in Paris," said Alex.

A week later, the camera arrived with the film already installed which supposedly required very little light to acquire good pictures. Early that evening, Markham drove his Ford Fairlane 500 convertible to the Hungarian Bazaar in Metz and parked his car at the curb of a street abutting commercial buildings separated by an alley. The entrance to the open air bazaar was approximately 150 yards from his parked car. Markham, dressed in slacks and a tight short-sleeve polo shirt, carried this rather bulky camera by its long handle into the bazaar and immediately started filming the people in each of the approximate 20 booths which sold all types of items from jewelry to clothing. Having finished filming the last booth, he started walking out of the bazaar when he noticed that two men dressed in suits, but no ties, were following him. Markham quickened his pace towards his car, but felt that they were getting too close for him to get into his car as he would be in a sitting position for at least a few seconds rendering him most vulnerable to attack. Furthermore, he didn't want them to know that this was his car, and he thought of a way to verify that they were in fact agents following him by walking past his car and into the dark alley. As he turned into the alley, he quickly ran to the telephone pole that abutted the wall of the commercial building about 50 feet away and hid behind it just as the two men appeared at the entrance to the alley. Hidden in the darkness of the alley, he could see the two men silhouetted by a nearby street light peering into the alleyway trying to locate him. One was hesitant, but the other convinced him to explore the alley and so they slowly walked down the middle of the alley while Markham, holding the camera by its handle as a weapon, waited anxiously for them to come within view. He realized that either one of them could have a weapon, a gun or knife, and he would have to assume the worst inasmuch as they were obviously pursuing him under threatening conditions.

As the two men side by side appeared nearly abreast of Markham, he lunged at the first one hitting him across the head with the camera which caused the other man to step away from his fallen comrade. The moon suddenly found an opening in the clouds which illuminated the steel blade of the knife wielded by the other man now threatening Markham, who switched the camera to his left hand. The man jabbed the knife at Markham, but each time missed his mark, then at the next jab Markham blocked the knife with the camera causing the knife's blade to slide outward away from him giving him that one opportunity to step in and deliver a right punch to the man's head that brought him down to his knees with the knife still in his hand, compelling Markham to punch him alongside the head, this time knocking him unconscious. With both men lying unconscious in the alley and the moon disappearing behind the dark clouds again, Markham walked away with camera in hand out of the alley, thankful for the moon's assistance, and seeing that no one was around, got into his car and drove away. He gave the camera with film to Alex Petrov without mentioning the alleyway incident which he felt was of no intelligence value.

Two weeks later, Alex informed Markham that some idiot at OSI headquarters had loaded the wrong type of film in the camera and as a result, his mission was an absolute failure.

The OSI was always made aware of any foreigners that entered Chambley Air Base, including American civilians and it came to Markham's attention that an American woman named Cynthia Berryman had arrived at Chambley from Indiana to visit her boyfriend, Sergeant Curtis Podoll in the United States Air Force Reserve unit assigned to Chambley. Markham and Ernest Meehan were at the NCO Club when they first saw her eating lunch with her boyfriend. She was a slim and rather frail looking young woman, while Sergeant Podoll was a rough-looking six-footer. Markham saw her once again when he held the door open for her to exit the Club, while her macho boyfriend behind her wouldn't dream of such courtesy.

Two days later in mid-afternoon, Markham was returning from Metz in his Ford convertible and decided to stop at the Coq d'Or café in Gorze for a ham sandwich with a glass of wine. As he entered the near-empty narrow café that had a long bar, but few tables, he noticed that there were two American Servicemen dressed in fatigues sitting at a table near the entrance. Markham walked towards the middle of the bar when to his surprise, Cynthia Berryman appeared from the back of the café in a battered state that made it difficult for her to walk. Both of her eyes were turning blue and her nose was swollen. Blood was also oozing from her bottom lip that was also swollen. As she saw Markham, she slowly went to him for assistance, and Markham readily obliged by helping her to a stool at the end of the bar.

"What happened to you?' asked Markham.

"It's my boyfriend. He tried to kill me," said Cynthia weakly.

"Where is he now?" asked Markham.

"He's in the room upstairs. He's drunk and he's asleep. That's when I was able to come downstairs. He tried to strangle me. He's gone crazy," said Cynthia.

"Well, don't you worry. He's not going to touch you now that I'm here. I've got to get you to the hospital and I'm calling the police," said Markham.

"Hey! Mister," said Markham to the owner/bartender. "I need to call the Air Police at Chambley. Can you connect me?" said Markham.

"Oh! No. No gendarmerie, please," said the bar owner.

"No, no. Not the gendarmerie, the Air Police at Chambley Air Base," said Markham, whose conversation was being overheard by the two American Servicemen sitting near the entrance to the café.

"Here's the phone. You can dial to Chambley directly," said the owner in French.

"Merci, Monsieur," said Markham, then called the Air Police at Chambley and told them that an American woman had been severely beaten by a Sergeant stationed at Chambley who was currently upstairs in the café and could be coming downstairs into the bar to continue the beating. He also said that this woman needed medical attention, and asked that they send Air Policemen to the café immediately. Markham was advised that a jeep would be there shortly. As soon as he had hung up the phone, he observed Sergeant Curtis Podoll entering the bar from the rear of the café and upon spotting Markham standing in front of Cynthia with fists closed for action, he avoided the both of them and walked directly to the front of the bar to join the other two servicemen, apparently from the same military unit. A few minutes later, the shortest of the three servicemen walked over to Markham.

"I'm Lieutenant Fowler," said the short young officer dressed in fatigues, whose rank was obvious to Markham by the two silver bars on his fatigue jacket.

"And I'm Mister Markham of the OSI," said Markham, inferring that he was not impressed by the Lieutenant's rank.

"I heard you call the Air Police. What goes on between a man and his woman is really not your concern," said the Lieutenant.

"Take a good look at Miss Berryman, Lieutenant. She's been severely beaten and she is in fear for her life. She asked for my protection and she's got it," said Markham.

"So he beat her up a bit. Some women need a good beating once in a while to keep them in line," said the Lieutenant, smiling with the expectancy of agreement from Markham.

"I don't know where you come from or how you were raised, but where I come from women are to be protected and cherished, not treated like animals. I'm taking this lady to the hospital and charges will be filed against your Sergeant," said Markham, visibly angry at the Lieutenant's cavalier attitude about the incident.

The Lieutenant returned to the table where he informed the Sergeant that the Air Police would be arriving any minute and it would be best if they were gone when they arrived, otherwise the Sergeant would be placed under arrest. About 10 minutes after the three servicemen had left the bar, two Air Policemen arrived and after being briefed on the situation, they escorted Cynthia into their jeep and drove her to the Chambley Air Base Hospital, while Markham drove his Ford directly to the OSI office to inform Alex and Ernest of the activity that had just transpired.

"We can't make this an OSI case unless her life was threatened. Was her life threatened Jim?" asked Alex Petrov.

"Yes. She told me specifically that he tried to strangle her and that he tried to kill her," replied Markham.

"Good, then you and Ernest go to the hospital and get a written statement from her to that effect and when you get back, I'll open an official investigation into the matter," said Alex. After Ernest Meehan took a statement from Cynthia Berryman in the presence of Markham, who served as a witness, Markham went to the NCO Club alone for a bite to eat. As he sat at a table in the dining room not far from the bar, four of Sergeant Curtis Podoll's friends standing at the bar turned their heads toward Markham and the shortest one walked over to Markham, who was eating his salad, and voiced his discontent.

"Curt's got a lot of friends who are not very happy about you interfering with his girlfriend. I'd watch my back if I were you," said the airman, dressed in casual civilian clothes.

"Don't let your mouth overload your body, and that goes for your friends too," replied Markham, and he started to stand up, at which time the airman turned and walked back to the bar to join his friends. Markham sat back down to finish his salad. He ordered a T-Bone steak as a shot of protein for the battle he expected to take place outside the Club. Strangely, he hoped that these macho men would assault him so that he could release his built-up anger at all of these women abusers who have for so long been getting away with their sadistic behavior. Markham didn't care how many there were as he had learned from a Spaniard bouncer in a London night club who successfully took on five attackers, that the key to dealing with a group is to position yourself in a corner with your back to the wall so that only one or two at a time can come at you, and if you have real punching power and speed, you can knock them down in a pile like cordwood.

However, the Club Manager was no stranger to fights in and out of the Club and was well aware of the brawling atmosphere that was brewing and had called the Air Police. As Markham stepped outside the Club to walk over to his car, he observed half a dozen Air Policemen with Billy clubs in their hands ready to use them on anyone that commenced a fight to the disappointment of both Sergeant Podoll loyalists and Markham who smiled at them as he nonchalantly walked over to his car and drove off. But this event reminded him of just how pervasive the dictatorial attitude of men in the military towards women had become, and he was about to learn that this attitude was not the exclusive domain of military men.

A few days later, Markham visited Lieutenant Jesse MacDonald, an electrical engineer in the Army stationed at the Army caserne in Metz, whom he had previously met and befriended while having a drink in the Army Officer's Club. Jesse had just purchased a brand new Austin Healy sports car which had been delivered from England that day and Jesse, who envied Markham's Ford convertible, wanted him to ride in his new silver-colored sports car which sat so low to the ground that Markham believed he would lose his muffler should he ride on one of the brick roads. Having ridden all over Metz with Jesse at the wheel, they finally called it a night and Markham got back in his car to drive back to Chambley, but as he passed a bar, the sign 'Les Miserables' caught his interest as it reminded him of the famous tale by the French author Victor Hugo. After parking his car in front of the bar, but several feet back from the entrance, he entered the bar and observed eight men and two women sitting on stools at the bar. Only a few customers were seated at tables around the spacious section that formed an L shape around the bar. Markham sat at the closed end of the bar. The cash register and the open end of the bar was at the other end. He ordered a beer and the waitress who served him stayed at his end and engaged in conversation with him, inasmuch as he had ordered his drink in French. There was no question that she was flirting with him and she revealed that her name was Jeanne. Markham, however, was not aware that she was living in the apartment upstairs with the owner of the bar, a stocky man in his early thirties who was working the other end of the bar. Suddenly the bar owner, angry at her flirtatious behavior towards Markham, grabbed Jeanne by the throat and started to beat her while she struggled to get free of him and in the process, they both worked their way to the open end of the bar.

Markham couldn't believe that no one was coming to her aid. Not one of the Frenchmen or the Frenchwomen for that matter even uttered a word of reproach. They all sat there on their stools at the bar watching the brutal event as if it was taking place on television. Markham couldn't control himself and ran around the bar to where she had managed to drag him, still holding her by the throat and right wrist near the door entrance to the upstairs apartment. Markham grabbed the owner by the throat with his powerful right hand and pinned him against the wall adjacent to the upstairs doorway while he held his right hand by the wrist against the wall also. But the owner refused to release Jeanne, whom he was still holding by her left wrist with his right hand which Markham held against the wall.

"Let her go," said Markham to the owner in French, but he refused. He thought of squeezing his neck a bit, thereby reducing the flow of blood to the brain which would cause him to weaken his grip on Jeanne, but he feared that he might accidentally strangle him. The thought came to him that he could quickly release his throat and punch him in the jaw, knocking him out, but then charges of assault could be filed against him and he didn't look forward to a French prison. All he could do was hold him immobile until the owner got tired of holding Jeanne and she could then run to safety. Markham noted that no one from the bar made any attempt to intervene on Jeanne's behalf, but from the table area Markham observed a middle-aged man slowly approach him from his left side. He readied himself to temporarily release the owner's right hand to strike the intruder with a karate chop to the upper lip or throat, when the man spoke to him in French.

"Why don't you let him go?" said the Frenchman.

"Why don't you ask him to let *her* go? What'sa matter with you Frenchmen? Don't any of you have the decency to help this poor woman, or are you all cowards?" yelled Markham so the entire bar would hear him.

The embarrassed Frenchman turned and walked back to his table in silence. Markham started squeezing the owner's right wrist until he lost feeling and the strength to hold Jeanne, who quickly closed and locked the upstairs door behind her. He then released the owner and faced him to see if he wanted to attack him which would then give him license to defend himself and thus punch his lights out, but instead the owner walked over to the bar and grabbed a wine glass with the bottom part in his palm, closing his fist over the stem which he then broke against the edge of the bar. He then faced Markham with the broken glass stem sticking out, but Markham felt and showed no fear of him. The owner stood there looking at Markham's clenched fist visibly ready for action and pondered whether it would be wise and safe for him to initiate a fight with a man who had so easily pinned him to the wall and who now invited him in French to assault him.

"C'mon you cowardly bastard, you woman beater, you don't even have the courage to fight me with a broken glass in your hand when my hands are empty. I guess that's the way you Frenchmen are, all talk and no action. Frankly, the whole lot of you disgust me," said Markham.

The owner knew that he was no match for Markham no matter what weapon he had in hand, so he slowly backed away and threw the broken glass in the trash can and returned behind the bar, while Markham nonchalantly walked out of the bar, convinced that not one of those Frenchmen would dare come after him, even after all of his insults. As Markham reached his car about 25 feet from the bar entrance, he observed that two of the Frenchmen at the bar momentarily stepped out the door to look at the vehicle Markham was driving then stepped back into the bar. He drove back to Chambley, concerned as to what would happen to Jeanne when she eventually unlocked the door to the apartment. It saddened him that he couldn't protect her even though she meant nothing to him personally.

Four days later, Jesse MacDonald and Markham were standing near the entrance to the elevated floor section containing the long bar in the large restaurant at the main train station in Metz. There was a wooden railing around the elevated platform that held the bar from which Jesse and Markham were looking over the people seated at tables in the spacious restaurant, when a short, portly man dressed in a grubby suit walked up to Markham.

"You look like a strong, tough guy. How would you like to fight him?" said the swarthy man in French, pointing to his companion, a six foot six inch, lean young man dressed in slacks and a long-sleeve shirt.

Markham looked into the face of his potential opponent and saw disdain in his eyes and a readiness to fight him, which didn't worry Markham as he sized the man as being tall, but not particularly muscular and from his stance, very vulnerable to fast combinations. He was confident that one powerful punch to his stomach would definitely bend him in two like a pretzel and the rest would be perfunctory. He was more concerned with the portly man who kept both of his hands in his pockets, probably holding a weapon such as a knife or even a handgun. Markham knew that he couldn't count on his skinny friend Jesse who wore thick eye glasses and probably had never been in a fight in his life. He figured that there were two ways to handle this situation. One was to oblige them in a fight, in which case he would have to disarm the portly man first by smashing him in the face, then turn his attention to the tall man. That scenario would certainly invite police intervention. The other way was to avoid the conflict by portraying himself as an American who doesn't understand French and calmly leave the scene with Jesse. Markham suspected with good reason that these two men were hired by the owner of the bar Les Miserables to cause him grievous bodily harm for humiliating the bar owner in front of his girlfriend and the bar patrons. All of these thoughts passed through Markham's mind in seconds and he decided that under the circumstances, the latter option was the most sensible choice.

"I'm sorry but I don't speak French," said Markham to the portly man, who said nothing as Markham kept his eye on him and his companion for some reaction. The portly man appeared puzzled and frustrated by Markham's unexpected response. He stood there in silence looking at Markham and Jesse without uttering a word to his companion. Markham was now standing at the railing next to Jesse looking over the restaurant crowd for any signs of the bar owner whom he thought might be there to watch and enjoy the fruits of his disbursement, but there was no sign of him. He informed Jesse of the situation and cautioned him not to look at them as they walked out of the area and the train station. To insure Jesse's safety, Markham had him leave the area first with Markham following directly behind him to cover his back and bring up the rear, as they say in military maneuvers, which went smoothly without either Frenchmen interrupting their exit.

As they drove away, Jesse agreed with Markham that the two hired Frenchmen found him by the presence of his distinctive and unmistakable automobile parked immediately outside the restaurant entrance to the train station. Jesse suggested that they alternate cars, by using his Austin Healy in Metz and the Ford when they went outside of Metz, which Markham appreciated, but didn't find necessary. In fact, a third option occurred to Markham as they were driving to the Army caserne.

"What would you have done if the guy had not bought your story of not understanding French and you had been compelled to fight the tall guy?" asked Jesse.

"You have to understand, Jesse, that I detest violence and I really don't like to fight. But if it's for a worthy cause or I'm compelled to fight, then I give it my full attention. You know, the thought just occurred to me that I could have told them that I don't fight for nothing and what he was getting paid was peanuts. I could have suggested to the portly one that he should get together with you, my fight manager, and arrange for a large place where his fighter could be advertised as the Frenchman versus the American in the bare knuckles fight of the decade and charge admission and collect on bets as well. Now we'd be talking real money and I'll bet they'd have gone for it," said Markham, now believing he'd missed a golden opportunity.

"Man, you're something else. You'd have me to manage you as a bare knuckles prize fighter to take place in a seedy part of Metz where the entire audience would be composed of people with anti-American sentiments? We'd be lucky to get out of there alive, especially if you won the fight, and with all of that money," said Jesse. "Would you really do it, Jim, if that opportunity did come about?"

"Sure, why not? We'd advertise the fight to American Servicemen as well. That would even up the odds, don't you think?" said Markham. "But, hey! It didn't happen and it's not likely to happen. Just a thought...that's all Jesse. Don't get nervous on me."

"I don't think I'll ever meet anyone like you. That's a fact," said Jesse as they arrived in front of the BOQ at the Army caserne where Jesse resided. Markham laughed at Jesse's remark and drove out of the main gate to the Army caserne. About 500 yards down the street from the main gate, Markham heard a loud 'POW' that sounded like an explosion coming out from under the rear of his car and the entire left rear of his car was now lying down against the rear wheel, forcing Markham to stop the car. A group of five young Frenchmen were standing across the street laughing at Markham's predicament.

"The great American piece of junk, ha! Ha!" they cried in French, not knowing that this American understood French. Markham said nothing as he examined the rear of his automobile. Apparently the leaves on the rear left spring had broken, causing the body of the car to be resting on the left wheel.

"Why don't you call for a tow truck to take your car to the junk yard?" yelled one Frenchman.

Another said to his friends in French, "When he leaves, let's take the radio," not realizing Markham's fluency in French.

Markham took the jack out of the trunk of his car and jacked up the rear high enough to examine the damage. He then removed several empty beer cans from the trunk of his car which he crushed together with his bare hands then pressed further with the heel of his shoe. Markham then placed the crushed beer cans between the V-shaped hard rubber protrusion on the body of the car and the axle directly beneath it. Using the jack, he slowly lowered the body of the car which came to rest on the beer cans against the axle, thus elevating the body to its original position allowing the wheel to turn freely. Satisfied, Markham threw the jack into the trunk and closed it. As he opened the door to his car to drive off, he yelled to the stupefied Frenchmen in their own language, "American ingenuity triumphs again," and he proudly drove off in a blaze of glory, even if the ride was hard on his rear end.

Back at Chambley, Markham had a real dilemma in that parts for an American automobile were not available in France, but there was a Ford dealer in Kaiserslautern, Germany, some 140 kilometers from Chambley. Markham knew a Lieutenant pilot who needed to get his four hours of flight time this month and Markham convinced him to use that flight time to fly the jet trainer to Kaiserslautern to pick up a set of springs for his Ford, which he agreed to do. In two days time, Markham had the springs in hand and a motor pool mechanic to install them, putting his Ford back on the road by the week's end.

Markham's busy schedule and affair with Mireille had obscured his memory of Hildegard Hunslinger until he received a letter from her informing him that she was disappointed in his failure to write to her. Under the circumstances, she had accepted an offer to work for the Nigerian Embassy in London, England and that by the time Markham would receive this letter, she would have already departed for London. She invited him to visit her in London, should he ever decide to see her again, by merely contacting the Nigerian embassy where she works. He felt he had been given a reprieve and sighed with relief.

Alex Petrov and Markham had already met with the DSM Colonel Gaston Dulong on several occasions, but on this particular occasion, Colonel Dulong brought four of his young Lieutenants to dinner with Petrov and Markham in a private room at a French restaurant in Metz. The Colonel sat at the head of the table with his four Lieutenants seated to his right and Petrov followed by Markham seated to his left. During the dinner, one of the Lieutenants was especially vocal about the grandeur of France which was expected, but he also found pleasure in debasing the United States and its culture in particular, stating at one point that President John Kennedy was the first United States President who had any culture, and his wife Jacqueline Bouvier Kennedy of obvious French heritage, played a major role in that regard. As Markham interpreted the Lieutenant's diatribe to Petrov, Colonel Dulong made no attempt to curb his young Turk's remarks and in fact, appeared to be amused by it. Unhindered, the Lieutenant continued his criticism.

"America is still a land of cowboys and Indians with a nineteenth century mentality. They should look to France as an example of a society of haute culture," said the Lieutenant with a pride that was only exceeded by his arrogance.

By the time Markham had finished interpreting the Lieutenant's discourse, Petrov's face had become flush with resentment and anger.

"Jim, I want you to translate my response word for word and don't pussy foot," said Petrov. "When the Romans occupied France, they considered the Gaulles barbarians and forbade their soldiers from fraternizing with them, and at that time the Aztecs were a thousand years ahead of the Romans," said Petrov with Markham translating every word.

With a stern face, Colonel Dulong stood up straight, threw down his serviette on the table, did an about face and marched out of the room followed by his four Lieutenants without saying a single word.

Petrov looked at Markham, then they both broke into laughter. "Have another glass of wine Jim," said Petrov as he poured red wine into Markham's glass, then his own. Petrov then held up his glass to Markham's and made a toast, "To American culture."

The following day, Petrov received word from the RG Andre Lazzard that they had developed information regarding the three individuals involved in the incident with Petrov and Markham and he desired a meeting to discuss the results. This time the meeting was to take place at Lazzard's office in Metz. Andre Lazzard was a very pleasant and informal person who had a genuine affection for Americans, some of which of course was due to the 'presents' that Petrov would occasionally bring him. On this occasion, Petrov brought him a box of Havana cigars which he cherished like gold rods.

Lazzard revealed that Petrov had uncovered a substantial ring of spies that targeted not only United States bases, but French bases as well. The leader was identified as Colonel Viktor Lukacs, formerly in the Hungarian Intelligence Service which was taken over when the Russians invaded Hungary. He was recruited and sent to the Intelligence school in Moscow then assigned to France via an Argentinian passport. The woman was identified as Krisztina Toldy. She was also in the Hungarian Intelligence Service and Leon Krazinski was actually from Poland and used his real name inasmuch as he had no previous record in the Intelligence community.

In addition, one other person employed in the ticket office at the Metz train station identified as Lucien LaPorte, a French National member of the Communist Party, was apprehended as part of the espionage team. Petrov had Markham write down all of the information provided by Lazzard, but Petrov didn't tell Lazzard that the CIA, through the photographs taken by Markham and the OSI Report of Investigation, had already identified Colonel Viktor Lukacs. However, it was reassuring to know that the information provided by Lazzard had been confirmed.

Mireille, now in her seventh month of pregnancy, was hoping that Markham would ask her to marry him as she needed a husband and Father for her unborn child, but Markham was still struggling with his own emotions and went to the Eglise (church) Saint Michel in Noveant-sur-Moselle for spiritual guidance. There was a long line of people waiting to take their place inside the confessional booth where a priest was listening to each individual's recitation of the sins they had committed since their last confession. The priest then listened to their prayer of contrition and pronounced their penance, usually a long repetition of a certain prayer appropriate for the sins committed.

Markham stood in line until his turn came, then he entered the confessional booth closing the door behind him. On his knees facing the square screen that prevented the priest from identifying the sinner, Markham waited for the priest to slide open the wooden panel that prevented him from hearing the priest conferring with the sinner on the other side. Finally, the panel slid open and the priest blessed Markham and asked him to confess his sins. Markham explained in French that he was an American who had not been to confession in many years and had not had an opportunity to recite his French prayers, hence asked for forgiveness if he should mangle them a bit. Markham explained that he believed that he was in love with a French girl who was pregnant by another American. Yes, he had sex with her several times, but he was seriously considering marrying her and adopting her child. After listening to Markham, the priest gave him absolution and his penance. As he stepped out of the confessional booth where a line of at least 30 people were waiting, the priest opened his door and stepped out of the confessional to speak to Markham.

"You are truly a brave man. God bless you," said the priest in French to Markham with all of the parishioners looking on, wondering what great sin had Markham committed to warrant such a tribute. Markham, with head bowed in embarrassment, quickly walked away from the confessional booth to the other side of the church where he hid from view while he recited his penance.

Even though Markham drove an ostentatious American car, he sometimes liked to dress like a Frenchman wearing a beret and would visit La Maison Rouge, a restaurant and bar in the village of Montigny-les-Metz just outside of the city of Metz, owned by a former newspaper reporter turned restaurateur. Markham would sit at the end of the bar where he would eat dinner with wine while the owner Pierre Gagner engaged in conversation with him. They had become good friends, Pierre divulging his Second World War experiences with the Germans and Markham divulging his experiences in Canada and the United States. This particular evening was on a Saturday when a musical trio consisting of a pianist, drummer and bassist played from 9 PM to 12 PM to a regular group of young people from the village who enjoyed dancing. As the band played, Markham noticed that the French danced the waltz in a continuous circle that would make most people dizzy, but it was unpretentiously graceful, requiring little room to navigate and exhilarating.

As the evening wore on, four US Army Lieutenants dressed in civilian clothes, one of whom Markham recognized as Jesse MacDonald's buddy, walked into the restaurant and were seated at a table located within view of the band. For more than an hour, Markham observed each of the four Lieutenants attempt to get one of the French girls to dance with them without success, and as they continued to drink, their frustration was becoming apparent.

"Tell me Pierre," asked Markham. "Do you see anything wrong with these four young American Lieutenants? I mean, they are all clean-cut, well-dressed, well-behaved, young men with a good income. Why can't any of them get even one girl to dance with them?"

"Because the young Frenchmen in the village know that they can't compete with the wages of these Americans who can afford to spoil these young, impressionable French women, so they label any French woman who dances or fraternizes with an American a prostitute and she would never be able to marry a Frenchmen in this village," said Pierre. "You might say that it's unfair, but to those young Frenchmen it's their only recourse."

Markham got off his stool and walked over to the young Lieutenants and after explaining the situation, they all left the restaurant for a more cosmopolitan bar in the city of Metz.

Markham returned to his stool at the bar where Pierre always positioned himself unless he had to serve a customer.

"I get the feeling, Pierre, that women in France are not considered equal to men as they are in the United States. Am I imagining things?" asked Markham.

"No, you are quite correct and that is codified under the Code Napoleon," said Pierre.

"I heard of the Napoleonic Code. In fact that code is in place in the State of Louisiana, but I'll admit that I'm not familiar with its contents," said Markham.

"Well my friend, let me explain it to you. The Code Napoleon was named after Napoleon Bonaparte, the Emperor of France at the beginning of the 19th Century to unify the country with one code that would treat all of its citizens equally. However it does have its weaknesses, especially when it comes to women. For instance, a wife must be obedient to her husband and he has total control of their property. A man can co-habitate with his mistress for two years before his wife can sue for divorce. The wife can also obtain a divorce if her husband committed adultery within the family home. However, a man who finds his wife in bed with another man can legally kill her, but if the wife did that, she could be charged with murder. As you can see, the Code Napoleon treats the wife as legally inferior to her husband," said Pierre.

"Now I understand French behavior towards women. Thank you for that enlightening historical lesson Pierre," said Markham, recalling the Parisian couple who had a marital arrangement that precluded their affairs from taking place at their home.

Mireille often invited Markham to have dinner at her parents' home where she resided and Maman Jurain never failed to serve an excellent meal. She was a plain woman who had experienced many hardships, especially during the war years between Germany and France. However, she still possessed remnants of her beauty earlier in life . Papa Jurain, a heavy-set man who always sat at the head of the table, loved to dominate the table conversation with his pontification and Markham on several occasions found himself at odds with him over certain details regarding undisputed facts that Papa Jurain absolutely refused to acknowledge, especially when it involved the United States versus France. Oftentimes Papa Jurain's older brother Heinrich, a tall, slender man who bragged about his prize-fighting days as a young Frenchman, would pay a visit to the family home on Rue de Berceau, usually after dinner time to consult with his brother, who owned the vineyard where he was employed. Mireille suspected that Heinrich stole from her Father by withholding revenue from the vineyard sales which was placing her Father in an unhealthy financial situation that worried Mireille. One day, Mireille saw an opportunity to confront Heinrich with her suspicions in the presence of her Father and Mother, knowing that Heinrich would not dare hurt her physically while Markham was at her side, especially in her pregnant condition.

Everyone was sitting at the dinner table at the Jurain home, including Mireille's younger sister Margo and her husband Julien, relaxing after a tasteful dinner, when Mireille got up from the table and stood with her back to the lit fireplace. Markham followed her and stood to her left side as he didn't want direct exposure to the fire while he talked to her. Papa Jurain was as usual pontificating about something when the door to the dining room opened and Heinrich walked in and to preserve the heat in the room, closed the door behind him. He walked over to the head of the table where Papa Jurain was seated and started to whisper something in his ear which visibly upset Papa Jurain.

"What do you mean someone stole ten cases of grapes from the barn? I thought that after that happened the last time you were going to padlock the place," said Papa Jurain. "Well, did you?"

"Well, I forgot to lock it," said Heinrich sheepishly.

Mireille was frustrated over her Father's reluctance to question Heinrich's honesty.

"I know what you've been doing Heinrich. You've been systematically stealing from my Father, you bum," said Mireille.

"Listen here, you little twerp. How dare you accuse me?" said Heinrich, who started walking along the long dining-room table towards Mireille, fully aware of Markham's ready stance beside her. Heinrich came around the end of the dining room table and walked the few feet that placed him directly in front of Mireille with Markham standing within a foot of him to his right. Markham was ready to grab Heinrich at the first sign of physical movement towards Mireille and Heinrich's sideways glance at Markham confirmed his precarious position that required great caution and self-restraint.

"Listen little girl, you'd better get some evidence before you shoot off your mouth," said Heinrich, shaking his index finger at Mireille. Heinrich then paused for a moment, apparently lost for words, then he turned towards the corner of the dining room table to his left, grabbed a dinner knife and threw it against the dining room door while shouting, "This is what happens to people who mess with me," but the knife bounced off the door and fell on the floor, bringing a subdued smile to Markham's face who viewed this act as nothing more than French bravado. Heinrich stormed out of the dining room and things went back to normal as if Heinrich had never entered the room, with Papa Jurain resuming his pontification.

Relations between Markham and Papa Jurain, however, were becoming strained to the point that Markham avoided having dinner with them and only came to the house to pick up Mireille. But now her pregnancy had advanced to the critical stage where she had to take a leave of absence from her job at the Base Housing Office and it was only a matter of a couple of weeks before she delivered her baby. On the 14th of December 1962, Mireille gave birth to a baby girl who she named Christiane. Mireille blamed her Father's animosity towards Markham as the primary reason for his loss of interest in her. In fact, the similarity of the facial features between Mireille and her Father served to diminish Markham's attraction to Mireille. However, the deciding factor for Markham was his gnawing suspicion that Mireille had a constant need for a man in her life and should that man for any reason take a legitimate leave of absence, she would easily yield to the temptations offered by another man.

Markham felt that faithfulness and trust were synonymous and absolutely essential for a marriage to work and in spite of Mireille's wonderful personality and beautiful appearance, she would most probably end up breaking his heart. He realized that there were no guarantees in life, but his instincts persuaded him to err on the side of caution and adopt a wait-and-see attitude. Markham waited until after the Christmas holidays, then one evening when he arrived at her house on Rue de Berceau, instead of getting into his car with her, he asked her to take a walk along the street which borders the Moselle River. He attempted to tactfully tell her that he no longer desired to date her and that she should try to make a life without him. She ran to the edge of the dark, rapid waters of the Moselle River and threatened to jump in.

"Mireille, please don't do it. Think of your daughter Christiane. She needs you," said Markham in a desperate voice.

"You don't love me anymore. I don't have any reason to live," said Mireille crying. "Don't come any closer or I'll jump. I swear I will."

"Please Mireille, come away from there, please. OK! I take it back; I'll give it another chance if you just come away from there," said Markham, afraid that if she jumped into the fast-moving river that he wouldn't be able to save her in spite of his lifeguard training because it was so dark.

Mireille started to walk towards Markham and he gently helped her back to his car where they talked for a while, then Markham told her that he was tired and had to get back to Chambley Air Base. Mireille went inside her house knowing that she had lost Markham, but she could not accept it. Perhaps she could get him to love her again, she thought. Maybe Anne Petrov could give her advice on ways to get him back.

However, when she did meet with Anne, she was told that, "You can't force a man to love you. It's either there or it isn't, and you can't do anything about it. I'd advise you to let go. If he does come back, it has to be of his own volition."

Mireille tried to follow Anne's advice, but she found it most difficult. She started dating a French Naval Officer who had recently returned to Noveant-sur-Moselle after a long absence. He had always had a crush on Mireille who never in the past had paid any attention to him. Now that he was a Naval Officer with some standing in the community, he looked like a good prospect.

One evening, Markham heard footsteps in the normally quiet winding stairway to the third floor loft to his small apartment. He had just lain down on his bed dressed only in his jockey shorts when he heard a knock on the door. As he opened the door, he was surprised to see Mireille standing before him with a bag in her hand.

"Hello Jacques," said Mireille, who appeared gaunt and thin. "Can I come in just for a minute?"

"Of course," said Markham as he opened the door wide. As she closed the door, Markham dressed only in his shorts, got back into bed to cover himself and propped himself up on his right elbow to talk to her.

"I just came to return one of your shirts I found in the house," said Mireille, removing the shirt from the bag and placing it on the small dresser. She then squatted near the bed to be at eye-level with Markham.

"I really miss you Jacques," she said. Then Markham heard the sound of a car horn going off from downstairs in the courtyard.

"Who's that sounding his horn?" asked Markham.

"Oh! It's only Alain the Naval Officer I told you about. He gave me a ride over here," said Mireille.

"Looks like he's getting tired of waiting for you. If you don't go soon, you'll be without a ride home," said Markham.

"I don't care," said Mireille. "I love you Jacques, and if I still feel that way by the time you leave France...I swear I will kill you."

Markham knew that she meant it, but he also knew that time had a way of healing wounds. Markham heard the sound of a car motor diminishing as it left the courtyard.

"I think your naval officer got tired of waiting and took off," said Markham who walked over to the loft window and observed that only his Ford was now parked in the courtyard. "I guess I'll now have to drive you home. Better yet, perhaps I can drive you over to his house so that he doesn't get the wrong idea."

Mireille suddenly threw both of her hands around his neck. "Kiss me Jacques...kiss me," she said desperately, but Markham didn't want to encourage or take advantage of her emotional condition, hence gently pulled her hands down from behind his neck and told her he had to quickly get dressed so they could catch up to Alain.

Mireille guided Markham down a narrow street where they came upon a small MG convertible owned by Alain who upon seeing the headlights of Markham's big car, stepped out into the street. Markham remained in his car while Mireille stepped out and walked over to Alain, who kept staring at Markham. Satisfied that Alain wasn't going to hurt Mireille, he backed his car out of the narrow street and drove back to his apartment hoping that Mireille's relationship with Alain would work out.

A week later, Markham learned from Alex Petrov that Mireille visited his wife Anne in an attempt to renew her relationship with Markham. It turned out that Alain, the Naval Officer, was only on leave and had to return to his Naval base in Marseille, leaving Mireille without a man.

"She's determined to have you one way or the other Jim. I think we'll have to introduce her to some eligible bachelor and I think I know just the guy for her," said Alex, smiling.

"Oh! Yeah! Anyone I know?" replied Markham.

"In a way you do. You met him once in the Officer's Club with his buddy at arms. Remember those two CIC guys from the Caserne in Metz who posed as officers, but I knew they were enlisted men?" said Alex.

"Yeah! I remember. They're the guys who spend most of their time in that little cubby hole of an office reading comic books," said Markham, amused at the thought of these guys.

"You know? I always wanted to know what they're actual rank is. Why don't I assign Mireille to penetrate their office and gain that information?" said Alex. "I'll invite them for drinks at the Officers Club here at Chambley and introduce them to Mireille and she can carry the ball from there."

"What'sa matter Jim? You look very pensive," asked Alex.

"Yeah! You're sending Mireille to penetrate their office, but I'm afraid that they might penetrate her instead," said Markham.

"Perish the thought Jacques," said Alex, who sometimes liked to use Markham's French name for emphasis. "That certainly is one way to find out what she's made of."

A week later, Alex informed Markham that Mireille had started dating one of the two Army CIC agents named Stephen Lundell and she found out that his rank was that of a Sergeant and his CIC colleague was a Corporal and they both shared an apartment in Metz not far from the Army caserne. Markham felt relieved at the news, however six weeks later, Mireille called him at the OSI office and asked him to meet her. At first he balked at the thought of meeting her alone, and to insure that the meeting had at least the appearance of official business, he requested that they meet in front of the Base Housing Office where she worked. As soon as Markham arrived at the Base Housing Office, Mireille, who had been waiting for his arrival, immediately walked out to his car, opened the passenger door and sat down. She looked distraught and Markham sensed that the meeting had to do with a personal problem.

"I need to talk to you Jacques. Can you drive somewhere?" asked Mireille.

"Alright," replied Markham as he started his car and drove near the flight line where he parked the car and turned to face her.

"I don't know how to tell you this, but I need your help," said Mireille, avoiding Markham's eyes.

"It's alright Mireille…whatever it is, I'm sure we can work it out," said Markham reassuringly.

"I'm pregnant," said Mireille, embarrassed.

"Are you sure?" asked Markham.

"Yes, I know the symptoms and I took a test," replied Mireille.

"Who's the Father?" asked Markham.

"Steve Lundell," said Mireille.

"The CIC Agent from Metz!" exclaimed Markham.

"Yes, that's the one," replied Mireille.

"Well have you told him yet?" asked Markham.

"Yes, and now he's avoiding me. He won't see me," said Mireille.

"OK! Give me his address where he lives. I'm going to pay him a visit he won't forget," said Markham. Mireille wrote down Steve's address with directions which she gave to Markham, knowing he could be most persuasive.

Markham contacted Alex Petrov before visiting Steve, in case Alex had a better idea.

"Jesus, you're kidding me. She got pregnant again?" said Alex. "You'd think by now she'd know how to use a diaphragm or else insist on the guy using a rubber."

"She's been going through a difficult period and she's very vulnerable to forceful advances," said Markham, who felt sorry for her.

"Listen Jim. When you go to visit Stephen, you tell him that if he doesn't do right by her and I mean right now, I'm going to report the whole thing to his boss at Paris Headquarters, and he can kiss his career goodbye," said Alex, with a look that meant business.

"Don't worry, Alex, I'll read him the riot act. I'm going down there right now. I'll drop by the Chateau on my way back to let you know how I made out," said Markham.

"Good luck Jim," said Alex, who had grown fond of Markham like a brother-at-arms.

It was evening and the neighborhood was dark. Steven Lundell lived in a second story apartment in a wooden building whose narrow wooden stairway would have allowed no one to pass Markham as he ascended the stairs to the upstairs apartment. From within, he could hear the sound of music and the voices of males and females. Markham knocked on the door and Stephen himself answered the door.

"Stephen. I'm sure you remember me. I'm Jim Markham from the OSI."

"Oh! Sure. I've got company right now. This is a bad time for a visit," said Stephen.

"I need to talk to you right now Steve. Close the door behind you," said Markham in a commanding tone and Steve obliged.

"I'll come right to the point Steve. You got Mireille pregnant; you know that, don't you?" said Markham.

Steve nodded his head affirmatively.

"What are you going to do about it Steve?" asked Markham.

"I really hadn't given it any thought," said Steve. "Listen I've got to go back inside." He made a move to go back up the stairs, when Markham grabbed him by the arm and held him close.

"Mireille is a very good friend of mine. I expect you to live up to your responsibilities and do what's right for her. Otherwise, I'm going to be your worst nightmare. You got that?"

"Yeah! OK! I'll do what I can," replied Steve.

"You'll do better than that, because if I'm not satisfied, Mr. Petrov will pay a visit to your Commanding Officer at CIC headquarters in Paris and apprise him of your indiscretion and you can kiss your career goodbye. You understand me Steve?" said Markham.

"Yeah! I understand. I'll take care of it. I promise," said Steve, visibly shaken by Markham's naked threat.

Markham drove over to the Chateau de Berceau and informed Alex of his meeting with Stephen Lundell.

"We'll give Steve a few days to contact Mireille and if he doesn't, then we'll start putting the pressure on him," said Alex. "But I have a feeling you put the fear of God in him and he'll do what's right for Mireille."

"Time will tell," said Markham, who now realized that his initial instinct about Mireille's weakness for men was accurate.

Two weeks later, Markham called Mireille at the Base Housing Office inasmuch as he had not heard from her and he wanted to know if her problem had been solved. Without elaborating, Mireille thanked Markham for his help, stating that the problem had been resolved and that she had another call waiting, hence had to postpone further conversation to another time. Markham got the impression that she didn't want to discuss the manner in which her problem was resolved which could have been an abortion or even a miscarriage. Markham didn't want to embarrass her by further prodding, therefore did not pursue the matter, but as the months went by, no evidence of pregnancy appeared. *Best to let sleeping dogs lie,* thought Markham.

Winter was harsh in the Alsace-Lorraine area of France and the Chateau de Berceau where Alex, his wife Anne and their son Evan resided just couldn't retain the heat from the coal furnace that was using about three tons of coal per month. Evan contracted a severe case of asthmatic bronchitis necessitating that Anne, a registered nurse, cover his crib with plastic sheeting while she applied a steam nebulizer. Markham could see that Anne was very worried about Evan's condition and Alex was ready to pack him up and take him to the Base hospital, but Anne's remedy soon overcame Evan's illness and the little boy regained his usual high spirit and vigor to his parents' relief. This prompted

Markham to give Evan a model wooden sailboat of the same type and size he had gotten when he was a small boy, which became a useful and pleasurable enticement for him to take his bath.

Mireille was free again and she hoped that somehow, she would regain Markham's attention and affection, but Markham was avoiding her calls and referring them to Agent Meehan or Petrov. However, one afternoon, she appeared at the OSI office in person and found Markham alone in the office. He was courteous and friendly to her and she apparently mistook that as an invitation to pursue him by getting close which made Markham uncomfortable. He offered her a chair and walked back behind his desk where he sat down to talk to her with the desk between them.

She told him that her Father needed $1500.00 within the next five days to pay past-due taxes on his vineyard or else he would lose the property. She blamed her uncle Heinrich for her Father's financial predicament, but unfortunately he was insolvent thus she needed immediate outside help. Mireille asked Markham if he could lend her the money and Markham told her that his bank account contained no more than $300.00 inasmuch as he was still making substantial car payments with puny wages.

Mireille then mentioned that Captain Hamilton who had acted as Major Henderson's emissary during her pregnancy might be a good prospect and requested that Markham drive her to the BOQ to pay Captain Hamilton a visit, that she wouldn't be long and he should wait for her, which he did. Markham sat in his car for a half-hour waiting for Mireille to come out of the BOQ building, and wondered what was taking her so long, when she finally exited the building and walked over to the car and sat in the passenger seat, quiet as a church mouse with what he believed to be a guilty look.

"Well, Mireille. How did it go? Did he lend you the money?" asked Markham.

"Yes," she said, not looking at Markham, who noticed that the top button on the back of her blouse was unbuttoned. Markham empathized with her predicament, in that out of love for her Father, she did what she felt she had to do to save her Father's vineyard. Markham thought that Mireille was a remarkable woman in spite of her promiscuity, which nevertheless was an important issue for Markham.

Spring was blooming as Madame Andre returned to the Chateau de Berceau to enjoy the beautiful weather. She loved to sit on the back patio overlooking the garden while she drank hot tea. On one particular afternoon when Markham was visiting Alex at the Chateau, Madame Andre invited Markham and Alex for tea on the patio. Anne was out with Evan shopping. As they sat talking, the telephone in the Petrov residence rang and Alex went inside the Chateau to answer it. At this point, Madame Andre seized the opportunity to ask Markham in French a question that had been troubling her.

"Tell me Jacques, as a race, are black men as intelligent as white men?" asked Madame Andre.

"Yes they are. In fact we have a three-star general in the United States Air Force who is black. If they are given the same opportunity as whites, they will perform just as well, but there's still a lot of prejudice against them and that's a major problem," replied Markham.

"Well, there are a lot of Frenchmen who would disagree with you, I'm sure," said Madame Andre.

"And they are just as ignorant as the Nazis who considered the Jews as subhuman and exterminated six million of them, yet some of the world's greatest scientists are Jews. Madame Andre...you'll always find people who need to trample on others in order to elevate themselves. Your own Code Napoleon mandates that all citizens, regardless of race, be treated equally and the Catholic Church demands it, n'est ce pas?" said Markham who was astounded by such a question coming from someone of nobility and high education.

"Yes, I suppose that's true," said Madame Andre who took another sip of her tea, then turned her attention to Alex who was reentering the patio. Markham went inside the Chateau to find the bathroom where he could relieve his bladder, and in his search he opened a door in the hallway that led into a small room that contained two wooden boxes, each about eight feet in height and two feet wide by two feet deep with a wooden door that could be locked with a padlock. Near the top of each door was a four inch opening covered with thick wire. Markham left the room and found the bathroom on the other side of the hallway and upon his return to the patio he decided to satisfy his curiosity about those two boxes.

"Madame Andre. I mistakenly entered that little room in the hallway and saw two long wooden boxes with an opening at the top of the door to them. I can't for the life of me figure out what they would be used for?" said Markham.

Madame Andre looked at Markham, surprised at the question. "I really don't know what you are referring to," she said.

"Oh! I know what you're talking about Jim. Those are sweat boxes that the Germans used in the Second World War to torture prisoners. They would lock a man up in one of those boxes and leave him in there for days. The opening at the top was for the prisoner to breathe. You've got to remember that during the war, the German Gestapo made this chateau their headquarters and Madame Andre was forbidden from entering the chateau during the entire war. Heinrich Jurain told me about this place. You know how he likes to brag. Obviously he collaborated with the Germans and so did Papa Jurain. The cellar downstairs was used to store wine, but now it's empty. The entire floor to the cellar is dirt except for one area that was cemented over by the Germans. We suspect that there are people buried underneath that cement slab who never came out of the chateau. In fact, Madame Andre will confirm this. After the war she had a modern bathroom added to the other side of the chateau and during the digging they found the bodies of Russian soldiers from the First World War. I'm telling you Jim, this chateau has some sinister history," said Alex.

"Hey! I just remembered...I picked up the mail on the way out of the office and brought it down here knowing you'd be here. It's out in the car...let me go and get it," said Alex, who subsequently returned with two letters, one was a statement from the Chambley Credit Union and the other was from Germany.

"I noticed that you got mail from Germany...some fraulein no doubt," said Alex laughing.

In fact it was from Hildegard Hunslinger. Markham didn't think that it was polite for him to read the letter in their presence so he stuck it in his pocket for a later read.

"Oh! So you're not going to let us in on it, huh?" said Alex kiddingly, with Madame Andre understanding some of the Emglish language. "You can read it in our presence, we don't mind."

"Naw! I'll read it later," said Markham, "that's alright."

Back at his loft apartment, Markham opened the envelope and read Hildegard's handwritten letter which stated that she was having problems with her immediate supervisor at the Nigerian Embassy in London, therefore she returned to work at the Nigerian Embassy in Bad Godesberg which made her Mother and brother happy. She invited Markham to spend vacation time at her house in Bad Godesberg and hoped that he would respond promptly this time as she would like to see him. She left a telephone number at the Embassy for him to call her. Markham had some leave time coming to him and thought that this would be a good opportunity to see Germany with someone who knew its geography.

It was a sunny day when Markham drove out of Chambley Air Base with the convertible top down on his way to Bad Godesberg, Germany about 190 kilometers north of Metz. Upon arrival in Bad Godesberg, he followed the directions provided by Hildegard which brought him to a two-story stone apartment building. Her Mother's apartment was on the first floor and when Markham had parked his car in front of the building and rang the doorbell, Hildegard answered the door. After kissing him on the cheek, she invited him into the apartment and introduced him to her Mother Doris, a short, plump woman in her early fifties. Hildegard showed Markham a small room with a single bed that would accommodate him during his stay there.

That evening Hildegard arranged a rendez-vous with her girlfriend Monika, a reporter for the local newspaper in Bad Godesberg. Markham, Hildegard and Monika had lunch the next day at an eatery across the street from the News office in Bad Godesburg. Apparently Hildegard wanted to show off her American conquest to Monika, who came from a prominent family of lawyers, her Father being a judge. Monika mentioned that there was a ball at the American Embassy in Bad Godesberg the following Saturday evening and that Markham could use his United States military ID card to attend the ball and they could accompany him as his guests. Hildegard immediately jumped at the idea and urged Markham to accept the invitation, which he did, believing that no harm could ensue as a result of it, and so the date was set.

That afternoon, Hildegard took Markham to the town outdoor pool which was quite impressive in that it had a three tier diving platform with diving boards and the pool itself was of Olympic size. In addition, it had several elevated rows of spectator seats for swimming events. Markham, wearing boxer swim trunks and a towel wrapped around his neck, stood near the diving platform waiting for Hildegard, who eventually appeared from the ladies' locker room, wearing a bikini that accentuated her beautiful, sleek, but well developed body. The pool was not crowded and they found ample room in the pool to swim and frolic until Hildegard observed her older brother walk into the pool with a couple of male friends, all wearing bathing suits.

Hildegard had mentioned her brother Hans to Markham before, and that during the Second World War, Hans, as most other children, had joined the Hitler Youth Program and according to Hildegard, Hans still held a subtle grudge against the allies for defeating his idol Adolph Hitler. But that was now history, Hildegard had said, and her brother should get over it. Hildegard, followed by Markham, got out of the water and walked over to her brother Hans and his friends standing near the diving platform.

Hans was a handsome man, about five feet 11 inches tall, weighing in at about 180 pounds with blonde hair and blue eyes, typical of the Aryan race. His two friends in their mid thirties were slightly larger in stature than Hans. Upon being introduced to them by Hildergard, Hans was the only one of the three men who attempted to physically size up Markham as if preparing for a bout. As the five of them had formed a small circle talking to each other, Hans grabbed Markham by both biceps in an attempt to wrestle him to the ground to everyone's annoyance, including Markham, who resisted Hans' persistent pushing by planting his feet firmly on the cement flooring. Hans tried vainly to move him and in the process slipped and fell to the ground on his back staring up at four pairs of eyes within the circle condemning him for his stupid failure. Embarrassed, Hans got back on his feet looking at Markham with newly gained respect which no doubt was shared by his two friends and sister. However, Hans had not lost his competitiveness and challenged Markham to race the length of the pool. He declined as he did not want to further humiliate Hildegard's brother, but they all insisted, including Hildegard who knew her brother was a strong swimmer and needed to regain their respect. Markham decided to place himself to Hans' left so that he would see him each time he took a breath from his right side. That way he would be able to observe Hans' speed and progress. This was a 50 yard pool and they were to swim one lap only.

As Markham and Hans stood at the edge of the pool, one of Hans' friends called out, "On your mark, get set, Go!"

The two swimmers dived into the pool. Markham purposely hit the water like a pancake so that he wouldn't sink and thus could immediately start his American Crawl stroke of three flutter beats of the feet for every arm stroke, while Hans swam the overhand freestyle with irregular flutter beats. As Markham swam towards the other end of the pool, he occasionally turned his head to the right quickly to grab a bite of air at which time he observed that Hans was about six yards behind him. Markham quickened his pace and instead of stopping at the 50 yard line, he flipped around and swam back with equal speed to the other end of the pool where he first started the race. With one mighty heave, he pulled himself out of the pool where he stood with his large upper muscles gleaming from the water . Hildegard walked over to him and wiped his back with her towel in unfettered admiration while Hans walked back the length of the pool and passed them without saying a word into the men's locker room followed by his two friends where they got dressed and left the pool with no farewell.

The next day, Markham and Hildegard drove to Koblenz, a resort area along the Rhine River where they stayed at a hotel overnight. It was there that Markham learned of Hildegard's lack of passion in lovemaking and affection in their romance. It reminded him of the old cliché that beauty is only skin deep and you can't judge a book by its cover. However, Markham reasoned that not everyone is endowed with those attributes and surely Hildegard had other compensatory qualities that should be given an opportunity to manifest themselves, hence he continued to treat her with kindness without showing any signs of disappointment.

On their return from Koblenz, they had to stop at the edge of the Rhine River for the ferry to return from the other side to take them and the car across. While waiting for the ferry, Hildegard recognized two German men in a power boat at the foot of the dock next to the ferry platform. Hildegard excused herself and quickly ran down the embankment to the boat and after some time talking to her friends, returned to the car.

"I'm going for a ride in their boat. Would you like to come along?" said Hildegard.

Markham was astounded by her declaration and question. She knew they were waiting for the ferry to cross the Rhine River, yet she had already decided to go for a boat ride with the two men without his company if he declined to accompany them. He realized that Hildegard was loyal only to herself and used men as the need arose. However, this was not the time nor place to sever their relationship, so he acquiesced and went for the boat ride. It was apparent that the two men knew Hildegard quite well. After about an hour of riding up and down the Rhine River, Markham demanded in a calm voice that would not accept non-compliance that they put them ashore whence they came which they obliged, without objection from Hildegard.

That Saturday, Hildergard, dressed in a long, form-fitting silver dress, guided Markham through Bad Godesberg to a large three-story house occupied by Monika and her parents. He parked his car in the courtyard next to a Mercedes Benz sedan, a Mercedes Benz convertible and two Volkswagens. A butler answered the door and upon recognizing Hildegard, allowed them inside where they were quickly met by Monika, who was dressed in an ankle-long black dress. Monika led them upstairs into a large foyer where two young German men, both dressed in dark suits, immediately stood up as is customary upon seeing the two women enter the room. The taller young man, named George, was a Lieutenant in the German Air Force and the other young man, named Heinrich, was a medical student. As they were exchanging pleasantries, Monika's Father Judge Dietrich Meier entered the room and George immediately stood at attention, clicking his heels together with a loud sound that impressed Markham, who had only observed such greetings in the movies. Judge Meier turned his attention to Markham and engaged him in conversation about his visit to Germany and in the process learned that he was a French Interpreter-Translator for the US Air Force.

"James failed to mention that he actually works for the United States Air Force Office of Special Investigations," said Hildegard in an attempt to impress the Judge.

"Is that right Mr. Markham?" said the Judge.

"Yes that is correct Sir, but only as an Interpreter-Translator," replied Markham. However, none of those present believed that title to be his true occupation with the OSI.

"You are a very interesting young man. You must come and visit us again, soon," said the Judge, who then wished them a good time at the American Embassy. As they left the house, Markham took Hildegard aside.

"How did you know I worked for the OSI?" asked Markham.

"I called Chambley Air Base to find out your complete mailing address and they told me to address it to the OSI Detachment where you worked," replied Hildegard. "It's not a secret is it?"

"No, it's not a secret. I had never mentioned it to you so I was curious as to how you learned of it, that's all," replied Markham.

Upon arrival at the American Embassy, the live band had already started playing dance music and the place was filled with people, many dressed in tuxedos and gowns. Markham showed his military identification card and the Marine on duty allowed him and his guests to enter the Embassy where they were escorted to a rectangular table covered with a white cloth. He and Hildegard sat on one side of the table and Monika flanked by George and Heinrich sat opposite them. George was a very pleasant man whom Markham found both interesting and intelligent, but Heinrich demonstrated a dislike for Americans that he was unable to control, which made Markham wonder why he ever accepted Monika's invitation to accompany her at the American Embassy. Most likely, he reasoned, because he wanted to be with Monika and didn't care where she took him. However, at one point when George was asking Markham questions about the American Air Force, Heinrich interrupted Markham's answer with a request that the conversation be changed to something else. In order to preserve the peace and joyful atmosphere of the soiree, Markham agreed, at which time George asked Hildegard for the pleasure of a dance, which she accepted. Monika asked Markham to dance with her, leaving Heinrich alone to brood.

"I know that Hildegard is sexy looking, but she's not intelligent enough for you, Jim," said Monika, looking up at him. He was surprised by her remark and wondered if she was suggesting that she was the correct match for him. Knowing that she was Hildegard's friend, Markham chose not to respond to her remark.

"You don't have to say anything Jim. You know she's not the right person for you," said Monika. However, Markham didn't think Monika was the right person for him either, but wouldn't reveal that to either of them.

"I love this music. It just transports me to another world of make-believe," said Markham, changing the conversation to something less serious and more buoyant.

"You have wonderful rhythm and I sense that you're a strong leader," said Monika.

"I learned most of my dancing in London. A wonderful city, London. Have you ever been there?" asked Markham.

"Yes, but only for a week, unfortunately," replied Monika.

The dance ended for the band to take a 15 minute break. Markham escorted Monika back to the table where he held out her chair for her to sit, then sat in his chair while George the gentleman did the same for Hildegard. It was obvious that Monika was not happy with Heinrich's behavior and George definitely gained her favor that evening.

The next day, Hildegard invited Markham to accompany her to the Nigerian Embassy where she worked. There were no guards and Hildegard seemed confident as she walked through the main hall until she reached a large wooden door which she opened into a very large room that looked like a library. After Markham entered the room, Hildegard took a key out of her jacket pocket and locked the door behind her. She then pointed to the file drawers extending from floor to ceiling. "They're all yours James."

Markham came to the sudden realization that Hildegard was either a frustrated wanna-be spy or else part of a plan with the Nigerians to place Markham and the US Government in a compromising situation by having him take or copy files from the Nigerian Embassy while being filmed committing the act of espionage.

"Unlock the door," said Markham to Hildegard in a commanding voice.

Hildegard hesitated, indeed surprised at Markham's decision not to take advantage of the opportunity she was offering him.

"Unlock the door Hildegard," said Markham as he walked towards her and the door. Disappointed, Hildegard unlocked the door and Markham opened it wide, stepping out into the hallway to see if anyone had been spying on them, then he walked out of the Embassy followed by Hildegard who remained silent until they got into his car.

"I thought you'd be pleased," said Hildegard.

"I'm not a spy Hildegard, and you placed me in a very vulnerable position back there," replied Markham.

"I'm sorry James. You will forgive me?" said Hildegard.

"Yes, of course I forgive you," said Markham.

The next morning, Markham packed his bag leaving a note to Hildegard who had gone to work at the Embassy as her vacation days were over, stating that it was best that he return to France and go back to work at Chambley Air Base.

He had no illusions about his relationship with Hildegard which he felt had come to an end before the Embassy incident, which was frosting on the cake. The Nigerian Embassy incident troubled Markham who felt that perhaps he had been targeted long before his arrival in Bad Godesberg, thus he informed Alex Petrov of the incident, which prompted Alex to make an intelligence inquiry regarding Hildegard Hunslinger.

"Jim," said Alex Petrov. "I've just received information that Hildegard Hunslinger, while assigned to the Nigerian Embassy in London, got intimately involved with a Russian diplomat, causing him to be deported from England and her recalled to Germany. That gal's a frustrated Mata Hari. She's dangerous. You made a smart move by exiting that Embassy when you did, Jim. That could have been a trap," said Alex.

"Man, how do I find these women?" said Markham.

"You don't find them. They find you, Jim," said Alex with a laugh. "Hey! Don't be so hard on yourself. You did OK. You exercised good judgment and you handled yourself very well."

"My car engine's giving me trouble. I think it needs a complete overhaul and the only place that can do that is at the Ford Dealership in Luxembourg. My friend Jesse MacDonald is on leave of absence traveling through Europe, so I'll just have to drive the car up to Luxembourg and take a train back, which is no problem, but I'll need two days if you can spare me Alex," said Markham.

"Sure, we're not busy right now, so if you take your car up there tomorrow, you can be back by Thursday," said Alex.

"Thanks Alex," replied Markham.

The next day Markham drove his black Ford Fairlane 500 Convertible to the Ford Dealership in Luxembourg and they agreed to completely rebuild the engine for the sum of $325.00 in US funds. As an act of good will and performance incentive, he gave the manager a bottle of Canadian Club whiskey. Markham then found a small bed and breakfast hotel recommended by the manager of the dealership. The following morning, he took a taxi to the train station. After purchasing his ticket to Metz, France, he walked into the large restaurant in the train station and noticed that he was the only patron. He ordered breakfast and sat at a remote table near the rear of the restaurant where he could observe anyone who walked into the place. He was nearly finished eating his breakfast when an attractive woman entered the station restaurant and without looking right or left, walked directly towards Markham and boldly sat down at his table directly in front of him.

"You're an American aren't you?" she said with a smile, but he didn't answer her.

"I love Americans. I just put my daughter on a train to visit her Father for a week and so I'm all alone and would love your company," she said, watching Markham's reaction. "I've got a bottle of whiskey and we could have a good time you and I," she added almost imploringly.

Markham suspected that this was too good to be true and a set up by some intelligence agency to place him in a compromising situation. *Good grief,* he thought, *now I have to pass up every offer of female companionship on the mere possibility of an intelligence entrapment which could also be a test by the OSI as well.* He had no choice but to decline the offer.

"I'm sorry lady. I do appreciate your kind offer, believe me, but I do have to catch a train. I'm sorry," said Markham as he got up and walked past her in disbelief at the rejection. He didn't have to wait long for his train to arrive and he embarked it with regret and wonder.

A week later, Markham called the Ford dealership and was informed that his car was not yet ready. Three weeks later he finally got a call that his car was ready for pick up and this time, Ernest Meehan drove him up to Luxembourg. At the Ford Dealership, Markham was given the invoice written in French for the work performed on his engine, which came to a total of $715.00 US funds.

"The agreement was for $325.00 for the engine overhaul. This bill is more than twice that amount. Where is the manager Mister Bisset with whom I entered into the agreement?" asked Markham with Meehan standing next to him.

"Ha! He's gone on vacation, Monsieur," replied the assistant manager.

"Let me see my car," said Markham, and the assistant manager brought him to the other end of the garage where Markham's Ford was parked. Markham opened the hood and observed that several parts attached to the engine had been painted over to look like new, but were in fact his original parts, which he pointed out to the assistant manager.

"I want you to know that I work for the United States Air Force Office of Special Investigations and this is Special Agent Meehan. You and your dealership have committed fraud and I'll report you to the Prosecutor's Office in Luxembourg if you do not correct this bill to its original price of $325.00 immediately," said Markham in French, which took the assistant manager completely by surprise. The assistant manager excused himself and went back to the office where he conferred with two other men who appeared to be in a supervisory capacity, after which he returned with a corrected bill of $325.00.

"I am so very sorry for the misunderstanding. Please accept our sincere apologies. If you will pay us the $325.00 dollars, we will release the car to you as payment in full," said the assistant manager.

"Would you please let me have the keys so that I can test the engine first?" said Markham.

"Of course Monsieur," said the assistant manager.

"Good idea James," said Meehan.

Markham got into his car and started the engine with the hood up so that Meehan could inspect the engine and related parts.

"Sounds good to me," said Meehan.

"Yeah! The mechanics are OK. It's the management that's crooked," said Markham. "Let's get out of here."

Markham paid the dealership by check and drove his car back to Chambley followed by Meehan in the Simca.

Upon arrival back at Chambley, Alex Petrov informed Meehan and Markham that Joe Priestly, the polygraph examiner from Paris Headquarters, was due at Chambley that evening and was scheduled to polygraph the subject of his larceny investigation the following morning.

Joe Priestly arrived in his OSI sedan dressed in a dark, pin-striped, three-piece suit that included a vest which flattered his slim build. He was a friendly sort, but very impressive with his credentials as a polygraph examiner because there were so few of them around. The following morning, Priestly spent two hours conducting the polygraph examination on an airman suspected of having stolen a carbine from his unit. After collecting several polygraph charts from the suspect and analyzing them, he could not arrive at a firm conclusion, but nevertheless conducted a post-test interrogation of the suspect using the polygraph as a psychological lever to acquire a confession. However, the suspected airman continued to deny his culpability which ended the session.

After the release of the suspect, Petrov drove Priestly and Markham to the Officer's Club for a late lunch and on the way there, Priestly confessed that the results were somewhat inconclusive and he would have to further analyze the charts at Paris Headquarters before he could render a definite, conclusive finding. After lunch and Priestly had departed Chambley Air Base for his return to Paris Headquarters, Markham voiced his concern about the polygraph examination.

"You know Alex, I don't know much of anything about the polygraph, but I would have thought that Priestly could have come up with a definite answer as to whether the airman was truthful or not regarding the theft of that carbine. He just seemed so uncertain about his analysis of the charts that it makes me wonder either about his competency or the accuracy of the test or both," said Markham.

"Well, those machines are only as good as the operator and its definitely not an exact science," replied Petrov. "But Joe is supposed to be a very good examiner."

"There's no literature on polygraph in our office, so I guess I'll have to wait until I get to the States," said Markham.

The lull in intelligence activity was short-lived when Monsieur Francois Mitterrand, the French Military Coordinator for the Base of Chambley came by the OSI office unexpectedly to advise Alex Petrov that he had received information from his office that the American Air Bases at Chambley and Toule-Rosieres had been targeted by an East German Intelligence Agent named Gurgen Toth working out of Bitburg, Germany which also hosted an American Air Base. Monsieur Mitterrand told Petrov, with Markham interpreting, that their jurisdiction did not extend into Germany, but the OSI did have investigative jurisdiction due to its bases in both countries.

"Where can we find this man Gurgen Toth?" asked Alex Petrov.

"Our 'unofficial' surveillance found him using a bar frequented mostly by American Servicemen as his preferred place of business you might say," said Monsieur Mitterrand. "In fact, we have even procured a photograph of him taken surreptitiously by one of our agents, which you can have with my compliments."

"Do you have the name of the bar and its location?" asked Petrov.

"Yes. The name of the bar is Brewhaven and it is located approximately one kilometer from the main gate of Bitburg Air Base, on the main route west of it," said Monsieur Mitterrand. "You can't miss it. It's a big establishment with a large neon sign with the name of the bar on it and their parking lot is always filled with automobiles, both American and foreign, especially on weekends."

"I am most grateful for this important information and you can be sure that I will keep you informed of this man's activities and the progress in our investigation inasmuch as he seems to have extended his activities into France," said Petrov. After the meeting was terminated, Petrov immediately called in Ernest Meehan to apprise him of this intelligence information.

"Listen Ernest, Jim and I are going to Bitburg, Germany this evening. I'm going to leave you with all of the information that Monsieur Mitterrand gave us plus where we will be in case of emergency," said Petrov. "Jim, we're going in the Simca. Your car is too identifiable for this job. We'll get a bite to eat at the Chateau and then we'll get going. Bitburg is about 97 kilometers north of Metz, which will take us about an hour to get there, in time for the evening action."

"I think we should take a camera with us, don't you think, Alex?" said Markham.

"It won't hurt and you never know when we may have use for it," said Petrov, who was removing something from his desk drawer that looked like a blackjack.

"Is that what I think it is?" said Markham with half a smile.

"Yeah! That's Betsy, my favorite companion when trouble starts," said Alex smiling as he slipped the blackjack into his back pocket. "OK! Let's go eat dinner."

On the way to Bitburg, Alex confessed that he had visited the Air Base at Bitburg once before and was familiar with the route there. It was 9:15 PM when they arrived at the Brewhaven Tavern located on the route about one kilometer west of the main gate of Bitburg AFB as Monsieur Mitterrand had predicted. The parking lot was full of cars, but Alex found a spot to park his Simca on the other side of the Tavern which was not paved, but offered a quick exit to the main road. Alex led the way into the Tavern followed by Markham. Alex was quick to find a small unoccupied table for two in the corner near the kitchen entrance facing the bar. It was ideal as both of their backs were literally against the wall and they could observe everyone who entered and exited the tavern, including those along the entire length of the bar. They both ordered German beer and waited for their man Gurgen Toth to appear.

"It would just be our luck that our man would pick this night to go somewhere else," said Alex.

"Yeah! But I feel lucky tonight," said Markham.

"Too bad we're not in Las Vegas, you could try out your luck," replied Alex.

"Frankly, I'm not much of a gambler," said Markham. "At least not to the extent that I would make a special trip there for that purpose."

"I wouldn't either, but the entertainment is great and the food is cheap," replied Alex. At that moment, a man wearing a black hat and an inexpensive striped suit entered the tavern and after perusing the establishment, pulled out a German pack of cigarettes from which he extracted one and lit it with a soft match. He then sat down on one of the bar stools and ordered a glass of draft beer. He could see behind him by looking in the large mirror behind the bar, but it didn't reflect the far corner of the tavern where Petrov and Markham were seated.

"Is that our guy?" asked Markham as Alex Petrov looked at the photograph of Gurgen Toth.

"Yeah! That's him alright. Now let's see who meets with him. That ought to be interesting," said Alex as they were both pumped up with adrenaline in anticipation. A half-hour went by without anyone approaching Gurgen except for one obvious prostitute plying her trade to no avail. Then a man wearing a baggy dark blue waist jacket zipped in the front half-way up, in his late thirties, sat down on the stool next to Gurgen. Markham knew that he'd seen this man before, but couldn't place him. He was certain that he was an American Serviceman.

"I know that guy, Alex. I just can't place him yet, but give me a few minutes," said Markham.

"You're kidding. Think hard Jim," said Alex anxiously.

"Jesus, I don't believe it. Now I know where I saw him last. Camp Kilmer. Sergeant Anthony Pucelli. That's the son-of-a bitch who kept all of my civilian clothes and the $50.00 I gave him to ship my clothes to England. I never thought I'd ever seen him again, and here he is 11 years later and of all places, Germany," said Markham.

"He must be near retirement," said Alex.

"Some of these guys like it so much over here that they extend their tour of duty and their time in service so that they get a larger retirement, but he's not that old yet," said Markham.

"Let me think this out. Maybe we can make use of this situation between you and this Sergeant Pucelli," said Alex, who was then interrupted by Markham.

"Did you see that Alex? Pucelli pulled out a thick brown envelope from inside his jacket and passed it to Gurgen, who put it inside his breast coat pocket," said Markham. "They're so confident that they don't even bother to use a dead letter drop."

"Yeah! I saw it. Looks like your Sergeant is involved in espionage my friend. We've got a situation here that may need immediate action," said Alex. "But I didn't see Gurgen pass him any money."

"He may have and we just missed it," said Markham. "No, there it is. He put the money on the bar and Pucelli picked it up. Hide in plain sight…pretty clever."

"Listen Jim. I want you to go over to him and act as if you just recognized him and demand your money for your clothes with interest. Act mad and drag him outside. I'll cover you in case Gurgen gets into the act. The plan is that once you get him outside, you can make Gurgen believe that you're settling a personal beef between you and Pucelli and I'll make sure that Gurgen doesn't follow you and Pucelli."

"But I do have a personal score to settle with that thief," said Markham.

"Yes, I know, but you must use that opportunity to accomplish a more important goal and that is to bust this espionage ring, so keep that in mind Jim…we want him to cooperate with us and turn him against his German handler."

"Gotcha," replied Markham as he stood up and walked over to where Pucelli was seated at the bar semi-facing Gurgen. When Pucelli realized that Markham was looking directly at him as he approached him, he got a bit worried because he didn't recognize him, but the deportment of his muscular physique conveyed a readiness for battle.

"Well if it ain't Sergeant Pucelli. You don't remember me, do you Sergeant?" said Markham, looking into Pucelli's quizzical eyes.

"It's been 11 years since I last saw you Sarge. Camp Kilmer. Does that jog your memory? You were supposed to send me my suitcase full of brand-new civilian clothes to England which you never did," said Markham, watching Pucelli's face turn pale.

"I figure you owe me one thousand dollars for the clothes, plus 11 years interest which would now bring it to two thousand dollars. I don't suppose you have that money on you, do you Sarge?" said Markham.

"Hey! Man, I can explain. I lost your address and was stuck with your clothes so I gave them away," said Pucelli.

"Now you're adding insult to injury. How much money you got on you Pucelli? I know that if I don't get it now, you'll run and I'll have to chase you down again. So let's have it," said Markham.

"Hey! Man. I ain't got that kind of money on me, honest," said Pucelli.

"How much have you got on you?" asked Markham.

"Hell! Only about fifty bucks, that's all," said Pucelli.

"You're a lying son-of-a-bitch Pucelli. Let's step outside where we can discuss this privately. Maybe we can come to some sort of arrangement," said Markham, trying to get Pucelli away from Gurgen.

"I'm not going outside with you. Whatever you want to say to me you can say it right here," said Pucelli.

"I can punch your lights out right here or else we can go outside and talk it over like civilized people...the choice is yours," said Markham, who noticed that Gurgen was so far just an observer.

Pucelli saw Markham's big hands clenched and ready to decimate him while he was in an unenviable sitting and defenseless position.

"Alright let's talk outside," said Pucelli, getting off the stool with a look at Gurgen that silently conveyed a request for assistance.

Markham allowed Pucelli to exit the entrance door first with him following closely behind him. Alex had cautiously left the corner table and positioned himself at the bar just a few stools away from Gurgen whose back was facing him, hence he hadn't noticed his presence because of his attentiveness to the unpleasant situation developing between his source Pucelli and Markham, the apparent victim of Pucelli's prior dishonesty.

Pucelli walked out of the tavern so rapidly that Markham thought he was perhaps attempting to escape him, but as Markham got within a couple of feet of him, Pucelli suddenly turned around with a round-house punch that missed his head by no more than an inch. Markham stepped back then lurched forward with a combination of punches that drove Pucelli to the ground between two cars in back of him.

As Markham faced Pucelli, Gurgen had stepped outside the tavern to witness the fight. Believing that Markham had not seen him and was alone, Gurgen started walking quietly towards Markham's rear when Alex, who had been tailing him all the while, struck him in back of the neck with a rabbit punch that brought Gurgen to his knees, then hit him again in back of the head with his fist, knocking him unconscious so that he wouldn't observe their activity with Pucelli.

Alex joined Markham in dragging Pucelli down the row of parked cars until they were secure from view of the tavern's patrons. Markham propped Pucelli up against the hood of one of the cars and Alex slapped his face a couple of times to revive him. After several seconds, Pucelli regained consciousness and upon recognizing Markham was reminded of the trouble he was in. However, he became even more fearful when he saw Alex towering over him.

"Who's this guy? What's going on?" asked Pucelli.

"This is Special Agent Petrov of the OSI. We know what you've been doing Pucelli. What you owe me is nothing compared to what you owe Uncle Sam," said Markham.

"I don't know what you're talking about," replied Pucelli.

"Try espionage for openers Pucelli," said Alex Petrov.

Pucelli's body almost went limp with fear. He looked at Alex wondering just how much he knew and decided to test him.

"What do you mean espionage? I don't know what you're talking about," said Pucelli.

"Listen you amateurish moron. We observed you passing classified documents to that East German Agent inside the tavern and when I search you I'm sure that I will find more than fifty bucks on you," said Alex, and turned Pucelli around putting him in a frisk position for weapons and evidence.

"Well, well, what have we got here?" said Alex as he pulled out a wad of $100.00 bills from Pucelli's breast pocket. "I figure there must be at least two grand here. Not bad for one night's work, hey, Pucelli?"

"Let's take a walk to my car where we can talk in private," said Alex as he and Markham escorted Pucelli to the Simca. Alex got into the driver's seat while Markham sat in the back with Pucelli. Alex drove out of the tavern parking lot to a nearby isolated area before Gurgen regained consciousness and decided to look for them.

Having parked the Simca, Alex turned his attention to Pucelli.

"OK, Pucelli. You've got some choices to make. You can become a loyal American Airman again and cooperate with your government in smashing this Communist espionage ring or else you can be convicted as a spy and serve the rest of your miserable life in a federal prison…which is it going to be Pucelli?" said Alex.

Pucelli looked at Alex, then at Markham and put both of his hands up to his face and started to moan. "Oh, my God. I really did it this time. Oh, my God…what's going to happen to me?"

"Listen Tony," said Markham, using his first name in an effort to appear cordial. "You're only smart choice now is to cooperate with us, and time is of the essence…you understand Tony…time is of the essence."

"We know the German Agent's real name Pucelli. It's Gurgen Toth. He will be apprehended. He'll have no qualms about turning you in because his loyalty is to the Communist regime in East Germany. But if you give us all of the information that you gave him, it will go a long way to show your cooperation and I'm sure that the Air Force will consider that when they have to make a decision regarding your case," said Alex.

"Alright," said Pucelli. "I'll cooperate. What do you want to know?"

"What name did you know him by?" asked Alex.

"It wasn't Gurgen. I knew him as Peter Misner," replied Pucelli.

"What documents did you give him tonight?" asked Alex.

"I gave him a copy of the Code Red Alert Plan and he also wanted a flight line badge so I got him one of them too, but it wasn't easy to get. He's supposed to give me another five thousand dollars after his superiors have authenticated the information," said Pucelli.

"What was the classification of the Code Red Alert Plan?" asked Alex.

"Top Secret," replied Pucelli.

"Where do you work, Tony?" asked Markham.

"I work as an aircraft mechanic on the flight line," said Pucelli.

"Then how did you have access to the Code Red Alert Plan?" asked Alex.

Pucelli hesitated. "I don't want to get anyone else involved."

"Pucelli…unless you tell us everything…you're going down as the heavy in this espionage case…so you'd better spill the beans and save your own hide," said Alex.

"Alright. I know this Staff Sergeant in the Combat Operations Section who's got expensive tastes and always needs money, so I promised him a thousand bucks for the Code Red Alert Plan and he knows I'm good for it because I paid him in full for some other document he gave me."

"What's his name?" asked Alex.

"Staff Sergeant Eric Stromberg," replied Pucelli.

"What other documents did he provide you with?" asked Alex.

"A roster of the names and addresses of all the pilots and navigators, plus the specific armaments on the bomber and fighter aircraft…information of that nature," said Pucelli.

"OK! Pucelli. We're going to Bitburg Air Base and we're going to isolate you from everyone so that no one will know that you've been talking to the OSI. You understand?" said Alex.

"Yes I understand," replied Pucelli.

"We're going to visit with the OSI detachment commander at Bitburg who will want to debrief you further on this matter, and we'll want you to work with us to put an end to this espionage ring…OK?" said Alex.

"Yes, Sir. You have my full cooperation, Sir," replied Pucelli.

At the main gate to Bitburg Air Base, Alex showed the Military Policeman his OSI credentials and the Policeman gave Alex a salute, although Alex was dressed in civilian clothes, and waved him on through. Alex knew where the OSI detachment was located, but didn't figure there would be anyone there at this time of the night. However, he knew that a duty Agent was on call 24 hours a day, hence he drove to the Provost Marshals office. So as not to draw attention to Pucelli, he left him and Markham in the Simca while he went inside the station and asked the Air Police Sergeant on Desk Duty to telephone the OSI Agent on Duty and ask him to meet him at the OSI Office on an urgent matter. He then got back in the Simca and drove to the OSI Detachment to await the arrival of the OSI Duty Agent. Ten minutes later, a Ford sedan pulled up beside the Simca and a slim, dark-haired man in his mid-thirties stepped out of the Ford and greeted Alex, who motioned Markham to bring Pucelli with him inside the OSI Detachment office.

"Jim, this is Special Agent Steve Martin," said Alex. "Why don't you bring Pucelli into the interrogation room over there and close the door?"

Markham escorted Pucelli into the small interrogation room and offered him a cigarette, but he said he had his own and thanked him. Markham then closed the door and returned to where Alex was briefing Agent Martin.

"Jim is my French Interpreter-Translator," said Alex to Agent Martin, "but in this country my German is what comes in handy."

"I'd better call my boss Karl Eisenhuth who speaks fluent German," said Agent Martin. "I think he'll want to act on this right away. He'll probably want to alert the Base Commander that the Code Red Alert Plan has been compromised and the flight line badges will have to be immediately changed. We'll be in debriefing with Sergeant Pucelli for the rest of the night."

"Well, Pucelli is all yours now. I'll dictate a statement while we're here to Markham, who can type as fast as I can dictate, and then we'll return to Chambley. I'm sure that OSI Headquarters in Germany will provide you with whatever assistance you need when Karl briefs them. If you should find out that they conducted espionage in France, I'd appreciate it if you would notify me immediately," said Alex.

"For sure Alex, we'll notify you the moment we learn of anything that pertains to your area of jurisdiction," said Agent Martin.

As Alex was dictating his statement concerning the events that had transpired that evening and the admissions made by Sergeant Anthony Pucelli, the door to the OSI office opened and a slightly-balding, heavyset man , with a lit cigar in his left hand entered the room. He immediately recognized Alex and shook his hand, and after being introduced to Markham, shook his hand also.

"Sergeant Anthony Pucelli, an aircraft mechanic stationed here at Bitburg Air Base is presently in your interrogation room waiting to be debriefed. I have already apprised Steve Martin of all the information Pucelli has so far given us and I'm executing a statement right now incorporating all of that information. There's an East German Agent by the name of Gurgen Toth involved in this espionage ring and Pucelli has been giving this German spy classified information in return for sizeable amounts of money. We witnessed the exchange of Top Secret information for two thousand dollars in the Brewhaven Tavern tonight. Pucelli is willing and ready to cooperate with the OSI to set a trap and nail him and any of his conspirators," said Alex.

"Alex, I have to hand it to you. You're the Master of counterintelligence," said Agent Eisenhuth admiringly. "I'm going to confer with Steve while you continue dictating your statement."

Markham finished typing Alex Petrov's statement, and Alex read it,signed it, then gave it to Karl Eisenhuth.

"Steve and I are going into the interrogation room now to debrief Pucelli. I believe that we have everything under control. I'm sure you guys are tired and want to get back to France. If I should need anything else from you, I'll be on the horn, don't worry," said Karl Eisenhuth. "Thanks again for a tremendous job, Alex."

"Don't mention it Karl. Glad to be of help. Take care Steve," said Alex.

They all shook hands including Markham who then left the OSI premises with Alex to return to Chambley Air Base.

"You know Jim, I think you should apply for OSI Special Investigations School in Washington, DC. I think you'd make an excellent Agent. You apply and I'll give you a glowing recommendation. You'll have to take a written test of course, but you shouldn't have any trouble passing it," said Alex.

"Where would I have to go to take the test?" asked Markham.

"They would send it to me at Chambley for me to administer it to you, then I would send it back to Directorate in Washington," replied Alex.

"How tough is it, really?" asked Markham.

"It's got some math, basic science and English composition of course, but I'm confident that you'll pass it with flying colors. I would recommend that you study the Uniform Code of Military Justice and all of the OSI Bulletins that are in my office. That'll give you a heads up on everybody at the school," said Alex.

"I will start on that tomorrow and if you'll give me the application form, I'll have that completed by the end of the day," said Markham enthusiastically. *Finally,* he thought, *my career is starting to take shape.*

Three weeks later, Alex received the written test from OSI Directorate which he administered to Markham the following day, then returned the completed test to OSI in Washington, D.C. Later that day, Alex Petrov received a telephone call from Special Agent Karl Eisenhuth.

"I'm calling to let you know that we have concluded our investigation of the espionage case involving Gurgen Toth and Sergeants Anthony Pucelli and Eric Stromberg. Pucelli and Stromberg cooperated with us and the German Intelligence Service and as a result, we were able to nab not only Gurgen Toth, but his handler, an East German Agent located in West Berlin. They're now all in custody awaiting trial. A copy of our investigative report should be reaching your office any day," said Eisenhuth.

"Thanks Karl. I appreciate your call. I'll pass the info onto Jim Markham. I'm sure he'll be delighted. By the way, I've recommended him and he's applied for the OSI Investigative School. I think he'll be a damn good Agent," said Alex Petrov.

"I agree. He made a good impression on me and Steve. I wish him the best. Well, that's all I've got, Alex. Take care and thanks for the help," said Eisenhuth.

Alex Petrov sat back in his swivel office chair behind his desk and looked out the window overlooking a small parking lot with Quonset huts in the background, feeling a great sense of accomplishment in an otherwise unspectacular, morose environment.

It was a normal, but overcast day at Chambley Air base on the 22nd of November 1963. Alex and Markham were working on an Essential Elements of Information, also known as an EEI Report, to be sent to OSI Headquarters in Paris, when the telephone rang and Alex picked it up. Alex's face turned pale as he listened and Markham sensed that something grave had happened because nothing usually disturbed Alex's composure. Finally, he hung up the phone.

"That was Anne. She just heard on the radio that President Kennedy has been assassinated. He was shot in a motorcade in Dallas, Texas," said Alex somberly.

"My God," said Markham in total surprise. "I can't believe it."

"Neither can I," said Alex. "This day will be remembered long after we're all gone. Let's turn on the radio and see if we can get further details on this."

The French news agencies reported at length the tragedy of President John F. Kennedy's assassination and the various theories regarding the perpetrator(s) of this dastardly deed. While Lee Harvey Oswald was apprehended as the perpetrator of the assassination, subsequent reports of his untimely execution by Jack Ruby left a lot of unanswered questions regarding the proposition that Oswald was merely the patsy in a conspiracy by unknown entities who sought President Kennedy's removal with motives that centered around revenge. At that time the United States had some 16,300 troops in Vietnam, but it was not involved in direct conflict with the North Vietnamese government. President Lyndon Johnson's assumption of the Presidency of the United States appeared seamless to the general public, but his goals and style were quite different from John F. Kennedy.

Being in France, so far away from the homeland, Alex Petrov and Markham were not exposed to the constant reminders of President Kennedy's death which enabled them to resume their work sooner than their counterparts in the United States.

Christmas time at the Chateau de Berceau was a memorable event for the Petrovs, who invited the unattached Markham to spend the holiday with them. Evan was now two years old and the cowboy outfit and rocking horse he received for Christmas was as much of a pleasure for the parents to watch as the son to enjoy. The Petrovs made Markham feel like part of the family. Indeed he was now part of the OSI family of Special Agents inasmuch as he had just received his Special Orders assigning him to OSI District 19 at Travis Air Force Base, California, pending his scheduled attendance at the OSI Special Investigations School in Washington, D.C. However, New Year's Eve turned out to be a time of reflection for Markham who knew that he had only two weeks left in France. Being a non-commissioned officer, Markham spent the evening at the NCO Club mostly alone except for occasional conversations with other airmen while Alex took his wife Anne to the Officer's Club as was their tradition for the New Year's Eve event.

Markham felt like going to a nightclub in Metz to dance the night away. This was a time for romance and gaiety, but not just with any woman. It had to be someone who palpitated his heart and shared his quixotic attitude and what better way to express it all than in unified dancing to French melodies in a quaint 'boite-de-nuit' amongst a crowd of joyful revelers. Unfortunately, of all the nights, Sylvia's face kept surfacing in his conscious mind with each drink of Scotch enlarging his fantasy of her in his arms dancing the night away, until he finally came to the heartbreaking realization that she was just a memory. He never went to Metz that night, he simply retired to his loft apartment in Noveant-sur-Moselle, alone with a profound sadness.

On the eve of Markham's scheduled departure for the United States, he had been invited to dinner by Alex and Anne Petrov at the Chateau de Berceau. Shortly after dinner, Mireille appeared at the Chateau to see Markham for the last time and after an hour of small talk, she bid Markham farewell and left the premises. A few minutes later, Anne asked Markham why he didn't walk her back to her house.

"I don't know. The thought never crossed my mind. I guess I subconsciously didn't want to offer her an opportunity for an emotional scene as the French are so capable of doing," replied Markham, who truthfully didn't want to make his departure any harder on Mireille than she had already endured.

The next morning, Markham, wearing his dress blue Air Force uniform adorned with two rows of colorful ribbons on his left breast and Staff Sergeant stripes on both upper sleeves of his jacket and his garrison hat slightly tilted on his head, was met by Alex in the Simca in the courtyard of his apartment in Noveant.

As Alex grabbed one of Markham's two large suitcases, he exclaimed, "What have you got in there, books? Man, this is going to exceed the weight limit."

"I've got both my civilian and military clothes in those two suitcases. It represents all of my earthly possessions," said Markham.

With both suitcases loaded into the trunk of the Simca, Alex drove Markham to the train station in Metz. As they waited for the boarding of the train to Paris-le-Bourget Airport, Alex had not realized until then just how close their association and friendship had become, and although at times quite eloquent, he couldn't find adequate words to express his deep feelings of camaraderie. By the same token, Markham felt that he owed Alex a great debt in his successful effort to have him accepted for attendance at the OSI Special Investigations School in Washington, DC.

"Looks like my train is ready to depart," said Markham, reaching out with his right hand to shake Alex's hand. "Thanks for everything, Alex," said Markham, knowing that Alex knew what he meant by 'everything.'

"Listen Jim. The OSI is a small family, so we'll meet again. You can be sure of that. In the meantime, you take care of yourself, and watch those French girls…you're not out of France yet my friend," he added laughingly. "Drop us a line when you get to Travis."

"I'll do that Alex…..I'm going to miss you guys," said Markham with assorted emotions, leaving Alex, Anne and Evan, but starting an exciting new career in the OSI.

Wearing his Air Force dress blue uniform, Markham stood out among the passengers on the train from Metz to Paris. Seated in a compartment with three women and two men, all French nationals, he felt rather tired and wanted to rest during the four hour train ride, therefore he decided not to reveal his knowledge of the French language which would permit him peace and quiet throughout the journey. However, his reverie was frequently disturbed by unfavorable comments made of him and Americans in general by the French passengers sharing his compartment, which made it extremely difficult for Markham to remain silent. Nevertheless, he did, so that he could learn to the fullest extent the depth of their dislike of Americans and their culture. Upon arrival at the Paris train station, Markham, who was sitting closest to the door to the hallway, stood up with his suitcases in hand and upon opening the compartment door, turned towards the French passengers and in perfect French thanked them for their honest, but misguided opinion of Americans, which left them all aghast at the realization that he had understood their entire conversation, yet made no attempt to reproach them. He walked out of the train station feeling immensely pleased with what he felt was an effective Coup-de-Grace.

He had orders to report to the MATS Passenger Representative at the Paris Housing Annex (Littre), #9, rue Littre, Paris 6e, for transportation on TWA Flight T-854 departing at 1430 hours the following day. He checked in at an inexpensive hotel and after eating a light dinner, spent the evening walking around Paris enjoying the sights and the throngs of people preoccupied with their daily activities in the City of Lights. Finally, Markham boarded his TWA flight from Paris to New York with many pleasant memories of France, but also many disappointments in its people.

The End of Part I

Book Review by John Nash, Professor of English Literature, ECC, Buffalo, New York..
The Caul, A Trilogy
Part One: Born With A Mission
By James Allan Matte

Remember the name Markham—it may soon be a household term. Part I, the lengthiest of the three books in this trilogy, introduces the protagonist James Markham as a child born with the Caul of Destiny during the Great Depression in New York City who must suffer the tribulations of abandonment, poverty and expatriation to Canada where he experiences the harshness of gratuitous corporal punishment in the French Canadian schools. This prepares him for his repatriation as a teenager to New York City where he hones his survival instincts amongst the city toughs. The Korean War becomes his theatre of operation and the US Air Force his guardian and only home. The military takes him to England and France setting the stage for the fulfillment of his providential destiny in Parts II and III. Markham's coming of age is virtually a memoir of the experiences author Matte actually navigated. This is an odyssey from The Karate Kid to James Bond, only it really happened, a life so exciting that I had to reread it after I had first finished the entire three-part trilogy. This is definitely a book for people of all ages and maturity. The saddest part of this trilogy is that it had to end. Hopefully there will be a Part IV.

Book Review by Ellen Tanner Marsh, NY Times Best Selling Author.
The Caul, A Trilogy
Book One: Born With A Mission
By James Allan Matte

How do we recognize our destiny? How do we know when to act and with whom we should form our alliances? Is it a feeling? An event?

Sometimes, as with James Markham, the hero of James Allan Matte's ambitious autobiographical trilogy, The Caul, it's with the help of a caul, a rare and protective membrane he was born with. Legend has it that those born with a caul are marked for greatness or are gifted with the second sight—the ability to see into the future and perhaps change it for common good.

Because the past is almost always a prologue to future greatness, Book One introduces us to the young James and takes us along on his journey as he makes friends and experiences a number of adventures, all of which strengthen his character and his keen sense of faith and morality. From Montreal of the 1940s to Manhattan, Markham faces his own personal challenges, attending boarding school and discovering the joys of baseball on the simmering streets of New York City. But clearly his greatest challenge is about to begin as he grows up and enters the Air Force.

Based on the life experiences of the author, this deftly-paced novel takes you on an insightful journey, brilliantly detailing all the incredible events and exotic locales that help forge Markham's indomitable strength and courage. A deeply stirring novel about faith and Christianity, this is also the sensitively rendered tale of a boy growing into manhood, whose great destiny is still just a glimmer—cleverly presented so that we are propelled into anxiously awaiting Book Two of what promises to be a riveting trilogy.

Made in the USA
Lexington, KY
19 December 2010